THE ORIGIN OF THE BRUNISTS

Robert Coover

THE
ORIGIN
OF
THE BRUNISTS

A Richard Seaver Book
The Viking Press New York

Respectfully for Richard P. McKeon

*And see that you make them
after the pattern for them,
which has been shown you on the mountain . . .*

A Richard Seaver Book/The Viking Press
Published in 1978 by The Viking Press
625 Madison Avenue, New York, N.Y. 10022
Distributed in Canada by Penguin Books Canada Limited

LIBRARY OF CONGRESS CATALOGING IN PUBLICATION DATA
Coover, Robert.
The origin of the Brunists.
"A Richard Seaver book."
I. Title.
PZ4.C780r 1977 [PS3553.O633] 813'.5'4 77–21787
ISBN 0–670–52863–3

Printed in the United States of America
Set in Linotype Electra

Contents

PROLOGUE
The Sacrifice

*Write what you see in a book and
send it to the Seven Churches.*

—REVELATION TO JOHN 1:11

Hiram Clegg, together with his wife Emma and four friends of the faith from Randolph Junction, were summoned by the Spirit and Mrs. Clara Collins, widow of the beloved Nazarene preacher Ely Collins, to West Condon on the weekend of the eighteenth and nineteenth of April, there to await the End of the World. What did he really expect? The Final Judgment, perhaps. Something, certainly, of importance. What he did not expect was to find himself standing on the night of Saturday the eighteenth—the Night, as it turned out, of the Sacrifice—in a ditch alongside the old road to Deepwater Number Nine Coalmine, watching a young girl die. He had been prepared, as only a man of great but simple faith can be prepared, for profound and terrifying events, but he had not been prepared for that. He couldn't even remember much of it later on, so squeezed had his mind been by plain awe. The crowd all came out of their cars and stood around, some up on the lip of the ditch, others, like himself, down near the girl, down where the long grass threw black spiked shadows. Some stared as though not seeing her. Some wept hysterically, knelt to pray. None, surely, was unmoved. He recalled seeing Mrs. Eleanor Norton at one point lying in the roadway as though dead, her husband fanning her desperately with the hem of his white tunic. Yes, oddly, Hiram retained that pointless detail: Dr. Norton's fat knees planted painfully in the ruts and cinders of the old mine road, revealed like a secret signal with every flap of the tunic hem. But the rest of it remained forever obscure to him, lost in the mad crisscross of headlight beams, a dreamlike

3

conjuring of happenings that whirled in a fantastical circle with neither beginning nor end.

They had anticipated, on arriving that afternoon at the home of the coalminer-visionary Giovanni Bruno, a small group of believers, such as they had seen witnessing on television, but they encountered instead literally hundreds of people milling about. At least half of them, Hiram noted, were newspaper, radio, and television people: many cameras, much light, an unbelievable excitement. He went looking immediately for Sister Clara, found her speaking animatedly with a group of people, like himself dressed in streetclothes, yet with the unmistakable quality of the Church of the Nazarene about them. "Sister Clara!"

"Brother Hiram!" Clara cried, and hurried toward him to take his hand in both of hers. "How wonderful! You've come!"

"Yes, after all you told me, Sister Clara, I could hardly stay away."

She introduced him to the group, friends of the faith from New Bridgeport. Hiram had never seen Clara so inspirited. She spoke glowingly of all their plans, of all the wonderful people who had answered the call, of this great moment that was gloriously upon them. Hiram, in turn, told her he had brought five persons with him, including his wife Emma.

"Well, we still don't have tunics for everybody," Clara said. "We plain didn't expect so many folks, Hiram. But I can give you two now for you and Emma, and maybe we'll get enough more done by tomorrow for the rest." She led him to a bedroom close by and presented him with the tunics, took a moment to explain some of the marvelous things that had transpired in that room, that very room, in the turbulent fourteen weeks just past.

"It is so . . . so humble, Sister Clara," Hiram remarked. "So appropriate."

"Yes," she agreed. "This house has been like our second home." She paused, her strong face sunk for a moment in

4

memory and grief. "I lost my own home, you know, mine and Ely's."

"Yes, so you told me. And yet it is, as you yourself said, Sister Clara, but one more sign among the many, one more assurance in the contest with doubt."

"Yes, but I got to admit, it hurt me, Hiram."

"It would have hurt any of us, Clara. You have borne the strain of these awesome months like a true saint." She did not reply, seemed absorbed in her own thoughts. "These tunics, do we just put them on over our—?"

"No, but see Ben about that. He'll direct you where to change and all."

And so then he led Clara over to where Emma and the others were waiting. He was deeply impressed, observing the widow Clara Collins. She stood so tall in her tunic, so strong and self-possessed. He had heard her speak on other occasions at tent meetings and in company with Brother Ely, but always then in that great man's shadow, and he had never before observed such eloquence in her, such candid poise, such great personal magnetism and contained power; she was as though possessed by the Holy Spirit Itself—and, indeed, was this not precisely the case?

More of Clara's friends arrived, groups from Wilmer Tucker City and a couple from Daviston, distracting her once more. She pointed toward where Brother Ben Wosznik could be found, and Hiram led his people over there, explaining elements of the movement as he understood them. Ben greeted them warmly, recognizing Hiram and Emma from his visit with Clara the previous Monday, and calling them by their first names. He informed them of the regulation regarding the wearing of only white garments under the tunics, and shepherded them upstairs to show them where the bathroom was. On the way, he interpreted for them the meaning of the design on the tunic, the cross that turned out to be a sort of coalminer's pick, the enclosing circle, the use of the color scheme of brown upon white, and they talked about their expectations of the

5

Coming of the Kingdom, the Kingdom of Light. As for the wearing of white underneath, he said that one of their members had gone to town this very afternoon to purchase a wide assortment of white underclothing for those who, in understandable ignorance, might have come without. Hiram had liked Ben immediately, upon the very first encounter, and now, climbing the narrow staircase in this strange house, below him a most strange and disturbing excitement, confronting the strangest event in Hiram Clegg's life, he all but loved the man. Ben Wosznik breathed humility, compassion, loyalty, warmth. Wherever Clara Collins and Ben Wosznik are, Hiram thought that moment, there I belong.

Hiram, suffering from a mild seasonable cold, had dressed that morning in his old white longjohns, though the spring weather hardly called for it, and now he was glad that he had done so. The tunics were lightweight and it was easy to get a chill. Emma, on the other hand, was wearing her black brassiere, and the other articles were pink. "I feel so undressed, Hiram," she confessed, once into the tunic and the underthings removed. Her breath still came quickly, irregularly, as a result of the climb upstairs, poor woman—her weight had become a severe problem to her these last years.

"I'll try to find some things for you," Hiram said. "I certainly don't want you to have any pulmonary problems now, just at a time like this!"

"Oh, now, don't worry, Hiram." She smiled, panting a little. "It's not the exertion, it's the excitement." And that was true. All that day and the next, it seemed impossible for Emma to catch her breath, even while sitting quietly.

Ben showed them where to hang their clothes, and they descended then, all together, returning to the turbulent event, and now to the very heart of it, for by their tunics they had announced their commitment. Ben led them to the altar, where, surrounded by such relics as white chicken feathers, the Black Hand of Persecution, a Mother Mary with her heart exposed on her breast, and, in a gilt

6

frame, the famous death message of the beloved Ely Collins, the teacher Mrs. Eleanor Norton was discoursing to newsmen. Ben left them there to guide others up the stairs, and when the journalists, in their nervous and inevitably insulting manner, had moved on, Hiram introduced himself and his people to Mrs. Norton. Hiram found her every bit as gracious and wise as Sister Clara had foresaid. Her gray eyes were cool, but her friendship, once given, Hiram knew, was given forever. Around her neck, unlike the others, she wore a gold medallion, and Emma observed that the circle sewn around the cross on Mrs. Norton's tunic seemed to have straight edges, instead of being a true circle. Mrs. Norton explained that it was in reality a dodecagon, and then she elaborated briefly upon some of her private views, which Hiram found a bit complicated, but extremely interesting. Addressing herself to the uppermost segments of the dodecagon, she indicated that which pertained to ascent and descent, and, in some fascinating yet obscure way, to the disaster and the rescue. The succeeding terms were those of "illumination," "mystic fusion," and, finally, "transformation." Mrs. Norton gazed up at them, smiling gently, here eyes a-twinkle. *"Tomorrow!"* she whispered. And for the next thirty minutes, Emma could hardly catch her breath again.

Before the afternoon had passed, they met all the other original members—Mrs. Norton's husband, Dr. Wylie Norton, the world-famous lawyer Mr. Ralph Himebaugh, the Willie Halls, the widows, and so on—eventually even the prophet himself and the prophet's mother. Emma and the widow of the martyr Edward Wilson, a charming yet pious lady, like Emma heavyset and softspoken, became fast friends upon first encounter and were seldom seen apart in the hours to follow. With Sister Clara so occupied, Sister Betty—for that was her name—became a kind of patron to his Randolph Junction people, and through her who had seen it all they felt yet more nearly drawn to its true center. They learned of the severe fast and the pledge of silence that the prophet's sister, Marcella Bruno, was

7

keeping in her room alone, measures taken, Sister Betty implied, to expiate the evil brought upon them by the hateful infiltrator from the Powers of Darkness, Mr. Justin Miller of the West Condon *Chronicle,* who, against his own dark purposes, as it were, had, through announcing and exploiting their presences, strengthened and augmented the Army of the Sons of Light. She was said to be very weak, but her decline seemed almost to provide a balancing curve against the upward drive of the Brunists, the two destined to meet in final consummation, it was believed, tomorrow on the Mount of Redemption. As for Giovanni Bruno, he was a most imposing man, lean and austere, with long hair and cavernous eyes, and Hiram, in the prophet's presence, was uncommonly wonderstruck. He spoke not at all, for of course, as both Sister Clara and Mrs. Norton had observed, his purpose was unique and precise: to announce the Coming of the Light. He had done so. Further speech was superflous. His only mission now was to lead them. And this, with sober poise, he did faultlessly.

Hiram himself was interviewed on one occasion. He had stepped out onto the front porch a moment to catch a breath of air, and there had been photographed in his tunic. A man asked him, "How long have you been a member of the Brunists?"

Hiram meditated but a moment, then replied, "Perhaps all of my life."

"I thought this thing just got started this winter," the man said, scribbling furiously in a notebook.

"Yes," mused Hiram, "a man's physical life is numbered by days. But the life of his soul is rooted in the centuries!"

"Oh, I getcha," said the man, cracking chewing gum between his teeth. "You only meant that figuratively."

"No, son. Nothing that is true is merely figurative."

"Unh-hunh. Well, whaddaya think is going to happen tomorrow?"

"Tomorrow will see the conclusion," Hiram replied, "of an historical epoch."

8

"Yes, but I mean, is there gonna be spaceships or what?"

"My boy! Did Christ foresee the crown of thorns, the shape of the cross, the rolling of that certain stone? We march to meet God's call, prepared to suffer what we must. Your questions are like those of a child who asks his parents what he'll be or when he'll die."

Speechless, the foolish man left him. Hiram turned to discover Emma and Sister Betty at his back. "That was well said, Hiram," said his wife.

"Why, it was *beautiful!*" cried the other woman. "Mr. Clegg—Brother Hiram—you'd make a wonderful preacher!"

"Will we go tonight to the Mount of Redemption?" Hiram inquired of Sister Betty.

"I don't rightly know," she said. "Let's go ask Clara."

Hiram's question created, in fact, a certain controversy. Many of the newcomers, like himself, wished to see it, wished to have some picture of tomorrow's goal, the place of the Coming, but on the other hand, and especially among the native West Condoners, there were fears about their several enemies, the reporters and Mr. Miller, the mayor and the law, the so-called West Condon Common Sense Committee which had been harassing them, and, above all, the fanatical followers of Abner Baxter, the coalminer who had arrogated the local Nazarene pulpit following the tragic and untimely death of Ely Collins. Clearly—if accounts of him could be believed—he was a man consumed by a terrible hatred, yet his power as a preacher of the Gospel was never denied; it was only that, as some said, he seemed, with all his power and eloquence, to have no "radiance" about him. The suggestion that was finally accepted was that they in fact make a pilgrimage to the Mount, taking along box suppers, so that all might become acquainted with it, but that they depart late in the evening, at a time when such a journey would no longer be suspected by the foe. The suppers, then, were prepared by the women, Emma, God rest her dear soul, doing her share and more, as always.

At the same time, modest refreshments were brought out and consumed readily. Excitement, Hiram had found, always engenders a certain dryness of the throat and a nervous hunger. White underclothing arrived in enormous bundles, and Hiram selected drawers for Emma, his friends doing likewise, as necessary, in fairly certain hopes now of having their own tunics before the night was over, for Sister Betty had procured the materials and the two women were already busy with needle and thread. A rather stupid and embarrassing thing occurred at that moment. Holding up the drawers to be sure they would be large enough for Emma, Hiram had his photo snapped by a passing news photographer. Hiram saw himself in all the newspapers of the world, holding up a pair of ladies' drawers. Spying Sister Clara Collins nearby, he told her what had happened. She turned dark with indignation, asked him to point out the photographer. Then, quickly, she rounded up six other men, including Brother Ben, and they encircled the man, suggested he turn over all his film packs or risk probable damages to his fine camera. The victory was sudden and total. Later that night, on the Mount, the films were burned. A great and forever unquenchable sense of gratitude welled up in Hiram's heart.

As the evening deepened, the newsmen thinned away, much to the relief of everyone, and finally they were able to rid themselves of all the intruders; able at last to stand alone together, gauge their strength. It was considerable: well over a hundred persons already, not including nearly as many children, and it was still, they all recognized solemnly, only the day before. Hiram, accustomed to such gatherings, was able to be of much help, distributing things, helping to maintain order, taking his turn at the door to forestall any further trespasses. They were all taught the secret password, the handshake, and several other devices properly intended to close nonbelievers out of the circle of the select. From various persons of the inner group, they learned once more about the now-famous White Bird visitation in the disaster-struck mine, the early prophecies,

10

the Night of the Sign, and the other astonishing events. Mr. Himebaugh the lawyer, who was an incredibly active man, seemingly everywhere at once, even-tempered and patient to a fault, yet as though blazing from within with a terrible energy, then presented to them, in outline, the mathematical proofs for the event's inevitable occurrence on the morrow, the nineteenth of April. If there had been doubts before, they were now dispelled. Hiram was speechless—how perfectly revolved this universe of ours!—and he saw tears and amazement in Emma's eyes.

Then the teacher Mrs. Norton spoke on the meaning of the hill, of the Mount of Redemption, and this too was a deeply moving performance. "Although the transformation we envision is unrelated to the temporal and spatial dimensions of the dense earth," she said, "nevertheless, it is wholly appropriate at these times to receive the call for certain symbolic actions, not as a part of a divine dialogue, but as a means of providing a comprehensible metaphor for the rest of the world, so as better to prepare the way—" (from the others, "amens," the nodding of heads gravely) "—and, for us, as a way to exercise our spiritual discipline." ("Amens" again, applause.) "Thus, meeting on a hill, the highest point in this area, is not so much because our rescue depends on it, but because it fulfills all of these functions: it is in itself symbolic of the upward effort we are all making in order to free ourselves from our physical prisons—" (Hiram said: "True, true!") "—it is a public act and a spiritual calisthenic; it ties up all the elements of what has gone before, returning us bodily, as it were, to the site of the mine disaster, of the initiating action, and of the White Bird visitation." Again, then, the chorus of "amens" and an eruption of prayer, the start of a song, but Sister Clara stood and gestured for silence. Mrs. Norton continued: "Moreover, it is so clearly a divine request: my logs have foreshadowed it, Giovanni Bruno announced it, Mr. Himebaugh's computations provide proofs of it, and Mrs. Collins rightly interpreted it—independently, we reached the same conclusion, in other words, each through his own channels of inspiration. And, finally, it is so right a place, as all of you will soon see. A place in nature, away from man-made distortions, and, but for a single tree, a barren place, an ascetic site proper for our great spiritual drama!" Now there were cheers and prayers aplenty, a tumultuous excitement, yes, the excitement had been long building, Hiram too had sensed it, the milling about, the cameras, the white tunics, this great gathering.

And then a little man stood up, staring above and beyond them, and Hiram's heart began to race, and Sister Clara cried out, "Brother Willie Hall!"

"As it says in the Gospel," Brother Willie cried out, and there was a wave of shouting, "the Gospel of Matthew," and another wave, yet more impassioned, "the fifth chapter and the fourteenth verse," and now there were cries addressing Brother Willie and asking that he teach them the truth, which, of course, he had every intention of doing, " 'Ye are the light of the world!' " and the cries mounted and the tears began to flow, " '*And a city set on a hill cannot be hid!*' "

"No, it cannot be hid!" cried a lady, and then they prayed in earnest, they sang in earnest, they wept in joy.

And Sister Clara Collins rose tall and she said, "We go, we go to that Mount of Redemption," and how her voice rang! "we go not to die, *but to act!*" And oh! how they exulted! and oh! how their hearts leapt with a common hope! and oh! how the hallelujahs were sounded! "The Kingdom is *ours!* It awaits us! It awaits us on the Mount of Redemption! We have but to *act!* We have but to *go!* But to go and *to receive it!*" Oh! it was tremendous! it was electric! it was glorious!

O *the Sons of Light are marching to the Mount*
    where it is said
We shall find our true Redemption from this world
    of woe and dread,

12

We shall see the cities crumble and the earth give
up its dead,
　　For the end of time has come!

So come and march with us to Glory!
Oh, come and march with us to Glory!
Yes, come and march with us to Glory!
For the end of time has come!

And so, loading up with box suppers, they headed for their automobiles. On the morrow, of course, they would march out there barefoot, but tonight's pilgrimage was primarily to familiarize the new people, and the cars, they reasoned, would permit them a quick removal in the event the enemy—any enemy—should appear. Tomorrow they faced persecutions, suffering, perhaps even death. Tonight they wished only for peace, desiring not to push God's hand. The following strategy was decided upon. A guard would be posted throughout the supper, and, at the first sight of approaching car lights on the mine road, they would adjourn instantly to their autos. West Condoners, most familiar with the route, would lead the escape, forming a caravan and keeping their own lights extinguished until the last possible moment, in an effort to speed by their persecutors before these latter realized what was taking place.

It was really incredibly beautiful out on the Mount, one felt indeed quite in the palm of God's gentle hand, a dark sky above but clear, the tipple of old Number Nine silhouetted against it, a glorious taste of burgeoning spring in the night air. They built a large bonfire, there sang songs familiar to them all from campmeetings and evangelistic outings, heard important declarations of faith from many of the newcomers. "Oh, I thank God I am here tonight! I thank God my Mommy and Daddy were Christian people! I thank God I am ready!" As they sang, a kind of nostalgia swept over them and it astonished them all to discover, as if for the first time, the true power, the inspiration, the profound significance of their songs' collective message. Someone had had the foresight to bring marshmallows, which the children roasted in the flames of their fire, and their innocent gaiety soothed the grown-ups' fears: yes, surely, to such belongeth the Kingdom of God. Giovanni Bruno, who, Hiram was told, may have perished in the disaster that shook the very earth beneath their feet, and might now be inhabited by a superior spirit, thus accounting further for his fragile taciturnity, never participated directly with them, though he passed among them freely, now smiling approvingly, now nodding solemnly, now raising his hand in a sort of benediction.

Standing out there on the hill, Hiram was not ignorant of, nor did he shy from, the recognition of the sensual excitation that accompanied the spiritual one: the cool night breeze around their all but unprotected loins, the descriptive folds of the tunics, the inciting fragrance, and the strangeness—and, when one passed before the fire, his body was as though revealed to those behind him. And yet, though perhaps it enhanced the fervor of their songs and prayers, there was a total chastity, not merely of action but of thought, pervading them all. The human body, after all, was an instrument of lust, but it was also—could also be—must *always* be!—a divinely created instrument of grace, consecrated to the Lord's service, beautiful in all its parts, when all its parts were subservient to piety and prudence. The body of a woman of sin, even when perfectly proportioned, was a hideous abomination, a repulsive and malformed tool of evil—yet these women now silhouetted against the flames, though sunken like Mrs. Norton or gauntly bold and athletic like Clara Collins, though wizened like Mrs. Bruno or inflated like his dear Emma or Sister Betty Wilson, possessed bodies which, by their modesty and their holiness, were consummately beautiful.

Besides the old songs, they sang many new ones written by Brother Ben Wosznik, including his exultant "White Bird" ballad, that, perhaps more than any other single

14

thing, most immediately conjoined them all to this common cause:

> On a cold and wintry eighth of January,
> Ninety-eight men entered into the mine;
> Only one of these returned to tell the story
> Of that disaster that struck—

"Lights!" cried the lookout. "*Lights on the mine road!*"

They gasped, panicked, flew in a mad scurry back toward their cars. They knew not this enemy and what a man knows not, he fears unreasonably. People cried without cause. Clara stood on the hill and shouted to all of them their instructions. Ben, at the foot, shepherded each into a car, and it was most confusing. Hiram and Emma were somehow separated, Hiram's own car filling up with complete strangers, and just before pulling the door to, he heard the lookout cry, "They's fifteen or twenty cars of 'em!" Hiram watched the fire being extinguished, a little guilty that he had run so frantically.

And then it began. Darkly, the procession eased away from the Mount of Redemption and turned toward West Condon, toward that advancing column, and there was no choice but to fall into place quickly, else be left behind, indefensible victims. They drove in rather rapidly, a little *too* rapidly, Hiram thought, for he observed there was a deep ditch to either side of them, and for one dark fear-stained moment he saw it all as stupid, insane, a blind and foolish covenant with whimsey, what had brought him—?

Then he saw the lights ahead and he thought of nothing at all but the immediate danger, the car in front of him, the ditch to his right. Yes, indeed, there were many of them; these advancing lights guided them. And then there were their own lights and, his heart leaping to his throat, he threw his on, lights everywhere, and suddenly . . .

But how did it happen? If all of it seemed a dream, how much more so this jolting dizzying moment! If all a whirl, this was its violent vortex! Hiram remembered something of the later return: the thick flow of their great procession through that little town, the congregation of automobiles jammed in all directions around the Bruno home. Of that night, there remained scattered images, the vigil, the weeping, the mournful making of tunics and tunics and tunics. There were public confessions and old enmities were dissolved in prayer and awe. No one slept. There was that profoundly moving incident of the gold medallion, when, just before dawn, the hysteria abating and their great task upon them, the deeply grieving lady Mrs. Eleanor Norton—had she not been a spiritual mother to the girl?—stood, approached, in a walk more of death than life, Sister Clara Collins, and, wordlessly, hung that medallion around Clara's neck. Whereupon they embraced and wept like schoolgirls, and all who saw wept too.

But the Sacrifice itself: where was he? when was it? who was there with him? what did he do? what did they do? He could never remember. Only split-second, almost motionless pictures remained. He saw her body hurtling by. But could it have been she? No, given the position of his car when he stopped, the position of the girl where they found her, it was quite impossible. Yet, he was sure of it: he saw her body hurtling by. There was another picture: lights askew, beamed in all directions. This terrified him. It was too bright, too harsh, too anarchical, too resplendent. Cars wrecked, in ditches, piled into each other—the grill of his own was smashed, his knee banged up, but he never recalled the crash, never remembered stopping, did not feel for hours his damaged knee, though afterwards it plagued him to his dying day: he recalled only the deranged play of lights and the moaning. Another picture, but this one was at the end: the girl's body in the back seat of a car. Her right arm hung off the seat, her left lay pinched between her body and the back of the seat, her eyes open. He could never forget this, because he had helped put her there—where had he found the strength? it seemed incredible to him after!—and could have rearranged her,

16

closed her eyelids, but did not. They were a good while untangling that heaped disarray of autos and the girl was slight, had bled much. By the time they entered her into her house, she had rigidified in that peculiar position, and so remained those intense hours that immediately followed.

And, finally, there was his picture of the girl herself, Marcella Bruno, lying, face up, in the ditch: lovely, yet wasted, drawn, so small! so helpless! Her face was serene, her eyes closed, her lips slightly parted, but her small body, enshrouded in its white tunic with the brown embroidery, was grotesquely twisted . . . one of her feet seemed even to point the wrong way. There was, he was sure, talk of rushing her to a hospital or of calling an ambulance: in such a situation, there was always such talk, and perhaps he himself even made a similar suggestion. And he seemed to remember the fear expressed that if she were turned over to any authority, even a doctor, she would be unable to join them on the Mount and thus could conceivably forfeit her eternal salvation. Though all of this may only have been re-created in later conversations (the fear of authority in some form or other was there, certainly, for Hiram himself knew a great anxiety). Anyway, this did happen: the girl's eyes opened suddenly and her lips parted as though to speak. All leaned forward—he himself must have been quite close—but instead of a sound, all that emerged was a bright red bubble of blood that ballooned, burst, and dribbled down her cheeks. These things Hiram Clegg—who was to become Bishop Clegg of Randolph Junction, the first President of the International Council of Brunist Bishops, the man to nominate Mrs. Clara Collins as their first Evangelical Leader and Organizer, and who would be, some years later, the Bishop of the State of Florida—carried away from that humbling experience: the body hurtling by, the mad play of lights, Dr. Wylie Norton's plump knees in the cinders, the bubble of blood, the girl in the back seat of a car.

Perhaps other occurrences of note transpired. Some seemed to remember a luminous white bird, perched high

17

above them on a telephone cable. Others spoke in later years of a heart-shaped bloodstain on the breast of Marcella's tunic, just where the circle and cross were. Many vouched that a priest had passed among them, solemn and ashen. There were those who recalled that the prophet dipped his fingers in the blood of his sister and therewith marked his forehead with a small dark cross, and some believed he so marked all those present. Hiram, it was true, did find blood on his forehead after, and so he was never in a position to deny this account. Yet if it occurred, he had wholly forgot it. The most persistent legend in later years—and the only one which Hiram knew to be false— was that the girl, in the last throes of death, had pointed to the heavens, and then, miraculously, maintained this gesture forever after. This death in the ditch, the Sacrifice, became in the years that followed a popular theme for religious art, and the painters never failed to exploit this legend of the heavenward gesture, never failed to omit the bubble of blood. Which was, of course, as it should be.

PART ONE
The White Bird

Do not fear what you are about to suffer.

—REVELATION TO JOHN 2:10

1

Clouds have massed, doming in the small world of West Condon. The patches of old snow, crusted black with soot in full daylight, now appear to whiten as the sky dulls toward evening. The temperature descends. Slag smoke sours the air. Only eight days since the new year began, but the vague hope its advent traditionally engenders has already gone stale. It is true, there are births, deaths, injuries, rumors, jokes, matings, and conflicts as usual, but a wearisome monotony seems to inform even the best and worst of them.

Schools exhale the young. Not yet convinced they care to take on the hard work of the world, most of them gather and disperse around pool tables and pinball machines, in drugstores and down at the bus station, or simply on corners. Basketball games are got up in schoolyards and back alleys. The members of the high school varsity work out briefly in the gym, then go home to rest up for tonight's game. Superboys wing cold-fingered through trees in the cause of justice while, below, slingshot wars are waged. Little girls play house or give injections to ailing dolls, while their older sisters pop gum, slam doors, gossip, suck at milkshakes, or merely sit in wonder at the odd age upon them. Gangs of youngsters fall upon the luckless eccentrics, those with big ears or short pants or restless egos, and sullen hates are nursed. Rebellious cigarette butts are lit, lipped, flicked, ground underheel.

Out at Deepwater No. 9 Coalmine, the day shift rise up out of the workings by the cagefuls, jostle like tough but tired ballplayers into the showers. Some will go to homes, some to hunt or talk about it, some to fill taverns, some to

21

card tables; many will go to the night's ball game against Tucker City. In town, the night shift severally eat, dress, bitch, wisecrack, wait for cars or warm up their own. A certain apprehension pesters them, but it's a nightly commonplace. Some joke to cover it, others complain sourly about wages or the contents of their lunchbuckets.

On Main Street, shops close and soon highballs will be poured at kitchen sinks, cards dealt at the Elks or the Country Club. Business is in its usual post-Christmas slump. Inventories are under way. Taxes must be figured. Dull stuff. Time gets on, seems to run and drag at the same time. People put their minds on supper and the ball game, and talk, talk about anything, talk and listen to talk. Religion, sex, politics, toothpastes, food, movie stars and prizefighters. Fishing, horoscopes, women's clothes, automobiles, human nature. Circles and squares, whores, virgins, wives, daughters, time and money. Boredom and good times. Putting on weight, going steady, cancer, evolution, parents, the good old days, Jesus, baseball trades. Sadists, saints, and eating places. Tick talk tick talk. Smoking cures. The job, better jobs, how dumb the kids are, television, coalmining, the hit parade. Indigestion cures. Jews, Arabs, Communists, Negroes, colleges. Impotence cures. The Holy Spirit. The state tournament, filters, West Condon, West Condoners—mostly that: West Condoners, what's wrong with them, what dumb things they've done, what they've been talking about, what's wrong with the way they talk, who's putting out, jokes they've told, why they're not happy, what's wrong with their homelife.

Some of the talk, though not the best of it, gets into the town newspaper, the West Condon *Chronicle*, which now young carriers fold and pack militantly into canvas bags, soon to fan out over the community on bikes on their nightly delivery of the word, dreaming as they throw that they are aces of the Cardinal staff. Up front, publisher and editor Justin Miller, himself an ex-carrier, cradles the telephone, pivots wearily in his swivel chair, stares out the window, unwashed in fourteen years, on the leaden parking lot. It is scabby with dead weeds, gray ice patches. On the other side of the lot: colorless hindside of the West Condon Hotel. His assistant, Lou Jones, hammers out copy for tomorrow at the other desk. He'd ask Jones to cover tonight's basketball game, but he knows Jones resents assignments that have anything to do with adolescents. Doris the waitress emerges from the rear door of the hotel coffeeshop with slops, empties them into the incinerator, pauses there a moment to pick her nose. Miller wonders why Fisher, the old guy who runs the hotel, manages to find only these blighted moldering dogs to work for him.

Behind the window of an old gray weatherbowed house in the town's cheap housing development district, a former buddy and high school basketball teammate of Miller's, Oxford Clemens, stands staring out. Children in the dirt street outside push their game of kick-the-can into the gathering dark, shrieking full-grown obscenities in shrill glee. Clemens yawns, scratches his crotch, chances to be looking when the streetlight goes on, grins at it. He turns and reaches for a pair of pants heaped up on a chair. There is a large rip in the seat of his jockey shorts; the khaki pants are war surplus, limp and long unlaundered. At 5:12, one hundred thirty-eight minutes before game time, a blowzy postwar Buick dappled with rust rattles up in front of the old place, sounds its deep-throated Model T horn. Oxford Clemens shambles out, buttoning a yellow silk shirt up against the skin, carrying a leather jacket and his bucket. He piles in back with Tub Puller, who is snoring. "Evenin', ladies," Clemens greets as he pulls the door to. Pooch Minicucci who is driving says nothing, but Angelo Moroni, Clemens' faceboss at the mine, turns around and says, "Hey, Ferd, is that the only fucking shirt you got?" Clemens grins faintly, lets it go.

The short drive out to Deepwater No. 9 is dominated by Moroni who talks without cease. The subject matter is getting out of the mine, getting out of West Condon, getting out of this whole useless life, and getting into

23

women. Oxford works his long arms into his leather jacket, accidentally jostling Tub Puller. Puller lashes out irritably with his stubby right arm, slams Clemens in the chest. Puller is an airdox shotfirer by trade, has a body and face the immensity and consistency of an iceboxful of bread dough, says next to nothing all day long. Moroni is a short muscular man with a cocky round face, wideset eyes that turn down smilingly at the corners, short upper lip, broad nose, and twenty-seven years in the mines. He wears a hat on the side of his head and has a habit of tipping it down toward his nose when having a drink or playing pinochle with his buddy Vince Bonali, or talking to women. Minicucci is thin, with a ridged Roman nose. He has a speech defect so that he cannot pronounce his "r's" and in the mine he is a triprider. Clemens is a timberman, tall with tousled yellow hair and narrow bloodshot eyes. At this moment he is coughing, a smoker's airy wheeze, doubled forward. "You cocksucker, Puller!" he rasps gamely through his teeth, leaning back. Puller unceremoniously whacks him again, squinting all the while out the window into the night, clearly disgusted to be awake. That's what a man gets who's born to be Ferd the Turd. Clemens lights a smoke. He's used to it, but that doesn't cheer him.

"They ain't no place to pouk," Minicucci complains, arriving at the mine.

"Go on up under the watertower," Moroni says.

"Gee, Ange, it's agin the wules. I don't—"

"Fuck the 'wules,' Pooch! You go park there and anybody asks, you tell them Ange said for you to, hear?"

It is 5:28. There is only one light burning in the front office building, more lights on toward the portal. The tipple is barely visible against the starless sky. The watertower, silver-bellied above them, is of course not obscured at all.

In the washhouse, Clemens removes his leather jacket, his yellow silk shirt, his loafers, and his khaki pants. He bends over, exposing the rip in his shorts, and a broadchested man, dark with yet darker heavy eyebrows, smiles, takes aim, cracks his butt with a wet towel. Clemens yelps, spins and throws himself savagely on the man with the towel. Angelo Moroni and Tuck Filbert pull them apart. "You fatass catlicker wop, Bonali! I done licked you wunst, I'll lick you agin!" Clemens' thin face is awry with his fury.

"Lick this, crybaby," says Vince Bonali, clutching his genitals with one thick-wristed fist and thrusting his round belly forward. He is laughing, but without humor.

At the gym, they'll be turning on the lights. Old Patch the janitor and a couple of the freshmen will be sweeping down the floor. Clemens can feel the polish, taste the hardwood, smell the sheer joy of it. He dresses and thinks about that, tries to forget about Bonali and Moroni and all the rest. He pulls on his stained bluish jacket, frayed at the cuffs, shoves heavy gloves into the pockets, picks up his bucket. For all his effort, tension still presses at his eyes and holds his jaws clamped. Bonali is dressed but is still horsing around, has just blistered the thin ass of a tall bony miner named Giovanni Bruno with his towel. Bruno says nothing, barely flinches, simply turns pale and stares coldly at Bonali. Several laugh. "Hit him agin!" cries Chester Johnson. "I think he likes it!" More laughter. Bruno's buddy and sole protector, Preacher Collins, has already gone below and Bruno is left alone.

"Hey, listen, you guys!" Bonali bellows in his deep-chested baritone. He waves a scrap of yellow paper. "I gotta give you bums a little *cool*-chur! Boys, I got a *poem!*" Bruno claws for the paper, but Bonali shoves him away.

Clemens pauses, returns to his locker, fishes in the pockets of his pants hanging inside, as Bonali reads: "*My Mother!*"

Now everybody is laughing and shouting. "*Give me that!*" Bruno cries, his voice strained like a child hurt in play, but three grinning miners hold him back, Johnson grabbing him around the middle, Mario Juliano and Bill Lawson pinning his arms back.

"*From out of thy immortal womb—*"

There is a roar of hooting and laughter, and all the men

25

crowd around to see and hear. Bruno, encircled, is crying. Johnson pumps his fist in front of Bruno as though masturbating him. Clemens gives no least damn about Bruno, but he can appreciate his position. He lights a small firecracker and tucks it into Bonali's hip pocket, exits for the lamphouse, tag in hand.

The tag is brass. Stamped on its face are a small 9, a much larger 1213, and at the bottom the letters G.D.C.Co. All the tags have the 9 and the letters, but only Oxford Clemens' bears 1213. Like the numbers on basketball jerseys, it tells you who the players are. At 6:03, he hands it over to old Pop Hendricks and receives in exchange his lamp and battery, similarly numbered. Pop hooks the brass tag on a large board which schematically describes the mine workings.

As Clemens is fitting the lamp into the groove in his helmet his faceboss, Angelo Moroni, stomps into the lamphouse, steel-toed boots sounding off the dry wooden floor. Moroni is laughing still about Bruno's poem, but when he sees Clemens, he wipes away the laugh with a bunched flicker of his thick grimy fist, growls something about the cracker. "I oughta take away your fucking butts, Clemens," he says, but low, not loud enough for Pop to hear. Moroni and Bonali are old wop buddies.

Oxford grins, exhibiting a missing eyetooth, changes the subject. "Ain't seen Willie Hall?" Hall is Clemens' assigned buddy in the mine.

"No. Whatsa matter? Ain't he here?"

"Ain't seen him."

"Trouble is, he can't stand working with you, Ferd."

Clemens shrugs, grins again. Moroni hands his tag to Pop Hendricks. "Want me to wait for him, or—?"

"No, wait a minute," says Moroni. "There's a new kid here tonight." He takes his lamp and battery, clumps with them to the door of the lamphouse, cranes his head out. "Hey, Rosselli? C'mere!"

Unwanted dead or alive, that's how it always was with

Oxford Clemens. They called him Ferd, Ferd the Turd, and either let him alone or let him have it. He didn't know his old man and his old lady wanted him croaked, wanted his Aunt Marge to kill him soon as he came out, but Aunt Marge never killed anything, not even cockroaches or chickens, for she believed in the peace everlasting and God's infinite mercy and eating the bread. And the teachers cracked his head with rulers and the kids at school, all younger than he, called him Bully and Ferd and Hayseed and threw rocks at him, ganged up on him. Only way they'd ever beat him. And they threw iceballs at him and tore up his books and threw spitballs at him and busted his tooth once with a bottle. That's how it was. He learned to take it easy and keep his eyes open. He stole himself a good gun, did a lot of hunting, caught squirrels on the run, then stomped their heads to stop them flopping around in the brush, but left them lie: people don't eat squirrels anymore. And he stole him some good line and a couple hooks, used grasshoppers, worms, plain old houseflies, and pulled bluegills out of the fat muddy streams on humid afternoons, setting world records till his arms got tired, and he strung them up on a piece of wire hanger, stuck them back in the water to stop them flopping around in the weeds, and left them there: Nobody likes to clean bluegills. And he stole him a basketball from the high school one night after a ball game and, being tall and rough, he could bully the young boys at Lincoln School of an evening. He got fancy with his hands and hooked them in from thirty feet, but nobody would stick around long with Ferd Clemens hogging the game, so he'd say to hell with them and go on popping long ones by himself, setting world records until the sun was long since gone, and then he'd have him a smoke and drop by the poolhall, shoot him some snooker, an ace from the age of eleven, and cuss like crazy, making those old guys split their sides.

Tony Rosselli introduces himself, and Oxford grunts in reply. They board the cage together, take hold of the rings.

Clemens now wears gloves, but Rosselli, without, flinches, not having realized the rings would be cold. Joe Castiglione, Mike Strelchuk, and a couple greasers named Cooley and Wosznik get on with them. They switch their lamps on and Castiglione trains his on Rosselli's new blue denims. "Hey, boys, who's the dude?" he shouts, and the others put their lamps on him too as the cage hurtles through blackness some five or six hundred feet to the bottom.

There, a half dozen miners are waiting for the mantrip, sitting idly on their buckets, and the arrival of the new man enlivens them. Foregoing their usual accounts of the arts of Ferd Clemens' sister, they turn instead on young Rosselli. Somebody suggests they maybe ought to initiate him. Rosselli grins awkwardly, full-faced brown-eyed boy of eighteen, maybe nineteen. Rare to see a young fellow like Rosselli starting in the mines these days: the assumption is that someone must have pulled strings to get him the job. Bill Lawson stares at the boy and stuffs a wad of tobacco in his cheeks. "Old Willie get fired, Ferd?" he asks, and spits through his teeth. Lawson pitches semipro ball in his off hours, and the tobacco is part of his style.

"Make room for the dude," says Juliano.

Oxford Clemens sits on his bucket and gazes dully at a far wall, nibbling a matchstick.

"Hey, kid, whose ass did you suck?" asks Joe Castiglione, whose brother has been out of work almost two years. "Who'd you little buddy suck, Ferd?"

At the gym, they'll be coming through the doors, filling it up with noise and color, waving, shaking hands, shouting at each other. Boys in aprons will be selling Cokes, and the cheerleaders, orange WCs on their black sweaters, will be bouncing up and down and clapping their hands, no matter what. Oxford can hear the buzzer and it makes his hands sweat and tingle. In that gym, one day his sophomore year, he was fooling around with a basketball when the team came in to practice. He was feeling hot, so he said to hell with them and just kept on shooting. A tall rangy kid with dark brows jogged up and caught the ball under the basket and pitched it back out to him. He popped another and the tall kid grinned and flipped the ball out to him again. It reached him going like ninety—that guy could really let go that ball. Oxford aimed and popped another. The kid pulled it out of the nets and walked out and said his name was Justin Miller, and he said his name was Oxford Clemens. Then Justin—well, his real name was Tiger, of course—Tiger introduced Oxford to Coach Bayles and he worked out every night with them after that. Tiger showed him how to rebound and tip in and jump shoot and bounce pass and they gave him a suit, and one day Tiger said, "Come on, Ox baby, pop one!" And after that they all called him Ox, he was skinny as a rail, but they called him Ox, *Big Ox*, and all year long he and Tiger Miller threw basketballs at each other and into nets. There was one night against Tucker City when Big Ox laid in 34 points and tied what was then Tiger Miller's high school record. It was the last minutes of the game and he and Tiger broke away with the ball and ended up a mile in front of everybody under the basket all alone. Tiger passed the ball to shoot, but that meant the new all-time record, so Ox grinned and handed it back to Tiger, and Tiger grinned right back and said, "You tip, Ox!" and he laid it up on the rim and, everybody pounding down on them, Ox arched up like a tall bird and lifted the ball light as an egg into the hoop. And it was a new all-time record and they carried him around on their shoulders after and wrote him up in all the papers, and his sister Dinah, even though she couldn't come, she read all about it.

Oxford and the others gathered at the bottom board a mantrip at 6:33 and ride toward their working places in the maze of black-walled rooms off New Main South, ninth to sixteenth entries. The light from bare bulbs glistens off the rough cracks in the roof as the iron box rocks and sways, rattles and shrieks, making too much noise for talk.

In its urgent rhythms, Oxford can almost hear his old Aunt Marge, who raised him and Dinah, letting go at the Church of the Nazarene:

"*. . . and oh God you have mercy on them children God (amen) show them the everlastin' peace (in Jesus' name) stop that boy acussin' warsh his feet (oh yes amen) and God stop Dinah seekin' men so as she might seek Thee (yes tell it Sister Marge) warsh her feet (amen amen) and God do stop Oxford asmokin' and adrinkin' You show him the way warsh his feet (hear her Lord) for the Day of His Judgment is at hand (yes God) and verily the Son of Man is acomin' in the glorious light of God the Father (yes) with all His angels (they are comin') and outa his mouth they comes a sharp sword (yes yes) and all these here sinners and false prophets shall be cast alive into the fire and brimstone (oh save us) and all things shall be made new and the poor and the true shall inherit (we shall inherit) and so for the love of Jesus Christ oh God save my Dinah and Oxford from their adulteratin' ways warsh them clean in the blood of the Lamb (oh God) let the dove of Grace descend on them (warsh them white) lead them home oh God teach them the love and the everlastin' glory oh God I'm callin' to Ye kin Ye hear me God warsh 'em warsh 'em all over God warsh their feet (amen)!*"

When the mantrip stops at the ninth entry and there is a moment of silence, Tony Rosselli turns to Clemens and asks, "Say, wait, ain't you Ox Clemens? Didn't you play on the team that went to State?"

Yes, and he wore silk shirts and stopped screwing his sister's friends at Waterton, made out with all the fancy-pants high school girls instead. He'd still stop in for a round of snooker now and then, but just to let the old men clap him on the back and call him Big Ox. And he and Tiger took the team to State that year and only lost the final game, getting named, both of them, to the All-State All-Star Team, and just sophomores. Only the next year it turned out Oxford was ineligible for being too old. He could hardly believe it, but when he found it was really true, he gave them all the royal digit and went down in the mines. Tiger had a new buddy he played ball with and Oxford almost never saw him, except when he went to see the games, had to put up instead with his bucktooth mine-buddy Willie Hall, who went to church with his Aunt Marge and was too scared of the mines to work more than half the time. Oxford never got written up anymore and those fancypants girls hung up on him if he tried to call. His Aunt Marge went completely off her head and fell down in a froth in campmeeting one night and died of a stroke. He had the blues something rotten all the time. He went to Waterton every week, drank with Dinah till he was sick, and tumbled her girlfriends when they weren't busy.

Clemens and Rosselli leave the mantrip at the eleventh entry because Clemens wants to speak to somebody in that area, a buggy runner named Eddie Wilson. Bill Lawson and his buddy Mike Strelchuk follow them off. They wait for Oxford to turn down the entry, and then they sidle up next to Rosselli. Each takes an elbow. "C'mon, Tony," says Strelchuk with a toothy big-jowled grin. "We'll walk you up toward the working area."

A few feet away, Wilson is saying: "No, Ferd, goldarn it, I'm tellin' ye, I ain't lettin' ye have the borry of my dog, and that's it. I got me a hankerin' to maybe take the pup and go huntin' myself this weekend anyhow." Clemens spits, gives it up.

Sitting there alone at a cracked creamy table one rainy week night, then, about midnight, and so desolate even Mrs. Dobie had waddled off to bed, the two of them sharing a sour beer, Oxford got to talking on about how he was feeling so very down, how his life was all used up, he might as well quit, and there weren't even any girls in the place tonight. Dinah showed deep age scars cutting through her forehead and under her eyes and around her mouth, and it made Oxford feel miserable and sick. He wished to hell he had some money to give her, send her off on a vacation somewhere, out West maybe, or buy her a new silk dress, spruce her up—Jesus! he was very sad. And while he was staring at his sister very sad she said, "C'mon, Oxford, you might as well stay here with me tonight." Nobody was around to notice, so they went upstairs, joking and feeling a little like dumb kids. In bed, she played with him a little, but he couldn't get it up, it just wasn't any good, so they laughed and dropped off to sleep, and then they both woke up in the middle of the night, humping away to beat hell. . . .

When Clemens arrives at the fourteenth, he discovers Rosselli down on his stomach, Strelchuk and Castiglione sitting on him, pinning his arms. The boy's face is smeared with blood and coal dust, and Strelchuk and Castiglione are rubbing coal dust into his new clothes. Jinx Pontormo kicks the stuff into his face. Tuck Filbert stands a few feet away with a big grin on his broad-jawed face. Strelchuck's buddy Bill Lawson comes up with a compressed-air hose. "Pull down his britches, boys, and we'll treat the baby dude to a little initiation goose!" he shouts, and lets fly a chaw of tobacco.

Ely Collins, the Nazarene preacher, emerges tall and gray from the entry, frowns, warns: "You boys oughtn't to clown around like that. It ain't right."

Clemens essays a couple steps forward, but Filbert, Pontormo, and a couple other guys get in his way. Strelchuk and Castiglione try to roll Rosselli over, but in the effort lose their grip, and the boy breaks free of them. Lawson runs over to help, and Rosselli, lashing out wildly, catches him on the side of the head with his new steel-toed boot, sends the older miner sprawling. Strelchuk and Castiglione leap on Rosselli cursing, pin his arms and legs. On his back, the boy keeps twisting and jerking, but they have him good now.

"Okay, get his pants!" Strelchuk gasps.

"Little shit," Lawson crabs, his hands trembling. He has a long bleeding gash on his face, and his false teeth are knocked awry. He and Pontormo unbuckle the kid's pants and rip them down off him.

The boy's struggling flesh, leaping like a chicken with its neck wrung, is a strange creamy white against the black earth. Strelchuk and Castiglione try to force the boy's legs back—Strelchuk clips him in the belly with the side of his hand, and the boy doubles up. They force his knees up against his chest, Rosselli still not giving up.

Collins steps into it. "Now, stop it, boys! Somebody's gonna get hurt! Please! In the name of Jesus Christ, I ask you to stop!"

But there is too big a sweat up. Collins gets elbowed aside. "Okay, Bill!" grunts Castiglione, "she's looking at you—*ram the fucker in!*" Lawson, pale, almost white under the coal dust with hurt and rage, seizes the air hose.

"*Hold it!*" Oxford Clemens slams his way past the four or five guys in the way, his bare blade flashing in the wavery light of the dull bulbs and gleaming headlamps. "Bill, baby, you make one move with that there hose and I'll dig me a hole in your fat belly so deep they kin dump six loads in there!" Lawson freezes, stares icily at the knife less than two feet from his face. Clemens' hand is tense, controlled, inches forward as though hungry to perform. "Okay, you ladies have got your wad off, now git your fat fairy asses off'n my buddy before I gotta dock me a few balls."

Castiglione and Strelchuk let go their grip, Strelchuk grinning and brushing himself off, but Castiglione stands half crouching, facing Clemens. "You think you're pretty fucking smart, Ferd, with that blade," says Castiglione, edging toward him.

Young Rosselli stands, pulls his pants up, buckles his belt. He moves over behind Castiglione.

Clemens smiles. "Jist regulatin' the odds, fatso. Anytime you wanna go it alone—"

"*Hey! What the fuck is going on here?*" It is Angelo

Moroni. All turn toward him except Clemens, who takes a sideways step to get the faceboss in the corner of his eye, while keeping his gaze locked warily on Lawson and Castiglione. There is a general relaxation. Moroni glances at the knife, at Rosselli, at Lawson, sizing things up. He has been in the mines for twenty-seven years. "Gimme that blade, Ferd," he says quietly.

Clemens flicks it shut, drops it in his own pocket, turns his back. "C'mon, Rosselli," he says, and puts his hand on the boy's shoulder to lead him south, toward the fifteenth.

"Better get your face doctored, Bill," Moroni is heard saying, and somebody lets a grumbling curse.

Well, shit, Oxford thinks, Moroni is right. He's got to get out of the mines. He's not the kind of guy to break his back down here. Better get out as soon as he can, time is running out on him, and if he doesn't make the move quick, he never will. Figures maybe he ought to get him a car one way or another and go out East or out West and take Dinah, and anybody ask him his name, goddamn it, he'll tell them it's Bill or Jack or Danny.

He and Rosselli turn right out of New Main South into the fifteenth crosscut, then right again down the fifth north air course. At the sixth east stub entry, Rosselli sees the other men and starts to turn in, but Clemens nods: "C'mon."

They angle left a few feet, then right, huddle up behind a pillar of coal. A cutter lies like a long-dead animal up near the abandoned face. Falls betray a slow squeeze. It is 7:32. At the gym, the game has probably begun. Clemens' fingers itch for the tip. He leans back on the pillar, pulls a pack of cigarettes out of his jacket pocket. Rosselli grins. "Gee, Ox, I wanna thank you for helping me out back there. I was in a bad spot, and, well, shit, I—"

Clemens shrugs if off, offers the pack to Rosselli. "Light up and fergit about it, buddy."

Rosselli hesitates, looks around, his headlamp slicing through the unfamiliar blackness, bringing timbers and tunnels and strange equipment into momentary view. He accepts a cigarette, fits it in his mouth. His lips are puffy, cracked, and there is blood, crusted with black dust, on his chin and right cheek. The mine is silent except for the distant scrape of machinery and voices, and what seems to be a sound nearby somewhat like that of bees.

2

There was light and
post drill leaped smashed the
turned over whole goddamn car kicking
felt it in his ears, grabbed his bucket, and turned from
the face, but then the second
"Hank! Hank Harlowe! I cain't see nothin'! Hank?"
Vince Bonali knew what it was and knew they had to
get out. He told Duncan to keep the boys from jumping
the gun and went for the phone in
saw it coming and crouched but it
"Wet a rag there! Git it on your face!"
seemed like it bounced right off the
Red Baxter's crew had hardly begun loading the first
car when the power went off. Supposed the ventilator fan
had stopped working, because the phone
"Jesus! Jesus! Help me! Oh dear God!"
came to still holding the shovel but his
looked like a locomotive coming
One of the firebosses was telling the night mine manager
a story about a nun who sat on a crucifix, when the phone
rang. "Wait a minute," laughed the night mine manager,
reaching for the phone, "I got a new one Lou Jones was
telling about— Hello? Yeah, speaking."
The voice from the tenth east shop stretched up pinched
and attenuated and leaked out into his ear a copper whine:

"Ain't no power down here, and they's a lotta dust. Seems like the air ain't movin'. Can you check the—?"

"Okay, okay. Hang on." The night mine manager leaned up from his desk and then again the phone

Mike Strelchuk had just clapped his buddy old Bill Lawson on the shoulders, reminding him it was just a gag, forget it, but Bill was hopping sore and swore he'd even it up with Rosselli and that goddamn hillbilly. Bill had walked over toward where the green light marked the first-aid gear, the gash on his cheek looking pretty mean, and Strelchuk had turned into fourteenth west. He had bumped into old Ely Collins, the holy-roller preacher lately given to seeing white birds winging around down here, and together they'd got right of way into the working area. At the stub entry they had come on Collins' useless buddy Giovanni Bruno, leaning up next to a pillar mindlessly scratching his ass. "Christ, go play with yourself somewheres else! We got work to do!" Mike had shouted, and had just taken a grip on Bruno's elbow to jostle him along when all of a sudden it felt like his ears would burst, but he didn't hear a thing. He still had a grip on Bruno's bony elbow when the second one hit—hard. Floor seemed to heave, threw him off his feet, top crashed down, chunk batted off his helmet, face bit into the cinders. Still had ahold on something and he cried, "Bruno! Hey—you okay?" But Bruno didn't answer. Strelchuk was scared maybe he had yanked the guy's elbow off . . . or maybe what he held was now just a piece of a dead man. He switched his light back on, didn't know how it got switched off, maybe it wasn't on before, and aimed it down on Bruno. His goddamn face was white as the Virgin's behind with feathery black streaks on his cheekbones, but his eyes were open and blinking—his mouth gaped, but nothing came out. Strelchuk hauled him to his feet, though they both had to crouch because the roof was down aslant. It was hotter and smokier than the griddles of hell.

A ritual buzzer alerts the young athletes on the West Condon court and strikes a blurred roar from the two confronting masses of spectators. In a body, all stand. The mute patterns of run-pass-leap-thrust dissolve, congealing into two tight knots on either extremity of the court, each governed by a taut-faced dark-suited hierarch. Six young novices in black, breasts ablaze with the mark of their confession, discipline the brute roars into pulsing chants with soft loops of arm and skirt, while, at their backs, five acolytes of the invading persuasion pressed immodestly into sleek diabolic red, rattle talismans with red and white paper tails, seeking to neutralize the efficacy of the West Condon locomotive. Young peddlers circulate, selling condiments indiscriminately to all. A light oil of warm-up perspiration anoints the shoulders of the ten athletes chosen as they explode out of their respective rings to confront each other. Some of them cross themselves, some clap and cry oaths, others tweak their genitals.

Eddie Wilson didn't know what it was hit him. He still couldn't think. He was overseas again and the earth was alive with powder going off and he was scared to die. Then he thought it was a plain fall. Pain was a small hot stab behind him, but he knew it was worse because he couldn't move. Couldn't even move a finger. He tried to cry out. Couldn't make a sound. Did the others know what had happened to him? Where was his buddy Tommy? Didn't they care? He felt as though he had shrunk, now sat bunched inside his skull. He wanted his wife Betty. He opened his eyes. His lamp arrowed a cloudy ray out into the darkness—*the lights were out!*

Bonali had told them to stay put when he went for the phone, but with the power gone and the vent system off, air scorching with suspended dust that could flame up any second, the need for action grabbed at them. Duncan, left in charge, couldn't hold it back, and they started to break away. Brevnik, choking with terror and screaming

"It's coming!" was the first to go, and Georgie Lucci followed on his heels. Pooch Minicucci couldn't find his buddy Cravens and raced after Brevnik and Lucci, thinking he was getting left behind. "Lee! Lee!" he cried, and ran head on into a timber. He scrambled, screaming, to his feet, not knowing who or what was trying to kill him, sending Brevnik and Lucci off on a dead panicked run, and Lee Cravens, thinking Minicucci was hurt, went chasing after. By the time he had caught up with him, Lucci and Brevnik were gone. Back in fourteenth west, Duncan shouted but no one listened. He wanted to run too, but he stood in a swirl of beaconed dust as though rooted and shouted until his lungs ached.

All Strelchuk could see was smoke. "Bruno!" he cried, "we gotta make a run for it, man!" But he heard some voice back of him and he hollered out, "Who is it?" There was topcoal and rock down everywhere, timbers smashed like matchsticks and rails twisted up, power gone, a roiling scummy dark—and then he saw old Joe Castiglione with a piece of timber stove clean through him and Tuck Filbert smack up against the roof, his head upsidedown staring down at him, his eyes open, and blood dribbling out his big square jaw. *My God! who is it?*" Strelchuk screamed, the goddamn smoke clawing his lungs to shreds.

"Here," a wretched thin whisper said. "Collins."

And there he was, the poor goddamn bastard, his right leg pinned between the floor and a dislodged timber. "Preach! Jesus, man, you—but don't worry none! We'll get you out okay!" he cried. "It's me, Strelchuk, buddy! We'll make it!" But God Almighty, he didn't know what he was going to do. Collins' whole leg must have been no more than a quarter-inch thick from the knee down. Terror gripped Strelchuk and made him shake.

Thrust up by a whistle burst, lifted by the taut jack of forced silence, the ball leans over its zenith, sinks briefly, then springs from a finger's jar toward the Tucker City basket, into the hands of a black-jerseyed West Condoner. A roar. A bounce. A pass. Gyrating patterns as fingers trace spiraling fences around the black-trunked bodies. Drive. Retreat. Pass. Jump. Shoot.

Parked in an unlit corner of the lot outside the West Condon High School auditorium, the two received the Word:

She is spreadin' her wings for a journey,
And is goin' to journey by and by,
And when the trumpet sounds in the mornin',
She will meet her dear Lord in the sky!

They had switched the radio on to keep up with the ball game, under way not a hundred yards distant, but, waiting for the old coils to warm, had become distracted and failed to tune it in. Instead, American evangelist messages of love, death, and chiliasm, transmitted through the nose all the way over from Randolph Junction, leaked into the old Dodge and dribbled recklessly over their young Italian-Catholic lust. These reached their indrawn senses, now rendered in five ways tactile, as curtains of alien irrelevance, permissive because it constrained in the wrong inflections; the glow of the radio was a distant worm that warmed them. . . .

When He comes descendin' from Heaven
On the clouds that He writes in His Word,
I'll be joyful, preparin' to meet Him
On the wings of that Great Speckled Bird!

Their bodies formed a convoluted "X," the figure of a Greek *psi*, he seated, boy's unchastised legs pushed forward under the dash, she curled across his lap and facing him. By thrust and retreat, they advanced their investigations: the circuit established by their mouths, his hand prowled into the rustle of her skirt and petticoat, while her hand rubbed and clawed his neck, proxy for the stalk wedged

39

against her underhip; parting to breathe, they fell motion-less, only their eyes pursuing the game, keeping it alive. Yet, though their hands and mouths pressed forward, toppling old resistances, dispersing ancestral phantoms, they had no clear idea of what the next inch would bring. If Angela Bonali's defloration was to be the consummation, neither of them guessed it.

For a long time, the smoke was so thick Eddie Wilson saw nothing else in the beam of his headlamp. He prayed into the radiant cloud for deliverance from despair. He tried to think of Brother Ely assuring him of his soul's state of grace. He should have told Ferd Clemens he could use the dog. He didn't mean to hunt this weekend. He prayed that he be saved from greed and covetousness. Then, slowly, grotesquely, a crushed human shape emerged on the floor at the ray's end: Tommy Catter, his buddy, staring at him from under an overturned pit car. Tommy's lamp was shattered. Eddie prayed that Tommy's sins be forgiven and prayed for his own salvation, and, hoping only to see his wife Betty once more, closed his eyes.

Strelchuk had thrust all his weight onto the timber that pinned Ely Collins' leg, but there was no budging it. That idiot Bruno was in a state of shock and no good to him at all, and Strelchuk cursed him. Then somebody coughed, deep thick old man's cough, not like Bruno, and Strelchuk spun: saw two headlamps wavering through the smoke! "Hey! Who is it? Strelchuk here! Who's there?" Jesus, he was damn near screaming!

"Juliano," said one of the lamps, and the other, still gagging, said, "Jinx, Mike! What the goddamn is hap-pened?"

"This wasn't no plain fall!" Mario Juliano said.

"No, there was a shock before. Something went off."

And Jinx Pontormo cried, "Hey! We got to get the hell out of here!"

"Wait!" Strelchuk shouted. Choking so he could hardly

40

breathe. "What do we do with Collins? He's pinned here by a timber!"

"Listen, if we don' get out of this merda," shouted Jinx, "it ain't going to matter none who is pinned and who ain't!" He flashed his headlamp all around and said: "It seem to me like it thins out toward the west! Maybe we can get out by old Main!"

"But we can't leave Preach here!" Strelchuk yelled. He was miffed that Pontormo was making to leave him. "Come on, you two bastards, give me a hand!"

"All right, goddamn it!" snapped Mario Juliano. "Where the hell is he?" They went back and turned their lamps down on him. "Jesus Christ, he's in a bad way!"

Mario helped and they tried again to work the timber off Collins' leg, but it couldn't be done. It had all five hundred feet of mother earth piling down on it. Pontormo came and tried to help too, didn't relish heading off by himself, the old man was scared, they were all scared.

"Barney? This is Dave Osborne out at the mine. You better come out. I think the southeast section blew up."

The night mine manager, though pierced through with a dread that, oddly, made him want to giggle, reached out calmly, reached down calmly, brought them up, brought them out here.

"Something awful has hit down here!"

"I know. Little trouble. Come on up." Told them how. But he didn't tell them what. Didn't want them to lose their goddamn heads.

"Bonali here. Been trying to get you. What the hell has happened?"

"Take your crew due north up Main, Vince. Due north. You hear? Bring them up the number two shaft."

"Jesus, Osborne, that's over five miles!"

Superintendent. Mine rescue crews. Sections north of the shaft. Radio station. Expanded, making the phone system one with his own, his messages throbbing through its channels with impulses of action. His mind mapped out

41

the possibilities, and, as when a boy pulling the toy train switches, he synchronized the movements, then opened all the circuits.

Collins was moaning something horrible. His face was black and cut from smashing into the cinders, and it was all screwed up with pain. His hands clenched dirt. He was praying. Then he twisted his neck and looked, white-eyeballed, up at Strelchuk, and he said in a fragile faraway old voice, "Mike! Git a ax!"

Strelchuk gasped. Jesus, I can't do it, Preach! he cried, but only to himself, and he went hobbling over the chunks of coal, banging his helmet on the broken roof, stumbling over the rails, and found his own hatchet just inside third north. He grabbed it up and came running back. Juliano and Pontormo had already started to move away, Bruno blindly following their lights. "*Don't you goddamn bastards go away and leave me!*" he screamed, and he thought for God's sake he was going to cry. They turned back, Pontormo swearing like a bishop, and Strelchuk said, "It's the only thing. If we leave him, he'll die. You and Bruno grab his arms and hold him so he don't jump or get them in the way, Jinx. And, Mario, take a grip on his other leg there." His voice was high and squawky; he didn't recognize it himself.

"It's okay, boys," Collins whispered up at them. "I kin take it." And he took to praying again.

Strelchuk lifted the ax in the air and thought: Jesus! what if I miss, I've never swung a goddamn ax much, what if I hit the wrong leg, or—?

"Goddamn you, Mike!" Jinx screamed, losing control. "Quit messing around! This gas is knocking me out, man! We got to get us out of here!"

And while he was screaming away like that, Strelchuk came down with the ax, caught the leg right where he aimed, true and clean, just below the knee, and the blood flew everywhere, and Juliano was crying like a goddamn baby, and Bruno, his face blood-sprayed, went dumb, mouth agape, and broke away in a silent fit, but the leg was still hooked on, they couldn't get him free. Preach was still praying to beat hell and never even whimpered. Mike raised the ax again and drove down with all the goddamn strength he had, felt the bone this time, heard the crack, felt the sickening braking of the ax in tough tissue, and he turned and vomited. He was gagging and hacking and crying and the blood was everywhere, and still that goddamn leg was hooked on. Mario ripped away Collins' pant leg, took the wedge he had in his pocket, pressed it up against Collins' thigh. Strelchuk whipped off his leather belt and, using it as a tourniquet against the wedge, they stopped the heavy bleeding. Pontormo whined Italian. Strelchuk grabbed up the ax once more. His hands were greasy with blood and it was wet on his chest and face. He was afraid of missing or losing hold, and the shakes were rattling him, so he took short hacking strokes, and at last it broke off. They dragged him free. And Preacher Collins, that game old sonuvabitch, he was still praying.

There was a comforting fullness about the room. Elaine Collins, listening to the high school basketball game while she ironed, wished to be there, yet knew she was always frightened outside this house, and once out would wish to be back. Out there, with the others, she would sit alone, persecuted by noises and events she did not understand, afraid of—she didn't know what. She knew Hell by her Pa's portrayals of it, but understood it by her own isolation and the fearful sense of disintegration she suffered out in public. Just as she understood God's peace by this house, by this room with its rich and harmonious variety of loved objects. Braided rugs her Ma had made lay like large soft flagstones over the polished floor, and out of them stemmed warm masses of stuffed furniture, tables stacked with her Pa's reading materials, lamps with opaque shades that showed white in the daytime and a mottled gold at night, two silver radiators that knocked and sighed, bookshelves hammered together by her Pa and painted oxblood brown to hold more of his small books and pamphlets and the family Bible, her Pa's straw-backed rocker and her Ma's footpedal Singer, baskets of clothing, and the ironing board where Elaine worked. The stuffed furniture, nubbed and musty, now served mainly to hold the stacks of laundry her Ma took in for the house money, though Elaine could remember when her older brother Harold, killed in the war, sprawled long-legged over it and struck softly at a banjo, singing popular religious tunes for her. On the ivory-papered walls hung last year's calendar still, with Christmas circled in red. Also a plastic crucifix, photographs, a gold star, two plaster of Paris plaques that said *He loveth the smallest sparrow* and *Prepare the Way of the Lord!*, a small corner shelf bearing small glass knickknacks, a kind of certificate or award her Pa had received once from the mining company during the war, and a number of prints framed in black, including Jesus preaching to the multitudes, alone at prayer in Gethsemane, lying dead in his Ma's arms after being lowered from the cross, and—surrounded by blue and white birds and standing on a cloud—ascending into Heaven. Most of the knickknacks on the shelf were gifts over the years from Elaine to her Ma. Missing was this year's Christmas present, a small porcelain statue of Jesus' Ma with a bright red heart on the outside of her breast. Her Ma had explained that it was mainly a Catholic statue, though it was very nice, so she kept it on her dresser in the bedroom, rather than out here where visitors might see it and misunderstand.

The photos were of Elaine, of Harold as a boy and in his uniform, and of her folks at different times. One was a newspaper clipping of her Pa preaching at a camp-meeting near Wilmer. He had received the call only a few years back, a little while after Harold got killed, but he had quickly become a great revivalist, for his talk was always simple and direct and powerful with conviction. If they heard him once, they always came back. He stood tall and calm and his clear steady voice spoke assuredly of salvation from our sins through Christ Jesus; in every sermon, he always said, "Grace is not something you die to get, it's something you get to live!" Almost every Sunday for over four years now he had been preaching and baptizing at the Church of the Nazarene here in West Condon, where her Ma had become leader of the Evening Circle. Elaine liked it when her Pa preached, because it was the one occasion that placed her among people without fear. He was there and she was his. Especially the tented campmeetings she liked.

Tucker City made a basket, and the score was tied. The crowd, in response, made a strange kind of animal noise—maybe the announcer had cupped his hand over the microphone. Elaine kept the volume low. Below, in the basement, her Ma sang revival hymns while she ran the washing machine.

Duncan was glad when Bonali returned and took over again. He was hoarse from shouting, and though he didn't have the goddamnedest notion what he had said, it had somehow worked, because after Brevnik, Lucci, Cravens, and Minicucci, nobody else had split off. Bonali was pissed to get the news about these four, but he wasted no time getting the show on the road. They took the intake air course but ran into smoke and dust, had to get back on the return air course. Against the rulebooks, but there was nothing they could do. They considered bratticing off, but then the air got better. They came across a little wooden propeller that told them the vent system was on again.

Masque: Exchange of roles as Blacks fade to enact static counterparts to Reds now bearing down in interstitched configurations. Red One crosses meridian, confronts tableau of Blacks, slows, signals placement: Red Two to his left, Red Three to center, Red Four and Five to the corners. Blacks dance lightly, buttocks oriented to netted eye. Red Three slaps thigh, shouts, and Black

45

Three leaps, slashes meaninglessly at empty space. Chants instruct. Red One holds, weighs forward, keeping the pendular (*down the corridor he comes*) scissoring of Red Three in the corner of his eye, juts young jaw, hoots; cued, Black One strikes, misses, as Red One withdraws. Black One flails, presses: Red One, laughing, delivers out to Red Two. Red Two (*and through the double doors into the auditorium like a bird bursting from its cage in alarm*) dissembles a return to Red One, but it is Red Three, momentarily stationary on a central black cross intersecting a black circle, who receives (*then down the aisle in flying leaps batting wildly against obstacles*) off the gleaming floorboards. He shams bounce to Red Four in the right corner, drawing Black Three out of the circle toward the foil, and then, alone and lit on his varnished disc, assumes his role: the Hook. A semicircling sweep, chassé, fade (*and white shirt aflutter leaps the rail to alight on the hardwood floor*), stretch—but circle breaks as Black Two and Three puncture its rim in assault. Collision (*past the players and pallid up to the scorekeeper's table*). Whistle. Roar. Buzzer, unexpectedly prolonged.

The throbbing paeans of the crowd within, seined but not trapped by the auditorium's drafty walls, washed over the old Dodge in the parking lot like surf, gathering ascendancy over the Randolph Junction radio station, which had begun to fade and grow fuzzy. For Angie Bonali, the shouting was both exotic and paternal, a distant tidal bath of freedom, and a proximate refuge if she needed it. . . .

I been gatherin' flowers from the hillside,
To wreathe around your (*ground?*),
But you've (fade) (*baby, I'm knockin' on your . . .*)
(*The flowers?*) *have all withered down . . .*

As they, chests heaving, leaned apart, she gazed up past his dark head, burred and ridged like a goat's, to the tattered roof of the old car. Under the tatters, in daylight, there was rust; now, behind them, there seemed only cosmic space. She closed her eyes. A width, less than three inches, of damp fragile nylon was all that kept his fingers out, and even now threatened to become less her buckler than his gauntlet. "It's nearly eight," she guessed, gasped. "Don't you think we'd better—better go—see the game?"

He sighed and gazed, pleasantly pained, down at her lips, full and appealing, as she knew, and now slightly bruised. Their *psi* plunged shut once more, her fist snarling eagerly in his cropped hair, his pawing savagely in her bared thighs, butting her body against the spiny fish that wriggled and plunged in his lap . . .

> (fade in) . . . *were in bloom,*
> *I shot and killt my darlin'*
> (static) *be my doom (all of God's children*
> *seem to gather there) to wreathe around your* . . .

"Please!" she sobbed.

"Angie!" he pleaded, freed his own hand a moment to tug hers down across his chest. She buried her face in his shirt, her hand at the buckle without strength. "Oh hell!" he snapped, and flicked her skirt down over her thighs.

She whirled away, sat up, stared out the fogged-up windows. "What is it!" Her heart pounded with the discovery of real place around her. The people were streaming out of the auditorium.

"What's going on?" he asked irritably, hand clinging to her knee in rote strategy.

"Is the game over?" She couldn't get her breath.

"Can't be," he said. "It just started." He flipped the radio dial, looking for the West Condon station.

The crowd, protoplasmic, flooded through the double doors and inundated the parking lot. Lamps on poles and swerving car lights made the onrushing mass seem translucent, unbodied. As individuals, nearing, emerged from it, Angie rolled down the window and called out, "What is it?"

"Number Nine blew up!"

The radio crashed on, piercing her breast. "We repeat:

All persons other than doctors, nurses, and members of mine rescue teams are urged to remain in their homes. Bulletins will be—"

"Hey! You got room?"

"Sure!" shouted the boy with Angie. "Get in!"

Angie slumped forward to let the three squeeze past her into the back seat. Her bruised lips against her knuckles cried *sin!* as her father's loved presence invaded the Dodge.

"Hey, Angie! Was your Dad on tonight?"

"Yes," she whispered, but she was already crying. Oh, Daddy! *I'm sorry!*

Parked at the outer edge of the lot, the advantage was all theirs, but even then they soon found themselves bumper to bumper on the old road out to the coalmine.

The three men jerryrigged a stretcher with brattice canvas and hustled Ely Collins into it. They'd been too long about it. The gas was so dense now, it felt like their goddamn clothes were floating free from their bodies. Strelchuk remembered Bruno, didn't see him anywhere. "Hey, Bruno!" he shouted, but go no answer.

"Come on, goddamn you, Strelchuk!" Jinx Pontormo cried, so nervous his old Italian voice squeaked like a boy's. "I have enough of your jackass games!"

"Bruno, we're going!" Mike called, but they were already on the move as he said it, Pontormo leading, fat round shoulders bulled forward in an anxious charge on the void ahead, Strelchuk and Juliano bearing the old mechanic on the cloth between them. With his buddy Collins nailed to the earth and maybe dying, Bruno had cut out to save his own skin—if he got in a hole, he goddamn well deserved it. "Jerk must have gone on," Strelchuk muttered, covering his vague sense of guilt.

She felt, as in dreams, to be running without gaining ground, willing acts she could not perform. Iron to its metal stand. Plug out. Around the far thrust of the ironing board. Through the wilderness of looming chairs, stirring pamphlets, whipped laundry. Past the pleading eyes stuck on the walls. Over cracked linoleum to the wooden basement stairs. Down half of them, knees feathery. "Ma!" Basement was lit hollowly by unsmoked bulbs. Her Ma was singing and didn't hear her. "Ma!" The washer churned like someone choking. "*Ma!*"

Her Ma glanced up from the machine, thrust another armload in, and walked over to the stairs. "Can't hear nothing with that machine going," she explained. Her arms were scabbed with suds.

"It's the mine, Ma!" Elaine said. She didn't know how to act. She feared what might happen when her Ma knew. "It's blowed up, Ma! I jist heard it on the radio!"

But all her Ma said was, "Git your coat, child," and turned back to unplug the washer. "And don't fergit your boots!" she called back over her shoulder. But later, as they ran along together toward the Deepwater road, Elaine saw it was her Ma who forgot hers.

Like ravens fly the black messages. By radio, by telephone, by word of mouth. Over and through the night streets of the wooden town. Flitting, fluttering, faster than flight. Crisp January night, but none notice. Out hatless into the streets to ask, to answer, to confirm each other's hearsay. Women shriek and neighbors vulture over them, press them back into shingled houses with solicitous quiverings. Three hundred are dead. They all escaped. God will save the good. All the good men died. Flapping. Flustering. Telephones choke up. Please get off the line! This is an emergency! Below the tangled branches of the gaunt winter elms, coatless they run, confirm each other's presence. No one remains alone. Lights burn multifoldly, doors gape and slap. Radios fill living rooms and kitchens, leak into charged streets, guide cars. The road to the mine is jammed. A policeman tries to turn them back, but now they approach in a double column and there is no route back. Everything stops. All cars hear the beatless music, the urgent appeals, but nothing yet is known. Down roll windows and again the ravens flit.

After supper, Eleanor Norton had performed her usual exercises but received no messages. Wylie was out on a house call. She curled up on the living room sofa to wait for him, catch up on some back readings in the *Phaedrus* myth. She heard noises in the street but was so absorbed in her reading that she barely registered them. "He would like to fly away, but he cannot; he is like a bird fluttering and looking upward and careless of the world below; and he is therefore thought to be mad." But the noises persisted. They entered and scratched their alarums on her emptying page, scraped on the nerve ends of her living tomb. She looked about her, put the book down, stepped out on the front porch. The temperature had dropped and the hard chill has a dampness to it. Cars were roaring and rumbling out of driveways. Everyone was out in the street, shouting at one another. Something about a shift. The noise of radios at full volume crackled into the restive street. The mine had exploded! Hundreds were dead or trapped!

Trembling, Eleanor groped behind her for the front door, fearful for one freezing moment it might not even be there, spun herself back into the house, pressed the door shut behind her. Even there, her shoulders to the door, the street havoc reached her, menacing. The radio! She turned it on. Boyish voice, taut and urgent. It was true! She felt weak, adrift, beset with a terrifying thought from some dark and uncleansed corner . . . *betrayal!* She had not been told! Oh no! no! she cried over and over, striking blows at her suddenly willful ego, a misunderstanding, must be! She turned on all the lights in the house, then took her journals to the kitchen. One essence! she cried, but was not reassured.

Strelchuk, taking the rear grip, had Collins in front of him, and each time his ducking headlamp grazed the stretcher, he was shaken afresh by the pulled gray face, scratched and sooted, of the old preacher, by the gaunt stretched knuckles of his fists and the white plastic gleam of brutalized thigh. Collins murmured ceaselessly, and stared moronically into the darkness behind Mike's shoulder. That darkness, hot, rubbery, breathed like a ravening mouth on Mike's back, and each time Collins' awed face leaped up in front of him to stare at it, it damn near swallowed Mike up. Although he could almost touch Juliano's broad young back ahead, and though Pontormo was no more than another four or five feet beyond, still the beams of their headlamps, licking ahead into the tunneled dark, seemed to spring them forward suddenly, leaving Strelchuk stranded, alone with the mutilated Collins, too far behind ever to catch up.

Strelchuk knew he was close to breaking, and he knew, too, that if he broke, they would go on without him. He tried to force his thoughts topside. But each attempt struck on a face that pitched him down in the mine again. Old Joe Castiglione literally spitted. And Tuck Filbert, that good old guy! Jesus! Lem and his Dad would take it rough. They had been trying for months to get Tuck to quit. And Strelchuk's own buddy Bill Lawson: what had happened out there in the main haulageway? Not minutes before, he had clapped old Bill on the shoulders, and now—

Suddenly Collins said, "Wait, boys!" and Strelchuk started so violently he nearly lost his grip on the stretcher. His hands were awash with sweat.

"What did you say, Preach?" he asked, his voice strangled and raw. Realized he was getting winded, too.

"Smoke, Mike. Dust."

"Yeah, I know, Preach. But nothing we can do."

"Mike . . ." He was trying like hell to say something.

As Strelchuk dragged, Juliano and Pontormo spun on him irritably, their lamps batting fiercely into his eyes.

"What the Jesus you waiting for now?" Pontormo demanded.

"If you don't like it, Pontormo, take a grip," snapped Juliano.

"It's Preach," Mike said weakly.

"So what?" growled Pontormo, and turned to move on.

"What is it, Ely?" Juliano asked. They eased him to the ground to rest their shoulders.

"Intake air," Collins whispered.

"Hell, he's right!" said Juliano. "Where's our damn heads? We ought to be in the intake air course!"

So they located a trapdoor into the north air course, and, sure as hell, the air seemed cleaner, not much, but some—enough anyway to lift the sodden weight of nameless fear off Strelchuk's shoulders. "Thanks, Preach," he said.

Vince Bonali kept his crew talking to make the long walk out seem shorter. For Duncan's sake, and Duncan knew it and loved the sonuvabitch for it, Bonali called frequent halts. They sprawled around, drank water from their buckets, and Duncan took the weight off his swollen miner's knees. They pushed forward, rested, pushed, rested, Bonali quarterbacking. It was going to be a long tough night, but, to keep cool, Duncan drew imaginary poker hands. When he felt threatened, he drew a pair of aces in the hole, with a loner showing, and goosed the ante with a frigid bluff, making old Lou Jones squint his beebee eyes. About a mile on, they crossed paths with Abner Baxter's section, and that loosened them all up some. They numbered forty now, including Tub Puller, the biggest bastard in the mine, and they figured not much could stand between them and topside that they couldn't push over.

The mayor of West Condon, pinned in traffic, fumed. All the way from the ball game he had cursed his cops and tried to believe the jam would work itself out. But they were stopped dead. In front of him, a carload of kids raised hell. Had half a mind to haul them out of there and throw them all in the jug. But he recognized one of them as Tommy Cavanaugh, the banker's son, so he got out and slogged up to them. Ground was frozen, but the heavy traffic had warmed the dirt on the road to mud. He batted the window with a pudgy knuckle, and the kid driving was about to give him the finger when Tommy's broad ball-playing hand swatted the guy on the back of the head and stretched over the seat to roll down the window. "H'lo, Mayor!" Tommy said.

"Tommy, would you do me a favor and drive my car the rest of the way out? I'm going on ahead to see what's holding up the circus."

"Sure, Mr. Whimple!" Tommy pushed out, still wearing his basketball suit and sweatshirt. A girl followed him. Goddamn, that's all he'd need now. Mayor Pimps for Banker's Boy. He didn't tell them not to, though.

The mayor found he wasn't the only one walking. It was like a damned parade. Some cars were locked up and standing square in the middle of traffic. Both lanes were full, so nothing could leave the mine if it wanted to. The farther he walked, the madder he got. At the end of it, he found Monk Wallace all by himself. "Where's Romano and Willie?"

"I dunno, Mort," said the cop. "Probably sitting at the other end of that shit."

Whimple noticed Justin Miller, the *Chronicle* editor, shinnied halfway up the goddamn watertower shooting photographs of the jam. Oh man! Mayor Muffs It. Historic Mess Muddles Mayor. "I'll go get a buncha guys to help."

The air course was not a straight track; the four men kept running into falls, would have to backtrack, sometimes as much as a hundred or hundred fifty feet, locate another course, and travel down that one as far as they could before they struck another fall. No markings, no light, air laden with a torpid calm that argued with their own urgency—they kept flashing into stupid arguments about which way they were going, got confused, swore at each other. Strelchuk didn't mind the blood or the thigh stub so much now, but carrying Ely Collins was hard work, and old Pontormo refused to help, said he'd wrenched his shoulder when the thing went off. "We better loosen the tourniquet again," Juliano gasped, and Mike didn't argue. They set him down, not so gently as at first. Didn't matter. He was completely out. Strelchuk felt for Collins' pulse: still there.

"He ain't gonna make it." Juliano sighed, breath husky.

Strelchuk knew what was on Juliano's mind. It was on his mind, too. But they wrapped the corners of the battice-cloth around their wrists again, hefted the old man up between them, and started off. "Come on, Pontormo!" Strelchuk cracked through his teeth. "We're getting goddamn tired of always waiting around for you!"

———◆•◆———

By the washhouse, Mayor Whimple found three men and sent them back to help Wallace. The grounds were swarming with miners, women, kids. In the offices, he commandeered the phone and called the state highway police and the National Guard. Took him nearly a quarter of an hour just to get the operator. When he swore at her, he could hear her break down and cry. He told her he was sorry and to relax, but no matter what to keep this line open at all times. In the lamphouse, he borrowed lights to guide the traffic. They told him about a hundred guys had come up already, so there were less than two hundred down there now. Pop Hendricks showed him the board full of tags. Most of the ones who had come up were waiting to go back down on rescue crews. One group was going down bareface now. Another hundred from the day shift had shown up. They said that mine rescue teams from five or six towns around were on the way, but they'd never make it through the traffic on time. One ambulance had arrived, beating the pack, bringing a doctor and some nurses. Then a Salvation Army woman in a uniform that reeked of mothballs got his ear and complained that they had a tent set up and food was on the way, but it was stalled somewhere in the jam. Miller's assistant, Lou Jones, overheard a nurse tell him that the hospital panel bringing bandages and medications had not arrived, and the guy nodded significantly, asked him what he was doing about it. Whimple felt like telling that fat snoop to go to hell, he didn't like him anyway because Jones always called him Pimple, but instead he replied, "Everything we can."

They inched. And finally they stopped. Between gospel songs and André Kostelanetz, the radio told them there had been 307 men on the night shift and that the cause and extent of the disaster were unknown. Angela Bonali prayed fervently, counting on her fingers. The others in the car respected her private ceremony; they talked only to each other.

Then two women ran past them, panting like horses. Angie recognized the girl, Elaine Collins from her freshman class at high school. Angie jumped out of the car, called out: "Elaine!" But the girl, whether she heard or not, did not turn around. Then, for the first time, it occurred to Angie that her Daddy might not be dead after all, that he might yet be saved. But she had to hurry. Ahead of her, the two women set the pace, but it was tempered by the longer distance they had had to cover. Angie could still pass them. She had to, to save her Daddy. She broke into a dead run.

While men heaped oxygen tanks, timber, shovels, and canvas alongside the cages, mine supervisor Barney Davis led the first crew down. Night mine manager Dave Osborne, two firebosses, and miners Pete Chigi, Sal Ferrero,

Ben Wosznik, and Carlo Juliano. Juliano and Wosznik had brothers on the night shift, Ferrero was Angelo Moroni's brother-in-law, and Big Pete Chigi was an old standby in emergencies. Pressed soaked rags against their faces. They had to get fresh air into the hit workings.

Mario Juliano said he thought he saw another light flick off a near wall. Strelchuk said that carrying the old preacher was turning him batty, referring of course to the birds. It was a trick the bounce of lights often played, but nobody ever expected an old vet like Ely Collins would ever be bugged by it. Juliano swore he'd seen it. And then, a couple minutes later, they all three saw it: a pair of head-lamps bobbing toward them in the dark. Didn't realize how dusty it was until they saw what was between them and those lights. "Hey!" they cried out. "Hey! Who's there?" They lowered Collins and ran to meet the two coming. It was Lee Cravens and his triprider Pooch Minicucci. Jesus, was Mike glad to see those guys!

"Where you'uns headed?" Lee asked, soft Southern slide tilting his voice, though he was a West Condoner by birth. Little guy, angular, goodnatured, but not the brightest lad in the county.

"We thought we'd try to reach the old number one portal, or otherwise go south to the fifteenth and take Old Main out," Strelchuk explained. It began crowding in on him then that these guys were coming from the way they were going.

"Ain't no good thetaway," said Lee, whipping his lamp momentarily back over his shoulder, then pausing to spit through his teeth. "We jist come from there. All fulla gas and we seen they was a lotta flame down toward the fifteenth. Doors all busted out and guys dead. Me'n' Pooch is lucky even to be here."

"It was a wough sonuvabitch," confirmed Pooch.

"Well, we can't go back neither," said Mario Juliano. "It's all caved in back there, and the gas is washing in in buckets."

"It musta wiped out the whole mine!" whined Pooch.

"Where's the rest of your outfit?" Juliano asked. "Bonali and the other guys?"

"I dunno," said Cravens. "They was foolin' around. I don't reckon they made it."

"If you damn bastards had only hurried!" Pontormo cried bitterly, and then he calmed down and said, "Well, it don' make no difference."

They led Cravens and Minicucci back to show them Ely Collins, and explained how they had lopped the leg and all. Cravens was pretty upset by it. He examined Collins' leg carefully, eased the tourniquet, fussed with the bratticecloth. "I know you done what you could," he said, as though apologizing.

"There wasn't nothing else to do," Strelchuk said. "I didn't want to leave him back there."

"No, you done good," Cravens said softly. Seemed like he might be crying a little.

Air blast at the door into the main air course was so stiff, they had to shove and tug each other through it. Like crossing some terrible threshold. Even Tub Puller needed help. But from there on, they knew, it was a coast home. Cokie Duncan even thought his knobbed rheumatic knees felt better. Bonali informed him with mock sarcasm that there never was anything wrong with them, all they had needed all along was exercise.

Old Red Baxter, gravelly voice rumbling acidly out of his deep belly, agitated in the old style, waxing blistery on the lousy mine management, the absentee swindlers in the East who fattened themselves on the flesh of the workers, and that criminal Barney Davis—Baxter said they ought to march out in a body and straight into the offices, grab the first one of them they found, if it was that traitor Davis so much the better, and lynch the devil. Jowls atremble, long red hair curling under the back of his helmet, small eyes lit with wrath. Antiquated fans, no dust down, not one piece of equipment that might not set the

57

mine off, worse lighting and stupider timbering than they had thirty years ago.

Excited the young boys, and one of them even came on a piece of rope, threw it over his shoulder, but Duncan knew Baxter's wind was nothing but gobpile oratory that blew feeble in the cleaner air topside. Anyway, Duncan hated the hot-eyed bastard since the day a quarter of a century ago, during the IWW riots, when Baxter punched his ribs with a rifle barrel and tried to make him kiss the ass of an old mule. In later years, Baxter tended to muddle his old political vocabulary with the saints-and-demons gloss of the local holy rollers, but the message was still fermented in the same tortured bowels. Duncan was glad when Bonali, cool for once, brought them down off that angry mountain by changing the topic to how they should celebrate getting out.

As Barney Davis and his rescue crew pushed deeper, they ran into worse damage and bad air. Where they could, they closed the blown-open airlock doors, adjusted the regulators. But they were bareface and it was getting too much for them. Ben Wosznik was getting sick. So they brought out the first two bodies they found. One was Lawson, the other looked like Moroni; check his battery number when they got him topside, if it was still readable. Both were burnt black and had suffered from impact.

The five men sat there around Ely Collins feeling pretty rotten. "Well, boys, I guess that's about it," Mike said. He felt very weak and tired. He thought about just stretching out there and dropping off, forget the whole fucking mess. Several times already he had thought it might only be a nightmare, and now the idea crept into him again. The sleepier he got, the more convinced he became that he was in the process of waking up.

Collins came to long enough to ask them if they had burlap up. "Yeah," said Lee Cravens, standing, "we gotta string us up a brattice, boys. Keep the bad air from

58

gittin' to us an hour or two anyways, and maybe somebody'll git through by then."

The project enlivened them. They hunted around, found
burlap, nailed it up on the timbers. They began taking
turns burning their headlamps. They guessed they had
between forty and fifty more battery hours among them,
using one at a time, and that was ten times what they
supposed they'd need. They sat around Collins as though
sheltering him, or maybe it was they who were seeking
shelter. He was awake more of the time now and was feeling the pain more. Strelchuk gave him all the aspirin he
had, and the other boys chipped theirs in, too. Collins
recognized Cravens now, and he asked Lee to help him
sing religious songs to keep his mind off the leg.

Angela Bonali arrived alone, breathless, surprised to find
so many she knew. She had never caught up with Elaine
Collins and her mother. The closer she had got, the faster
they had seemed to run. Now her chest hurt, and a troubling lonesome fear gnawed at her. People asked her about
her Dad. She didn't know. They didn't know. She walked
among the intent people, under strings of yellow lights.
Her brother Charlie was there, acting bored and chewing
a toothpick, but worry told on him because he couldn't
keep still. Snapped his fingers like always, but there was
no rhythm in it.

Then her Daddy's friend Mr. Ferrero came out of the
mine, his black face crying, and Angie started to cry, and
he came and told them that Uncle Ange was dead, that
they had just brought his body up. Angela had been
named for her Daddy's other friend, Angelo Moroni, and
she had always called him Uncle Ange, though he wasn't
an uncle. They always kidded her he looked more like
her father than her own Daddy did, and until recently she
had supposed his paternity reasonable and had half believed it. Uncle Ange's sister was Mr. Ferrero's wife.

Charlie came up and asked about their Dad, "the old
man," he called him, and Angie saw that Charlie had

59

started to cry too. Mr. Ferrero didn't know, but he said he believed he must be okay. Angie believed so, too. Uncle Ange had died, so she could keep her real Daddy. It made sense. There was food and coffee arriving at the Salvation Army canteen now, and they all went there together to have a doughnut.

They keep coming. Families, miners, officials, newsmen, police, civil defense, state cops, priests, Legion, Red Cross, television, psychiatric service. Fully equipped rescue teams now enter the mine methodically. Trucks arrive with oxygen tanks, stretchers, and tents. A bank president moves from group to group, bringing hope. At the city hospital, beds are cleared and nurses alerted. The West Condon radio station asks for and receives permission to stay on the air twenty-four hours a day. The high school gymnasium, still, is brightly floodlit. The electric scoreboard reads: WEST CONDON 14, VISITORS 11. Its clock is stopped. In a few hours, it will host a new activity: already the gym has been designated Temporary Morgue. The janitor, alone, spreads a tarpaulin on the floor.

He heard them coming, and then they went away. Eddie Wilson stared down the dusty beam at his dead buddy Tommy. It was awful. God's fist had closed on the mine-hive and shook it. God hated him. God loved Eddie's bird dog, and Eddie always kicked it. Sometimes, right in the nuts. The more God hated, the more Eddie grieved, the more he loved. Won't kick it again, won't! A foot materialized between his eyes and dead Tommy's stare. Hadn't heard it coming. Almost scared him. It turned toward Tommy, then back to Eddie. Approached.

"Hey, boys, come help! It's Eddie Wilson! He's still blinkin'!"

—*I once was lost, but now I am found,
Was blind, but now I see!*

They slumped in a group and listened. Sometimes they dozed. Lee Cravens' voice, gentle and musical as a girl's, flattening the vowels with the insertion of nasal *a*'s, glissandoed over them like a fluttery shield against the tons of black earth above their heads. Underneath, in short punched squawks of raw sound, Ely Collins followed painfully the principal beat. Pontormo muttered something once about saving breath, but Cravens asked for whom was breath if not for God, and Ely said, "Amen."

Mike Strelchuk, who never attended church but always supposed he believed that something or somebody was out there, reacted ambivalently to the singing. It distracted him and gave him hope: they were connected by it somehow to the outside; on the other hand, there was something eerie about the way the sound floated off. They were pretty depressing songs, too, for the most part. He wished to suggest something more cheerful, but it was mainly for Collins' benefit.

"Lee!" Collins whispered, when Cravens paused. "Agin!"

> '*Twas Grace that taught my heart to fear,*
> *And Grace my fear relieved—*

What about it? Mike asked himself. If I die, what's going to happen to me? He had no clear idea. He had always joked a lot about being hellbound, but he had never really doubted that God would take care of him when his time came. But what did he mean, "take care"? And what was grace? Did he have it? Who got it and how? Was it fair some didn't? He wished to hell something would happen to take his mind off it.

> *—How precious did that Grace appear,*
> *The hour I first believed!*

And then Mike felt it coming. The grace. He didn't know whether to resist it or not.

Up they came. Jesus, it felt good! On top, the air was cold, about sixty degrees colder than the air they had been breathing in the mine, but it tasted sweeter than honey in their welcoming lungs. Wives, brothers, fathers, kids, mothers piled on them, and, as Duncan had foreseen, most of them scattered immediately. Baxter the plotter himself wandered off peaceably, noosed by his wife and five children. Well, by God, they had made it! Duncan, without family, felt so weak suddenly he had to sit down. Just sank to the ground. Somebody gave him a smoke.

Beside him, standing, Bonali had just received his hysterical daughter. The kid was blubbering something about her Uncle Ange. Bonali's boy swaggered up, apparently regretting his old man's escape, and, around the cool stab of a toothpick that pricked out of his mouthful of flashy white teeth, dropped the tidings that Angelo Moroni had been killed. Sal Ferrero, smeared with soot, came up and confirmed it, half in tears, he and Bonali embracing like women. Bonali told his daughter to hurry in and inform her Mom that he was okay, and that she should go stay with Angelo's wife tonight. "Mom'll be at the church," Bonali said. He gave the girl his handkerchief and she ran off, emptying her excited tears into it, made awkward by the big word she bore. The boy had already disappeared without another nod between him and his old man.

Bonali said to come on. Duncan stubbed out the butt, stood cautiously, unlocking his sore knees, and followed his faceboss to the Salvation Army canteen. They located Lucci and Brevnik there, munching apples. Bonali showed he was glad to see them, but gave them hell for losing their heads and bolting the section. They looked pretty sheepish but tried to cover by saying they were going back down soon on rescue crews. Bonali asked them where Cravens and Minicucci were, but they didn't know, they had come out alone.

Outside the canteen, Bonali discovered Cravens' wife, Wanda. First time Duncan had met her, frail and weary type with nothing between the bones. She said there was still no word.

Seven men more are retrieved, but this time four live yet: Martini, Wilson, Sicano, Cooley. Wives gather, cluck and weep. Two white ambulances receive them horizontally, under face cages that pump oxygen purely. It is all, really, that Sicano and Cooley, uninjured, require. Martini's sleeve is empty below the elbow. Wilson's spine is wrecked. He revives briefly. Does he recognize his wife's quivering smile? It is hard to tell. He cannot move and can barely speak. "Dog," he says. And then: "Ely." With that, he loses consciousness once more. The dead, meanwhile, Catter, Wosznik, and Harlowe, join Lawson and Moroni inside a hastily thrown-up tent—already dubbed "the basket"—where they are officially identified and tagged by a company representative, a union man, and the company doctor.

The ambulance doors snap shut, the drivers leap behind the wheels. Red fists on top wheeling and sirens howling, the two carriers ark down the mine road toward town. Traffic is still in a snarl in spite of an army of angry bellowing cops, but the appearance of the ambulances breathes an urgency that works miracles. Now people ditch their cars without even being asked: peeling quickly like playing cards into the cuts on each side of the road. But not quickly enough for Eddie Wilson.

"I see Him, boys!" said Ely Collins, though his eyes were closed. "He's beautiful! And He's gonna take good care of us!"

Lee Cravens asked, "Who, Ely?"

"Why, the white bird! He's spreadin' His great wings over us, yes, I kin see it! and He's smilin' down!"

The other five looked at each other, but nobody laughed. Strelchuk saw Lee Cravens looking up, and he looked up too. The slabs of black rock still hovered there, but they seemed not so heavy somehow.

Collins' breath started coming in short gasps. "Pray with me boys!" he pleaded.

Juliano glanced up at Pontormo. "You think it's okay?" he asked.

"God's a good God," Cravens said. "It's what Ely always said. He's got room in His heart for everybody."

"God, be with Clara tonight, and Wanda, and all our wives and loved ones," the preacher said.

"He ought to take it easy," Pontormo urged, but more gently than usual.

"Give them courage and strength and . . ." Collins' voice faded. Mike and Lee edged toward the old man, Mike reaching for his wrist to check his pulse, but just then Collins' eyes opened and fixed on Mike. The old man smiled feebly, closed his eyes once more. "And, God, whatever happens, take good care of Mike. He done more than any man need t've done for anybody." Strelchuk felt a wash of pride and embarrassment pass through him. "He's a good . . ."

"Now, you just better rest a little," Strelchuk said awkwardly.

Collins began to sing. "So I walk with him . . . and I talk . . ."

Lee Cravens, eyes damp, picked it up:

> ". . . . and I talk with him,
> And I tell him I am His own;
> And the joys we share—"

"Boys!" gasped Collins. His breath was coming hard and his face was screwed up with pain. "Y' got any more water?" Strelchuk gave him what he had, but giving up the last of it made him worry. He held it to Collins' lips himself, careful not to waste any of it, since the old man's hands were shaking badly. Collins licked his lips, then asked, "Where's Giovanni?"

"Who?" asked Cravens.

"He means Bruno," Strelchuk said. "I forgot all about him."

"He's running around down here somewhere," Mario Juliano explained to Cravens and Minicucci. "He was with us at first, but he busted off while we was cutting Collins free."

"Is that so?" said Cravens. "We never seen him."

"Didn't come ou' way," Pooch confirmed.

"Could've took a different course," suggested Strelchuk.

"God, be with Giovanni . . . ," Collins whispered.

"He's a funny guy, that Bruno," Juliano said.

Ten more bodies are recovered, and hope wanes for the remainder. Nearly two hundred night shift miners have surfaced, turning in their tags, or gone back below to seek survivors, leaving about a hundred still in the mine. Ministers and priests keep vigil. First National Bank president Ted Cavanaugh continues his restless rounds, huddling here with a team of sweating, sooted miners, there listening intently to the wranglings of state mine inspectors and UMW officials; now turning a heartening phrase or two for Greater Deepwater Coal Company people, then offering hope and consolation to waiting or grieving mining families. The surfeit of volunteer rescuers gather in the Salvation Army canteen, await their turn, speak in whispers. Many of the merely curious have, since there's really nothing much to see, gone home. Rescuers, coming up, report greater and greater violence the farther south they push.

Dr. Wylie Norton, the veterinarian, arrived home from his house call to find his wife Eleanor in the brightly lit and silent house, poring through her logbooks. "Eleanor!" he said with alarm. "What is it? You're pale!" He set his bag down, approached her tentatively.

"Not a trace." She spoke gravely, evenly. "I have been all the way through, Wylie, and . . . there is not a word."

He sat down at the kitchen table across from her, adjusted the glasses on his narrow nose. "You mean about the mine?"

"Yes," she said. "There's no denying it, Wylie. I was not told a thing. Not one single word suggests it."

"Well," he said. His voice was hushed, his eyes, avoiding hers, fixed on the journals. He rubbed his hands, pressed together the fleshy tips of his supple tolerant thumbs. "Well."

"Why do you suppose Domiron did not . . . did not enlighten me?" Her voice, against her will, slipped a pitch higher. "Do you think he's . . . he's leaving me? Wylie! What have I done? Have I—?"

"Oh, well, now," cautioned Wylie, shifting in his chair.

"Wylie, the mine, this town's life, its *essence, our* town, Wylie, it blew up, it all blew up!" Her voice was leaping and breaking and pitching like a wild animal. Lost!

"Yes, dear, but—"

"*Men* are down there! Hundreds! *Dying!* Perhaps beneath our very feet!" Tears sprang. She bit down on her lip. "Wylie, we have come here, found a pattern, and in one split second it has all been destroyed and we did not receive so much as a *hint* of it!"

"Eleanor," said Wylie calmly, his eyes bending up to meet hers now. "I think maybe it's a little too soon to jump to conclusions." His damp blue eyes, holding hers, somehow took the edge off her panic. "I think, well, I don't know, but there must be, there's probably some purpose."

"Do you? Oh, *do* you, Wylie?" She grasped at this, and found it held her. "Do you think so?" She paused. He smiled faintly. "Wylie, let us hope so! I don't know what I'd do if . . . if I . . . stopped . . ." She couldn't pronounce it.

"I feel pretty sure you'll get a message soon," her husband said. "You'll receive a clarification soon enough." He reached across the table and patted her slender hands.

And, true enough! Wylie was right! They went into the

living room together. She sat on the sofa, Wylie in the easy chair. Through all the houses and furnishings they had passed, through all their trials and uprootings, always there seemed to be this situation: she on the sofa, he in an easy chair in front of her and slightly to her left, somewhat shadowed. They did not turn on the television. Loosed by her return from panic, her mind floated free. Images from her long life bubbled up and disappeared. Ten thousand years must elapse, how many had she known? Quietly they sat, Wylie glancing over at her from time to time. Her mind drew lots and passed through ageless epochs. Distantly came the street sounds, an occasional shout, radios, a car racing. And then, suddenly, she started up out of the sofa, grasped her journal, locked herself in the bedroom, and emerged about fifteen minutes later with the message.

Wylie was waiting for her in his armchair. He looked up at her questioningly. She nodded. She was exhausted, and her face felt damp with perspiration. He smiled, pushed the glasses up on his nose, and followed her into the kitchen, where she read the message to him:

"Do you hear? Do you see? Do you think? Then, why do you doubt still? Elan has lost discipline and moves darkly among alien forms. Cling in recollection to the abiding universals! Seek my light without seeking, guileless and true, do not resist! Domiron hails Womwom for his superior insight: all praise to him who shall be called a Saint! Let it be guarded in memories that false portents are sprung from too hasty knowledges. Time is for all events, all passages are brought to light. Cosmic purposes of enormous importance are to be illumined soon. Further direct contact between worldsouls and higher aspected beings may be anticipated to transpire very near future. Elan is to confront with courage and inward serenity the history that is to come and to comprehend with grace the bitter obligement of suffering. Levity has

67

intruded upon your meditations and vanity distorts your actions! Awake! Beneath you, the earth has leapt in protest. Proceed henceforth in resolute accord with the duty of your enlightenment! You will comprehend more intensely soon. Domiron bids you!"

Wylie sat very heavily in his chair. He peered up at his wife over his spectacles. "Eleanor," he began softly, "don't you think perhaps . . . ?" But then he stopped. He stared down at his square practical hands. He scratched some clay off one finger. After a moment, he looked up at her and smiled. "That's fine," he said.

Her Ma led them all in prayer. They sang "Beulah Land," "The Old Rugged Cross," "The Ninety and Nine" . . .

> —Sick and helpless, and ready to die;
> Sick and helpless, and ready to die!

The words made them cry. The cinders bit into their knees, and the cold air stung their wet faces. Elaine Collins wept shamelessly and prayed amen to all her Ma said, prayed to save poor Eddie Wilson in the hospital, and to be tonight with Tessie Lawson, who had lost her belovèd Bill, and Mary Harlowe, who'd lost her Hank. But Elaine wasn't afraid now. Her Ma was here, they had run out here together, and she could tell from the look on her Ma's face that her Pa was okay, that he was alive and would come back to them. . . .

> —Rejoice, for the Lord brings back His own!
> Rejoice, for the Lord brings back His own.

The air worsened. They all noticed it. They knew the answer, but had been putting it off. They had to build a better brattice. Strelchuk and Juliano led them. They scouted around and discovered a room inside what looked to be about seventh south that was relatively clean and not hard to brattice off. They lifted Collins in there and set about the task of barricading themselves in. They erected temporary stoppings to hold the gases back as long as possible, collected all the tools and canvas and boards they could find. Collins, the veteran, came to from time to time and instructed them in short choppy gasps how to short-circuit the return vent system, and also reminded them to leave a bucket or something outside with a sign on it. Minicucci volunteered his undershirt and they wrote on it with a ballpoint pen: COME AND GET US!, drew an arrow, and signed their names. It cheered them to pass the shirt around, yet there was the disconcerting quality of a tombstone about it. They tacked it up on a timber about a hundred yards away, chalked some large arrows on the roof and walls.

They had few boards, had to make do with coal and slate, but Collins said that was the best thing anyhow. He hauled himself up against a wall, he seemed improved, and pulled out a scrap of paper he had in his pocket. He tried to write something on it with a stub of pencil, but his old freckled hand was shaking terribly.

While Strelchuk was hunting for chunks of loose coal and whatever else he could find, his headlamp flashed over a body. "Jesus!" he squeaked. He was afraid to beam it that way again, but his head twitched back in a kind of reflex, and his lamp had to follow. He could hardly believe what he saw. *"Bruno!"* he cried. "Bruno, you sonuvabitch! How the hell did you get here?"

Bruno didn't answer. He was stretched out on a sort of ledge or groove in a recess. His eyes were big as saucers and his white lips were pulled back, showing his clenched teeth. Dried blood on his face. Twitching all over. He reminded Strelchuk of rabbits he had shot and wounded, just before he finished them off.

"Hey, it's okay, Bruno! It's me, Strelchuk!"

But nothing; the guy just stared at Strelchuk with those

buggy eyes. He was trembling like he might have a fever or something.

Strelchuk ran back and told the others, and they all went to have a look, but they couldn't budge him either.

"Maybe we ought to drag him in here," said Pontormo. Jinx enunciated with a peculiar precision, a careful thickening of the consonants that betrayed a shift of language somewhere in his past.

"Aw, let him be," said Lee Cravens. His soft voice always took the edge off things. "He ain't doin' us no harm there, and he sure ain't no kinder help."

Together, the five of them built two walls, a couple inches apart, and filled the space between with shovelloads of fine stuff. They pissed to make clay and plastered up the chinks in the inner wall. They worked a long time. And when they were all done and feeling suddenly very beat down, they noticed two things: one, that they were all out of water, and two, that old Ely Collins was dead.

3

Tiger Miller on a Saturday night. Out at a coalmine, no place to be. Physically exhausted, otherwise restless. He'd planned, knowing he'd need to unwind after the disaster pressure, to make the usual roadhouse circuit tonight, but now he didn't know. Three days and only about half the bodies recovered. The official toll was now ninety-eight dead or trapped, almost surely dead. Yet hope, the forgivable madness, kept the friends and families out here, doggedly waiting; kept the tired frightened rescue workers digging away.

Black bodies, burnt and gas bloated, had been his dismal fare since Thursday night. Had they moved him? He thought not, yet details were etched deeply. There was one without its head. Normal, except for the missing head and the body's scorched nakedness—in one brief instant of flame, all the clothes, but for one shoe and a pant leg, had been burnt or blown off. There might have been some shirt fragments pasted to its shoulder, it was hard to tell. Peculiarly, part of the jaw was still intact. Body hair, hairs in the crotch, in the armpits, they were all carbonized, but stood rigid. He supposed they would crumble like cigarette ash if you touched them. Yet, he had discovered that the roots of the hair on one man's head, one who still had his, were a soft blond. They removed the one remaining shoe from the headless one— the torso had seemed familiar to a woman who said she had dressed her husband's right foot that afternoon with a corn plaster. The shoeless foot stuck out screaming nude on the end of the black leg, a blistery glowing pink vegetable thing attached to the charred leg stump like a mushroom. There *was* a corn plaster, too, but the woman didn't think it was the same kind. Not exactly horrible finally. Ironic form of ultimate definition. Square corn plaster. Round corn plaster.

Miller sat in the Salvation Army canteen, drinking chlorine-scented coffee to keep warm, eating gummy packaged doughnuts and bruised apples to pacify if he could—and he couldn't—his nervous stomach. Lou Jones was due to relieve him at midnight, and was already overdue. Maybe he wouldn't show up. Miller couldn't blame him if he didn't. Except during the midday deadline hours, he and Jones had maintained a 24-hour watch out here. They weren't alone. Some hundred and fifty newsmen and photographers on hand, though the number had fallen off considerably as the rescue dragged out. He sometimes joined them in the bar at Wally Fisher's hotel, or wherever else they chanced to congregate, feeling a vague nostalgia for the old days. After graduating from West Condon High years ago and making the usual university/military cycle, Miller had turned wire service correspondent, and probably

71

would still be one had he not returned to West Condon a few years ago for his mother's funeral and found the *Chronicle* up for sale. He'd always wanted his own newspaper, had a lot of untried ideas for one, and here it was, a good buy and everyone anxious to make it easy for him, a working knowledge of the town, even his folks' old house to live in. Why not? And so here he was, years later, the prince become a frog, living grimly ever after, drowned in debt, sick to death of the disenchanted forest, and knowing no way out.

Miller sipped the hot black coffee. Mere habit. He reached into his trench-coat pocket, pulled out a pint flask, emptied what whiskey remained into the coffee, realizing as he did so he was being watched. One of the new widows, Mrs. Lee Cravens—still not technically a widow, actually, since Cravens' body had not yet been recovered. She sat on a wooden folding chair in one corner of the tent. She smiled at him when he glanced over, but he pretended not to notice, let his gaze drift on past and out the door. Glanced at his watch impatiently, but paid no attention to what it said. Mrs. Cravens was a spindly nondescript young woman, but the tragedy had brought her bloom. Miller's photographs chronicled the transformation from Thursday's formless cotton print hung baggily, shabby loafers, and sparse hair limp over pale crabbed face to the present pert act: now, a nightly pressed indigo skirt swathed her rear in hooked silhouette, breasts arrowed up in a starched white blouse, color tipped faintly fingers, lips, and lashes, and her hair coiled instructed under a woolly cap. Ingeniously, to this caparison she had added her husband's bunchy black and orange high school letter sweater. Three infants had whimpered this morning at the wind's gnaw, augmenting that aura of mournful innocence that so attracted the foreign newsmen and photographers, but tonight she was without.

Though he had never seen her before this disaster, Miller knew her: she was the disconcerting epilogue to all his high school eroticism here, his fatuous taste then for the dumb poppy that ran to seed with the first tentative wound. In spite of the intoxicating touch of their taut adolescent bodies and the fragrant heat of the sweaty prefatory scramble, the conquest was always a comedown—in the end, they laid for want of imagination. Freeing himself was painful, but seldom difficult; curiously, they had usually led him to the next one. They married for the reason they laid, and when the famous bane of progeny poisoned it for them, there was nothing left—a few empty infantile motions and instincts, absently clung to. They peopled West Condon, these pricked flowers of his, and getting used to them was his first hard work on coming back here. Often they had recognized him, even those like this one he had never had, and something persistent in them had seemed to freshen briefly. It was illusory, of course; not even they knew what it was. He had blundered a few times before he had learned to see past that false rebudding—maybe the will to blunder had been part of what had brought him back here—and each indiscretion had punctured his privacy with the nuisance of mild scandal. He had learned to look elsewhere, out in East Condon generally; they watched him here.

Jones showed up, after all. Jones was his salvation: his dogged attending to the task made the silly game almost pleasurable. A slow copywriter, but a genius out in the field: always in the right place at the right time, and he always knew everything. A real find. But then, of course, Jones had found him. Blond stubble frosted the man's pale jowls and his small creased eyes were marshy with blood vessels. The blond wiry hairs that fringed his upper face below the hat gave him a moronic look. "You look like an advertisement for the black death, buddy," Miller told him. "Sure you don't want to call it a night?"

"And miss all the fun and glory? I'm okay." He patted a topcoat pocket that bulged with a fifth. "What's the story?"

"Fifty-six cadavers up and tagged. Two rubberbag cases. Forty to go."

"That makes ninety-eight, one down. They find somebody?"

"Yeah, they found Willie Hall working on a rescue crew. Turns out he didn't show up for work Thursday night and nobody noticed."

Jones grunted. Miller drank off the coffee and whiskey. Cold. Nearly made him gag. He crumpled the cup, took aim at a scrap barrel across the length of the tent, fired. Deadly. The Tiger. He turned to find Mrs. Cravens at his elbow. "You wouldn't be goin' inta town, wouldja, Mr. Miller?"

"Well, yes . . ."

"D'ye mind?"

Miller glanced up at Jones, attempted to suggest a shrug of total indifference, but saw it only added to Jones's deadpan amusement. "I suppose not."

Night's damp had deposited fog and the drive in from the mine was painfully slow, cramped at his shoulders. The fog came at him in waves, curding into a dense bright mass, then suddenly tearing like tissue. The road's dirt ruts were frozen hard and jagged. Occasional gray hulks in the ditches to the right and left reared as monuments to Thursday night's crises.

The woman beside him, in a show of weariness, slumped against his shoulder. Of course. It disgusted him, yet in spite of himself, he started picking up messages from below, and there was a stirring there. She was too obvious and there was a cheap-soapiness about her, but he was oddly agitated by the cushiony feel of the thick sweater with its bright WC—"Water Closet," said Lou Jones— and the yellow glow of her knobby adolescent knees in the light of the dashboard. He tried to put his principles in order and found, in short, he had none. He felt overworked and unrewarded, tired of the game he played, the masks he wore. West Condon, community of Christians and coalminers, and he its chronicler: if they were mad, how much more so was he? So, screw them; when in hell, do as the damned do. Besides, it was almost thirty miles to the nearest roadhouse, and what would he find? Maybe nothing at all, arriving so late; at best some pimpled telephone operator or listless store clerk. As for scandal, Jones would be sure to make something of it no matter what he did now, so what difference did it make? The Chevy plumped out of the ruts onto asphalt. As though jostled, Mrs. Cravens slipped down, tumbling her hands and face into his lap and deciding the issue once and for all, bringing a few curses of his own down upon his head.

Miller reached home about five, staggered into the shower. He was nearly blind with fatigue, eaten up with a vague sense of betrayal, though of whom or what (prudence?) he couldn't remember, and drunk as a skunk to boot. "Let us all learn," he said aloud in the shower, raising Montaigne from the dead, "from stupidity." His next station was the bed, but, fallen there, he found that the room leaned and turned, and remorse troubled his imaginings. He decided he must be hungry, went to the kitchen to check the refrigerator. Not much there. Punched open a can of beer. Hair of the dog. Cockroach skittered out from under the refrigerator. He jumped to stamp on it and spilled the beer, got squashed cockroach all over the sole of his foot. "Do not despair," he said drunkenly to the roach as he scraped it off on the edge of a cardboard box used as a wastebasket, "for our Lord Jesus has changed the shape of death." He thought about maybe frying some bacon for a sandwich, but the frying-pan reeked of onions he'd burned in it several nights ago. So he had a peanut butter sandwich. Again. On stale goddamn bread. Took it to bed with him. He sank, forgetting everything, awoke moments later with a mouthful of peanut butter sandwich and an earful of telephone alarm. Nauseous, he crawled across the bed, dragged it off the hook. "The number you have just dialed has been disconnected—"

'You're home." It was Lou Jones. Something in the tone said that Jones had been calling for some time.

"West or east, home's a beast." Miller hung up, took a bite of sandwich. The phone rang again. He tried to figure out what the bastard's angle might be. He picked it up: "Jones—"

"They've found some maybe live ones."

"What!" Miller stirred, propped himself on an elbow. "Have they got them up?"

"Not yet, but they know where they are. Found a T-shirt tacked up with six names on it and arrows drawn."

"What's the matter they can't—"

"Big fall in the way. They figure it must have come down after they bratticed themselves off."

"Do they know who—"

"Well, besides Lee Cravens," Jones said wryly, hesitating a moment to allow the blade to twist, "there's Ely Collins, Mario Juliano, Paul Minicucci, Guido Pontormo, and Michael Strelchuk."

Miller slumped back into the pillows. Oh man. "I'll be out."

4

The veterinarian Dr. Wylie Norton sat in the kitchen in his pajamas, sipping coffee and milk and waiting for Sunday to dawn. Upstairs, his wife Eleanor slept fitfully. Perhaps none in all West Condon had escaped suffering this raw January weekend, but this was little consolation to Wylie, who had hardly slept and saw worse times ahead. Others, after all, would sooner or later adjust, but not Eleanor. Therein lay her greatness, to be sure, yet . . . Wylie sighed and sipped. He hoped only that, whatever happened, they would not have to move again. They had had to change towns eight times now in the past fifteen years, and the frequency seemed to be accelerating. They had left Carlyle to come here to West Condon just a year ago, and they had only been in Carlyle fourteen months before that. Just long enough for him to get a small practice established, begin paying off debts, then—knock! knock!—the inevitable committee.

He had just dozed off in front of the television when they came to their door in Carlyle one year ago, and for a woozy moment he hadn't even been able to remember, staring at the men under his porch light, what town he was in. There had been four of them, their pale mordant faces puddled blackly under the dull bulb. He had invited them in, but they had hesitated, frowned at one another. Eleanor had stepped up behind him, and knowing all too well why they were there, had asked, "What is it, Wylie?"

"These gentlemen . . ."

"What we got to say won't take no time, Norton," one of the men had said. A big man, over six feet tall, with a heavy stomach underbelted, wearing a sport coat with wide lapels, green checked shirt buttoned at the collar, and peering baggily down at them: Mr. Wild, young Larry's father. A man much like this one had once blackened Wylie's eye in another town, claiming a similar offense.

"In plain talk, we want you two to get out of Carlyle," another had piped up, a man named Loomis who owned three beagles that he whipped with gun butts, or so Wylie, who had had to treat them after, had been convinced. Though much shorter, he had stood behind Mr. Wild, and all you could see were his little red wet eyes and thin blond eyebrows over the big man's padded shoulder.

"I don't rightly understand, fellows," Wylie had said, drawling a little like he had learned to do, showing that he was just a quiet peaceful man . . . and he was. "We've always tried to be—"

"Norton," Mr. Wild had said bluntly, "you know why."

Wylie had turned to face his wife, becoming, as it were, their intercessor. "Eleanor . . ." She had stood pale but erect. The others perhaps had seen only the defiance. Wylie had seen the pain, the fortitude draining away, the higher she lifted her chin.

"But who are you gentlemen?" she had asked. "What is your authority?" A mere delaying tactic. They always had a way, ultimately. She had placed one hand on Wylie's shoulder, and he had stood firm to support her.

"Excuse me, Mrs. Norton," a third man had said, a man whom Wylie had recognized as the owner of one of the town drugstores, tall fellow with rimless glasses, a "mercurial" type, as Eleanor would say, oval and merchantlike in the face. "We are not a what you call, ah, *legal body*, Mrs. Norton, as I am sure you can appreciate." He had chuckled abruptly, continuing soberly: "We are only you might say interested citizens of this—interested citizens and *parents* of this community. We have, well, we have been requested by our, ah, our good neighbors to speak briefly if you don't mind for a few moments with you. Mrs. Norton, frankly, we—that is, *all* of us, have been frankly asking—have *repeatedly* asked you to terminate your, ah, your activities as regards all the—as regards the *youth* of Carlyle, and you have nevertheless persisted. Now, in view of—"

"We're asking you two to get out of town!" Mr. Loomis had snapped.

"Now, now, take it easy, Loomis," the druggist had scolded. "Dr. and Mrs. Norton are, that is, they are reasonable people. I am sure that we can be too."

The short man had grunted, glaring schoolboyishly at the druggist. Mr. Wild had peered down on them all and had said, "I think they get the picture."

The druggist, while apparently engaged in observing a lone unseasonal gnat knocking at the bulb overhead, had then coughed and dropped the phrase "certain, ah, *medical* procedures, which might be taken," and Wylie, turning to Eleanor briefly, had seen that her fight was over. "All right, gentlemen," he had said, looking at each of them in turn, though only Mr. Wild had returned his gaze. "We liked Carlyle. But we'll go."

And so they'd disposed of everything again, everything but what they could pack into the small luggage trailer he had wisely picked up at a country auction about five years before, and had driven out of Carlyle. Young Larry Wild, one of Eleanor's pupils, had dropped by before they left, the only one in town to do so, admitting that he'd had to sneak away from home, his father having promised him a stiff belting if he turned up at the Nortons'. But he didn't care, he'd said, he'd wanted to tell them how unfair it was and how he'd always believe in her and in Domiron and in all she had taught him, and that he'd practice all the exercises faithfully. He had shown them then, shyly, a word his hand had written the night before. It was SAD-NESS, but he'd said he didn't really know for sure if it came from some other aspect of intensity or not. He had admitted that he felt like he had thought the word before writing it. Eleanor had encouraged the boy to continue to try, but to obey his parents whenever possible and to love the Good. She'd counseled him not to worry too much about his message, sometimes the spirits from other aspects of intensity did act through thoughts instead of, or prior to, writing, and Wylie had admitted he'd not even gotten that far. "Let thoughts pass through your mind," Eleanor had said to the boy, quoting one of her own favorite messages, one Wylie had heard countless times, "like fluffs of dandelion afloat on an errant breeze, like migrating birds, like purposeless foam appearing and disappearing, but let your mind dwell on none of them. The surface must be barren, the page white, the water placid, the room of the mind empty." Larry had helped with the last part of the loading, had walked them out to the car to say good-bye. He'd said it didn't matter if people did see him, they would all find out someday anyway, wouldn't they?

And now: Was it about to happen all over again?

Wylie shuddered, walked to the window. Dark still, and a fog had rolled in. He wondered what Eleanor would make of that. In one thing, they were lucky: there were no kids involved this time, not yet. Or virtually none: it was true, she did have one pupil at the high school, a senior named Colin Meredith, who was now designated a Chosen One and receiving other-aspected instruction, but it was a relaxed and natural sort of relationship, with none of the strain of seeking converts or educating young men from scratch, and luckily he was an orphan. And there was still hope that Domiron would define the disaster as insignificant; after all, he'd said nothing about it before it happened. And certainly she was getting tired of moving around, too, would think twice before carrying things too far again.

On the other hand, the disaster at the mine was anything but a promising sign. Eleanor had not been forewarned, and had been badly shocked. She had hardly slept or eaten since Thursday night, and vivid cacophonic messages now vibrated from her fingertips almost hourly—as though the disaster might have set off shock waves that were buffeting the entire universe, rebounding through Eleanor's fingers. And just here it had to happen, where things had been working out so well.

They'd liked West Condon. They'd found inexpensive housing and easy credit, enough clients to keep Wylie busy, and Eleanor had been able to obtain substitute teaching assignments at the high school. In fact, she was teaching practically full time, and they had told her only her lack of a State teaching certificate prevented her from being named permanently to the staff—toward which end she was now taking correspondence courses. Domiron, for his part, had urged caution and continued striving for inner self-knowing, and both of them had been greatly relieved. Eleanor's long life as a communicant with the higher forces had taken its toll on her, Wylie felt. "It's the price of the intensity of a Scorpion's passage," she always said—and it gave them both great consolation that her voices were at last permitting her this much-needed rest. As Domiron counseled:

Fly with birds as a bird, swim in the sea as a fish, behave in the world as the world would have you, for all is illusion but illusion itself, and only the wise can exist in it with tranquillity.

And then the mine blew up.

It made Wylie recall something Eleanor had said on their way here to West Condon a year ago. As usual, they had stayed in inexpensive motels on the edges of towns, while seeking a settling place. Wylie would check the telephone directories to count the number of veterinarians in the area, would make inquiries about the extent of farming, animal husbandry, and so on. He had, in the past, worked as a lab assistant in hospitals, as a salesman and store clerk, and even, during one depressing period, as a janitor in the high school where Eleanor was substitute teaching. Usually though, he had been able to find work in his chosen field, especially in small and otherwise unattractive Midwestern towns.

They had made several stops before coming on West Condon. In Springer, for example, there had seemed to be too few vets for the amount of farming that was around, but they hadn't liked the community somehow. A taste of degeneracy, a crabbed and wounded look about the citizens. More stops and then in Wickham they'd stayed a week, liked it, had even begun the house search, but Eleanor had chanced to see on the street, of all persons, the tall Carlyle druggist. They had left hurriedly (eventually to arrive and remain here), Eleanor biting her lip and breathing heavily. Maybe the druggist had had relatives in Wickham. Or maybe, as Eleanor had insisted, there had been more to it. But it had in any event been enough to awaken a worry in Eleanor that had apparently been lurking just under the surface. "Wylie," she'd asked, as the car licked and snapped at the blacktop beneath them, "how many men came to see us that night in Carlyle?"

"Four, I think. Or three. No, four."

"The druggist and—"

"The Wild boy's father, Mr. Loomis, and—"

"And *who*, Wylie?"

"Funny. I can't remember."

"Nor can I, Wylie, but the fourth was there, there all the time!"

"Yes, but—"

"Wylie, I don't think now that was the real person of the Carlyle druggist who appeared to me on the street in Wickham." She'd paused, placed her hand on his arm, sending goosebumps to his flesh. "It was a sign, Wylie . . . *we're being sent!*"

5

The wind's edged lick badgers the shifting thickening crowd, provokes from it a chronic babble of muted Sunday morning curses. Marcella, at the mine, blows her nose. Her reflections are pierced from beneath by omens of sickness: tomorrow, maybe even today. But these omens do not undermine her thoughts so much as provide a setting for them. It is as though once-disparate things are fusing, coalescing into a new whole, a whole that requires her sickness no less than the explosion that set the parts in motion. A puzzle oddly revolving into its own solution. The huddled round-shouldered figures, their bleak white faces of disaster, the pale fog of morning crawling sluggishly like a wet beast out of the yellow-bulbed night, the measured raddling of helmeted men, the toothed patterns

*chewed in the sky by the once-whitewashed buildings and
the rust-red machinery—the both laminated with ages of
soot, the raw shreds of gray slate masking the earth: all of
it—each pain, each cry, each gesture—is somehow conjoined to describe a dream she has already dreamt. She
knows first the curse, then hears the passing miner utter it;
recognizes the platinum disc of the emerging sun behind
the watertower, then observes it there. If one among the
present looks over at her, it is clearly a look of recognition
—not of her, but of what is happening. The Salvation Army
lady who has countless times already offered her a blanket
now passes dutifully with another, and this time Marcella
accepts it—but no, not from the cold. And, as she reaches
for it, she feels her hand write an arc through the air, like
a word without letters, yet for that all the more real—feels
suddenly wrenched apart from herself, staring down, observing that act, that arc, that bold single sign in an otherwise stark and motionless tableau . . . she trembles slightly.
The Salvation Army lady hesitates, observes her silently
with heavylidded eyes. Although the woman has before
been extravagant in her pity, the three gray dawns have
humbled her. "Poor child," is all she says, and then she
turns away. The olivedrab blanket is thin and coarse, chafes
Marcella's skin, but it dulls some the wind's hunger. She
drapes it over her head and shoulders like a shawl, and
waits.*

Miller, the rash and intemperate, woke from acid dreams
crying "Mercy!" and wallowing in peanut butter and bread
crumbs, half strangled by the phone cord. He lay there,
trying to recall who and where he was—then Jones's
phone call came to mind and he leaped from the bed,
phone, crumbs, and all. Dressing, he telephoned his frontoffice chief Annie Pompa—their Girl Fried Egg, as Jones
called her when he wasn't calling her worse—and asked
her to go down and open up the office, put the backshop
force on alert.

In the front seat of the Chevy he found Wanda

Cravens' woolly cap, authenticating his folly. He pushed it into one of his trenchcoat pockets. Word was out and the mine road was alive with traffic. Fog gone, Miller pushed the Chevy up to ninety and stayed in the left lane. Twice, other cars lurched out in front of him to pass creepers, and, braking, he nearly spun to the ditch. He swore, lay on the horn, and gunned past them when they ducked sheepishly back in line. He was past caring.

He swung into the yard, parked in the restricted area, leaped out, Speedgraphic in hand, locked the car. Checked his pockets, on the run, for film, notebooks, pencils, felt the woolly cap there. Grisly vision of Wanda Cravens throwing herself, sobbing, into his arms in front of all the popping shutters, haggard husband, fresh from the pits, staring incredulously on. Miller supposed Jones would be up at the Salvation Army tent, but didn't want to face the man cold. Maybe it was all over. He paused to get a photo or two as he crossed the yard—gray sooty day: perfect tone—and exchanged words with those who waved or called out to him. He learned: not there yet, but hope was gone. They had driven pipes through to the different rooms behind the fall, and had got no response. Miller calmed, photographed. Children keeping vigil. The dark stoic mother of a boy named Rosselli whose first night it had been to work in the mine. Tuck Filbert's old father, refusing to give up hope, fighting to get on every rescue crew. He saw Wanda Cravens. She seemed undone by the news: in spite of the renewed attention given her, she had faded back into the baggy cotton print and run-down loafers. He stayed clear.

Circling wide to avoid her, Miller came across a prayer meeting. A clique of West Condon Nazarenes, powered by a squat ebullient man with thick red-maned head, and including several women widowed overnight, had seized the temporary Red Cross shelter pitched near the portal for the miners' families, and from it now issued hymned plaints, remorseful cries, and bristling execrations upon the community's sinful damned. Miller floated experimentally at their outer edge, but sensed his presence bedeviling them; even those who knew him seemed to resent his curiosity, or, at best, stared back at him apathetically. The jowly man leading them, he learned, was Abner Baxter, a faceboss who had led his section out Thursday night standing up. Though men prayed among them, most of his group were women, pale lumpy sorts with sacklike bodies draped blackly, kneeling in cinders and ashes. Baxter lacked eloquence and subtlety, but he had a compact bullying style of his own and a volcanic delivery. *"Serve the Lord with fear!"* he cried. *"With trembling kiss His feet!"* Their prayers defined the disaster as a judgment upon West Condon and a trial for God's faithful. What massed them up and charged them, apparently, was the expectation that Ely Collins—their man of tested faith—would emerge with messages, and it was with no small awe that they now awaited him. Miller knew of Collins. A seasoned mechanic within the mine, he was a locally celebrated evangelist without. He'd run the guy's photo a few times. Mrs. Collins was not among the group, he learned, but her daughter was: a plain gangly girl—pubescent gangliness —named Elaine. She wouldn't speak to him. Then Baxter suddenly interrupted the meeting, roared at Miller to kneel with them or be damned. Miller rose and, holding Baxter's raging gaze, slowly lifted the Speedgraphic before his face and popped a photo, exiting casually before Baxter could get his wind back.

He saw Jones bulge out of the Salvation Army canteen up to his left, hulking face expressionless except for the eyes, falling away with their familiar as-though-pained squint. Miller waved; Jones nodded. Miller stopped to shake a miner's hand, wish him luck, offer a smoke—and caught sight of something off to his right. Stared a moment, strangely moved, then thought to get a photo.

Up at the canteen, Jones stood waiting, looking like a great stone Buddha that had just stood up for the first time in eighteen thousand years and felt like hell for doing so. "What do you think?" Jones asked. "Gonna put the old bitch to work tonight?" Jones had a professional greed for special editions.

"Maybe. If something happens." Miller, feeling guilt for having turned out so late, meant that remark to imply coming any sooner would have been a waste of time. "I've alerted Carl and the boys, put Annie to the task of digging up what bios she can on the six."

Jones grunted, sipped coffee, thin brows arching up away from the brown heat. "We'll know soon. Chigi's team is down there. Is twenty-five bucks okay?"

"For what?" Miller's mind was on doughnuts and coffee and the girl he'd seen. He reached in his trenchcoat pocket for a pack of smokes, absently pulled the woolly cap out instead. Looked at it, blanched, stuffed it back.

Jones, fighting back a grin, drank down his coffee, spat out the last mouthful, crushed the paper cup in his squabby hand and pitched it at a scrap barrel, missing it by a yard. "I offered it to Chigi for a firsthand story, if there's one worth telling."

"Sure, cheap at twice the price." Miller lit a cigarette, dropped the match to his feet, stood on it. "Who's the girl with the shawl?"

"The one you been taking pictures off?" Jones shook his head and sighed, grinned. "Hang tight." He padded a few yards away, hands rammed into his broad misshapen topcoat, conferred briefly with a miner, padded back. "The name is Bruno. She had a brother on this shift. One of the rubber bag cases the FBI had to identify. But, apparently, she doesn't buy it."

"Bruno," Miller repeated mechanically. He stared off toward where the girl stood, darkly turned into herself, yet somehow radiant, some distance away from anyone else, a young girl, probably not much more than nineteen or twenty, under an olive-colored shawl—well, not a shawl, of course: a blanket.

*The watertower—"DEEP" is what she reads of the familiar
eponym—beats its silvery breast against the lightening sky
like a proud but headless colossus. The cast of the sky is
constant, immaculate, innocent of any raincloud blemishes:
sober monochrome white, except for the singular phos-
phorescent eye of the sun, a cutout cemented to this side
of the sky. It is a soft sky, a papyrus sky, on which, at this
moment, a single black bird, a crow, inscribes silent in-
decipherable messages, erasing them as he goes, flapping
his ragged wings in an occasional fury of punctuation. Thin
efforts of gray soot struggle upwards from dying slag
heaps—the earth striving to keep back light—but they disappear into the vastness of the arching overwhite. The
infinite absorbing the finite, and, mercifully, without
ridicule. Below: all is gray. The color of: transition.
Marcella watches the woman running toward her, clutching her broad skirts with one hand, waving wildly the
other, watches the multitude of expanding faces pivot
toward her as though a button has been pressed, watches
the sudden crushing mass against the portal, watches
them fall back as the door swings open, watches the woman
gasp for breath—yes! how she wishes to tell! "It's your
brother!" the woman cries when she is able. "Yes, I know,"
says Marcella.*

Big Pete Chigi emerged, blinking, trailing a smoky
dust, ahead of the stretcher and let fall the bolt: "Bruno.
We were too late for the others."

Bodies mashed at the portal. No one seemed to understand. "Who is it?" they cried. "How many?"

Miller, in the press, held the Speedgraphic high over
his head, sighted by guess, caught the prostrate figure of
Giovanni Bruno being carried out, Father Baglione, the
Catholic priest, coal-smudged and helmeted, following.
Mine supervisor Barney Davis. The company doctor.

"Collins?" they cried.

"Juliano?"

"Dead. Dead. Dead," said the exiting miners.

87

Miller saw a white face amid the blackened: Jones. Good man! Saw Chigi turn aside, glance over at Miller, then slip away with Jones. Bruno! Not even on the list!

Bruno! Miller changed film over his head, pivoted just in time to see the girl, her head still covered, standing isolated and as though unaware, about thirty feet away. Miller elbowed free of the mob, sighted hastily, but just as he fired, a Salvation Army woman thrust her broad ass in the way. He cursed aloud, sidestepped toward the waiting ambulance. They were easing Bruno into it. The girl started forward and he raised his hand.

"Pardon me, miss!" he said, and punched the shutter, just as the blanket settled to her narrow shoulders. He reloaded and said, "My name is—"

"I already know it, Mr. Miller."

"Can you—?"

"I'll be at the hospital with my brother." She spoke briefly with the ambulance driver, and he jumped out to clear a way for her. Inside, in the back, Giovanni Bruno stretched unconscious. Father Baglione and a couple miners had crowded in. The miners clambered out, let the girl replace them. And they were gone. Miller had forgot to get a second photo.

Someone jostled him hard, nearly knocked the camera from his hand, and a voice said, "I seen Tuck, Paw!" Miller lited the Speedgraphic steadily, focused, recorded the tall silent grief of the two men, Lem Filbert and his Dad, both in miner's clothes though both had left the mines, both with damp black faces.

Miller got Barney Davis aside, asked about Bruno.

"I don't know, Miller. We found him knocked out, up on a ledge, away from the others. Like they didn't know he was there or something."

"What shape is he in?"

"Terrible. Should be dead of afterdamp like the others." Davis eased off his helmet. His burry white hair was black from just above the ears down. Miller offered him a cigarette, lit it for him. Davis had a way of gazing off like a movie hero contemplating the sunset as the curtain falls.

"What do you figure?"

"Luck."

"What about the others?"

"They'd been dead awhile." Davis gazed off.

"You going to reopen, Barney?"

"Can't say. Probably. Haven't thought about that yet." He flicked his smoke's ash with one finger nervously. "Oh, by the way, you seen any of the Collins people out here?"

"His daughter." Miller glanced around, spied the Nazarene group at prayer, but Elaine was not among them. "Looks like she's gone."

Davis stuffed his fingers into his shirt pocket, came out with a small scrap of paper. "I picked something up down there. Maybe you'd like to deliver it." He handed it to Miller. "Found it by Ely Collins' hand. One of Collins' legs was gone, apparently something had fell on it and broke it off. Looked like he'd been dead for some time."

Miller read the scrap, pocketed it, smiled. "Thanks, Barney, that's great." Took a couple informal shots of Davis.

"Fair shake on the coverage, Miller."

"Sure, Barney. As always." Davis meant the company was not to be blamed for the disaster and he was not to be blamed for the delay in reaching the trapped men, but Miller played no sides, took favors like Collins' note in stride and let the chips drop. "Come by the office tomorrow or Tuesday, we'll have a talk."

Davis nodded and gazed off.

On the way back to the Chevy, Miller was stopped by the correspondent from UP, just arriving. "Hey, there, Scoop!" he shouted, virtually in Miller's ear. "Jesus! What's up, buddy? I just heard—" His eye were red-rimmed, still baggy with sleep. Cigarette trembled in his fingers. Miller knew just how he felt.

"Brought one up alive, just took him to the hospital."

"Yeah, shit, I know that, Chief. But who was it?"

"Guy named . . . guy named Lou Jones."

"Lou Jones? Where've I heard that—?"

"Out here probably. You maybe met his wife, fat old—"

"Oh yeah! I know the one! Big fat one. They had some kids or something, didn't they?"

"Eight, I think. No, nine. I'm not sure. Better say nine."

"Yeah! Nine! Great! Jesus, these fucking mining families, eh? What's their address?"

"I don't know, but they're at the hospital. Press conference first thing tomorrow morning."

"Not till tomorrow."

"Right. Jones is in sick shape."

"I'll bet. I couldn't live through a conference now anyway." He laughed and, because he was expected to, Miller joined him. Miller turned to go, but the UP rep grabbed his arm. "Hey, wait, Chief! I forgot! Was he conscious?"

"Who—Jones? Hell, no!"

"Jesus, thanks, scooper! You don't know how I appreciate it!" He pounded Miller cheerily on the back, turned to run back to his car. Miller had seen the portable phone hookup in it.

"Hey! Hold on!" Miller called. The slap on the back had pissed him off. The UP guy braked, swung around, staggering like a wounded pigeon. "I forgot to mention that Jones was apparently reading his prayerbook when he fell unconscious. They found it beside him when—"

"Oh yeah? Hey, shit! That's a helluva great angle! Thanks, Chief! Come on over to the town flophouse tonight, I'll buy a round!" And he ran off at full gallop toward his car.

Gray trees wail flying by, cars blink. Inside the ambulance, all is white, preamble to the race's object. Only her brother is black, his long gentle fingers black, his fragile eyelids black, his distant breath comes: blackly. His face is spattered with dried blood. Whose—? Then West Condon bursts upon them with a thump and a scream. Out the back window, she sees a small scrap of white paper lifted in the wake of the ambulance—suspended, it flies away from them and turns a corner. Does it fly still? It is impossible to know.

Big Pete was standing like a mountain, still in greasy work denims, still reeking of underground sweat, just inside the door of the *Chronicle*, when Miller arrived. Miller greeted him warmly, shook his thick hand. Jones bumped through the swinging door from the back shop, lit with one of his uncommon smiles. Changed his whole goddamn face. "Four columns," he announced.

"Terrific!" Miller said. He asked fat Annie, who bulked by her frontoffice desk like an obedient recruit, to make out a check for twenty-five dollars to Chigi, and, waiting for it, made an impatient moment's small talk with the man. Enormous guy with black curly hair and big Mediterranean eyes, his face minstrel-black with coal soot, and when he blinked, as he just did, his eyelids looked starkly white. The digging out of mashed and rotting bodies made most men sick, but Chigi was a stoic down there and much admired for it.

As soon as he had left, Miller hurried to the back, found Jones there, standing over the linotypist's shoulder. Miller scanned the opening lines of the story in a hot galley that sat on a stone about four feet away, counted the galleys already set, gave Carl and John makeup instructions. Carl's fat back protested with shouldered silence. "No paper next Saturday," Miller said. "Long weekend." Carl, enlivened, commenced a round of whore stories, and his hands woke.

Miller, en route to the newsroom, pulled a Coke from the machine, dumped his exposed film in the darkroom. Driving himself now. Front page forming up. No time to ready the photos. Just as well: need them during the collapse next couple days. Put Annie on getting sandwiches and beer sent over from Mick's, setting up distribution of the Extra. She had already obtained notes on Bruno and his family, following Jones's arrival with the news, and her information on the other six was longwinded but useful. Good goddamn girl, he had to admit it.

Jones wheezed in and together they worked out a front-page layout. Jones dug up a pile of old cuts, including a couple Miller had shot down in No. 9 about two months ago that they hadn't used yet, and wrote up a rough summary of Big Pete's version of the rescue for Miller to polish. Decided to banner it with MIRACLE IN WEST CONDON just to wow the homefolks. Jones seemed to be carrying his belly a foot lower than usual, so Miller told him he could do the rest alone; a moment later, the jobroom sofa received Jones's hulk with a sigh that was no doubt meant to strike envy into the benefactor's heart —Jones never took a favor with grace.

Miller called the hospital, learned from Dr. Lewis that Bruno, in a coma, was still hanging on, but that complications, as expected, had set in. In short: "critical." Read Annie's notes. Parents born in Italy, old man a retired coalminer. Five children, two sons killed in the mines and a daughter dead of diphtheria, Giovanni and Marcella remaining. Marcella. He printed the letters on his desk blotter, lit a cigarette, and stared down at them. Marcella Bruno. Agreeable images roamed randomly through his forebrain. Eyelids weighted. He smoked. She knew his name. Turns— Christ! Blinked at his watch: nearly two! Attacked the old Underwood. Cursed, typed, cursed. Stubbed out smokes, lit new ones. Food came. Slowly, the bog of his mind hardened and the way became easier. On the jobroom sofa, Jones snored.

When she calls, Rosalia from next door answers. Marcella hears threats and intermittent gunfire. Rosalia says Mama is in bed and resting peacefully after praying at the church all day. Papa watches the television like usual. "I got plenty company here and don' worry about nothing." Sure, she knows all about Papa, she has changed him once already, no trouble. More gunfire. "He don' even know they's been a accident, child."

92

On his way to the Collins house, Miller kept the car radio on to make sure they announced his special and the pickup points. Heard it three times on the short run. Most of their musical library inapt for the funereal occasion, they apparently appreciated anything out there that would eat up time. He found the Collins place, sturdy old yellow frame, broad porch bellying out, big trees in the yard.

He was met at the door by the girl Elaine. Miller introduced himself, asked if he could speak with her mother. The girl was reluctant, but finally pushed the screen door open for him. Her eyes looked clawed and her hair hung loose. Inside, there was a stale vegetable scent that reminded him of his carrier days, those wrecked Saturday mornings when he had to collect for the week's newspapers, had to step inside cabbage houses and choke while the wide housecoated women searched absently for their purses and fifteen cents and old men in undershirts scratched their beards and glared. While Elaine went for her mother, Miller roamed the room. Not much choice, for the furniture was buried under stacks of laundry. A sentimental religiosity prevailed: evangelist pamphlets, dimestore plaques, cheap Biblical prints. A gold star tokened a war death, and from the pictures Miller gathered it was an only son.

Elaine returned, said her mother was coming. They stood awkwardly to wait. The girl's front teeth were crooked; she covered her mouth when she talked. She said almost nothing and could hardly be heard, just stared mournfully into corners. She was frankly homely, strawlike hair, patch of freckles on her nose, sallow unhealthy pallor about her skin—her hands were coarsely pink, hands of a woman of forty. A simple print dress hung on her slight frame limply.

Mrs. Collins, dry-eyed, stepped broad-shouldered into the room, put her hand on her daughter's frail back, said she didn't want any publicity.

"My reason for coming, Mrs. Collins, was only to bring

you this." He handed her the note. "It was found in your husband's hand."

Mrs. Collins accepted the note, faint tremor in her roughly reddened hand, studied it. "Child," she said, "go get my glasses." She shifted a stack of laundry—Miller noticed now it was tagged with people's names—and sat on the couch, squinting at the note. She was gangly like her daughter, but large-boned, stouter. Same straw hair, even more freckles, but her skull was larger, her neck thicker, her body more massive, her hands tougher. She, too, wore a print dress, but unlike Elaine's, it was dominated by her form. She had quick nervous eyes, wider set, more determined and aggressive than her daughter's. And she spoke with the absolute authority of a longtime matriarch. "I cain't understand it," she said. "It don't make sense that Ely should die."

Elaine returned with the glasses, fragile rimless spectacles with thin gold bridge and earpieces. The woman hooked them on cautiously, unused to the feeble claws, and struggled with her husband's dying hand. Collins must have been very weak when he wrote it; the scrawl staggered almost illegibly and fell away at the end.

" 'Abide in Grace,' " the woman read. She looked up at Miller. "If they was any man alive a saint," she told him firmly, though her eyes had misted and contracted behind the lenses, "it was that man!—He walked amongst the blessèd, Mr. Miller!"

Miller, on his feet still, found himself nodding in agreement. "Mrs. Collins, I wonder if you—"

"Ely Collins did not deserve to die like that, Mr. Miller!"

"No, I believe you. I'm truly sorry." Miller ventured on, aware he might be trespassing family ground. "But can you tell me what you think he means about having disobeyed?"

"They was a bird in the mine."

"A bird?"

94

"A white bird, like a dove. He seen it." She paused, eyes testing his sincerity in asking. "He knowed he was maybe jist seein' things, like you ofttimes do down there, but he was afeerd too as how God might be tryin' to tell him somethin'. He was afeerd God was tellin' him to git outa the mines and go preach." Tears rolled down her broad cheeks and her voice quavered, but she held on.

"You mean he was afraid there would be a disaster?"

"No, I don't think he thought of it like that. He only thought as how he might be sinnin' agin the Lord, might be committin' greed and avarice, to go on workin' for money when the Lord was callin' him to go do His work." She swallowed. Her hands shook. "We wanted to git Elaine growed first," she said, and now the tears were streaming. "He was a good man, Mr. Miller!" she cried in sudden protest. "He done no wrong! He didn't deserve to git killt like that!" Swallowed sobs shook her. Miller felt her grief, but was helpless. "Ifn he died like that, they must be a reason! The Good Lord would not take Ely away ifn they weren't no reason! Would He, Mr. Miller? *Would He?*" Her wide tortured bespectacled face seemed to be accusing him. "Why did Ely die and his partner live? *What is God tryin' to tell me, Mr. Miller?*" Tears flowed; she didn't even see him now. "*Why?*" she screamed.

Miller stammered something about being sorry. Elaine, weeping, begged, "Ma! please don't cry! *Ma!*"

The woman, clutching her husband's note, slumped from the couch to her knees on the floor. She wept so huskily, so brokenly, that Miller was certain that, though perhaps she prayed often, she wept seldom. "*Oh God! help me! help me!*" she cried. Her great body quaked with wailing, and her red hands clawed in the braided rug. Elaine wept hysterically, her face buried in her mother's armpit. Miller took the moment to step over the two women and get to the door. He had already photographed the note, and he'd call later by phone to ask about publishing the damned thing.

It was after nine before he reached the hospital. Stopped short at the entrance: realized he was still running. Hadn't slowed since the rescue. Paused to calm himself. Flicked his cigarette into the bushes, wiped the sweat off his upper lip: coarse growth of stubble scraped his hand. Pocketed his hands and shouldered through the door. He knew the girl at the desk. She told him: "Third floor. Dr. Lewis."

On third, he was barred by the floor nurse, narrow-waisted girl with an award-winning hind end. Must be new. Dr. Lewis stepped out of the small lab nearby and his greeting cleared the way. Short even-tempered man in late middle-age, thick gray moustache, heavy brow, white jacket. Miller gave him and the nurse copies of the special, asked about Bruno.

"We're not encouraged, Miller, but that's not a quote. The man absorbed what should be a fatal quantity of carbon monoxide. It tends to accumulate, you know, doesn't get passed off like most gases. Hemoglobin sponges up carbon monoxide two hundred and fifty times as fast as it does oxygen, so what happens, the CO prevents the blood from taking in the oxygen it needs, even if there is plenty present. The other six men in the same space with him obviously died earlier from just this cause."

"Have you made autopsies, or is there—?"

"Blood samples have already told us the story."

"How is it you think Bruno survived?"

"Frankly, I don't know. Maybe your headline makes a . . . valid diagnosis." Lewis smiled faintly: fellow skeptic's gentle prod of hypocrisy. The nurse winked. "One thing, he was separated from the others, though no one knows why, and he may have received a much more gradual dosage. The others could have spread out more, there was room, but fright probably closed their circle. Important to stir the air, too, and they may not have moved around much, especially after their light gave out."

"But if they knew the gas was there, couldn't they—?"

The nurse stood, smoothed her white skirt down over the pubic knoll, and switched into the small lab nearby.

"Probably didn't know. Hard to detect. They just dropped off to sleep as they normally would and didn't wake up after. Or, if they did, they probably lacked the strength in their limbs to move or were too groggy to think things out." The nurse lacked nothing in her limbs, which, beyond the door of the lab, she stretched for him to see. "Peculiar reversal of the dream process: meant to serve us by protecting our sleep, it more likely than not kept these men confused about reality, might well have convinced their vertiginous minds that the disaster was a dream."

"Served them after all, then," Miller said. The nurse was loading medicines on a tray.

Lewis smiled. "In a way. But if Bruno lived, then maybe they all could have."

"Can I see him?"

"Nothing to see. He's still in a coma."

"Is that a bad sign?"

The nurse reached for medicines high on a shelf: made her skirt ruck up and her fanny bobble. She glanced back over her shoulder and saw him looking. He smiled.

"I'm afraid it is. His chances of recovery diminish the longer he remains in it. Usually they come around within the first couple hours, once they've got into fresh air or are fed oxygen, if they do at all. If he does come around, the delay increases the likelihood of pulmonary complications. He is still getting transfusions, respiratory stimulants."

"Can he have any other troubles?"

"Asthenia." Lewis paused. "Temporary stupor or maybe amnesia. This isn't for print, of course."

"No."

"Carbon monoxide poisoning, Miller, amounts to oxygen lack. And oxygen is the one thing—it and glucose—that the brain cannot do without, even for short periods of time. So some damage is conceivable, and there have been cases of permanent mental illness, although almost always, I should say, in cases where there was a predisposition for it."

Miller pushed: "Bruno has some of that in his background?"

Lewis hesitated, then replied, "I don't know, Miller."

"Is he alone?" The question he'd been saving.

"No, there's a young girl here. His sister."

"Can I see her?"

"Rather you didn't. She's exhausted and pretty frightened. She has been out at the mine, almost without sleep, these entire three days, and I'm having to keep a close eye on her as well as her brother." The nurse was doing phallic things, though maybe unintentionally, with a syringe and needle. "We have her on a spare bed in a room that adjoins his, and I was just preparing a light sedative when you came. I've kept everyone away from her, of course, and will do so tomorrow, too. However, if you want to drop around, you might call me first, and—"

"Thanks, I will." Miller gave them spare copies of the special edition for the girl and her brother, as well as for the other patients, stopped in a moment to visit Bert Martini, the guy who'd lost an arm Thursday night. Martini caught on Miller's semipro baseball team. Used to. Martini was in good-enough spirits, but Miller felt his smile cracking, and left depressed. He wondered what he could do for the guy. Make him the coach maybe.

When he went out, the nurse was gone, busy apparently, and he missed seeing her. Too bad. She was something worth seeing. He thought about the miner's sister, pajamaed and small in the hospital bed. Tomorrow. Felt the woolly cap in his pocket. He laughed, and the girl at the downstairs desk smiled back.

And the fatherly man with the gray moustache pats her head and wears a white jacket starchy and dark brows a turned-up trenchcoat collar though his face is black dear God! black! and he can't breathe but smiles dark eyes and wears silk bright shorts silk shirt with a number on it —can't breathe! oh please! and runs like the wind white jacket number fourteen soothes but soot in his hair and can't white eyes face like the wind silk mouth and turned-up can't breathe! the number on it can't breathe! *she screams and he holds her wrist brows with a gray jacket needle fatherly white pats her head and a nurse*

6

This book of the law shall not depart out of thy mouth, but thou shalt meditate thereon day and night, that thou mayest observe to do according to all that is written therein. . . . Have not I commanded thee? Be strong and of good courage; be not affrighted, neither be thou dismayed: for Jehovah thy God is with thee whithersover . . .

The Baxters' family worship Sunday evening was interrupted by an unexpected visit from Sister Clara Collins and her daughter Elaine. Abner frowned in concern; Sarah too was surprised: they had brought up Brother Ely's body only that morning. The simplicities of Sarah's recent life were fragmenting this weekend, changes had touched her that she could not yet cope with, so she now felt something excessively intrusive—if not improper—about Sister Clara's unannounced call. Still, no sooner had she arrived than Sarah, almost against her will, began to weep for the other woman. So hard to believe so good a man was gone. Sister Clara clutched a note; she was terribly agitated.

From the day's commencement, Sarah Baxter had been sorely tried. Abner had slept but poorly, rose early. He had kept to himself, bellowing alone in the closed front room in preparation for the early-morning service, could not even help her with the children. Now that the five were grown so, they all trod over her, especially the three boys, she couldn't help it, and when Abner withheld his hand they blew their disobedience into open malice. Their oldest girl, Frances, usually some help, had had to pass the last three nights on the canvas cot in the shed, and so had waked sore and sniffly, poor child. It was too cold and damp out there and the mice made a fright of sleep— Sarah dreaded the week to come. Abner's austere insistence on the practice vexed her, but the Good Book guided him and he was not to be moved. And as the girls grew, the problems mounted. Already, she and Franny had crossed dates a few times, and it would not be long before little Amanda, already ten, would be complicating the sorry matter even further.

But, although breakfast had been a persecution for her, curiosity to see their father preach for the first time had finally chased the five into their Sunday clothes and had cowed them to unwonted silence in the church. The Nazarenes had grown accustomed over the recent years to Brother Ely Collins' tall eloquence in the Sunday pulpit, and Sarah had feared this morning that her husband's blunt red wrath would whip them with too alien a chill. Brother Ely had saved their church, had built a roaring fire here and tended it with devotion. Although his message, no less than Abner's, had been of the Lord's awesome plans for sinners, his voice had been comfortingly paternal, and he had offered wonderful salvation in Christ Jesus. He had baptized all the Baxters, though they had been baptized before, and Abner himself had always agreed: Brother Ely was a saint.

Abner had stood, round and glowering, behind the rostrum this morning—it had surprised Sarah how stocky and aged he had seemed there, blunt hands gripping the rostrum, red-shocked face with its wide down-drawn mouth just visible above his knuckles—and after they had sung the fearsomely appropriate "Ninety and Nine," which Abner had selected just for its relevance, he had raged forth astonishingly: *"Belovèd! Think it not strange con-*

cerning the fiery trial among you, which cometh upon you to prove you, as though a strange thing happened unto you!" The congregation, almost as a body, had started. Some had snickered in embarrassment afterward, and Sarah had seen with horror that her two oldest boys, Junior and Nat, were giggling furtively into their songbooks. How she had hated them then! She herself had felt near to tears: poor Abner! But, suddenly, the cry had become a prophecy! A boy had burst into the auditorium with the announcement that Brother Ely Collins might still be alive! Sister Clara and Elaine had rushed out and the congregation had bolted up to chase after. There had been a scattering, a rude disorder. *"Hold!"* Abner had thundered. *"Have you forgotten that this is the House of the Lord?"* They had hesitated, lashed to a respectful hush. "Let us all pause before departing," her husband had commanded them, "for one minute of silent prayer that our belovèd brother Ely Collins might soon be among us again!" The minute, abided by, had passed like an eternal judgment upon them, Abner's final "Grace be with all of you! Amen," releasing them somehow miraculously blessed.

Sarah had taken four of the children home, while Abner, a terrible and inexplicable tension crowding his red brows, had with Junior followed the others out to the mine. She had telephoned the Collins place, and Sister Mary Harlowe, poor woman, answering, had confirmed that Sister Clara was waiting at home. She had left Franny with the three younger children and had gone to sit a spell with Sister Clara. Many had come: poor Tessie Lawson, Mabel Hall, Betty Wilson, whose Eddie had died in the hospital, almost all the women from Sister Clara's Evening Circle. She had learned then that Sister Wanda Cravens' husband might also have survived. They had cried together a great deal there. Worried finally that Abner might return out of temper and find the children untended, Sarah had left before any word had come.

Arriving home, she had overheard from the front porch the two youngest, Amanda and Paul, taunting Frances in

the kitchen with the hateful chant Junior and Nat had
started last summer:

Fran–ny! Fran–ny!
She's got red hairs on her fan–ny!

Sarah had slammed in and upbraided them unmercifully, shouting at them that they would hear from their
father on that score that very night. Franny had insisted
shyly that she didn't mind the teasing, and had begged her
not to tell their father, but Sarah had replied she was
anyway mad at both of them still for the way they had
carried on at breakfast. Then Franny had told her that
Nat had run off, presumably to the mine. Franny was less
charitable toward Nathan. They all were. Sarah had heard
before Nathan even came about the curse of the third
child, and certainly that boy was the devil's own. Well.
She was wearied of whipping the child, and now he was
so grown, husky for an eleven-year-old, it usually took both
her and Franny holding for Abner to manage it. And Lord,
it did no good. Abner would not admit it, but that was
the plain truth of it. Nathan could not be saved.

Franny had dragged about all faint and teary, so Sarah
had told her to go lie down until her father came home,
she would finish the kitchen and get Sunday dinner. The
girl hadn't argued; behind her glasses, her eyes had been
red-rimmed, her round cheeks flushed and feverish. Poor
Franny! Such a good girl, and to suffer so! And then the
other children humiliating to make it worse. Franny was
fifteen, she shouldn't have had to endure that trial, but
what more could Sarah have done to stop it? It had been
Abner that hot summer night who had judged the girl's
refusal to tattle on the little ones an act of disobedience,
and all Sarah's wailing had not constrained him. Abner
had not thrashed Franny for a long time, so he had laid
the razor strop to her. Tears had spilled and Abner had
sweated, but the girl had not complained. And the others,

witnessing the scourging, had discovered what now they sang about. How could they be so dreadful, those children? It grieved Sarah. Junior, who had started it, no longer mocked, of course: Sarah had noticed, giving him his baths recently, that he must sooner or later fall prey to his own malevolence. Her poor white goose, he was such a soft one. They were all redheads, all but Amanda, and that was probably why she was her father's favorite.

Abner and Junior had come home shortly after noon, Abner somber and uncommonly gentle. Ely Collins was dead, he had told her softly: horribly dead. She had wished to weep then, but had been unable. Now, he had said, much work lay ahead. Had he meant for her, too? The vague foreboding of ordeal had dismayed her. They had eaten Sunday dinner in virtual silence, all but Nat, who had not returned home and who had not been seen by Junior at the mine. When Abner had retired to the front room, Junior's plump white face had turned to her and he said, "He was frightening out there! Everybody cried! He *made* them!"

More omens of disruption had touched her during family worship. Abner had passed the afternoon studying the Holy Bible, and by evening he had fallen strangely meditative. He had listened with curious patience as the children had recounted their evil doings, and instead of administering the usual castigations, had spoken solemnly with each of them about duty and led them, individually, in prayer. "The fear of Jehovah is the beginning of knowledge," he had told Franny, "but the foolish despise wisdom and instruction." To Junior, he had explained proverbially: "He hath made a pit, and digged it, and is fallen into the ditch which he made; his mischief shall return upon his own head, and his violence shall come down upon his own pate." And he had instructed Junior how the ruthless avarice of the mine owners would bring disaster upon their pates, just as vice and waywardness had brought retributive death to many miners. Nathan, typically, had refused to say where he had been all day, or what it was he had brought home in a paper sack, would not even answer his father. Abner's face had contracted darkly. "The eye that mocketh at his father, and despiseth to obey his mother," he had rumbled ominously, and for a moment the familiar thunderheads had seemed to be forming and Sarah had breathed easier, "the ravens of the valley shall pick it out, and the young vultures shall eat it!" But he had pursued the matter no further, had turned to little Amanda to receive her admission of mocking her sister Franny that day and disobeying her mother, and had, with alarming tenderness, lectured the confused child on love, admonishing her to make love her aim, and to "desire earnestly spiritual gifts, but rather that ye may prophesy!" What had he meant by that? Unnerving portents everywhere! Praying with Amanda, Abner had cried upwards to the Lord: "Oh deliver not the soul of Thy turtle-dove unto the wild beast; forget not the life of Thy poor forever!"

The children, disoriented by their father's altered manner, had gradually grown more unruly, testing the new limits, and Sarah had feared for them. Only little Paul, whose turn was last, had remained wanly mute, apparently too young to perceive the shift. Once Nathan had whispered something in the boy's ear, and he had begun to cry softly. That Nathan! She could have beat him herself! Abner had turned then to Paul, and whimpering, the boy had repeated what Amanda had revealed just before him. And then the doorbell had rung, bringing Sister Clara Collins and her tagtail daughter into the awry room, and Sarah had commenced to weep.

Abner invited Sister Clara to join them in prayer, but she impatiently thrust her note into his hands, saying, "I need your guidance, Abner! It's from Ely!" Sarah wished to see it, but feared Abner's rebuke if she asked; Sister Clara determined the matter by snapping it out of Abner's hand the moment he glanced up and planting it in Sarah's. In tortured script, it read:

Dear Clara and all:

I dissobayed and I know I must Die. Listen all-ways to the Holy Spirit in your Harts Abide in Grace. We will stand Together befor Our Lord the 8th of

Even before Sarah finished it, Sister Clara was demanding: "But what can it mean? What do you take it to mean?" Sarah was too confused even to hook the words of it together sensibly. She waited anxiously, staring hard at the note, for Abner to remove the burden of that response from her, and at last he did: "I think it means that it's better, if the will of God should so will, that ye suffer for well-doing than for evil-doing." The words touched Sarah familiarly: she had awakened to them. They were to have been a part of Abner's sermon this morning.

"Maybe, Abner, but it ain't all of it, it cain't be. I know, God was tellin' him to leave the mine and go preach, and Ely he didn't do it, and so in a way he done wrong. Maybe. But what is troublin' me so, Abner, is what does he mean about listenin' to the Holy Spirit and standin' together—"

Abner, interrupting, growing nervous, explained that the Holy Spirit was the inspired word of the Holy Gospel; we must study it in our hearts and abide in Christ Jesus, so that our consciences will be clear when we must stand before Him "that is ready to judge the living and the dead—" The children were growing restless and noisy, but fell silent instantly before Abner's sudden buffeting glare. "The living and the dead," he repeated, then added, though his mind seemed to be on the children: "For the end of all things is at hand—"

"*That's it, Abner!*" Clara cried and Abner's white face spun toward her, pinched inward in consternation. "The end of all things *is* at hand! Don't you see—?"

"Now, Sister Clara—"

But the woman was in a frenzy and wouldn't be hushed, though Sarah saw that Abner's temper would not long be contained. "We will stand together before the Lord the eighth of—the eighth of when? Of *when*, Abner? *That's* the point of it, don't you see? *Ely was tryin' to tell us that God's final judgment is near upon us!*"

A tremor of dread convulsed Sarah's heavy body, iced her spine: *the end!* "Oh, Abner!" she cried, and reached for him. He shrugged her off sternly. The children had stood, stirred, and tears floated now in Franny's eyes.

Abner calmed them. He reminded Sister Clara that the accident had happened on the eighth of the month, that Ely had probably only meant to date his note to her.

"Maybe," Sister Clara said, clearly not convinced. "But ifn he died today, why did he put the eighth? And they ain't a period there before. God's signs to Ely seem terrible urgent to me, and I— Well, anyhow, I wanted both you folks to read it and meditate on it. Me and Elaine, we been showin' it around tonight to all the friends. I mean to bring it with me to Evenin' Circle next Sunday night, so's we can all talk it over together. I hope I kin count on you two bein' there."

Sarah nodded, of course, she always went, but glimpsed Abner's sudden reprehensive glower—and understood then what it was he had been demanding of her all day—and why he must hate her, knowing she wasn't able. "Yes," he said, for them both.

Sarah thought, as Sister Clara and her daughter departed, that the family worship would be considered ended for that night, but Abner shoved shut the door and spun enflamed on little Paul. "A whip for the horse, a bridle for the ass," he recited thunderingly into the now-recognizable terror-riven room, "*and a rod for the back of fools!*" His freckled white hand, pinked with fine red hairs, grasped the razor strop and cracked it across his thigh.

"No, Abner!" whispered Sarah. "Please!"

With frightened fingers, Paul dutifully unbuttoned his pants. Abner, twitching with impatience, reached to tear them from him just as, in terror, the boy made water. It sprayed out in frantic spurts on Abner's hands and knees—reflexively, Abner's right hand whipped and the razor strop cracked like a rifle shot into the child's wee fork. Paul screamed. Sarah cried, "No! *Abner!*"

Abner, implacable, gripped the boy's frail shoulder. "If thou beat a child with the rod," he blustered, "he will not die!"

But Franny, sobbing, covered Paul's body with her own like a mother hen. "Beat *me!*" she cried.

Abner was in a froth. Paul shrieked insanely under Franny's shield. Sarah saw a horrible smile flirt at the corner of Junior's mouth. She stood. Though terrified, she would not allow it again!

But then Abner did a wonderful thing: he ordered them all out of the room but for Franny. Sarah wouldn't even let them hear the flogging, she sent them straight to bed. Paul's peewee was strangely flushed, but he had quieted at least, and she could hear him talking with Nathan in their room. Alone, outside the door, Sarah listened to the blows fall.

When Abner came to bed, his anger had abated. She was fearfully disturbed, but he was disinterested in her explications. She lay awake hopelessly, not knowing what it would all come to. In spite of Abner, Sarah had been cruelly penetrated by the prophetic vision in Brother Ely's deathnote, and only one sinister mystery still vexed her: Why had the Lord chosen to take Brother Ely just the second before he would have completed the terrible message?

7

Until the lightness passes off, she sits on the edge of the bed, as though at a beginning place. Then she slides to the marble floor and pads in bare feet into her brother's room. Withdrawn he lies, absorbed into the bed, one with it, dark etching on the immaculate sheets. "Giovanni!" she whispers. No sign is given her but the determined pulsing of a vein in his neck. His skin has shrunk taut over his high skull, exaggerating the recession of his hairline. His black hair is long on the neck, feathers dark and wild on the pillow. He is . . . somehow . . . changed: yes, a new brother must come of it. She fears for him. So white! The dried blood she'd seen on his face seems to have sunk beneath the surface, now mottles with rose the flesh's pallor. For the first time since the night of the disaster, black doubts peck at her.

Miller was met on Monday midmorning arrival by an officeful of comedy and the miner Willie Hall, who'd been waiting there since eight, Lou Jones having left for "Mick's Dispensary," leaving the message that the doctors advised complete rest and not to expect him for a week or two. His prank had been a complete success, and the wirecopy which he retrieved from the wastecan testified to UP's subsequent panic. Someone had run over to the bus station to buy up the early morning editions from the city, and all but one carried it, one of them happily subheading the prayerbook episode. Miller equipped his ad force with copies to entertain the businessmen they called on that morning, and wrote up a boldface box for that night's front page on "this strange and inexplicable lapse in East Condon journalism." He wondered if the UP rep was still in town—man! the dumb bastard had even embellished his cribbed account with praise of Jones's "long and worthy experience" in the mines and his "model Christian fatherhood"! Such are history's documents! He laughed. Miller had been seeking this vendetta ever since Jones had jockeyed through his latest typo a couple of months ago on "the new *Chronicle* subscription rates, announced this week by publisher and editor Justin Milker," which eventually made *The New Yorker*. He'd been burned more than once by Jones's propensity for the rigged typo, his worst being

108

when Mrs. Ted Cavanaugh, wife of the banker, was named "Lay of the Year at the Presbyterian Church." Only by the grace of Ted's fear of court publicity had they escaped being sued. Now he had squared it and had twitted the sloppy East Condoners as well.

But, pleased as he was, he had little chance to enjoy it. His Monday edition lay blank before him, plugged only in part by the two full-page ads of condolence from businessmen, professionals, and organizations, and the uphill ritual of his newsday now had to be compressed into half the time. Yesterday's special had devoured all his standing copy on the mine, leaving him at best some eighty or ninety column inches of unused miscellany lying idle. Yesterday's photos were not printed, but there were a few old ones he could use a second time. Hastily, he plotted a six-page layout and sent back a pageful of wirecopy. He asked Willie Hall, seated stoically deadpan in the vortex of a pandemonium he didn't understand, to give him five minutes more and raced over to Mickey DeMar's Bar and Grill to deposit copies of the UP story with the morning klatchers. Found Jones in there with Ted Cavanaugh, dimestore owner Burt Robbins, and the Chamber of Commerce secretary, Jim Elliott, town's tireless prince of gossips. Miller had a rushed coffee, while Mick and the others enjoyed the tale. It was a great entertainment, and others who arrived joined the laughter. Robbins, dependably acidic, tagged Jones with "Father" and the rest delightedly picked it up, all but Cavanaugh, who almost always excepted himself in the banter and who in any case had been cool toward Jones since the typo that had humiliated his wife. To escape the worsening consequences, Jones agreed to return to the stable, and that eased some the day's increasing stress.

While Jones issued wearily forth like a jaded elephant to collect the routine tidings, Miller hurried back to the waiting Willie Hall, and Hall had no sooner left than in came mine supervisor Barney Davis, and he was followed by Vince Bonali, one of the facebosses on at Number

Nine Thursday night near the blast in the southeast section. It was after noon before he got his breath and ate the doughnut Annie had bought for him.

From Hall, he picked up a small feature on the events that kept him home from the mine Thursday night and away from death. Spare stunted man in his early fifties, married but childless, with a long record of absenteeism in the mine, Hall explained that he had "had a hunch" about that night: it was on the eighth of the month, and one of his cousins had been hurt by a fall on the eighth of July some years back, and his bird dog had died the eighth of last December, just a month ago.

"Now, I ain't superstitious, Mr. Miller, I don't hold no truck with black cats and suchlike, I ain't no old woman. But, see, them mines they is always dangerous in the winter, now I'm fatalistic about it, I figger when the Good Lord He says my day is up, well, it's up, but then in the summer they's always these here falls. The roofs, why, they jis fall in. You kin usually hear them, they's a kinder stretchin' sound, a kinder crackle, oh, it ain't near so bad in the winter. I don't mind workin' in the—but, see, in the winter then, everything it gits all dried out and they's a powerful lot of dust, and, you know, that dadblamed mine, they don't lay enough rock dust, Mr. Miller, I'm tellin' you the Lord's own truth, they don't give a care about us miners, they don't give a care about nothin' except makin' money. Why, the coal dust gits so bad you cain't even see them machines, them big machines, you jis trip right over them, your lights right on them and all. And that's how it is that it's winter when all these here explosions takes place. I don't mind it in the summer so terrible much. But, you know, I don't think I'm gonna work no more down in the mines. No, sir, I don't think so."

Hall squirmed buglike in his chair, twisted his visored cap in his slender hands, pale mapped with blue veins. He refused the cigarette Miller offered him. "No, thanks, Mr. Miller. It's right kind, but I don't smoke none. No, listen, I got all this here coal dust down in my lungs, see, cause once you breathe it in, why, it don't never come out again, and I'm afeered that smokin' might touch off a kinder explosion right there in my lungs and, you know, smokin' causes TB and this here dust it sticks to the wet part of the lungs, now a doctor told me this, Mr. Miller, it's the Lord's truth, and the lung it gits as tough as the backside of an old mule, and you start coughin' and ifn you smoke, you git TB. Oxford, he smoked all the dadblamed time, and I always says to him, I says, 'Oxford, dadblame it—' Oxford, he's my buddy, he *was* my buddy, he got killt down there, Oxford Clemens, they all called him Ferd, but I called him Oxford, oh, he weren't worth a hill a beans, he come from pretty poor stock, and that man he cussed and smoked all the time, but I ain't one to use nicknames, see, I think it's downright unfriendly, and, why, nobody called Jesus by no nickname, did they? But Oxford, he didn't pay me no mind, he went right on smokin'. He had a cough, too, I weren't surprised none. He even smoked down there in the mine, oh, it was agin' the rules and all, but he never gave no care about no rules, when he wanted him a dadblamed smoke, he was gonna have it. Shoot, everybody else done the same, it weren't jis Oxford. But our faceboss, that's Angelo Moroni, Mr. Miller, he got killt, too, well, he didn't like the idea none, and he always said, 'don't lemme catch none a you guys smokin' down here or I'll have you outa here on your tail fast as scat,' that's more or less how he put it, but he never took the cigarettes away, so what happened is all these guys'd duck off in some room where they'd stopped working and sneak them a smoke now and agin, and, well, Mr. Miller, ifn they'da smoked out in the haulageways in the open, it wouldn'ta been dangerous at all, but these here abandoned rooms, they's plumb fulla gas, and everybody told Angelo that, but he jis said, dadblame it! I don't want none a you guys to smoke at all and that's period! That's pretty much how he put it."

"How many years have you been a minor, Mr. Hall?"

"Thirty-six years, Mr. Miller, thirty-six years, off and

on." The man had small eyes circled with worry lines, an overbite, very little chin. A light gray grizzle furred his cheeks.

"Do you know Bruno well?"

"No, I seen a lot of him, he was on my shift and all, but, no, I cain't say as how I really know him. Always I felt sorry on account of the others they all picked on him a lot down there, but you couldn't never git friendly with him, he was a kinder *inter*-verted type, ifn you know what I mean. Like you'd say it was a nice day, and he'd jis stare back at you. He was a funny bird." Hall tilted his head to one side a moment as though listening, himself resembling for that instant a "funny bird," and then he continued: "Knowed his buddy well. Wasn't it a pity, Mr. Miller, how Ely Collins had to suffer? Don't seem right somehow, man like that, he was our preacher, you know, how his leg got chopped off and how . . ." Hall's voice trailed away as, gazing off, he suffered Collins' mutilations. "He took a lotta trouble with Bruno, he was always tryin' to save him, build him up."

"You mean he was trying to convert him from Catholicism?"

"Not exactly, on account of he weren't no Catholic, or leastways none a them other Roman fellers cared to claim him. They said he'd split off or somethin' and I guess he's sort of nothin' at all."

"Did Collins talk to you about leaving the mine?"

"No."

"Or seeing white birds in the workings?"

"Seein' birds? No, not Ely, musta been somebody else."

"And now you're thinking of retiring, Mr. Hall?"

"Well, now, I won't exactly say that, Mr. Miller, but I'm gonna be lookin' around. I ain't too old to learn a new trade. My wife Mabel she thinks I oughter start over in somethin' where I kin work out in the open. I ain't afeerd none a the mines, a miner he ain't skeered about goin' down, else he'd never go, you git fatalistic, but it's jis they's so dadblamed unhealthy. Besides, that there bed

112

is playin' out, and now they's this mess down there to clean up—you know, they don't give no care at all about the poor miner what gits throwed outa his job, they jis only reckon up what it's gonna cost them to fix up all the damage, and they reckon up how much they kin make off the coal that's left, and they add and subtract, and it all depends on the number they end up with, see, no, it's the Lord's own truth, Mr. Miller. It don't come to their minds none about us poor miners, outa work and too dadblamed old to start over again. Why, I don't know *what* I'd do now, see, I'm over fifty, and you cain't learn an old dog, as the feller says, why, they're jis leavin' us to rot!"

"That pansy!" Davis grinned later, when Miller described the interview. "Why sometimes right in the middle of a shift, he'd start bellyaching about the smoke and cry around there was going to be an accident and he'd refuse to work. He hasn't got the nerve for the job."

"Maybe," said Miller, "but, still, there he was, right afterwards, volunteering for rescue crews and taking twice the risk of usual work."

"Feeling guilty probably," said Davis.

"Here, Barney, before I forget. I saved you a couple extra copies of the special. Your ugly mug made it again."

"What the hell! Two nights running! I'm getting famous!" Davis opened the paper, searched out his photograph, studied it a moment, then tossed it down on the desk with an effort at indifference, handsome square jaw set in disdain. "Think you'll win some more prizes with it?"

"Maybe. If your picture doesn't stop them." Barney laughed and Miller asked, "What caused it, Barney? Have you figured it out?"

"Smoking, Tiger. I'd bet my last buck on it. We located two or three possible areas where it might have been touched off. Trouble is, the first blast set off secondary ones, so you can't always be sure which is the first one. But we're pretty convinced one of those guys or more was smoking."

"Who's 'we,' Barney? You mean the operators?"

"Well," said Davis with a loose laugh, touching the bridge of his rimless glasses, "you don't figure the union's gonna volunteer that, do you? Anyhow, we already found some cigarettes."

"Whose were they?"

"I don't want you to print any of this now, Miller, it would only prejudice the inspections, but we found them next to a new kid, his first night down there, kid named Tony Rosselli, by him and a timberman, Oxford Clemens." Clemens was out of Miller's own generation, and his violent death, like a breath of his own approaching doom, had preyed on Miller more than any of the other ninety-six. Ox had been his adolescent effort at rehabilitation of the downtrodden, and though Clemens as hero had disconcerted him, the emotions and indistinct yearnings of that sophomoric time had their claws in him yet. "We didn't find any matches, but they may have got blown up or maybe one of the rescuers snuck them out."

"Why was there so much fire, Barney?"

"You're getting at we didn't have enough rock dust down," Davis said defensively, adjusting again the glasses on his small sharp nose. "I know, that's what the union propaganda's trying to establish. Sure, it could have been better, it always could have been better, it's one of those things you can never do enough. But we passed all the inspections, Miller, and we'd just ordered some more, figured to lay it down in February, but, well, it just didn't work out the best possible way—we didn't want those guys to die, Miller."

"No, I know, Barney, but—"

"I wish to hell we *had* had more rock dust down, I can tell you that, I'm goddamn sorry how it has turned out. But that's a small thing, you don't need any rock dust at all if you don't have fire in the first place. Why, we hold safety meetings every month, and do you think it does one goddamn bit of good? Those bastards go right on smoking—what can you do?—and not taking care of their

114

machinery, just asking for trouble. Sometimes, it's just like they're daring the goddamn mines to fall on their heads and half hoping it will, like that's gonna prove something or something."

Miller asked the question he supposed he'd be asking for weeks to come: "What about it, Barney: think you'll reopen?"

"Can't say yet, Miller. I hope so. It's my job, too, after all. After the official inspections, we'll survey the mine, consider its potential, and if there's any goddamn chance at all it can be profitably reopened, why, we'll do it. There's too many people around here depend on that mine, Miller, and we don't want to let them down. We're not a charity, but we're not pigs either. If you're gonna print anything, I'd suggest you say that at this time the company has no intention of closing the mine. I think you can say that." Davis got up to go. "And, say, I just want to mention, we didn't think too much of that story by Chigi. He was just one guy of hundreds out there working their asses off and it seemed like his story made it out he went down there single-handed and carried Bruno out on his goddamn back."

"Really? I thought it was pretty fair, Barney—"

"Well, I'm exaggerating. But I just wanted you to know—and it didn't exactly paint the mine as the prettiest place in the country to work, either, if you know what I mean."

"Well," Miller laughed, "it isn't."

They stood, and while they were shaking hands, Vince Bonali walked in. Greetings were exchanged. Bonali wallowed a cheap fat cigar around in his mouth. "You got a real parade today, Miller," Davis said.

"Hell, you can't hog it all," Bonali said.

Davis laughed unconvincingly and, with good-byes, left.

Miller took down Bonali's account of the night of the disaster. Bonali was faceboss over eighteen men in twelfth west off old Main South, not too distant from where

Bruno and the other six had entombed themselves up in fourteenth east; he had been in the zone of impact and only yards out of the sections where the fire had reached. With the habit of all facebosses Miller had ever known, he provided an extensive preamble on his own merits as a miner, punctuating with stabs of his mutilated cigar. As he talked he grew excited, nearly shouting. No longer looking at Miller, he seemed to be concentrating on some point about five or six feet out in front of him. Big barrel-chested guy with a voice that filled the office. Impressive man. Probably a good faceboss, all right. "So I run back and already the shit's so thick you can't see. I find out there's four guys have bugged out. Two of them, Lucci and Brevnik, they got out okay, though I gave them a royal chewing afterwards for jumping the goddamn gun. The other two who left was Cravens and Minicucci. They must have gone the wrong way." He paused to consider them, then went on to describe enthusiastically exactly how they had used the ninth east air course, crossed over on the overcast to the New Main South air course, running into Abner Baxter's section, and exited the mine about two and a half hours after the explosion.

"What kind of guy is Baxter, by the way?" Miller asked. "I called him for a routine interview and he flapped into a rage on the wealth of the wicked and the sanctity of the poor, but refused to come down for an interview and wouldn't let me quote him."

Bonali hesitated, bit down on his cigar. "To tell you the truth, Tiger, that guy's been a pain in my ass since the day I was born. Nothing was ever enough for him. He and his buddies nearly wrecked the union movement through these parts. Every time we organized, he'd disorganize, and then holler at us for lack of guts. Stirred up a lot of bad feeling toward . . . toward our people, too. For a while, it was like one union for Italians, one for Americans. And he made a lot of noise but he was scared of fighting himself and he always packed a gun. Guys got killed in those days, and it wasn't only the scabs. Of course, I don't need to tell you that, Tiger. Your Dad was a great guy. A buddy of mine got it, right in the brains, one of the toughest union men we ever had, and just about everybody knows it was Baxter shot him, but there was no way of proving it. Back then, we blamed it on the operators because we needed evidence against them, and we was afraid of busting up our own ranks, but everybody knew. Now he's grown him a fat belly and has got religion and lets his steam off on the holy rollers. We brought our sections out together Thursday night, and this is just between you and me, but he wanted to drag Davis out of his office and lynch him. He's a nut."

Miller asked him what he thought caused the blast.

"Gas, Tiger. Only thing that can cause one like that. Damn mine is full of it." Bonali squashed his cigar murderously into an ashtray, thick dark brows crossed into an angry frown. "Needed better control, better ventilation. All those abandoned workings up in fifteenth and sixteenth were full of caves, pumping out methane by the tankfuls. Should have either ventilated better in there, or closed it off. Spark off some motor, maybe even just the goddamn friction of one piece of machinery rubbing up against some other one—and then, there wasn't any rock dust down in that firetrap, Tiger. It's a wonder we didn't all of us get killed."

"Barney said they'd passed all inspections."

"I don't give a shit what Barney Davis says, there wasn't any goddamn dusting done. Listen, sometimes those inspectors don't even trouble their asses to come down into the mine. They just have them a big fancy dinner somewhere and lots of drinks with Davis and the rest of those bastards, and the next day they file their report, hell, I've seen it!"

"Pretty serious charges, Vince."

"Yeah, and there's ninety-seven dead buddies of mine to make them more serious, Tiger, including one of the greatest facebosses that mine ever saw." A tear came to that strong man's eye, and he brushed it away. "But, hell, don't quote me, I'd never get another job in this country."

"Say, somebody said something about some horseplay in the washhouse Thursday night, something that had to do with Bruno."

Bonali flushed. "Well, there wasn't nothing, it was— no, there wasn't any horseplay."

Miller laughed. "Hell, I'm not running court, Vince. What I want to find out is about that poem."

"Oh, that." Bonali grinned, shifted heavily in his chair. He rubbed his jaw with his hand, the little finger of which was missing. "Yeah. Bruno wrote a poem."

"Do you still have it?"

"The poem? Naw, I gave it back to him. What would I want with the goddamn thing? Poem about his Mother." Bonali laughed loosely. "That silly bastard!"

Rosalia brings Mama. The veil she wears to funerals she is wearing and her feet are compressed into the old black shoes too small for her. Sia fatta la vostra volontà. Stands so darkly singular, small hurt blemish in this sterile white. Tears glinting like prisms tumble out and wet with light her crinkly brown cheeks. "My boy!" she says to the nurses who enter. "My boy! my Chonny!" Her Mama, whom English frightens, is the only person to Marcella's knowledge who has called Giovanni by the English equivalent of his name. Mumbles, rootlike fingers rattling the rosary. Curved light ekes out of radiators, bending perception. Adesso e nell' ora della nostra mòrte. Marcella repeats the words. Giovanni, the tall boy whose shy protective love has brought her safely to womanhood, lies suspended in a mechanism of light and steel, generated by his own indecisive pulse. "My boy! povero Chonny!" The old black shoes melt into the marble floor. Boots, really, with hooks instead of holes for the laces. Brittle and black and cracked. Reflecting the white room, condensing it into a minute pattern of glitter deep in the hard black polish. Nonna's shoes. Così sia. Her Mama thinks Giovanni is already dead.

Shaved and lightly barbered, the Monday edition sand-bagged with everything short of leftover Christmas carols and put to bed, Miller drove to the hospital. Over the phone, Lewis had told him Bruno was still in a coma, no change in his condition, but that Miller could speak this afternoon with the man's sister if he wished. Bright cold day—prinked faintly with a widely scattered dazzle of frost crystals—chiseled the town's usual tumble of casual boxes into planes of rare precision. He drove through these hard streets feeling himself peculiarly distinct, as though watching the processes of animation that slid him, white outlined cartoon figure, past the fixed drop of white outlined cartoon town. The Speedgraphic lay, as always, on the seat beside him, but it was unlikely he would use it. Formulated questions, but images of her fragmented them. He was surprised to discover that his hands were sweating on the wheel.

The hospital, usually a dead white inside, was today somehow blurred and hopeful, a contrast to the frozen clarity he had just driven through. Uncommonly, neither the blood of birth nor the knock of death jolted his mind this afternoon as he entered, but rather a flush of pleasure in visible human progress warmed him. We move on. Things can be better. There are goals.

This bud of well-being was threatened momentarily by a near-encounter with Wesley Edwards, the Presbyterian minister, out dispensing his crinkly-smile consolations, but luckily Edwards didn't see him, turned into somebody's room. Actually, the man Edwards, while unimaginative and soft-souled, was no worse than the rest of the West Condoners—no, what rankled was his goddamn presumption. All his breed galled Miller, but especially the complacently doubtful types like Edwards—he blanked out this town's small mind with his codified hand-me-down messages, and when you pushed him he would slyly hint he didn't believe it himself, goddamn ethical parable or some crap of the sort. Well, you're still the old fundamentalist at heart, Miller accused himself. Miller had noticed that Edwards, awkward among ailing men, spent most of his time giggling with the hospitalized women. They were prone and all but naked, yet safe, and so was he. Maybe the bastard got a buzz out of their bedpans. The thought made Miller smile, and it was this smile he carried into the third-floor convalescent lounge, where Marcella Bruno awaited him.

He arrives, in crushed light, bringing with him the air of old storybooks, things wanted, things with a buried value in them. As a child, she watched him run, a man to her, though they called him a boy, a man with long legs and strong shoulders. He ran for them and was praised, he leaped and was loved. And now it is for her he comes smiling, a man to her still, long and strong, with something about him of forest greenness and church masonry and northern stars. They speak of her brother, of her family, he asks about her. A man to be praised, yes, a man to be loved.

Back in, the cartoon town had fuzzed once more into lumpy solids, and the cartoon man was singing. A healing was happening. Sore, worn, he had found a young girl's affection and had plunged in wholly. Where would it end? He didn't care, he would see her again. The lumps glided recognizably by, and he found he hated them less. "You arrogant shit!" he said out loud, and laughed.

Still high, he left the Chevy in the plant lot and went straight to Mick's. Hadn't had anything but Cokes and a doughnut. He found Lou Jones at the big round table near the bar, apparently into some story, and he thought of some Jones could be telling that put him ill at ease. With Jones were the hotelman Wally Fisher, the lawyer Ralph Himebaugh, and Maury Castle, who had a shoe-store in town, three of Mick's most dependable klatchers. Although Fisher had a coffeeshop and bar in his own hotel, he was always in here afternoons. "Two with onions,

Mick, and a beer," Miller said, and damn if it didn't sound like a feast to him.

Jones, disgruntled at having his story interrupted, leaned back and lit a cigar. The others cheered, reluctantly but sincerely, yesterday's special edition, and exulted once more in the Father Jones escapade. Castle rattled tonight's paper and read Miller's "inexplicable lapse" box aloud for laughs, then Wally Fisher rumbled, "So, come on, Father, tell us what the sonuvabitch did."

"Lou was just describing one of the gentlemen at your newspaper," Himebaugh said by way of explanation. His quaint precision tinkled discordantly in the dark plain bar. "He has a rather, shall we say, individual manner of demonstrating his passions."

Castle heehawed.

"Who's that?" asked Miller.

"Carl," said Jones.

The pressman. Miller grinned. "I should have guessed. Schwartz is the world's most disturbed cocksman. What now?" Mick passed a glass of beer over the counter and Castle slid it across the Formica tabletop to Miller. It was well after lunchtime, and the place was quiet. Only the sizzle of hamburgers in the yard-square kitchen off the bar. Mick had the television on as always, but the volume was off. Grand gestures of a bigmouthed guy pushing deodorant.

Jones drank off his beer, nodded at Mick for another. "Says he was worldweary after his unusual Sunday labors yesterday, so to restore the spirit he toted body and soul over to Waterton to Mrs. Dooley's. He meets with this—"

"Mrs. Dobie's," interrupted Miller. "You can see how often Jones gets over there!"

Jones didn't share in the laughter, chose to relight his cigar instead. His eyelids slowly drooped the table to silence. "He meets with this pigeon he has in the past plucked, and he flaps over to bicker with her the tariff. But this birdie is grounded. Very down in the beak. Just slopping up a drink or two, she says. Carl inquires what can the matter be, and she informs him tearily she has lost a brother in the mine accident." Miller glanced up, winced inwardly. That bitter breath again. Had to be her. "She has decided she is gonna take a week off from the ranch, fly the scene, try to forget. She's sniffling blowsily, and Carl is afraid she's gonna break into some noisy lament and ruin his whole fucking night. He scans the club, but the others are all paired, have eggs aplenty."

"You would think they would do less business on such a night," Himebaugh interposed softly, but they ignored him.

"So finally he says to her, let's go to your room, have a quiet drink there, you can tell me all about it, I'll buy the bottle. She's a sorry-looking red-eyed droop, but, as I say, he has no choice. She shrugs and says okay. She leads the way, and at this juncture in the narration, Carl consecrates a quarter hour or so to the immortalizing of her butt as it joggles up the stairs a few inches in front of his face, her skirt rucking and rippling, and bringing on, in Carl, a certain agitated enlargement."

While Castle hollered about that, Miller asked, "Hey, Mick, what about those hamburgers?"

"Hunh? Oh, Jesus, Tiger! Hold on!" Mick ran to the kitchen, called out, "Just in time!" Which meant they were black, not white, ash.

"Round of beers, too, Mick." The bigmouth guy on television, who had earlier been urging fragrant armpits, now spun a large wheel, while a muss of little mousy women stood by mockbreathless, clutching their handbags. Whole goddamn American populace was becoming a bunch of actors.

Mick handed the hamburgers, fresh from cremation, over the bar to Castle and went to work on the beers. Jones puffed on the cigar, took a long swallow of beer, continued: "So they get to the room. He, she, and her prize wazoo. Carl pours out two tumblers. There's only one chair in the room, and, just his luck, while he's dispensing whiskey, she's planting her buns on it. Carl seeks a scheme to decoy her off the chair and onto the bed. He puts her drink on the dresser, thinking she'll come and get it. No. She sits there looking run-over and commences to stare at her feet. He suggests she go lie down, as she looks a mite peaked. She hears nothing. He finally concludes he will have to use force, and that is just the which he does not care yet to do." Jones drinks to the rapt silence.

Mick hung over the bar with a big foolish grin on his broad Italian face, finally came around and joined the others at the table. "What do you mean?" he asked incredulously, without dropping the grin. "You mean he aims to lay this miserable broad?" Mick was a large guy, but he had a funny high nasal voice.

"Well, so he's thinking about this and he is just about to screw the gentility act and go heave her off, when the goddamn whore herself gets blithely up and humps off to weewee. Carl hastily claps her whiskey down on the night table aside the famous scene of action and appropriates the chair for himself. And, true to form, she staggers back in, still out of the plot, and plumps down on the bed. She picks up the glass, drinks it off like it was water, sets it down again. Still, she hasn't looked once at our hero, hasn't let a peep."

Himebaugh was giggling softly, eyes squinting slightly under his bushy black eyebrows. There was a prudery in him that usually drove him from such gatherings as this— he was a common visitor to this table, but seldom stayed long. Now he tittered and stared at his hands, nervous on the tabletop. Fisher, a flabby old man, sat leaning back on two legs of his chair, chin tucked in the soft fleshfolds of his neck, a smile on his poker face—he frankly enjoyed the story, rarely interpolated. Castle guffawed abruptly from time to time, but not in strict cadence with the tale. He had round leathery cheeks that ballooned when he laughed. Castle could tell at a glance where a man bought his shoes, and, if they weren't from his place, it didn't pacify him to explain you had to spread your business around.

"Meanwhile, our man in Waterton is taking it easy with the alcohol. He pumps in a couple stiff swallows, avers it prolongs the action, but too much and he might not fire off at all—"

"Yes, that's true!" Mick sang, then flushed when everyone roared. Fisher even had to ease his chair down on all four legs momentarily for fear his convulsions would spill him.

Jones smiled around his dead cigar, continued: "Patience pays its way. The whore spreads on the bed and commences to chatter. Carl learns who her brother was and some miscellany about him. She kicks off her shoes. Carl, coolly denying still his throbbing rod, pumps her more about the brother. She tells all. Tears. Very touching scene. Carl waxes sympathetic. It is very sad indeed. He even works up a kind of tear and rubs his eye red. Advises her she ought to turn in for the night, forget all about it, head off tomorrow on that trip she's been thinking about. She's grateful. Says by Jesus he understands her. She tells him nighty-night and flops over to the wardrobe, stopping by the dresser to puddle out another tumblerful. Sets the tumbler on the floor by the wardrobe, hauls off her blouse, skirt, and bra, drops her drawers, wriggles into a traditional scrap of lingerie." Jones paused to light the cigar again, while the others exchanged commentary. Lou could never keep a cigar going and tell a story at the same time.

Miller had finished the hamburgers, delicious in spite of the charring, and wanted another beer, but Mick was hunched over the table in such unabashed absorption, he didn't have the heart to break the spell. Fisher smoked and chuckled drily, leaning back. Castle brayed and shouted, "Come on!" and beat the table. Himebaugh giggled to himself and stared at his glass, still full of beer.

"She squats for the tumbler and is surprised to discover

our boy still in the picture. Look, she says, I'm going to bed. Like you said. Good night. Thanks, but good night. Carl shrugs, tells her don't mind him, he's just finishing his drink, and before she can object he switches back to the belovèd brother, jaws on like he has known the poor bastard all his life. So she doesn't complain now, just quaffs the rye, then nests into the sheets, her famous bun to the breezes, and listens to him. Carl says she holds her goddamn hand curled up against her mouth and reminds him of how his little daughter sucks her thumb at night."

"A detail only a doting father could provide," Miller interposed. Fisher laughed drily, but the others seemed not to have noticed there had been an interruption. Jones downed his beer. Himebaugh's glass sat untouched in front of him. The man's soft flabby titter was nearly inaudible. Seemed in some world of his own. On the screen above, pain pills were Bigmouth's product now. Disturbingly graphic.

Jones said, "Carl's knob, caught wrong in his pants somehow, is paining him, so he decides the time is come. She is gazing placidly and weepily through the far wall, so he quietly slips his pants off and, talking all the time, hooks them on the foot of her bed. Then, just as the whore seems about to emerge from her distant focus, he jumps her, pins her arms behind her, and says: *'Your brother was the biggest shit I ever knew, he deserved to die!'* "

"Jesus Christ!" cried Castle, slamming the table, half out of his chair.

Mick was stunned, jaw slack, and even old Fisher lowered his chair, smile sliding to frown.

"Mad!" whispered Himebaugh, glancing at the others. "The man is a psychopath, a lust murderer!" But, strangely, it was as though he were still giggling.

"That cocksucker!" Castle thundered, as always the most vocal. "Why, he's a damn, a damn, a goddamn—what did you say, Himebaugh?" With that, they started to laugh again.

While Jones relit his cigar a fourth time, Miller ducked behind the bar and pulled five more beers, omitting Ralph. Castle, Fisher, DeMars, and Himebaugh stared at each other with astonished half grins and exchanged condemnations. "No, what I mean, that sonuvabitch oughta hang!" Mick declared in summation.

"Well, the hapless lady is too shocked even to fart," Jones resumed. "She starts a fierce struggle to break loose, but Carl is twice her size, and, besides, she's at a real disadvantage there on her belly with two hundred and fifty pounds of hot raging beef saddling her, pinning her wings. And all the time he keeps rubbing it in what a cheap rotten punk her goddamn brother was." Castle banged. Fisher was over the table. "Only trouble is, Carl complains, he can't get his reamer in the slot from behind, nice inspirational view of these great nates butting and flushing, but from the style he has her pinned, he can't jack her up enough to bore in without losing his hold. He tries to tap the devil's porthole, but there's too much angry muscle there." Himebaugh, wide-eyed, watched it in his beer glass. Mick gaped. On the screen, Bigmouth was panned offcamera and a sniveling grandmother admired her new prizes. "Carl clamps both her wrists in one hand, perforates and diddles her with the thumb of the other. She screams and bawls and then suddenly she twists out of his grip and they punch and wrestle and peck and claw, but Carl downs her finally and plunges it in and she shrieks like she's been stabbed for the first time. Carl's getting edgy about the cops or Mrs. Dopey, it's a scene like that, figures you can hear her all the way to West Condon, but he has locked the door and the time it'll take them to break it down he reckons will be time enough and he doesn't give a damn. He digs her how her brother was queer and about the fruity silk shirts he always wore in all kinds of nigger colors, she'd just cut him in, see, on how she had bought the boy all these silk shirts, and that the brother sucked everybody at the mine, and on and on, and she's screeching and flapping and belting the shit out of

126

him, and now he says there's a real sweet stink rising, and she tries to pitch him out, but he's got his talons deep in her tail and doesn't let go no matter what, and she twists and doubles and sweats and even somehow gets her feet once against his chest, and, boy, he says he is flying blind but there is nothing like it!"

Jones drank beer to let Castle and Mick get a few choice pent-up expletives off their chests. Himebaugh was pale. "I'll be goddamned!" muttered Fisher, now smiling broadly.

"So they're crashing around on that bed, blood and feathers flying, she clawing at his eyes, him grabbing a fistful of her hair and arching her head back so she can't take good aim, and first thing you know they're whamming away in rhythm and she's clutching him in the ass and warbling his goddamn name and they both come in a tremendous simultaneous explosion and collapse in a tremor of secondary spasms."

Castle whapped the table and Mick, in his peculiar twitter, cried out the name of the Savior over and over. Beer was spilled. Jones calmly examined his mutilated cigar. Himebaugh's eyes lacked focus. "I'll be goddamned!" Fisher rumbled again, reaching for a wet pack of cigarettes on the table.

"But, Jesus, Lou! Do you mean to say—did she—?" Mick lacked the words for it.

"Yeah," said Jones. "She liked it."

"Goddamn!" boomed Castle. "It's too much!"

"They both admit it was the greatest fuck they've ever had, if not indeed the greatest in world history. The rookery is a wreck, all whipped and shredded, blood here and there. Carl is nearly blind, but he can see that those flawless haunches are brilliantly striped and maybe for good. He apologizes about what he'd said, explains he really never knew her brother, he was just trying to snap her out of her doldrums. She says never mind, doesn't matter. He says he is sure he was a great guy, the greatest, had to be: brother of a woman like her. And silk shirts

127

were his favorite kind. She agrees and cuddles up in Carl's arms and he ends up passing the night there. They couple three or four more times during the night and this morning. No comparison to the first round, but it is warm and satisfying, quoth our hero. He adds that his old lady really has her feathers up when he appears for breakfast this morning, clawed and bloodied and reeking of strange persons, but he's feeling so afloat he doesn't even take the bother to apologize, just eats his Wheaties in blissful silence, and wafts on down to the shop, advising everybody it is spring." Jones pulled Himebaugh's untapped beer toward him, leaned back and drained it, turned his attention to relighting the cigar: all signs that the tale was told.

It was too much for Castle's restricted vocabulary. There was no expletive to do it justice. Finally, he just shook his tanned jowls and said, "What a story, man!"

"If it don't beat all!" chirped Mick, mopping up the beer on the table with his apron. "Sometimes I think most of us poor bastards just don't know how to live. This corrupt lunatic is—really!—" He paused for effect and looked around at the others: *"He's a goddamn genius!"*

"Yeah, you said it!" laughed Wally Fisher. He propped back on two legs again. "Goddamn genius!"

"It's a fucking outrage, that's what it is!" Castle laughed, relocating words. His voice banged in the still room. On the television, somebody won $33. Camera panned on the audience. Pasty sheep-faced smiles. Hands silently and dutifully slapping each other. "But goddamn if it ain't true to life!"

"And twice as beautiful!" added Mick over his sopped apron, and they all laughed. He still sat, but now Miller's interest in another beer had passed. He couldn't help but keep Himebaugh in the edge of his eye: the man sat silently, shaking his bony head, his thin old legs crossed, hunched in such a way that his elbow was pressed into his groin.

"Miller," said Fisher, "you oughta publish this!" The thought delighted them all.

"What'll we call it?" Miller asked drily. "A Child's Visit to a Whorehouse?"

"Now don't take the fun out of it?" said Castle.

"What if this sort of animal madness were set up as a precept for humanity?" Himebaugh asked earnestly. He cleared his throat, shifted his position, straightened up. "What would we all turn into? It's ghastly!"

"Aw, shit, Ralph," Castle protested, "that's stupid!" Himebaugh glared at the shoe salesman from across the round table, soft underlip turned in. "That's goddamn plain stupid!" Castle repeated, rankled to have had such a good story tainted.

"Stupid! But this is grotesque! This disaster—I mean, in the middle of all this horror, this tragedy—that, that man—that beast—you're *all* beasts!" Himebaugh was losing control.

"I thought it was pretty funny," said Fisher.

"You're a beast," Jones said to him.

Himebaugh glanced darkly at their laughter.

Mick butted in: "Who do you suppose that'd be, Tiger? Reckon that'd be Oxford Clemens' sister?"

"Sure," said Miller. Bigmouth had given way on the screen to a smoking hunter. Miller lit one. "Dinah. I always wondered where Ox got those fancy shirts. I thought he stole them."

"You used to get a little of that, didn't you, Tiger?" Castle asked.

Miller smiled. For several days, he had felt his past sticking to him here like shreds of flypaper. "Well, she wasn't the toughest teacher we had in high school," he said, "but she was the sincerest."

Mick stretched himself through the loose laughter to his feet and gathered up the beer glasses, lining them up on the bar. He got a bar rag to finish mopping the table. "That was sure one goddamn story," he coded.

"Beasts!" bleated Himebaugh insistently and wiped his mouth nervously with a clean handkerchief. Castle snorted, and they started in again.

For an instant something seems to hover . . . enters him: his eyes open. They turn to her, blink in recognition. A hand faces its pale palm to her and she takes it. She assures him.

The phone rang. Everyone was gone. Miller, dozing upright in his swivel chair, listened to it jangle. Wouldn't answer it. Looked at his watch. Seven. Home was an empty icebox and an unmade bed, didn't feel like going there. Too bushed to go elsewhere. Still it rang, jarring him. He looked at it. Angry black fish, eyeing him with one gleam of reflection. He took it off the spit. "Hello?" He'd tell them it was a wrong number. But it was Marcella. He awoke. Giovanni was conscious and his condition was satisfactory. He listened to her voice, dreamed up questions to keep her talking, knew now there was a better place to go. But there was little more she could tell him. Except that Giovanni had been visited in the mine by the Virgin, a vision, so to speak. Yes, he could publish that. She had come to him in the form of a white bird.

PART TWO
The Sign

The first woe has passed;
behold, two woes are still to come.

—REVELATION TO JOHN 9:12

1

While the mine disaster reduced itself to numbers, repercussions, and causes, Eleanor Norton turned all her time—for school was closed of course—to a review of messages received in Carlyle and West Condon, reasoning that it was the Carlyle crisis that had driven them here, so a relevancy might well be expected. On the first page of each of her logbooks were the words, which she took from the apocryphal book of Baruch: "Walk in the presence of the light of this book, that you may be illuminated." On a first reading, she found only familiar admonitions to live a deeper life and lessons in the cosmological verities . . .

A flower plucked, a fish's leap: the distant star is tortured!

. . . preceded in Carlyle by simple warnings of imminent danger. But by Saturday she had read them all six times, and had begun to discover, beneath the placid surface, an emergent design of revelation. There was, for example, that peculiar reference of a year ago December to

. . . the one who is to come.

At the time, already harassed, she had supposed it to be merely another in the succession of warnings in Carlyle, for the "one" was to bring her suffering and injustice, and Domiron had urged her not to fear him. But now she remembered that she had received similar cautions three or four times in the past—she searched them out, astonished to discover the almost identical wording. Had she misread them all along?

> Do not despair if One should come. Faith and truth have fled away, to be replaced by evil and violence and the lust for illusory things of the body. Oh men of the earth! only a cleansing can preserve you! Wash the earth from your hands and feet, and cast your eyes to the limitless stars!

Did this confirm her theory that the earth had formerly enjoyed a higher aspect of intensity? Was a cleansing to occur? And she, was she to be the agent? And then there was that exceedingly strange message, only a month old, that told her to

> . . . look to the east! look to the west! the feet tug downward, but the spirit soars!

The east: the source of light, of course. The west . . . West Condon? And the tugging downward, was that the miners? These messages troubled her, yet consoled her as well; nevertheless, it was altogether clear that more remained to be revealed.

On Saturday night, learning that there was no longer any hope left for the men still in the mine and that the toll was fixed at ninety-eight, she opened her mind to the Teacher and received the following message:

> As the body suffers, so is the mind cleansed. The seven starred image of life's oscillation from abysses to cusps shadows forth in morning's east, but a firmness is forthcoming. Is nine a number? Is eight a number? Lead men to numberlessness! In the earth a harsh tremor, above . . . an infinite repose. Avoid the illusory, the present accident of conjoined particles, and seek wisdom with love! For a time is to come, and the soul will swim in the vast and empty

sea of enlightenment! Does the body tremble? Chastise it, mind, with mocking laughter! Domiron bids you!

She was disturbed to discover that this new message was largely composed of parts of old ones, but the new ordering of these parts not only provided her startling insights into the events of the moment, but also revealed to her how blind and complacent she had become. It was there all the time, and she had not seen it—had virtually *refused* to see it! And it was she who had accused Domiron of betrayal! And now other wonders came to mind: the frequent minor accidents she had suffered recently around the house, the disappearance of objects, the unseasonal autumn blizzards and the strange damp January, not to mention the increasing turbulence of the messages, the ruptured syntax and enigmatic juxtapositions, all a kind of static, as it were, electromagnetic countersignals from malfeasant forces. Customarily, Domiron instructed her through her right hand, though occasionally through her left, and, in certain urgent situations, directly through her voice.

By my light, thou shalt flee the darkness!

he had cried in her throat more than once.

She had attempted, over the years, to assist Wylie in attaining a communication with the higher forces in the universe, but, though he honestly tried, he had almost no success. Domiron explained privately to her that

. . . if even the faithful are few, how rare then the master!

and that passive natures, themselves noble and receptive, if not supremely spiritual,

may find subtler paths to wisdom.

135

In any event, it was common knowledge who Womwom (Domiron's name for Wylie's soul at the seventh aspect) once was—when the time was ripe, he would play his significant role.

Have faith! All that is, I am, I am all that never was. All that shall be, I have been.

Sunday, the eleventh, a thick fog pressed at her morning windows. Fog pleased her usually, misted the hard forms that so often deluded and misled her, provided fleeting images of the essential emptiness, but today it betokened her own uncertainties, her difficulties in finding the true way. It curled and wisped through the black branches of their tall elms, like her thoughts floating elusively through the stretched fingers of her mind. Now an object took shape, became an inference, a cipher for action, but then it faded behind the fog's nervous curtain. She sought a clarification of last night's message, but none came. She considered it. Last night she had understood it, but now she wondered if it were really anything more than the customary exhortation to maintain spiritual discipline. She understood, of course the next ascendant sign—now befogged!—but what of the forthcoming firmness? For herself alone or for others? Lead men, the message said. Was she to lead them to the "firmness" in the time that "is to come"? Or is the firmness merely the vernal closing of the cycle? Doesn't the message in fact dismiss the mine disaster as irrelevant? The "harsh tremor" in the earth does not disturb the "infinite repose" above, in the higher aspects. And "the time to come" is nothing more than the soul's return to its source, is it not? Was Domiron trying to tell her that her own death was near? But then why would he ask her to "lead men"? Or might it have to do somehow with the "One" to come? And why should he draw especial attention to the sun's sign? A signal to free herself from the merely phenomenological, or was there a more destructive intent, a parabolic reference to former devastations upon the earth? And there were the numbers to be considered, the number of miners who perished, of course, ninety-eight, but if thought of in a series, nine and then eight, then the next number would be seven . . . but what of that? For it is to "numberlessness" he asked her to lead men.

She inspected the whole band and all channels, but neither radio nor television provided her clues, although the radio repeated frequently the toll of ninety-eight miners missing or dead. She copied down what names they gave, but they proved meaningless to her. Now, if something of cosmic significance *were* to happen, how would it be signaled? Isn't a fire deep in the earth as telling as a prodigy in the sky? Perhaps, but there were few precedents. Of course, there was the evidence of lithomancy, and even the scales of fish had prophesied. Nevertheless, the message seemed to discount a cosmic event:

> . . . an infinite repose.

Outside, the fog lifted, but the day remained overcast. Lunch came and went, but she had little appetite. Wylie napped after, then went for an afternoon walk—she had been greatly blessed: she knew she could never have survived the humiliations and suffering of the last fifteen years without Wylie's belief in her. She read once more the past two years of communications, and struggled with the enigma of these present words. Impulsively, she counted them . . . *ninety-eight!* She started, counted again. Her heart raced. No doubt about it!

> Lead men to numberlessness!

Of course! Domiron was trying to tell her to lead men away from . . . from a head-count of mortalities to his message! to the limitless and unnumbered truth of his word! "Does it matter these have died?" he was in effect asking. "Bring all to wisdom!" She nearly leaped for excitement! And it was in this state that she found herself

137

when Wylie came back from his walk with a copy of the special edition of the West Condon *Chronicle*, announcing in headlines the miraculous rescue of Giovanni Bruno. "Wylie!" she cried. "I knew it! I knew it! I knew it before you came back! Domiron told me!"

"What! You mean about the rescue?"

"Yes! It was all there! I wanted to shout it out, but I was alone!"

"But how—?"

"It started with the numbers. Nine and eight in a series. Next comes seven, and it—"

"Seven?"

"Yes, and it is seven that leads to numberlessness and to the One!" She was so excited she hardly knew what she was saying. Everything fit at last! It was happening! She even felt certain she had begun thinking about Bruno before Wylie came in.

"That's funny," said Wylie, as though disquieted.

"Yes, don't you—?"

"Eleanor," he said softly, "there were other men trapped in a room with Bruno, but they died." He paused, but his gentle blue gaze, aglitter with a kind of awe, was on her unwavering.

She lowered herself slowly to sit on the sofa. "How many?" she asked in fear.

"There were six others," he said. "With Bruno, they made seven." They said nothing more for a long time. There was much to consider.

A fine snow, more like frost, flecked the land overnight, and Monday dawned bright and cold. Eleanor dressed in warm wool and, after poached egg on toast, slipped on her winter coat and galoshes, fur cap, gloves and scarf and walked out to the mine, she had decided upon it last night, walked out, as it were, to the point of origin.

The town, as she passed through it, or at least this northwest segment of it, seemed strangely unaffected by the disaster that had rocked its very underpinnings and widowed so many of its houses. If anything, there was a fresh renewal, a mocking sense of gladness, brick and painted homes adazzle under the harsh blue sky, toys and bikes in a gay scatter, naked elms casting long graceful shadows on the gilt pavement.

But what was an exhilarating crispness in town became a bitter cold at its edge. Wind smarted her eyes, tears converting the blue radiance into a blurred and angry glare. She pinched the scarf up tight against her throat, but the cold blew through it. The mine road was rutted and her booted feet made poor progress on it. After about ten minutes, she stopped, looked back at the town behind her. She had barely begun. It would take her at least an hour. She faltered. What was the point of it, anyway? But something vital in her, something more than mere will, some deep-celled quality forged in some other life's trial, pivoted her once more and thrust her forward down the old road to Deepwater No. 9.

The road, like the barren yellow-stalked fields, was of a brownish clay the color of bruised fruit. Short bushes grew wildly along the ditches to either side of her, and occasional tree sprouts stuck up like stripped switches, but desolation and death were mostly what she saw through her tears. Much of the time, she walked with eyes closed, her face a numb mask, the air gathering in icy pockets within her lungs. Her legs grew very weary, then indifferent, then seemed even to strengthen, discovering a needled warmth in motion. She walked head down, staring at her feet, counting the steps. She began to see the burdened feet of humanity, treading through their endless centuries of despair. Each gray-booted foot appeared before her like a birth, and died just as quickly as the other materialized to replace it, a ceaseless recurrence, and yet each step was different, unique, fell on different soil, angled away from hazards, delayed a moment longer or perished in a quickened stumble, and always, cushioned by soft earth or tormented by frozen corrugations, there was pain and, in spite of the progress . . . a loss. The voice beside her

139

took her wholly by surprise. "I'm sorry," she said. "What did you say?"

"Can we give you a lift? It's a cold morning." Inside the old car there were two men, both in miners' clothes. They looked to be Italians, the driver a large dark man, bold-jawed and perhaps intemperate, the other slender with a generous hooked nose and crinkly smile.

"No, no, thank you," she stammered. "I . . . I'm just out for the walk." How foolish that sounded! Timidly, she smiled.

"Are you sure?" asked the driver. He had a large voice, resonant and willful, but friendly. "It's a pretty rough hike."

"How much farther is it?"

"About ten, fifteen minutes more. You can see the small rise up there ahead, that hill. The offices and portal are just to the left."

She could see nothing, but she nodded. "I'll walk," she said. "But thank you very much."

They shrugged and left her. She watched the car lurch and rattle away from her, then turned her eyes once more to her feet. She had been close to something and had lost it, but still she could hold before her that which she had had and investigate it with her mind. The unthought thought that the men in the car had blocked was this: Though each step, each appearance and disappearance, was singularly unique, the spirit lodged in them was of an unalterable whole, inseparable from past steps, a part of future ones—it was not the mere passage of finite existences themselves with which one had to reckon, but with passage itself; motion, not the moving thing. And though opposites her feet—this, too, had been at the edge of her broken thoughts—though apparently isolate and contrary, at their source they were a single essence, there their duality disappeared. A triangle occurred to her, but something suddenly unpleasant about it repulsed her. She looked up, wearied of her feet, and discovered the mine buildings just ahead of her, crouched in a sparse grove of barren trees. To her right, distantly, a small rise, itself almost treeless. Above, a potbellied watertank that over-lorded the squat buildings; beneath it, cars sat in a gravel lot, including that which had passed her. She was glad she had walked the whole distance, yet an edge of disappointment frustrated complete satisfaction: her meditations had not equaled the promise of the previous direct experience.

An odor of sulfur here, soot in the air, and near the buildings the sky seemed to yellow. Slate like black jasper crunched underfoot. Behind the watertower reared an insectlike structure, housed in at the top, about four stories high. She guessed it was where the coal was processed—was it sorted or cleaned or something?—for a chute yawned from it over railroad tracks. She stared at the building, letting its eccentric shape sear into her underconsciousness—there was nothing like it in her memory—while her thoughts sputtered and bubbled away. A line came to her suddenly from somewhere, she fumbled in her coat pocket, found paper and pencil:

Out of fog: new signals; in clarity: the gathering of . . . fog.

She seemed to wake, discovered for the first time there were people about her, mostly miners, motion was minimal, there seemed to be nothing happening, some glanced at her, but none paid attention. She sighed, secretly relieved, for the sense of awakening in public had startled her. She read the message. It did not seem to be from Domiron. Some lesser aspect probably. Of these, she trusted few, and doubted now. On the contrary, she reasoned, fog is a false emptying that adds interest to the mystified forms, while clarity, simplifying perception, liberated the mind from counteractive effort. Nevertheless, she pocketed the note . . . it was foolish to be too hasty.

Over one grimy brick office building, a wind sock jabbed rigidly. A northwest wind, and it pierced her thoroughly. The sock poked its signal at the nearby rise, which lifted its nubbed crest just over the fretwork of denuded trees to the east of the buildings. Too squat for a hill really; a hummock, a soft knoll. On a concrete wall, next to a steel door, she found a sign that read: CAUTION! NO SCUFFLING OR PLAYING! NO SMOKING! *This is a Closed Light Mine—Smoking in or Carrying Smoking Materials into This Mine is a* VIOLATION OF THE LAW! Scratched on the wall with coal was: *Look! This Means You!* with an arrow aimed at the word "Scuffling." A few adolescent obscenities, cartooned nude women, male genitals, no clues. In red: JEU AVE! *Why don't you? 1st Nat'l Bank.* She counted the words on the printed sign: twenty-eight—it meant nothing to her. Four sevens. Well, so what? The first five words, true, contained a certain meaning applicable to her: to be careful not to become childish about this crisis, nor to seek unnecessary trouble; but, given the rest of it, it was probably merest accident. What was a "closed light mine"? She didn't know. Were the lights enclosed, or was the mine defined somehow as "light"? Perhaps there was, in a sense, light trapped in the mine that needed now to be released. But all these directions seemed futile. And then, suddenly, beside the steel door, as though it were materializing, appearing there now for the first time, she saw a telephone! So certain was she that she had marched this bitter way to receive a message, that she impulsively lifted the phone off the hook and put it to her ear.

"Excuse me, lady, can I help you?"

She nearly dropped the phone in fright, fumbling returned it to its cradle, apologized to the tall miner beside her. "No, no! I'm sorry! I was only curious, and—"

The miner smiled. "Oh well, go ahead and listen, if you like."

Eleanor calmed. "Thanks," she said, "but I'm just getting in your way, I'm afraid. I hope you'll pardon me." They exchanged smiles, and she walked away.

Unexpectedly, she came upon a Salvation Army canteen,

still operating although the two women inside were packing things away into carton boxes. There was coffee, though, steaming hot against the chill in her, and they seemed delighted to have a customer. They apologized that the doughnuts were from Saturday, but, suddenly hungry, Eleanor accepted one anyway. It was rubbery and tough, sugarless, but sweet to her. When the women learned she was not herself a widow, had lost no one out here, they grew talkative, but Eleanor was too weak to listen. A sense of displacement was overtaking her; exhaustion threatened to buckle her knees. She sat on a wooden folding chair. She could never walk back again. The women told her that all the bodies had been recovered and were being prepared by morticians at the high school gymnasium. They described the hideous condition of some. Funerals tomorrow and Wednesday. They produced anecdotes of rescue, which Eleanor pretended to attend. Their hollow voices clucked and moaned at the horror. Well, did they think they would escape it? Sensational slaughter made people count death exceptional.

The two miners who had offered her the ride entered, and she asked if they might be going back soon; she would like to take them up on their offer. They laughed and said, "Sure," introduced themselves as Mr. Ferrero and Mr. Bonali. They had coffee first, and Eleanor received an account of Mr. Bonali's escape from the disaster.

The ride back into town was surprisingly brief. On foot, it was a healthy hike, of course, but the cold wind had distorted the distance. She told the two men that she was a teacher at the high school, and Mr. Bonali, the driver, said he had thought so when she had told him her name, because he had a daughter, a freshman this year, who had mentioned her. Angela. Angie. Eleanor said, oh, of course, Angela Bonali, but she couldn't bring the girl's face to mind. Mr. Ferrero said it must be a tough job, he wouldn't have the courage to face up to a pack of teen-age monsters every day. She replied that she enjoyed her work, but regretted the absence of spontaneity and receptivity in

143

today's youth. Of course, she didn't mean Angela, she was only speaking generally.

"No, I know what you mean," Mr. Bonali concurred. "She's a wise kid, thinks she's pretty smart. They all do."

"Well, we weren't angels," observed Mr. Ferrero, and Mr. Bonali, laughter booming, agreed with that.

Eleanor explained to them that she had to pick up some papers to be graded in her office at the school, so they dropped her off there, although of course her purpose was to visit the gymnasium.

The mine company guards at the gymnasium door would not allow her to enter. Beyond their bulked shoulders she could see the dark cadaver lumps on the floor under army blankets, fewer than she had expected, white light raying in on them from the opaque windows back of the bleachers, dust hovering gloomily. On the basketball scoreboard: WEST CONDON 14, VISITORS 11. Eleanor rarely thought about numbers—she respected the numerologists, but the ever-present prime numbers were too vague to satisfy her—but, out of an old prejudice from childhood, multiples of seven always caught her eye. Seven, fourteen, twenty-eight, thir—well, yes! of course! the toll! *incredible!*

As though on cue, Colin Meredith appeared before her, a tall supple-limbed boy with guileless eyes and perceptive brow whom Domiron had led to her. His long blond hair, soft and silky, flopped loosely on his pale brow. He seemed extremely excited. Colin's discipleship, if it could be called that, had thus far disappointed Eleanor faintly: he was too playfully interested still in flying saucers and green men from Mars to grasp the profounder truths of essence, transience, emanations, and reabsorptions. Nonetheless, the soil was fertile, his was an aristocratic spirit, and, though cautious (she suddenly thought of the sign at the mine!), she entertained large hopes for him. Now, he said he had been looking for her, had come here hoping to find her. "Mrs. Norton," he gasped, once they had slipped out of earshot of others, "do you remember the message you gave me, the one from, from . . ."

"Domiron." It was not to tell him, for he knew it well; only he feared yet to speak it aloud.

"Yes, the one that said about the long uphill struggle one must endure, out of—do you remember?—'*out of the abyss of darkness*,' you said!"

She nodded, accepting his child's awe, and saw that his true growth had begun. "I received perhaps the most important messages of my long life over this past weekend," she told him solemnly. "Cosmic purposes of enormous significance are to be revealed to us soon. Can you visit me later this week?"

"Sure! Would Friday be soon enough?"

She smiled. "I hope so," she replied.

Eleanor and Wylie returned home from the Tuesday mass funerals, depressed and, for her part, confused. So many deaths at once, the irregular and paradoxical messages she was receiving, the bitter weather—Eleanor was frightened, felt weak and light-minded before the challenge, but could not resist its excitement. She had tried to visit the rescued miner, Mr. Bruno, yesterday, but was told he had not awakened from his coma. She would try again tomorrow, if he lived still. Yet, she was sure he would. She understood at this point all too little, but she was convinced that Giovanni Bruno was somehow a part of it.

She hung up her coat, fixed sandwiches for both of them, but finally didn't eat her own, decided first to read the evening paper. Wylie sank sleepily into the armchair. She felt a kind of peculiar dizziness as she reached for the paper. She glanced at the headlines—and started up, her heart pounding: not only had Giovanni Bruno recovered from his coma, *but he had announced a visitation by what he called the Holy Virgin during his entombment!* She had appeared to him, he said, in the form of a . . . a white bird!

A *white bird!* the image of the soul, the volatile principle, *life itself!* messenger of peace and prodigies! symbol

145

through man's story of spiritualism and sublimation! of thoughts and of angels! the color and creature of mystic illumination! *ecstasis* out of time and freed from space! *"O Domiron!"* she cried, and fell to the floor. *"Let me have light!"* She rolled onto her back, and the chandelier above her lit, swayed, expanded, burst into flame like a skyrocket.

She was on the couch. Her head throbbed. Wylie was leaning over her, patting her hand. She breathed as though against resistances. He withdrew the thermometer from her armpit, shook his head as he read it, gazed compassionately down upon her over the pale rims of his spectacles, his round chin doubling. "Over a hundred," he said. "You've got to slow down a little."

"Wylie . . . what happened?"

"You were reading the paper. Then you . . . you cried out, and, well, you sort of passed out."

"Did you read about it?" He nodded. "Wylie, what did I say?"

He hesitated, looked away from her. "You said, first you said, 'Domiron,' and then, 'Let me have light.'"

"Yes . . . ?"

"And then you said, 'Ask and thou shalt be confirmed.'"

"Ask and thou shalt be confirmed."

"That's right."

"What do you think . . . what do you think it means, Wylie?"

"I . . . I don't know, dear."

"I do." It had been on her mind since Sunday night, since Thursday, perhaps even before. "I must see Mr. Bruno tonight," she said.

"Eleanor, please! You have a fever!"

"It doesn't matter. Nothing else does." As she sat up, a chill vibrated through her. "I have to go, Wylie."

He pressed his lips together, his eyes pained, but then he smiled. "All right," he said. "I'll go with you."

The heated rhythm of fever disturbed the uniformity of Eleanor's perceptions, and what happened at the hospital had afterwards to be reconstructed. People, there were many, though she noticed few in particular. The clocking knock of heels on the marble floor. Whiteness, the antiseptic odor. A fat dark priest was there, old women. One of these, wizened and brown, gnarled with misery but not with great wisdom, was the rescued miner's mother; she spoke no English. Eleanor, impelled by forces far greater than herself, had reached his bedside. He was gaunt and spectral, high-browed with hollowed eyes and fragile as she had known he would be, still passing, thought Eleanor headily, into substance. There were other women outside, a coarse mulelike woman named Mrs. Collins, whose husband, Giovanni Bruno's working partner in the mine, had been killed by the disaster. One of the seven, Eleanor learned, and another chill rattled through her. Other widows, the Collins child—Eleanor knew the girl from school, a shy and weak-minded student. And Giovanni's sister Marcella—when their eyes met, Eleanor discovered a friendship already eons old. "Wylie!" she had whispered. "The girl! She is one of us!" A remarkable innocence, so profoundly seated it could never be excised, opened wide her brown eyes, taught delicacy and gaiety to her ready smile, graced the motions of her limbs. The old woman said her boy had died and come back to life! Marcella translated it, her warmth transforming it, elevating it to essential truth. Marcella, like Eleanor herself, lived, she saw, in a responsive universe. By his bedside, Eleanor contemplated the strange and inexorable processes that had transported her here, suddenly envisioned the confused complex of her past as a series of concentric circles, each smaller and pulling toward the center . . . and wasn't this the very sense of aspects?

Shards of old prophecies broke kaleidoscopically on her mind, as memories of old conflicts, old conquests, streamed out into pattern, rationally ordered. He opened his eyes and looked at her. A sudden terror gripped her: he was

Italian, a Roman Catholic, a stranger, she knew nothing about him, a laborer in the mines, would he find her mad? Hostile faces of old crises appeared, floated, rippled over his gaunt face like watery masks, and if she were wrong . . . ?

Ask and thou shalt be confirmed!

And, indeed, hadn't Mrs. Collins all but confirmed it? That message had excited Eleanor, even though a reading of it was disappointing. A simple Christian admonition finally, which the Collins woman with equal simplicity equated to stale dreams of a Last Judgment. Eleanor could not help becoming impatient with the Christians and their adolescent clubbiness, their absurd dualities, concern with the physical body, their chosen-people complex . . . even though the Bible itself, before Domiron, had been her chief guide. Now, the woman believed that something— perhaps even the Second Coming—must happen on the eighth of February, finding this implication in her dead husband's note, and she was bullish and tense and she had power. She led a group called the "Evening Circle"; Eleanor was invited to attend the Sunday night meeting, but, for the moment, on the pretext of precarious health, Eleanor declined. She understood clearly, in spite of her feverish state of mind, the threat that the Collins woman posed: it was the threat of ignorance. But, in any case, she had to agree with the woman, events of supreme importance were in the air, although the function and date hardly appealed to her, especially since they had never been mentioned by her own sources. Of course, Mr. Collins had been a preacher, it was quite natural that his imagery should be lower-class Christian (and misspelled at that!), he could not be blamed, and there was above all a prodigious, an awesome, coincidence of interest in Giovanni Bruno.

Ask and thou shalt be confirmed!

In that brief moment beside his bed, before they discovered her there and ordered her away, in that instant when he looked up at her, through her terror she drove the question: "Are you the One who is to come?" His eyes burned through her. His breath came shortly. He nodded. They found her leaning against the foot of the bed, eyes closed. Wylie explained calmly to them about her fever, and she apologized, saying she had come in here looking for a place to rest.

Marcella had invited them all to return Friday evening, but by Thursday, Eleanor could wait no longer. Though free from fever, she now suffered from a head cold and sore throat, and had stayed home from this first day of school. Messages since Tuesday evening had appeared one on the heels of another, and all arrowed upon the same incredible event, long foretold, but terrifying in its realization: Giovanni Bruno's body had been invaded by a higher being! *Contact had been established!*

She had to take extreme care. So far as she knew, she was the only person alive who realized it, the entire burden of keeping the connection alive was on her shoulders—a foolish move and it was lost! She hardly slept, though feared sleeplessness that it might weaken her. She distrusted antibiotics: they muddled her, and she could not afford that now. It would be difficult, in the transpiercing of aspects there would be problems. Had it ever really happened before? Surely, but always there must have been final failure, the contact interrupted, its significance distorted, the agent body destroyed; and always the walls were built, introceptive minds buried behind the rubble mounds of power and dogma, the charismatic moment forgotten, misconstrued, the light hopelessly flickering out, extinguished by the terrible density of this earth. And now, over fifteen years of resolute intransigent preparation —no! more! *centuries!*—were coming to bear upon this delicate moment, visible within the fragility of human time and space! Every breath she breathed seemed fraught with peril, yet starred and eternal as well, each a *cosmic* breath. And no sooner had the connection been established, but from somewhere, from within, or from denser aspects, from something malefic in the universe perhaps, something she did not understand, there came resistance: fever, disease, attacks from all sides on her body, on her mind, confusion, a blurring of vision: *so frail a fortress!* She trembled, searching out a greater strength. Her mortality shadowed her, clung to her ankles . . . yes, she would die soon, she must make haste, a second lost and it was for nothing— *she must go tonight!*

The hospital stood on its vast acreage, distant from West Condon's center, under a bright glitter of stars. Eleanor examined them hastily: all seemed in order. A glance at her watch told her Leo, invisible, was ascendant, not the most favorable of signs. Wylie panted along at her side, opened the hospital door for her.

Unhappily, Marcella and her brother were not alone, additional proof to Eleanor of the sudden gathering of malign forces, particularly since the intruder was a newspaperman, Mr. Miller of the local paper. She knew him not at all, but one glance warned her to be on guard. Her life had been so often disrupted by newsmen, she had come to regard the trade as itself an inherently evil one. He seemed courteous and intelligent, but a cruelty lurked at his mouth's edges, and his smooth face's manly mask did not conceal the ravenous gleam of his dark eyes. Yes, yes, she knew him. She spoke idly, stalling for time. What was she doing here? Hah! let him wonder to the end of his days! She sensed that he already had reached the girl and she was in danger. Yet, there was a well-disposed order to the man: she would watch and wait.

Wylie engaged Mr. Miller in aspects of the precomatose phase of carbon monoxide poisoning, and Eleanor, tense, but concentrating her tension in the grip on her damp handkerchief, asked Marcella about her brother.

Marcella looked at Eleanor's glasses, at her graying

hair: "You must be the lady my brother has been asking about," she said.

Eleanor caught her breath. Her sore throat contracted. They went in. Apparently he slept, but then his eyes opened. When he saw her, he nodded, raised one hand weakly in recognition, dropped it, Marcella left them. "Am I to call you Giovanni?" she asked. He nodded. "Giovanni," she continued, seeking the direction, "from whence came you?" He did not reply. His eyes closed. "Giovanni!" she whispered anxiously—she must hold on to it!—"*Giovanni!*" Again his eyes opened. "Giovanni, did you come a great distance?" He nodded. "From another aspect?" He hesitated, then nodded. He trusted her! She licked her lips, tried to grasp the difficulties the other faced in communicating to her, kept her unwavering gaze locked on his. "Have you . . . have you any messages?" He did not reply, but continued to stare at her. So tenuous! She swallowed and felt them at her throat. "The white bird," she ventured, "does it signal . . . a new life?" He nodded. "May I come often?" Again the nod. "There is time then!" she whispered, and at his nod a great relief washed over her. With time, she could do it. She felt the malignant bodies disperse and retreat.

Reentering to stand beside her, the girl Marcella watched. She seemed undisturbed, somehow even pleased. Wylie, she noticed, had also come into the room. The newspaperman was gone. Giovanni Bruno seemed weary, but she wished a confirmation with witnesses present. "Are you the One who is to come?" she asked. He nodded, shut his eyes. In a moment, he was sleeping. But it was done. Eleanor looked at Wylie and at Marcella, and saw that they had understood. In part, at least. The burden was lighter.

2

"One a them cutters makes the goddamn bugdust fly around like grass outa a electric lawnmower," said Vince Bonali. In the mine, voices rose and fell peculiarly, bouncing off a face of coal here, disappearing down a channel there, going dead where it was dry, echoing near water. Miller walked in a slight crouch, the hunching slump of the adolescent feeling his new height: there was headroom down here, but it had to be taken on faith. Always, out in front, the roof seemed to cave downward. The lamp on his head, like the illuminative middle eye, shot its dull beam wherever he looked, was as jittery as his head was, steadied on nothing unless he could hold still, and that, plus the helmet's weight, was giving him a stiff neck.

"What? The climb? Well now, Senator, that's due to the slant in the layers. In these parts, they always dip toward the northwest." Under the shelling of the miners' bitching, Davis remained outwardly calm, gathering influence over the know-nots of the inspection party.

"I see. Uh, the northwest."

"That's right. If the seam is known to slope, why you always put the shaft in at the slope bottom. That way, the loaded cars run to the bottom of the shaft under their own weight and are pulled back up empty."

"Oh yes. Very good."

Any goddamn topic to free the mind's eye from the hovering mass. There were splits in the roof, carvings, grooves, it was oppressively close, always tested Miller's nerve, had since his first visits as a boy, but more so today in this mine that had seen so much violence, heaps of rubble here and there, an all too plentiful evidence of falls: Chicken Licken's panic. He knew Ox Clemens' urge to have a smoke, caught in this black hive of tight deep stalls, found his own fingers more than once at his emptied shirt pocket. On edge, he got a distorted view of things. The shadows pitched by the whitewashed timbers turned into black crucifixes. The equipment, pieces of wood, cable, rubble heaps, wallowed in their own shadows like mangled bodies, and he kept hearing falls, seeing dead ends ahead, smelling gas. As they pushed on, they encountered increasing disturbance, whole rooms spilling out their insides, fractured timbers, the men uneasy, feeling the roof, knocking at it gently, only Big Pete Chigi seemingly unconscious of the threat, wallowing and plunging like a big fat seal, willing to carry the earth above on his nose like a ball, if need be. Heavy equipment lay upended, cables swooped like streamers at a dance, chatter from several corners crisscrossing, varying in volume.

". . . was sunk and put down in the coal in 1923. The coal was shot up on the solid, brung from all the . . ."

"No, we don't use powder, always for a long time now we been employing compressed air, what you call . . ."

". . . a slab there which should oughta be took down or else timbered."

Names. Guys Miller had known, had interviewed, gone to school here with, guys he played baseball with in the summer. Bill Lawson. Tuck Filbert. Mario Juliano. There was still a sick sweet smell down here.

". . . and I was standing there in the engine room, see, when the fuse on the . . ."

". . . gas and smoke, bodies bleeding at the mouth and nose, but they wasn't no other signs of . . ."

"Who? Bruno? No, we come on him and the others back there a piece, Tiger. I'm sorry. I thought you noticed."

"Lemme see here the . . ."

"Well, yessir, that's the rock dust. You don't see it so clear on account of how it is coked over from the explosion." Pedantic precision to Davis' delivery in the effort to score as the present authority. Had his Dad sounded like that? "How's that? Well, it's usually mostly limestone. Should be the same specific gravity so as to rise

153

in suspension with the coal dust, light in color to reflect light, nonhygroscopic so it don't ball."

"The pattern is always the same in these gassy mines," the engineering professor in the party explained. "An accumulation of methane, ignition, usually by sparks off faulty machinery or by smoking, the explosion confined or extended in scope, depending on the effectiveness of the rock dusting." No, *that* was his Dad, right to the point.

"*What* rock dusting?" Bonali's voice came through loud and clear. The whole walk he had been edging in his gripes, but Davis had kept the inspectors' ears, and Bonali himself, in spite of his reputation, seemed edgy, over-cautious.

"Any inspector ever been down in this mine, they've bragged on the place looking like the inside of a goddamn hospital, Vince."

"Which room, Davis? I take it you mean the morgue."

The deeper they got, the blacker it got, the whitewashed timbers coated with soot and coke, the rock dust all but nonexistent—in Miller's mind, as surely in most, the issue was settled, regardless of Davis' rhetoric. The black walls sucked up the light from their lamps. Drip of water. Distant thump. Crickety-crick sound: scamper of rats maybe.

". . . gob, rails, ties, props are piled too close to the track here, don't you see?"

"All your stoppings has got blowed out by the violence, and so your air doesn't . . ."

". . . a spray stuff that helps some, but it don't kill it all. Finally, you just gotta throw up and go on back to . . ."

". . . as how they was apt to blow up the cable. You couldn't hardly possibly see nothing, Professor, the machinery neither."

"And, man, when my buddy seen all that shit flying around out there, why he commenced to plug her and put the brakes on, but . . ."

And then he was standing on the spot, before he understood properly where they were, that they had arrived at what was objectively referred to as "the ignition area." Some contended for another room where drills lay with cap screws missing, while Davis and Osborne snorted at the electric arc theorists by drawing lines of force, declaring for ignition by cigarettes found alongside Clemens and Rosselli. Bonali, a little puffed up from his victories on the walk here, ridiculed: "You can't light a fire with cigarettes, Davis." But the absence of matches or lighter did not impress the inspectors. The former could have been consumed by the explosion, the latter picked up during rescue—or perhaps might still be in a dead man's hands . . . it was doubtful anyone had checked.

What did impress the inspectors was that work had been going on in a squeezing area. An unnerving blue cap now crowned the yellow flame in the safety lamp. "Who declared this room safe?" a visiting UMW man asked angrily, and there were no answers, Osborne the night mine manager sneaking out of earshot, although Barney Davis did protest that the methane was normally vented out of the area, but since the disaster this section was now largely short-circuited. Besides, this face wasn't being worked; Rosselli and Clemens must have slipped back here for the smoke, against orders. Nevertheless, most agreed: the area should have been sealed off. Miller followed the lead of others and put his ear to the face: soft buzz like a fine bubbling.

And here, in this tight black pit, which was crushed and shaken down, damp and dusty at once, in a gloomy intangible nimbus of CH_4, his legs cramped from kneeling, ducking, spine pinched, the air dead and stagnant, among furtive black faces mostly alien and isolate, Tiger Miller suffered for one febrile moment the leap and joy and glory of the state basketball championships—bright flash of meaning, a possible faith in a possible thing: that they could *win!* and there were globes of white light and wide-open space and a thundering excitement, a fast responsive body, patterns that *worked,* challenge, rescue, always a resolution, redemptions tested and proved in the scoring columns . . . a grace on him. Standing straight, he knocked his helmet against the roof: drums rolled funereally, blunt reminder, from the insensate earth, of the real.

"But the evidence?"

"Well, we first notice for soot and coke, Tiger, burnt fibers, paper, for polished surfaces. Here, you see how this rib has got rounded off? Well, that's by coarse pieces flying by, and you can tell the direction plain enough."

Coarse pieces of Oxford Clemens.

"And then, now look at this: see how the dust is streamlined here? The front side of this post is like sand-blasted and then little eddy currents travel to the rear here—see?—and leave them little dust deposits. Way these here mines is cut up, the forces they go ever which way. But when you come on a point where all the forces go *away* from it in *ever* direction, why, you know something went off here."

From this point, Oxford Clemens traveled off in ever which direction. They raked up the pieces and deposited them in a rubber bag. The bag was light and they guessed it was a little man. But the fingerprint expert identified the remains as not one but two persons, both once sizable. Clemens and Rosselli, like ultimate lovers cellularly conjoined, descended as one to their common grave.

"And look here, Tiger. You see how the materials here on the floor is all different sizes? Well, it makes sense, don't it, that the coarser stuff is gonna get dropped first by the forces. And then it goes until you reach the dust point, and that is what is called sizing the materials. So, that's the way you can tell how the flame and forces traversed along here. . . ."

Expansion and white light, a thundering excitement: did Ox go out in a hot dream of the gilded past? It hardly mattered. Out was out. Miller chose not to size the materials too finely. He was giddy enough down here as it was. Kept feeling like he was walking around on a litter of human fatty tissue.

She heard them as a child, a voiced flutter of angels at her
bedstead. Marcella, frail and often ill, watched for them,
and they sustained her. But a hatred in the house frightened
them away. Growing, she rediscovered them at the altar
and in nature. No longer words, but whole sensations
were what they brought her. An indivisibility to life, an
essential sympathy: then, everything mattered. Giovanni
heard them too. In truth, perhaps they were his, not hers.
Of age, she lost them, seeking them. They fled from being
understood. "It is grasped whole, Marcella, but never
learned." Thus, with tenderness and patience, Eleanor
leads her back to her abandoned voices.

Voices. Out of mouths, over phone cables, on the streets,
in his office, out of letters, from other papers, over the
Teletype. Day in, day out, they battered at Miller's eyes
and ears, throbbed convulsively through him, emerged at
his fingertips as the West Condon *Chronicle*. Births and
deaths. The forecast of snow, low pressure, high pressure,
the unseasonable seasonable cold warm rainy dry front
over front . . . process revealed. Twelfth Street under
repair. Rotary's district governor visits, is "favorably
impressed." Six or eight pages twenty inches deep by eight
times wide, 960 to 1,280 column inches, upwards of 50,000
words of space, a decent novel, six days a week. Miller
filled them up. Threats of war. Bingo at St. Stephen's.
Burglary in a supermarket. Cuts, heads, ads, syndicated
features rescued him daily, but only from crisis, not from
thrall. Afflictions, ball games, comic strips, and drunken
drivers. The endless reiteration of sundered instants,
grounded in the subject's abject nature. He wanted to
stop it, but once you turned it on, there was no turning it
off. Grocers' specials and Sunday services. Assassinations.
High school prom. That's where Miller's January went. He
didn't want to see it go, but the next thing he knew, it
was gone.

Always tomorrow's deadline: but he no longer wished
to lose today. Goddamn Clemens and his cigarette! The

mine disaster had touched off something latently restless in him, and now he could not be satisfied. Miller felt rotten, edgy all the time. Snapped at Annie, wrote wearily, fell sullen at Mick's. His stomach rumbled and burned and his gut softened and sank. But he had no time to think. The fleeting whimsy became a recurrent wish: he wanted to stop it. Should never have invented the written word. Kept folly hopelessly alive.

Hopelessly alive: epigraph of the day.

And as for folly, goddamn it, he hadn't learned a thing. It took him a week to discover the classified ads Jones had planted, nearly on top of each other, in the *Chronicle*, and by then he was the last in town to do so:

FOUND: *Lady's wool cap. Intimate circumstances. Inquire in person to* Chronicle *editor.*

LOST: *One husband and one wool cap, same night. Reward for cap. Box "Woolly."*

They called him "the widow-warmer" in Mick's and asked him if he'd collected yet the reward of the woolly box. He reminded them that, as St. James had said, the consoling of widows in their affliction was the stamp of a religion that was pure and undefiled, and, since he was the only one in the Christian crowd who had ever bothered to read the Good Old Book, no one knew enough to append: "and to keep oneself unstained from the world."

Stained and stung, daily abused, Miller sought relief —even a redemption of sorts—in the company of Marcella Bruno. At first, in the days following the disaster, he saw her almost daily on one pretense or another, almost always in connection with her brother. No problem that, for Bruno himself was news, nationally as well as locally: his escape story, white bird vision, precarious health, prolonged comeback, even his peculiar taciturnity. Miller's own interest in the man soon dissipated: what he saw there was the browbeaten child turned egocentered adult psychopath, now upstaging it with his sudden splash of glory—a waste of time. But he made good copy, and Miller sold some of it nationally. With Marcella, it was another story. For one thing, she flattered the hell out of him, the way she looked at him. And there was a grace about everything she did, laughed, walked, turned. Bright, too. And she was beautiful. Coming or going, she caught a man's eye.

But, finally, there was something that got between them. She lacked her brother's laconic self-exaltation— open innocence was in fact the quality that best described her—but shared with him the old fiction of the universe as a closed and well-made circle. It ran deep in her, colored every phrase, and he began to hesitate in the pursuit of his obvious advantage: how did she in fact see him and what did she expect? There could be consequences he didn't want. And he stopped being flattered by her affection when he realized how much she admired her nut of a brother. Understandable, of course: she was born into a family already centered around him, and all she had done all her life had been one way or another related to him. And there was the weight of racial habit, the deep-rooted Italian family traditions, especially those of the beleaguered immigrant families. Nevertheless, she was old enough to judge him rightly. Roman Catholic, too, but as with all mystics, a mild disdain for the establishment, and Miller had seen Giovanni go somehow cold and angry whenever Father Baglione, the local priest, showed up. No, mainly it was her child's view of the plenum—until she accepted it as the mad scatter it was, they could never get beyond banalities and sex play. Did he *want* to get beyond? Apparently, though it surprised him, he did.

So, though caution braked his assault, he nevertheless kept the phone lines open, when with her did not reject and maybe even emboldened her long glances, and somehow felt certain that, sooner or later, they'd share a couch, whatever the circumstances of it might be. She, in turn, supposed his continuing interest in her brother, gave him status reports on his health, and talked of the people who came to see him. A recently arrived veterinarian named

Wylie Norton and his schoolteacher wife were the most frequent visitors. Miller gathered that the Norton woman was a practicing medium of some sort, an automatist and old-fashioned sibyl. He had met the woman and found her harmless. More dramatic were the regular visitations of the Widow Collins and some of her Church of the Nazarene friends. These openly emotional but eminently practical people made an odd contrast with the introverted Catholic Bruno, though he welcomed them. It was mainly the accident of the work relationship between Collins and Bruno in the mine that now conjoined them. Collins, Miller learned, had accepted Bruno as his buddy out of Christian charity toward the rejected misfit, and maybe a little bit out of wonderment at rejection itself. Seeking sainthood, Reverend Ely Collins had probably been surprised that he had had it so easy. Collins, to be popular, must surely have touched more than once on the never-dead chiliastic expectations of the lower-class Christians, and so the violence of his death, the ambiguity of his final message, the singular rescue of his buddy, and, above all, the odd coincidence—if it was that, and it surely was not—of the white bird vision he shared with Bruno, now made these people—especially the suddenly widowed —wonder if something disastrous, perhaps worldwide in scope, might not be in the air. Their immediate fear, apparently, was the eighth of February. Their speculations amused Miller—who himself at age thirteen had read Revelation and never quite got over it—so he printed everything he thought might help them along, might seem relevant to them, amateur space theories, enigmatic Biblical texts, filler tripe on peculiar practices and inexplicable happenings elsewhere, as well as everything they wished to give him. Once the emotions had settled down and the widows themselves had established new affairs or found mind-busying work, their eccentric interests of the moment would be forgotten, of course. Which, in its way, was too bad. As games went, it was a game, and there was some promise in it.

Games were what kept Miller going. Games, and the pacifying of mind and organs. Miller perceived existence as a loose concatenation of separate and ultimately inconsequential instants, each colored by the actions that preceded it, but each possessed of a small wanton freedom of its own. Life, then, was a series of adjustments to these actions and, if one kept his sense of humor and produced as many of these actions himself as possible, adjustment was easier. And so it was that, on his way out of the hospital on a Sunday night, first day of the runt month and the day before Giovanni Bruno was due to be sent home, gamester Tiger Miller, not a wee bit agitated in the fork after a quarter of an hour with Marcella, used his wanton freedom to reject impulsively an old precept about bedding down with the locals and picked up a nurse at the doorway, took her home with him. He had noticed her the night of the rescue, sandy-haired Tucker City girl, now more or less of West Condon, family a mixture of immigrant Englishmen and East Europeans, he learned, bright-eyed and quick to banter. Mainly it was her long slim waist and plump butt that had drawn and kept his eye; privately, he called her Happy Bottom, and, in bed later, she laughed gaily when he told her. What was something so great as this doing in West Condon? Only a fool would stop to ask.

3

They have moved me to jealousy with that which is not God! They have provoked me to anger with their vanities!

Abner Baxter paced the front room fretfully Sunday evening, waiting for Sarah to get the children dressed for the family's evening worship. His knuckled white fist belted the desktop, slapped at the open Bible, thumped into the back of an easy chair. "Strive thou, O God, with them that strive with me!" he whispered hoarsely. He paused before a large reproduction of the great bearded Peter, standing over the convulsing Sapphira, enemy of another day. White with righteous indignation, quivering with holy rage, swollen with the power of the Lord, the mighty Peter in one volcanic gesture had shown the true glory of God. "Why hath Satan filled thy heart to lie to the Holy Spirit?" asked the caption.

Well, Sister Clara Collins' "eighth of the month" heresy had harrowed them all, but Abner restrained his wrath, biding his time. He preached in the church on the faith of Enoch and Noah, Abraham and Moses, and let them read what they would into it. Time would do her in. But for now, she still had most of them with her, prideful and perverse as her foolish message was, and his duty to the Lord was to remain steadfast in the faith and wait for the woman's inexorable fall.

Not that she'd challenged his right to the pulpit—it was rather that she didn't seem to care about it. She attended his services, but seemed detached. Even in prayer, down on her knees before him, there was an arrogant willfulness about her that seemed to lift her above the others. And it was at her Wednesday Evening Circle where she most sorely vexed him. Their prophet and master in the Sunday pulpit, he was nothing at her Evening Circle. There, even that spineless chinless little fool Willie Hall had the presumption to contradict and interrupt him. Abner had counted on his wife Sarah assuming the leadership of the Circle, but once again that wretched woman had proven more burden than blessing to him. He'd upbraided her unmercifully for her faithless trepidation, but she only cowered and whimpered and begged that he forgive her.

And now tomorrow, the grand and triumphant homecoming for Mr. Giovanni Bruno! What a mockery! What an outrage! Why, even his own people knew him to be mad—how could Clara be such an imbecile? If she could only have seen that silly man, held naked and blubbering while his fellow Romanist Bonali read that poem—! No, she'd been blinded by her grief, had given in to her selfish whimsy, and only shock and punishment could now bring her once more to the true path. And this was Abner's task. He cracked his palm with a razor strop, gazed up once more at Peter.

There was a knock: he ordered them to enter. Sarah and Francis came first, the others trailing reluctantly. And tomorrow there would be hosannas and dollars strewn like palm branches: the irony of it stuck in Abner's flesh like cruel barbs. I, too, was saved! "Cursed shalt thou be when thou comest in," he cried aloud, and his family shrank before him, "and cursed shalt thou be when thou goest out!"

Bruno's big homecoming was Ted Cavanaugh's idea. There was a national—even international—focus on the man, why not put it to the whole town's service? Already, Bruno had emerged as something of a town hero, a symbol of the community's own struggle to survive, so why not make the most of it? True, as a hero, he was a little short on style maybe, but this town was long accustomed to making do with less than the best.

So Cavanaugh had talked to the Rotarians at their regular luncheon meeting, called the Chamber board together, conferred with Mayor Mort Whimple. They'd set 2 February as the date, since that was the anniversary of the town's incorporation, even though Doc Lewis had said that might be pushing it a bit. A special statewide relief-fund drive for all the families of miners lost in the disaster had already been launched, and now Whimple had agreed to double the effort, enlarging especially on Bruno's needs. Ted had got at the Jaycees through an employee at his bank and to the BPW and Eastern Star through his wife. His son Tommy had activated the youngsters at the high school, especially those of Hi-Y,

Job's Daughters, the Lettermen's Club, and the like. Alderman Joe Altoviti had carried the project for Ted into the Knights of Columbus, Lombard Society, and the Eagles; Burt Robbins and Jim Elliott had worked on the Elks and the Legion; and Cavanaugh's minister Reverend Wesley Edwards had involved the West Condon Ministerial Association. The Catholic priest was, as usual, more grudging, but he agreed to appear on the scene at least. Father Baglione was an old Italian whose loyalty to Rome, as much racial and provincial as organizational and pious, so outweighed any local considerations that he was really still a foreigner here. Didn't even speak good English. Cavanaugh had been trying for years to get him promoted or some damn thing, get a young American fellow in here in his place.

Cavanaugh had also run into some resistance in the least-expected quarter: among Bruno's fellow Italian coalminers. At first, he didn't know what to make of it. Then, slowly, he had come to see that there was a kind of class embarrassment toward Bruno, and a certain amount of scarcely concealed resentment that if only one could have made it, it had to be someone like Giovanni Bruno. Unmarried. Belonged to no clubs, had no friends. Not active at the church. Maybe even a negative attitude there. Standoffish and peculiar. Well, Cavanaugh had made them forget that. He had pushed the idea that in the eyes of the world, Giovanni Bruno represented this generation's victory over hatred and prejudice, and that they could all stand taller today, not because of who Bruno was personally or what he'd done, but because of the way others saw him. And, even more important, for the moment—no matter how arbitrary it might seem—he stood for West Condon, and they all had to help lift West Condon high!

He had written a couple articles more or less to that effect and had planted them in Miller's newspaper. Not that it was easy: Miller was getting hard to get along with. There was a time when Miller would have written them himself and been all too glad to do it, but something had gone wrong. Tiger wasn't panning out. Cavanaugh had thought, back when he first got Miller to come back here, that he'd get married, settle in for good, become a leader here, mayor for a while maybe, or even better things. He had a good head, plenty of drive and spirit, and a big following. Should have been a sure thing. Instead, he couldn't even make the goddamn paper pay off. Oh, he'd won a number of meaningless prizes, had sold some articles nationally, had introduced a lot of spectacular though finally pretty silly innovations in the *Chronicle*, most of which had long since been abandoned, but the paper was losing money, and, what was far more serious, Miller didn't seem to give a damn.

Of course, Miller was a spoiled kid, only child, raised by his mother, pampered in school, and so his ego made it hard for him to blend in. Still given to adolescent just-for-the-hell-of-it storm-raising. His Dad was a mining engineer who was killed accidentally while trying to arbitrate a management-union struggle in the early thirties, a friend of Ted's Dad, and maybe this had made Tiger grow up with that peculiar fascination for conflict—he always said it was what had led him into journalism as a career. Maybe Ted should have thought about all this before he encouraged him to come back and buy up the *Chronicle*, then loaned him the money to do it. From the day Tiger took that money, they'd been at odds. And he'd antagonized his best advertisers with tasteless stories, true or not, had ducked all responsibilities in the community, and had developed an annoying habit of mocking those very customs and traditions that most folks here revered. What was the matter with him? Maybe it was Jones's influence. Cavanaugh didn't know where the sonuvabitch had come from, but as far as he was concerned, he could move on any day. Jones's irresponsible anything-goes virus could eat up a community, strike it with a kind of moral encephalitis, and goddamn it, Ted Cavanaugh wasn't going to see that happen.

Miller's private life was something less than exemplary,

165

too, and now this latest scandal involving the Cravens widow had finally got Cavanaugh to wondering if Miller might not be best off leaving with Jones on the same train. Miller had a way of always getting his prick in the wrong place at the wrong time: Jesus! when was that guy going to grow up? It worried Ted, too, that his own son Tommy admired the man so. Came from the old days when young Tiger, as athletic hero and top student, was the town prince, but now Ted wasn't sure what lessons Tommy might be learning from the man's gathering ruin.

Still, on this project anyway, Miller had been cooperative enough, had run stories nightly, had done all he could to lure out-of-town—what Miller and now the whole town liked to call "East Condon"—newsmen to the scene: the hotel was filled up Sunday night and there were even a couple national television cameras on the Bruno front lawn Monday morning. Bunting was up and a welcome sign on the front porch. Inside, neighbor women were giving the house a thorough cleaning. The outside had been freshly painted by high school students. Cheerful day, couldn't be better. Ted had seen to it that schools and businesses would be closed for the morning, that the high school band would be on hand, and that the ceremonies would include a number of state dignitaries. Town spirit was the theme. Wes Edwards, for one, had a speech ready that was just the ticket: would call on everyone in earshot to join him in a pledge for community renewal. Edwards was a quiet intellectual guy, tremendous organizer, good golfer, moving speaker, a sharp cookie. Best they'd ever got here. Cavanaugh planned to get Bruno and his parents out of the ambulance and into the house as quickly as possible, let the girl represent the family in front of the cameras. Cute girl, shy but charming, just the right mixture of pride and humility.

Before things got under way, Cavanaugh stopped by the hotel, hospital, school, city hall, made sure everything was ready to go. Along the way, he learned whom Tiger Miller had slept with last night. Well, hell, why not? Might be just the girl he'd been needing all along. He'd have to check her out, not a local girl, but she looked good. In fact, at the hospital, where she worked, Cavanaugh looked twice and decided she looked very goddamn good. Lay of the Year at the Municipal Hospital. Inwardly, he grinned a wry grin. That damn Jones is getting to us all, he thought.

Vince Bonali woke Monday morning, before dawn, wound up in the sheets, face sweating, eyes wet with tears, breathing like a steamboat. He'd been down in the mine and the going was tough, he was beating his way through it, smoke, dark, things tripping him up—*bodies?* Oh God! God Almighty! The place was all turned around, everybody had bugged out on him, lamps flickering meaninglessly, distantly, sonsabitches wouldn't listen! "Hey, you guys! Goddamn!" He'd sidled up somehow, pulled the lights nearer, got them going right. The head, buddy, use your goddamn head! "Both ways!" he'd cried, felt like he had to shout. "That way some of us'll be chosen!" Jesus! he hadn't meant that, he'd meant some would get out—"Get out!" He'd separated them and they'd headed off. Yet, God, it seemed all wrong! What the hell was he doing? Lights blinking down unseen channels, cut off now—all gone! He was alone! But wait! He couldn't remember which way he'd meant to go himself! Knew before, knew one of them was wrong, but which—? "Hey, Cokie! Ange!" Tried to change the scene, knew he'd done it all before, wasn't real, but it only got worse. Then he saw Pooch—old Pooch Minicucci! "Hey, by God! I thought you'd bugged out on me, Pooch!" Jesus, he was glad to see him! "Come on, man, it's you and me!" He'd get Pooch out now, just tear ass down the—but what the—? Jesus Christ! The dumb bastard was jacking off! "Oh *no!*" Couldn't believe it! "Hey, Pooch! What are you doing, man?" The idiot was just squatting there on a heap of gob, eyes blank like mica, prick long as a damn timber, pulling himself off! "The old snake!" roared Ange Moroni in the washhouse, big laughter booming out, and Vince

167

laughed, everybody was laughing, and for a minute he was out of there. "Cut half of it off, maybe he could talk plain!" Jesus, that was funny! Good old Ange—but no! There he was still: "Pooch!" Pooch's jaw went slack, twitched like he wanted to talk only couldn't. Whole face caving in like the bones were breaking, going dark, and bastard kept pumping away with his right fist. Never saw it stiff like that before, couldn't even see the end of it, seemed to reach right up to the— "Pooch! I ain't gonna say it one more time! If you don't come, man, it's your own goddamn fault!" Jesus! Maybe he'd loosen it all, bring the whole fucking mine down! Noise of topcoal splitting, some fell somewhere. Distant screams. Vince was running, trying to run, a shifting under his feet, hollow echoing emptiness, ears ached, hard to breathe, air thick as cotton—gas! *Gas!* Don't think about it, just *run*, man! Couldn't see the sides, couldn't see the timbers, machines, couldn't see a goddamn thing. But didn't bump into anything, going like ninety, but somehow nothing got in the way. Felt stuff brushing by, tight spots here and there, pushed, turned, faked, okay, okay, buddy, racing to beat hell, just a—hot! hot as hell! smoke! what's *that?* a glow! *glow* ahead! *fire!* Wrong way, oh my God! *he'd been running the wrong goddamn way!* No! No! Coming, it's coming! Tried to turn back. Couldn't turn back. Heat! Done for! *Done for!* Turn! Turn, goddamn it! But hard, hard to get, to get swung around. He struggled. Things in his way now. Legs heavy, tired. Goddamn tired. It was too much for one man. At his back now. Done for. Legs flabby. Out of shape. Too late. Up against a wall. Thick. Oily, like soft clay. Trapped! Clawed his way into it. Air gone. Get through! Choked.

"It's okay," Etta said.

Vince unwound himself, still choked up, wiped his face with the sheet. "I'm sorry Pooch died," he said hoarsely.

"Sure," said Etta.

"Etta?"

Alongside him, her big hind end turned toward him, his wife grunted.

"Etta, I ain't never going back down there again."

And then he was able to sleep. Slept like a log. When he finally did wake up, Etta already had breakfast ready for him. Over his eggs, trying to remember his dream, he asked, "Where's the kids? Angie off to school already?"

"No school today," Etta reminded him. "Both she and Charlie were up early. I think they were going over to Tony and Emilia Bruno's house. Their boy is coming home from the hospital today, you know."

"Oh, yeah, that's right. That's today," Vince said. "Think I'll drop over there too. They're shelling out a lotta dough and maybe they'll have some left over."

Etta took that crack in grim silence. She was down to just about nothing in her grocery budget. But, by God, things would be different now. Once he'd got him a good job, never mind what, just so it wasn't coalmining, they'd never have to fret these long layoffs again. He felt strong, left with his shoulders squared.

Townsfolk had already massed up on the Bruno front lawn when Vince arrived. Bright sun, though the day was crisp, holiday air. Shops, school, everything closed. Vince moved around, talking with old buddies, joking about Bruno. Still, there was nothing sour about it, and everybody was feeling good. Mort Whimple, the mayor, arrived in a new black Chrysler, accompanied by Father Baglione, some state politicians, and one of the Protestant ministers. TV guys dollied around on the sidewalk, shooting everybody. Jesus, the crowd was really big! Officials from the Red Cross, the UMW, the coal company, members of the city council, and representatives from other civic organizations pulled up behind the Chrysler. Vince said hello to his alderman Joe Altoviti, and they kidded around a little.

A sign on the mayor's car said: GIOVANNI BRUNO —WEST CONDON SAYS—GET WELL SOON!!! Everybody cheered as Whimple, in his trademark tweeds and sportshirt buttoned at the neck, moved among them,

169

flanked by the congressmen, the whole group smiling toothily in all directions. Whimple was a homely little guy, used to be fire chief, and before that a car salesman. Vince found himself with a big smile spltting his own face. A piece of the high school band arrived, tooted a bunch of marches on the lawn. Lot of excitement. Well, in spite of everything, by God, it was a great goddamn town, and when the chips were down—

Then a distant siren alerted them, drew shouts from the crowds. The band broke off, then started up again. The dignitaries, with self-conscious shrugs and private jokes nobody could hear, arranged themselves on the front porch, while the cops, Dee Romano, Monk Wallace, and old Willie, cleared the sidewalk. Vince helped. He felt a part of it. The sun shown bright and here in the crowd there was a warmth. A couple ladies appeared at the storm door, noses pressed on the panes, neighbor women. Probably had got the house ready. The band played "For He's a Jolly Good Fellow." Vince saw Georgie Lucci's face grinning at him, and he grinned back. Everybody was grinning. The siren was getting louder. All necks craned toward the siren now. It was like a distant cry of good cheer, yet an anxious one, too—always something of terror and the unexpected in the pitch of an ambulance siren.

Then it swung up, bright white. The music was loud and there was a lot of noise, a lot of enthusiasm. They brought Bruno out on a stretcher. Poor guy looked scared to death. Television cameras were grinding away. Vince saw Tiger Miller, the *Chronicle* editor, popping photos along with all the other newsguys, gave him the nod when he chanced to glance his way. Vince had not been too hot on this big show for Bruno, but Miller in his paper had made it seem almost reasonable. Bruno's family, his folks and his kid sister, walked beside the stretcher. Vince hadn't seen old Tony in years and he was shocked by what he saw. Trembling, a sickly white, nearly blind old man with a bandaged nose. Had to be helped along. And he used to be such a tough hard-fisted bastard. What was worse, the poor old guy had wet his pants. It was embarrassing, but people overlooked it. Tony's wife was small and wizened, looked now like a lot of old ladies who had lived on too long.

The kid sister received the check, represented the family during the big ceremonies. She did a good job of it. And Vince thought, If everybody in the goddamn country is going to be looking at West Condon, it's sure a helluva lot better to have her up there than her brother. He realized he still wasn't too happy about its being Bruno. The speeches were full of praise for West Condon's great community spirit and its stamina. Whimple, the congressmen, Ted Cavanaugh, the preacher, everybody scored the same theme. The band played the high school fight song. Vince remembered with pride those team huddles, back when Ted Cavanaugh captained the squad and ran his famous offtackle plays over Vince, remembered the slaps, the spirit, the power, how they spat water and dug in their cleats and pounded away. Jesus, it's a great place! he thought, and he knew then he was right in getting out of the mine, right in coming topside to play a real part, knew by God he'd make it.

After the ceremonies, everybody still milling around, not wanting to go home and lose this thing, Vince ran into Barney Davis, the mine manager. Barney asked him if he'd mind delivering the charity drive checks to Cravens' widow and Minicucci's folks. Vince said okay, make a nice farewell gesture.

"What do you mean, 'farewell'?" Davis asked.

"I'm getting out."

"What? You mean you're quitting the mines?" Davis laughed. "Shit, Bonali, it gets in the blood. You can't quit easy as that."

"Yeah? Well, watch and see, Davis."

Davis laughed again. "I'll believe it when I see it in the *Chronicle*," he said.

4

Once a day, six days a week and sometimes seven, year in, year out, the affairs of West Condon were compressed into a set of conventionally accepted signs and became, in the shape of the West Condon *Chronicle*, what most folks in town thought of as life, or history. Compactly folded into a soft, damp, aromatic pouch, it fluttered onto porches nightly, was gathered in by the several citizens to easy chairs and kitchen tables, there to open its petals like the proverbial lotus, providing, if not exactly wisdom, at least plenty to talk about and maybe a laugh or two. That its publisher and editor, Justin Miller, sometimes thought of himself as in the entertainment business and viewed his product, based as it was on the technicality of the recordable fact, as a kind of benevolent hoax, probably only helped to make the paper greater, for it was certainly true that although the *Chronicle* was as old as West Condon and as much father of the town as child of it, it was only when Tiger came home to take it over that it became a real institution.

Miller himself was something of a local institution even before that, having been the greatest athlete to pass through West Condon High School. Small towns like West Condon seldom reached the state basketball finals, but Miller had taken them there twice, to this day a kind of Golden Age to the town's middle-aged and old-timers, a legend for the young: number 14; jersey retired. He had, meanwhile, captained both the track and baseball teams, edited the school paper, presided over his class twice, made mostly A's, and, surprising no one, vanished from the premises immediately after graduation. Nobody asked why he left: anybody with any sense did. So, his extraordinary decision to return a few years later, giving up his freewheeling life as a correspondent in order to resuscitate the defunct *Chronicle*, had come like a breath of new life: hey! Tiger's back in town! things are moving again!

And there were prodigies: the highway was widened by the state, two mines resumed operations awhile, and a new factory making plastic toys was established on the outskirts, though this operation later folded. The newspaper, of course, was great, if Tiger had anything to do with it it *had* to be great, won a lot of prizes, put West Condon on the map. The basketball team won the conference title and Tiger started up his semipro baseball club, never had a losing season. And whenever the town fell into the dumps, people looked to the *Chronicle*, counted on Tiger to pull them out, and he usually did.

So now their communal eye was on the *Chronicle* again. Deepwater No. 9, last mine in the area to keep operating, was closed since the disaster, and rumor was, it was going to stay that way. No new industry, business was poor, and people were moving out again. Hard winter. But was Tiger still with them? Most folks thought so, but there were bad signs. Rumor was that the paper was losing money, and Miller didn't seem to care. Some of the Rotary Club meetings had been treated pretty unpleasantly, punch lines left out of speeches, names misspelled, that kind of thing. The traditional Christmas spirit had got knocked, too, when Miller started running parodies of the best-loved Christmas songs and gave the Yuletide charity activities almost no space at all. Some said, that's the trouble with Miller, he keeps going soft just when you expect the best of him. A lot of jump, but not much of a miler. It was still a matter of town curiosity that Miller had led the basketball team to State his sophomore and junior years, but had been unable to get them past the regionals his senior year. Some said he was screwing around too much that year; others thought they saw "some spark go out of him," as though he'd become just plain bored; others blamed the coach. And that was why, while most people saw his return to take over the *Chronicle* as a heroic kind of yea-saying, if not indeed an act of grace, there were those, even then, who wondered if Tiger might not simply have run out of wind out there in the world and returned to rest up awhile in a place where heroism was still possible without sticking to training rules.

And now, since the mine disaster, people wondered why this big play to the spookier side of the Bruno rescue and all those peculiar little squibs about religious eccentrics? Miller was a skeptic, didn't go to church, everybody knew that: so why this sudden interest in so-called miracles and visions? When Reverend Wesley Edwards first came to town to take over the Presbyterian pulpit he had, prodded by some of his elders, sought to reactivate Miller's interest in the church. Miller's skepticism hadn't bothered him, he was a skeptic in most ways himself, and in fact he'd got a kick out of arguing with that romantic rationalist. But there was no getting him back to church. Miller was an atheist, and a fundamentalist to boot, who couldn't see past the end of his own flesh-and-bone nose, to put it politely. And then Miller had started throwing some of his own remarks back at him, and Edwards had realized he'd compromised himself in the course of their talks. So one day he had just taken the pipe out of his mouth and said, "Justin, make your peace with God, surrender to His will." Miller had snorted, and that had been the end of it.

Then, on this otherwise calm sixth of February, a Friday, when church news was customarily printed, there appeared, right on the front page in a small neat box, a paragraph which announced that the Evening Circle of the West Condon Church of the Nazarene would convene on Sunday evening at the home of Mr. Giovanni Bruno. "All interested townsfolk are invited to attend this very important meeting." Edwards smarted. Nothing the Presbyterians had ever done had made the front page, not even his own election to the chairmanship of the Ministerial Association. What was Miller up to? Edwards sensed it: it's me he's after.

Actually, Miller had toned the story, giving Mrs. Clara Collins much less than she'd asked for, a bare announce-

174

ment where she'd wanted a screaming banner. He'd just
come back from Mick's and his daily late-afternoon ration
of hamburger-ash and beer the day before, Thursday, having left his assistant Lou Jones behind, regaling the boys
with horror stories from the history of coalmining. Jones
had a knack. He'd turned a grisly tale of management
goons working over a hapless unionizer into a goddamn
song-and-dance act that had had the whole klatch laughing
and crying at the same time. Miller didn't know much
about Jones, he'd just turned up one day announcing he'd
decided to seek his fortune with the West Comedown
Comical. Miller had laughed and taken him on. There had
been some hint of a job as an all-night disk jockey that
he'd just involuntarily surrendered ("Obscenity was the
uncouth charge," Jónes had said), but on the other hand
that might have been several jobs back. Jones was, in brief,
a complacent drifter, gifted with an uncommonly facile
feedback system, making his way any way he could, keeping a perverse eye out and telling good stories about what
he saw. Miller was glad to have him, and though his humor
sometimes had a way of biting too deep, he generally
enjoyed the guy.

Clara Collins had not only wanted more attention for
her announcement, she'd wanted Miller to attend the
Sunday night meeting. She'd jumped up when he entered,
nearly knocking the chair over. Her purse had swung,
sweeping a stack of copypaper to the floor. "I don't mean
to trouble ye, Mr. Miller, I only stopped by a minute—"

"No trouble, Mrs. Collins. Good to see you." He'd
picked up the copypaper, tossed it carelessly on the desk.
"Sit down." He'd hung up his coat, dropped into his
swivel chair, pulled out his pack of cigarettes, but, catching
her look, had tossed them on his desk without lighting one.
The beer, as usual, had made him drowsy.

She'd sat awkwardly beside his desk, knobby knees
apart, had glanced around nervously at a restless activity
she was ignorant of. "We're all meetin' Sunday over to
Mr. Bruno's house," she had said, boldly yet somehow

175

whispering it. "We'd be honored ifn you could see fit to come."

"That's very kind, Mrs. Collins." He'd suppressed a yawn, reached again for the pack, stopped himself. "But I'm afraid I'm tied up. Is there some special reason—?"

"Well, that's jist it, Mr. Miller." She'd straightened up, smoothing the plain print dress out over her broad thighs. He'd known of course what was coming. "Sunday's the eighth of the month. Mebbe . . . mebbe it's the end a the world!"

"Oh yes. Your husband's note."

So she'd explained again about that, had told him what had been happening at Evening Circle. He'd heard the pressman Carl Schwartz's voice out front saying good night to Annie—like Lou, he called her Anus Poopa—and it had set him to thinking of Carl's disaster story, the assault on Dinah Clemens. Miller could still picture vividly the room as it was the first time he went there. Aqua-blue with pink and white lily pads, the walls; bed an old iron antique, lumpy mattress, a single sheet stretched tautly on it. Dinah had a certain sense of order. There were pillows and blankets in the wardrobe, which she'd got out later. It had been Ox's idea.

"Willie Hall? That's the fellow who used to be Oxford Clemens' buddy at the mine, isn't it?"

She'd said it was, talked about Willie and his wife Mabel, Oxford's late foster mother Marge Clark. Miller, watching Clara, had realized she had something in common with Dinah—not just the rawboned hillbilly part, but something attractive, too. Also had realized he was getting a hard-on. "It was Willie's idea, Mr. Miller," she'd said, "to meet at Mr. Bruno's."

"Why this Sunday, Clara, and not some other month?" Why had he called her by her first name, why the tenderness? Horsey woman, well along in years, tough reddish hands, not his type at all, and yet there was this throb between his legs. Maybe it was just the beer.

She'd told him why she was counting on February, but

176

he could see she was troubled, not all that confident. He had listened to her voice, hearing Dinah Clemens. They'd gone the night they won the regionals. Five green guys ages fifteen to seventeen, Miller the youngest. Ox had taken them in the back door so they wouldn't have to face any of the old guys in the bar who might recognize them. Ox had kept insisting that Tiger go with the one called Dinah. It was the one thing Ox had been set on, and Miller hadn't seen the point in arguing. He'd assumed Ox Clemens knew better than anyone which one was best, and if it was all some kind of gag, well, hell, he didn't have to go through with it. That in actuality it had been the very opposite, had been virtually an act of consecration, Miller hadn't found out until they were climbing the back steps to her room, the girl telling him she'd heard so much about him from her brother. "And then I read about that there shepherd boy, Mr. Miller," Clara had said, "and it all seemed to fit."

"And you talked with—?" He'd realized then that he had a cigarette between his lips. What the hell. He'd lit up.

"I went by right after the meeting and asked, and his sister she said, 'Sure, come along. We'll be expectin' you.' Y'know, Mr. Miller, I think Mr. Bruno he already *knows!*"

"It's possible." When he'd glanced at the large shadowy space between her knobby knees, he'd been repulsed by a sense of a-sexuality there, yet the erection had kept drumming away. What was it? Was it plain sincerity that was exciting him? Or only the provocation of his waterjugs? He'd undressed by the bed. Dinah had hung her few clothes in the old wardrobe that leaned up against one aqua-blue corner, had frocked her strong freckled shoulders with a pink robe. Miller had looked at Clara's shoulders: yes, she almost certainly had freckles there. "Will Abner Baxter be there?"

Clara had slumped a little, relaxing some of that raw aggressiveness, her taut belly briefly softening. "I dunno, Mr. Miller. I hope so."

"Is he a real minister, or—?"

177

And she'd commenced to tell him about how one gets the call and gives testimony of it to the local church board, and he'd kept hearing Dinah telling a young kid who was asking all the wrong questions how a girl got to be a whore, and the difference between local preachers, district ministers, and elders. Her voice had had a husky soothing quality, all the harsh sounds of the words rounded off; it was rustic nasal from the mountains, all right, blue-grass in cadence and twang, but the warmth and kindness and earnestness in it were all her own. She'd rubbed his chest and abdomen. "You're a good boy with my brother. I'm much obliged."

"So Baxter still has to wait a year?"

"That's right." Clara had seemed confused. Her hands had pressed nervously on her thighs. Of course, if you thought the world was ending, what sense did it make to talk about next year? "Well, all we kin do, Mr. Miller, is hope for the best."

Miller had swung around to his old Underwood, had run copypaper in, and had rapped out the one-paragraph box about her proposed meeting. "I can put that on the front page for you."

"But do ye think it's . . . enough?" He'd felt a shrink-ing.

"Any more than that, Mrs. Collins, and I'm afraid you'll get a lot of people you don't want."

That hadn't entirely satisfied her, and he'd felt like, with Dinah, trying again, but she'd finally agreed it was the best. When she'd left, Miller had called Happy Bottom at the hospital and, holding on, had made a date. Off at nine. They'd have sandwiches somewhere, spend the night at his place.

At home later, he'd just undressed to shower when the phone rang. It was Marcella, calling to tell him of the planned Sunday night meeting, and repeating Clara's invitation to come. Her soft Catholic voice was something else: instead of cornfields, terraced gardens, secret and undiscovered. Yes, he thought, but no, the Nazarenes

178

were too much for him, Baxter especially, that was a pose he could never fake. So he again refused but pretended great interest, and asked her to tell him afterwards all that happened.

Hanging up, the phone cord snaked momentarily around what Happy called his gaff—already starting to dance at the sound of Marcella's voice and the vision of Happy here, soon, the speared whale, white tail flipping—then slipped off, just a touch, a taunt, just enough to bring his entire attention to bear briefly on that obstreperous machine, filament and didymous anther, feel himself that instant only an extension of the mechanism, accouterments of defense and motion: sperm carrier. It wasn't sex that whipped him, whipped them all, it was the spook behind sex, that thing that designed him, reshaped him, waked him, churned him, thought for him even: Jesus, when was the last time he'd committed a wholly rational act! He felt the engine drive his legs to the bath, hoist him over the edge, felt his balls sensitizing his fingertips as he turned on the water, his prick reach for the soap, heard the tubes boil and sigh as the hot water struck and soothed. Wesley Edwards had once chided him for his "romantic attachment to rationalism." Rationalism indeed! Christ! Old Edwards would laugh his ass off if he knew!

5

"God," said Tommy Cavanaugh, *alias* Kit Cavanaugh, *alias* the Kitten, known in the bleachers and back seats as "the boy with the paws that refresh," youngest son of the town banker, starting forward on the basketball team and class officer, owner at sixteen of his own set of wheels, "wouldn't hurt people."

Reverend Edwards argued that while God was surely just and benevolent, He was still capable of righteous punishment, and that sometimes when a man thought he was being hurt, he later found out it had been for his own benefit, as when a father chastises his son, for example, or when a coach makes you go to bed early at night. Everybody snickered at that, since it was already out in closed circles that Tommy had the very night before broken training rules to take Sally Elliott out parking at the ice plant. Bushwhackers had come on a scene of some disarray, the implications of which Tommy had not, though perhaps he should have, denied. "God is good," said the minister in that talk-down tone of his that always bugged Tommy, "but sometimes He makes us to suffer experiences we might rather avoid. Remember the stories of Adam and Joseph, of Abraham and Noah. Remember that, as good as God is, this is a God Who could say to Noah, 'I have determined to make an end of all flesh, for the earth is—' "

"I can't believe all those stories," said Tommy flatly. He looked around at the class and saw that they were with him. Usually Mr. Robbins or Sally's Dad taught their Sunday school group, and then they talked sports. Reverend Edwards was an aggravation. For Tommy, though God was a distant elusive substance difficult to envision, He was nonetheless guardian of what was good in human affairs, a kind of president, as it were. "Anyway, you said we weren't supposed to take them literally."

"No, that's right, but I didn't mean you were to ignore them altogether either. Just reflect, fellows, how God made His own Son to suffer, and how He promises a terrible judgment upon those who turn away from Him."

Tommy knew nothing of terrible judgments. He knew that God was generally satisfied with a token pledge of allegiance once a week, a more or less solemn pause to consider the moral virtues, and that anything more than that would suppose a pride in God only imaginable in men. He supposed that some day, after a happy life on this earth, he would pass an even happier eternity in God's country, a place spatially distant but not entirely unlike West Condon. "All I'm saying is that I think if God wants us to believe in Him, He makes us believe, and if He wants us to do something, He knows how to get the job done without a lot of faking around. A coach is just a man, you know, he may be a pretty smart man, but he's just a man, he doesn't know everything, but God is, well, God is *God!*"

Reverend Edwards smiled, as the other guys giggled and wheezed. "That's right, Tommy, but sometimes God may think that you learn a lesson better if you learn it by yourself. As the Bible says, 'For the moment all discipline seems painful rather than pleasant, but later it yields—' "

"But *why?*" demanded Tommy, getting exasperated. "Has God got control over things, or hasn't He? You know, if He has to pass signals to me by blowing up a mine and killing a hundred guys almost and then not bother to tell me why, well, He isn't even much of a coach!"

"Well now, let's not be impertinent," scolded Reverend Edwards, no longer smiling, chewing on his lip like he always did when he got bothered. "As for all that seems evil in this world, you're forgetting about the devil and—"

"That's the other team," interrupted Tommy. "I don't play for them." Again the convulsions of snorting and snickering. Tommy himself giggled without being able to hold back.

Reverend Edwards looked at his watch. "Well, fellows, I think it's about time . . ."

"One thing's been bothering me, though, Reverend," said Tommy, "and that's about sin."

"Well now," said Reverend Edwards with a sly class-is-over smile, "have you been sinning, Tommy?"

Everybody laughed. Tommy grinned, accepting the laughter as praise, having in fact set himself up for it. "What I mean is, if God knows everything, even before it happens, and has all that say-so over everything we do, well, if we sin, it must be because He wants us to sin, and if He wants us to sin, then how is it sin?" He paused, a little breathless. "If you see what I mean."

"Yes, I do, Tommy, though I'm afraid it gets us into the doctrine of predestination," said Reverend Edwards gravely, again consulting his watch, "and I doubt we can cover all of that in the two or three minutes we have left. But let me say that, as Presbyterians, we do not believe that man is without free will. Perhaps, Tommy, God in His infinite wisdom has granted man the one freedom to turn away from Him, and that is what is really meant by sin."

"Oh yeah? Well, why would He want to do that?" Tommy asked, and when the minister showed no signs of answering, added, "I don't know, I can't see giving up something you already got or playing spooky games like that with people who are too stupid to know what's going on. If it's all so indefinite and weird and shaky like you say, well, that's a pretty scary idea."

"I think God is a pretty scary idea," said Reverend Edwards softly, and he smiled. The bell rang and they all went outside, even though it was cold, eighth day of February, to horse around ten or fifteen minutes before they had to go to church.

"Comin' at you, Kit!"

Tommy pivoted to receive the morning's church program, wadded into a loose ball, as the guy who had pitched it made a hoop behind his back with his arms and faded like a football end. Tommy the Kitten mock-dribbled, wheeled, cupping the paper ball in the broad long-fingered hand that was his on-the-court trademark, and hooked it gracefully through the receding hoop, bouncing it off the guy's butt below.

"Hole in one, Kit baby!"

"Well, a hole in one is better than no hole at all," Tommy gagged and they howled with laughter. Old standby of his Dad's. His father was, in fact, at that very moment on the other side of the church lawn surrounded by the older guys. They were laughing and that meant his Dad had a new story. His Dad was a great storyteller, if not the greatest of all time, but he never told a sacrilegious joke, and he never told a story that made fun of West Condon. Those two things went together for his Dad: the community was sacred and religion was there to keep it so. For Tommy, both were pretty boring and restrictive, but he didn't really mind either. If you really had to, there were ways of getting around both. The ice plant, for example, was outside the city limits. His Dad, he thought, had a few pretty old-fashioned ideas, but everybody's Dad did. For one thing, he would always lecture Tommy that although property was in itself a kind of virtue, it carried with it an equal responsibility, and Tommy could never get it out of his mind that he would *have* the property, whether he was responsible or not.

"Hey, you seen Kit's girl? She's a real dog!"

"Whaddaya mean, man?"

"Haven't you seen how she drops her pants whenever she sees his bone?"

"Ow!"

Another thing his Dad had told him was that the girls would only come to him as clean as he went to them, and he had found out that this wasn't exactly true either. That little Elliott girl, for example, as far as she knew from the way everybody joked around about him, he was over in Waterton or had somebody in his back seat every night and had syphilis and everything else from so much sex, and yet there she was, letting him drive her right out to the ice plant last night, popping into the back seat with him, and, my gosh, not knowing anything about anything, just letting him do what he wanted to do, a complete dumb cherry, though really kind of nice, and only if he had *known* what to do, known for *sure*, why, he could have made her right then and there. Even as it was, they had had a pretty hot time, but finally he got a little scared. He was afraid of making a mess of things. One trouble was, he never felt like going out with a girl unless he could like her well enough to marry her, and if he liked her then he didn't want to hurt her any way. Of course, Sally Elliott came from a good family, her Dad being the Chamber of

Commerce secretary and all, so even if something did happen it couldn't be too horrible. Yes, he was a darned kitten, all right, and the more he thought about it, the more it made him mad. Boy, Tiger Miller wouldn't wait around—you gotta grow up, man!

"Hey, Kit! What's worse than your old man with a jag on?"

Tommy thought. "I don't know. Your girl with a rag on?"

"Naw!" the guy howled through the laughter. "Your old lady with a jig on!"

Tommy laughed with the others, but he didn't like the joke. He was sensitive about "old lady" jokes ever since his Mom had got humiliated last year in the newspaper. It had really made his Dad sore, because he thought at first Tiger Miller had done it on purpose, and here he had been the one who had brought him back to West Condon in the first place and then to pull a rotten trick like that. Tommy had been badly upset by the event, since three of the people he loved the most were involved, but finally it turned out that Tiger probably wasn't at fault.

Actually, though none of his buddies knew it now, Tommy had received his nickname upon Tiger Miller's return to the town. He was about eleven or so when Tiger came home, and everybody said then that Tommy was going to be just like him, and they started calling him Tiger's Kitten. Now it was plain Kit, and when anyone asked, he would say it was the girls who had started calling him Kit Carson, the Irrepressible Explorer. After graduation, he looked forward to playing on Tiger's baseball team in the area semipro league. Even though Tiger was a pretty old guy now, he was still the best first baseman in the league and a regular .400 hitter. Tommy was glad he had learned to play shortstop, because they would have a chance to play together.

Tommy noticed Sally Elliott over by the vacated Sunday school building, staring over his way. "Excuse me, men," he said, catching the wadded program and flipping it back into the guy's crotch, "but my services are in demand."

"Hey, Kit," one guy whispered, "you getting some of that?"

"Well, uh, let's say I'm looking into it." He strolled out of their laughter and over toward the girl. Wow, just seeing her standing there so awkward heated him up—he hoped it wasn't going to show. Man, it *had* to happen soon! And she was so nice, there was something really soft and great about her. If only she had known the score, and he—well, he knew what it was that held him back. Sometimes he envied those poor bastards with their nobody fathers. Man, they could do it in full public and it wouldn't matter.

Charlie Bonali, making laborious toilet, listened to his old man in the living room bitching and moaning about his bad luck. Well, he was a goddamn failure and he wouldn't admit it. Just about everybody Charlie knew was a failure and that was the goddamn truth, a bunch of saps. Everywhere he looked, nothing but saps. And his old lady was even worse, trying to drag him off to Mass and yap-yapping about the horrors of hell. Charlie had skipped Mass this morning and had had to take a lot of guff off her and he was still sore about it. Man! he'd sure got dropped by a pair of squares! Showered and shampooed, Charlie stood naked in the bathroom, rolling on deodorant and applying cologne. He cocked his dark brow and curled his thick lip down. "You handsome fucker!" he said and flashed a white toothy smile. Held it. Looked closer. Yeah, they needed brushing again.

Saps. God, the place was rotten to the core! Pray, pay, and get blown to hell. Jesus, when would they ever learn? Take the disaster. Okay, so his old man got out, but what the hell was he doing down there in the first place? And old Ange. There was a smart one. Thousand laughs, punch in the ribs, knew all the answers. Now he rots, burned black to the bone. Smart, very smart. And now what was Charlie's old lady saying? That Uncle Ange was lucky: he'd been to confession the Sunday before. Charlie nearly laughed out loud. He could hear old Ange himself say it, it was Ange's favorite line: "Lucky, my lily-white *ass!*" It was hard to figure. A dumb guy gets nailed up on a goddamn cross, and they all think that's so great, they want to get up there and hang with him. What a bunch of misery-loving nuts! Man, that was *one* line Charlie Bonali was not going to stand in! He didn't even know if he could stomach another Easter season around this dump. He had cleaned his fingernails and toenails with a brush in the bath, and now trimmed them with a clipper. He had one foot up on the stool, his bare ass to the door, when his kid sister Angie knocked.

"Aren't you out of there *yet?*" she demanded. "You're worse than a girl!"

"Come on ahead, if you're in such a hurry," he shouted back. He hoped to hell she would, she'd shut up then, and he stood a little straighter just in case she did.

"Not with *you* in there!" she huffed and went away.

He sighed, put his foot down, filed his fingernails. The old man was howling about all his hard work in the mines having brought him to nothing but a big fat dead end, a favorite crybaby routine of his these days, and how there was no justice in it. The old man was very hot on justice and injustice, and thought a man should get what he worked for. Jesus God, he was dumb.

Charlie fingered tonic into his wavy black hair, devoted ten careful minutes to a strand-by-strand arrangement of it. Damn hairline was edging back, he was sure of it. Work, my Jesus. Well, Charlie could tell the old man things. If a punk weighed in at a hundred pounds, could he play tackle on a varsity team? Hell, no! And take it from a big man. Some guys had it, some didn't. So much for justice, old man. Now, the guys that had it, the smart guys, how did they get it? By being tough. None of your bellyaching about justice, man. If the other guy was born dumb or weak or sick or poor or old or unlucky, well, fuck him.

186

Make him work for you, make him kiss *your* ass, *that* was the message from the cross. Charlie flexed his meaty shoulders, smashed his fist into his palm. Yeah, man. Snapped his fingers, the old sign for action.

He brushed his teeth, leaning up against the lavatory. The sleek pressure of the cold enamel delighted his rod and groin. As he looked down to spit, though, he saw that his belly ballooned out over the lip of the sink. Goddamn beergut, he was going to pot. He stared glumly at that pale bag, shaggily coated with curly black hair. Another sign of the bad times. All he did now was drink beer and sometimes pick up some middle-age stuff in one of the joints. They had to know a lot of tricks or he couldn't even pop off, he was so depressed. He had to get out of here. Nearly all his buddies who graduated with him last year were gone now, and the ones who'd stayed were in worse shape than he was. The new high school kids looked like little babies, like that bitchy little runt of a sister of his, and the upper-class girls acted scared of him. Jesus, he was looking like an old man, that's what. He sucked in his gut and whacked it hard with the butt of his hand. Have to toughen up, goddamn it! He whacked it a couple more times, then looked away irritably as it sagged again.

He pulled on his clean T-shirt and repeated the ritual of the comb. Couple of his buddies had joined the Marines. Shit, that sounded pretty stupid, but maybe he ought to, too. Something to tide him over until he found his way to the top. If he hung around here any longer he was going to go off his nut. By God, why not? He'd do it, he'd join the goddamn Marines and get away from his old man and his old lady, away from the bitching and nagging and away from the mines and West Condon and God and all His fucking paraphernalia. He flashed the smile. Yeah, man. Then, reluctantly, he pulled on his shorts.

Thou didst crush the head of the wicked,
laying him bare from thigh to neck . . .

187

One difference between Nathan Baxter and his father, now the Reverend Abner Baxter of the Church of the Nazarene, was that while his father believed in the eventual redistribution of all property equally to all people (or anyway all saints), no matter how it had to be accomplished, and as Jesus Christ, he preached, had intended, Nat Baxter recognized no property rights at all. "Whatever the eye sees and covets, let the hand grasp it." At the high school gymnasium the Sunday of the mine disaster, Nat's eye saw and coveted a beautifully gnarled black hand that lay, carbonized and unattached, among the bodies and other refuse, and, covertly, his hand grasped it, stuffed it in a paper sack.

For a long time before, he and his little brother Paulie had played Batman and Robin, flying dangerously through the trees, destroying wild beasts, and doing God's will amongst the ungodly. Bad guys were not always easy to come by, of course, and sometimes, to keep the game going, Robin himself had to display a streak of perversity, so he could be dealt with by the hard arm of the law, but there were usually some little kids in the neighborhood they could catch and tie up and bring to proper retribution. Or, if not, they could almost always talk their sister Amanda into it. She was ten and bigger than Paulie, but so weak that Paulie—Robin, that is—could usually catch her and pin her down by himself. The trouble was, she sometimes tattled, but that only added danger to their game, and whenever she did, she always knew she would get it double next time.

Paulie had grown a little too smart, though, about playing Robin; he seemed to consider that it was even better than being Batman. So one day, as a lesson, Nat had shot a real robin with his beebee gun and had made Paulie watch it die. "Me, Batman," he had said, standing over the bird. "You, Robin." The bird was still blinking its heavy gray lids, but it had stopped trying to fly. As Paulie, scared, squatted down close to see where the bird had been hit, Nat had placed his foot on the bird's head and slowly

188

crunched its skull in. That had stopped Paulie being cocky about the part he played, but also it had almost stopped the game altogether. Paulie was too big a baby all the time.

But finding the hand had solved all that. That Sunday, when he came home, he put on his sweatshirt, and pulling his left hand up into the sleeve, carefully fitted the left cuff around the wrist of the dead hand, holding it inside by the bone that stuck out. He left a note where Paulie would be sure to see it: *Beware the Black Hand!* and then waited until he had him alone in the bedroom to spring it on him. Paulie screamed and nearly fell into a frothing fit. Nat could hardly keep from giggling. Lowering his voice in imitation of their father's, he warned Paulie to keep quiet about it; if he said anything to anybody, the Black Hand would get him. When, later that evening, Paulie got his peter whopped by their father's razor strop, Nat told him it was God's punishment because he had acted so scared he had almost given it all away. But, Nat said, he had proven himself, and now he could be the assistant to the Black Hand. What did he want to call himself? Paul suggested the Black Finger, but Nat rejected the idea: if they painted it black with ink, everybody would see it and ask about it. Paulie said, what about the Black Peter? That was where God had hit him, and you couldn't see that. Nat agreed, provided Paulie would promise to be careful and wash it off every time before their mother gave them their baths.

So, after that, the Black Hand and the Black Peter stalked the neighborhood. It was a million times better than being Batman and Robin, because now they were on the other side, and they could do whatever they wanted to. They stole and put poop on porches and tortured victims and broke bottles and burned birds they shot in gasoline and one night they strangled Widow Harlowe's cat. With ink, Nat drew pictures of the black hand on little pieces of paper, which they left behind whenever they completed a really good job.

They began making plans for initiating Amanda, but
their father was home almost all the time now, what with
the mine closed and the sermons he was always having to
prepare, and they were afraid about her tattling. She was
their father's favorite, and he could get pretty rough if he
thought she was being victimized. But then, one Sunday
night early in February when he'd had the hand just about
a month, both their parents had to attend some important
church meeting called by Widow Collins in some man's
house, a wop man named Mr. Bruno, and they left Franny
in charge. Nat now had the idea that his father did not
like Widow Collins anymore, so he put her on the list
for future visitations. Once their parents had left, their big
brother Junior wandered off to town to play the pinball
machines, and then one of Franny's girlfriends came by
and they went for a walk, so Paul and Nathan had Amanda
to themselves. An opportunity like that could not be
passed by. Pitilessly, the Black Hand and the Black Peter
struck.

6

A month of anguish and ordeal. A month of hope. Oh,
the upward straining! Oh, the despair of nonfulfillment!
Rarely had conviction so wholly failed her. Struck down,
Clara Collins wept. Hardship-afflicted though her life had
been, always there had been something, or someone, to
comfort her, to guard her from grief's last defeat. Always
in crisis—even at the worst a month ago when Ely got
killed, and earlier when Harold died in the war—she had
discovered, through her enduring faith in God the Father
and the Lord Jesus Christ, new inner rivers of resolve.

But now, in this strange house, in inexplicable legion with these strange persons, at this strange and empty hour—emptier than she had ever conceived an hour could be—of midnight, the midnight that cleft the eighth of the month of February from the new ninth, as Abner Baxter hurled his implacable curses and all her friends walked out on her, Clara suffered a total collapse of strength. Everything just dropped out. Even faith failed her. She could not pray. It was as though they had walked out taking her very spirit with them, and now the hollow shell of her could but sit, utterly powerless and forsaken, in this bewilderingly darkened Italian living room lit only by its irreverent television —sit whimpering like a lost child.

The hour had been striking still as she followed them out of Giovanni Bruno's bedroom, through the dining room with its alien pungency, into the shrouded blink and rasp of the living room where the old father sat, foul-smelling and raking his throat, staring mindlessly at an old movie, followed them, held by a mere thread to the edge of the awful cliff, to the very door. Out they had marched, indignant, inflexible, even as though frightened, the Baxters and the Coateses, all those people, the widows Lawson and Harlowe, the Willie Halls and Calvin Smiths, the Grays, Gideon Diggs, everybody, all the friends of the faith she had known and so devotedly served, even her truest friend Betty Wilson. Out! If only *one* could have—*"Please!"* she had whispered desperately to Betty, and Betty, crying shamelessly, had begged her forgiveness, then left with the others. The thread parted. She dropped, head spinning. Nearby: a sofa. It received her. There she wept.

And the worst of it was: she no longer felt Ely's presence. Throughout this month of terror and trial, he had stayed by her side, had seemed closer even than he had been while living, had guided her, inspirited her, given her strength and singleness of purpose . . . and now he was gone. Gone! Ely! How? How had it come to pass? "Puffed up with conceit!" Abner Baxter had cried, passing through the door. Oh no, dear God, it was not so!

191

So utterly, so frankly and wholeheartedly, had she believed that the portentous thing was truly happening, that now it was as though it *had* happened and had left her behind, behind in the strange-scented emptiness with its blue flickering light and tinkling hollow voices. She had not doubted, no, indeed all her life had seemed to come to bear on this moment, all good Ely had taught her, and all the signs this month—especially his suffering—had insisted upon it. "For our light affliction, which is for the moment only, worketh for us more and more exceedingly an eternal weight of glory, because we look not at the things which are seen, but at the things which are not seen!" So *many* indications of the Spirit at work! Ely's message and the appearances to both him and his companion Giovanni Bruno of the mysterious white bird, then the startling coincidence of the story that appeared in the evening *Chronicle*—had not the whole world seen it?—about the shepherd boy who had been visited centuries ago by a white bird that had also changed into the Mother Mary, telling him then to lead a Holy Crusade. Even little Elaine's innocent gift at Christmas of the small porcelain statue of Mary with the bleeding heart now seemed almost terrifying in its hidden portent. Then, too, there was poor Eddie Wilson with the broken back, suffering like Ely a saint's end, dying in Sister Betty's arms with Ely's name on his lips and something like "God" before—and he had not even been near Ely in the mine! And what of the puzzling "black hand" slaying of Mary Harlowe's cat? Was it not another sign? So clear! So foreboding! And how excited Willie and Mabel Hall had become when she showed them the note! Willie had turned pale as a ghost, told Clara he had stayed home from the mine that night just *because* it had been the eighth of the month. Oh, true! true!

And with such seeming irreversibility had it all proceeded! The Evening Circle meetings so well attended, so much spiritual excitement, the anxiety of all to learn— not even Brother Abner's momentary sullenness could dull their zeal for the Lord and their eager faith in Ely! "Forgetting the things which are behind, and stretching forward to the things which are before, press on toward the goal unto the prize of the high calling of God in Christ Jesus!" Yes! yes! they had been as one! She and Ely had lived among them, mostly hardworking mining people, almost all their lives, and they had responded ardently to her call. Sorely afflicted, they had found hope in a faith renewed by love: her love and Ely's. The eighth of the month! The moment had grasped them all, each and every one! Even Abner Baxter, swept by the current, had called on them all to "run with patience the race that is set before us!" and had preached in church on the faith of the prophets.. Like a thunderclap of doom had come his inspired message the week before: "And by faith Noah, being warned by Almighty God concerning events as yet unseen, he took heed and, moved with a godly fear, prepared him an ark to the saving of his house, *and by this he condemned the world!*" Dear old Gideon Diggs had leapt right up in the church and cried out, *"Lord! I believe!"* And the whole congregation had stood with him and prayed as a body. And it was these who had come, rejoicing . . . and had left, reviling.

Why, it had not even been her, but Brother Willie Hall who, when informed that Giovanni Bruno was too weak still to attend their special February eighth meeting, had made the motion to assemble this night in the Bruno home. In spite of doubts expressed by Abner and a couple of the menfolk, Giovanni Bruno's presence had seemed somehow crucial to them all. She had met him and so had reassured them that, though silent and in his illness withdrawn, he had shown himself no less profound and sensitive than Ely had so often said he was, and Betty and Mary had backed her up. But a Roman Catholic? No, he was *not* one, and she'd told them of his enthusiastic response to Ely's teachings and had reminded them of his vision of the white bird—*Ely's* white bird. Aye! Aye! Unanimously, they had agreed, and Clara had obtained that very night, from the man and his sister, the invitation. The way was made straight.

And then, finally, the best of all possible signs: almost none had stayed away, not even Abner and Sarah Baxter, and all had come with fear and great joy in their hearts. "The darkness is passing away and the true light already shineth!" But what was this? She had seen that there were no children, as if by agreement they had all been left at home, and if tonight were—? But it was Abner's work, she had learned—what *was* it had turned so true a man? And Clara had prudently avoided making an issue of it. Meek Mary Harlowe had ducked her eyes on greeting, and Betty Wilson had seemed fretful, anxious to speak of something, but the press of time had not allowed it. A few moments, then, at the outset, of awkward silence and muffled introductions, the harsh unresponsive stare of Giovanni—"He's got a fever," Clara had alibied—and his sister's gentle but faintly hostile shield, the aroma of medicine, of bedclothes, of something foreign, something like sin, yes, there *was* sin here, wine and television and tobacco and Roman Catholic pictures and crosses, and the sister, sensuous, too pretty really; and not to mention the long preliminary march from the front door through the living room with its disconcerting noises of senility and illicit entertainments even before *getting* to the bedroom, and then the Nortons—oh, *why* had they come?—he kindly enough and at first conversational, but that brittle icy woman, so openly annoyed, so imperiously silent, refusing to participate yet placing herself at the very head of Giovanni Bruno's bed—what did she think they wanted? What did she fear?

But her people had crowded in and soon the room was as if the world and they as if its people, united in faith. A natural reticence at first, of course, but Clara had marshaled them quickly to her side. Emboldened by the truth she carried and the grace upon her, she had led them in opening prayer, beseeching and exhorting them to open their hearts to Christ Jesus and earnestly prepare His way.

194

For in just such manner, behind shut doors, He had appeared to the Eleven, had He not? Yes! Yes! "Oh why are ye troubled? And wherefore do questionings arise in your hearts?" None rise, Lord! No! None! "For yourselves know perfectly that the day of the Lord so cometh as a thief in the night!" Yes! He comes! He is coming! "When folks say, 'Peace and safety,' then sudden destruction cometh upon them, as travail upon a woman with child, and they shall in no wise escape!" Come, Lord! Come! "O spirit of holiness, on us descend!" Their voices rose in fervent song. "But ye, brethren, are not in darkness, that that day should overtake you as a thief, for ye are all sons of light!" Amen! Amen! "For God appointed us not unto wrath, but unto the obtaining of salvation through our Lord Jesus Christ!"

How they'd worshiped! How they'd praised! Knowing not the form of the event, they sought only a readiness and a unity of spirit. Sister Tess Lawson, so slow to submit, had fallen to her knees to confess her sins. Ready, Lord! Clara, on her knees, had thought then of her friends in distant places, had begged God that He have mercy on them and others who could not be present. "In Him it is always *yea!*" Giovanni Bruno, too, though silent, had been ever watchful, joining them, she could see, in spirit, trembling faintly as they called in tearful joy upon the Lord. "For the Lord Hisself shall come down from heaven above! with a shout! with the voice of the archangel! and with the sound of the trump of God! and the dead in Christ shall rise first!" After ten o'clock! Oh dear God! They sang, they prayed, they read. Brother Gideon stood and broke into inspired prayer, admonishing them to rejoice in the Lord always and in all ways, and to "put on the whole armor of God!" His melodic old voice rose and, falling all to their knees now, they chanted their amens. Clara, in her blur of terror and joy, saw in one brief alarming moment all the frustration and anger of the terrible powers of evil in the glittering eyes of Mrs. Norton—knew suddenly with whom she contended! "And, above all, take

up the shield of faith, wherewith ye kin quench all the
fiery darts of the evil one! and take the helmet of salvation—yes! and the sword of the Spirit! yes! which *is* the
word of God! O sisters! hear me! brothers! pray! Pray at
all times! pray in the Spirit! pray in the Glory! pray in the
name of Lord Jesus! 'If ye shall ask,' He says, 'if ye shall
ask *in my name,*' He says, 'well, that will I *do!*' And
rejoice! rejoice in the Lord always! I say, *rejoice!*"

Eleven chimed the wall clock. They sang. "The Old
Rugged Cross." Her daughter Elaine, at her side, lifted her
sweet timid voice in courage and pride. "Oh Beulah Land,
sweet Beulah Land!" Tears welled in Clara's eyes. Oh,
Ely! Ely! Ezra Gray called for repentance, and Sister
Thelma Coates led them in a new wave of confession of
love for the Lord Jesus. And Clara read Ely's message
aloud and Giovanni Bruno clapped his hands as though
in benediction and even in that hard woman's eyes the
anger dimmed and Elaine called, "Oh, Pa! Pa!" and
Brother Abner, whom Ely himself had converted and baptized, even Brother Abner joined them then with all his
heart. "*Behold!*" he thundered and they all praised. "The
Judge standeth before the door! *The coming of the Lord
is at hand!*" They shouted and wept. "Let the lowly
brother *boast* in his exaltation, and the rich in his humiliation, he will pass away!" And they clapped and cried in
unison with him. "Come now, ye rich! Weep and howl for
your miseries that are coming upon you!" Perspiration
pocked his pale brow and his jowls shook with righteous
fury. "Verily, verily, I say unto you, the hour cometh, and
now *is,* when the dead shall hear the voice of the Son of
God! *And them that hear shall live!*" Yes! We shall live!
Mercy! "But *woe* to him who heapeth up what is not his
own! him who getteth an evil gain for his house! him that
buildeth a town with blood and establisheth a city by
iniquity!" Woe! Woe! Yes, Brother Abner! Amen! Clara's
heart leaped: 11:45! "For, I tell you, he shall drink of the
wine of the wrath of God!" O Lord, save us! O Brother
Abner, tell us! "And he shall be tormented with fire and

196

brimstone in the presence of the holy angels and in the presence of the Lamb!" Abner paused to breathe and Sarah Baxter's whimper trickled into the gap: "Have mercy on the children, Lord!" But Abner roared above her: *"And the smoke of their torment goeth up forever!"* Yes! We shall see it! *"And ever!"* Repent! Clara felt suddenly a something, a hand, gripping her elbow! Assured now, yet possessed with a holy fear, she turned: but it was only her little Elaine, tears washing down her pale cheeks, bravely smiling—

"But do ye beware, my friends, of false prophets, deceitful workers, disguising themselves as apostles of Christ!"

Clara turned, looked, appalled. The room, as though itself a living body, shocked and terrified, fell silent, its whole breath caught. Abner Baxter stood, shook his head, the red hair wild as a lion's mane, and glowered down upon her. No doubt: it was she he meant! Something empty and hollow bloomed and began to grow in her. Five minutes remaining still, and what was he—?

"But be not deceived: *God is not mocked!*"

"Abner!" She could hardly believe it. "Abner, they's jist five minutes! *Don't close your heart agin' the Spirit, Abner!"* Her voice was hushed and faltered. "Ely said—"

"I tell you what the *Lord* says, woman! *He* says, 'Woe unto the foolish prophets that follow their own spirit and have not seen nothing!' Now you listen, Sister Clara! *The Lord He has not sent you,* and you've made all these here people trust in a *lie!"* He paused, this man blessed by Ely's love and lifted up by Ely's blood, paused: for the dread hour was near upon them.

"Who are you to judge another's gifts?" asked a gentle voice with a calm, a mildness, strange to this awesome hour. With unbelief, Clara saw that it was Mrs. Norton who had spoken.

Abner Baxter glared, astonished, at the little woman by Giovanni Bruno's bed. "You shall see for yourself!" he bellowed, and taking his wife Sarah brusquely by the arm, he turned to leave the room. At the bedroom door he halted, spun on them once more. "This day shall end and the false prophecy shall be disgraced! Do you hear me? *You will be put to shame, Clara Collins, and so will they all who stay here with you!*" And, with Sarah, he departed.

Roy and Thelma Coates hesitated just a troubled second, then followed them out of the bedroom. The clock began to strike the hour. "Wait!" Clara cried. "In the name of Christ Jesus, *wait!*"

But none had waited, not a one. With each throbbing chime of the midnight hour, they had stood and left her, slowly at first, uneasily, lacking conviction, then, as though somehow fearing to be in the house after midnight, more and more hastily, until at the end they were running, the men clumsily light-footed out of their mining boots, the women scraping and clacking their heels across the wooden dining room floor, carrying their coats, Clara running after, pleading, and Abner's chastisements roaring back at her from the front door like a terrible tide she had to struggle against, until, with the last hollow knock of the hour, she found herself alone, alone and weeping like a child, betrayed, crushed down, and for a long time, as she lapsed lifeless on the sofa, the last peal of the clock echoed and resounded in her head like a mockery of trumpets. Alone. Alone and forsaken in a foreign place. Forsaken even . . . even by Ely.

The voice, then, was in the air, speaking, before she heard it. She stored its syllables in her despairing mind, then contemplated them. "Have you forgotten, Mrs. Collins, what the Bible says? 'Do not regard lightly the discipline of the Lord,' it warns, 'nor lose courage when you are punished by Him. Consider Him Who endured from sinners such hostility against Himself, so that you may not grow weary or fainthearted.'" The woman stood in the open doorway between the living room and dining room, the light at her back, only a pale bluish flicker from the television playing on her face. Elaine crouched stricken near her against a wall, soft sobs barely audible breaking from her small chest like fitful punctuation. "Now, will you please come back? Giovanni has asked to show something to you."

She lacked all strength to resist. Mechanically, walled in by her grief, Clara lifted herself from the couch, took Elaine's frail shoulder, followed Mrs. Norton back, through the dining room, into the bedroom. It was empty, but the heat and odor of an anxious massing were still present. Giovanni lay, as before, on his bed, propped by pillows, but now a Bible—Clara's own Bible—rested in his lap. With his finger, he was pointing to a passage. At Mrs. Norton's urging, Clara approached him and read. It was the Gospel according to John, chapter one, verses ten and eleven: "He was in the world, and the world was made through him, and the world knew him not. He came unto his own, and they that were his own received him not."

"Giovanni, to whom do you mean this to apply?" asked Mrs. Norton. "To Mrs. Collins?" Giovanni Bruno nodded solemnly. "Indeed perhaps, each in his own way, to all of us here?" Something in her voice of awe, a kind of God-fear sound, when she spoke to him. And again he nodded. Mrs. Norton turned to her, and Clara observed now a patience, a compassion, in her face, a face, she saw instantly, that had known hurt and suffering like herself. "As Jesus is said to have told His disciples, Mrs. Collins: 'If the world hates you, know that it has hated me before it hated you.' Marcella dear, is there any coffee?"

The girl smiled openly. "Yes, I'll get some. Do you take cream or sugar, Mrs. Collins?"

"No, but Elaine—"

"We'll bring everything." The girl took Elaine's hand, and together they went to the kitchen.

"I . . . I'm sorry," Clara said, addressing no one in particular, except God Himself maybe. Her eyes were still full of tears, but she felt all cried out. "I don't know. I don't understand. I thought . . . but, well, you seen it. I jist don't—"

"*Giovanni Bruno, hear me!*" The woman was again addressing the sick man, and again that hollow sound to it. Clara watched, not knowing quite what to make of it, yet fascinated just the same. "Is there any reason why . . . why nothing has happened tonight?" Again: the solemn affirmative nod. "Is it because . . . is it because there were perhaps hostile forces of darkness present?" Giovanni Bruno nodded. The woman relaxed, sighed, turned again to Clara. "It may be, Mrs. Collins," she said, "that our night is not yet over."

The two girls returned, smiling as though at something just said, Giovanni's sister bringing the coffee, Clara's daughter Elaine following with a tray of cups and cream and sugar. For the first time since the mass exodus, Clara was reminded of the other presence in the room: Mr. Norton, chubby and humble-spirited, stepped out of a corner and came over to accept a cup of coffee. He smiled cordially at Clara as he spooned three heaps of sugar into his coffee and added cream. "I hope you're feeling better," he said.

"I'm feelin' a mite like a fool," Clara confessed frankly.

He smiled again at that. "Well," he acknowledged in a familiar drawl, "I don't know anybody who has expressed himself more eloquently on being a fool for the truth than the apostle Paul himself."

"Well said, Wylie!" avowed his wife, and Clara had to admit, too, that it was so. She sipped the hot black coffee, finding it good. The girl Marcella helped her brother, lifting a cup to his lips. He was apparently still very weak. It was a little curious how he had got ahold of her Bible, in fact. Elaine, sitting meekly by the Bruno girl, smiled over at her, and Clara smiled back. "Who is this Mr. Baxter?" Mrs. Norton asked. "Do I understand that he is the minister at your church?"

"Yes, that's right," Clara said. "Now he is."

"But your husband was the minister before."

"Yes." She felt the tears returning, concentrated on the coffee.

"What does the Bible say, Mrs. Collins? I confess, I'm not very good at quoting it offhand. But doesn't it say something about those who preach from envy and rivalry?"

"Yes, they's something like that, I think. But you mean . . . you mean, you reckon Abner's jealous of—? But Ely . . . he's passed away, Abner ain't got cause to—"

"True, Mrs. Collins, but you live still, and, through you, in spirit, lives your good husband yet. Isn't that so?"

"Yes. Yes, I allow it is. I hadn't thought of it like that." For the first time, the vague hostile rumblings of the past month, especially those touching her leadership of Evening Circle, began to make sense to her. Why hadn't it occurred to her before?

There was a silence, then, as they drank their coffee. Clara began contemplating the bitter walk home to their empty house. Mrs. Norton glanced over at Giovanni from time to time, and, absently, Clara soon found herself doing the same. What? Did she expect something? Marcella poured more coffee. And then the doorbell rang. Everybody started, looked wonderstruck at each other. Marcella went to answer . . . and returned with Betty Wilson!

Betty burst weeping into the room and came to take Clara's hands. "Oh, I'm sorry, Clara! Lord, I jist don't know whatever come over me! I was skeered is all! It was— oh, Clara, please, I'm—"

"That's okay, Betty," Clara said. "I almost felt like goin' out on myself myself." With that, everyone smiled a little, and Betty stopped her crying. "How about a cup of coffee?"

"Well, I . . ." Betty wiped her eyes, glanced around her now, uneasy in the presence of these strangers. "Ifn you think . . . ifn you think it's all right . . ."

"Of *course* it's all right, Mrs. Wilson," Mrs. Norton said warmly. "We're happy you have come back. It's a *very* good sign." Dr. Norton carried over a chair. Marcella brought coffee.

And then it happened.

Giovanni Bruno lifted his hand.

Mrs. Norton, with a gasp, flew to the foot of his bed.

Dr. Norton stood rigidly, expectant.

Marcella set the coffeepot down, slipped over by the bed.

Weak but yet resonant, Giovanni Bruno's voice entered the still room for the first time: *"The coming . . . of . . . light!"*

Mrs. Norton drew a quick sharp breath. Clara stood, felt Betty and Elaine fearful at her side. *"When?"* asked Mrs. Norton.

There was a long pause. Giovanni's eyes moved among them, returned to stare upon Mrs. Norton. *"Sunday . . ."* he said, *". . . week."* He dropped his hand.

Clara started to speak up, to ask what this was about, but Mrs. Norton held up her hand for silence. "The coming of light?" she repeated, and Giovanni nodded. "Sunday week?" Again, he nodded. "Giovanni Bruno, hear me! Is there anything . . . is there something more?" A pause. And then he shook his head no, the first time Clara had seen him do so. The movement made his hair splay out on the pillow, and Clara was astonished to see how really long it had grown. Mrs. Norton relaxed, but when she turned from the bed to face them, Clara saw tension and worry on her face still.

"What is it?" asked Clara, though she had already begun to grasp it. Though frightened, she was ready: she had been tested, she realized, and found true.

"I don't know exactly, Mrs. Collins." Then: "May I"— she fingered a small gold medallion that hung around her neck on a chain—"may I explain something to you?"

Clara nodded. She sat, in awe, but feeling Ely close at her side once more.

7

Vince Bonali stopped up at the Eagles one night for a whiskey, keeping nothing at home but beer these lean days. From the minute he walked into the place, he was reminded of old Angelo Moroni, and from then on he couldn't get his mind off him. They had gone to school together, hunted women together, broken into mining and drunk together, were best men at each other's weddings, had worked their ways up simultaneously to be facebosses out at Number Nine. And they had always teamed up to play pitch and pinochle. Ange with his hat tipped down to his nose, Vince deadpan with a mouthful of cigar, unbeatable goddamn combination: that was mainly what hit him when he walked in.

Sal Ferrero was shooting pool with Georgie Lucci. Vince carried his whiskey over, sat down on a stool to watch. They bandied sober hellos around. Sal and Ange and he used to make a trio, ever since Sal married Ange's sister. In recent years, Sal only worked as a repairman in the mine, and in a different section at that, so they'd kind of split apart, but family functions always saw them together again, and he and Sal had seen a lot of each other since the disaster. Sal was a small wiry guy, kind of Jewish-looking, but a good goddamn man, knew how to joke around with the best of them, always on hand when help was needed. He was one of the first guys down into the mine after the explosion, told Vince later he'd mainly gone down to look for him and Ange. He'd found Ange, okay. Lucci was one of the four guys in Vince's gang who'd panicked after the blast and run out without knowing where they were going. Lucci and his buddy Brevnik had lucked out. Lee Cravens and Pooch Minicucci had gone the wrong way. Tomorrow, Vince had to deliver the relief checks to their families. Happy Valentines. He didn't look forward to it.

"Want in?" offered Sal, straightening up. He had just muffed a shoo-in on the ninespot.

"No, thanks," said Vince. "I get a bigger charge outa watching the exhibition."

"Then keep your eye on this'n, Vincenzo old culo," growled Georgie down the length of his cue. With a soft *thuck*, followed by a tight pair of *clicks*, he pocketed both the nine and the fifteen, then proceeded to clean the table.

Sal plunked a half dollar on the table while Georgie was still lining up the last ball. "Never could do any good on Friday the thirteenth," he said.

So it was, Friday the thirteenth.

"Find anything yet?" asked Georgie, leaning into his shot.

"Not yet." Vince had found himself caught up in an odd sense of nervous exhilaration the past week or so, but it was starting to fade on him. What kicked it off was saying out loud what he'd wanted to say for thirty years: he was through with coalmining. He'd put in a couple applications around town, talked to different people, boasted how he was commencing the new life, fifty years or no. Everybody'd agreed that yes, by God, he was doing the right thing. Took a lot of nerve to try to learn new tricks when you were staggering into your second half century, too; they all appreciated that. In fact they sometimes harped on it so much, Vince would get a little jittery. Just what the hell *could* he learn to do? he'd ask himself; then, just as quickly, he'd shove the dumb question aside: let's see what they *ask* him to learn first.

Georgie plucked the coin off the felt, emptied the far pockets as Sal racked. "I hear Guido Mello got on at the garage where Lem Filbert's working," he said, and chalked his cue.

"Yeah, that's right," Vince said. He'd tried there, asked too late. Awful lot of guys seemed to have the same idea he had.

Vince's kids, the two still at home, Charlie and Angie, had showed right off they were pleased, had talked up the change, they made big plans for the future. Charlie, actually getting halfway friendly to him for the first time in the kid's useless life, would flash his big toothy smile and ask from time to time what had turned up. Vince always returned the boy a healthy line. Give the kid a little ambition by example. Began to consider taking him fishing when spring came on, Charlie had never taken an interest like the other boys, go upstate for a couple days maybe, sleep out. If he'd just stop snapping his goddamn fingers.

Georgie broke the racked balls with a tremendous *splat*. Vince himself preferred to break soft, but Lucci liked the wide-open game. "Pretty big show last week," Lucci said.

"Yeah?" asked Vince mechanically. Heard some cards rattling loosely against each other over near the bar, then the *flick flick flick* of the deal. Caught himself glancing around for Ange.

Lucci, trapped in the wide scatter of balls, had to use two cushions to get at the one, sitting like a pale orange near a sidepocket. He escorted the ball with twists of his hips, grunts and Italian obscenities, but missed just the same. "Yeah," he said, picking up the chalk. "I think the least our Big Number One Hero could've done is share some of that fucking loot with his old buddies."

At first, Vince didn't know what the hell Lucci was talking about. Wasn't paying attention. "Oh, you mean Bruno," he said after a moment. "Well, buddy, those are the breaks."

Sal stared across the green expanse of the table toward Vince, then looked down as though studying his shot. Vince knew what it meant. Sal was feeling it, too. Things were upsidedown. Self-consciously, Vince swallowed down his whiskey, moseyed back to the bar for another.

He leaned on the bar awhile, staring glumly into his sweating glass, wondering why the hell he didn't just go on home. Felt out of place. Like an old man at a kids' party.

What was wrong? He had tried to talk it out with Etta, but she never said anything. That's the way she was, he hadn't expected otherwise, been just like that for the thirty years they'd been married. She'd absorb his harangues and projected joys into her big-spread 300-pound body, return some little joke or other, then leave him to make his own decisions. True, he sometimes wished she'd turn on a little enthusiasm once in a while, but on the other hand, whenever the kids with their interminable questions began to get to him, it was a large relief to have her friendly silence around.

They had both of them broken all the old family traditions, Etta the German ones, Vince the Italian, when they got married. Her folks over in Randolph Junction weren't so bad, though they hardly ever got over to see them, but Vince's old man had nearly pitched him bodily right out of the goddamn house when he found out. Finally, things had settled down, of course, as they always do. Etta was Catholic at least, helluva lot better one than Vince or most of his family for that matter, and that had made it easier on Mama. She worked hard, had got all the kids through their catechisms and their schoolwork, kept them clean and looking neat even through hard times—and they'd known plenty—never failed to keep hot food in the whole family. So, eventually, his family had got used to her, made stale jokes about the difference between potatoes and pastas, even slipped and spoke Italian at her sometimes, and then they'd all laugh. Underneath, it probably pissed Etta off a little, Vince figured; she was still a German, even if her name did come to be Bonali, and it seemed like sometimes she got the idea they did it as a kind of insult. But Etta had decent manners, always knew when to take it easy; really, by God, they got along fine. And he felt troubled now that he couldn't give her more to hope for in her old age.

When they married, Etta was a pretty exciting catch, tall and ripe-bodied and country fresh, though making a family had quickly ballooned her into the big woman she was now. Together, the two of them had brought off seven kids, all of them still alive and all well reared—well, all but Charlie maybe. The first five were married, living in different parts of the United States, and Angie, the youngest, was still in high school. It was Charlie who really burned Vince's ass, just swaggering around all day, snapping his fingers, cracking his knuckles, dangling a butt in his thick lips—but still, goddamn it, Vince understood. He understood how it was to grow up in a house where the old man was out of work half the time and where there didn't seem to be any real future. As Charlie himself had put it, hurting Vince more than the kid knew: "You saw how Ange got it. *That's* the real future, man!"

A chair scraped behind him, someone called out his name. Vince took a drink, lazed around, keeping one elbow on the bar. Rattle of cards. "Chair open, Bonali," came the twang. Chester Johnson, toothy hillbilly, another guy from Vince's shift, but a different part of the mine. They were all hanging around up here, Jesus, the whole damned mine. What there was left. Johnson fluttered the cards in a loose-wristed shuffle. "Wanna sit in as my partner a hand or two?"

No, thanks, Vince thought, but there was something in the soft tease of the shuffle, persuasive presence of jacks in that thin deck, that could set the moment aright if not the times . . . and next thing he knew, he found himself straddling an old metal folding chair, staring half-blind at harsh little cardboard faces who this night said just nothing to him. Johnson kept yakking away, couldn't keep his goddamn mouth shut five seconds, talked off every play he made, kept overbidding. Vince lit a cigar, glared through the hovering smoke at Johnson.

"What really grinds my ass," Johnson was whining, "is that outa ninety-eight possible guys, that fuckin' crybaby had to be the lucky dolly."

Vince looked up sharply. The other two guys said nothing, stared at their cards. So at least he wasn't the only one, that was plain. He'd been feeling guilty about his resentment at the fanfare surrounding Bruno, but maybe if the other guys like Lucci and Johnson felt like he did, there was cause. Still in his miner's clothes, still black with that stinking soot, Vince had made his visit that night to the gymnasium, had gone there to see Ange Moroni's cadaver. One of four long black lumps laid out side by side with a fifth in a rubber bag. On a tarp on the basketball floor. Ange's uppers were missing, black eyelids half-open, showing a watery white stuff below that didn't look like eyeballs. Vince, though he rarely did now, had prayed for Ange. And for himself and all the other guys.

"Jesus, Bonali!" cackled Johnson. "You remember that fuckin' poem?"

"Three," snapped Vince, cutting him off. Both red jacks.

"Aw, four," Johnson drawled, topping him. Tipped his scrawny head one way, then the other, shrugged, grinned. "Spades, I reckon. Sure hope you got the jig, buddy." They went down fast. Vince shuffled, cracked the cards roughly. "They makin' all this big fuss, but shit, I bet he never knowed what hit him." Johnson pushed on, the others nodding absently. Theme of the week apparently. Harsh nasal voice that pricked the ear: "Too many good goddamn guys got it." Vince's hands shook as he dealt the cards around. Johnson watched. "Guys like old Lee Cravens and old Ange Moroni and—"

"One good thing about Moroni," Vince butted in. "He knew how to keep his fucking mouth shut in a card game."

Johnson leaned back on two chair legs, stared at his cards a moment, then flipped them down on the table. "I dunno, boys, I think I've had enough," he said, flicker of a grin crossing his wide lipless mouth. "Air's got a mite sour."

"Suits me," said Vince, and shoved his chair back. Tossed down the rest of his whiskey, walked out. Friday the thirteenth. Felt rotten, really rotten. Hated Johnson, hated Bruno, hated even himself. Down the hill, man. "What a fucked-up world!" he muttered.

Even with the welcome money in his hand, Vince got no fun out of the idea of visiting the Minicucci and Cravens homes next morning. Stirring up the ashes, that's all. He'd seen nearly all of the families at the mass funerals about a month ago, had steered clear of them since. Just didn't feel comfortable, didn't know what to say, knew they couldn't help but resent that he had got out.

Pooch wasn't married—as old Ange used to say: why waste all that artillery in just one little mousehole?—but his folks more or less depended on him, so the charity committee had awarded them a full share of the money. Vince tried to take care of the business out on the front porch, but they dragged him on in, said it was too cold, sat him down in one of their overstuffed chairs, gave him wine, talked about Pooch and how he'd looked so fine at the funeral, and how badly they did need the money.

The room was overheated, bore that weighted odor of old people, old food, old dust, made Vince recall his Mama the last couple years before she died. Vince only understood about half the Italian. Slipping away from him. The old woman sucked her dry withered lips, spoke of God's ominous ways, how important it was to be ready at all times, one never knew, *un giorno o l'altro*, life was brief and inscrutable. Vince nodded gravely, growing sleepy. "*Si, una bolla di sapone,*" he acknowledged, a soapbubble, his Mama's pet commentary on life in this world. Vince fidgeted in the chair to keep awake, covered up best he could, finally had to admit he hadn't been to Mass in over three years. *Tre anni!* Ever since the kids had grown up, he said, but, yes, she was right, he figured to get started back, you never knew, any moment, *a qualsiasi ora.*

"*ECCO il momento!*" the old woman said, wagging her finger. And as she rattled on, Vince remembered his old blind grandmother telling him about hell when he was a boy. She was an expert on hell. If Vince ever ended up there, he was sure he'd find his way around, she'd imbedded forever in him a mental map of the place. He had nearly forgot, but now he found he was missing not a word of the old lady's Italian, it was all there, he felt once more the claws on his flesh, the pincers plucking out his nails, foul mouths sucking out his eyes. Rapt but edgy, a boy again, he listened. The dwarfish television set pitched a silent nervous image into the room. Pooch's old man was nodding off. *"Tre anni!"* He apologized, thanked her for the wine, left somehow oddly grateful.

But in West Condon's old housing development, hell lost its charm, turned gray, and he grew old again. Old and tired and cold. He'd got overheated in the Minicucci living room, and the cold was bitter. Get this over with, get home, take a hot bath. Wanda Cravens met him at the tattered screen door with a baby in her arms, toddler hanging on from below. Another kid whined somewhere inside. Never a very big girl, she now seemed more drawn than ever. Must not weigh even a hundred pounds, Vince thought. He felt sorry for her, glad he was bringing some money. He told her what he was there for, and she asked him on in.

Her living room was a wreck of cluttered junk, far from clean, far from warm, winter crawling across the bare floor, cockroaches scrambling alongside the wallboards. It looked more like a house after somebody had moved out than a place someone was living in. Vince found an arm of a waddy chair he thought would hold him, sat down gingerly against it. Wanda dropped the baby and toddler on a ragged throw rug in a corner with the cockroaches, shooed the older one, boy about three or four, on out the door, turned wearily toward Vince. She sure had it tough, okay. With a thin white hand, she pushed back a snarl of sandy-colored hair from her forehead, accepted the check he held out to her. They exchanged only a few words. Her voice was thin, had a hopeless lost distance about it.

"I'm sure you can use it, Wanda," he said clumsily.

She stood in front of him, a wooden table behind her. She sighed, nodded, then turned around, shoved aside the gray heap of clothes on the table, laid the check down, leaned over to examine it.

Vince tried to come up with a couple remarks about what a swell guy he'd always thought Lee was, dependable and goodnatured, but her dress, the starch out of it, hung with limp descriptiveness over her small hips, and talk about old Lee seemed weirdly irregular. The back of her left thigh touched his knee. "Lee was one of the greatest guys I ever worked with, Wanda," he said, confused by the silliness of it: "It was a honor . . ." She leaned further over the table onto one elbow, closed her eyes, rubbed them. Jesus, the poor kid! Her back trembled. Her legs were apart and the dress, folded wispily down the cleft of her buttocks, vibrated gently with her crying. If that was what she was doing. Vince stood up, unavoidably against her, laid his broad dark hand on her back. The bone was right there, hadn't felt a back like that for years. "I . . . I guess I'd better be shoving off." But she butted back against him with a kind of sob, and he thought less about shoving off. His fingers slid to her waist and she curled around like an old routine into his arms, gazed sadly up at him. Her eyes were a little red, but probably from the rubbing, he got the idea right away she was faking it. Thing that surprised him most was how he was staying so goddamn cool. Felt keyed up, okay, but like a spectator caught up in some movie.

Her tiny chest heaved a little against him. "Vince!" she whispered, and it could have meant just about anything. Gentle-boned face, eyes a little close together like old Lee's, cheeks dotted with mud-colored freckles, mouth a soft thin line with a slight overbite, her teeth a bit— They kissed. Vince yanked her in tight against his hard and heated body, clutched the whole of her ass with one big hand, went grabbing down for the lean thighs, felt the taut flesh snap back at him through the wilted cotton, a tautness he'd nearly forgot in women. Wished he still had the little finger on that hand, felt like he was missing something. She broke away, buried her face in his chest.

He looked down at her hair, coarse and dry like yellowed grass. An act, he thought, but he said, "I'm sorry, Wanda, this is all wrong. Hell, I'm not the kind of guy ever to . . ." He tried his damnedest to think of old Lee, that swell guy, but just couldn't bring him well to mind, smelled the hair, odor of sweet soap, reluctantly let go her neat cranny, but she held on to him.

"Don't leave me, Vince!" she whispered.

"Wanda, listen—"

"Vince, I'm so terrible alone, you cain't know how it is for me!" That sounded real enough. The toddler had left the baby squalling on its back in the corner, had crawled over to where they stood embraced, and now had a grip on Vince's pant leg. "Vince, it's Valentine's Day!" she whispered into his mouth, then jammed her lips against it, her hand pulling mightily on his fly. He jerked up her dress, drove his hand down between her thighs as the three-year-old banged in through the front door, letting in a sharp gust of winter.

Charlie announced that night he had joined the Marines. They were sitting in the living room watching television, Vince and Etta, and Vince said, "If you're gonna butt in on the program, why don't you tell us something important?" Both he and Etta made a lot of wisecracks about the Marines being the right place for a shaggy zootsuit bum like him, and Charlie wised back that at least he'd get a decent meal now and then, and he wouldn't have to sweat getting nagged at every five minutes. Vince snorted, said he sure had a helluva lot to learn about the Marines. Charlie shrugged, tucked a butt in his mouth, moved out the door snapping his fingers. Vince watched him parade out, then turned to Etta to remark what a useless cocky grandstander that boy was, but checked himself just in time. Etta was crying. "Hey! what's the matter, chicken? Was it something Charlie said? I'll go—"

She shook her head. "I don't care how bad they are, Vince," she whispered through her tears. "I just hate to see them go."

Angela came in from her bedroom, where she'd been doing her homework. Music from her radio piped in to muddle with the television. "What's Mom crying about?" she demanded.

Vince stammered a moment before he realized he wasn't guilty of anything, then said, "Nothing, baby. Go on back to your studies."

"I believe I have a right to know," she insisted.

Vince supposed she'd got the line out of some goddamn movie. That girl could get under a man's skin sometimes. "It's just that Charlie is going into the Marines, and your Mom—"

"Oh, is *that* all! Well, that's *hardly* something *tragic!* I'd say it was good riddance of bad rubbish!" She clamped her pencil between her neat white teeth, then apparently thought better of it and fitted it carefully over her ear, fiddled with a hairpin. There was a pause, filled only by an overemotional argument on TV and music from Angie's radio that sounded to Vince like some guy having a public orgasm. Etta checked her sniffling, smiled feebly at Angie, and the girl went back to her room.

Vince walked over, patted Etta gently on the shoulder. "Care for half a beer?" She shook her head. Vince figured maybe they ought to try to work something up tonight, been a long time and he felt she deserved a share of his rediscovered potency. But later he fell asleep watching an old movie on the set, and when he woke, Etta had already long since turned in.

One night in bed with Wanda not long after that, he happened to mention that he had a boy going into the

213

Marines. "You already got a boy growed up, Vince?" she asked absently.

He swallowed, felt it shrivel. "Yeah," he said. Decided not to mention the other six.

At the bus station on Ash Wednesday, last week of the month, they made stale jokes about the snowstorm predicted and how Charlie, the lucky bastard, was headed south. Vince noticed how much taller the boy looked all of a sudden, and then, trying not to be nervous, said good-bye to Etta instead of Charlie. And from then on, there were just the three of them in the old house.

8

March tore into West Condon on a sudden savage snowstorm. The lawyer Ralph Himebaugh, brooding over the sinister state of affairs in the world, pushed through the swirling drifts, fur-capped head down butting the wind, feet secure in heavy galoshes, but still cold, cold to the bone. In the whine of wind and snow, there was little to see or hear. Ralph was a man removed, and it was as though the world were remarking the continuing aggravation of his isolation, as though nature herself were persecuting him, the victim, the sacrifice, the outcast. Disaster whistled at his wraps and portents stung his ears.

Discord, famine, war, cruelty, deaths, rape—couldn't the fools see it? Every day, mounting, tragedy upon tragedy, horror succeeding horror, oh my God! It was too plain! Yet their blindness was a part of it, was it not? For years it had been clear to him, the pervasive current of mantling terror, discernible through the scrim of false and superficial reportage, and for years now he had kept records of its progress, scrapbooks of calamities and disasters, deathtoll lists, maps of its movements. Everything about it absorbed him: the scope, the periodicity, the routes of passage, certain correlativities, duration and instantaneity, origin and distant derivative effects, expenditure of energy, parallelisms and counteractions, and, above all, its wake of mathematical clues. Oh, he was *wise* to have done so! For although at the outset the incredible complexities had pitched him into a hell of confusion and despair, by disciplining himself, by virtually chaining himself to the task and pummeling himself to greater wakefulness, he had at last mastered the necessary technology. No, it had been no delusion, not at all! Almost immediately, he had discovered the steady intensification of the disaster frequency, the irreversible course toward cataclysm.

Suddenly, as his own mind was on the terror, a car fluttering through the snow about a hundred yards away went into a spin. Ralph stood transfixed, appalled, as the black machine, mindless, yet possessed by its own inner necessities, lazed through wide chaotic circles in the unbounded street, then bumped up and stopped against a telephone pole that reared out of the shifting snow like a black cross. Oh my God, my God! How much time? A man got out, startling Ralph. He had somehow forgot to expect a man. Ralph felt the old impulse, the impulse to flee, but he overrode it; the recent years, while sobering, had engendered a new kind of courage. It was what emerged and took over, he supposed, when the old irrational constructs of hope and their false comforts were cut away. He stumbled through the snow toward the man, wind nearly blinding him.

The man looked up, smiled, shook his head. "Damn!" he said. "Just like a merry-go-round!"

"Are you all right?"

"Yeah." The man laughed nervously. "But I'm gonna leave her stuck right where she's at and walk the rest of the way. Boy! She really come in like a lion, didn't she?"

Ralph nodded, but did not return the stupid smile. The man's indifference to the experience angered him. They

215

shook gloved hands, and the man left him. His heart still racing, Ralph considered the car and the pole. When the man was out of sight, Ralph glanced about to assure himself of the snow's effective screen, then kicked a dent in the door. "God*damn* you!" he whispered. The rest of the walk home, the machine coiled and spun in maddening sweeps before his eyes.

On his porch, he mechanically checked the mailbox, then remembered it was Sunday. He tugged off the galoshes and stepped inside to greet his cats, Grendel, Nabob, Melpomene, Nyx, and Omar. They were hungry and so attended his presence. Nabob twisted and coiled, rubbing against his moving leg. It was not love. Their emotional range was between indifference and pure hate. He could accept that, yet at times it hurt him, for, against his will, he could not help loving them. He turned into the kitchen and Nabob nearly tripped him up—he brought his foot down on a paw. He removed hake from the freezer and put it to boil. He poured them some milk, but they lapped at it distractedly, their minds on the fish. Nyx sulked. He slipped her a piece of chicken liver. Nyx was a big pure-black animal with a long straight nose. Ralph feared her. "You hot black bitch!" he whispered at her.

While the fish thawed and cooked, he sat down at his desk in the front room and recorded the car accident in the P.O.—Personal Observations—journal. While constructing an essentially objective system, Ralph did not entirely reject subjectivity from it: the mere fact that it was he who had assumed that responsibility of this task was in itself a subjective element, and he recognized it. It was not proven, after all, that the force was mindless— the purity of its mathematics would in fact argue the contrary—and were it not mindless, he could well expect to be regarded as its enemy. He unwrapped last Sunday's *Guardian* and *Times*, sent to him airmail, clipped out pertinent articles, recorded data from them.

The cats protested. He returned to the kitchen, poured the boiling water into the sink, dumped the fish on the cats' plate. With his foot, he blocked Nyx's approach to the plate, made sure the other four had got their share. She clawed his ankle, but he laughed and held her back a little longer. "One day . . . !" he warned her.

At his desk once more, he withdrew his scratchpad, did some hurried calculations. Still, the augmentation, the emergent numerical pattern, the cyclical behavior. Incredible! He sighed, chewed meditatively on the pencil, then began the task of carrying his figures all the way out. No, there was no escaping it. At the present rate of severity increase, mankind would necessarily be overcome within the next six or seven years. *Six or seven years!* Meticulously he rechecked his figures, and with graph paper he described a varied set of conceivable curves based on the slightly different scales he used in the different journal categories. And each time, it resulted in the same forecast—or suggested an even earlier date. Grotesque! It would be grotesque!

This had happened before, of course, signs leading to the immediacy of catastrophe, and dates had in fact been passed, but always he had uncovered some fundamental error in the schematism itself, some critical factor omitted in ignorance from his computations. For example, at the very beginning he had simply listed all events as numerically equal, an appalling lack of sophistication that now amazed and embarrassed him in retrospect. But time and error had brought wisdom. Now, he was convinced, the system could not be more complete. There was no hope in it, given the human condition, for omniscient finality, to be sure, but it had to be taken seriously.

The phone rang, startling him. What now? But it was only Jim Elliott, the Chamber of Commerce secretary. He was working at home on the new industrial brochure and needed information on certain zoning ordinances, which of course Ralph had at the office, not here at home. Elliott was a stupid arrogant ass. Himebaugh explained the problem. "But listen, Jim, if you really need the ordinances, I'll go get them for you."

217

"Aw hell, no, Ralph! Not out in *that* fucking mess. I just thought you might, you know, have them at hand, or something."

"No, but I really don't mind. It *is* a nasty day, but—"

"Don't think twice about it! Anyhow, there's a game on TV, and I'm sick of this goddamn brochure anyway. We'll do it tomorrow."

"Well, if you insist. But do come in the first thing tomorrow. You know I wish to help all I can. How's your family?"

"Oh, everybody's fine, thanks. Fat and lazy. Sally's sore at me because I wouldn't let her go out in the storm to a movie, but I think she'll get over it."

Ralph chuckled cordially, chewed irritably on his pencil. Would the fool never shut up? He and the mayor were the two men Ralph hated most in this stupid town. They never wearied of imposing on his good will with their infantile little games and incredibly insignificant problems. And, God, they monologized without cease. Now it was that hateful brochure. And it was useless, utterly useless. They would never recover from the mine disaster, of that Ralph was sure. But what good would it do to tell them? They were all sick.

"See you tomorrow then, Ralph."

"Yes, I'll keep the day entirely free for you, Jim. Give my best to your good wife."

"Thanks, I'll do that. Hang loose, now!"

Ralph laughed lightly, as he supposed he was expected to do, and cradled the receiver. The idiot! The cats, fed, had composed themselves about the house. One of them scratched in the sand in the pantry. Ralph stood at a window and gazed out on a gradually darkening world, vanishing under the deadweight of snow. The wind had diminished, but the snow still sifted down heavily. There would be accident suits and insurance claims.

He poured himself a snifter of cognac, brushed Omar out of the armchair, and curled up moodily in it, alongside his several scrapbooks and records. He started back about seven years, flipped slowly through, disaster after disaster, pausing meditatively at unusually significant events or peculiarly grotesque ones, letting his mind drift unanchored through the accumulating morass of woe and rot and grief. Slowly the black shape grew. It came to bear, as it had every day for nearly two months, upon the explosion at the Deepwater Number Nine Coalmine, seemed to hover like thick black fumes over that ravaged pit. What did it mean, why was it that single horror so impressed him? He knew full well it was purblind to place exaggerated emphasis on one event merely because of its proximity, yet he could not rid his mind of the possibility that this disaster, this one in particular, provided him, him in particular, some vital urgent message: as though—as though *he* had been the intended victim and had in some incredible manner escaped, and now he had one more chance, one more chance to find the way out, to discover the system that would allow him to predict and escape the next blow.

The number ninety-seven, the number of the dead, was itself unbelievably relevant. Not only did it take its place almost perfectly in the concatenation of disaster figures he had been recording, but it contained internal mysteries as well: nine, after all, was the number of the mine itself, and seven, pregnant integer out of all divination, was the number of trapped miners. The number between nine and seven, eight, was the date of the explosion, and the day of the rescue was eleven, two ones, or two, the difference between nine and seven. Nine and seven added to sixteen, whose parts, one and six, again added to . . . seven! Sixteen was, moreover, in the universe of the line, a fourth-dimensional figure, hardly less important than sixty-four, one more than the product of nine and seven. That product, sixty-three, also added to nine. And yet there was more: Though the acceleration curves for, as an example, energy expenditure and estimated cellular destruction were not the same, yet all of his curves tended to approximate the common parabola produced by the graph of $y = x^2$, on which, as the value of x is increased by one in a series of whole numbers, the value of y increases as the square of the numbers in that series, and the value of the *difference* between the successive lengths of the accelerating y ordinates forms a series of odd numbers increasing at the rate of two units between each whole number in the original x series. When the unit value of x has reached three—the quotient of sixty-three divided by twenty-one, the number of the day within the tenth sign on which rescue took place!—the related value of y becomes nine and the difference between that value and the succeeding one of sixteen is *seven!* It was through *this* astounding discovery that Ralph had been able to place himself with certainty upon the present moment of the parabola, lacking only a final calculation of the value or values of the single x unit. When he had *that*, he knew he would be invulnerable! And it was not beyond his grasp, for he was slowly learning to measure the area *under the several parabolas*, and the area-function sooner or later would lead him to the ordinate-function, provided only he could finally expurgate these area measurements of all arbitrary components, which he believed his current project of graph overlays would eventually do. His head spun. He uncurled, poured another snifter of brandy, watching Grendel licking her genitals. Suddenly infuriated, he doused her with the cognac; she started, scampered under the couch. Only Nyx could do that and not nauseate him. He poured another snifterful.

And then there was ninety-seven plus one: the infamous product of seven and fourteen. For years he had resented the emphasis placed on the number seven, supposing it to be the consequence of stupid obedience to the religionists' texts. Only late in life did he discover that these infantile texts were actually corruptions of older and infinitely more precise, infinitely less adulterated writings, now lost, and he now willingly suffered through the garbage in search of the sources, now willingly respected the generative powers of numbers like one and seven and twelve and fourteen.

Plus one: Giovanni Bruno. Who was he? Why was it he? John Brown! The very anonymity lent an unreal—or, rather, a *superreal*—odor to the occasion, a kind of terror, the terror inevitably associated with voids, infinities, absences, facelessness, zero. For seven weeks now, he had been contemplating a private conversation with the man. Ralph paced the living room. Perhaps he should go tonight. Yet, so much was at stake. His entire reputation in West Condon, for one thing. Nevertheless, a night like tonight, who would be out in it? Who would there be to see him coming and going? And, if apprehended, he could always explain himself in terms of some obscure legal matter. Even a will or something; God knows, the man should have a will. But how would he explain himself to Bruno himself? No, it was better to wait, to be certain, to have the questions precisely formulated. He poured more cognac, again stroked Omar out of the armchair, curled into it now with a thin jacketless book. He tried to read it, but could not concentrate. Why was it so famous? It was a pack of emotional ignorant ravings! He threw it down. The destroyer, damn it! *The destroyer!* They all saw it, but could not face it. Oh, the cowards! Oh, the disgusting yellow pigheads! Oh, the sniveling pissants! He again paced, cursing them, and drank his cognac. Precious ninnies! Asses! Babbling little chickenshits!

Mel came tearing through the room, Nyx at her heels, and they rolled and tumbled, bounded and raced. He shouted, but they ignored him. They tangled in the cord of his desk lamp, brought it down with a crash. Separately, they scampered, but not before he had grabbed the broken lamp and brought it down punishingly on Mel's sleek haunches. They hid. He crouched on his hands and knees, struggling to breathe. The room seemed to be afloat. He spied Nyx. With the lamp, on all fours, he stalked her. She curled her lip, emitting a kind of vicious snorting hiss. In his hand, the broken lamp shook. "*You goddamn nigger whore!*" he snarled. But he couldn't hit her. Dizzily, he stood. He got a broom, swept the broken glass into a dustpan, emptied it into the wastebasket by his desk. His hands were quaking uncontrollably. Better read something, something to forget about it, he thought, but then decided on a warm bath instead.

The water at least was hot and soothing. He lay in the tub, closed his eyes, struggled to free his mind from the terror— Was that how it would get him? Sink into his mind like a fungus? The bubbles were fragrant and oily. He let the hot water trickle into the tub to raise the temperature. It burned his toes, crept up past his ankles, advanced like a living thing toward his fork. "Destroy me!" he whispered, but it was only ritual. His mind was still in the living room, still with the graphs, still with the mine. He sat up, the water boiling hot now around his hips, and sipped cognac. "Mel!" he whispered. "Grendel!" But he got no response. He lay back. It was hot on his back and chest, and he flinched, but he stayed down. He tried to imagine the room, the fat mindless beast stalking her, circling, observing her from every angle. "*Your brother deserved to die!*" he hissed. He was breathing heavily, stroking, clawing, but still his mind refused to participate, still it watched him coldly, contemptuously, faintly disgusted. He sat up and turned off the hot water. In spite of a gathering nausea, he finished the snifter of cognac. He rested his head on the edge of the tub. "Oh, *damn* you!" he cried. He grew uncomfortable. Hastily, he soaped his armpits and genitals, rinsed, and got out.

He dried himself before the mirror, slipped into his lounging robe, returned to the living room for a cigarette. He decided to eat something, but poured more cognac instead. He pulled the blinds, turned on lights. Outside, it was dark, still blustery. He curled into the chair, patted his lap, and Mel hopped up, made herself comfortable. On her haunches, a streak of still-fresh blood. "Poor little sister!" he said, stroking her gently. Tears came, and he sniffled. He would kill Nyx someday. Yes, he would! Mel's fur was silky against him, but she fidgeted. Smell of soap, probably. Yet he felt too weary, too wretched, to bother to go get the fish oil. He sighed, shuddered. "Oh God!" he whispered, then grew suddenly angry. "What's the matter with you?" he cried.

He jumped up from the chair, flipping the cat to the carpet, and strode into the bedroom to dress. Enough of this babying around! He'd go tonight! To hell with the risks! He had to see Bruno and get this thing straightened out, and right now. Tonight!

9

Snow pyramided the old Chevy and drifted deep in the streets, so Miller walked over, feeling faintly ridiculous. Hark ye to the White Bird. Oh boy. In the wind, he chain-smoked, lighting from the butt end of the old the new. The snow flew, though he could see, during lulls, that not much new snow was falling. Maybe no one else would show up. There was that to hope for.

Many reasons, but all of the inopportune instant with no time to think them out, had prompted him to accept when Marcella had called to invite him: the germ of a salable story, his own everlastingly perverse amusement with eccentricity, and so on, but mostly, he supposed, it was a kind of sudden gamy wish to raise a little hell. West Condon was going stale on him, needed a spectacle. Moreover, he had been standing nude and elegantly if awkwardly protracted, having been drawn to the phone from under knowledgeable hands, and had too self-consciously seen himself as for the sweet moment suspended between two female hungers (Golgotha: that timeless ubiquitous image!). Happy Bottom, with characteristic impatience, had lobbed a pillow, bringing down his tacked-up list of ever-ready phone numbers: hastily, then, he had acceded to the request of one thief, not to forfeit the voracity of the other.

House lights laid down luminous trapdoor patches on the snow here and there, but mostly, on the walk to the Brunos', there was just a darkness and a lot of blowing snow. A leonine first of March: which led to the possibility it might go out with the Lamb. Miller laughed, stepped up his pace, enthused once more by the chance to look in on these types. After all, they needed him, for he believed he might have been indirectly responsible for having set the date. Marcella had called him the day after Clara Collins' eighth of February pageant to tell him all that had happened and what her brother had said, though this time she'd asked him not to print it. They were planning to meet again the following Sunday in response to her brother's pronouncement, she had said, but Miller, already committed with Happy for that night, had suggested an alternative reading of "Sunday week": a week of Sundays. He had had vaguely in mind seven weeks from the eighth, but it had apparently got interpreted finally, by way of Eleanor Norton's arcane sources, as tonight, seven Sundays from Bruno's rescue.

Marcella, who was the other and no doubt most telling reason for his coming, met him at the door, stood backlit by a dull hall bulb while he struggled with his boots. He tossed them with the others—he would not be alone—and flicked his cigarette out into the drifts, brushed the snow from his shoulders, entered. Marcella closed the door behind him, turned toward him, touching an index finger to her lips for silence as she took his coat. Her blouse, even in this poor light, was incredibly white. Alive. With it, she wore a coffee-colored skirt, pleated, a little juvenile maybe, but he was too caught up in the way her gently molded hips disturbed the pleats' verticals to want it otherwise. She stretched up to toss his hat on the shelf above the coats, causing a new play of lights and shadows in the blouse. He touched her elbow gently, took the hat, laid it on the shelf, had the pleasure of her forearm's lingering slide down through his fingertips. He'd forgot, in all the grosser scrabblings, that he could still enjoy things like that. He smiled down at her, feeling four-handed without either the camera or a body trained to his touch. "Am I late?" he whispered.

"No," she said. "Mrs. Collins isn't here yet. The others are in my brother's room. I don't think they're tremendously happy you're coming. They seem awfully afraid of publicity or something, I don't know why."

"Don't worry," he assured her. "I'll be careful."

She led him through the living room, behind her old father Antonio slumped in a chair before the television screen, coffee can on the armrest beside him: homemade cuspidor. On the screen, three splay-pelvised girls dressed in animal skins did a kind of warped jazz ballet, the cheap set stunting their legs. Gabriel's sisters, no doubt.

A large fancy cake sat on the dining room table, neatly encircled by plates, forks, cups, spoons, and napkins. He asked with a gesture if she had made it, and Marcella replied with a smile and a nod that she had. An antique cut-glass chandelier with electric candles, overbearing in this simple room of simple things, provided the light, left the room virtually shadowless except right under the table. Marcella showed him to a door leading off the back of the dining room: the downstairs bedroom which had been her brother's since his return a month ago from the hospital. She knocked. Miller licked his lips. The game was on.

The door cracked open. "What is your message?" inquired a hushed male voice, so faint Miller barely understood it.

"Hark ye to the White Bird," Miller replied, and then Marcella echoed him. The door opened, and they were admitted.

First thing he saw was Giovanni, sitting halfway up in bed, supported by a mound of pillows. He wore dark pajamas that exaggerated his pallor, had two or three blankets piled up on him to the waist. He turned his head

—one thought of it more as a mechanical toy than a living man's head—to look as Miller and Marcella entered. The others in the room did the same: pivoted silently toward them. The room was lit by a nightlamp beside the bed and a few candles placed about; aroma of tallow. At a small table near the foot of the bed, facing the door, sat Eleanor Norton, the high school teacher who had become Bruno's spiritual counselor, and across from her, a squat pillowy woman in a cheap shiny dress. Black: must be one of the disaster widows. But which? When she turned to peek at him over her shoulder, he found her face familiar, but he couldn't place it. Two young boys sat stiffly in chairs next to the far wall. The doorkeeper, of course, was Eleanor Norton's husband, Dr. Wylie Norton. And it was very quiet.

"Good evening, Mrs. Norton, Dr. Norton," Miller said into the silence. "How are you feeling, Giovanni? Much better, I hope." He smiled at the others, added with measured concern, "I hope I haven't interrupted any . . ."

"Not at all, Mr. Miller." Wylie Norton smiled, extending his hand. "We're glad you've come!" With Norton's welcome, there were traces of relaxation all around. The two boys stood, came over, were introduced by Norton as Colin Meredith and Carl Dean Palmers, seniors at the high school. They were both shy, slow to commit themselves in any way, but Miller spoke frankly with them, and they were soon friendly. Meredith was a tall gangly boy with loose blond hair, a pink flush to his cheeks, tendency to stoop as he walked; Palmers was shorter, stockier, had a bad case of acne, seemed more mature, more aggressive. Miller noticed Palmers' missing tooth and asked if he were the Palmers who played guard this year on the varsity football team. The boy grinned awkwardly and nodded, obviously pleased to have been recognized.

The name of the other one in the room came suddenly to mind, and he turned to the plump widow. "Mrs. Wilson, I'm Justin Miller. I don't know if you remember me, but we—"

"Oh, yes," she said quickly, kittenish little whimper of a voice. "You wrote up such nice things when I lost . . . when I lost . . ." And she began to pucker up.

"Now, now!" intervened Eleanor Norton. "Please remember, Mrs. Wilson, we must all stand firm!" She glanced up sharply at Miller, partly accusing, partly as though seeking—but seeking what? Some kind of signal, or—?

Miller nodded firmly. He thought of saying something like "I'm sure that's how Eddie would want it," but it was just too cornball, he might start grinning, so he kept silence. He let his gaze lift past the two women toward Giovanni, fixed, he hoped, with an adequate awe. For the moment, at least until he understood better what was going on, what had happened, what was expected, it was the best he could do for Mrs. Norton. On the wall over the headboard of the bed, there was a crucifix. Other things framed here and there. What looked to be an old wedding portrait of Antonio and Emilia: something of the old woman in Marcella, all right.

"We have been discussing certain instructions, Mr. Miller," Eleanor Norton said suddenly. She had a precise gentle voice that cut cleanly through the silence. "Instructions from . . . from the worlds beyond us." She paused. Miller, coming back to the table, noticed now the book open on it between the two women, a blank book, bound, the kind used for record-keeping. "These are messages received over the recent weeks from . . . from them, by way of extrasensory perception." Miller didn't know what to say to that, so he merely returned, unsmiling but genuinely attentive, her gray-eyed gaze. This, he knew, was his worst test. Marcella's soft proximity bolstered him, yet he felt vaguely uneasy about her presence, witness to this act of his. "We are anxious, all of us, to comprehend what we can from them, and we are quite naturally . . . pleased, Mr. Miller, to have with us in our endeavors the sincere interest of all fellow beings whose motives are pure and who will . . . that is, who will participate in our meditations in a spirit of hope and honesty and . . . in a *positive* spirit, let me say."

"Of course, Mrs. Norton. Let me—"

"But do understand, we are not like . . . like evangelists, Mr. Miller. Quite the contrary. We believe in quiet unpretentious and unadvertised gatherings."

"Sure," said Miller. "I can understand that you're concerned about my being a newspaper editor. But I can assure you, Mrs. Norton, that my interest here has nothing to do with my paper, and I'll never publish anything in it unless you want me to. Unless," he added, feeling adventurous and addressing the whole room, "we all do."

The doorbell rang. "That must be Mrs. Collins," Marcella said, and left him to stand alone. Miller watched her go, moving lightly, a spontaneous gladness seeming to lift her up. She glanced back at him from the door and they exchanged smiles, surprised at each other's attention.

Miller pulled a pack of cigarettes from his pocket, turned to offer one to Wylie Norton, standing beside him, but Mrs. Norton came up, put her hand over his pack: "Please, Mr. Miller. No smoking." And she turned her head significantly toward Bruno, who watched them darkly.

"Of course," he said, returning the cigarettes to his pocket. Here but a couple minutes, and he'd already forgot that the sick miner was even in the room. As for Mrs. Norton, she seemed jumpy and peremptory, but Miller guessed it was at least partly due to Clara Collins' imminent arrival. Eleanor had had Bruno—and Marcella, too—entirely to herself until three weeks ago when Clara Collins appropriated him to her own vision. The February eighth show, as he understood it, was a kind of emotional steamroller, with Eleanor Norton finally outlasting them all and obtaining a tenuous kind of intellectual control over Clara.

After four times through the white bird routine, more ridiculous than ever from this side of the door, the widow Clara Collins strode noisily in with her daughter Elaine, the coalminer Willie Hall, and a woman who turned out to be Mabel Hall, Willie's wife. Miller had had no idea the Halls would be here, Marcella hadn't mentioned them, yet he wasn't surprised, recalling his interview of Hall, Oxford Clemens' buddy, just after the disaster. Hall, he remembered, lived by hunches.

The Halls were introduced to everyone. Talk was about the snowstorm. Some took it as a portent. The boys, also new here apparently, were introduced to Clara and Elaine, though Carl Dean said he recognized Elaine from a study hall they had together. While Elaine, hand covering her mouthful of bad teeth and small shoulders hunched, received shy attention from Meredith and Palmers, her mother swung horsily around the bedroom, greeted Bruno, the Nortons, Betty Wilson, never waiting for a reply. She seemed intent, nervous, self-important, yet respectful. She lugged a large shiny patent-leather handbag out of which she now pulled a man's handkerchief, blew her nose stoutly. As she strode long-legged—Miller thought of trotters—over to him, he realized she was nearly as tall as he was. Then he saw that she was wearing heels tonight. White ones, odd for midwinter. Nylons wrinkled, sparkled above the ankles with melted snow. "It's a good thing you come," she said to him, and he understood immediately that he would suffer no challenges from her. Somehow from the beginning, maybe because of his interest in her husband and the note, she had clearly supposed him friendly to any cause of hers. "We need folks like you here."

"I'm sorry I wasn't able to come before," he said.

"Well, maybe jist as good you didn't." Trace of a smile touched the corners of her mouth. "We had a couple purty rough nights. But this'n's apt to be a mite better." The Halls tittered nervously.

Miller asked about the meeting on the eighth, but she didn't seem to want to talk about it, except to repeat Bruno's six-word message. As for the small and uneventful gathering on the fifteenth, she only shrugged, said that Mrs. Norton had received a "kinder prophecy like" that something was sure to happen this night, the first of March. "Something, uh, final? Nope: It ain't the eighth." He pursued further the matter of Mrs. Norton's talents, seeking skepticism, but saw clearly that Clara was impressed by them, thought Eleanor "a fine Christian woman," believed that it was God who had brought them all, each with his different gifts, together. "She's been a great comfort to me, Mr. Miller, and she's taught me more about the Holy Bible than I ever knowed before." He wondered if she'd changed her mind about the Second Coming, but before he could ask, she was gone, trotting away from him as abruptly as she had come, her feet broad and knobby in the white pumps.

Marcella stood at his side, and in the moment they had together he asked her what exactly they were expecting tonight. "I don't know," she said. "Perhaps . . . the coming of light." Was that irony he heard? Was she, like him, having fun with all this? He wished to know what she meant, but feared to risk too much. Instead, he asked her why she had told him that tonight's password was designed "to keep out the Baxters." Did Abner Baxter have something to do with it?

"He's the one who hates Mrs. Collins. He's the man who turned all her friends against her and made his own wife the president of Mrs. Collins' Evening Circle."

"Was he here on the eighth?"

"Yes. He's a fat man with red hair and a furious temper." She made funny puffing gestures of fatness and fury. "He made everybody walk out and leave her alone. He's with the enemy."

"The enemy? Who are they?"

"Why," she said with a smile, as though surprised he should ask, "the powers of darkness."

He smiled in return, but it made her stop smiling, and that confused him. "Don't you think it's kind of funny," he said to cover for his smile, "that a redheaded preacher should be the devil's advocate?"

"If you saw him, you wouldn't think so," she said, and there was no smile at all.

Elaine Collins and Carl Dean Palmers had become engrossed in a quiet argument about religion. Colin Meredith, severed, walked over to join him and Marcella. Affected, the boy's walk, but not effeminate exactly. The nice child, the ever-willing friend, the shy young man who would fade into the shy old bachelor, fastidious, moody, kindly, especially toward small children. He explained that he had known Mrs. Norton for several months, that she had been helping him establish contact with superior spirits. He had introduced his friend Carl Dean to her, and although Carl Dean was skeptical at first, they had both come to have a lot of faith in her. She was extremely sincere and intelligent and unselfish, and she had done a great deal for him, not so much yet for Carl Dean maybe, but she had made a whole new person out of *him*, leading him away from the love of earthly things to love of things of the spirit. He had brought an end to all his bad habits, and had even discovered that sometimes he did attain to a kind of communication with the other world. Well, maybe not exactly a communication, but something very much like it. It took literally hours and hours of meditation and humility and self-searching and seeking without thought, but once in a while something happened, something really unbelievable, it was like—like a light turning on inside. Afterwards, after this kind of terribly exhilarating experience, he couldn't explain it, or even describe it, it was beyond the capacity of human language, like Mrs. Norton always said. But, really, it was wonderful, a truly extraordinary experience—but then, Mr. Miller probably already knew what he meant. Beside him, Marcella nodded for him; she seemed pretty caught up in what this silly kid had to say. Also, Meredith said, he sometimes received—like Mrs. Norton, through his right hand—messages from his dead mother and father, but that was mainly thanks to another woman he had known a couple years before in the orphanage; Mrs. Norton didn't seem too excited about these writings from his parents, though of course she said they were surely true. She herself, she had told him, had received her very first communications from recently dead earth people, or spirits that assumed their parts. Now, with her help, he was learning how to achieve much greater things.

Willie and Mabel Hall came over, disrupting the boy's monologue. Marcella excused herself, left the room. "Well, as the Good Book says," said Willie Hall, " 'the poor has good tidings preached to them!' " Hall looked at no one when he spoke, just gazed off and let fly.

"You know the Bible well?" Miller asked.

"And 'somethin' greater than the temple is here!' "

Mabel Hall, though not too big, outweighed her husband by a good thirty pounds and had a couple inches on him, but Miller's first-sight estimate of her as the muscled tyrant proved far from the case. She was as submissive as Willie was impulsive, as mute and secretive as he was loquacious.

"Excuse me, Mr. Hall, but what do you think is going to—?"

"As the Good Book says, Mr. Miller, 'in malice be ye babes, but in mind be men!' And 'many are called, but few are chosen'!"

It was useless, so Miller gave it up.

"Watch ye, stand fast in the faith, quit you like men, be strong—"

Marcella came in and announced that refreshments were ready. She smiled over at Miller, and he winked in return. Everyone stood and moved with polite gestures toward the dining room, sweeping Marcella in ahead of them. All but Giovanni, of course: he watched them exit, expressionless. His eyes were what you noticed: glittering, black, restless, the flesh around them sunken, making them seem to protrude abnormally.

Miller held back, let the others go ahead, and he saw, as he'd more or less anticipated, that Eleanor Norton was also delaying, fussing with her logbooks. When the others had filed into the dining room, she approached him. "I saw you were talking with Mrs. Collins."

"Yes, for a moment. I must say, she seems very impressed by you. She says you have been a great inspiration to her."

Mrs. Norton sighed, absently rubbed a small medallion that hung from her neck on a chain. "She's a sincere woman, Mr. Miller, but . . . a frightful amateur." She smiled up at him, accepting the sympathetic smile he returned her. "Tell me," she continued without transition, "do you believe in communication with spiritual beings at higher levels?"

Marcella had explained enough of what had happened until now to prepare him somewhat for tonight's experience, and he had even half expected this woman's very question, yet when she put it directly to him, he discovered he didn't have an answer for it. He reached again for his cigarettes, checked himself just in time. Chatter trickled in irrelevantly from the dining room. Giovanni looked on from his bed. "It's a subject," he managed finally, "in which I have long had a serious interest, Mrs. Norton."

"Good," she said simply, apparently accepting that, lame as it was. "Oh dear, we really have *so* much to do!" She focused on some great distance, sighed. "I do hope we shall be ready!"

He ventured: "For what, Mrs. Norton?" All he had picked up so far was that she claimed to be able to receive messages, through writing and sometimes, in emergencies, through her voice, from superior spirits, spirits at what she called "higher aspects of intensity," and that now she had reached the seventh such aspect, perhaps the last, whence she received periodic communiqués from a teacher known to her as "Domiron." This Domiron presumably existed, not exactly in a different place or a different stellar system, but somehow in this same space, but at a different density level, as though his atoms were lighter or something.

233

"I don't know," she said slowly, after a pause. "I hope . . ." But her voice trailed off. She glanced at her watch, and he instinctively checked his: 8:50. "Mr. Miller?" She looked up at him. He guessed her eyes to be gray or gray-blue, though in this dull flickering light he couldn't tell for sure. But they had that faded, indistinct, introspective quality of gray eyes. "Do you believe that Giovanni Bruno was miraculously rescued from the coalmine disaster?"

"Yes, I do." No more hesitations, boy.

"I don't."

"Really? But—"

"I am convinced, Mr. Miller—more than that: I have received specific information on the matter—Giovanni Bruno perished in that mine disaster!"

What could he say? From over her small graying head, Giovanni Bruno's eyes shone at them, as though . . . as though he were assenting, inciting her. "But then, how—?"

"His own mother has confirmed it. She said she saw him dead. And everyone has agreed on one thing: that this is a very different man now from the one they all knew as Giovanni Bruno."

"Then you think—?"

"Not think, Mr. Miller! This kind of insight is never achieved by thinking!" She seemed suddenly angry. He realized that, for all her modest manner, there was something ever seething underneath. She frowned, as a mother might at a forgetful child, then continued matter-of-factly: "Giovanni Bruno died and his body is now inhabited by a superior being. This is the meaning of the . . . the vision of the white bird."

At a loss, he replied, "I see," and then, in the ensuing silence, added, "Well, I'm certainly learning a great deal!"

She assented. "We all have much to learn," she said.

"And Mrs. Collins?"

A barely perceptible little sigh of exasperation, a pause. "We felt extremely fortunate that Mrs. Collins joined us three weeks ago. There is every reason to believe that

234

the . . . the being, let us say, the being now struggling to establish communication with us through . . . through the body and person of Giovanni Bruno"—a thoughtful hesitation, a brief glance Bruno's way—"might originally have intended to utilize Mrs. Collins' husband."

"But why do you think—?"

"The . . . the condition . . ."

"Ah. And does Mrs. Collins herself . . . ?"

Again the impatient sigh. "Grasp it? I don't know, Mr. Miller. I hope so. But she is slow to learn, is overemotional and impulsive. And she is too hemmed in, I am afraid, by her own . . . her own prejudices, if I may so speak."

"Her Christianity."

"Yes. I have had to employ all the frightfully dull simplifications and bumbling writings to which she is accustomed in order even to communicate—I hope I don't offend you . . . ?"

"Not at all."

"Righteousness and salvation, the so-called Second Coming, the terribly overworked parable of the cross, angels and devils and sin—*sin!* Good heavens! Finally, Mr. Miller, we are all of us emanations of the world soul, are we not? Ultimately we all partake, like it or not, in what is commonly called the divine, and the only conceivable sin in such a case is to be willfully ignorant of one's proper condition. Isn't that so?"

He assented, remarking privately that that was not unlike the line by which he often made out with the reluctant.

"But what can I do? And I simply can *not* share—that is, *we* cannot share—her morbid expectations. I admit, it is possible, at least another thing somewhat like the disaster she expects is possible, but, well, there is a logic to everything, Mr. Miller, even the irrational, don't you think?"

"By all means."

"I have received no single message to confirm such an extreme interpretation, though it is true, there have been hints implying *something* of cosmic importance. . . ." She gazed off, her mind momentarily elsewhere, bit her lip. She seldom let go her grip on the medallion. "Mr. Miller, I cannot believe that my . . . my sources . . ."

"Domiron, I think you—"

"Why, yes! How did you know?"

He perceived an answer that would really bowl her over, but he passed it by. "Marcella mentioned . . ."

"Oh, yes. Of course." She looked up at Miller, her schoolmistress sternness melting for a moment. "She's a truly marvelous pupil, so kind and sincere, the finest in all my years as . . . as a teacher. We're deeply fond of her, Wylie and I. And she is making such extraordinary progress!"

Inwardly, he frowned at that but said, "She's a wonderful girl."

"Yes, yes, she is." Fadeout again.

"Mrs. Norton, I'd like to arrange for, sometime at your convenience, of course, some private instruction, too, if I may."

"Of course, Mr. Miller," she said, then added gravely, "It is my duty for those who ask." She cast a glance toward Bruno, then turned to enter the dining room.

"Oh, and Mrs. Norton, what do you think, what do you believe Giovanni Bruno—or the voice within him—meant by 'the coming of light'?"

"I'm not sure," she said, looking at him quizzically. "But we shall know tonight. Shouldn't we go in? I'm afraid there'll be no cake for us."

The coming of light! Do none of them perceive it so well as she? So plain! Her knife licks into the cake, his cake, light dances on the blade, on the frosting's glaze, spoons reflect it, eyes sparkle with it, light decorates her laughter, her motions flow in it. Are not their pasts so shadowed as hers? Does not a storm blow through their present? Do not their morrows flash with promise? Is not this very room bursting with light? Are they blind? Are they all so old? Need they their terrors? Must they distort it? Oh, come! she

236

cries. Yes, there is plenty for all! for seconds! take more!
Gaily, she serves, pours, helps, hands, gives . . . gives!

Around the table a cheerful tumble of voices, forks
clicking plates, compliments on the cake, modest pasts in
halting revelation, the boys talking basketball and animal
care with Wylie Norton: could be a party anywhere. Willie
Hall, his jaws in motion as always, but now with cake
damming the sound, listened, eyes asquint, to Eleanor
Norton. Mrs. Wilson and Mrs. Hall sat flatly on chairs,
overlapping the edges, nibbling at the cake, Mrs. Hall
whispering furtively into Mrs. Wilson's ear. Miller located
Marcella behind the broad shoulders of Clara Collins, delivering cake to Elaine. He maneuvered so as to catch her
eye, showed her his empty hands. She smiled, stretched
over the dining room table, starched blouse snapping taut,
under the yellow—almost amber—glow of the chandelier,
sliced him a wide wedge, laid it neatly on a plate. He knew
it was unwarranted, but he couldn't rid his mind of the idea
she had baked the cake especially for him. Anyway, why
not think of it that way? Watching her was a feast in itself.
More than anything, it was her poise, her unfailing delicacy
of movement, her radiance, open smiles, frank gazes, all
without visible effort, operating on some internal principle
of—well, he was tempted to say *Joy.* But maybe that was
merely an instance of projection. Certainly *he* felt like
blowing the goddamn roof off. She brought him the cake
and a cup of coffee. "I don't suppose you take cream or
sugar."

"No." He smiled, a little surprised at the way she'd said
it. He could hear some thin music trickling in from the
television. He motioned toward it. "We can't escape it,
should we join it?" Wanted it to sound natural, but it
didn't: could almost feel the goddamn whiskers sprouting
and bristling. He expected the worst.

But she smiled and said, "Okay. Let me get some
coffee."

In the darkened living room, they leaned back against a wall, just inside the door to the dining room, facing the television set. Her father sagged in his chair between them and the screen, his back more or less to them, snorted restlessly from time to time, ran his old white hands trembling through his thinning hair. There was no bandage on his nose tonight, and the large sores showed black when they caught the bluish-white glare of the television.

Miller, sipping coffee, looked down at the clasp on Marcella's head. He couldn't distinguish the outlines of the televised picture exactly, but the motion of the screen was reflected in it. Nervous back-and-forth twitches of light. Her hair had a fresh smell that reminded him vaguely of some distant event, something beyond his mere recollections, some fragrant imprecise time he had possibly never really known. A lock of her hair had come loose from the clasp, arched out now over her smooth forehead. She looked up and, not smiling, held his gaze. He lowered the cup. A strange thought intruded and he wondered where it came from and if it were truly a thought or already an irrevocable decision. She had large wideset sensitive eyes, he knew them to be brown, a small fine-boned—and, in sudden need, their mouths drew together, he felt her warm breath flickering over his lips just before they touched hers—and it was only a touch, a brush: plain unskilled reception, and he thought, I'm the first to come here! She held his gaze as he leaned away and they were both still for a moment. Then she smiled. Her smile broke the last bolts. He watched her dancing through his once-gloomy house.

"Here," she whispered, and took the plate of his hand, set it on a table a few feet away, put her cup there, too, returned to his side. She took his free hand, clasped it firmly but not in ownership exactly, a kind of eager gratitude, affirmation, and she leaned against him. He knelt, set the cup on the floor, lifted his eyes the full length of her young body, all those subtle curves of thigh and belly, and as he rose to—he thought coolly—enrich her experience, the doorbell sounded. He started, and she laughed gaily. "Excuse me," she said, and her amused smile tweaked him faintly. "You giddy adolescent ass!" he accused himself as she walked away, but he had to grin. Goddamn, he didn't know when he'd been so wildly high!

When Marcella came back in, she was with *Ralph Himebaugh!* Miller almost laughed aloud. What a night! Himebaugh! Ralph didn't see him at first, kept his coat on, fur cap in hand, peered anxiously into the shadowed corners, blinked, twisted his cap, man being chased, nodded at old Antonio in the chair, who of course ignored the newest intruder as he had ignored them all, bumped into Marcella, who had paused, squinted at the television as though seeking a clue there, eyes flicked across Miller, frowned toward the lighted dining room and its noises, whipped back on Miller, and he stopped dead in his tracks. "Evening, Ralph," said Miller, smiling.

"My God!" stammered Ralph. "M-Miller, you—? Is that—? What— My heavens, *what's happening?*"

"I don't know, Ralph. It's not certain. Step in and have some cake." Couldn't hold back the grin, flowed all over his goddamn face; hoped it looked like welcome only.

Himebaugh finally summoned the will to take another step, squinted anxiously over his shoulder once more at the old man, then again at Miller, hurried on at last into the dining room, still twisting hell out of his cap. Miller hoped Marcella would linger behind, but of course she didn't, so he picked up his cup from the floor and followed them in. What the hell, he reasoned, there would be time now. Don't push it.

Himebaugh was introduced to all present and, in snatches, to the general purpose of the congregation. He seemed dazed, eyes dilated still from the dark walk over, ears bright red from the cold, flabby old lips moving foolishly, unable to understand the whirl around him. A lot of commotion, as a matter of fact, in spite of the group's professed caution. Miller didn't quite understand it himself. Ralph stammered something inanely aimless about a will, finally blurted out he had come to see Bruno, a personal, that is to say, only a routine visit, in order to discuss his, er, his, let us say, press releases (hopeful glance at Miller), how's that? Vision? Yes, his vision, and chose tonight by merest accident, well, not by merest accident, but he had had no idea, none at all, that there would be, that so many people, that is to say, and he almost turned back because of the snowstorm. He removed his coat, gave it to Marcella without even observing who took it, unlocked the fur cap from his hands and thrust that at her, too. She left the room with them. Himebaugh accepted a cup of coffee, turned down the cake.

Miller turned to pursue Marcella into the privacy of the hallway, but Eleanor Norton intercepted him. Her face had paled, her eyes were pinched from below with anxiety, a kind of horror or foreboding. Perspiration on her forehead. Miller assumed concern. Clara Collins loomed, alarmed, at their side. Mrs. Norton looked up at the two of them, first at one, then at the other. "Don't you see?" she whispered. "He is the twelfth! The circle is complete!" And she moved away again, spreading the word.

An uneasy silence sank into the room. Himebaugh plunked three or four spoonfuls of sugar into his coffee, stirred, spoon scraping the china. His hands trembled. Everyone watched. He glanced around anxiously at all the eyes as he sipped the coffee, his dark shaggy eyebrows arched up at the middle, asking What? *What?* his eyes popping with shock. Since a boy in school, Miller had known the old guy but had never seen him in this light. And in this snowstorm, with nothing to go on— Alongside Miller, Clara Collins, breathing noisily, clenched and unclenched her fists.

"Perhaps," announced Eleanor Norton ominously, "we should return to Mr. Bruno's room."

Miller could hear, from the living room, guns and horses' hoofs, tinny shouts of mock anger, soul-legend of the nation, and then the clanging voice of an announcer telling where good tobaccos come from. It was probably permitted to smoke out here, and he'd forgot. Marcella was cleaning off the table. He asked her softly what Eleanor had meant by "completing the circle."

Marcella thought a moment, then said, "Well, there were six of us before, not counting Giovanni, and we were all supposed to bring somebody tonight. But Mrs. Wilson's guest couldn't come because of the bad weather or something." She smiled up at him, returned to stacking plates. He started to help, but she shook her head, nodded toward the bedroom. "I'll be there in a minute," she said.

She carried the plates into the kitchen, and Miller took advantage of his momentary solitude to enjoy a prolonged unobserved regard of the easy cadence of her hips. Where Happy Bottom pinched in at the waist, bulged tremulously in the buttocks, Marcella tapered finely, arched firmly. There was a conscious challenge, a proud taunting thrust to Happy Bottom's stagy shamble; Marcella swung loose-limbed and light of heart, stunning but chaste. Difference between a hurdy-gurdy and a pipe's soft capriccio. But he liked both.

He was the last but for Marcella into the bedroom. Wylie Norton eased the door shut behind him. It was 10:45. Eleanor Norton posed priestesslike at the foot of Bruno's bed. Bruno sat as he had sat before, staring out straight in front of him, and thus, as she had planned it, at Mrs. Norton; his dark scooped-out eyes, though, now seemed blank and unseeing. Worn out probably. The others gathered around his bed: Wylie, Clara, young Meredith, the Halls, Betty Wilson. Marcella entered quietly. She touched Giovanni's head, measured some medicine in a teaspoon, offered it to her brother, who accepted it without expression. Carl Dean Palmers and Elaine Collins hung back slightly, she in shyness, he as if hesitant to commit himself. Himebaugh, still carrying the coffee, tiptoed over beside Miller. He was breathing rapidly,

abjectly terrified. The cup rattled on its saucer. His eyes
blinked with a kind of nervous tic. "Wh-what for God's
sake *is* it?" he rasped.

"Relax," Miller whispered. "Watch and see." He nodded toward Eleanor Norton.

Mrs. Norton now lifted her slender arms slowly before
her, a kind of benediction, as it were. He understood well
enough her task: she had called this thing and was under
pressure to produce; if she didn't, she'd likely lose the mace.
"Hark ye to the White Bird!" she commanded, shattering
the silence and causing some to start. Himebaugh caught
his breath sharply. "Giovanni Bruno! The One to Come!"
The widows and Mrs. Hall whispered mewing amens. "We
look to the east! We look to the west! The feet tug downward, but the spirit soars!" She had a fine voice, strong and
clear. "A firmness is forthcoming! A cosmic repose! Hark
ye! We avoid the illusory to seek wisdom with love! For a
time, we know, is to come, and the soul will swim in the
vast and empty sea of enlightenment!" Betty Wilson had
begun to whimper softly. Elaine and Carl Dean had
joined the group at the bed. Slowly, Himebaugh edged
away from Miller's side toward the others. "So hark ye,
hark ye to the White Bird of wisdom and grace!" At this
familiar angelus all the Nazarenes, in Pavlovian response,
amenned. "From out of the abyss of darkness, *lead us to
light!*"

Colin Meredith caught his breath. He opened his
mouth as though to speak, but nothing came out. Instead,
it was Clara Collins who cried out, "Hear us, o God!"

"In the name of Christ Jesus!" added Willie Hall as
though reciting, apparently emboldened by Clara's cry. "As
it says—"

"*Hark ye to the White Bird!*" Eleanor demanded, her
voice pitched up a notch.

Clara, undaunted, or maybe ignorant of the other
woman's meaning, opened her mouth to speak again, but
just then Giovanni Bruno lifted one hand and brought a
sudden hush down on all of them. They waited. "*The*

tomb . . ." he said, and it was weird how the sound emerged as though forged in some inner and deeply resonant cavity, then heaved whole through his open but utterly passive mouth, *". . . is its message!"* Hand down.

Message, tomb: all eyes turned on Clara Collins. *"Oh God!"* she screamed, thrusting high her husband's note. *"The Day of the Lord is at hand!"*

Betty Wilson bubbled into tears, plumped to her waddy knees, commenced to pray wildly. Eleanor Norton had paled, seemed confused, unbelieving: betrayed. Wylie watched her. Himebaugh, beside himself with panic, shrank back, found Miller's side.

"I say, the day of salvation is upon us!"

"Yes, Lord!" chorused Willie Hall. His wife sank apprehensively to Betty Wilson's side, and Elaine Collins knelt dutifully behind them. They chanted amens and their voices rose, and now the boys joined in.

"We must walk with God and *believe!"* cried Clara. "We must listen always to the white bird in our hearts! Abide in grace! The Son of God, *He is comin'!* We will stand—"

"Caution!" cried Eleanor Norton with tremendous power.

Even though he'd been expecting it, having realized that Clara was quoting her husband's message and was now nearing the controversial phrase about the eighth of the month, nevertheless, like everyone else, Miller started. Clara stood transfixed before the other woman's intensity. Betty Wilson began to whimper again, and Clara shushed her. Silence, troubled and fearful, settled, out of which the heavy breathing emerged like an invisible animal. Miller, seeking concealment, too tall to stand alone in the room without notice, found a corner chair and edged back into it. Himebaugh stood marooned in the room's middle. The poor sonuvabitch, Miller knew how he felt and supposed he could rescue him, but was having too goddamned good a time to want to break the spell. Jesus! Lou Jones should be here! He'd love it!

243

"Mrs. Norton," said Clara submissively, almost tenderly, "lead us to light!"

Eleanor turned stiffly to the chair at the foot of the bed, slowly sat down upon it. Wylie watched, frowning worriedly. No one talked. All looked on. Mrs. Norton stretched her arms forward. She placed her hands on the table, palms down, thumbs touching, fingers spread apart. She stared, breathless, at the opposite wall, and for several tense minutes nothing happened. Then, slowly, almost imperceptibly at first, her lips began to move. There was no sound except for a little hissing noise that came from them. Then it stopped. Her lips closed. Her eyes widened as though focusing on some extreme distance. The candlelight beamed off her gold medallion like a tiny sun trembling there on her dark dress. Her mouth fell open and a strange almost masculine voice emerged. Her lips closed down around the sound, almost a gargling, and produced:

Hark ye to the new voice among ye!

The invisible animal gasped. Eyes turned. Himebaugh came into focus. Miller leaned forward in his chair, pressing his cheeks into the palms of his hands, his hands in a kind of prayer position. A laugh leaped in his diaphragm, but he was now Ralph's backdrop, the eyes on Ralph saw him, so he managed to keep his face poker-stiff. Himebaugh, the poor fucker, literally shook. His body seemed to shrink, his clothes to bag. His cup tinkled in its saucer. Eleanor Norton collapsed on the tabletop. A great act, but —Miller glanced quickly at the other faces—was he the only one who knew she had failed? Wylie stepped over, patted his wife's hands. He knelt beside her, looked back over his shoulder at Himebaugh. Marcella stood, pressed against the wall at the head of her brother's bed. Now, for the first time, she saw Miller again, and as though in imitation of him, she brought her hands together before her face. Her eyes sparkled . . . goddamn it, were there tears?

244

"I came," said Himebaugh suddenly, his precisely mannered voice now half growl, half squeak, "if you must know"—he swallowed—"in fear of . . . of the *destroyer!*"

"*Oh dear Jesus!*" wailed Clara Collins, and dropped like a brick to her knobby knees: ka*whump!* Again the Nazarenes took over. Christ, they were irrepressible! Miller had to admit, though, that Himebaugh had, under the circumstances, performed well.

Eleanor Norton came around, opened her eyes, appeared lost. "Mrs. Collins!" she appealed, stumbling over to her. "Come! Tell me what happened!" She led the widow to the dining room, apparently eager to learn, but effectively—at last—breaking up the revival meeting. The two boys began to argue quietly, Wylie engaged Willie Hall in talk, and with these distractions the rest of the Nazarenes lost their zeal. Soon the room was full of chatter and motion again, and Miller felt free to leave his lair.

He slipped quietly from group to group. Everyone had his own opinion about the meaning of events. Wylie Norton seemed upset, but Miller couldn't pin him down on anything. Norton was a heavy sad-eyed fellow with glasses on the end of his nose, so suppressed and polite a voice one had to lean far forward to understand him. Willie Hall quoted the Bible irrelevantly, seemed to have seen nothing that happened, proved to be little more than a desensitized loudspeaker, emitting endless textual nonsense from his self-enclosed inner world. Miller guessed that nothing in the world would really surprise the man.

Mrs. Norton returned, sought written explication from Domiron, but finally gave it up when few attended her. Himebaugh shrank to a corner and stared at Bruno. Miller wondered at the message, so-called, with which Bruno had so dramatically torched the meeting. The tomb is its message. Meaningless, yet loaded. He remembered that "tomb" was probably the word that rhymed with "womb" in Bruno's lost poem, Bonali had finally remembered that much. Had Bruno really had Ely Collins' deathnote in mind, though, as everyone assumed? Miller doubted the guy even understood there *was* such a note, wondered if he even grasped the brute fact of Collins' death. Then, what was he getting at? If the guy were rational, he might have been responding to the night's question: What is the meaning of "the coming of light"? with the answer: Death; or: Christ's resurrection. But was Giovanni Bruno in any sense rational? Miller frankly thought not, not from what he'd seen so far. No, the more likely explanation was that he had heard something more or less like that from Mrs. Norton, or from others here tonight, and had produced his own abbreviated paraphrase. Miller decided he would spend some time with Mrs. Norton's logs as soon as possible.

The two widows discussed Bruno's grace with Mabel Hall. Clara insisted that God was indeed speaking through him—"The Spirit has took on flesh!"—and the others, though eyeing him uneasily, had to agree: it all seemed to fit, just like Ely had said. Colin Meredith was sniffling, his long-lashed eyes damp and reddened, and Carl Dean Palmers seemed irritated with him, looked embarrassed when Miller passed by. He ducked his head from the others and whispered, "I don't see it, Mr. Miller. They're making a lot outa nothing."

Restlessness grew, more shifting between groups. Something unimaginable was to have happened by midnight, and now only some twenty minutes or so remained. Miller joined Marcella near her brother, but before he could ask her, she asked him. He said he didn't know, didn't know what to make of it. Eleanor Norton sat studying her logbook. Miller supposed she was preparing now to find the buffer message to explain why the undefined event did not occur, or how it *did* take place but was not properly grasped by all.

Marcella, beside him, spooned more medicine into her brother. Miller's main wish now was to have another moment alone with her before the night's program was over. He watched her bent back, fascinated by the narrowness of the white blouse on her shoulders and the single starched pleat, now opening down her back as though to smile. He felt he was at the brink of some fundamental change, and, strangely enough, he welcomed the sensation. Bruno himself was obviously exhausted. His long high-domed face, gleaming with a clammy perspiration, sagged, and he slumped lower and lower into the pillows. A feverish glow still lit his eyes, but his day was just about done. As Marcella leaned back to cap the medicine bottle, the curve of her hip bumped Miller's thigh: she looked up, smiled.

Footsteps!

All started, stood, stiffened. Anxious glances, eyes agog. Short breaths. Frowns. Was this it?

"Mama," Marcella explained. "She's come down to turn off the television."

Everyone relaxed some. Miller longed for a smoke. Soon. He considered that it was curious Bruno's parents did not participate here. Just too old, probably. Carl Dean sighed, an undisguised protest—and then the whole house was rent with a terrible throaty scream!

For a moment, in group terror, no one moved.

Then, almost simultaneously, Miller and Marcella turned and ran for the door, then on through the dining room to the front room. In confusion and with frightened shouts, the others stumbled and clattered behind.

The living room was dark, as before, but for the television screen. There, a man on a dark horse pulled a kerchief up over his mouth, turned to his two companions and said, "There he comes!" Emilia Bruno whined insanely. Stiff upright in his armchair in front of the television sat Antonio Bruno. He was dead.

Lights came on. People cried, "What is it?" Miller heard himself explaining it. It was Clara Collins who first lost control. She fell in a kind of sobbing fit to the floor, calling out her dead husband's name. Elaine started bawling. Others cried then, kept shouting, hurrying in, hurrying out. Marcella, in tears, ran back to her brother's room. Miller trailed a short distance behind, arrived to find

247

her weeping quietly on the edge of the bed. "Go with Mama," Giovanni whispered, his plain voice altogether unlike that which had uttered the message. His eyes were perhaps a little wider awake, but otherwise he was the same as before.

Miller stood unobtrusively in the shadows by the door. Marcella passed him on the way out, but didn't see him through her tears. Bruno stared at nothing. Was he smiling? In the dining room, Carl Dean was stammering, "If, if, why, if this d-don't beat all!" Colin said, "I told you so! I *told* you so, Carl Dean!" They were both very white. On a chair, BettyWilson slumped waddily. "Oh my God!" she whimpered softly. "I didn't think it'd be like this!"

Ralph Himebaugh and the Nortons stood in the dining room on the other side of the table from Miller. He could still hear Emilia Bruno and Clara Collins keeping it up in the living room, and it looked like the Halls were in there, too. Eleanor Norton held her small face in her hands, gazed upward toward the cut-glass chandelier. For some reason, people all turned toward her. Well, had she not, by calling this meeting tonight, prophesied its denouement?

Marcella, her face streaked with tears, but outwardly calm and protective, led her old mother out of the front room, started toward the stairs in the kitchen with her, paused. The Halls, holding each other up, stumbled in, she weeping, he talking to himself.

After a long while, Eleanor lowered her hands. "Death as a sign," she said gravely, her voice breaking, seeming very old, "can mean only one thing." She hesitated, as though afraid to continue. A small sob caught in her chest. "*The end of the world!*"

"*Oh no!*" cried Himebaugh. "I—I *thought* so! I knew it! It's what I thought all the time! *It's why I came!*"

Clara Collins stood, shaken, big square-jawed face wet with tears, hair snarled, heavy mouth agape, in the living room doorway. "Yes!" she gasped. "*The eighth of the month!*"

Well, not the eighth, of course. Elan, Domiron, the One to Come, and time itself soon took care of that. But the course was set. And Tiger Miller had his game.

10

With the storm that hit West Condon the first part of March blew in the first distinct rumors that Deepwater Number Nine was going to be closed down. As soon as the rumors started circulating, Vince Bonali knew, goddamn it, he wanted to go back down. If you were born to be a coalminer, there was no point in fighting fate. A kind of anxious humor swept around town. Everybody made a big joke about how bad the air was up on top and how when they took baths these days they felt like they were wasting water. And then on Monday, the second, old Sal Ferrero slipped on the ice in front of his house and broke his arm, and that got everybody cracking how they wanted to get back down in the goddamn mine where it was safe.

So, as soon as the roads were cleared, Vince drove around to a few of the mines in neighboring counties. He put in his chit with the offices, looked up relatives, chewed over the situation with union bosses, but it was anything but encouraging. Got an earful of sympathy, of course, but he found a helluva lot of other guys out of work, just like himself. Bad as it was, though, he discovered that at least a half dozen guys from Number Nine had got on at other mines: goddamn it, he had started too late! *Too late!*

All day, the old car lapped up the long stretches of greasy asphalt, and all for nothing. Passed a lot of strip mines along the way, whited over with snow, and they depressed him all the more. Not only fucked up the countryside, but they meant fewer jobs, too, and jobs he didn't know how to handle. And now all this talk about gasification of coal beds—he swore and slapped the steering wheel. "Come on, God! Get me outa this one!" he said out loud. Vince had always imagined God as a tough dark old bastard who lived a good ways off, but had a long rubbery arm, spoke street Italian, gave the sonsabitches their due, and for some inexplicable reason had a peculiar fondness for Vince. His vision hadn't changed much, except he was beginning to suspect God maybe had come to lump him in with the sonsabitches.

Talking to God made him recollect the joke or something he'd been hearing around town about the end of the world or an invasion from Mars or some goddamn calamity due up next weekend. Boy! what was the matter with this town? As far as he could make out, it had something to do with that nut Bruno again, or maybe it was just that everybody assumed it. Well, that just went to show what a smart cookie that Father Baglione was. Bonali had never given the old priest too much credit, but a couple months ago when all the old gossips at the church had wanted to canonize the guy because of his so-called visitation, the old man had just chewed his cigar and kept his peace. From what Etta had found out, it wasn't long before these same old women were getting shunted out of Bruno's hospital room and told, in effect, to go to hell. And now the end of the world! Man, what next? Well, what the hell, maybe it wasn't a bad idea at that—might be a relief to have done with this moronic business once and for all. He laughed at the idea of the world going up in a puff of smoke. Then he remembered he wasn't ready, saw again the unblinking stare of Pooch Minicucci's old lady. Sunday, for sure, he was going to keep his resolution and tag along with Angie and Etta to Mass, get himself on the right team again.

At home, beat down and depressed, he dropped into a chair facing the TV. It was off, but he didn't feel like turning it on. Etta came in and sat down on the sofa near him. The fatness and silence of her presence irritated him all the more, but, hell, she didn't have it easy either. He got to talking out loud, said the way things were going, it sure didn't look to be a very hilarious goddamn thirtieth anniversary for them this year, did it? and how he figured they were really done for. Why was it turning out like this? Thank God, they still had the old house, but, shit, they'd probably have to mortgage that, too. And then, all of a sudden, he saw Etta was crying. He got half out of his chair, took her hand, said not to cry like that, he was just mouthing off, hell, things'd work out, they always did. But she handed him a letter.

He glanced at the envelope: from their oldest boy, Vince Junior. He was working out on the Coast, worked on airplanes. Vince supposed something terrible must have happened, one of the grandkids or something, and, Jesus, just now—! He was almost crying and he hated to look inside. But when he opened it, there was a nice friendly letter and scribblings from the grandkids and a check for $300. The boy said he figured things must be a little close, what with the mines closed down, and, since he had a little extra, he was sending it along, keep beer in the icebox and Angie in pretty clothes, and so on, have a happy anniversary, and to let him know if they needed more.

"Jesus, Etta," Vince said. "That sure was nice of Junior, wasn't it?" And he got out his handkerchief and blew his nose.

Vince had always gagged along with the rest about getting old, but nowadays he found it hard to smile, found that cracks about his fifty years only made his stomach turn. Couldn't land a new job and he began to see it wouldn't even be easy to get on at the mines now. Trouble was, though he hadn't wanted to admit it before, people hardly ever hired a new man old as Vince was. He could do the work of five or six young guys, understand, especially in the mines, he had the basic skills down and that's what really counted these days, but, hell, it still didn't matter. It was just the dumb attitude these people doing the hiring took. Vince hated even to look into a mirror. A thick gray depression was crowding down all over him.

One Tuesday at Wanda's—he'd fallen into the consoling habit of passing afterdark Tuesdays there—when there wasn't much to do but talk, he tried to explain it. He had been feeling his goddamn half century all day, and now, mainly because before coming over he had got a little too tanked up at the Eagles, he couldn't seem to stiffen the old pecker up enough to get the trick done, and that made him all the more miserable. "Wanda, I have to tell you, I'm getting old," he confessed simply. He was goddamn sorrowful. The hall light was on, just outside the bedroom door, and it spread a harsh sallow glare over their side-by-side bellies.

"It sure is somethin' how time gits on," she replied. She sounded worn out. Life was no picnic for her either, goddamn it.

"It sure is a tough solution to worry about. I just don't know what the hell I'm gonna do." His tongue was thick. Room was slipping a little toward the left. And he'd never felt so weak and shriveled. "The future looks to me just like a big goddamn empty hole, Wanda."

She yawned. Her breasts filled up a little, and then slid off to each side again like wobbly little airbubbles. Then she giggled.

"No, listen! I mean it, Wanda! What's gonna come of me?"

There was a long idiot span of silence, filled only by the squeaky sucking noises that the baby in the crib at the foot of their bed was making on his bottle. Wanda dug at one ear with her finger. The coarse pale hairs of her crotch poked up like dry weeds, pitched long sharp shadows across her right groin. He felt dizzy. He closed his eyes. And finally she said, "Vince, hon, d'you believe in talkin' with spirits?"

11

What does it matter that secrecy has been decreed? the Spirit is made manifest by signs. Else, how account for the uprooting of the widow Mrs. Wilson's hollyhocks, excrement on her front porch, a signature from the "Black Hand"? Or the theft of the widow Mrs. Lawson's porch swing, the dead rat left on her window ledge? The inexplicable death of the coalminer Mr. Hall's young bird dog? The town veterinarian, Dr. Norton, diagnoses: internal bleeding. Or how explain the suddenly fierce gossip of the dour old women in the nave of St. Stephen's?*"Fatti del diavolo!"* Or the revival of St. Peter gags in clubs and bars and on church lawns Sundays? Or the excited nonsense of boys in high school locker rooms? "Gee whiz! the end of the world already, and me almost a virgin still!" How else shed light on the anonymous phonecalls received at the home of the coalminer Mr. Bruno? the appearance in the city newspaper of strange tales of medieval seers and wizards? the inflamed preachments against heresy from the pulpit of the Church of the Nazarene?

Or who can say why else this town's collective fate darkens so? The last of the area mines seems sure to close. The streets of the business sector grow desolate. Glumly, the shopowners visit each other. The mayor declares a one-month moratorium on parking meters to encourage downtown trade. The winter is bitter and long. The families of ninety-seven dead coalminers huddle around old habits, their empty futures hovering like birds of prey. Some marry again, some leave. Most wait, not knowing for what. Young people desert, breaking up families. A motel closes. The basketball team loses. A strange virus cripples half the community. The whole town seems to age overnight.

Children grow rebellious. TV reception is often bad. A dance at the Eagles is canceled. People die. The rate of harassment crimes rises.

Who is the "Black Hand"? Opinions vary. Italians, including Police Chief Dee Romano, fear the revival of old blood enmities, of old extortions and death by night, but, strangely, few Italians are struck. Some blame out-of-towners, even rival cities. Others the Klan. A maniac. Communists.

The mayor recognizes the adolescent style: some high school prankster.

Coalminers observe uncomfortably that the victims are usually coalminers or their families. Not even widows in mourning are exempted. The Nazarene pastor Reverend Baxter, his own congregation often the prey, passes thundering judgment upon false prophets and apostates who, with their black signature and foul deeds, confess their allegiance to the Devil. "These here people they are *murmurers!* they are *malcontents!* they are walking after their own *lusts!* ungodly folks turning the great grace of our God into *lasciviousness,* and denying our only Master and Lord, *Christ Jesus!* These here people, I tell ye even weeping, they are the enemy of the cross of Jesus! Their end it is *perdition!* their god it is the *belly!* and they do *glory* in their shame!" Rumors of Black Masses.

Actually, a clandestine high school club or gang, not just a single boy, the mayor explains to a meeting of the Chamber of Commerce board members.

The schoolteacher Mrs. Norton attributes the attacks to "the powers of darkness," and when the widow Mrs. Collins contends it can *only* be the work of "Baxter's people," Mrs. Norton reminds her that the specific agents utilized by the dark powers are less significant than a recognition of the existence and activity of the powers themselves. To friends in private, Mrs. Collins admits frankly that she doesn't understand what Mrs. Norton means, and she sits up nights hoping to catch one of the "people" redhanded and prove her point.

The mayor announces in the city newspaper, the West Condon *Chronicle*, that the frequency of the recent "Black Hand" incidents makes it clear that it has become a new teen-age fad, a game, and he asks cooperation from all parents. With that, it does in fact become a teen-age fad, proving the mayor a prophet if not a consummate analyst, and culminates with a "Black Hand Blast" up at the youth center, which is converted at the last moment by the adult supervisors into a "Black Magic Party," and, as usual, is not much of a success.

"Black Hand" phonecalls tie up the circuits, and letters from same arrive daily at the newspaper office, city hall, private homes. When the newspaper releases the report of two other signatures, the "Black Peter" and the "Black Piggy," it sets off a rash of new calls and letters, etc., by everything from the "Blackhead" to the "Black Bottom." "The Black Maria." "The Blackboard." "The Black Widow." "The Blackball." "The Black Armpit."

Yes, the mayor admits with a rueful sigh when the suggestion is put to him by several civic leaders: it is really a reflection of the town's whole general deterioration, and is at the same time contributing to it. A community-wide moral problem. Monstrous. A cancer. Something has to be done, says one. The mayor agrees. A little common sense, says another.

At the city hospital, a nurse, idle, picks up the telephone, waggles it indecisively in her hand a moment, glances down the empty corridor, sighs, finally dials a number.

"West Condon *Chronicle*."

"Is Mr. Miller there, please?"

"Whom shall I say is calling?"

"The Black Hand."

"!"

"Hello?"

"Just—just a moment, please." Clump clump, clump. "(Mr. Miller! it's some woman says she's the Black Hand!)"

"Hello, Miller here."

"This is the Black Hand."

"Hello there, Black. What a nice voice you have."

"Do you know why my hand is black?"

"No, why?" Scratch. (Lighting a smoke.)

"Blackness, you will agree, is the absence of light."

"That's reasonable."

"But what is light?"

"I wish I knew."

"Light is the radiant energy which enables the corresponding organs to perform their proper function. It is transmitted by an undulatory or vibrational movement, the velocity of which, uh, need not concern us here."

"Aha." His loose laugh. Makes her catch her breath.

"Tiger?" She rubs her nose to block a sniffle. *My whole me is going black!*" She swallows. Don't get sappy.

His easy laughter trickles through the wires, makes her relax again. Anyway, she hasn't made him mad. "I'm sorry, Happy. But what more can I tell you? I'm up to my ears in this goddamn project and it just doesn't give me a minute."

"Is it about these people who think the Last Judgment is about to happen?"

"How do you know about that?"

"I'm probably the last dope in town to find out. One of my hernia patients told me all about it."

"Well, yes, that's it."

"Any pretty girls?"

Laughter. Too quick. "Nothing but old widows."

"Unh-hunh. Well, when's Jesus going to come and get it over with, so I can see you again?"

Laughter again. He likes to laugh. He has told her that no one else makes him laugh so much, laugh so well. "Middle of April or thereabouts, I think. It's not sure."

"A whole month!" She pauses. "Listen, Tiger, can I anyway write letters to the editor?"

"Sure." A little awkwardly. "Listen, Happy, I mean it, I really am sorry. I warned you, though, I had a knack for getting hung up like this. But it can't last much longer, God knows I'm getting sick of it, and then we'll see if we can't do something about that poor hand and so on of yours."

"It won't be easy. It's very very black." That laugh. "Especially the so on." She nibbles at the phone cord, hating to let go of him. Any excuse. "But if I write the letters, will you at least bring me the postage?"

A hesitation. "Sure."

"Cross your black heart and hope to die, never to rise again?"

A pause. "Listen, if my office girl weren't listening in, I'd even promise to take it out for you and drop it in the slot."

The nurse giggles, rubs her nose. "Beware then," she hisses, "for the Coming is at hand!"

"The *Black* Hand, I assume," he replies, and, giggling, she hangs up, runs paper into the typewriter beside her.

Common sense. Common sense tells the former coal-miner and now small-time farmer Ben Wosznik that where there's an effect, there's a cause. Sometimes more than one. A good fertilizer and crop rotation bring on a good harvest. But planting by the almanac helps, too. Maybe somebody's cigarette caused the disaster that killed his brother, maybe not. The cigarette might have been only a part of it. Now they are having bad times. Common sense tells him it's no accident, nothing is. He hears about the man who says the world is coming to an end. The man survived the disaster and everybody else, including Ben's brother, died. Has to be a reason. There always is. Maybe there was more oxygen where he was or maybe he had more resistance. Maybe both. Maybe more. Common sense tells him it's smart to go see what the man has to say. Can't hurt. Might change his life. Might save it.

Taking a shower at the high school, Tommy (the Kitten) Cavanaugh kids Ugly Palmers. "Ugly, if you think the world is coming to an end," he says, "what are you wasting your time here at this jail for? You gonna need American history up there?"

Ugly, soaping his feet, turns crimson. He never really blushes, his acne just flares up. "I don't know what you're talking about," he says. A short guy, kind of a tube, small hump in the shoulders, almost no butt at all. Pretty well hung, though.

"Aw, come on, Ugly, don't kid me!" Tommy winks at a couple other guys at nearby lockers, lathers up his belly. "The little Collins girl told me all about it."

"*You leave her out of it!*" Ugly yells, going red halfway down into his chest. Boy, he is suddenly mad as all get out! Just a lucky guess, too.

Tommy figures he could whip Ugly, but he doesn't want to get into anything down here, so, as though to soak better, he pivots under the hot spray until he has his butt to the guy. Never shoot a guy in the back. His Dad has a dirty joke about it. A couple guys are grinning, looking on, so he winks again. "Well, so what's the story, Ugly? Is it really gonna happen, or isn't it? We need to know, man!"

"What's it to you, Moneybags?" Really sore, all right.

"Well, gosh, Ugly, I don't wanna go to hell, do I?" He gets some snickering on that, but not much. Most of these guys are scared of Palmers. He hears Ugly's shower turning off, decides it might be better politics to face the guy. He assumes a modest grin, and, working the soap between his legs, turns, just as Ugly slaps flatfooted by.

At the edge of the showers, where the lockers begin, Ugly spins around. "I suppose you just think that this is all just a buncha nuts!" he blurts clumsily.

"Who, Ugly?" Tommy counters, blinking innocently.
"You know who."

"No, listen, Ugly, we don't know anything. You gotta save us, man!"

Palmers hesitates, his jaws working. "Okay, smart guy, I suppose you never heard of Tiger Miller."

This time the blink is real. "Sure I know Tiger Miller," Tommy says. "You're not trying to kid me that he comes to your meetings."

"He sure does!" Ugly snaps, gloating now, though his acne is still a bright vermilion.

"I don't believe it."

"Wanna bet?" Ugly thrusts out his hand. "C'mon. How about a thousand dollars?"

"How you gonna prove it?" This thing is rankling Tommy now. He wishes he hadn't brought it up.

"Come and see for yourself." Ugly is grinning. "C'mon. A thousand bucks. Your old man's got the money." He pokes his hand toward Tommy's midriff.

"I'll bet a quarter."

"C'mon. A thousand bucks. Put up or shut up."

"Okay, Ugly, I believe you. But that's just one. Who else?"

Ugly backs down. "Lotsa people," he says.

"Yeah? Like who?"

"You gonna soap that little thing all day?" Trying to get out of it.

"Like who, Ugly?"

Outwardly, the signs are few. Intimately, the message radiates. At a meeting, ministers are warned. Over Cokes, a talent is described. In a bed, someone is invited. A child overhears his parents denounce an old friend. A priest, making a house visit, is bluntly turned away. An impeccable lawyer becomes irascible and unreliable. At an evening meeting of a Baptist youth group, "what if" questions are posed. Chiliastic warnings appear among the graffiti of boys' rest rooms. MARCH 8. Erasure. MARCH

259

21 (in ink). Rotarians are informally entertained by a Presbyterian minister with new rumors. The newspaper, except for anonymous letters to the editor, is silent, but the editor is known to be intently absorbed in a new "project." A neighbor darkens her kitchen and sits by the window. Observes the furtive arrivals. The sinister preparations. The burning candles. The sheets hung over the windows. Hears the screams. Who knows how the old man died?

The banker, phone cradled between jaw and shoulder, draws a square on his tablet. A cross inside the square gives him four small squares. Two diagonals: eight small triangles. He blacks in alternate ones with a vertical stroke. Then the remaining ones with a horizontal stroke. To one corner of the now all-black square, he attaches the corner of another large one, adds in the cross and diagonals. On the other end of the line, the high school principal is saying, "She's just a substitute teacher, of course, but one of the finest we've ever come across. I'm glad you brought her name up, Ted. I wanted to mention her before, but she doesn't have a certificate yet. With the board's approval, of course, we hope to—"

"Unh-hunh. Well, don't do anything too definite just yet, John. We want to—"

"No, no, of course not! Is something wrong?"

"No, I don't think so. You know. We just want to run a routine check before we commit ourselves."

"Something in the past?"

"Can't be sure, John. Just want to be careful, that's—"

"Of course, I had no way of knowing, Ted. I felt she qualified professionally, and, ah, but of course, I'll wait to hear from you."

The original square, blacked in, has another square, comprising eight triangles, attached to each corner.

The police are summoned by the Reverend Abner Baxter, irate. The city mayor Mr. Whimple is present during the call, so he accompanies two of his police, Mr. Romano and Mr. Wallace, to the Church of the Nazarene. Boxy building with artificial brick siding. Smell of mildew inside. Seething with rage, the redheaded preacher leads them to his pulpit, a plain rostrum on a one-foot stage, and, with a trembling white finger, stubby and fuzzy with fine red hear, directs their attention to the floor behind the lectern. The city mayor and the two policemen stare down at the little heap of feces. "*Sacrilege!*" the minister thunders. "*Desecration!*" And commences an oration on the theme.

The police chief Romano stoops and extracts a half-buried note, holds it between fingertips at arm's length. The three men study it. THE BLACK PIGGY. "Looks more like a toe to me," drawls Romano, his other hand resting nervously on the butt of his gun.

"Seems to be operating independently now," observes the mayor.

The preacher whirls on them, red with wrath, and demands they remove their hats. "*This is the house of the Lord!*"

Sheepishly, the three do so. The policeman Wallace, abashed, stoops as though to inspect the feces. The other policeman and the mayor also stoop.

"*There!*" roars the preacher, pointing to an open window, through which, no doubt, the Black Piggy has come and gone. He marches over to secure it.

"Looks like baby shit," Wallace whispers. "Whaddaya think, Mort?"

"I dunno, looks like it," the mayor acknowledges in a hushed voice. "Whaddaya think, Dee?"

"Whaddaya asking me for?" Romano whispers in reply. "I don't know nothing about shit."

"Lemme see that thing. No, just hold it out there. Does look a little like a toe, all right."

"I dunno, Mort," drawls the ploice chief hoarsely. "Maybe we oughta call the FBI."

Ben comes on a Friday night. Like a gift. The widow Betty Wilson knows the minute he walks in that he's that strange dark man Mabel Hall found in her tea leaves, that "man of honor." All night, in her breast, there is a flutter like a caged bird, like a fish in a net.

It is an exciting meeting because when they arrive they find the Bruno front room all fixed up like a church sort of, the television in the bedroom, and Giovanni sitting up in the living room armchair, the one his father died in. So pale! it frightens Betty even to look at him, so she hardly ever does, but when accidentally her eyes do happen to light on him, he is almost always staring straight at *her*, and that scares her all the more. But the room is very nice and they are all pleased, especially Clara, who has been using her own house for Sunday services for folks who don't want to go hear Abner Baxter. There's a little table fixed up with things like old Mr. Bruno's gold pocket-watch and so on, and Mr. Himebaugh asks everybody to bring something to the next meeting that is precious to them to include there. Betty thinks right away of Eddie's dentures, which she still to this day has kept in a glass on the dressing table by her bed in memory of him, but instead she decides she will bring his war medals. Mr. Himebaugh asks for Ely's last note to hang there in a pretty frame he has brought, and Clara hates to give it up, but she is honored, too, and they all have a little ceremony there, putting it in the frame, and Mrs. Norton reads it to all of them so nicely.

Well, just then, in the middle of all that excitement, the doorbell rings. Mr. Norton says it is somebody who doesn't know the password, and they are all afraid it is some dirty trick again. Mr. Miller gets up and goes out there. Whenever they have trouble, they always depend on him, such a fine strong young man, even if he isn't too religious. When he returns, he brings this man in with him, and the man says his name is Ben Wosznik, and that's when Betty's heart starts to sputter around so. She looks over at Mabel and Mabel looks back at her. It is he. She was afraid the stranger might be Mr. Himebaugh, and now her fear is relieved. He says he has heard so much about them and he read the letter in the newspaper that said everybody was welcome (that was Clara's letter), and, well, here he is. He is big and thick-shouldered and has black burry hair and heavy brows and kindly eyes and a man's broad smile that creases his tan cheeks in many folds. He used to be a coalminer, he says, though now he is just sort of a farmer. He knew all their husbands. He says he always admired Ely Collins and is glad to know that Mrs. Collins is here. His brother who used to live with him was also killed in the disaster, he says. No, he says, he isn't married.

The Girl Fried Egg of the West Condon *Chronicle*, opening her editor's Saturday morning mail, discovers an envelope bordered in black. A death! she gasps inwardly, and eagerly opens it, but is disappointed by its unsigned contents. Doesn't even understand it. She shows it, perplexed, to Mr. Miller. He smiles inexplicably and instructs her to pass such envelopes on to him unopened henceforth. She sighs, feels for some reason like crying or something. So much has been happening lately which she doesn't understand.

The terrifying cataclysms anticipated as a prelude to the Last Judgment actually did not take place. No explanation was given; perhaps they were merely overlooked in the press of last-minute details. Whatever the reason for it, however, their absence helped provoke a universal apathy to the event which even the prospect of sensational personal revelations failed to dissipate. It improved tempers only slightly that

*the affair, held in April, was moved from Jerusalem
to West Condon, which, sitting like a mote on the
fat belly of the great American prairie, was properly
thought to be, like God Himself, utterly remote from
anything human.*

.   .   .

*No one had anticipated that the Judgment would
prove such a complex business, least of all the Orga-
nizers Themselves. After one frustrating day of hearing the petty petitions of the condemned, the
Supreme Judge was heard to mutter: We shoulda
pulled this goddamn thing off a long time ago. It
began to appear that the process might prove interminable, but finally a stopgap solution to the increased cramming of the judicial calendar was found
in condemning all politicians, welfare workers, postal
employees, physicians, and journalists forthwith. Not
without bitter protest, of course: Someone has to
keep the world going, they wept. Therein, replied
their Judge, lies the seed of your damnation. . . .*

"But you aren't listening to me, Reverend Edwards,"
Tommy interrupts. Kit Cavanaugh is at his best when
playing their own game with preachers and teachers. He
is famous for it. Not that he doesn't respect them. He does.
But it's so easy to string them along, he can't resist it.
Snickers, like those he hears now, are his best reward. "I
asked you if the Last Judgment *could* happen *here* and
happen *now*, and you said it was not impossible, and so I
asked you, then what would it be *like*? I don't think it's
gonna happen either, I mean, I *agree* with you, Reverend
Edwards, but what I'm saying is *if* it happened, *what*
would happen?"

"I'm sure I don't know, Tommy. And God would probably consider the question an impertinent one." The
minister is a little bit riled.

"Like here in the Bible, see, it talks about all kinds of

264

dragons and tremendous beasts and things. Would we get to see some of that?"

"I don't think I would interpret all that too—"

"And what about that poor, uh prostitute? Boy, she really gets it! *That* must be something to see!" Rolling in the aisles.

"The harlot is an image of a city, Tommy, of a literal historic enemy, and, ultimately, of all the enemies of Christ."

"And all that blood everywhere—*whoo!*" Tommy shudders visibly and gets a new rise in the suppressed hysterics.

"But now you're not listening to me. The Book of Revelation teaches us simply that Christ will have the final victory over all forms of evil. Instead of worrying about dragons, young man, which is an idea that no longer has much meaning for modern man, you should be worrying more about the salvation of you own soul. That's what this story is trying to tell you. That each man, to find salvation, must, in a sense, pass first through a kind of terror—"

"Oh yeah?" Tommy nods studiously, gazing down at his open Bible, reading not it, however, but what he has concealed there. "I see what you mean." A pause for effect. "Is that what happened to you, Reverend Edwards?"

The minister blushes before the ducked snorting heads of the boys' Sunday school class. "Something like it," he replies bluntly, glancing at his watch.

"All I can say is I get the feeling here that God really hates us. Man, it's really murder!"

"He hates evil, Tommy." The minister relaxes slightly. "And He no doubt hates impudence." Freed, the boys laugh openly. "I see you've read Revelation well. Have you bothered to read the rest of the Bible?" More laughter.

"Nope. This was enough to scare me!" The bell rings. The minister leaves hastily to dress for the main service. The class erupts into horselaughs. Tommy preens on them a moment, then ducks out. Must see Sally Elliott, make a date. An eight-page comicbook, concealed in his Bible, has told him at last all he wants to know.

Sunday night, March fifteenth, is a sad night, and everybody is very depressed. Just one week ago, on the eighth, when they thought it was the End, there were so many folks. Gideon Diggs was here, and the Calvin Smiths, and Tess Lawson came and Wanda Cravens and two high school girls and Mary Harlowe, so many. And now they're just about back where they started. Only Wanda, Mary, and Tess have stayed on, and now there's Ben Wosznik with them. Betty Wilson knows how bad the others are feeling, and she'd like to cheer them up somehow, but she feels as awful as they do. Besides that, Clara and Mrs. Norton aren't getting along tonight. Clara insists now the end is coming on April 8, and Mrs. Norton is saying, no, it will be next Saturday, March 21, but nobody really knows. Trouble is, as Betty knows well enough, Sister Clara talks too loud. And then Sister Tess Lawson gets angry with both of them and calls them both spooky and just walks right out of there. Somehow that kind of frightens them.

Then, as if things aren't bad enough, they start getting the phonecalls again. Seems like it's always worse on Sunday nights. That poor child, the Bruno girl, that she should have to suffer such abuse! Clara says they ought to just take the phone out, but Mrs. Norton says, no, you never know in what manner or by what means enlightenment is to be received. One night, after midnight, for example, they all sat for an hour watching "snow" on the TV because Mrs. Norton was convinced some message was going to appear there. Trouble is, Mrs. Norton has too many different ideas at once. But now even their old friend Brother Gideon calls and asks them to forget their foolish ways, and then Cal Smith calls saying the same. Mrs. Norton tries to receive an explanation in her book, but the phonecalls make it impossible. And Giovanni Bruno isn't any kind of help either. He seems kind of sick. Maybe he's been getting up too much.

Finally, Clara takes the phone off the hook and says flatly the sources will just have to get through some other way tonight, and Mrs. Norton pinches her mouth in, but she doesn't argue. Sometimes you can see when it's best not to argue with Clara. And then, just as everybody is feeling so awful and nobody is talking for fear of making somebody mad or something, why, like a miracle, Ben Wosznik starts to sing. His soft vibrant baritone floats out over their despair like an embrace from Jesus and they all listen. Betty closes her eyes.

"*Ama-azi-i-ing Grace, ha-ow sweet the-e saound,*
Tha-at saved a-a-a wretch la-ike me!
I-I wu-unce wa-a-as lost, bu-ut naow I am faound,
Wa-as blind, bu-u-ut naow I-I see!"

As he sings, he touches them, touches her. Tears come. The great hymn and the great voice pierce to the very core of her being, where now she sits, withdrawn, in the dark, for her eyes are closed, in the saddest joy she's ever known. Her childhood, her mother, church camps and revivals, damp spring nights and cold winters by a coalstove, snow on her father's mining boots, Eddie and the war and the mines, all her dear friends, her children scattered over the world, trees lit for Christmas and the pink frock she danced in, prayer and love and Ely and Jesus, all her life seems like a beautiful instant, miraculously captured in the divine moment of this song, this man's voice. Slowly, as though under its own power, out of the dark core, her own voice emerges, gentle, tempered, truer than she's ever heard it, to harmonize in a tender humming plaint behind his radiant refrains:

"*'Twa-as Grace tha-a-at taught my-y heart to-o fear,*
A-and Grace my-y-y fear re-elieved;
Ha-ow pre-ecio-ou-ous did tha-at Grace a-appear,
Thee-e haour I-I-I first be-elieved!"

267

And there are sighs as they sing and soft amens and she knows Ben is watching her, but her eyes will not open. She can hear Wanda Cravens sniffling, thinking of how Lee used to sing that song in his sweet tender tenor, and Clara crying softly in a kind of faint almost, on account of it was Ely's favorite hymn. And now, at the chorus, they all join in, filling the room with their harmony, though it is she and Ben Wosznik who lead them. Even Mr. Miller and the little Bruno girl sing, and finally the Nortons. It is beautiful. It is the most beautiful moment in Betty Wilson's life . . .

> *"Ama-azi-i-ing Greace, ha-ow sweet the-e saound,*
> *Tha-at saved a-a-a wretch la-ike me!*
> *I-I wu-unce wa-a-as lost, bu-ut naow I am faound,*
> *Wa-as blind, bu-u-ut naow I-I see!"*

The hotelkeeper Mr. Fisher and the Chamber of Commerce secretary Mr. Elliott whuff into the hotel coffeeshop through the lobby door Monday morning, the sixteenth, and there discover the city editor finishing his morning coffee.

"Hello, Tiger!" greets the Chamber secretary with a clap to the trenchcoated shoulders. "Say, what do you know about Ralph Himebaugh?"

"What do you mean?" The editor stands, hands a dollar across the counter. Doris the waitress fumbles with his change, drops a quarter into the dishwater.

"Well, I don't know, the guy's been kinda peculiar lately. Promises to work with me on the industrial brochure and we set up dates and he doesn't show up. When I call him up at home, he always puts me off and hangs up. Now, that's not like old Ralphie."

The editor shrugs, while the waitress fishes in the dishwater. "Beats me, Elliott. Why don't you—?"

"Aw, shit now, Miller!" rattles the old hotelman, pink jowls folded into a kind of grin. "What we wanna know is has that old sonuvabitch got hisself mixed up somehow with this troop of religious monkeys over at that wop miner's house?"

"How should I know?" The editor smiles innocently. "Why don't you just ask Ralph the next time you get him on the phone, Jim?" The waitress comes up with a bottle-cap.

"That might embarrass him," the Chamber secretary says. "I don't want to get him teed off at us or nothing. We're just, you know, curious. That's all." Wide greeter's grin.

"Listen, Doris, goddamn it! Just give me another quarter!"

"You won't tell, hunh?"

The editor pulls out his cigarette pack, finds it empty, crumples it, tosses it in the pecan jug, bringing an indignant glower to the hotelman's face. "What makes you think I even know anything about those—?"

"Well, for one thing," growls the hotelman with a smirk, "you got a Chevy with a license ending in 7241."

The editor laughs. "Okay, I admit I've been trying to see what's going on over there, but they're pretty secretive. I—"

"Listen, Tiger," the Chamber man butts in, grinning as always. "Will you tell me I'm wrong? I say Ralphie is one of them. Do you say he's not?"

"Why should I tell you anything?"

"Okay, that's good enough by me. He's in it."

The old hotelman cackles.

The editor shrugs, reaches over the counter, and appropriates a pack of cigarettes from the display there. "Keep the quarter, Doris," he says. "Tip from your boss."

"The hell you say!" grumbles the hotelman, and goes behind the counter to help fish for the coin.

In his office, the editor discovers in the morning mail further messages from the lady Black Hand . . .

269

The Mayor of West Condon, upon being asked why, when the moment of the Judgment arrived, he was discovered by the Angel of Death masturbating in his own bathtub, replied that the Chief of Police was using the official one at City Hall. Although there was general laughter, the face of the Divine Judge remained utterly immobile. I, too, have a sense of humor, He said when the laughter had subsided, and, in demonstration of it, He forthwith dispatched all who had laughed to hell and sent the Mayor to heaven, thereby depriving him forever of his audience.

.   .   .

The Pope, justifiably fearing the worst, slipped away from the proceedings and approached the Gate with his own set of keys, forged through the centuries. Yes, they worked! Just as his predecessors had always claimed! St. Peter seemed to be on the nod, so the Pope shut the Gate quietly behind him, signed the register, and tiptoed on down the path. Hee hee hee! Everything was just as he'd thought it would be, everything! Except, of course, for the strange peculiarity of St. Peter's three heads.

.   .   .

A famous lawyer was brought before the Divine Court and accused of sodomy. When asked what he had to say to that, he stammered in apparent incredulity that he was not guilty. Of course, replied his Judge, but if you were guilty, then what would you say? Thus challenged, the lawyer delivered an eloquent and moving defense, no doubt the greatest performance of his career, and it was not without effect. Under all precepts of orthodoxy, his Judge said leaning toward him, you would have condemned yourself to eternal perdition with this address. So enchanting was it, however, we might yet offer you one final path to salvation. . . .

"Hello, Ralph! Ted Cavanaugh here. How's it going?"

"Oh. Hello, Ted. Fine, fine. Yourself?"

Loose chuckle. "You're sure a hard fellow to find these days!" The five blacked-in squares form an X of sorts. This X is converted to a diamond by adding four new squares: top, bottom, and two sides.

"Yes. I've been . . . busy. Eh, how's the wife?"

"Wonderful, Ralph. Matter of fact, she was just re-marking at dinner yesterday that it had been a long time since we'd had you over." More casual laughter. "I think she sees herself as a kind of patron saint to all bachelors." The four new squares touch the four outside blacked-in squares at two corners each: that is, a sort of checkerboard pattern is emerging. "What do you say to tomorrow night?"

"That's very kind, Ted. But I've, uh, been a little under the weather. Flu. I wouldn't make a very good guest, I'm afraid."

"Oh? Sorry to hear that! Listen then, how about next—?"

"Ted . . . maybe you'd better, eh, let me call you."

Four crosses, eight diagonals: thirty-two new small triangles. The banker frowns. "Ralph . . . Ralph, you know how much we all think of you here. We'd hate . . . believe me, it's simply out of personal concern that I bring it up . . . but we'd hate to hear that you, that you got mixed up somehow—Ralph? Ralph?" In the uppermost square of the diamond, half the triangles have been blacked in with vertical strokes.

Reluctantly, smelling warmly of winter hay and after-birth, vitamin D and hogsweat, Womwom the guardian of holy places, no less than the living reincarnation of Noah, and compassionate apostle of Kwan-yin, drives back toward West Condon, returning from outlying calls. There is an unwanted commitment there of which the country frees him. Not that nature is beautiful, certainly

271

he has never thought so, only that, as pure process, it absorbs all catastrophes, relaxes him when the paradox of his own ego terrorizes him. Unlike Elan, he has never succeeded in neutralizing it. What does he want? He doesn't even know. But the point is, out here in the country, he doesn't care.

Signs. Womwom has been having to make his own breakfast. Not that he minds, but it is symptomatic. Elan gazes the mornings long out on the snow, on the rain, on the sun, on the wind, and finds words like "structural dissolution" and "the coalescence of polarities" leaking out her fingertips. He has heard them before, knows what must surely follow. Again. But not just again. Something new this time. Of course, it's obvious what it is. It is the unprecedented participation of the Other. There have been large groups before, but the nucleus has always been his wife. Now, several nuclei seem, as though by accident, to have become attached, forming an almost organic something larger than any of them, and though his wife is still its most important member, she is now, for the first time, truly a member, depending on the others as they depend on her. If there is a center, of course, it is Giovanni Bruno, the One to Come. Little matter that he is so enigmatic a figure, Elan has led Womwom to expect such a mystery at the middle, but the point is, this abstract thing which has dragged them through the years is now suddenly upon them, and what he never expected is that the core thing should be outside his wife herself.

West Condon pep talk and sales pitches appear on billboards, defiantly tawdry above the patches of crusty snow, signaling the town's proximity. Working hard these days. Has to get what he can. He is not an avaricious man, anybody can tell that by a single glance, but always they need it. Money. And never more than at times like these. And so he has to push, though he has no heart for it. Of course, he enjoys his work, but, as his wife has always said, he is too much an artist. Wastes whole days in the country, and meanwhile the easy money is in town. Sick dogs. Dogs with worms. Worms! A farmer bets on value when he calls a vet. Pet owners care nothing for economics. Keeping a pet is an affront to thrift in the first place, not to mention that it's an affront to nature to boot. So, they pay up. "Ten bucks? Sure, Doc!" Beaming grab for the pocket. And little brats gazing raptly on, learning patterns that will make successes out of medical frauds for generations to come. Leeches. Why can't he be a happy leech like the rest? An artist. Well, he is. But times of stress push him and he undertakes, against his own nature, the disagreeable.

Indications of West Condon can be seen a couple miles outside of town: a steeple or two, some smoke, and so on. But the town itself springs into being only at the city limits. There's just enough soft roll to the land around, a settling over the coal beds, that no great distances can be seen from ground level. Then, too, things block the view— trees, humps of raw land shoveled up by strip-mining, barns and motels and the like, the usual brash fungi of billboards—block the view or flick distractingly in front of it, such that the city limits sign is a kind of guarantee you have made it, a lever you trip in passing that pops the town out of the yellow soil like a jack-in-the-box. Nothing special about it. Town like many they have lived in. But he likes it, has liked them all, and here in West Condon, as the only fully qualified veterinarian, he is especially needed. So, he feels an urge today, tripping the lever and feeling the town spring up to embrace him, to drive his roots in so deeply here that no crisis could ever tear him out.

At home, his wife is seated at the kitchen table, as usual, with Rahim the lawyer. Papers, logs, graphs, tools out in front of them. Late afternoon sun glows there. "Wylie!" she exclaims when he enters. "Giovanni said, 'A circle of evenings'—of course! It means *another seven Sundays!* And seven Sundays after the first of March is the *nineteenth of April:* the last day the sun is in the sign of *rebirth!*" Rahim, excited, is frantically constructing new graphs.

"That's good, dear," Womwom says with a smile, and he goes in and lies down on the couch. The nineteenth of April.

But he has work to do. Can't waste a minute. He gets up and goes out to straighten up his garage-office. Things are in a mess. The more he cleans, the worse it seems to get. He shows a fellow there through the pens, where he is growing worms, using dog intestines as hosts. Important experiment. Many of the worms are, as though magnified, snake size, but their morphology is strictly vermicular. "Lyttae," he puns, but he sees the fellow fails to grasp this. A scorpion has got in and killed his best worms. Carnage. It is grotesque. Afraid of the tail, he kicks it in the head. The scorpion's legs, detached by the blow, twitch in death throes, look almost like chicken claws. The head wanders about autonomously. "Make the best of it," he cautions himself, and attempts to study the scorpion's incredible head. But it terrifies him. The fellow is gone. Wylie is alone. With the dead worms and the scorpion head. It seems to be enjoying itself. He is afraid to kill it.

"I'm cold, Tommy," whimpers Sally Elliott at the ice plant. A thawing rain drums the roof of the big Lincoln, securing them from parents, police, and bushwhackers. Tommy has found that girls jump in the back faster when he uses his Dad's Lincoln instead of his own jalop. Something psychological. "Somebody'll come and catch us."

"Use a little common sense, Sally. It's Monday night and it's raining pitchforks. Nobody's gonna come." He has talked the slacks off her, but not the panties. He kisses her neck, strokes the sleek flesh of her tummy. Boy oh boy, does it feel good! "I told you I know what I'm doing," he whispers. He insinuates his fingers under the elastic band, slithers toward whatever it is that's down there.

She twists away, curls up in one corner, staring out at the rain. "Tommy, please, let's go home."

She wants you to do it, she just doesn't want to feel guilty, wants you to make her do it so it's not her fault. He sets his teeth. "Listen, Sally, if it was the end of the world tomorrow, I mean really, if this was our last, like our last chance, would you let me do it then?" He is on his knees beside her, staring at her almost edible everything. Sheen off the silk panties. White as a ghost.

"Why do you talk like that, Tommy? Do you believe that?"

"No, I just mean, *if*." Boy, she's dumb! She deserves it! If he can just get her down on her belly somehow.

"I guess so," she says then, surprising him.

"Sally!" he whispers, kissing her ear. He moves in. "You're beautiful! You're Eve!" His own mark of Adam, so taut and prickly he almost wants somebody to bite the end off, prods her softly in the side.

That scares her and she jumps away, scrambles for her slacks, pulls them on. But anyway she finally sees what he's got. He figures she's pretty impressed, because she forgets about being mad and gets cuddly again on the way home. "If the end of the world *does* come," she whispers, "will you hold my hand all the time?"

"Sure," he smiles, Hey, this Judgment thing is pretty rich, he decides, and can be mined for more. He'll have to plan it out. Meanwhile, he lays hold of a plump breast and says, "We'll have to practice, though."

Rain falls. Clerks are laid off. A creek outside town overflows its banks. A three-hour power failure blacks out the town. A nice old lady rolls down a flight of stairs and breaks her neck. Signs all, and the signs are bad. And on the door of a stall in the boys' rest room at the high school: APRIL 19. Carved with a knife.

"Mrs. Norton, this is a friend calling."
"Why can't you people leave us alone?"

"I'm not calling to trouble you, Mrs. Norton, let me assure you." The diamond shape has reverted once more to a square, a large checkerboard, composed of twenty-five smaller squares, thirteen of which contain eight small triangles each, all blacked in, although the alternating vertical and horizontal strokes preserve the separate identity of each triangle. If the light is right. "Why I called was simply to tell you that I have good reason to believe you have a, shall we say, a pretender, in your midst, who may in fact mean you considerable harm." The other end of the line remains silent. Diagonals are passed through the white squares, giving them four triangles each. "And perhaps harm to our community as well. I speak of Mr. Justin Miller. I am sorry to say that I fear his intentions may be opportunistic ones."

A prolonged pause. Then, snappishly, "We have long been aware of that. Thank you for your interest."

The common sense thing to do, the mayor reasons, is to tell those people to stay home, they're creating a public disturbance. Neighbors are complaining about the noise. But he hopes it will just solve itself somehow like the "Black Hand" thing, which has at last died out. Everybody seems to be out after his neck as it is, blaming him for the town's troubles, even for bad business and power failures, when there's just nothing he could ever do about it, and he doesn't need any more enemies, even crazy ones. He pretends he has solved the "Black Hand" affair, hinting that the boys involved may well come from well-to-do families in town, and he has seen fit to bring it quietly to an end his own way. People say that's good common sense. He even starts believing it himself. Sometimes he wishes he was back in the fire department.

Four men, all Italian Catholics, play pitch at the Eagles. The first, thumbing his cards into order, says, "It's common sense. I'm not exactly cheering my ass off, I can't even sleep nights. But that mine ain't never gonna open up again. I pass." The second man bids two, as the first codas, "That's all I'm saying. Anybody with any common sense can see it's never gonna open up again."

"Common sense!" snorts the third, partner of the first. "To hell with common sense! Listen, if that mines closes, I'm dead. I can't let myself think that. I gotta believe it's gonna open up, or I'd go off my bat. There's some things, buddy, common sense ain't no good for. Three." The fourth man passes.

And more signs. Elan the teacher senses estrangement from the rest of the faculty at school. The principal, while by no means hostile, forgets now to smile, does not mention the permanent appointment. Students grow lax in their homework, seem amused at her austerity. Her two boys suffer endless humiliation and she must pretend detachment.

Up early one morning, the skies broken up for a change, she takes a stroll before going to school, passes a small frame church with yellow brick siding. Outside, a signboard reads:

GAL. 1.9: *If any man preacheth unto you any good gospel other than that which ye received, let him be anathema!*

She shudders, recognizing she has wandered into an alien place. A redheaded boy sits on the steps eyeing her coldly, cradling a root or something in his lap. Can he know who she is? She hurries by, feigning interest in something across the street.

At school, there is an obscene drawing on her blackboard. Supposedly an angel, or so it seems, it nevertheless possesses two stringy bare breasts, buckteeth, large spectacles, and frizzy hair. From its naked bottom rises a flag that reads: REPENT! Below the figure: ST. ELLIE. The children are hysterical, their faces buried in books. Elan, suddenly near tears, feels utterly helpless. Her back is to the students, and she cannot turn to face them, nor can she bring herself to erase the angel.

Her two boys enter then, Karmin and Ko-li. They stand and stare. Karmin slams his books to a desk, marches to the board, and erases the drawing. *"Boy!"* he shouts out. *"Whoever did that is really rotten!"* His face is afire with righteous anger. *"If he's got any guts, he'll go outside with me right now!"*

Elan is to confront with courage and inward serenity the history that is to come and to comprehend with grace the bitter obligation of suffering. "Thank you, Carl Dean." Wash the earth from your hands and feet and cast your eyes to the limitless stars. "Now, please take your seat." She is able at last to face the class. The giggling diminishes. Some blush. By my light, thou shalt flee the darkness.

Kit Cavanaugh, crusing back into town from the ice plant with Sally Elliott, is sore. Boy oh boy, how can any guy get so far and not get in? He must be the biggest idiot, the biggest chicken, in the whole United States. It was so beautiful, that whole Last Judgment line, they were already off the earth and *flying*, man, stretched out there near-naked in the back seat of the Lincoln. Boy, there were flames everywhere! Her skirt was up, her blouse off. He slipped from her embrace to ease her panties down. And he was just ogling that fantastic black place below her bum and wedging his nervous fingers down inside there, when he heard Sally talking to herself.

"What'd you say, Sal?"

"I'm praying."

"Praying! Whatcha doing that for?"

"I'm praying to Jesus not to let you do anything wrong, Tommy. If it's gonna be the Last Judgment, I don't want you to go to you know where."

He thought she must be kidding, but there were tears running down her nose. "Aw, Sal," he said, and took a last hungry look at the bum. He already had the rubber on: what a waste! Glumly, they headed for home.

The trouble is: how do you keep kissing them and get on top there at the same time?

"Tommy! Look at that!" Sally cries now.

He'd almost driven by without noticing, but now he sees the big gang of people. "My gosh! it's a big fight!"

"Don't stop, Tommy!"

"I'm just going slow to see. Hey! there's old Ugly Palmers! Hey! look at him go! Man!" Maybe it's be a pretty even fight at that, him and Ugly. "Say, you know what, Sal? That must be Mr. Bruno's house! The guy who says it's gonna be the Last Judgment!" Sally squeezes toward him. "Holy cow, wait'll Dad hears about this!"

"Tommy, please don't stop! I'm afraid!"

"But, gee, I think I oughta help old Ugly out. They're ganging up on him." Doesn't mean to, though. Just whip old Sal up a little bit.

Suddenly, a window breaks with a tremendous crash. People start to run. "*Tommy!*" Sally screams. He guns it out of there, shaking just a little bit. Ho-lee *cow!*

In front of Sally's house, they get in a hot clinch. Sal is trembling, sort of. Man, if he could just keep her mouth stopped, he could do it, just hold the kiss until he was in there. But how would he do that without breaking her neck? Something is wrong.

It is the last day of winter, the twentieth of March, a morning heavily overcast like many of late, and Betty Wilson is going to Mabel Hall's. She slips out the back door, so Sister Clara, who lives down the block, is sure not to see her, past her torn-up hollyhocks and Eddie's old bird dog nosing at a corner of his pen, and goes to see Mabel, knowing, though nothing has been said, that the other girls, anyway Mary Harlowe and probably Wanda Cravens, will come there, too. A new element has been added and now it must be appraised. Cards will be consulted, or else tea will tell what otherwise might be missed.

Like when Mabel saw "an evil event" and "love destroyed" in January, and she even says now she made

279

Willie stay home that dreadful night, and who can say it isn't so? it's possible. And certainly it was Mabel who saved them all from despair when the Judgment failed to come the eighth of March like Clara had said, and it was Mabel who found "the man of honor" that knocked on their door just one week later. As for the eighth, they had met at Mabel's the Wednesday before, and she had foretold it: "adversity," "deception," and "vain expectation." So, in a way, they knew it all along, all the girls, knew it wouldn't happen that night. Sometimes, in the excitement of a meeting, or when Clara was telling them how it would be, how they would see Ely and Eddie and Hank and all of them again, they forgot, and then the end was surely coming that night again, the eighth. But probably, deep down, they all knew a postponement had been ordained. Of course, Mabel was very close to that Norton woman these days, and, though they all believed Mabel, they listened to her with two ears, as it were, and she was certainly very quick a couple days ago to find the nineteenth of April in her cards, where it had never been before. Clara could be, in a way, wrong, and she could be stubborn in her wrongheadedness, but Clara could always be trusted. Betty never doubted for a moment a single word Brother Ely ever spoke in his entire life, he was truly the greatest man she ever knew, maybe even a living saint, nor does she nowadays doubt a single thing that her best friend Clara says, but sometimes, well, the same word can mean twenty different things, that's all. Of course, Mabel is a little batty sometimes and she probably wouldn't recognize the Coming in her cards if she saw it there, there's that to consider, but one would at least have expected something like "a long journey" or "an unexpected visitor"—not even to mention the awesome trump twenty—and not "vain expectation." So, they probably knew. Not the eighth of March, not yet. Mabel always used to read tea leaves, but more and more she has been turning to the cards, ever since she bought that fancy set in Mr. Robbins' dimestore.

Now, the new element is the hill. "The Mount of

Redemption." They are going out there tomorrow night, since Mrs. Norton thinks something still could happen the first day of spring. It all started last night when Abner Baxter led his people over to sing revival songs on the front lawn at Giovanni Bruno's. He gave them no peace now. Only this time, Sister Clara shot right out there and shook a finger at Abner and said, "Abner Baxter, you're only doing this on account of you're afraid it might be *true!*" It made Betty so proud, it was just like Ely was back with them again. Oh, and there was a lot of shouting and Mr. Miller took pictures because he said he wanted to humiliate them and they all sang as loud as they could, everybody singing different songs, and Mrs. Norton wanted everybody to come in and lock the doors. Willie Hall wanted to go home right then, only Mabel made him stay. Mr. Himebaugh went upstairs to the bathroom and never came down for a whole hour.

Abner Baxter raised a terrible fuss then and shook his fist and said the power of the Lord was upon him and somebody started throwing rocks and then Ben Wosznik walked out there and he said, "Now, who threw them rocks?" and Roy Coates said back, "What's it to you?" and that high school boy who's taken such a shine to Clara's daughter went out there and Dr. Norton, too, and it looked like there was going to be a big fight. And Ben said, "Well, I just don't think that was a very Christian thing to do!" and Roy said, "What do you wops know about Christians?" even though Ben wasn't a wop, isn't even an Italian. And the Palmers boy said nobody was going to call a friend of his a wop, and he cocked back to take a poke at Roy, but Ben held him back and said they had to turn the other cheek like the Good Book says and then Roy Coates hit him. Right in the eye he had just turned. They all went running out to help Ben and the Palmers boy was swinging at everybody and Mr. Miller was taking pictures and Mrs. Norton started crying that the police were coming and a rock smashed the porch window and the Baxter people all ran away.

281

So they went back in, creeping like they were guilty of something awful, but they didn't know what, and everybody was nervous and upset and crying, and poor Ben, his eye was swelled up and his nose was all bloody, and Wanda Cravens was dabbing it with a wet dishtowel, Betty wanted to help, was hurt that Sister Wanda was doing it, but was just too weepy and trembling. The Palmers boy, though, said he hit at least five of them and he showed off his bruised fist to little Elaine to try to stop her crying so. Dr. Norton felt it and said he didn't think any bones were broken. And then the police *did* come, but Mr. Miller went out and sent them away.

For some reason, then, they all started watching Giovanni Bruno, or whoever he is. Something special was coming. He was still in the armchair, wrapped in blankets, just like always, like nothing had happened, even though the window in front of him was all broken in, but he was jittery, scratched all the time at the arms of the stuffed chair, darted his peculiar eyes around so, Betty grew a little frightened. And suddenly he lifted his hand and said: *"Mount of Redemption!"* And after that, Mr. Himebaugh came down from the bathroom.

"Mount of Redemption." What in the name of heaven could it mean? Always riddles! Just like with "Sunday Week" and "A Circle of Evenings." Betty complained one night to Mrs. Norton about it, how the spirits never said things plain, but Mrs. Norton said of course they talked plain, it was just that we weren't always smart enough to understand them, and that's why we have to study and work hard. Betty knew that, she'd known that all her life, every preacher she ever knew said so, but she also knew she'd never *be* smart enough, and that made her feel sad, made her feel cheated, and sometimes, God help her, even made her angry at the spirits. "Mount of Redemption." Mrs. Norton said it must mean some place, perhaps where they must await the Coming, but she was utterly perplexed about where. But then Clara jumped right up like something had stuck her and cried out, "Why that there hill out

282

by Number Nine! You know, that one right over where we worked!" And what got everybody so terribly excited was how Clara said "we" instead of "you" or "they" so spontaneous like. Mrs. Norton was so wrought up she was almost weeping, and she cried, "It's your husband! He has reached you!" And poor Clara, she was trembling all over and had to allow it must be so—where else could it have come from? And so they all prayed and sang and had goosebumps about it, and Mrs. Norton received a message.

And that is why Betty is going to Mabel's, because she wants to know what it means. Is it still going to happen? Will it happen out there at the mine? Will it happen in April? Will something happen tomorrow night? But mostly, to tell the truth, Betty really wants to know more about the dark stranger, the man of honor, who has entered her life. It starts to sprinkle.

It was widely assumed that Christ would preside at the Final Judgment. Imagine one man's astonishment, therefore, when he found himself confronted by his first wife instead. Well, he smiled with an insouciant shrug upon recognizing the old girl, you can't win them all. Don't be ridiculous, admonished his Judge; the one fault of which the Divine can never be accused is the perpetration of a bad joke. You have said it, the man replied.

.   .   .

A middle-aged woman, in the flash of total insight granted those at the Last Judgment, discovered that the intense jealous hatred she felt toward all humanity, male and female alike, was not really due to the corruption of her soul by the Devil, but to the embarrassment her flat breasts always caused her. She was therefore only mildly surprised, when, upon being arraigned, she was accused only of the sin of having failed to exercise her breasts properly. When she protested that her fault was hereditary, that her mother also had had small breasts, her Judge replied that that was hardly a defense, that as a matter of fact, her mother had preceded her to hell.

. . .

Most souls lost all hope for salvation when, upon being asked, they remembered their names. Thus it was that a sad-eyed old drunk, forgetting his in the confusion of the moment, received, perhaps by mistake, the earth as a gift.

. . .

Bankers and businessmen, as the whole world could have predicted, were, without exception, condemned, Go directly to hell, the Divine Judge would roar upon being confronted by one of them; do not pass Go, do not collect $200. The egalitarians were also sent to hell, of course, but they were allowed to collect the money. Sometimes, even the Divine Mind is scrutable . . .

"West Condon Chronicle."

"Mr. Miller, please."

"Whom shall I say—?"

"It's the Black Hand again."

"Oh. Well, madame, Mr. Miller can *not* talk to you. He is a *very* busy man, and he doesn't have time for your sort."

"Don't I know it."

"(Who's that, Annie?) (Oh, it's just that crazy lady who keeps calling up saying she's the Black Hand. I already told her to—) (That's all right, Annie. I'll take it.) Hello, Black Hand." Scratch. Drag. "(Annie, get off the phone!)" Click. "Say, I always knew you were hilarious, Happy, but I didn't realize you were such a goddamn genius. If you don't mind, I think I'm going to run your Judgments in our Good Friday issue."

"I'm not looking for fame, Mr. Editor, I'm looking for the payoff."

"And the poor unendowed ladies! You are indeed pitiless!"

"Just cleaning out the competition. Is Annie a cute girl?"

"Oh yeah, very. Certainly not hellbound by your rules."

"Oh?" She's not quite sure how she's supposed to take that. Calls for a visit. "You already owe me a fortune in postage, you black heel."

His laughter. "You're right. Listen, I promise, I'll at least stop out to see you a minute, if not today, tomorrow at the latest."

A pause. She ought to forget it, not mention it, but she says, "Say, Tiger, is it true about all those wild orgies you're having over there with those Christians?"

He laughs. "Sure, it's great! Just me and Johnny Bruno and an ecstatic houseful of naked old widows!"

"I heard some of those widows weren't so old."

"What do you mean?"

What is it makes her open her big mouth? She hesitates, then says, "Oh, a guy called. Said he was a friend and told me things he thought I'd like to know. About Mrs. Cravens, for example."

"Oh yeah? Sounds like some friend. Listen, Happy, that's a lot of crap, there's nothing there. I don't know why anybody's so goddamn adolescent as to—"

"He said he thought I might be able to persuade you to get out of that group and away from that woman, be better for me, for you, and everybody else. He said."

"Well, he's got it all wrong, whoever the hell he is. Besides, that woman's got the melancholiest bottom I ever saw."

"You've had a good look?"

"Sure. At all the orgies."

Womwom pours orange juice, boils eggs, makes toast. Elan, gazing out on the rain, eats distractedly. "Wylie," she says, looking up at him, her pupils shrunk to pinpricks by the long look at too much light, "do you remember how, after the powers of darkness had chased us from Carlyle, we could not remember who the fourth man was?"

"Yes."

"Do you recall what he looked like?"

Womwom munches toast meditatively. "Not very well."

"He was dark, Wylie, and rather tall. I remember how his glittering eyes frightened me so."

"Yes, perhaps that's so." He doesn't remember.

"Wylie . . . I think I know now who he was!"

It is Friday, the day for fish. It is March, the month of the fish. The destruction of the world by water, the dissolving of prevalent structures, the liberation from things merely seen or touched. The fish. The unconscious. The cyclic renovation. Fertility of the spirit. "Come ye after me, and I will make you fishers of men." Mana's closed and perfect circle, a gift from her childhood, assumes a new dimension, a new beauty. Elan's primordial energy now whirls upon it through measurable phases. The soul is spun upon it, falling now into matter, climbing now toward its source, wriggling through the twelfth moment toward its rebirth. Unity fragments into multiplicity upon it, multiplicity reassembles itself to unity. All is in it, on it, leaping, turning, cavorting, promenading, falling, climbing . . . swimming. The fish. She consumes it. Defeat? Reclusion? Negation? No! Mana awaits with excitement and with certainty her turn on the wheel, her inexorable rebirth! Outside, it rains. Dissolves.

Rain. The banker stares out on it from his office window on the second floor. It reflects his own depression. He remembers how, after the war, there was so much hope here, so much promise. And now it's all going sour. "You're not in the nineteenth century, son," his Dad told him, dying. "Get your money out of here. Coal's on the way out." But he couldn't. It was home. Not that he's in any real financial trouble, he's hedged properly on all bets. But that's not the point. This is his home and his home is sick. He believes it is really a matter of spirit. Ted Cavanaugh has faith in the spirit, or, as he puts it, in will. A community of men of good will: his ideal.

So, he has been looking for something to stimulate the community spirit again. Something they could all believe in, rich and poor, miners and merchants, Italians and gentiles. Working together, they can make West Condon as great as any town in the United States, he's convinced of that, highblown as it may sound. But something has to provide the spark, something has to unite them. This little cult at the miner Bruno's house occurred to him as an idea, but it seemed too negative. Tried to work up a Special Commission on Industrial Planning. Not much interest. Searched for new industry. So far, nothing: bad labor history. He tried at least to keep the mine open. He offered money. He couldn't offer enough. It's not official, but he knows they will close it. And so, he is back at the cult. It has given him an idea. A committee. Communal exercising of a little common sense. Start with it as a specific problem, get the town enthused, as many people into the thing as possible, then subtly convert it into something positive, a kind of all-community WPA and sales team, so to speak.

But, on principle, he just can't fight anybody else's religion, no matter how absurd it is. They had to *do* something first, hopefully something offensive. And now, what do you know, that old Wobbly agitator Red Baxter has done it for them. For him. Created that old vacuum, the filling of which is every American's first nature: the need for a third force.

He picks up his phone, dials. The checkerboard on his pad is now, virtually, one huge black square, though, within the blackness, a pattern is still discernible. "Hello, Maury? Maury, this is Ted calling. I'm getting in touch with several of the fellows, ones I can count on. I've just been thinking, Maury . . ."

So unobtrusively, the point of no return is passed. No one has expressed it, yet everyone knows it. Nor can any really doubt that this knowledge is now general, distorted in places perhaps, but widespread. Rahim—barrister, adviser, procurator, scrivener, sacramentalist, mathematician, and historian—is the last to concede it. He continues to press for secrecy, but observes that it is futile. On the streets of West Condon, he is avoided. Ugly phonecalls are received. Letters. Well, good riddance to the fools! Soon enough, it will be his turn to laugh! Hah!

He shuns the common meeting places, spends less time at his office, takes no new cases. He catches up on his filing, ridiculous task, of course, yet an old habit here impels him. His cats still give him solace, but more and more he is passing his days with Elan or at the Bruno house. He is quick to perceive the weaknesses of the others, of course, but the very lack which he fills—almost, one could say, with mathematical exactitude—is, as it were, the final proof of the veracity of his calculations. Thirty days.

Rain keeps him home this noon. No matter. Rain is just too appropriate today, and Elan would be passing out cheap zodiacal preachments again. How she dupes them with that nonsense! Still, to be honest, it is really only the harmless residue of her core genius, and Rahim supposes she must find excess in him, too. But this will be no moral victory, it will be a cold victory of the human mind. He has tried to explain that to the others, but they refuse to grasp it. Except for little Mana perhaps. There, there is still hope. Thinking of her makes him curse the rain that keeps him home. Perhaps he should go anyway. Her room, though she doesn't know he's been there, delights him. It has a charmingly eccentric shape, walls turned and cornered to fit the needs of adjoining rooms, part of the ceiling aslant from the roof's angle, one large window nearly floor to ceiling . . . it is perhaps its *lack* of logic that most appeals to him. But, no, it is always awkward, he has no clear purpose there, and he still, in spite of the total breakdown in security, resists the daytime visits.

He removes his streetclothes, dresses in the new piece of silk underwear and his own lounging robe, curls up meditatively in the living room armchair with a snifter of brandy, listens to it rain. The cats rub by, but he deflects their efforts to hop up. Thirty days! Sipping the brandy, he passes his hand over the silk, her silk, and contemplates the End. Hah! It will be lovely! It will be grotesque!

Two of the girls, Mary Harlowe and Lucy Smith, are already in Mabel Hall's kitchen when Betty Wilson arrives, running in from under the rain, and the cards, stacked, are on the talble. Lucy is explaining how she has begged and begged her husband to take back her to Bruno's, but how Calvin is afraid of Abner Baxter. Lucy doesn't say "afraid," of course, she says "swayed," but the other three know what she means. She tells them that everybody at the church is just disgusted with both the Baxters, how Abner and Sarah just stole the Circle right away from Clara and nobody could do anything about it, and how stupid Sarah Baxter is. Mabel informs Betty they have just been reading the cards, and Lucy and Calvin will join them again one day. They talk about Mr. Himebaugh being up in the bathroom all the time last night, and Mabel explains he has the flu. Mabel hardly ever talks, but she knows what's going on before anybody else.

Mary asks if they all were noticing how Mr. Miller and the Bruno girl, the prophet's sister, were getting so lovey-dovey, and, in a whisper, says she saw them kissing back in the bedroom when she went looking for her kids. Mabel says very bluntly that Wanda Cravens is also doing everything but lifting her skirts to get Mr. Miller's eye, and at that Lucy Smith starts giggling so she can't stop. "He *is* kinder cute," she says in a titter.

"Well! if you knew what I know about that young man and dear Sister Wanda—!" says Mary Harlowe, and then she tells them.

"Wanda always has been man-crazy," says Lucy. "I don't know how poor Brother Lee ever put up with her so long."

"And she was even flirting one night with that silly

289

blond high school boy, poor child," Mary adds, "and she certainly didn't waste a minute trying to get her hooks in Ben Wosznik, either!"

Betty Wilson's weak heart leaps dangerously to her throat, and she exchanges a terrified glance with Mabel, who, with a little shake of her head, warns her to say nothing. Betty guesses then that Wanda Cravens is not her only threat, that even her old friend Mary Harlowe has got ideas.

Just then, Wanda Cravens herself arrives with Thelma Coates, Thelma sneaking away from home and that horrible tyrannical husband of hers, Roy. She tries to say how sorry she is about the other night and starts crying pathetically, and they all cry together for a while.

After that, they speculate on the meaning of Giovanni Bruno's pronouncement about the Mount of Redemption, while Mabel shuffles the cards and says they should be quiet if it is going to work out properly. Sister Thelma asks what is the Mount, and Mary tells her about the hill at the mine, but Thelma and Lucy are admonished to keep utmost secrecy so as not to cause more trouble with Abner Baxter. A Bible is found and they swear on it. Mabel lays the cards out. She fingers each one before revealing it, studies each development, gasps, sighs, broods, smiles, purses her lips, squints her eyes. For a long time, an almost endless time, she gazes at the exposed cards. Outside, the rain falls steadily shushing mysteriously against the roof. "A controversy," she says at last. Betty looks for it, but the faces are forever strange to her. "Two blond queens," says Mabel, indicating them, "but," another card, "the controversy is resolved," yet another, "by time." They all nod.

"But the *end*, Mabel," Lucy insists, "is it coming?"

Mabel turns up another card, places it upper right. "It is not certain, but it is probable," she says.

"Is it still April nineteenth?"

Mabel stares, her eyes running over the exposed cards. "I don't know, but, yes, I think so," she replies at last.

"Here's a five . . . black. Perhaps: a black hand . . ." A pause while they catch their breaths and glance at one another. Mary Harlowe is pale. ". . . And the number . . . the number . . . seven."

"What does it mean?" Mary asks.

Mabel, not replying, turns up another card, places it just below the last one. "A reunion," she says. "Perhaps to discuss the controversy." Another card. "A distant place."

"The hill!" Thelma whispers.

Mabel nods. "It can be," she says.

Betty steals a glance at Sister Wanda Cravens. She is very young and slender with a cute freckly face, and Betty loses heart. Of course, she is *too* young and *too* thin and she is silly and fickle, but will Ben see that?

Mabel turns up a new card and catches her breath sharply. They all stare at it. "The Judgment!" she whispers, and one ringed finger points to Gabriel and three naked people: a fat lady with oversized breasts, a thin lady showing her bare behind, and an elderly man praying. Fascinated by the card, Betty barely hears the rest, only scattered phrases reaching her: ". . . ordeal . . . will subjected to wisdom and prudence . . . evil men . . . victory over opposition . . . false friends . . ." and so on. Trump twenty. Judgment. God has spoken.

"Who are the false friends?" Mary Harlowe asks. She would.

Mabel hesitates. "A dark man." She glances up at Betty, who withers. Of course, all the men Betty can think of are dark, except maybe the Meredith boy. And Abner, who is no friend in the first place. But, still, a cruel doubt has stabbed her, hurt her deeply, and inwardly she grows faint. "And perhaps a child," continues Mabel, eyes flicking over the cards. "And a married woman."

After the session, one of the best they have ever had, when the others have left, Mabel reminds Betty that Wanda Cravens has three small children and Mary Harlowe five, no obstacle perhaps to a beast of lust, but hardly attractive to a man of honor. Betty thanks her, weeping gratefully, and, as the rain lets up momentarily, leaves, her joy renewed.

12

West Condon came alive as Miller walked through it. First day of spring and, on impulse, he'd decided to leave the Chevy at home, walk to the *Chronicle*. Still needed the trenchcoat, but he wore it open. Women appeared to sweep porches, men laughed foolishly from autos, children ran and shouted. Bicycles bounced down off porches. He heard the *whump-whump* of a basketball bouncing on cinders. The cool rains of the last couple days had sunk a fragrance into the soil that the sudden vernal sun this Saturday morning exploited gaudily. Who would think some here saw an end to it all?

The new time springs forth! Sun splintering through the windowfrost sprays the truth of the new evangel upon her bed. She stretches, feels old constraints squeeze out her sinews to run fingering down her arms and out into oblivion. Make way for light!

Downtown, people opening their shops hailed him. He took off his trenchcoat, carried it over his shoulder. West Condon showing its best face, momentary denial of the gloomy omens. Exchanges of witless banter, easy laughter. Maury Castle, rolling out the awning of his shoestore, made a dig about widows and orgies. Miller only laughed and told him he'd better join up quick if he wanted to get a little of that grace. Castle heehawed.

The worst of it was still in front of him, but he felt

292

ready for it. Admittedly, it was pretty harrying, and now that the cult had become a more or less public phenomenon, there was more to keep an eye on than merely the little group itself, and that pushed him all the more, but as long as they didn't move the date up on him again, he felt he could make it to the end. Or close enough anyway, for what he wanted out of it. The cult itself had not grown much since Miller's first night—an ex-coalminer named Ben Wosznik and two or three more disaster widows—but its force had. The town was now awake to them, and the members themselves felt this awakening. There was always a tension as they faced out of the Bruno house, and even their own homes now sometimes seemed alien to them.

The Nazarene preacher Abner Baxter, made jealous it would seem by the loss of some of his own congregation, had been the first to make the cult public by his open denunciation of it. Squat red-maned head butted forward, copy rolled up in his freckled fist like a truncheon, he had invaded Miller's office one afternoon, accompanied by two of his flock—introduced to Miller as Mr. Roy Coates and Mr. Ezra Gray—to deliver a formal handwritten repudiation of the "false prophet Giovanni Bruno" and the "sorcerers and impostors" who surrounded him. His thunderings on apostasy and women—"Women they gotta keep silence in the churches! they ain't permitted to speak out, like the law says! Anything they need to know, Mr. Miller, let them ask their menfolk!"—had made it clear he saw Sister Clara as the real marplot behind the heresy. He had raged there in the darkening office to the clacking rhythm of the wireservice Teletypes and the distant thump of old Hilda the press, his stubby legs set martially apart, his two lieutenants now conciliatory, now indignant, now sinister, now apologetic. If Miller had been tempted to drop the project, it was Baxter who removed the temptation. Even Jones, watching on deadpan from his desk, had had to admit he was impressed. The office girl Annie Pompa, moonface blanched to a pale olive, had stood stunned in the doorway, staring at this exhibition as though at green-

293

skinned monsters from outer space, had squeaked in fright as the three men had wheeled suddenly—in mid-damnation, as it were—to bulk out past her. In a half-faint behind her desk afterwards, plump hand pressed into the sponge of her bosom, she had been voiceless, able only to shake her fat head fearfully, as though to affirm that the world was, in truth, in danger.

The heady spring weather today whetted Miller's appetite for baseball and golf, for the feel of damp grass as he knuckled a ball and tee into the earth or fielded a bunt, for different places he'd been on different spring openings, even for West Condon in the spring, but the old West Condon with track meets and pickups and late evening ball games, tennis and Indian rubber, picnics, bonfires, furtive assaults under burred blankets that scratched agitatingly on the uncalloused flesh—whetted, in short, his underappetite, and, truth to tell, he was hungry enough. Here, the cult had robbed him utterly. At Bruno's house, neither he nor Marcella was left alone five minutes now. As their chief scribe, his presence was required at all times and at every break he got set upon by one or another of the factions, each seeking to convince him of their own peculiar point of view. All knew it without understanding what they knew: he was the only one present without convictions.

As for Happy Bottom, well, she was impatient and surely she tempted him, but he just didn't have the time free. Trouble with that girl was that the act was no five-minute project with her, it was an epoch. Sometimes it almost seemed to him there was something suicidal about her leap into bed: a hot mole. Not that she looked like one—nor sounded like one: her Judgments gave him as much pleasure as he got these days. Still, he wasn't able to make a whole kingdom of a mattress, and that was the kind of circle she seemed to chart for him. And, what was more to the point maybe, he wanted to stop lying to Marcella. Her total ingenuous belief in him gave him a kind of responsibility he hadn't had before: didn't especially want it, but he couldn't help but recognize it. Commitment was a real thing to her, solid as a door, specific as a threshold, and so, unavoidably, had become so for him as well. He knew that weaning her away from the cult and her brother would not be easy, but he meant to try, and he knew the consequences of success, knew and accepted them. In fact, goddamn it, they even appealed to him.

She skips, singing to the bathroom, peeling off her pajamas, shedding old skins. Everything new, everything clean, and, for the day, a bright yellow frock with the rustle of spring in it. Rebirth! Water splashes in the tub, exciting her, sunlight splashes on the floor. And then, just as she's stepping into the tub, Mr. Himebaugh walks in, looking ill—"Oh, I'm sorry, dear!" he says. "That's all right," she smiles, ducking down into the tub, and he leaves.

Father Jones sat, fat polyp, alone on a stool in the hotel coffeeshop, belly butting the bar, before him an oval platter stained with egg yolk and dusted with toast crumbs. Jones sometimes ate as many as eight fried eggs in a morning. Miller flung his hat onto a wall hook, took a stool one removed from Jones to give the man elbow room, and they exchanged dry grunts of recognition. "Pecan waffles, Doris," Miller said to the woman who wandered blearily behind the counter. She poured a cup of coffee, bopped the counter with it before bringing it to abrupt rest in front of him, thrust a grubby hand into the pecan jug, which still contained the crumpled cigarette package Miller had thrown there five days ago.

Cup at mouth, hat tipped back, eyes asquint, Jones said, "Lucky you happened in just now. Strange as it must seem, I was just contemplating as how, now that we've copped all the goddamn prizes being passed out this season, you'd probably be anxious to give your old Dad here a fortnight off. See, my poor old Mother is ailing, and—"

"Jones, don't kid me, you never had a mother," said Miller, pouring the coffee in the saucer back into the cup and sheeting the saucer with a paper napkin. "I will say, though, your appetite sure seems to have gone to pot from all the overwork."

"Yeah, that's it. Whoo! I feel awful." Jones sagged.

"How many eggs did he eat this morning, Doris?"

"Same as always," she said and poured stringy batter on the waffle iron, rained upon it broken pecans. "All we had."

Miller laughed. "Okay, it's a deal. But give me just four or five weeks more. Until this Bruno thing is over."

"What? Haven't you laid that chick yet?"

"Jones, that gang is full of women, and I can only handle one at a time," Miller said, as Doris, dropping the lid of the waffle iron, turned a puffy eye on them. The lid lifted, batter bagged out and dribbled, turned hard. "In fact, you can help me out if you've got a couple minutes free tonight."

Jones lit a cigar, grunted interrogatively.

"I haven't been able to get good pictures of the group yet, but tonight may be a good time. They're going to meet out at that little rise next to Deepwater Number Nine. You know it?"

"Yeah. Cunt Hill."

"What! Are you serious?"

"Somebody told me when we were out there for the disaster."

"But how did it get a name like that?"

"Looks like one. The east, or belly, slope is gradual, and there's even a slight abdominal dip before the last pubic rise— Stretch out there on the bar, Doris, and lemme show—"

"Not me," grumbled Doris. "My slope ain't gradual," and she slapped her belly, making them laugh.

"Then, on the west side," Jones continued, "it drops off sharply into a grove of trees at the edge of the mine buildings. But it only really got its name, I understand, when the company for some goddamn reason cut a clearing in the middle of all that vegetation, went digging for something or other, and left an incredible gash right in the old alveolus of love!"

"Right in the old olive-oilus of love!" exclaimed Doris. "What the hell is that?" She left them, shaking her head, to continue her mindless wandering behind the counter, smudging a clean glass here, dropping bread on the floor there.

"This fissure is now the repository of used condums, thrown there, it is said, in the belief that such oblations prolong the potency of the communicant."

"Jones, you're kidding!"

"There is, in fact, a sizable orifice in the crack, driven no doubt by some wag with an electric drill and a compressed air hose, though many in the heat of a drunken brawl have claimed to be the Man Who Deflowered Cunt Hill."

Marcella, fresh from the bath and into the frock, flies gaily down the steps. Flagstones of sun lie bright in the living room garden. Out! out with the sackcloth! let the new day in! Marcella sings swings leaps skips whirls through the musty old house, heaves open the windows, brings the green air in, brings smiles to the faces of Elan and Rahim, huddled over writings at the kitchen table. It is spring! And she is in love! And then, from outside, a bird's liquid laughter sends wildflowers shivering up her spine, and out she dances to drench herself in the hot and holy sun!

Passing through the hotel lobby on his way to the plant, Miller ran into Wally Fisher and the Chamber secretary Jim Elliott. Elliott wanted to talk about the industrial brochure and the new West Condon Common Sense Committee being set up. Miller agreed to print the brochure at cost and help with the layouts, listened noncommittally to the Common Sense idea. He had bet

Cavanaugh would get into this thing, was glad to see it finally happen, but wouldn't be able to participate. Fisher, for his part, had a wild story about an out-of-town couple that had come through last night, registering as Mr. and Mrs. Washington; they had slipped out before dawn without paying, leaving deposits of shit all over the bed. "Some spring," he said.

"Happy first day of spring!" Annie his office chief sang out as Miller pushed through the front door.

"Same to you, Annie!" he said, so boisterously that Annie started. They both laughed.

"Mr. Miller, the plaque came today, the award for the disaster special!" She was giddy with possession of it.

"Well, hang it up!" He smiled.

In the newsroom, he plumped his hat on the spare chair beside his desk, tossed the trenchcoat over the back of it. Crossed to the Teletype and snapped the switch. The carriage jumped as though goosed, bringing the room to with its familiar clacking thumping heartbeat. Thing he liked. In his morning mail, besides the award plaque, he found another black-bordered Last Judgment communication from the lady Black Hand:

The Devil, to no one's surprise, turned out to be a woman. She roamed the tight streets of West Condon during the drawnout Judgment proceedings, servicing weak souls. Mother, complained the Supreme Judge, you are depopulating heaven! Your paradoxes drive me nuts, she responded with a dry scoffing cackle, and gave her skirts a kick.

• • •

Seven thousand philosophy professors were assembled simultaneously and told that if they could produce one truth among them, they would all be pardoned. The seven thousand consulted for seven days. At the end of that time, they presented their candidate, who, standing before his Judge, said: God is just. This philosopher was immediately sent to heaven to

298

demonstrate the stupidity of his statement, and the remaining 6,999 were consumed by Holy Wrath.

. . .

A poet, seeking favors at the Judgment, composed a brilliant ode to Divine Justice, and presented it. It was so enthusiastically received that the poet was proclaimed Judge of the Day and granted Supreme Authority for twenty-four hours. So ingenuous and sweet-natured was the fellow, however, that he unhesitatingly absolved everyone who appeared before him. God finally had to call an end to the poet's franchise for fear of being laughed at . . .

He shouldn't go out there, just fog up the vision, but he'd promised yesterday. He'd better go. He would. Picked up the phone, dialed the hospital. Though it was what he lived by, he regretted the one-track specificity of all action, of all choice, what time made you do when you came to a fork in the path . . . or two forks at once. Eleanor Norton's seven aspects were the thing, by God! While he waited, he hummed "Just as I Am," an old revival tune, and doodled on his desk blotter. He noticed that all the doodles lately looked alike: *M*'s. Since his own name had never fascinated him that much, they could only stand for one thing. Some were peaked and shaded heavily, gone over and over until they looked like a flock of shaggy black birds in flight in a green sky. Others were rounded like two hillocks, or like one hill cleft, insignia of all three feminine distinctions at once. As if something were lacking still, some of the *M*'s had even been enclosed in a circle. "And that Thou bidd'st me come to Thee," he sang into the phone, "O Lamb of God, I come! I come!"

Marcella digging in the dewed earth by the old apple tree, sings revival songs of her own make. She punches open the gaily colored seed packages. Thirty days! The sun is gloriously hot on her spring-frocked back. He comes!

299

After loading up the hooks with wirecopy, Miller took the panel out to the hospital. Stalled at every stopsign, clanked even on new asphalt. Old rusty-smelling wreck. One year old. Stopped for gas at the station where Lem Filbert worked, asked him if he was keeping in shape. Filbert played a creaky shortstop on their semipro team. The guy grinned broadly, then sighed, spat. "Ahh, shit, I'm gittin' too fuckin' old, Tiger."

"Yeah, we all are. Where's all the young talent?"

Filbert's grin faded. "They're smart. They're all gittin' outa this deathtrap before it's too fuckin' late."

"Is that Mello in there working on that Ford?"

"Yep, he's one a the fuckin' lucky ones. Come on a coupla weeks ago. Been at least fifty fuckin' guys by here lookin' for a job." The valve on the gas hose burped shut. Filbert squirted enough more in to round the charge off, hung up the hose, capped the gastank, spat again. "Gonna be a lotta fuckin' holes in the lineup this year," he said flatly, and stared off.

"I know." There was nothing else either of them could say, so Miller paid and left. Lem's brother, Tuck, killed in the mine disaster—about all they were able to bring out were his head and feet—had played a great center field with them for six or seven years. There were others, too, too painful to think about. Lorenzini and Calcaterra. Their pitcher Bill Lawson, whose widow had been in and out of the cult. Mario Juliano. And Bert Martini with one arm gone now. Martini caught and Miller had known one-arm catchers before, and he hoped to rehabilitate the old guy. But it was going to be a pretty glum season. Man. Down with spring.

Inside the hospital, the white was perhaps a little whiter, but past that there was nothing to let you know spring had got turned on outside. Miller picked up the traffic list. Seven admitted, five released: even the batting average was bad. He went back, took the elevator up to second. As he stepped out, the first thing he saw was Happy Bottom's happy bottom. Her back was to him, her head down studying the diet and medications lists, and she was absently pinching through her skirt to tug down the legband that forever gaped upward. A useless effort, he had told her, being able to prove that the band's natural position, given all stresses, was exactly five picas above her thigh's best wrinkle. So what? she would say, and, turning from him, tug it again. "Now, how did you know I was coming?" he asked.

Her hand twitched away in reflex as her head came up, then stroked back toward its tugging cranny, again pincered the white skirt. Her arm relaxed, the hand sagging, pulling the taut skirt yet tauter. She turned then to look at him. "Oh," she pouted, "I thought it was one of the doctors."

A bell rang and a light came on down the corridor. "Say, I can't stay," Miller said. "I just dropped up a second to—"

"Post office is in room 24-A," she said with a challenging smile, and left him to go answer the patient's signal, switching her hips not too subtly at all. He could almost hear the old barrel organ root-toot-tootling away.

Of course, he should just wait here since he wasn't going to stay, but he didn't, wandered instead down to 24-A, empty as he had supposed it would be. He leaned back against the bed, waited, a few fantasies flowering from the root below.

Happy entered, glanced back behind her, eased the door shut. All those M's, my God! M for mountains. She met his smile with one of her own, approached, everything moving at once. M for everything moving at once. "At last!" she growled. A wisp of sandy hair poked out under her nurse's cap. "You are in my clutches! The Black Hand strokes again!"

Miller grinned. "Mother," he complained, "you forget the gravity of the situation. Men are dying!"

She smiled up at him. Her breasts had that rare muscular thrust that made them look, from above, like a pedestal for the head. Or a platter. "Dying indeed. You've been around those awful morbid people too much, Tiger."

301

"They're not morbid, they're ecstatic."

"Listen, I saw that poor boy Bruno. He had so many scars on and around his unfortunate joint, it looked like he'd been rebuilt there by a quack plastic surgeon."

"Who, Giovanni? You mean he had some accident—?"

"You bet, accident. Whoever flayed him, flayed by patterns. Or maybe he used a knife. He was a real curiosity out here. All the nurses took turns with his baths to get a look. Of course, as soon as he was strong enough, we couldn't get near him."

"Really?" Miller laughed. He'd guessed as much, but now he had information he hadn't known otherwise how to get. "Who bathed him then?"

"His sister." If she caught his inward jolt, she gave no sign of it. "And as for dying, well, nobody tries any of that funny business up here unless I let them. Of course, on off days, why, I don't really care. I just forget and they drop off like flies." The platter punched his chest as if to roll his own head upon it, and, below, her hipbone curled in to knock once. Enough. "Tiger, there's thirty-six people up here whose lives depend on you!"

"Hand," he grinned, "you're even blacker than I thought." And, as if in thanks for that, as her mouth dampened his grin, her hand trickled in a liquid gambol down his spine to midthigh, then back up the front where a wild demand had stirred. "But there's no lock on that door," he whispered, her lips biting his words.

"I've got the key to the upstairs X-ray room, and it just happens to be time for my break. Won't be anybody up there all morning." There was spring light in her smile and a glitter in her eyes' mischief that chased all phantoms, even the most recent, while from his fingertips, pressed urgently into the soft swells that had won her her name, there radiated a message of scorn for the highflown moralizing of his morning walk and a sense of cosmic pandemonium that made him laugh. "We shall take inside pictures and sell them secretly to zee leetle boys," she murmured. "We shall make a *meellion!*" He didn't know if she meant dollars or pictures, but knew better than to ask.

Marcella sits on a stool under the scrawny apple tree in the grassless backyard, her hands full of damp dirt, the sun on her bright yellow back. Before her: a plot of troubled earth, about four feet square, marked off from the world's vague extension by four corner stakes and a piece of wrapping string. Four or five sticks poke up in the plot like its first people, broad-shouldered, wearing empty seed packages, but headless. The gaiety of their uniforms delights her, but what will express the joy they think? She spies a clump of new dandelions in Rosalia's yard next door. She picks a few, punches little holes in the tops of the seed envelopes— really the bottoms, for they are upsidedown, of course—and inserts the dandelion heads. She laughs. The fact is, Marcella doesn't exactly believe in the cataclysm. At first, she had some doubts about her brother even, for she had never confused love with worship. But she has grown greatly in these few weeks, has discovered the true solidity of truths she previously only suspected, or thought might just be creatures of her own inturned foolishness. For example: that Jesus is not salvation, but only a single path among many to a higher condition that ultimately must even exclude him. Or: that true knowledge is the discerning of pattern, and wisdom is its right interpretation. She has been greatly helped by them all. By Eleanor and by Mr. Himebaugh, even by Clara. And most of all by Justin. Though silent, apart, calm, singular, he is yet at the heart of the Plan, moving with hidden fingers, fulfilling with unspoken words, gentle, responsive, aloof from the human frailties of the group. Justin is—in a sense—their priest. She feels it. Perhaps they all feel it. She thinks of his silence as like the ardent silence of the sun, his apartness as like the enfolding apartness of the stars, his calm like the contained explosions in her chest. But the cataclysm: well, it's a matter of definition. God is terrible, but as beauty is terrible, not horror. So, if she prepares the earth for Him, even four little square feet of it, it is not to deny His coming, but to affirm the love that motivates Him.

Impulsively, his Saturday edition thrown shoddily to bed, Miller decided to go see Marcella. Go see her now, while his seed machine, old despot, was utterly drained of need, and make up his mind about that thing once and for all. Without the Chevy and the panel out, he had no choice, walked over. Didn't mind. Loosened him up and gave him time to think. It was a little brazen, this midday visit, but there were few ignorant now of his involvement with the cult and, therefore, with any or all women in it. That was the trouble with this goddamn village, there was just no way to let an affair ripen on its own, it inevitably got put on a stage to be applauded, hooted, laughed at, or second-guessed. Even the high school kids suffered this kind of daily intrusion—how long had he known, for instance, that Ted Cavanaugh's boy Tommy had been taking little Sally Elliott, Jim's daughter, out to the ice plant several times a week? Only guy in town who refused to listen to that rumor was Coach George Bayles, who was afraid if he acknowledged it, he'd have to bench Tommy for breaking training and lose every game left on the schedule. Miller had in recent years resigned himself to pickups in roadhouses and distant dance halls—had the advantage they were usually young—but he was growing away from secretaries and phone operators, had trouble setting up anything worth more than a second listless event.

He passed the Lincoln School yard, where a gang of youngsters were playing basketball. Lot of pushing, elbowing, fumbling, shouting. Found himself unconsciously trying to pick out the ones that might have promise. The ball escaped them, trickled out of bounds. A fat boy chased it, and the others let him. "Hey! Hi, Tiger!" shouted one of them, one of his carriers down at the plant. "That's Tiger Miller, the baseball player!" the kid shouted at the others.

"We know it," said the fat boy irritably, then turned his hungry smile on Miller. "Take a shot, Tiger!" he called, and heaved the ball. Three bounces. Miller reached down for it. Felt good in his hands.

"From way out here?" Miller asked, grinning. "I don't think I can make it."

"Aww," said the fat boy, and the others joined in. "C'mon, Tiger!"

Miller sucked the ball with both hands to his forehead, his old shot: believed in thinking the ball into the basket. Hell of a long distance at that, though. He relaxed, brought the ball down hard against the pavement, half step forward, ball eased up against the palm of his right, the impact that converted mere force into a subtle control system, and as the ball's momentum pushed his hand up, his left glided up, struggling against the bind of his trenchcoat, to guide—thrust off the asphalt with the calf muscles, felt old muscles snap awake, at jump's peak, ball at the brain, shoved himself back to earth again. The ball arched away—*fffft!*—didn't even touch the fucking rim going through. Hah! Only the stiff clock of his leather soles batting thinly on the asphalt whipped him back out of the stadium to this present scene, where small boys cheered the old baseball player who ran the town newspaper.

"Shoot another one, Tiger!" they cried.

Miller laughed, but knew when to quit. Still felt the knot in his legs from that short tight jump. "Let's see you guys try it," he said, and he left them excitedly imitating him.

As luck would have it, it was Eleanor Norton, not Marcella, who met him at the door of the Bruno house. Unprepared for her and with no excuse for being there, he said lamely, "Looks like good weather for tonight's trip to the hill, doesn't it?"

"Yes," she replied, reluctantly admitting him. He recognized a growing distrust in her, especially since his photographing Baxter's assault night before last. He knew his days were numbered, was a little surprised he had lasted so long—well, people accepted what they wanted to accept, and they wanted to think the city editor was on their side.

"How's Giovanni? Will he be able to go out?"

"He's doing well, but I don't think we'll risk it." She sighed, rubbing her medallion. "It's a delicate business, Mr. Miller."

He agreed with that solemnly, and they passed through the meeting room and dining room into the kitchen. Giovanni's door was closed, but he pushed away the thought that crowded in, accepting what he wanted to accept. Ralph Himebaugh was in the kitchen. Logs and papers were spread on the kitchen table. Ralph muttered a greeting. Another reason why Eleanor had come to distrust him, surely. Miller had always got along with the man, but, in the new context of the cult, Ralph could only hate him, whether he was being sincere or not. And now that Ralph had fallen victim, like the rest, to the informal harassment campaign on in town, he seemed to suggest he saw Miller as the man who had let the word out. A glance out the kitchen window into the backyard: Marcella was out there, mourning clothes off and now into a starchy yellow dress, bright as the bright day. She was working a small plot of earth, garden or something. When he glanced back at Mrs. Norton, he saw she was watching him. Himebaugh, too. Well, screw 'em. He smiled blankly, then, without excuses, walked out back to the girl.

The small yard was barren. Garbage pails by the back door. Small twisted fruit tree, fruitless, where Marcella sat now, back to him, on a stool. Wire incinerator in front of the alley. Fenced on one side, open to the neighbors on the other. This was his stage and something in the challenge from the kitchen, the warmth from the sun, the tug in his calves, the rumpled delicacy of her seated figure, made him shrug off caution and strut it like a cock.

The soft pulsing fine-boned feel of her shoulders—knew it, enjoyed it, even before his large hands wrapped them. The dress was fresh and crisp to the touch. She gazed up smiling—delighted, but not surprised. He had never succeeded in surprising her. Some way of divining his presence, split second of presentiment. He relinquished her shoulders, knelt to inspect her garden. They laughed at its seed-package keepers with dandelion heads, though Miller's perverse eye turned them right side up and saw something else there. His gaze traced the expressive tapering of her right forearm, resting on her crossed knee, the bone-bent turn of her wrist, the fragile fretwork of veins, fingers smudged with earth. They talked nonsense, but under that sun out on this stage with that fragrance in the soil, anything else would have sounded pretentious. Anyway, he was watching her, curious about himself. If his artless inspection troubled her, her poise and easy gaiety gave no sign of it. The poise, that was part of it. The gaiety. And her eyes, brown, doelike, yet bright and awake, and eagerness there, and love for him. But he'd seen that intense gaze, been loved before, and painlessly had turned his back. Still, there was something there, in her eyes. Sensitivity, yes, and intelligence, though he'd hardly challenged either enough to prove them. He felt then, watching her eyes and warmed by the sun, a flicker of exaggerated tones and comforts from a distant innocence of his own—yes, the innocence, the astonishing uncomplicated ingenuousness that gave her such a nice clean sphere to live in, all harmony, and with him at dead center, that must be it. And it was what had been troubling him all day, even in the heat of that frantic bull-like assault on the X-ray table: that his own motivations had become fragmented, that Marcella and Happy, the newspaper and dead buddies, West Condon and East Condon, baseball, sociology, saviors, and sex, all existed isolated under uniquely different legal systems; Ellie Norton's seven aspects hardly covered the field. And now, unexpectedly, he had knocked up against a simple yet all-embracing view whose every action was a direct manifestation of it. Purity. Saint's eyes. And, goddamn, he had a yearning to share it. He glanced down at the seed-package soldiers. Back to the garden. He had spent a decade rooting it out of himself, and here, happily in hell, he'd wandered right back to the gate.

He stood, feeling weak, and she stood to face him, sun bright on her upturned face. He realized that the decision was actually already made, had been made long before, and this was only a ritual: drawn to her sphere's center, he had long since agreed to stay. There now remained for him only to redescribe the sphere itself for her, make a few holes and let real air in; and relearn himself the integrity and continence that belonged to her view of him. He asked her to have dinner with him tonight, and she, radiant, accepted. The scene, the moment, called for an embrace, but the old cock was feeling himself public again. He was, too. A glance back at the house revealed Mrs. Norton and old Himebaugh posed rigidly in the window: stony-faced American Gothic. They had come for lunch, Marcella said, smiling apologetically, and she had to get it ready. Would he stay? Something told him he should, but he hesitated to face those two, couldn't run the risk yet of a direct showdown in Marcella's presence. He told her he had to get the paper out if they were to have dinner together, walked her to the back door.

Eleanor and Ralph were waiting for them. Marcella, smiling, slipped on by them. "Don't forget the wirecopy tonight," Ralph snapped, drumming a metal rule on his knuckles. Himebaugh had decided the evening paper was neither soon enough nor comprehensive enough for his purposes, now demanded the Teletype copy in its entirety every evening.

"And please, Mr. Miller, no photographs tonight," said Mrs. Norton bluntly, fingering the gold disc.

"No, of course not," he said. "I'm sorry about the other night. I thought I was being a help. But, if you like, I'll bring the negatives and turn them over to the group."

"I'd appreciate that," she said, but there was no melting there. He left before they could progress beyond these petty complaints to the real thing that was irking them. Off to Mick's. For charred hamburgers.

The blossoming spiritual affair between Ralph Himebaugh and Eleanor Norton was, to be sure, one of the more
fascinating products of the cult. And it was odd, because
under ordinary circumstances, they would probably never
even have spoken to each other. Both avoided others, were
excessively polite and formal when necessarily in public.
She, childless and middle-aged, was a good teacher, but uncompromising and not a popular one. He, a bachelor a few
years her senior, was a brilliant file cabinet lawyer who
avoided cases that must come to court, and Miller could
never remember having seen the guy do more than tip his
hat and mutter a delicate "hello" to a woman. But a
disaster had thrown them together, two innocents surprised in a fever, and now their logbooks, their respective
systems, were drawing their timid souls together in holy
intercourse. In fact, their two systems did fit together in
the mating posture, one embracing from above, the other
reaching up from below. The funny thing was, though,
Ralph's system was the one on the bottom.

Because they were reading each other's logbooks—
excitedly, voraciously, as though they were loveletters—
Miller had to take what was for the given moment left
over, jumping back and forth in time and between the two
authors. The disrupted chronology was no problem in
Eleanor's case, for behind her writings of fifteen years ago
there was the same essentially whole ontology that governed
her most recent messages; if there was a difference, it was
one of gradual growth, greater profundity, a stripping away
of early pseudoscientific imagery related to space travel and
biological transmutations, and an approach to that kind of
all-embracing mysticism that characterized the poets of all
faiths. But, read out of order, it was hard to make any
sense at all out of Himebaugh's schemata; their parts arose
separately from their several points of origin, founded
always in some concrete event in the world, discarded as
they curved away from each other, altered, revised with
each discovery of new data. Stylistically, Eleanor's writings
changed as a young author's might, from an early awkward

manner whose mystery was provided by broken phrases and harsh juxtapositions, through a florid "literary" period, acquiring finally her present mastery of vocabulary and syntax, a unique, albeit eclectic, style of her own. Himebaugh's writings, at least those Miller read, covered a much narrower time span, only about four years, though he had disaster clippings that were a lot older, and his writing ways were constant: pedantic, precise, and abbreviated. The only change of note was a gradual adoption of new symbols, shrinking yet more his ever-spare use of language.

There were enormous differences between them. While Eleanor was, essentially, a gentle mystic who found peace of soul in the denial of all dualisms, particularly that of life and death, Ralph was terrorized by a haunting vision of the worst half of all dichotomies, obsessed by the horror of existence *qua* existence. In Eleanor's messages from the higher aspects, Miller found, through all personal trials, an uncompromising rejection of constructive thinking: wisdom could only be intuited; contrarily, in Himebaugh's disaster scrapbooks and derivative graphs, one encountered a total commitment to the precision tools of logic, of science, of mathematics, the patient step-by-step addition of simple premises or single actions to arrive, hopefully, at complex totalities, the larger truths beyond phenomena.

So, what was it united them? Partly, to be sure, it was the lonely need for compurgators they both felt, and partly it was their mutual recognition of superior intellects. They both shared, as well, that extreme intensity in the private project that characterizes all introverts, and both had staked their lives on some unspecified but cataclysmic event to which they believed their own destinies linked—each lent credence, that is, to the other's central hope. And it was also true that, though Eleanor championed the intuitive life, her behavior was reassuringly rational, while Ralph's rationalism reached to the superreal, became a kind of rational advocacy of the irrational.

But yet it was more than that, for there was a structural objective bond between them, too, as Miller had begun to perceive in conversations with each of them separately and in watching their behavior at the nightly meetings. Requisite to any understanding of either of them, of course, was an acceptance of their canonical faith in their own private ways to truth. It was all too easy to see Eleanor's self-styled divine dispatches as mere responses, conscious or unconscious, to her own psychic needs of the given moment, and forget that she herself never doubted that they truly came to her from higher forces in the universe—by way of her gift of "extrasensory perception," as she described it. Her transports were real, and though the envisioned truth was too grand for memory to contain it, she was convinced she had brought back with her from ecstasy partial images of it, and these she and the dense world possessed forever in her logbooks. If she did not live in perpetual communion with those mighty souls of the seventh aspect, it was only because of a fault in spiritual discipline. In like manner, while composed of what looked like arbitrary first principles, founded upon ambiguities he did not see as such, flawed by the confusions of the numerologists, and limited by his emotionally derived specter, "the destroyer," Ralph's system was nevertheless for him a new science, and if he did not yet embrace the whole truth of the universe, it was only because he still lacked all the data, lacked some vital but surely existent connection—in short, had not yet perfected his system. They shared, that is, this hope for perfection, for final complete knowledge, and their different approaches actually complemented each other, or at least seemed to. Eleanor's practical difficulty, after all, was in relating her inexpressible vision of the One to the tangible particulars of in-the-world existence, and it was here where Himebaugh's constructions and proofs, founded on the cold data of newspaper reports, seemed to be of value, providing her shortcuts, as it were, to the relevant material within the impossible superfluity of sense-data, and enriching her own vision with new and useful kinds of imagery. Similarly, Himebaugh's major frustration, as he had explained it some time ago to Miller, was that his additive process never

311

seemed to end, it was apparently impossible ever to ascend to that last telling sum, and he had welcomed this final figure, so-called, toward which he could more accurately direct his computations.

Moreover, for Ralph Himebaugh, the One, if his universe of screaming particles could be so described, was the mindless spreading blot of death—the emptiness was not beautiful but black—and Eleanor, the mystagogue, had provided Ralph, the beloved disciple, a new kind of hope: if that blot, what she called "density" or the "force of darkness," were indeed mindless and random, how did he account for the very mathematical system he himself employed? If all were haphazard, where did order, however tenuous it might seem, come from? If all were irrational, how explain reason? As day, she covered and penetrated his night. Couldn't he see that there must be an affirmative, an ascendant, a disciplining force in the universe? That if there were darkness and density, there must also be light?

Light: not the image but the substance radiates within her, from her. These weeks she has dutifully cloaked it in black to hide it from the mourners, from Mama, from Rosalia and the prying dark-eyed neighbor ladies, from the old priest, from the fearful many who congregate now at her brother's bed. Papa died and she could not weep, for sheer joy had overwhelmed her. The wailing widowed women omen the end, but for her it is a magnificent commencement. Only Eleanor has understood. "Love," she has told her, "is not a goal, Marcella, it is a given. Love is the soul and the soul is love. It is our irreducible portion of the Divine, of the One, of Light." Gaily, she prepares their lunch. His eyes today: how they opened! how they touched her! how they laughed! She smiles at Eleanor's gloom, impulsively kisses her cheek. "It's spring!" she whispers. Poor Mr. Himebaugh, irascible with his flu, eats without appetite. When he walked in on her this morning—the second time it's happened now, poor man—he was clearly in pain:

*how strange that common illness should travel with them
to the end! Her Mama, she knows, kneels still in St.
Stephen's, befuddled and bleak, her troubled old head
bowed to her gnarled and knotted hands, the pews sullen
and musty and empty, and would, untended, kneel there to
her death. So Marcella eats hastily, her own appetite undone by excitement, by love, and rises to go bring Mama
home, her daily midday ritual. Eleanor trails her to the
door and there says a strange thing, so strange and unexpected Marcella cannot at first believe she has heard it:
"Take care, Mama, for his mouth is the mouth of a cruel
man!" Over the gentle lady's shoulder, Marcella sees the
old lawyer, nodding paternally. Light flashes golden off
Eleanor's medallion and compassionate tears mist her eyes.
"Listen!" Marcella, though afraid, waits. "There is known
to be one among us," Eleanor whispers hoarsely, "sent by
the powers of darkness!"*

After a can of soup and a couple hamburgers at Mick's,
Miller hurried back to the office, goosed by guilt. But back
by old Hilda, he was surprised to discover all the forms
locked up and in place. Maybe they didn't need him after
all. Carl Schwartz, ink-smeared, told him the story, obviously filtered through Jones and thus elevated to a classic,
of the George Washingtons who came to the hotel and left
a deposit of shit to cover the bed if not the board, while
two paperboys lurked behind the press to overhear it. Still
another enduring contribution to American folklore: Jones
had done it again. Miller used the toilet, washed up,
glanced over the pegged layouts trying to remember what
was going into the paper, nickeled a Coke from the
machine, nodded to old Jerry the janitor as he shuffled in
for work.

At his desk, he answered a few phone messages that had
come in during his several long absences, took notes from
a book on the Dutch Anabaptists which could be turned
into a small feature piece for tomorrow's edition, cleaned
the excess clutter off his desk. Felt sleepy. Too much exer-

cise. He dragged the manila file folders out of his bottom desk drawer: they contained the accumulation of his notes on the Brunists . . . hmmm. He jotted that down: the Brunists. Hilda's muffled rhythm and the Teletype (mustn't forget the goddamn copy for Himebaugh) nearly had him dozing over his notes, when Reverend Wesley Edwards dropped in. Tweed overcoat, Sam Snead hat, leather gloves, smirking smugly around the stem of his briar pipe. Gregarious cleric of the new confession, seer of the secular Christ. All of which meant that once again the priests, having something to lose by risking the challenge, were rolling with the punch. In one breath, Edwards would ridicule "Mother Goose parsons" and boast of man's "progress toward independence from any transcendent boss," then, puff-puff on the pipe, turn right around and defend myth as "an image-language reaching out beyond the particulars of appearance toward the transcendence." Today, it turned out, Edwards was not happy about the recent millennial features in the paper, felt they were adversely affecting the impressionable young, who were asking him questions, the answers to which they weren't intellectually prepared to grasp.

"Well, Edwards, news is news."

"Even if it's from the fourteenth century?"

Miller laughed. "Well, of course, that's not why—"

"No, I know it's not why. If news is news, how did it turn out you missed that fight the other night on Mr. Bruno's front lawn?" Miller shrugged. Edwards assumed a look of concern. Pipe out. Eyetooth nibbling his lower lip. "Justin, it's just that sort of thing, I'm afraid, that's beginning to worry me."

"Unh-hunh. You think maybe we ought to use a little, uh, common sense . . . ?"

"Well." Deep flush. Puff-puff on the pipe. Edwards played the part of the Christlike servant, holding no direct power or wealth like his class before him, nor seeming to want any. But he was just more sophisticated. What had any hierophant since Aaron ever been, give or take a few awesome franchises, but a witchstick for the power man against the masses? The Reverend. "Of course, I suppose it will all be over in another month."

"Maybe, maybe not. They're already committed to the irrational, what's to make them change their minds?"

"Well, if what they think is going to happen doesn't happen . . ."

"Do you think Christ rose?"

"Well," fumbled Edwards, "yes, of course." He emptied his pipe into the wastebasket, reached into his coat pocket, withdrew a tobacco pouch. "But anyway, that's not the point, it doesn't matter—"

"Exactly! It doesn't matter! Somebody with a little imagination, a new interpretation, a bit of eloquence, and —zap!—they're off for another hundred or thousand years." Miller passed his hand over the heap of manila folders on his desk. "Anyway, it makes a good story."

Edwards gazed down at the folders. "But, Justin, doesn't it occur to you? These are human lives—one-time human lives—you're toying with!"

"Sure, what else?"

"But to make a game out of—"

Miller laughed. "You know, Edwards, it's the one thing you and I have got in common."

Edwards stood there, indignant, dead pipe in hand, glaring down at the folders. "The only difference," he said finally, curling his mouth into a patronizing smile, "is that I know what I'm doing."

They stand by his bed, Elan, Rahim, and Mana. Elan questions, her brother's nods condemn, fracturing her vision. Alone in her room afterwards, Marcella prays. She's convinced there's been a mistake, and that a new day, a new hour, will restore consonance. She does not yet, however, see how that will happen, and so pleads now for help. And meanwhile, in her garden, the sunny heads of her seed-package people wilt to a disconsolate brown.

Miller returned to the plant from a haircut and a purchase: a collar of roughly hammered pieces of old brass, primitive, magnificently simple, colors taken from the earth. The colors on her fingers this noon. Late afternoon, press run over, long but inviting night ahead. Where should they go? Perhaps his own place, a good steak or something. But on his desk, he found a pink message to call Miss Bruno. Uneasily, foreseeing that Eleanor might have spread her mothering wings already, he did so and proved himself a fair prophet. Mrs. Norton had called a small supper meeting of certain members in preparation for tonight's expedition to the Mount of Redemption, and Marcella now had to stay to prepare for it.

"You can't get out of it?"

"No." Then, hesitatingly, as though perhaps being overheard, she added, "Tonight . . . please . . . be careful!" And she hung up . . . without inviting him to the supper.

Disgruntled, he dropped the phone in its cradle. The first day of spring was fading outside, gathering to a gray chill that matched his inner turn. The thought occurred to him to drop the whole thing. His morning seemed an age ago. But he had invested three hard weeks, and he needed at least that many more to have anything really exploitable. He stared at the manila folders: yes, there was a story there. More than one. And even his struggle to stay in the group would provide him new materials, wouldn't it? It would. Then, there was the brass collar in his pocket. He took it out, held it in daylight. Did it really matter who established the choice for her? Let them do it, let them victimize him, let them crack her circle, and with patience the pieces would be his. Grinning malevolently at those two old specters in the back window, he took up the gauntlet, and, doing so, realized he had to hurry. Tonight. He'd begin tonight.

Before supper, dusk hanging still, they gather, the select. Giovanni slumps pale in the front room armchair, pale but life now waxes beneath the filigree of eggshell ribs. Eyes aglitter with the flames of early candles, they form community with him in a circle: Giovanni, Womwom, Karmin, Ko-li, Elan, Rahim, Mana. The absent one is missed silently by all. They lock hands to meditate. Privately, Mana repeats her prayer. She has felt her own security totter, fears now for what might yet come, though love has invested her with a strength none has accurately reckoned. The challenge, she realizes full well, is her own: to bring him back, to bring them back to him. Veins ripple electrically in Eleanor's temples. Both hands Marcella grips shed a damp cool clamminess: it is as though both hands were the same man's. But her brother's hand is rigid, a frozen metallic claw; Mr. Himebaugh's fidgets, squeezes her fingers absently, strokes her thumb. His eyes are closed and he shows his teeth. Eleanor gasps. Hands drop. Domiron speaks:

I call thee now to courage! Though each hour bring thee a new test, persist! Through all plights, against the blind, despite all mischief, persist! Though the powers of darkness pursue thee, yea, though they clasp your hands and share your table and strike at your innermost heart, persist! In self-denial, austere and venerative, persist! Persist, and unto new aspects shall the vernal winds of regenesis blow thee! Domiron bids you!

And so, where this night she anticipated joy, she confronts asperity and fear. Hints of betrayal. Divisions. Justin rises above the conflict, smiles silently upon it. Then, the journey to the hill: it reunites them. Her mother remains with Giovanni, the rest leave in cars: Mr. Himebaugh with the Nortons, Mrs. Wilson and Mrs. Harlowe with the Halls. Mrs. Collins, Elaine, and Colin with Carl Dean, Mr. Wosznik and Mrs. Cravens with her and Justin. His right hand rests on her knee. She takes it into her lap. It is a large hand, not coarse, yet full of strength. He glances at her, smiles reassuringly. His fingers grip her thigh, giving her strength, then he returns the hand to the wheel. The Mount of Redemption. They arrive to find it dark. Colder than they had expected. Why: they are so few! It shocks them all. Justin eases the crisis: they line the cars up facing them, turn on all the headlights. Mr. Wosznik says that he will make torches for their next meeting. They sing, but their voices are swallowed up in the night and they seem, each, to sing alone. Without her brother, they seem strangely purposeless. Mr. Wosznik and Carl Dean build a small fire, blotting out the last of the stars, but bringing a moment of warmth to their small community. Below them, past a patch of firs and naked elms, the mine buildings squat darkly, unspecific threat that somehow, in its inanimate crouch, draws tears from the eyes of the women widowed here. Only one thing seems certain: they have come to the right place. Suddenly: car lights on the mine road! They huddle at the fire and watch in silence, in fear —yes! again!—it is Reverend Baxter and all his people! More of them than ever! Cars and cars! How did they know? The Nortons insist they must get away. But they are all afraid to leave the little fire. Mr. Himebaugh is trembling. Mrs. Collins is angry with Mrs. Wilson and Mrs. Hall. Taunts and shouts from below. Justin speaks with Mr. Wosznik and Carl Dean and Colin. And still another car. But this time the driver, Mr. Diggs, comes running up the hill. The men brace for him. "Clara! Clara!" he cries. "It's your house! It's burnin' down!"

PART THREE
Passage

The second woe has passed;
behold, the third woe is soon to come.

—REVELATION TO JOHN 11:14

1

Thwock! The Black Peter administers justice upon the Evil One. Thwock! The Black Peter is tough, boy! He can really lay it on. Thwock! The Evil One bawls, but the Black Hand has gagged his filthy mouth. "Again!" the Black Hand commands. He holds pinned the Evil One. Thwock! "Switch him again, Paulie! Right on the peewee!" *Thwock!*

The Black Piggy is a sissy. A scaredy-cat. She administers justice like a baby. She always cries and runs away. Boy! they'll get her now! They'll make blood come.

They tell the Cravens boy if he will stop crying they will let him go home. He stops, but he keeps choking like. The Black Hand peeks out the shed door. "All clear!" he whispers. "Now, you shut up, Davey, and not a word, or we'll deal with you again!"

"We mean it!" the Black Peter avers, whistling the switch through the air. But they're not scared, because Davey Cravens is just three and hardly talks yet.

The Evil One, sobbing remorsefully, leaves. "Good job, Black Peter!" says the Black Hand. The Black Peter, swelling with pride, switches an old inner tube. Carefully, the Black Hand pushes his own hand out his sweater sleeve and slips the black one into a paper sack. The black one is beginning to fall apart. Already, the little finger has got lost and pieces chip off all the time. "Button up, Paulie."

When the Evil One is out of sight, the Black Hand and the Black Peter, now disguised as Nat and Paulie Baxter, slip out of the shed and down the alley toward home, discussing proper retribution for the Black Piggy and plotting further astounding adventures.

Abner Baxter, Jr., helped his Mom as he always did on Saturday mornings, burning trash, filling the coalbin, cleaning the yard, and so on. Warm sunny day, a perfect first day of spring. The ground was damp and spongy from yesterday's rain. His sister Franny was cleaning the kitchen, the other three were out playing. They got it easier than he ever did. He was already a freshman in high school, and he shouldn't have to do this kid stuff.

Junior stared into the flames of his trash fire and watched the boxes melt, flare up, collapse. He built his fires like cities, then consumed them with his fiery wrath. Sodom fell beneath the flames every Saturday, an epic, and better even than in the movies. He put ants and bettles inside the boxes, watched them scramble out and to the top, just like people running to the roof. They scurried about up there, helterskelter, until, doomed anyway, they finally tumbled off and died. Sometimes he would catch a frog for his fires. Sometimes the frog died; sometimes, like Lot, he got away.

His little sister Amanda came down the alley. She was crying. "Whatsa matter?" he asked, Not that he cared.

"Nothing," she said, and went on by. She was always crying.

A cornflakes carton tipped precariously as flames licked into its lower stories. The lettering turned cloudy black like the box, then shiny in contrast to the box. Miraculously, the carton did not fall, burned to a fragile black ash in that half-topple. Miracles happened all the time in Junior's trash fires.

His Mom came out. "I been calling you," she said.

"Fire ain't out yet." He watched her closely now for change, whenever she wasn't looking, but she was still the same. Fat women don't show for a while. It disgusted him to think about it. "Awful dry today, and you cain't take chances."

She sighed and went back in.

He'd always thought his Mom was pretty, but now he didn't think so. She was big and old. Maybe that was the kind of change that was happening.

A big black ant appeared on a milk carton skyscraper. Junior imagined it was Carl Dean Palmers. Carl Dean was a senior at the high school, a bully, and possessed by the Devil. He made fun of Junior in the shower room, and pushed him around outside classes, knocked his books out of his hands. The carton burned slowly, being heavily coated with wax. The wax began to melt and it made the ant run faster.

Carl Dean was having carnal knowledge of Elaine Collins. Elaine was only a freshman like himself and too young for seniors, but her Mom was arranging it. Junior's Dad all but said so, and right in church on Sunday mornings, so it had to be true. When Junior went with his Dad to sing on the Bruno lawn night before last, he had hoped he might get to see it. He wondered if only Carl Dean did it to her, or if they all took turns. But his Dad made so much noise he scared them, and they came out and got in a fight.

The ant peeked over the edge, his feelers wobbling around. He was probably thinking about jumping. Junior watched with his hand in his pocket. Last year, when Reverend Collins was still alive and everybody was friends, Junior used to go by Elaine's house at night, because she sometimes left her blinds up. The thing he always wanted to see was if she was getting hair yet like him, but he was never able to make sure. Now, she wasn't at home so much, and anyway her Mom seemed awfully suspicious suddenly about Peeping Toms. The ant stopped running. It was surrounded by torturing flames. The roof of the skyscraper began to buckle. The ant bowed its back like a cat raising its fur. Then, as the skyscraper tipped, the ant rolled into the fire. Junior tried to watch it, but he lost sight of it in the ashes. Did God watch each single Sodomite to be sure he burned? When his dad's side finally won out and they took holy retribution on the apostates and

323

impostors, Junior hoped he could be responsible for Carl Dean Palmers and Elaine Collins.

Franny Baxter knew who the "Black Hand" was. But she discovered that the two little ones were also mixed up in it, and she didn't want them to get into trouble with her father. He had preached so furiously against whoever it was, she was sure he'd just about kill them if he found out.

Her mother shuffled about gloomily in the kitchen. Franny thought she should be joyful about having another baby, but she wasn't. Maybe the truth of it was that the Sarah in the Bible wasn't happy either, her husband only thought she was, or should be—the Bible never told the woman's side of things. Maybe her mother was afraid: she wept all the time now. She was an old woman, after all, nearly forty. Franny wondered if she would ever have a baby, and, if she did, what it would feel like. She had never even had a boyfriend, but her mother always said that their father was her first beau, and she was over twenty when she met him. Franny thought she would like to have babies, but she didn't want a man very much. Unless he was very nice and very quiet and loved her just as she was. If someone like James Stewart or Gary Cooper asked her to marry him and have babies, well, she would do it.

Amanda came in, in tears, and Franny decided it was time for a serious talk with the girl. She followed her into their room. Amanda threw herself on the bed and pushed her face into the pillow. But she wouldn't admit anything, wouldn't tell about it. Franny wanted to know why they used those peculiar names. She'd never seen them in comicbooks or in the movies. "You'll get in trouble."

"I don't care."

Franny never knew how to reason with Amanda. She could handle the boys, but there was always some kind of friction between her and her sister. She gave up, went back to her housecleaning. Really, she didn't care. Let them do what they wanted to. It was little Paulie she was worried about. Paulie could grow up to be like James Stewart, if only he didn't get going the wrong way.

Junior came in then from burning trash. She watched him at the high school, always felt a pain of disappointment. He never seemed to grow up. He slouched around the halls, looking lost and scared, his hands in his pockets, his head ducked, didn't have any friends, didn't join any of the clubs, didn't study, didn't do anything. He was just a wad of nothing. And he was going to get fat. He was already getting fat.

He was glancing sideways into the kitchen at their mother. Franny recognized that Junior was going to be jealous of the new baby. Amanda and Paul already were. Only she and Nat wouldn't care. She smiled to think she coud have something in common with Nathan. Junior looked up at Franny watching him and blushed, went into the bathroom. And that was another thing. Their mother was too careless about getting undressed and using the bathroom with the door open and everything, and she still gave all three boys their baths. No wonder Junior was like he was. Franny believed simply that people shouldn't use the bathroom when other people were in there. But it did no good to argue. Not in this house. Junior didn't butt in on her anymore at least, but everybody else did.

She saw Nat and Paulie outside. Nat with that paper bag. She knew she could count on Paulie. "Junior," she called. He flushed the toilet and came out, looking kind of red-faced like he a lot of times did. "Go make Paulie come in. I want to talk to him."

"What for?"

"Never mind. Something serious." Junior was sullen, but she knew he would always do what she asked.

It was a hard thing to be the Black Piggy. She sought their admiration, but she always got crying at the wrong time and ruined it. Like when they fed that little long-eared doggy of Mister Brother Hall the hamburger with the broken glass in it. She just couldn't believe a dog could be bad like people, even if bad people touched it, and when it started to twitch so funny and drip long stringy drips of blood from the mouth, she got all sick and sorry and had to run home. And when they switched the little Harlowe girl who was just two and made her go home in the snow without any clothes on, she just couldn't stand it, it was too terribly cold, so she went right out there and dressed the girl in front of the whole world and took her home to her mother. Ow! She really got it that time! They took her into the shed and tied her on the old cot and hit her harder even than her Daddy did, because they said it had to be a blood punishment. And she had to prove to them she was as brave as they were by having a b.m. behind her Daddy's pulpit, all alone, in the middle of the day. She nearly got caught and had to jump out a window and skinned her knees all up. And after that, they had to be pretty careful for a while, because their Daddy was really mad and it seemed like he might have some idea who did it. But they let her be the Black Piggy again, instead of one of the Evil Ones.

And now today, she did it again. She wouldn't hit that little boy. He looked sick or something to her. They would get her again. And there was nothing she could do. Unless she could think of the bravest thing of all. Against the worst enemy of all.

At supper Saturday night, their parents gone, the Black Hand smells danger. Sees it in his big sister's eyes. Their parents have gone to a church meeting or something, and Junior went, too. At some hill. The Black Hand tries to beat it after, but she catches him outside. "Nat!" He slugs her in her soft cowardly gut, but she hangs on. "What's in that bag, Nat?"

"Nothing. Candy."

"Nat—"

"What do you care?"

"I know what it is. It's awful, Nat. I'm going to tell."

"Go ahead and tell. You fat old tattletale! It's nothing. See if I care."

She tries to grab it, but he kicks her in the legs, hits her on the ear. "I'm going to tell them as soon as they come home," she says, still hanging on. She's just like a pillow. You can hit her all day and nothing happens.

"You're stupid," he says. "You got red hairs on your fanny." Schemes of bloody revenge race through his mind. "You'll be sorry, you'll really be sorry!"

"Not as sorry as you."

"Who said it was anything?"

"Never mind who said."

He knows. The Black Hand always knows. That stupid little sissy baby. They should never have let her join their gang.

Franny drags him back into the house, makes him go to the room. He kicks and punches. A pillow. She pushes him inside. The Black Peter is there, looking scared.

"Piggy squealed," the Black Hand says when the door closes. "We gotta get rid of the hand."

"How?" Peter is nervous. A punk, after all.

"Let's dump it on old Widow Collins." Number one enemy. He likes that hand. It hurts to give it up. But it's getting old anyhow and a finger is broken off. He can be the Black Hand without it.

"Put it in her pants?"

"Don't be stupid! We'll wrap it up, give it like a present. We'll *scare* the pants off that old whore!" The Black Peter giggles. "C'mon!"

Through the window.

In the trash, they find a box only partly burned. They put the hand in it, wrap it in newspaper from the shed. Warm night. Stars. Thin moon, though. Good night for a job.

The Collins house is dark. So much the better. They case it, approach from separate angles, recognize each other with soft clucks of the tongue, meet on the front porch. Steps creak as they mount them. They stiffen, crouch, slip up behind the swing. Minutes pass. Still okay. They scout around. Nothing to steal. The old whore has got smart. Black Hand tries the door. Locked. Slices up the screen, opens it. Inside door locked, too. Could smash the glass. Taps it. Too much noise. Quiet night. "Got any poop?" he whispers.

"No," says Black Peter. "I already went."

"Well, keep a watch out."

The Black Hand lowers his pants, squats in front of the door where they'll be sure to step in it when they come home. The poop is just half out, when the Black Peter gasps: *"There's somebody there!"* and bolts down off the porch. The Black Hand pulls up his pants on the run and follows wide-legged after. What a mess.

Behind a tree, Hand stops, considers. Keep cool. Don't let it drop and you're okay. There'll be a place. Peter slips up stealthily. "Do you see? There, at the back!"

"Yeah, you're right. Shut up." He winces into the black night. Can't make out a thing, except some vague motion back there. "It's only a dog, I think." If it is, he's going to rap the Black Peter, but good. And then he sees it. Like a star out of place. "Hey!" he hisses. "Somebody's setting fire to the house! We gotta get outa here!"

Later, safely back in the room, the Black Peter asks, "What did you do with the hand?"

"I dunno. I don't remember."

2

Warm night in old West Condon. Still a chill there, but it was moving on. Vince Bonali, mildly looped, passed through this night, this town, on a Saturday night stroll. Spring had come on this morning hot and fragrant as a young girl in heat, and he still hadn't quite got over it: bad as a man felt, how could he hate a day like that?

He'd spent the morning puttering around the house. The thaw and the cool March rains had left a damp soggy ground, easy to work, at least the first few inches, so he had loosened it up, planted some grass seed. He had knocked together a little picket fence about a foot and a half high, had painted it a bright white, and posted a sign to keep the kids in the neighborhood from gouging it up with their war games. The big elm over his head was budding, some sparrows in it, late morning sun seeping greenly through its branches, warm on his neck and arms. It was the kind of day that used to please Vince's Mama so, break her gloom, set her mind turning about the Mediterranean and her old home there. Vince had always doubted that she could really remember it, left it too young, got the idea afterwards from calendars and fairy tales, talk with other Italians, movies later on maybe, but it didn't matter. It was enough that it contented her that Italy equaled spring days. Rocky run-up-and-down hills terraced for the vines, cool breezes sliding through the umbrella pines, spongy beaches and necklaces of seashells and towns radiant white—and the sun: *her* sun of Italy. For a long time, Vince had actually been convinced his Mama really had *owned* the sun back in Italy, part of that mythical family estate all the Italian families joked about or something. Vince, as a young guy, had always hated the idea he was an Italian, but lately, last few years or so, he'd got to thinking maybe it wasn't too bad, might even be nice to go back there, see where the old folks came from, see that sun.

After lunch, he'd gone out to admire his work, had seen that the bright little fence put the rest of the house to shame, so he'd wandered on downtown, picked up some housepaint on credit, borrowed a ladder from Sal Ferrero, and by evening had the front finished, plus a patch on the south side. Only night coming on had made him quit. Once inside, though, he'd wondered why he'd pushed so hard. Felt like ninety, not fifty, his back split down the middle from shoulderblades to ass, short pricks of pain stabbing the back of his head. Too long out of work, he was getting soft. Etta had asked him how much he'd got done, and he'd snapped back at her to stop asking dumb questions and just get the goddamn supper on. They had traded a few bad words and Angela had come in from her bedroom, had told them to stop carrying on like that, the neighbors would hear, it was just disgraceful.

"I'll disgraceful your fanny, by God, if you come butting your nose in one more time!" he had roared at her. "You've sure got awful damn wise lately, kid!"

"Don't be *vulgar!*" Angie had said, thrusting one shoulder at him and prancing back to her room. It had been all Vince could do to hold himself back from grabbing her and tanning her smart-alecky butt right on the spot.

He had shouldered on past his wife into the bathroom to take a hot shower. Had turned it up hot as he could stand it, letting it beat down, melt the hard knot of muscles bunched up in his shoulders and back, and, relaxing, had begun to regret jumping all over Etta and Angie like that. First day of spring, too. But, Jesus! he hadn't ached so much since his first day down in the mines. He had tried to explain that after the bath, apologizing to Etta, and she had understood and had gone out to see his work. Angie, too. They'd come back in saying it was going to be just beautiful, they were pretty excited about it, even made him out a kind of hero, and had been very sympathetic when he'd said after supper that he needed a walk and maybe a drink or two to loosen up.

So he'd gone up to the Eagles for a couple drinks, the place being unbelievably dead for a Saturday night, and had wandered out feeling giddy with the spring and all he'd got done that day and with a big erection from thinking about Wanda. She wouldn't be expecting him, but she was always glad to see him. He felt very goddamn good, tired but tough, and he walked relaxed but firm.

When he reached the housing development where she

lived, however, he saw that her place was dark. He guessed where she was, and that made him madder than ever. He wondered if Bruno was getting into that girl. There were some pretty wild stories going around and he wouldn't put anything past Wanda. Maybe old Bruno wasn't a complete nut after all. Might have something going there. Vince had always been secretly aroused by accounts of Black Masses.

Well, home to big Etta. He did not fail to notice that the erection had gone limp again. Maybe there'd be a good war picture on the TV midnight movie. And then he heard the sirens. Bells. Didn't seem far off, so he wandered toward where it seemed to be coming from. Began to notice a glow over the rooftops. Hadn't seen a good fire in eight or nine years, ever since the lumberyard near the railroad station went up. But a siren at night is deceptive; the chase was longer than he thought. Some ten, twelve blocks finally. He got there winded, feeling pretty sober, a crowd already gathered. He shouldered his way to the front line, located Mort Whimple, the mayor, all decked out in his old firechief's slicker. "Need help, Mort?"

"Hello, Vince. Maybe. May have to put some barricades up if this crowd builds up."

"Jesus, it's going up like a matchbox! Whose place is it?"

"Ely Collins' widow."

"Oh, yeah? Jesus, that's tough. Did she get out okay?"

"Nobody home."

Flames lapped at the dark sky. Windows were smashed. Hoses snaked around and there was a lot of shouting. There were people running up all the time, and now it was Tiger Miller, the newspaper editor. Lot of nervous drive to that guy. He showed up everywhere. Vince had always liked him. "What started this fire, Mort?" Miller asked point-blank. He seemed a little out of breath.

"Beats me," Whimple said. The guy worked his jaws funny. What was up? "She probably left something plugged in or something."

"Sure. Like a Christmas tree," Miller suggested.

Then Vince heard it behind him somewhere: the Black Hand. And with that, he suddenly remembered that the friend who had talked Wanda into joining the weirdies at Bruno's house was Widow Collins. It was all falling into place. Jesus Christ, he'd stumbled onto something! "Hey, you mean this is one of those Black Hand jobs?" he asked Whimple.

That stung the mayor somehow. Vince felt people cluster at his back. "Naw," Whimple grumped. "That's got all cleared up." And he walked away. Aha.

Just then, a couple women jumped out of a car and came busting through the crowd. He recognized Widow Collins. The other was a young girl. They went flying right at the blazing house. Vince shouted at them to stay back. Tiger Miller chased after them. The door was already busted in. All three disappeared into the house. Smoke seeping out like a kind of sweat. Vince hesitated just a moment, then, with three or four other guys at his heels, followed them in. Darker inside than outside. Spotlights beamed through the front windows. Living room wet and the windows broken, but no flames here yet. The smoke stung, but it wasn't too bad. Made him think of the mine disaster—had a brief flash of panic, then it lifted. He felt at home. The women were grabbing things off the walls and out of closets. Miller and the other guys were helping, loading up and running out. The widow headed for a back room and Vince followed. Bedroom. Fire there all right. Still, goddamn it, he almost enjoyed it. A spray of water slammed through a broken window. "Load me up!" he cried. She looked up at him, her face wild with shock—Jesus Christ! she's really mad! She yanked stuff out of closets and drawers, dumped them in his arms. He was crying from the smoke. "Let's get outa here!" he shouted. He staggered out under his load, coughing like a sonuvabitch. Somebody had spread a blanket out front near the street, and he dumped his armful on it. Ground was wet and soggy from all the water flying around. Vince dipped his handkerchief in the mud, tied it around his face. People watching agog. Lot of them now. Real community function. He recognized buddies from the mine, business guys off Main, teachers from the school, they were really piling in. Weird light from the flames playing on all their gaping faces.

Going back in, he met the rest coming out, all loaded down, all gagging. Widow Collins leaning on Tiger Miller. Didn't see the girl. Pushed on in. He heard a crash to the rear, felt a puff of hot air in his face. Christ! what an idiot! maybe he was all alone in here! But then he saw the girl, sitting on the floor behind a stuffed chair with an armful of pictures and crap. He tried to grab the stuff away from her, but she wouldn't let go, so he just grabbed her up, loot and all, lugged her out of there. About Angie's age, he guessed, though she didn't have what Angie had, and for a minute there it was like his own house was burning, the house it took him seventeen goddamn years to pay for and all afternoon to paint the front side of—he felt the pain of these people's loss, just like it was his own, knew the emptiness that would come over them when the shock was gone, and, Jesus, he felt sorry for them and let the tears, pricked out of him by the smoke, flow freely.

On the way in this time, he'd noticed something somebody had dropped by the front door, so, on the porch, he set the little girl down, picked the thing up. Just a shoebox wrapped with newspaper. The girl slumped in his arms as he helped her down the steps, and Widow Collins, standing like something dead over her sad heap of dumped possessions, watched as though she wasn't seeing anything. Oddly, she held a little porcelain Sacred Heart Madonna in her hand. Friends circled her, a lot of them bawling. Vince wiped his own eyes with his shirtsleeve.

The street was packed with townsfolk. He saw guys like Hall, Smith, Mello, Johnson, Baxter, Lucci, nodded to all of them. Lucci asked him if this was a Black Hand job, and Vince told Georgie that's what he'd heard. He listened to his answer travel out in waves through the people. He spotted Whimple and Miller in a huddle near Widow Collins, Ted Cavanaugh there, too, and he wandered over, not out of a sense of seeking importance, but because there was something reassuring about them. Cavanaugh tossed him a nod. Old football buddy.

"What do you have there, Vince?" Tiger Miller asked.

"Hunh?" He'd forget he was carrying the box. "I dunno. Found it by the door there."

He started to hand it over to Widow Collins to put with her things, but Whimple grabbed it out of his hands. Tore off the paper, opened the box, which was partly burned on the inside somehow, turned stone white and fainted dead away, knocking two guys down as he fell.

There were screams and the crowd pressed on all sides. Vince took up the box from where it fell, shook out on the blanket what was inside. A carbonized human hand. One finger missing. Same finger that Vince had lost. He felt dizzy and sat down.

People shrieked out what it was. Some girl started to vomit and Tiger Miller held her head. Widow Collins grabbed up that thing and held it high. "*Ely!*" she screamed. A piece of it fell off and everybody ducked. Jesus, the whole place went crazy! People wailed and hollered and people prayed and people got sick and people shouted and pushed, going in every direction at once, man, it was awful! Vince stared at his own hand with the little finger gone, feeling like he'd just seen an apparition. Widow Collins went completely off her bat, bleating out crazy stuff about the end of the world and the horrors of the last times, and her daughter was howling and groveling around in the stuff on the blanket something terrible. Vince, sitting still, glanced up and noticed that Ted Cavanaugh was looking down at him. Somehow, oddly, that calmed him for the moment. He sighed, got to his feet.

"Vince, you usually home weekdays?" Ted asked.

"Sure." He realized, standing, how much he was trembling. His throat was parched and his chest hurt.

"I may drop by sometime during the week, if you don't mind."

"Any time."

Cavanaugh left him then and he felt alone and the scene was just too wild for him. He had to get out of there. He pushed and bullied his way through the crowd. They seemed to respect him. He broke free, made his weak knees hold long enough to get him down the street a half block or so, then sat down against a tree. He looked back at the crowd, at the house burning. No stopping it. It was burning clean to the ground. The noise was farther off now. He began to feel a little better. The roof collapsed on part of the house, sending a big orange cloud billowing up into the black sky like a message. The sweat was cold on his face. He rubbed his hand to be sure of it. Did old Collins have a finger gone? He couldn't remember. He did recall, though, that the Preach didn't get burned in the disaster, but died trapped with Mario Juliano and the others, with Lee and Pooch. So what did she mean it was Ely's hand? Anyhow it was so small, looked almost like a woman's hand, and Ely Collins was a pretty big man.

There were a lot of guys back there in the crowd that he knew and could kid around with, but for some goddamn reason he was scared to go back. Scared of the panic maybe. At home, there would be Etta and maybe Angie, but he didn't know if he could make it. He felt weak and the street looked treacherous. He wiped his mouth, discovered he still had the muddy handkerchief tied around it. He took it off. Felt better then. Felt freer.

Damp was creeping up his ass. He stood. He was stiff from all the day's work, but not so shaky now. Then he noticed Guido Mello and Georgie Lucci leaving the scene. They lived near him. He waited for them. Mello was a chubby type, mostly nose, not too bright but a willing sort who always did his share. Worked as a garage mechanic now. Lucci, one of Vince's boys in the mine, was tall, something of a clown, but goodnatured; Vince had felt a

335

lot closer to the man since the disaster, since Ange Moroni's death, and he and Sal and Georgie quite often did things together now.

"Hey, whatsa matter?" Georgie asked. "You shit your pants back there?"

Vince had been noticing the smell, too. At the streetlight, they looked: all over his ass. "Jesus, there must have been something by that tree where I sat down," he said. He took a branch from a tree and scraped off what he could. Mello and Lucci laughed like idiots and made dumb cracks about it.

The rest of the way back to their neighborhood, of course, they talked about the fire and the hand. "You think you know what the fuck is happening in the world," Vince told them, "and then suddenly you find out there's a lot more going on than you ever guessed." They both agreed. They were pretty shaken up too. They talked about the mayor fainting away and Widow Collins going off her nut and about the end of the world and Bruno.

"Hey, you remember when we stole that wine?" Mello asked.

Lucci laughed. "What wine?" Vince asked.

"Once when we was kids," Mello said, "we stole a case of communion wine outa the church. Me and Georgie and Mario Juliano and his brother and a couple other guys. There wasn't nobody else in the place except for Bruno. He was a kind of Father's helper back then."

"Jesus!" snorted Lucci, "you remember how he puked all over the Father?"

Vince laughed with the others. "You mean on the priest?"

"We talked him into going with us," Lucci explained. "He hung back but you could see the poor sonuvabitch was lonesome and wanted to go, so we sorta dragged him along."

"We took the wine out to the outdoor basketball court," Guido said, "and opened it. Mario Juliano had snuck some alcohol outa chem lab just in case we couldn't get the wine, and now he slipped a load into Bruno's wine."

336

"Christ, he got happy as a fucking lark," laughed Georgie. "And five minutes after that he was out on his ass!"

"Then we went and told the Father," said Mello, "and he went out and found old Bruno stretched out in the middle of all that stolen wine. He tried to bring Bruno around—"

"And that's when he got puked on," Georgie said. They all laughed. It was good to have something to laugh about. "The Father really gave that poor bastard hell. I don't think he ever showed his face around the church again!"

Etta had already gone to bed when Vince got home, but he woke her up to tell her about it. He couldn't get over how that hand had been missing the little finger just like his own, and he repeated that detail several times over, until Etta told him he'd better try to forget about it. He was too tired, too excited, too shaken up, and he slept badly, but his dreams were pretty good. Several times he was in Italy with his Mama and she was very grateful. Some problems about how he got there, or how he would get Etta and the kids over, but it seemed like all of these would get worked out. That morning, he got up with Etta and Angie and went to Mass.

He calmed down, but the hand kept haunting him. Like somebody was trying to tell him something. Like maybe his days were numbered or some goddamn thing. He tried to keep busy and when the good weather kept up Monday, he crawled back up the ladder to pick up where he'd left off with his paint job. But Sal Ferrero, his arm still plastered up in the cast, dropped by, having missed the fire, and Vince came down to tell the story. He tried to explain about the hand, but Sal only laughed. "Go ahead and laugh, you bastard," Vince said, "but I got a feeling if I go back down in a mine, it's gonna get me, that's all."

Sal told him about his boy Tommy making sergeant in the Air Force, and asked how Charlie liked the Marines. "He's only wrote us once," Vince said. "He said he managed to get his ass in a sling right off the first day, but they were gonna let him come home Easter anyhow. That goddamn wise-off. He's lucky they don't flog anymore."

"Charlie's okay. He'll make out."

"Yeah, Sal, that's what I'm afraid of. Anyhow, he finally admitted there was worse food in the world than his old lady's cooking."

"That's a helluva grand thing to say. I suppose Etta loved that, being compared to the—"

"Shit," Vince laughed, "she bawled like a baby. And now she don't talk about nothing except Easter."

Etta brought them out a couple beers and joked about them being loafers and they both ought to break their necks instead of only their arms. Sal kidded back it was anyways better than breaking the old universal digitary, wasn't it? and Etta went back in laughing her big laugh.

Then, over the beers, he and Sal started chewing over the old days, about how it was to be an immigrant kid in a place so loose and without any history, about the almost daily fights with the Polacks and hillbillies and Croats, nobody understanding anybody else, about how the old folks were always saving up to beat it back to the old country, how really it kind of scared them over here sometimes, and about how the Klan started up when they were just kids, he and Sal, and all that rum and Romanism crap and the stinkbombs they set off in the church.

Sal related again how his old man came out of a tavern one night and ran into a whole goddamn mob of hillbilly Americans filled out like spooks, and how they took him out to a tree and said they were by God going to string him up, and they even tossed a rope over a branch before they finally let the poor guy go. The hillbillies stripped him and chased him bare-ass down Main Street with firecrackers and shotguns, a real goddamn party. And then Vince told Sal again how he and Angie Moroni and Bert Morani stood off seven goddamn sonsabitches out back of the high school one night after football practice, and how Bert

338

got clobbered with a piece of lead pipe and died. "Jesus, Sal!" Vince said. "I'm the only one left!" The idea sent a windy chill through him and called up again the specter of the black hand.

Sal started in then on how it was down in the mines in the old days, about the crazy things he and Ange and Vince used to do down in those gassy deathtraps, not an ounce of goddamn sense, and so on. He and Sal had talked about these things hundreds of times, so now Vince just sort of tuned out. He sat there on the soft earth in front of his car, his back to the front fender, sipping the cool beer, smoking the cigar, feeling a little drowsy in the noonhigh sun, staring up at the front of his house. Bright yellow here on the front side, sun beating off it, ground out front turned over, the little picket fence, white and cheerful.

"You know, Sal," Vince cut in suddenly. "I'm just for the first time in my goddamn useless life getting to feel like I live here!"

Sal stared up at the house too then. "It sure has took us a long time to come home, Vince."

They sat there staring awhile, finishing the beer, and listening to the sparrows fussing over their heads. Finally, they stood, shook left hands on account of Sal's fractured right, and Sal walked off, both of them saying they sure were damned glad they had had this talk, and how things were bound to work out for them in the end.

But then, goddamn it, the next afternoon he stopped by the garage where Guido Mello and Lem Filbert were working, and he got depressed again! Lem had got out of the mine just in time, and the only occasion he'd gone back down was to help with rescue parties in January. He'd come on his brother Tuck pasted up against the roof by a buggy, split clean in two, and since then he couldn't talk enough about what a rotten job coalmining was, and how any man had to be a fucking idiot to go down in one of them fucking holes just so some fucking out-of-town rich bastard out in the East could live it up on fucking twenty-dollar dinners and hundred-dollar whores. Sure made a man feel pretty sick of being what he was, okay. Vince told Guido and Lem that he for one had seen his last of it, he was through. Lem said that at last he was getting some fucking sense, and Vince went away from there feeling just pretty miserable, because he knew it was all a goddamn lie. Lem and Guido were just young guys, hardly in their thirties, they didn't know what it meant.

He tried to explain it to Wanda that night, it being one of their Tuesdays, but it was useless. As always. It really burned Vince how he had felt such a tremendous goddamn sympathy for her after the disaster, helped her all he possibly could, even gave her a little money now and then that he couldn't afford, listened respectfully to her problems—mainly that: at least he *listened* to her—and now, when *he* was having problems, all she could find to yap about was talking with spooks and having wienie roasts out on some goddamn hill and building up that nut Bruno like he was a goddamn saint or something. Vince was almost positive that bastard was getting into her now. Boy, it really pissed him off!

There he was, the whole stupid scene: stretched out chilly bare-ass on her lumpy bed in that drafty dusty shanty, still sweaty from just having made it with her, feeling so miserable he thought he was for Christ sake going to cry— and all she could find to say was, "Y'know, Vince hon, what if Lee's right here in the room with us now, lookin' on, whaddaya think he's thinkin'?"

"*Oh Jesus GOD!*" Vince roared. He shoved her away, sat up abruptly on the edge of the bed, began pulling on his undershirt. "He's probably thinking what a goddamn idiot you are to be screwing around with those lunatics!" he cried.

That woke up the baby in the crib and it started raising a ruckus. "*Now* look whatcha went and done!" whined Wanda. She sat up and her poochy belly wrinkled up like a washboard. She sure had one baggy stomach for such a skinny little girl, Vince thought angrily. The brat's screams were getting on his goddamn nerves. He kept imagining neighbors busting in on them, subject of a number of nightmares he'd had since this thing got started. He stamped over, shook the crib. It howled worse. The three-year-old appeared in the doorway. "Now, Davey, you git back in bed, y'hear? It's late," said Wanda, pulling the sheet over her belly, but letting her tits dangle. The kid stared hard at Vince's crotch. "Least ye could do," Wanda complained, "is put your pants on."

"Yeah, it sure is!" said Vince. He turned his ass to the kid's dogged stare and pulled on his shorts. This was it, man, he'd had enough.

"Now, Davey, I'm tellin' ya, git back tuh bed or Mommy's gonna paddle, y'hear?" She had to talk loud over the baby's squall. Jesus God, what am I *doing* here? Vince asked himself, buttoning up his shirt, confronted by his own utterly unreal image in the bureau mirror. He could see in the mirror that the boy hadn't moved, was still staring at him. The kid always had a lot of bruises lately, Vince noticed. Wanda probably really belted him around. "I dunno what I'm gonna do with that boy," she complained, apparently to Vince. "He needs him a daddy to teach him some manners now, I declare."

The next day being rocker weather, that was how Vince spent it. Out on the front porch, rocking slowly back and forth, thinking about that hand and feeling sorry for himself. Didn't even feel like going on with the painting. Sorry he had left Wanda in such a bluster. Sorry he was an old granddad with all his kids scattered. Sorry he was so fucking poor he couldn't even buy a bucket of paint without going into debt— No matter how they tried to cover it up, by God, the big guys still made all the dough, the little bastards knocked themselves out to get enough to pay their taxes, it was the goddamn truth. The Constitution was okay, or the Declaration of Independence, whichever it was, but goddamn it, it just wasn't getting understood proper! That was it. If the people knew what was there and used it right, those big sonsabitches would get sat on mighty damn quick. Vince thought of becoming a congressman and changing a few things, by God, or a senator or governor or something, voice of the workingman, nothing for himself, just see to it for the first time in world history that everybody got a fair shake.

So that was what he was doing, rocking there in the spring, the twenty-fifth day of March, contemplating how he'd straighten things out once he was governor, how they'd cheer, when Ted Cavanaugh's big Lincoln swung up at the curb. Ted got out, waved. Vince returned it, said to come on up, and he stretched out of the rocker to greet him, remembering then that Ted had said he might drop by this week. Ted was a rich bastard, but a good guy. They'd played football together back in high school, Vince was left tackle, Ted the best goddamn fullback in all football history. They were a real team, Ted always ran his offtackle play, the play that made him famous, over Vince: helluva great combination. Even though Ted later became a big name up at State, while Vince went anonymously down into the mines, they had always stayed friendly, calling each other by first names and talking casually when they ran into each other on street corners. In bad times, Ted had always seen Vince through on house payments and the like. He was still a powerfully built man, though his hair was thin and white on his big skull now, and there was a kind of settling around the middle.

They shook hands, said something about the weather, laughed about nothing in particular. Etta brought beers out to them. Ted kidded with her a minute, then he and Vince sat down on the porch together, completely relaxed. A good guy. They talked, of course, about the fire and the black hand. Ted had got pretty shook up too. Vince told him how the missing finger had been pestering him ever since. Ted understood. He told him a little bit

342

about what was going on between Bruno's group and Red Baxter's holy rollers. Vince didn't know about Baxter's part in it, but his chitchat in Wanda's bed had made him a mild authority on the inside workings of Bruno's gang, and he was able to impress Ted with a couple tidbits. The business about how they were meeting outside of town now, for example, and how there was apparently something kind of immoral going on over there.

They used that up and just started reminiscing about the old football team, about life in West Condon, all the ups and downs, wound up at the disaster. Vince asked if Ted had heard anything definite about whether or not No. 9 would reopen. Ted said, no, but he still had hopes. He went on to explain some of the plans he'd been working up, how he'd got the city to buy up some unused property out by the old mine road to offer rent-free to industry, how they had drawn up a proposed bill to get another highway diverted through here, how he'd talked a university group into making an objective survey of the area's industrial potential, how he and some other fellows were working up a special brochure in their spare time, and so on. Vince even began to feel pretty good. But then they drifted back to the business about the fire and the hand and Bruno and all, and they got gloomy again.

Ted sighed. "Sure going to be hell trying to impress some bigwig at DuPont or Westinghouse if they get wind of all this."

"Yeah, ain't it the truth?" Wow, that was pretty big-time! "Seems like something oughta be done." Vince stroked his chin thoughtfully. He was thinking about getting a few of the boys together and just booting Bruno's ass right out of town, but he didn't know if Ted would be too impressed by the idea.

"You know, I just had an idea," said Ted, cracking his fist—smack!—into his palm. "Something occurred to me at the fire the other night when I saw you, but I couldn't quite put my finger on it. Maybe, by God, what we need here is some kind of third force, something to bring a little

343

common sense into the community and some peace between Baxter and Bruno. You know what I mean?"

"Yeah, that might be a good idea," said Vince, staring
meditatively down at his beer glass. He wasn't sure Ted
was including him in his idea, but he thought he ought to
say he was available. "We could get the whole town in on
it maybe, get some life here."

"By God, you're right!" Ted beamed. Jesus, the guy
really looked pleased. Vince drank off his beer. "Get up a
kind of committee or something, and, like you say, the more
people the better. I think if these people saw how the
whole community felt, they might start showing a little,
you know, a little common—"

"Common sense."

"Exactly. Hey, wait! That's great! A Common Sense
Committee!" Ted slapped the porch rail. "How does that
sound?"

"Sounds great!" Vince suddenly felt very goddamn
bright, very much on top of things. "When do we start?"

"Hell, why not right now?"

"I'm ready."

"Let's see, today's Wednesday, what do you say about
Friday night? How many people do you think—?"

"How many do you want?"

Ted laughed. "That's the boy!" Vince grinned. "Where
can we meet, do you think?"

Vince thought about that, stroking his chin. "How
about the old auditorium at St. Stephen's?"

"Not a bad idea. How many does it hold?"

"Couple hundred, I guess."

"I can probably round up a hundred or so. Think we
can fill it?"

"Hell," said Vince, "we'll have them standing outside."

Cavanaugh laughed, slapped him on the shoulder. Over
Bonali. "Good man, Vince! By God, I'm glad I stopped
over!"

With Etta's help on the telephone, plus evening visits to the Eagles, the Legion and VFW halls, a couple key taverns and filling stations, and the Knights of Columbus, Vince managed to round up some hundred and twenty people who promised to show up. Ted called him a couple times to see how things were going, and Friday stopped by a few minutes to brief him on the meeting. He told him he'd got the support of the Rotarians and the Chamber board, the Protestant ministers, a couple women's groups, Father Baglione, the PTA, just about all right-minded West Condon groups. He reminded Vince again how things like this Bruno nonsense could get out of hand, produce mass hysteria, make West Condon an object of national ridicule, but Vince didn't need reminding, told Ted that was what he'd been telling the others. Ted asked him what he thought about making the mayor chairman of the committee. Vince said it sounded like a good idea. Made it plain this was an all-community affair. Exactly! Ted was really leaning on him.

As soon as Vince and Etta arrived at the Friday night meeting they found themselves surrounded by the people they'd contacted, wanting details, wanting to find out what the pitch was going to be, wanting in on the center of things and apparently figuring Vince was the route. The little auditorium was packed, must have been more than two hundred squeezing in, Jesus, it was just as good as he'd said it would be. And here in St. Stephen's, Vince and his people felt right at home. He left Etta with a gang of them, told her just to talk and keep their interest up, while he looked for Ted.

He knocked into Chester Johnson, who asked him, "Hey, Bonali! We gonna have a lynchin', baby?"

"Yeah." Vince grinned, barely pausing as he moved through. "We're gonna clean out the lousy pitch players in this town."

He worked his way over toward where some of the town politicos were buzzing around Mayor Whimple. Felt a tug on his arm, turned: Ted Cavanaugh. "Come with me a minute, Vince."

He and Ted shouldered their way through the crowd, a lot of eyes on them, respectful mumble, stepped into a little room just outside the auditorium proper. Couple businessmen in there. Vince recognized them, but had never met them personally. They turned toward him. "Maury, Burt, this is Vince Bonali. Maury Castle, Vince. Burt Robbins." Vince greeted them, gave them a hard handshake. They said they knew him. Joe Altoviti and another guy stepped into the room. Altoviti was alderman from Vince's part of town. The other guy was introduced as Jim Elliott, Chamber of Commerce secretary. "Man, Ted, that's a real crowd out there!" Elliott said.

"Vince here had a lot to do with it," Cavanaugh said simply. They all turned and looked at him. He pulled out a cigar, clamped it in his teeth, reached for matches, but Castle lit it for him. "We don't have much time," Cavanaugh went on. "I'm going to get the thing under way by stating the main purposes, telling what I know of Bruno's group and the trouble that Reverend Baxter is causing, but we'll need motions to actually get the committee set up and really functioning. Burt, Maury, can you take care of that?"

"Sure."

"Who should we make chairman of it?"

The guys in the room looked around at each other. Vince didn't see what was wrong with Ted's idea. "Why not the mayor?"

Ted seemed to think about that a minute, like he'd forgot. "Okay. Will you take care of the nomination, Vince?"

Again the eyes. Vince nodded. Castle drew the second.

Cavanaugh: "Of course, this is as much a religious problem as a civic one. Maybe we ought to have a couple vice-chairmen. Father Baglione, for example. One of the Protestant ministers maybe. How does that strike you fellows?"

346

They assented, settling finally on Reverend Edwards of the First Presbyterian, since he also headed up the Ministerial Association. To emphasize it was all nonsectarian, Elliott was charged with nominating Baglione, Altoviti with naming Edwards.

On the way out, Elliott whispered in Vince's ear, "Say, I hate to seem stupid, but what's Father Baglione's first name?"

"Battista."

Elliott grinned, clapped Vince's shoulders. "Thanks."

Vince was thinking over what Ted had said. This was a town of Christians. Catholics and Protestants. We all believe in bringing up our children in our own faith, seeing to it that they get properly oriented to the life ahead of them here in this Christian country, that they learn what's good and bad, right and wrong. It was true. That was what held them together. It was West Condon.

Back in the auditorium, Vince felt all the eyes on him. He felt a little nervous about the speech he had to make. They all seemed to sense he had some key part to play. Etta winked soberly from across the room. Turned some phrases over. Youngsters of this town. Our young people. Threat to our community and its welfare. Our Christian community. Morals. Immoral. City's leading citizen. We all know him, know we can depend on him. Sense of responsibility. Vince nodded at Sal Ferrero and Georgie Lucci. Those of us who have grown up here. Has taken us a long time to come home. Home. West Condon is our home. Our lives are a part of. He saw a lot of his mining buddies. Taken chances. Invested our lives here. Bad situation. Explosive situation. Have to put down a little rock dust. Yeah, that was it. Your first blast can set off secondary ones. Depends on the effectiveness of your rock dusting. Contain the effect. Cavanaugh thumped him on the shoulders, moved his big frame up toward the front of the auditorium to call for order. Over left tackle. Vince ground the cigar out under his heel. Teamwork.

3

Mayor Mortimer Whimple's West Condon Common
Sense Committee burst upon the scene with unexpected
force. Its impact was felt in every corner of the town, and
its repercussions carried even beyond. The West Condon
Chronicle, still silent on the activity that had sparked the
Committee, nevertheless headlined the Committee itself,
printed the texts of all speeches, reported all that it did or
said it meant to do, and the wireservices and city papers
picked a lot of it up. Old-timers could remember nothing
quite like it since the long-gone days of Prohibition and
the interunion wars. It was like the town had been slowly
dying of blackdamp and only a good sharp blast could
really clear the air. As the Committee grew, its meetings
were shifted from the Catholic auditorium to the high
school auditorium, and finally to the gymnasium. "If something like this can happen here in West Condon," the
Italian coalminer Vince Bonali said during his famous
"rock dusting speech" before that mass assembled on
March twenty-seventh, "something is wrong! It's up to us
—you and me—to find out what it is, and *set it right!*"
There was a thunderous burst of cheering and applause,
and then the Presbyterian minister Reverend Wesley
Edwards rose to read from the Bible:

> *"There are six things which the Lord hates, seven*
> *which are an abomination to him: haughty eyes, a*
> *lying tongue, and hands that shed innocent blood,*
> *a heart that devises wicked plans, feet that make*
> *haste to run to evil, a false witness who breathes out*
> *lies, and . . ."*

The minister paused, gazed out upon the crowd, closed his
Bible with a resounding snap.

". . . and a man who sows discord among brothers!"

Solidarity was the theme, but it was not complete. Some abstained, others were effectively barred. The embarrassing fantasies of the coalminer Giovanni Bruno were flouted, but no less so were "opportunism" and "extreme and fanatical fundamentalism." Neither the *Chronicle* editor nor any loyal Nazarene follower of Reverend Abner Baxter could fail to recognize he was not exactly welcome. A famous proverb became the Committee's unofficial motto, and no one doubted which West Condoners were therein being rebuked. . . .

> *A worthless man plots evil, and his speech is like a scorching fire; a perverse man spreads strife, and a whisperer separates close friends; a man of violence entices his neighbor and leads him in a way that is not good!*

The mayor and certain business leaders urged prudence and restraint, emphasizing the Committee's potential for positive constructive activities, and set up a program of community renovation, which, hopefully, would establish a base of Christian fellowship and prosperity here that would make "these other sentiments" seem silly and inconsequential. The Ministerial Association together with the Roman Catholic Church issued a joint resolution on the first day of April calling all citizens to join them in a renewal of basic Christian faith and to make this Easter season an occasion for recovering those values and aspirations that had made this nation great and brought justifiable honor to it. It all made sense, good old-fashioned American *common* sense, and the townsfolk of West Condon went for it, few doubting the while that things would be so dull as the mayor and the business leaders seemed to think. Subcommittees were set up, plans made, responsibilities given.

Meanwhile, attacked on one side by the violent powers

of darkness, reviled on the other by a thickening mass of ignorance and prejudice, and even, as some feared, threatened from within by subversive or weakhearted elements, the followers of Giovanni Bruno decided it was time, as the former coalmine. Ben Wosznik put it, to brattice themselves off, to retire entirely from public view. "When something goes off," he said, "your first impulse is to beat it for the nearest exit. But you can't tell from where you are just where it happened, and you may end up running right into the middle of the worst of it. It's almost usually better to find you a safe place, wall it up, and wait there." Domiron concurred:

Imitate the prophet!

They determined to avoid all conflict, to vary and keep secret the time and place of their meetings, to seek for the moment no new members, and to prepare quietly, each in his own way, for the personal test that awaited them all on the nineteenth of April.

"Those who are ready will come without our seeking them," Eleanor Norton told them all, and they were quick to agree. "Let us only be certain to be prepared for them."

The lawyer Ralph Himebaugh introduced hand signals and special tunics to go with the White Bird password and, with Mrs. Norton and Mrs. Collins, redesigned the altar and developed a meeting format. His new tunics, which the women made and which they all wore at their gatherings now, were white (the White Bird, the Coming of Light) with brown (Bruno) ropes at the waist, and, embroidered in brown on the breast, a large circle (Evening Circle, a Circle of Evenings) enclosing a miner's pick, stylized to resemble a cross. The dimensions of this pick/cross were numerologically determined: seven units each for the arms and head, twelve units for the post or handle, totaling thirty-three, the life in years of Christ, not to mention an entire history of secondary meanings derived from important ancient writings. A banner was designed with the same emblem as the robes with the addition of a white bird flying above the embroidered cross and circle.

And there was given them to each one a white robe; and it was said unto them, that they should rest yet for a little time . . .

Mr. Himebaugh also designed a secret cross, utilizing the new secret name suggested to the group by their scribe and secretary Mr. Justin Miller, the "Brunists," in which the *T* of the name was the cross itself, with *BRUNI* across the top of the crossarm and an *S* on each side of the post under the arm. The *U*, being the middle letter of the five on top, had the effect by enlargement of turning the cross or *T* into a trident, suggesting the Trinity and other significant trichotomies, as well as the horns of the Ram, with *BR* to the left and *NI* to the right. Giving these letters their alphabet value in numbers, the number of the cross itself became 20; across the top, the numbers read 2—18—21—14—9, with two 19's below, on each side of the cross. The *U*'s number of 21 on top and in the middle was identified not only as three sevens, with all that meant, but also as 21 March, the first day of the sign of rebirth and the night Mrs. Collins' house burned, marking mystically the commencement of this their final trial; similarly, the 19's, repeated as though for emphasis, were quickly accepted as heralds of the 19th of April, the last day of the sign of Aries and the night the end of the world—"the ultimate transformation"—would come. Mrs. Collins, it was true, still clung to the notion this could happen, as her husband's note implied, on the 8th of April, but even she was admittedly prepared to accept Mrs. Norton's date fully if nothing did happen on the 8th. The most important number, of course, was the initial 2, which symbolized everything from the cosmic combat between the sons of light and the powers of darkness, to the two figureheads of the movement, Ely Collins and Giovanni Bruno. The number 18 was generally accepted as representing the first month

351

and the eighth day, the day of the mine disaster, but some, including Mrs. Wilson Hall, feared it omened a significant event for 18 April. The 14 and 9 of N and I also possessed a hierarchy of meanings, but the approved ones were those originally proposed by Mr. Himebaugh: the 14 stood for the number of weeks between Bruno's rescue and the end of the world (a "week of Sundays" plus a "circle of evenings"), while the 9 represented the number of the coalmine, and thus the Mount of Redemption, where they would gather for the end. But Mr. Himebaugh also added and subtracted all these numbers, introduced 7 in different and intriguing ways, gave the letters Greek and Hebrew alphabet values, superimposed elements on his own graphs and vice versa, and even integrated the birthdates of each of the members for personal interpretations. With so much to learn, there was little time left for making foolish quixotic charges upon the hostile and ultimately damned world, and in their prayers they asked only for the peace which would permit them to remain together unto the end.

And then, on the evening of Palm Sunday, the fifth of April, a surprising message was received from Domiron in the presence of all members:

Hark ye to the message from the tomb! Light comes upon the eighth! Let no evil heart block its passage Domiron bids you!

All were stunned. Mrs. Norton, as though in disbelief, looked up from what her hand had written at Mrs. Collins. Mrs. Collins turned pale. Mrs. Wilson began to tremble. "Oh, Clara!" she wept. "That's just three days!" said Carl Dean Palmers. "Friends," said Mrs. Collins, standing tall now in her white tunic: *"Prepare!"*

4

Idly, contentedly, Marcella stitches his white tunic. Dust, like a microscopic imitation of the universe, floats and revolves in the shafts of sunlight that penetrate the room through the south windows. Hanging up the phone this morning, she felt the gray unnamable anxiety that has shadowed her these last weeks let go its grip, lift, fade like a bad dream. A paradox has apparently resolved itself, and now, with her discovery of its resolution, comes a great calm. The discovery encloses a decision, yet it is so easy a decision to make—in fact, it is already made.

Miller knew he had it in his hands to heave old Water Closet around and set her on a crisis course, and on April 8, Wednesday of Holy Week, partly because he had no choice, he did it. Eight-page special on the Brunists, with photos, a 1,500-word release to the wireservices, and longer articles, previously accepted in précis, wired to three newspapers in large cities. The wireservices couldn't get enough, offered special rates for another 1,500 words the next day, plus continued coverage. He airmailed wirecopy to the weekly news and photo magazines, suggesting unique angles for each and offering complete picture coverage; similarly to the television companies, tendering his services as "consultant." Later, they'd get airmail copies of tonight's edition.

He'd been considering all along popping it on Good Friday, had thought it might be a more destructive moment. But Eleanor Norton, obviously convinced he was an infiltrator sent by the powers of darkness—and indeed, she was right, he was—had been out to get him for some time now, and he'd suddenly realized she'd set him up for the ax tonight. It was the only way to account for Domiron's sudden capitulation to the Collins faction last

Sunday night: after announcing the "coming of the light," on the eighth he had warned them to "let no evil heart block its passage." And, of course, when it didn't come, the heretic-hunt would have begun. Anyway, today wasn't bad: not only was it Clara Collins' celebrated "eighth of the month" and right in the middle of Easter Week, but it was also the Buddha's birthday, a day to "beat the drum of the Immortal in the darkness of the world."

The scene was ripe. The Brunists sat in hiding, intent only upon reaching the 19th without further harassment; Baxter and the loyal Nazarenes, furious as ever, had been effectively suppressed since the Collins fire by the Common Sense Committee and Whimple's police; and Cavanaugh's bund of Common Sensers itself had been using this time of silence to proselyte amongst belligerents and potential converts. As a result, Baxter's forces had been reduced and the Brunists were down to the hardcore members, having got no new ones since Ben Wosznik: the Bruno family, the Nortons, the two boys, Himebaugh, Clara Collins and her daughter, the Halls, Wosznik, and the widows Wilson, Cravens, and Harlowe, with eight small children among them. Not that the cult was disheartened: this paucity of believers only made them more convinced than ever of their uniqueness, their special status as God's select, and their group zeal and devotion couldn't be greater. All they needed, Miller felt, was to be thrown upon the world scene, and they'd have no choice but to "prove" themselves right by finding more people to agree with them. Baxter, too, was probably waiting for that moment, for what he needed most right now was a visible enemy. And, surely, the Common Sensers realized that, for they'd been to see Miller several times already to urge him to continue suppressing this story, and most of them had even begun to get the idea he was on their side.

His main worry was Marcella. He'd thought to have her safely out of it by now. Originally, discovering Eleanor's hostility toward him and her maternal sway over Marcella, he had thought it best to affect conviction and then tunnel out from within, share a carefully structured doubt, and then: conversion. Didn't work. Marcella's mind was complex and delicate, contained sweeping world-views that made cosmic events out of a casual gesture or a cloud's idle passage, and, in such a mind, the commonplaces he liked to use were not common at all and refuted nothing. He had even hinted at marriage and she had laughed, supposing he must be joking. Now, he was bringing it to a head. He had called, asked her to meet him here at the plant this evening, and she had agreed. He'd insisted on the urgency of it: yes, regardless of what anybody might say to the contrary, she'd be there . . . she understood, she said. And maybe, at last, she did. He hoped so. He would show her the night's edition, ask her to leave with him. He had no ring to offer, but he did have the brass collar still. He recognized that it might not be easy, but he believed, once the choice was clear to her, that her commitment to him would outweigh any other—Miller had that much faith in the gonads' clutch upon what folks called reason.

Eleanor calls with the news. Marcella tells her she is sorry. Eleanor believes it is really a blessing, a further sign. Marcella agrees. She says nothing of her discovery, of her resolution. It was Eleanor, after all, who first confused her with all her divisions of love. But now the confusion has passed, the fear has passed, for perfect love, it is true, casts out fear. Love, she instructs her needle, never ends. Prohpecy? it will pass away. Tongues? they will cease. Knowledge? it will pass away. But he who loves . . . abides in the light.

A beautiful spread! Goddamn, he had too much good stuff! Eight-column banner: BRUNISTS PROPHESY END OF WORLD! Four-column photo of the group on Cunt Hill, lit by the car lights he'd arranged and shot from the shaggy crotch by Lou Jones. Two-column mugshot of the Prophet in his new tunic, which Marcella had let him get for "inspirational" purposes. An inspirational it was:

wonderful dark head afloat in pale white light, forehead, nose, cheeks—all looked as though chiseled from granite or marble, while the uncombed black hair and dark shadows in the throat, mouth and brow seemed almost like concentric circles leading inward to the glittering black pupils of his fierce eyes. Other photos through the issue of the free-for-all on the front lawn with the Baxterites, of Clara Collins' house burning and the Brunists sifting through the ruins the next day for clues, of the Common Sensers assembled and excited, of the altar in the Bruno living room with its bizarre assortment of relics and instruments. There was an exquisitely grim three-column blowup of the Black Hand and, on the back page, some pictures from the Bruno family album, including a news photo from the late twenties of old Antonio Bruno bringing a gun butt down on somebody's luckless head during the union struggles— same glittering eyes as his boy and a grin splitting his tough lean jaws. Miller was working up ideas for a special Millennium's Eve TV documentary, if he could just sell the notion to one of the networks, and that picture of old Antonio was one he meant to use. Then, as if he wasn't already overloaded, the school board had provided him an unexpected bonus story by firing Eleanor Norton last night. He dug up a somber group shot of the board, never before used because they all looked so sour in it, and ran it with cutlines that all but made grand inquisitors of them. Except for these cum-incensed types, as Lou Jones called them, Miller's stories were essentially objective—meaning, he left it up to the reader to decide if the end might really be coming or not.

Of course, the greatest story would have to remain untold. Happy's description of Giovanni's abdominal scars had rung some kind of bell in his mind. She'd said they were all horizontal or vertical, but, though intricate, had no apparent design to them. It made him think of cracked wood and that made him think of the wooden statue of Saint Stephen in the local Catholic church—its patron. He'd first noticed it at Antonio Bruno's funeral a month

356

ago. The mere fact that it was a Roman Catholic burial had troubled Clara's people, but the excuse given that it had been the old woman's pious wish had pacified them. The strangeness of the Cathedral, in fact, was probably the only thing that had kept the Nazarenes from completely losing their heads back then—as it was, they got a sudden stiff injection of awesome grandeur that would no doubt color the rest of their days. Antonio had been properly Disneyed up for his jolly journey, it would seem, to lollypop land, his bloody nose cured and even straightened in death. In fact, it was his very artificiality, oddly giving life to the statues in the Cathedral, that had drawn Miller's attention to the boyish Stephen. Torso writhing, eyes turned inward to confront death, arms twisted up over his head, the boy was naked but for the usual loincloth—typically half-off, as though about to get raped— which hid away the prick beneath the soft girlish abdomen. Whereas old Antonio's flesh had been ivory-smooth, the boy's body was finely cracked, paint chipping off, joints separating. After Happy had tipped him off, he'd made a trip back to the Cathedral to see for himself: yes, the belly was that abstract fretwork of tiny scars she had described. Happy, when he took her there, had not only confirmed it, but located a kind of "LOF" in the right groin that had caused all the girls at the hospital to wonder if it stood for "love" or "laugh."

The whole shop caught the day's excitement. The ad force was instructed to keep quiet but to sell to beat hell, since there could be lean days in the offing. A boycott wouldn't surprise him. Cavanaugh had already told him that "too extreme an exposure" might jeopardize the paper's readership, might cause Miller to "lose contact with citizens here," and this exposure was going to be pretty extreme. The front office was abuzz with anxious whisperings and Miller overheard that a couple of the girls had been approached by somebody who had asked them to quit or at least to protest if the newspaper they worked for insulted their community or their faith. Lou Jones, long chafing for this moment and unable to grasp why Miller had waited so long, was ecstatic now that it was on, which was to say, he wore a kind of half smile and smoked cigars all day. For his typesetters in the back, it was all the same: war, markets, recipes, disasters, end of the winter, end of the world. On the other hand, his pressman Carl Schwartz was in high spirits: perhaps he saw another holiday in the making, or another bonus—or maybe it was just his elation at receiving a gift from a whore.

Once all the copy had been hooked and layouts sent back, he headed out for a quick lunch. Already feeling a little giddy with what was coming. He skipped Mick's, stopped in a drugstore for a sandwich instead, found Maury Castle and Vince Bonali in a booth there. Bonali had emerged as a new Cavanaugh protégé via the Common Sensers, and turned up on Main Street pretty often these days. Now a grin split his dark face from ear to ear.

"Hey, Tiger!" Castle boomed. "I was just telling old Vince here that story about the whore in Waterton, the one your boy laid the night after the disaster." A quick glance told Miller that the little girl at the soda fountain and two ladies at another booth had heard it, too.

"Funny thing happened last night," Miller said. "Dinah gave Carl a silk shirt."

Castle roared with laughter. "No shit!" he bellowed. "What was it, his birthday or something?"

"No," Miller said. "It would have been her brother Oxford's birthday."

There's a small green sprout in her garden. She examines it closely. No, not a weed—birth! She feels a hand on her shoulder. But not his. She smiles up at Mr. Himebaugh. He clasps his hands in front of him, as though embarrassed, makes his sad face smile timidly. Such a child, and yet he is so wise and kind. He has been almost a father to them both since their own father died, and though he eats here almost daily now, he buys all their food and has undertaken many of her own tasks. Especially those touching her

brother. "Is it a flower?" he asks. "I think so," she says.
He crouches down to see, loses his balance, steadies him-
self with a pale hand on her knee. "Yes, yes, I think it is!"
he says.

Mort Whimple was waiting for Miller in the office when
he got back, and said, glancing toward Jones, that he
wanted a quiet personal-like talk. They went into the jobroom. Miller wondered if he had heard somehow they were
breaking the story tonight. "What is it, Mayor?"

"Tiger, I just wanted to talk to you alone a minute."
Whimple was a small rolypoly man with a big nose, short
forehead, close-cropped hair, wore colorful clothes too
tight for him. Had a big idea of the swath he cut. Jones
called him Wart Pimple. "Tiger, I'm in a spot. You've
been a big help to me before, and maybe you can be again.
Even if only for a little goddamn advice." Whimple's narrow eyes got so sincere, it looked like they might cross.

"Shoot."

"Well, in a sense, now don't take me wrong, but in a
sense, I *am* West Condon, Tiger. I don't mean that in any
arrogant self-conceited way, goddamn it, you know that, I
just mean I sometimes feel this whole town inside me.
Organic like." Miller shuddered at the image. "When
something ain't functioning right, I get to feeling sick. You
know what I mean? Well, things ain't functioning right
now, Miller. And I'm feeling pretty cruddy. I'm sorry, but
that's the only goddamn way I know how to put it."

Miller nodded. "Mort, I think if you just—"

"Now, I'm getting letters. Bushels of letters. More
every day. Letters from crackpots. Letters from people who
are out to get me anyway. But, more important, Miller,
letters from sensible people here in West Condon. They
don't like this Bruno outfit. They're getting nervous about
what might happen next week. They don't like the bad
name the town is going to get if this thing gets out of hand.
They're good hardworking Christian people, Miller, who
just want to be left the fuck alone."

"Yes, I know. I'm getting letters, too."

"All right, let's face it, Miller. Bruno is a goddamn nut. I don't give a shit about your big line that if Bruno's a nut, Christ was a nut, that don't mean nothing to me. I got a feeling everybody in that whole fucking outfit is a nut, but no offense. I admit, sometimes people can get carried away by this or that. Anyhow, I don't give a good goddamn if Bruno thinks he's the Virgin Mary, but what I don't like is for the law and order in this town to get disturbed, see? People can belong to any goddamn religion they like, that's their business, that's their right, but what they can't do, by God, is turn a goddamn town upsidedown!"

"Yes, but, Mayor—"

"Don't but-Mayor me, Miller! Goddamn it! I want to make it clear how I feel. I ain't the mayor to set on my fat ass and let the town go to hell. I got a duty, I got my duty here, and I think it's pretty goddamn clear. I gotta nip this outfit in the butt."

"In the bud."

"I said *butt!* Now look, here's what, Miller. Let me be clear. I don't want to interfere with religion, see—"

"Yes, I've got that."

"Now, just *listen!* I ain't asking you to do a goddamn thing except just listen. And then tell me what you think I oughta do. I don't want to interfere with religion, but I gotta stop this pack of screwballs from blowing the lid off here. Now, wait! I don't mean *stop*, I mean, well, more like just hold them where they are. Jesus! if they'd only forget about this doom scare, so the people in this town could get settled down—"

"Mort, they can't forget, not if that's what they believe—"

"Oh, Jesus Christ, Miller! I *know* they can't! I just said, if *only*. Why can't you listen? I don't want to interfere in any way with the freedom of the press neither. I mean that, Miller. It don't mean a goddamn thing to me, to tell you the truth, but I don't want to interfere, not if it's in the Constitution. So you can go and write your goddamn stories

360

and in fact the whole fucking world can write all the god-damn stories they want for all *I* care, but I don't want to give them stupid embarrassing things to write about!"

"Listen, Mort, calm down. You'll—"

"Don't calm-down me, Miller! I'm telling you! I don't want to give you bastards stupid embarrassing things to write about! Can't you understand that? I don't want stupid embarrassing things to happen here in West Condon!"

The mayor was so red in the face, Miller had to smile. "But we're all human here, Mort. You can't expect—"

"Jesus Christ, I *know* we're all humans, Miller—what the shit do you *take* me for? But, see, I'm the goddamn mayor of these humans, and some of the humans think certain other humans are stepping over their rights as citizens of this town, and it's going to get worse. *That's* the point! *That's* what I've been trying to tell you! They want me to arrest Bruno and have him examined by a state psychiatrist and get him locked in a nutbin somewhere. But I don't want to interfere with religion, see?" His chubby face drooped, the anger flush draining away. He looked like a sad fat little dog. "Miller, please, what the fuck should I do?"

Miller stood, rammed his hands in his pockets, turned his back to Whimple. Might be the way out at that. If the guy were arrested and proven mad, even if only a few hard doubts were raised. . . . It would be one hell of a shock for her, but isn't she to get that shock sooner or later anyway? But she'd probably see it as some kind of affirmation. Some of the others might quit, but not Marcella. Could even push her over the line for good. Besides, all this time he'd put into this thing, and now just as it seemed ready to pay off, could he let them pull the plug on him? No, he couldn't. "It wouldn't work, Mort," he said, turning to face the mayor. "I know them. If anything, it'd only make them more agitated, more fanatic than ever. They expect things like this to happen as the date—"

"But, Miller, if we had that sonuvabitch in the jug—"

"You'd have twice the trouble you've got now. Bruno's not the whole team, Mort. You'd have to arrest the whole lot, and then Himebaugh would raise a storm, and there'd be hell to pay in the nation's press. God, you'd have every occult fanatic in the country piling in here!"

"I dunno, I got a feeling they're packing their bags and are on the way, as it is." Collapse was setting in. "Oh boy, sometimes I wish I was just a plain old smoke-eater again."

"Mort, let me give you the best advice I know how. No matter what Cavanaugh or the other people here in town tell you, your best move is to sit it out. I mean it. Anything else will only give you more trouble in the long run. Bruno expects the end to come on the nineteenth. That's just eleven days away, Mort. What can happen in eleven days? And, after that, it should all be over. Besides the Bruno family, there are only ten adults in this group. Why all this fuss about ten people?"

Mort Whimple sat like a waddy ball of bright-colored yarn on the leather sofa. He was quiet for some time, scratched his bur head out of habit. To the right of Whimple, the door of the darkroom was open, and Miller could see a photo of the Brunist banner hung up to dry. "But you really think we ought to just let them—?"

"I think it's all you *can* do. I'm afraid anything else will get your neck in a noose, Mort."

The mayor stared glumly at his pointed black shoes, his several chins beetling over his buttoned sportshirt collar. Finally, he stood. "Okay. Maybe you're right," he said. "But the first sign of any goddamn public disturbance, and I'm taking him in." And he stamped authoritatively out of the plant.

She breaks open the crackly package of white underwear, purchased out of the community treasury in response to the new regulations, selects white socks and a fresh white blouse, the coffee-colored skirt he likes. Entering the bathroom with these things, she perceives, out of the corner of her eye, a shadow—but when she looks more closely, there is nothing there. This sensation of being pursued by some-thing incorporeal has been with Marcella for two or three weeks now. Shapes in dark rooms. Shadows falling across her path. Disembodied sounds on stairways and under her bed at night. Sense always of a second presence, spectral and foreboding. It has worried Eleanor, who believes they must be manifestations of the powers of darkness—she, too, has been troubled more than a few times in the course of her long life. But Marcella wonders if Eleanor really grasps the intensity of her feeling, the oppressive frequency of the sensations. Frightened, she has asked Ben Wosznik to put hooks on all the bathroom and bedroom doors—but once already she has even hooked her own door at night and waked in the morning to find it unhooked. She has men-tioned it to Justin a couple times, but he only smiles at her fears. Well, perhaps she is being childish. Yes, she laughs, she has been a child about too many things. Drying, she sings to herself. The water gurgles gaily from the tub. Over her glistening body, alive and tingling to its least touch, dances the towel, a white flutter like the beating of wings. She will not be afraid.

Hilda was thundering away in the back shop, producing the bomb. Jones had gone to cover a car accident, would spend the rest of the day in bars and clubs, scouting out the reaction for features tomorrow. There was an agitated stir up front, the girls gasping and whispering, carriers arguing and trying to explain to each other what it all meant. The boy who had the Bruno house on his route was king for the night. Miller leaned back in his swivel chair, gloating over the edition. Better than he had ex-pected even, a work of art. He wished he'd had a copy to hand Whimple on his way out the door a couple hours before.

He knocked out some five or six galleys of stuff for tomorrow, taken in large part from the articles he was shipping elsewhere. He discovered he had enough photos, spacing them out, to last him right up to the 19th, though he and Marcella were in several of them. Anyway, as long as they were willing to convene out on the hill, there was no reason not to get more. Hooking the copy up, he asked the typesetters to help the other guys clean up the press after the run and knock off early tonight. He explained that they may have some busy days ahead. They offered to stay on, but he wanted them out of there. His mind was on the collar, and how to make of it an amulet against Christ and Domiron and all like fiends of the hag-ridden Western world. He planned to start out slowly, reasonably, parabolically, and if he saw he wasn't breaking through her shell, he'd throw it straight at her, hard right to that delectable midriff, the night's paper, the wireservice stories, his real motives, what he thought of her brother and all those other types, everything. He'd tell her bluntly he was through as of right now, would never go back. He loved her and wanted her to marry him, wanted her to leave the cult with him now. Tonight. No pretenses. Sounded too cold. And where did the brass collar fit in? Better write it out. He realized he was back at his typewriter, but he didn't recall having said anything when he walked away from the guys in the back shop. He rolled copypaper into his old Underwood, sat there for ten minutes, maybe longer, drumming his fingers on the keys. He wrote MARCELLA and added a comma. He heard Hilda groan to a halt. He x-ed out the comma, typed a colon. Maybe it'd be easy. Maybe he was making too much of it.

The phone started to ring and the populace to whoop and scream. He told the girls to take the phones off the hook and go on home. He wanted to lock the door after them, but couldn't until Marcella had arrived. He hoped she'd make it before seeing a copy of the paper. He helped the ad force wind up its day and get out, hurried carriers out on their routes, pushed old Jerry through his clean-up rituals.

Waiting for Marcella, he perched on a stool near the front door, behind the counter, peddling copies to people who pushed in, answering no questions, smiling absently at all comment. Most of them seemed to like it. One of his customers was Happy Bottom. Pert and fresh in spring green with a soft green cap atilt in her sandy hair, eyes full of challenge and unconcealable delight. She carried a black-bordered envelope. "Special delivery," she said, hanging on to it. "Postage in advance."

Miller smiled, trying to keep calm, hoping to get her out somehow without incident, showed her a copy of the paper. He glanced at his watch: didn't think he could make it. "Eleven more days," he said. "Christ, I'll be glad when it's over!" But he made no commitments.

She hardly glanced at the paper. "Listen, Tiger," she said, but just then Carl Schwartz and a couple other back shop guys passed through on their way home.

"Hey!" praised Schwartz, openly surveying what she had. Miller was half afraid the guy might goose her on the way by.

When they were gone, and he was suddenly alone in the plant with Happy, she said, "Tell me the truth. Am I just wasting my time?"

"No," he said, but then Marcella came through the door to contradict him. Young in a crisp blouse and the coffee skirt, a beige sweater over her narrow shoulders. Marcella gave the same distracted glance at Happy Bottom that Happy had given his evening edition, then turned her brown-eyed gaze full on him, exalting him with a soft smile.

Happy, whose eyes had not left the girl since her entrance, now tucked the envelope back in her purse. Her face was tugged gently downward in hurt, her lips parted. She folded the newspaper under her arm and clanked a nickel onto the counter. "Happy end of the world," she said softly, and left. It had to happen, he supposed, but he was sorry about it.

He sighed, got down from the stool, came around and locked the door. He asked Marcella if she would like a tour of the plant. With a smile, she said she would. Full hopeful ingenuous mouth, slight fault in the smile that perfected her face—he kissed it, felt her press up into him. Though she clung to him, he eased her away, led her toward the back. He showed her his news office, but her eyes were on him. She told him she had finished his tunic. The Teletype thumpety-clacked, repeating, he noticed, his story on the cult. They went on back, through the swinging door, to the composing and press rooms, where he pulled on a few lights, four-studded fluorescent fixtures big as desktops with blackened cotton cords, scant to the touch. He realized for the first time how dull and lumpy the back shop was, watching her pass through it. How was it the girl moved? Not a case merely of her legs propelling her, rather all of her seemed to participate at once, yet without effort, an easy light laborless motion. She seemed always to have been here, he the stranger.

On the concrete floor by a Linotype lay a small pile of lead slugs, rejected lines of type. He picked one up, showed her his type-reading trick, how you had to read it upside-down—

given into his hand for a time, tow times,

He had a talent not only for reading it at a glance, but for proofing it faultlessly as well. Had learned the knack back in his carrier days. He snapped the small rectangle of lead in two, pitched the halves into a metal bucket some six or seven yards away. She laughed at his accuracy and clapped.

Holding hands, he led her past the stone with its locked-up forms, his Brunist special, black, greasy, and all backwards. She studied it, or pretended to, her hips pressed back into the cavity between his thighs, his hands held in hers at her breasts. She fingered the long graceful arm of a Linotype, remarked on the patterns in a fontcase, asked how the old flatbed press had got its name, Hilda. He told her it was the name of the pressman's useless gun-shy bird dog. She laughed, but insisted Hilda was a sphinx, not a dog. In the basket there in front of her was the last of tonight's run, but she noticed nothing. All the time, he looked for entries, yet each mention of the subject got ignored by her. She smiled at everything he said, and he realized suddenly she wasn't really listening.

They returned to the jobroom, where he got out some Old English and set her name. She asked him to set his, too. He put twelve points of space between the two names, but she took the spacing out, pressed the type up flush. He inked it, pulled a trial. The *T* in his name was broken, and she made him change it. The next one, she liked. He pulled half a dozen proofs for her, conscious that she had stepped a pace away, was watching his face while he worked. There was the leather sofa in there and he couldn't get his mind off it. He laid the proofs out to dry. She stood against his side, cheek against his shoulder, corresponding metaphor to the proofs, to look at them. He started to put his arm around her shoulder, then remembered the ink on his hands. Some on hers, too. They both laughed, a little awkwardly, and, hands at their sides, kissed. He felt the sharp thrust of her young breasts against his ribs, felt the urgency in his groin as she squeezed into it, saw again the couch over her temple. It worked on him, undermined him. They washed at a small sink there. Apologizing for the coarse black soap, he stammered, caught himself losing his goddamn breath. Swore inwardly in a kind of amazement, then gave her the gift

She fingers each perfect fragment, turns it in the light: reds golds shadowy browns and soft brassy greens. She listens to its subtle music clashing somewhere in another century, watches astonished as it spills tumbles dives leaps in her trembling hands, flashing forth its bold prophecy of love. He takes it from her with strong hands, fastens it around her throat. An aroma present as of sacramental ashes from altarfires. His eyes from under dark brows gaze down upon her, burning her lips. She explains awkwardly, brokenly, how she loves him, accepts the benediction of his mouth. Do not be afraid, she tells him. His hands search

her body, found it trembling with a kind of wild excitement wherever he touched, her breast heaving against his, hands gripping his neck, pelvis thrust forward in immolation. Be careful! he told himself, but his hand, advancing on its own, glided down her thigh's side, then up the back, passing between her legs to animating focus and combing the cleft above it, then grasped in its broad spread the whole width of her vibrant waist. There, unheeding, his fingers poked down between blouse and skirt, seeking flesh —she reached down to one side, unhooked the skirt, and it fell to the floor at their feet. "Marcella, wait!" The plant was empty, but impulsively he pulled away, put the hook on the jobroom door, arguing with the bold thrust of his own wishbone, then turned

to face her. He looks strangely like a small boy. As she unbuttons her blouse, her flesh is stroked by his hallowing beseeching eyes. Not for one moment does she fear, not even when, as though confused, he again asks her to wait. She drops the blouse, momentarily chilled by the pace of distance between them, but the collar warms her. She encloses herself in his arms once more, pulls out his shirt so as to run her hands up his strong back

The shirt sliding up out of his trousers felt like the uprooting of his entire control system. Stop her, you ass! he cried, but their mouths were locked and his own hand was coursing hungrily down the sleek gloss of her taut and trembling hips, his nostrils filled with the sweet odors of a recent bath. No! he argued, as the couch received them, soughing gratefully. His eyes fell on a copy of the night's paper not three feet away, but his hands had already stripped her, found the place: wet with its own hot supplication. Wait! show her the goddamn paper! he shouted, as he removed his own clothes over her excited gaze. He kissed the hard erect nubs of her breasts, feeling her hands chase like a curious breeze over

his body, erect, strangely tense. She cannot believe it. She stares at it, trying desperately to understand, trying not to see the shadows gathering in all corners. "But what does it mean?" He seems drawn, spent, fearfully dark. "It means I'm leaving the cult, Marcella." Again he embraces her, but now, in terror, she shrinks from him. "It has been a mistake. But now I'm trying to undo that mistake. And I want you to undo it with me. I want you to marry me, Marcella. Right away. Tonight even. I know it will be hard at first, but—" She twists away from his grasp, her body damp with fear, cold with the shadowed wind. "But, but you promised!" she manages to cry, tears tickling her cheeks. She pulls on the skirt and

blouse, buttoning a couple buttons hastily without tucking it in, grabbed up her other things, ran barefoot to the door. He tried to block her. "Marcella, wait! I love you! Please! We'll leave together! We—we'll get a nurse for your brother—*Marcella!*" She was past him.

She runs, but her balance has been thrown, she falls, skinning her legs. Shadows chase, eyes watch, driving her forward. Rocks bite at her bare soles. She cries out, but nothing emerges from her throat. Elan and Rahim receive her, frightened—they have copies of the paper, bear them trembling. They clasp their arms around her and hold her tight, take the clothes she carries from her, lead her up to her bed. Later, Rahim brings warm soup.

Dressing, he discovered a sock she had left behind. He picked it up, squeezed it tenderly in one hand: soft and white, spongy. A small foot. A child's foot.

He went to the house, but it was locked and no one would let him in. He felt somehow oddly old and tired:

where have I taken us? he wondered. The smells of her young body lingered with him still. People stopped him to talk about the Brunists. Some protested, some laughed, some were curious, some indignant. The full Easter moon was up early in the twilit sky, but it clouded over. In his pocket, he gripped her sock. With the threat of rain, the streets gradually emptied.

One caustic star lights the black hill and a wind creeps by like death. She stands there in her tunic, silent and forever removed. Something in Marcella Bruno has revolved a final turn. Crowds gather to taunt. A cloud comes.

5

Tiger Miller's April eighth Brunist special hit the streets of West Condon like a blow in the gut. Reading it, Vince Bonali couldn't sit down. Kept jumping up, slamming his fist into his palm, making speeches at nobody. Man! it was like somebody had dropped a bomb right on Easter, right on Christ Himself! Cavanaugh called him. "Yes, Ted, I read it. It's awful." He didn't know the half of it. Cavanaugh clued him in on the stories appearing everywhere all over the goddamn country. "Jesus, Ted, it makes you sick!" But he'd never felt better. Nervous, pitched too high, feeling every minute like he had to hit out at something, but very goddamn good. Strong. In there. Knowing what he had to do. Everything seemed to be happening at once: the Committee, the Brunists, Red Baxter leading his hopped-up holy rollers all over town, Holy Week, and, as if to top it, Charlie's expected return on Good Friday. Etta had cleaned the house all over again, fed Vince and Angie on potatoes and sausage, so she'd have money for a big Easter spread. Vince was on the move all the time. He had been appointed by the mayor to head up a special subcommittee to visit the homes of miners and disaster widows, anyone in the community apt to be contacted by the Brunists. He had had Sal and Georgie and Guido Mello to help him, along with the First Baptist minister and a couple young fellows off Main Street. They had worked hard, harder than the other three subcommittees put together, had managed to visit over sixty families in a week, getting a hundred percent firm commitments from them to turn any proselyters away from their doors, and several of them had agreed to send letters to the mayor and the newspaper. Everyone thought their subcommittee was doing a whale of a job. Ted Cavanaugh had been by his place almost every day or else had called him on the phone, mainly to post him on developments, call a few new plays, and to tell Vince what a goddamn good job he was doing. Reminded Vince of those benedictory slaps on the ass Ted used to give him on the way back to the huddle after a good offtackle play, and sometimes, talking to Ted, he almost felt his butt tingle with the great sense of inclusion. Once, Vince had happened to be out making house calls when Ted had stopped by, and afterwards Etta had told Vince that Ted had chatted with her a few minutes and that apparently he had "great hopes" for Vince. "It was those speeches did it," she said with a big smile. She was proud as hell, Vince could tell. He had spoken at every meeting, reporting on calls and so on, and they always applauded after like hell.

Now, with the *Chronicle* special in the picture, Vince was invited to an emergency meeting of Committee leaders that Wednesday night. They all decided they had better try to break up the Brunists before they could get to their goddamn end. Mort Whimple refused to make any arrests yet, so Cavanaugh said they'd better go see each of them, one by one. Start day after tomorrow, Good Friday, with the weakest ones. The Halls, the Cravens and Harlowe widows, maybe Ben Wosznik. Vince went along with the idea, but he was sweating. Said he'd be tied up: Charlie was coming home that day, and, uh . . . But Ted said they needed him. What could he say to that?

Thursday interlude. *Giovedì santo.* Ninth of April. The Church was a flickering white, massed with lighted candles and white lilies. Together, they prayed to the Host. Murmur of sorrowful worshiping voices like a gently rocking sea. Angie, kneeling in simple pure white, prayed fervently at his side. Vince watched the words form in her mouth, slip through her moving lips. Their baby. She's a good girl, God. He prayed in silence for his daughter. Barest fragrance of incense, low hum, altar radiant. Somehow, it felt to Vince like all his long life, from his boyhood to now, was wrapped up in this moment, he was all himselves at once, here, facing the Divine. Etta placed her hand gently over his. Slowly, half-forgotten words broke in on him, caught on Mama's accent. Shadow of the priest moving among the candles, head bowed, God hovering above in the high dome like a reaching cloud. I've come back, Mama, he said to the cloud. *"E non ci inducete nella tentazione ma liberateci dal male. Così sia."*

Outside, he was encircled by a clique of dark old ladies, anxious and peering up at him, almost like he was the priest. "I don't know," Vince said gently, "I ain't superstitious. But you're right, there sure is a funny coincidence about the disaster and Bruno's operations."

"Eresia!" whispered one. *"Negromanzia!"* muttered another in an old masculine rattle, and the other women bobbed their shawled heads solemnly, fingered their rosaries.

Vince was still inventing excuses, when Ted Cavanaugh's Lincoln pulled up out front the next day. Even considered beating it out the back door. Etta went to meet Ted at the door, called to Vince from the front room. Well, hell, face up to it, he thought. Wages of sin and all that shit.

He worked up a careless smile, went in, shook Ted's hand, that of Burt Robbins, the owner of the dimestore. "Ready to go?" Ted asked.

"Sure. Say, you know, Charlie's coming home tonight, I don't wanna get held up or anything, it—"

"Don't worry, this won't take long. Who's going with us?"

"Sal Ferrero and Georgie Lucci. Sal's waiting at home. Georgie said to pick him up at the Legion Hall." Which was on the second floor over Robbins' dimestore.

"Fine, let's go. We wanted to have a minister along with us, but they're all tied up with the Good Friday services."

They said so long to Etta, hurried through the light sprinkle out to Ted's car. On the way to Sal's house, Ted remarked what a terrific woman Etta was. "You're a goddamn lucky man, Vince." Vince smiled and nodded. Be goddamn lucky to get out of this one, okay. He hoped Wanda knew enough to keep her mouth shut. They also talked about the publicity. The paper last night was even worse than the Wednesday edition, and stories, Ted said, were popping up everywhere.

They picked up Sal and drove to the Legion. The other three waited while Vince went upstairs. Pretty dead, just a few of the bachelors. He found Georgie playing poker with his old section assistant Cokie Duncan, who was as usual pretty drunk, and a few other guys. "Ready to go?" Vince asked.

"Shit, Vincenzo, I'm winning!" Georgie complained.

"Good time to quit, then," said Vince.

"Well, excuse me, boys and girls," said Lucci, getting up with a rueful sigh. "Gotta go burn a few crosses."

Another guy at the table, Chester Johnson, looked up. "Oh yeah?" Split his hillbilly face into a big smile. Bad teeth, spaced widely, gave him a beat-up look.

Vince and Georgie laughed. "Shit, I think he'd really like to," Vince said. Then he added: "Ain't nothing. We're just paying a couple social calls on some of the Brunists."

373

"Well, goddamn, Vince baby! count me in!" said Johnson, scraping back his chair. He turned to the others. "Wanna join the party?" None did. Vince wasn't happy, but decided not to argue.

In the car, Vince outlined the plan as Ted had given it to him earlier. Robbins inserted a couple remarks so as not to be left out. Shifty bastard with a razorsharp nose and tongue to go with it. Vince didn't trust him, didn't like the way he always brown-nosed Cavanaugh. "We don't want any rough talk, any threats, or any wising off," said Vince, turning his gaze on Johnson. "We just mean to explain in simple common sense why they're making a mistake that is gonna hurt them and is already hurting the community. It's Holy Week, and we wanna use the traditional feeling about it to maybe make some inroads with these people. Mr. Cavanaugh here is taxiing us around, but it's mainly our job. Any questions?"

"Yeah," said Johnson in that goddamn nasal country twang of his. "Anybody remember to bring the hammer and nails?" Even Cavanaugh grinned.

At Willie Hall's place, they got literally nowhere. They stood in the light rain at the front door and talked through the screen to Willie's wife, who said Willie was not home, while a whole goddamn bevy of women tittered and whispered in the back of the house. "We're all friends of Willie's, Mrs. Hall," Vince said, "and we just stopped by here for a minute to discuss with you both about this group you people have got that is talking about the end. We thought if we had a little—" And she shut the door in their faces.

Back in the Lincoln, wet and disgruntled, Vince suggested they maybe should have just gone on in there. His buddies backed him up, remarking that Willie was probably in there under the bed, and they could talk him out of anything. Ted shook his head, made it clear in a word that they had to keep calm, do what they could, not worry about it if they didn't succeed. They changed the subject, joked instead about what a big brute little Willie's wife was.

Widow Wilson they passed by, since Widow Collins was living there now. Since the fire. Ted told them Widow Collins had been somewhat deranged by her husband's death and was a hopeless case. Widow Harlowe, who lived in the old housing development, just a couple dozen doors or so around the circle from Wanda Cravens, let them in. She kept a neat little house, in spite of a bunch of little children. "This is Mr. Cavanaugh," Vince began, "from the bank. Mr. Robbins from Woolworth's. The rest of us worked down in the mine, Mrs. Harlowe. With Hank. We just only wanted to have a little personal talk with you about, about Giovanni Bruno and the . . . his . . ."

"Oh, that," said Mrs. Harlowe. "They ain't nothin' to talk about about that. Not 'less you wanna come'n' be members."

"Well, not likely," drawled Johnson.

"Let Vince handle it," said Sal.

"The point is," Vince continued, looking for the entry into this woman, "we just wonder if you fully understand the position you are putting West Condon into. Now, we all of us believe in God, Mrs. Harlowe, all of us in our own way, and we don't mean to interfere with that belief, with your belief, that's up to you. Only, you see, we think maybe this fellow Bruno, I mean we've all known him for a long time and he is a rather suspicious type, if you know what I mean, and we're afraid he might have got some of you people off the track like. Call it the devil, call it a little strangeness, call it how you want, but, see, he might be getting you into trouble, and if he gets you in trouble, why, its gets us all in trouble."

"Maybe," said the widow. "But maybe it ain't only trouble, Mr. Bonali. Maybe it really is the real end of the world. I know your Pope he don't like it none, but we been expecting that. See, maybe it's you all who's in trouble."

"If there was any reason for us to think so," said Ted

gently, "would we be here now?" Vince relaxed; somehow you always knew Ted could do the job, could carry the ball—he watched to see it happen. "Mrs. Harlowe, we're trying to save you from shame and embarrassment. It's not West Condon we are primarily worried about, or Bruno, or anybody else. We're worried about you personally. You and your children and your future here with us."

The widow weakened. She chewed on one reddish finger, stared out the window. A steady rain, now, fell in a tumbling hush on the low roof. "Well, I'll think about it more. I know I sure do have doubts sometimes, and even when I'm talkin' with Hank or whoever it is if it's anybody at all, why, I'm not sure I know what I'm doin'. I'll sure think about what you say, I promise."

Vince and the others got up to go. Good work. But Ted remained seated, leaned his big athletic body forward. "Mrs. Harlowe, could you make a decision right now? Could you turn away from these people and join us today, now, on Good Friday, in our efforts to keep West Condon wholesome and Christian?"

The widow hesitated, twisted her thin hands, then started to cry. Vince wanted to pat her on the shoulder, tell her it was okay, let her be, but Ted waved him off. The man sat there calmly and gazed at her. She looked up at him, tears streaming down her cheeks. "I don't know *what* to do!" she whimpered.

"Come with us. Now." Ted wasn't letting go.

"But the kids—"

"Do you have a phone?"

She nodded, pointed to the small passageway that led to the kitchen. Ted dialed his house, asked his wife to drive over in Tommy's car, gave the address. Ted and Burt talked to the widow while they waited. Vince suggested he could stay with the kids while they went on to the Widow Cravens' house, then could catch up with them there. While Ted was still considering that, Mrs. Cavanaugh arrived, smiling, to take over. Handsome woman from upstate that Ted had brought back from college with him.

On the drive around the circle to Wanda's house, Vince broke out in a cold sweat. Just so she didn't act too fucking friendly, but he doubted she had enough sense to fake anything. It was bad enough, but with that bastard Johnson along, just itching for comedy—damn! He chewed down hard on his cigar. Mrs. Harlowe snuffled all the way.

"This it, Vince?" Cavanaugh asked, slowing to a stop.

Vince squinted out into the rain. "Can you see the number?"

"This is the place, okay," Johnson said.

Mrs. Harlowe seemed reluctant to go with them, but Ted hooked one hand under her arm and she had little choice. They found the door open. Wanda would probably ask him why he hadn't just walked on in. That dumb bitch. Or: why hadn't he been coming by? Or: we done talked all this out before, Vince hon, what's the point a goin' through it agin? Sal knocked. Little Davey came to the door.

"Your mama home?" Sal asked.

The little boy just stood there staring at them. Vince had maneuvered to the rear, but the two guys in front of him for some goddamn reason stepped aside. The kid fixed his gaze on Vince: right on the fly. That goddamn kid was abnormal.

Sal beat on the door again.

"Must be out," Vince said, and turned as if making to go.

"I don't know, I think I hear somebody in there." Probably pulling some pants on. She slouched around in almost nothing most of the time, he'd noticed.

Georgie knocked, shaded his eyes, tried to see in. "Should we just go on in?"

Before Vince or anybody could say no, Chester Johnson jerked open the screen door, pushed past the kid into the house. Almost like he'd been here before, too. Old buddy

377

of Lee's maybe. Robbins and Cavanaugh edged down off the porch with Widow Harlowe, and Vince followed. Johnson came out. "Ain't nobody in there 'cept another little kid," he said.

"Let's go," said Cavanaugh. Vince was ready, damn near flew to the car. Oh man! he was glad now he'd been going to Mass! The worst was over. Vince noticed Ted was starting to keep his eye on Johnson. Seemed a little pissed off.

When Widow Harlowe learned that their next call was upon Ben Wosznik, she went white and trembly, said she wasn't feeling good and wanted to go home. Ted used the old arguments again, but this time they didn't seem to work. Vince guessed she was scared of old Ben. Maybe what he'd heard about the whips was true. When Ted drove on out of the housing development anyway, and toward the edge of town where Wosznik worked an acre or two, she almost got hysterical. Ted told her she could stay in the car if she wanted to, and finally she calmed down.

Wosznik welcomed them warmly, invited them into his shack to have a hot cup of coffee, get out of the rain. Big heavy-shouldered man, a little stooped now, the still-impressive remains of a powerful though very mild-mannered guy. Vince remembered the man from the days of the union struggles: quiet and easygoing, but one of the toughest bravest bastards in the movement. He could've gone places in the union, but always joked that he didn't have the brains for it.

"Well, what brings you boys around?" he asked, smiling good-naturedly. There was no place to sit down. Just a stove, a table, a rocker, and a cot, and the cot was taken up by a big dog, an old gray German police, who had Wosznik's sense of aging power, but not his friendliness. Johnson settled into the rocker, while the rest stood. Wosznik put a kettle on for coffee.

"Ben, we just come by, as old friends," Vince began, "to—"

"Wozz, old buddy," Johnson cut in from the rocker,

"why are you fuckin' around with them goddamn loonies anyhow?"

Wosznik frowned, looked down at Johnson, then around at each of them. "Well now," he said, "I don't like you talking about my friends like that. They're fine people, kind and sincere, and I don't think you've got any call to come in here and—"

"Mr. Wosznik," said Ted, calming the scene down, "you're right. Mr. Johnson was not speaking for the rest of us. Our only hope was that we might, as men, talk this thing over, using the common sense and good will that God gave us to—"

"Well, now as you mention that, Mr. Cavanaugh," said Ben, "I should tell you that's exactly why I'm associated with these people. We all thought it was a little funny that you folks should call yourselves a 'common sense committee,' when it was just that, common sense, that you was forgetting to use. Now, not one of you has had the common sense to come hear first what Mr. Bruno has to say. Not one of you has had the good will to listen to the other side of the story. Not one of you had the common sense to find out what it was poor Mrs. Norton believed before you went and fired her from the school."

"Maybe," said Burt Robbins, talking up for the first time. "But there's no need to now. We've read all about it in the paper. And now you'd just have to be pretty crazy to—"

"Just a minute now, Burt," Ted interrupted. Robbins' neck had started to go red, his face to blanch. Vince felt a smug pleasure at Robbins' comedown. "Well, then, why don't we talk about it right now, Mr. Wosznik?"

"I'd be glad to, Mr. Cavanaugh, on account of I think—"

"Listen, Ben," said Johnson, grinning from the rocker. "Let's not shit around. How many of those broads you been screwin'?"

Wosznik suddenly stood very goddamn tall and wide. "Get out!" he rasped. "*Get outa here!*"

Cavanaugh interceded. "Wait a minute, that's not what—"

"*Get out!*" The old man was really riled. The police dog lifted its head, snarled. Very deep in the throat.

"Now hold on, old buddy!" Johnson grinned. "That ain't no goddamn way to talk with old friends!" Maybe he didn't see the dog.

"Come on," said Cavanaugh to Johnson. "I think it's better to go." Robbins was already at the door, his eye on the dog.

"Aw, it's all right, Mr. Cavanaugh," said Johnson, rocking placidly. "We still ain't found out—"

Wosznik made a lunge at Johnson. Johnson sprang up, cocked his fist, but simultaneously the dog shot off the cot, made for Johnson's arm. Vince was the fourth one out the door, Georgie Lucci right behind him. Sounds of scuffling behind them, snarling and cursing, table falling, a groan. Johnson stepped out, a grin on his long face. "Shit, that old mutt ain't got no teeth, boys. Now, don't you wanna have that talk?"

"No," said Cavanaugh bluntly. He was plainly sore. They found the car empty.

"Jesus, she's got a long walk home," said Lucci.

"In the rain, too," said Robbins.

They all stared a moment down the muddy road. They couldn't see her. "That's enough for today," Cavanaugh said.

When all but he and Robbins had been dropped off, Vince said: "Jesus, I'm sorry about Johnson, Ted. He invited himself, and I didn't—"

"I know, Vince," Ted said. "Those things happen. Let's just hope Miller doesn't get wind of it. Forget about it." But he knew he'd chalked up a negative, and he thought he saw Robbins grin.

In walked Charlie Saturday afternoon, the eleventh, snapping his fingers, cap tipped so far down his nose he could've polished the bill with his tongue, and the door

380

hadn't even swung shut before he and Vince were into it again. Etta planted herself heftily between them, got Charlie maneuvered into the kitchen for a sandwich. When Vince asked him why he didn't show up the night before like he'd said he would, all he got from the boy was a wink. A few minutes later, Charlie passed through the living room again, sandwich in hand, tipping his cap, revealing his nearly bald head, and then—*snap! snap!*—right on out the door.

"Didn't stay long, did he?" Vince remarked sourly.

Etta sat down on the couch, big smile on her face. "Looks funny with that haircut, don't he?"

"Haircut can't change a boy."

"Vince, you're too hard on him. He's a good boy." Etta sat pleased and plump. She sighed. "I guess he'll be a big man on the town tonight."

Vince saw it was silly to carp. Anyway, it was good in a way to have Charlie home. Livened up the house. He wished the other kids would come home more often. Lots of room for them now. Grandkids and all.

There was a knock on the door.

"Jesus, he's in trouble already!" said Vince, getting up, stuffing his feet back into the shoes.

"Mr. and Mrs. Vincent Bonali?" asked the boy at the door. Holding a goddamn bouquet of flowers big as he was.

"Well, yeah, that's right," said Vince.

"Well, Happy Easter, Mr. Bonali!" the kid said with a big smile, and handed him the flowers.

"What is it, Vince?" asked Etta from the living room.

"Jesus, I don't know!" said Vince. He lugged the bouquet into the living room. "Somebody sent us this!"

"Oh my God!" cried Etta, jumping up. "It's *beautiful!*" She came hurrying over, but she seemed almost afraid to touch it. "Does it have a card or anything?"

Vince fumbled around the stems, found a little white envelope. "Yeah, just a minute." Fingers unsteady. The thing had really bowled him over. "Well, I'll be damned!"

381

"Who—?"

" 'To the Vince Bonalis, Happy Easter! Mr. and Mrs. Theodore Cavanaugh and family.' Wow! Whaddaya think about *that?*"

Etta, speechless, took the card from him and read it. "I can't hardly get my breath!" she said. "Why, it must've cost a fortune! But, but where can we put it?"

"Hell, I don't know. May have to build a new house just to have room for the damn thing!" Really, it was too great, it was a *great* thing to do! "There, let's clear off that end table, it's big enough, I think."

When Angie came home an hour later, they still hadn't got used to the thing, still kept fiddling with it, staring at it, putting the card one place or another, walking around it. She started to tell them she'd just seen Charlie, then stopped short: "Good golly, where did you get *that?*"

Vince shrugged. "The Cavanaughs," he said as casually as he could, though he felt like a goddamn blimp in his pride.

"Really?" Angie was tremendously impressed. "Gosh, Mom, Dad's really getting important, isn't he?"

"Say, Vince, that's some damn forest there!"

"Yeah, well, I told Ted he didn't need to go to so much trouble this year, just a few samples off the shelves down at his store would do fine, but I guess he didn't hear me."

Greatest Easter of all time.

Angie and Etta passed round the coffee and sweet rolls, some thirty or forty people milling through the old house. Place looked shipshape, too. Etta had worked hard getting it ready for Charlie. Outside, the front was brightly painted and grass was poking up. Vince caught Angie's eye, winked at her. He felt very damned proud of her. This after-Mass breakfast had been her idea.

"Ready for the Second Coming, Vince? Just got seven more days, you know."

"Now, you know I'm always ready, Joe. But me and

382

Georgie here, we've talked it over, and we've decided not to hold it for a little while longer yet. Still too many of you sinners around."

Vince had really enjoyed church this morning. First time he had really felt one hundred percent at home since he'd started going back regularly. Even Charlie had consented to come along, remarking in his fashion that it was a good place to search out skirts. He'd made a big splash, too, polished and shined to a spit, and Vince saw that the Marines had been good for the boy, had slapped his burgeoning beergut back flat again and given him a new stature. Angie, full of ideas, had made a cutting from the bouquet and fashioned corsages for Etta and herself, and then, just before Mass, all excited over her project, had gone along with Vince to buy the sweet rolls and to borrow an extra percolator from the Ferreros.

Mass itself had been something extraordinarily beautiful, he'd forgotten it could give a man so much pleasure, so much peace. His conscience completely clean, he had entered into this day of Christ's Rising with unchecked enthusiasm. Afterwards, Father Baglione had singled him out and, in front of everybody, had thanked him for his recent good works. His thick strong hand on Vince's shoulder, he had looked up with dark searching eyes. "*Dio vi benedica, Vincenzo,*" he had said gravely. A wonderful old man.

"Mr. Bonali, we think it is an excellent fine thing you are doing with this, how you call, Common Sense Club."

"Thanks, Mrs. Abruzzi. I really appreciate your support."

Etta moved with surprising grace among the people. She never failed to have something to say, and folks even seemed to seek her out. Cavanaugh was right. She was a great woman.

"Where's Charlie? Didn't I see him at Mass this morning?"

"Yeah, but the experience was too much for him. He was afraid he might get his halo bent around such a big crowd."

"How's he getting along in the Marines?"

"All they were able to do to Charlie was shave his head, but after Charlie the Marine Corps will never be the same again."

A big turkey was roasting in the oven in Charlie's honor, stuffed with apple dressing. Whipped potatoes, turkey gravy, hot rolls, big green salad. A man had to arrange his life, by God, so that no matter how great the present was, there was always something better sitting out just in front.

"Thanks for having us over, Vince. Nice idea!"

"Don't think a thing of it, Dom. Collection plate's there beside the door."

It wasn't until after two that the last of the stragglers pulled out. "Man, that was some breakfast," said Vince. "I thought I was gonna have to invite them to stay overnight." He kissed Etta's cheek. "Charlie here?"

"Not yet," she said. "I told him about two or so."

"You said noon. Well, as far as I'm concerned, it's his tough luck. What do you say, Angie?"

"Second."

"There, baby, you're outvoted."

"It'll take me a few minutes yet anyway. I've still got to mash the potatoes and put the rolls in the oven to heat."

Angie settled down on the floor to read the funnies from the city paper, while Vince thumbed through the sports section, glanced at the news headlines. Angie had nice legs. Lot of action in that blouse, too. She'd do all right. She was a great girl. Vince noticed a small boxed-in article at the bottom of the front page on the Brunists. Made them out to be a lot more than they were. Well, let them come and see for themselves. When they find out how Miller has been hoaxing them, maybe they'll string the bastard up.

At three, Etta came in looking down in the mouth. "I'm afraid it's all going to spoil," she said.

"Well, hell, chicken, let's eat without him."

"That's what *I* say," said Angie.

Etta stalled. "Just a couple more minutes," she pleaded. Vince stood up, put his arm around her. "Come on, Mrs. Bonali, I'm starved. If we don't start now, I'll have to eat those flowers. It will still be good when that boy gets here, no sense ruining this banquet for all of us."

Reluctantly, she let herself be led along to the table. It was all decked out with candles and fancy napkins and the best table linen. A little American flag in the middle. The front door opened. "There he is!" they all cried at once.

"Charlie! that you?" called Vince.

"Yeah!"

"Come on! You're late for dinner!"

Charlie appeared in the doorway. "Jeez, I can't stay. Got a date with a very fine number, a real pro-*test*-ant type. Man! Just whack me off a hunk of that bird, Mom, and stick it between two pieces of bread." He turned, humming, snapping his goddamn fingers, and went into the bathroom.

She's going to cry, thought Vince. Goddamn that little shit. Etta picked up the carving knife, sliced a thick slab of breast off the turkey, carried it to the kitchen. "Mayonnaise, Charlie?" she called, voice constricted, trying to hold up.

Vince shoved back his chair. Time to meet that boy head on. At the bathroom door, he lifted his hand to knock, then decided just to barge in. Charlie was sitting on the can, still wearing that goddamn cap tipped down on his nose. "Charlie, you get in there and you have dinner with us!"

"Jesus, old man, c'mon! Can't you see I'm taking a crap?"

"I don't give a damn *what* you're taking!" cried Vince. He tried to swallow down his fury. "Now, you look! Your Mom fixed a special meal today, just for you, boy, she's been planning it for two weeks, and I'm going to see to it that you eat it, you hear?"

"Look, at least close the door, hunh?"

"Now, when you're done, you get coming!"

Charlie unwound a big wad of toilet paper off the spool. "Okay, okay," he grumbled, "only just let me wipe my ass in peace, okay?"

In the kitchen, Vince found Etta spreading mayonnaise on a slice of bread. "Now, you put that away, damn it! That boy's gonna have dinner with us today, or, so help me God, he ain't never gonna step foot in my house again as long as I live!"

"Please, Vince. Don't shout." She was already starting. Big wet tear rolling down her round cheek.

"Well, okay," he said, feeling clumsy and hurt and angry all at once. "But I mean it." Angie stood in the doorway, her face pale, her lip turned down. "Now, don't you start, too," said Vince. The front door slammed. Vince ended up eating Easter dinner alone.

6

Who? Jones, Duncan, Fisher.

Poker game.

Day of the Bunny and the Risen Son.

Legion Hall, over the Woolworth.

Nothing else to do till traintime.

How? hmmm. Inebriatus. With large coins. Very large coins. But not large enough, no. And with very limber preadamite pasteboards. Jones with four of the prettiest boys in his hand he has seen all night.

"This place is deader than my hotel," observes Wallace the red-eyed Fish, he of the shiny pate and pink dewlaps. "Where is everybody?"

"Must be Sunday," responds Dunc the droop. "Raise ye three."

"So it is," Jones informs them, consulting his timepiece. "Five of the clock."

"Aha," says Wally wagging head wisely. "Morning or evening?"

"Make it five, then," ups the looselimbed Duncan, shoving two coins additional into the pot with his elbow. "Of the cock."

Fisher squints through blooded orbs as Jones meets five, raises five. "Fuck you, dear Father!" he declares parsimoniously and folds. "It is finished!"

"You are risen," Jones reminds the remaining bettor. Coke calls.

"Four infant jesi," announces Jones the eternally damned, spreading his jacks with ritual flourish. "Read 'em and lament!" Rakes in the gold and silver as Coca Dunca blasphemes beneath breath.

Jones deals, Dunc reels, Fish spiels: "I thirst."

Jones passes jug, coolly faces five: two Negroid damsels, the anus of spades, and a twosome of nondescripts. It is then he, Jones, who advances three pieces of silver, and it is they, Duncan and Fisher, who, emitting bodily threats, respond in kind.

Further negotiations are momentarily interrupted by the pitter-patter of boots on the stair.

"Hark!" soundeth Jones. "One comes!"

"Get some more money in this fucking game," smirks Fish, spreading cruel innkeeper's lips in undisguised avarice.

Indeed, such is the case: it is the jester Chester Johnson with ready if not ample funds. "By God!" he cackles. "I thought I seen a light on up here!" He is welcomed with tripartite joy: one rumbling belch apiece. "How many days you guys been up here?"

"Yea, unto forty-two generations," returns Jones and, retiring the two nondescripts from further participation, prepares to offer seconds. Of the which, Dunc reluctantly accepts an individual, whilst Walleye petitions with desperation for four.

John's chestless son, stirring the straw on knobby skull, lifts from the fundament two empty flagons bearing birds sinister, then two more, scrutinizes with beady balls. "Man! you guys done put it away!" is his typically superfluous commentary. Bald Fish produces a fifth fifth still vivifiable. This he straightarms into lean eager face, the which releases: "Well, by damn now! Whose party?" Jones nonchalantly slides four coins forward, covering the misfortune of two new nondescripts.

"Lou's," reveals the multiloquent hotelier, meeting the challenge of four.

"His last night in town. Wants some spendin' money to take with him up to the big city," is the more complex revelation of Cokedunk the old minero, and likewise replies with four, adds three.

"Hey, no shit, Lou baby? You all buggin' out on us?" interrogates Johnson, and tips bottle greedily in apparent fear of an immediate exodus.

"The eight thirty-five," says Jones, meets three, farts, raises four. "Passage is procured. It is a matter now of history."

"Aw, shit, I ain't got nothing," Fisher the flushed and fleshy affirms and fades.

Dunc eyes Jones, eyes cards, eyes Jones, eyes cards, eyes Johnson slaking interminable thirst, eyes own terminable funds. "I gotto piss," he trows and cedes. Jones gathers.

"Tonight! Well, what the hell, Jonesy? You git a offer summers or somethin'?"

"Cheese, old comrade, I have been fired."

"Fired!"

"Fired. Dismissed. Bounced. Cashiered. Exiled. In brief, this is farewell. Summarily, I have been passed the shaft."

Fisher flings five to each while curses are laid upon the head of Just-in Miller. Jones discovers two hoary old studs and a pair of sevens, promising, if not the end, at least an in. They wait. Duncan, however, returns not. Chester, still motile, investigates. "He's sawin' 'em off on the crapper'' is his not overly voluminous report, and once again they are three.

Hands pass.

Fog descends.

Gains are lost.

Heads weigh and sag.

"Hey, Lou baby," reaches Jones from afar the seedy voice, "I ain't anxious to see ye cut out, man, but it's eight-thirty."

Jones, with incredible fortitude, stands. Straight proceeds he unto the crapper, deposes the Duncan, and employs the venerable instrument. Returns.

"Say, listen, Fish, let's us see old Jonesy off, whaddaya say?" It is the irrepressible Johnson, as usual, talking.

Fish, bleary, seeks Johnson's face, nods, and "Great idea!" cries before collapsing backward to the floor.

"Well, Jonesy," Johnson concludes, "it's you and me."

"Never, my friend, have the prospects been more cheering."

Concludes, of course, is imprecise. That lean sonuvabitch never concludes. Unto the frugging station he without cease declaims. He has employed Good Friedegg in visitation upon the Brunuts and must intricately reveal the data of his consequent sainthood. "You're leavin' this fuckin' town jist in time, Jonesy. It's the goddamn end a the world in jist seven days."

"West Condom, Cheese, is not the world."

Soggy and lumped stand Jones and Johnson afoot the termite-crudded platform, awaiting Old Destiny. She arrives with a wheeze and a blackgrease groan at 9:17.

Jones boards her, as Johnson fades in a chorus of effusive well-meaning obscenities. "We'll git ol' Tiger for ye, Jonesy!" is the last he hears. The old girl leaps forward with a jolt, topples Jones over possessions. Fat conductor splits worthless goddamn sides in contemplation of the Fall. Jones recovers, shoves bill into laughingbuck's quaking midriff. "Just plant those bags somewhere," he belches, "and cram it." Then, briefcase under arm, he lurches, pissed, to club car.

Jones alone.
Meditation.
Festival still of the goddess Eastre, last year of our Lord.
Destiny's club car.
Why? The authoritative source withholds further comment.
On his butt, rye beside. High as a bloated angel.
Jones is goddamn glad to get out, says Jones. Upward and onward to the big city, man. Tips rye to that. Water Closet. Pull the chain.
Opens briefcase, flips caressingly through photos. Hayseed bandy-legs in, Jones covers. Hayseed reposes bony hunkers at distant end, minds own matters, whatever they might horribly be. Jones re-eyes photos.
Story: that fabled day of the boom's lowering, the Brunist special. Jones is in darkroom just off jobroom working up gore pix of car wreck. Enters heroic protagonist to jobroom, quiff in hand. Jones observes, unseen, through Speedgraphic viewfinder and darkroom window. Little gift, touch here, touch there, big itch all around. Protagonist struggles with conversion-from-cult pitch which twitches quiff to drop drawers, switching protagonist's premises the which can only lead to syllogistic fuck: beautiful beautiful beautiful! Jones nearly leaps ecstatic out to congratulate, but lovingly operates instead voyeuristic camera eye. Splendid prelim thrashing about very photogenic and then, little quiff delirious afloat on cloud of imminent glory sacrifice, protagonist suddenly stands off (human interest shot of deceived crotch pathetically petitioning) and resumes with unanticipated fury his from-cult brief, accenting phoniness self-delusion marriageneed and godmadness, all of it an exquisite torture, Jones the while seizing his own balls and jumping silently for joy—but then, instead of quashing the quiff, protagonist stands

390

ladylike by as she jumps into rudiments of clothing and barefoot staggers out door, and then, and *then*, O farewell manly virtues! protagonist *weeps. Ugh!*

Epilogue: Jones presents set of prints as Happy Easter Bunny oblation and receives compensatory walking papers. No goddamn sense of humor.

Jones swigging rye in club car now resumes review, confers blue ribbon on one titled "Quiff Couching at Forty-five Degrees." Hayseed passes on rubber legs, gawks, flushes. "Hey, them's purty hot pitchers you got there, mister!"

Jones belches wearily. "Three bucks apiece," says he. "Thirty silver dimes."

7

Easter Sunday, after dark. The phone rings. Eleanor Norton answers. "Yes?"

"This is Jesus Christ calling."

She blanches and those watching blanch, too. These are the Last Days and even harassment must be taken for a sign, must be exploited for concealed meaning. "Why are you troubling us?"

"I have an important message for you all."

"Why don't you bring the message personally?" She tries to be stern, but her voice fails her.

"Well, actually, that's what I'm doing. To tell the truth, I am here in the room with you right now, but you can't see me. My only means to cross the, uh, aspect barriers between us was by utilizing the electronic amplification system provided by this instrument you hold in your hand."

"Ah!" It is too reasonable to be denied. Hand covering

the mouthpiece, she explains to the others, now crowding around, all, like her, dressed in white tunics. "But what . . . what is your message?"

"We have waited too long. The publicity campaign being waged against us by our enemies is muddling up the frequencies. We cannot risk any further delays. We have decided the end, that is, the transition, must come tonight."

"Tonight!" she cries, her voice breaking with a squeak. She covers the mouthpiece. "He says the end is coming *tonight!*"

Mary Harlowe, paling, to Mabel Hall: "You *said* it could be Easter!"

Willie Hall: "As it says in the Good Book—"

Jesus: "Can you make it out to the hill in twenty minutes?"

"Yes!" Eleanor is already standing, waving at Wylie to get ready to go. She hears the sarcasm, knows it's wrong, another horrid prank, yet doubts what she knows, for how can one be sure? And there is no time to think. "In twenty minutes!" she cries to them all, not covering, and there is a flurry of activity.

"Uh, just one thing. You must rid yourselves of everything that belongs to this world or you won't be light enough to pass through to the next. Do you understand?"

"Yes, yes! Everything!"

"Roger. No possessions, no clothes, no jewelry, nothing."

"No—!"

"Eighteen minutes." (*Click.*)

She is frantic. She explains. Clara snorts. An argument ensues. Time passes. Even Wylie resists. But dare we take chances? Clara says flatly she isn't going to go stand stark naked on that hill just on account of some telephone call and Elaine isn't either. Carl Dean Palmers is strangely spotted with his acne-centered flush, but he refuses to support Eleanor. On the other hand, Ben Wosznik agrees they had better do it. They are grown-up people and common sense tells you you won't be wearing clothes in

Paradise anyhow, so why be embarrassed about it now? The widows pink and stammer, but seem to agree. Clara retorts she's not embarrassed, she just doesn't want to go put on a show for a townful of practical jokers.

The phone rings again. "Yes?" Eleanor's hand trembles. "Thirteen minutes." (*Click.*)

"Thirteen minutes!" she cries. "Giovanni Bruno! Hark ye!" He is excited, alert, fingers digging into the scruff of the old armchair. She is suddenly terrified at the realization that he will say yes, they must go, that something awry could break forever the fragile circuit, that she herself really does not believe—or was that his inner voice on the phone—?

It rings again. Eleanor shies, watching Giovanni, and Clara jumps for it. "Hello, who is this?"

"Ten minutes—"

"Don't hang up Now listen, if you are who you say you are, and if you're here in the room like you say you are, then you don't need to dial our number to reach us. Even if I hang up on you, I shouldn't be able to disconnect you, ain't that so?"

Eleanor is breathless with the brilliance of it, awed by Clara's majestic calm.

"Uh, the electronic mechanism is such that—"

Clara plunges her fist down on the cradle, gazes around at all present, then lifts it. She listens, smiles. They all listen: the dial tone . . . *burrrp* . . . *burrrp* . . . *burrrp.* They relax. Clara is praised. But they decide anyway to visit the hill.

Around town that night of Easter Sunday, April twelfth, the collective eye is on the hill. The great vernal celebration of the Risen Christ concluded, West Condon has no choice but to turn and face the week before them, the week of the Brunists, the prophesied end, the Mount of Redemption and of humiliation. For four straight days, the West Condon *Chronicle* has headlined the bizarre story. For four straight days, the city editor has exploited

393

the event in special articles and photo features released to the world. As Vince Bonali put it, talking to his buddy Sal Ferrero one day: "History is like a big goddamn sea, Sal, and here we are, bobbing around on it, a buncha poor bastards who can't swim, seasick, lost, unable to see past the next goddamn wave, not knowing where the hell it's taking us if it takes us anywhere at all." And so now, thanks to the city editor's all-round betrayal, the leaky raft of West Condon rises on a crest, and if it cannot perceive, it is at least perceived. All the way from the Antipodes to the Balearics, Curaçao to Dahomey. Wire-photos, news stories, television and radio broadcasts, those tawdry flares that randomly light up pieces of that sea, burst now over West Condon, exposing it to all the Peeping Toms of Egypt and the Fijis, the Ganges and Hong Kong . . . indeed unto Zion. A month and a half ago, it was all about coalmines and violence and economics and death, and there was an innocence about it. Today it is faith and prophecy and cataclysm and conflict, and it is outrageous. Why did it happen here? How will it be stopped? Where will it end? Luckless mariners adrift, none can know.

At Easter Sunday Evening Circle at the Church of the Nazarene, Lucy Smith is telling all the girls about the lovely new tunics the Brunists are wearing now and how the prophet's sister has neither spoken nor eaten in four days. There are rumors of something unspeakable that might have transpired between her and Mr. Miller, the newspaper editor, who has turned out to be the dark false friend that Mabel Hall found in her cards. President Sarah Baxter listens, as excited as the rest, yet oppressed by a terrible melancholy, hoping only that Abner is not listening in on them again. She feels so inadequate, *is* inadequate, and Abner has so reviled her for it. She liked Circle so much better when Sister Clara did everything, when she herself, like Sister Lucy now, was merely a belovèd anecdotist, free to have her tea leaves read by Mabel and to complain with the other girls about why the Circle wasn't better than it was. Abner has grown so distant through this struggle, so austere, so crossgrained and vindictive, she feels quite desperately alone in the world with this new life stirring like a terrible condemnation in her aged womb. She cries every day. She just can't help it. And Abner doesn't care, he doesn't even punish her for it. He just hates her.

Thelma Coates tells them now about Sister Clara's travels through the neighboring counties and how, if the world should still exist in some form or other after next Sunday (they all giggle nervously), Clara has been authorized by God Himself, she says, to carry His new word and appoint His new bishops, and, what is more, Mabel Hall believes that Brother Willie may become the bishop of all West Condon, which is very exciting news.

Mildred Gray tells them how they are all selling everything they own and sharing the money as a single community, enjoying grand banquets and who knows what all, and how one night they all ate a whole leg of lamb apiece. Mr. Himebaugh, who is a *very* rich man, has given them all his money and is selling all his possessions and they say he is a true and living saint. Of course, she says, when it's all over, they won't have a stitch to their name. If they need one.

Lucy Smith then informs them with very tight meaningful lips that, speaking of not having a stitch, under the tunics all they wear is their underwear, and Sister Thelma whispers that *she* has good reason to believe they don't even wear *that*, but she won't say more. Utterly without any reason whatsoever, then, Sarah Baxter starts to weep uncontrollably.

Earlier in the evening, before the phonecall from the man who said he was Jesus Christ, Carl Dean Palmers has attended the Baptist Youth Group meeting. He used to be president of it and he is still very much looked up to. He is courageous in his questioning, and yet at the same time he is not conceited about being a senior and is not ashamed to believe, not ashamed to pray. Ashamed of Jesus! that dear Friend/On whom my hopes of heaven depend? Not Carl Dean! Tonight, as usual, Carl Dean has pressed the claims of his new affiliation. Reverend Cummins, who has always made it very difficult for him and has even threatened to bar him from attendance at the BYG meetings, was not there, so the eight kids who showed up were glad to listen to Carl Dean. "What have you got to lose?" he asked them. "You don't even have to come until next Saturday, if you don't want to, and you can all come together so you won't feel alone. Listen, you got nothing to do next weekend anyhow. And what if it's true? What if it really happens? You don't want to miss out, do you?" They did not! And he reminded them how he was never one to get mixed up in anything crazy, was he? And he told them again how swell all the people were and how, if anybody in town just tried to get the least bit smart with them, they'd take care of them, and then he prayed out loud that they all find the grace in their hearts to be saved in this moment of trial, and with that they agreed to come. Saturday night. Carl Dean said he would get them all the materials they needed, and the girls promised to make the robes. They were very impressed and excited about the robes. He told them that there were many secrets they would learn, and, as a starter, he taught them the secret password and one of Mr. Wosznik's new songs:

> *March on! march on, ye Brunists!*
> *March on and fear no loss!*
> *March on beneath thy banner,*
> *The Circle and the Cross!*
> *In spite of all adversity,*
> *March out upon that mine!*
> *The Cross within the Circle*
> *Will make the vict'ry thine!*

March on! march on, ye Brunists!
Forever shall we live!
The Cross within the Circle
Will us God's Glory give!
So know ye are the chosen,
The gold among the dross!
March on beneath thy banner,
The Circle and the Cross!

And now, marched to the Mount (from their cars at the foot of the hill), standing courageously atop their origins and confronting a hostile world, dressed in pure white tunics embroidered in brown and tied at the waist with brown rope, the Brunists sing around a small campfire.

> *. . . Risk not your soul,*
> *it is precious indeed . . .*

Ben Wosznik, guitar strapped around his neck, wanders tall and melodic among them. How is it that this mournful and uneducated, yet strangely reassuring man can to one be a father, to another a son a brother and lover all in one? Such, one might suspect, are the sort of mysteries that lie at the heart of and propagate all faiths.

> *. . . Sinners, hear me, when I say:*
> *"Fall down on your knees and pray!"*

Fearing not the Baxters, for no man with the truth fears, yet unwilling to evoke the Last Battles prematurely, they have left the car lights off, such that the lonely fire dramatizes the fragility of God's spark in the world of men, and the holy glow that warms their hearts, as their bodies, which they soon will shed, grow cool.

"Oh, Ben!" sighs the widow Betty Wilson. "It's so lovely!"

To that, amens are heard, and even that austere schoolteacher has two tears that gleam in the corners of her gray eyes.

. . . I was a stranger there, intent upon my way,
But when I saw the crowd, I had the urge to stay . . .

By habit, and perhaps by instinct, they have always gathered near a small lone tree on the Mount, hardly more than a sprout, some distance from the grove of trees down near the mine that surely fathered it. The tree is like another member of their group, so familiar has it become: a promise and a shelter. Now, Dr. Wylie Norton, sitting as always at the edge of the group and nearer therefore to the tree than the others, chances to look up into its young branches and sees what looks like a kind of package up there. He stands, approaches it, peers more circumspectly, and, as he does so, the other members of the group watch him curiously.

He reaches up, grasps something. "That's odd," he says softly. The others crowd around. He is holding what seems to be a sort of tag, tied by a string to a bulky object above. He adjusts the glasses on his nose, squints, reads: PULL ME. Rather, he lets go of it, gazes blankly at the others. "What should we do?" he whispers in his tiny voice.

Ben Wosznik strides forward, takes a look at the tag, gives it a yank. There is a soft pop and then hundreds of white feathers cascade gently down upon their heads.

"The White Bird!" cry several women at once.

There is a rustling and whispering down in the grove of trees. The Brunists hastily stamp out the fire and flee to their cars. But before they do so, in spite of an inner certainty that this has been but another in the long succession of harrowing pranks, they gather up all the feathers.

The white bird: image of light and grace and the Holy Spirit, signal, as Eleanor Norton learned upon asking the One to Come, of a new life, another age. Has so radical a wonder ever happened before? Have mortals before been

398

invaded by beings from higher aspected spheres? Or, as a reasonable man might ask: have men, known to be basically so reasonable, ever before anticipated with such unreasonable assurance such unreasonable events, behaved with such unreasonable zeal to obtain such unreasonable ends? A thoughtful question, and the sort that a reasonable man like Mortimer Whimple, the much-harassed public servant of this quiet reasonable little community, might fairly ask. Or Theodore Cavanaugh, that most reasonable businessman, whose cornerstones for the great community are old-fashioned hard work, good will, and common sense. Or a fellow like Vincent Bonali, that good-willed hard worker of incomparable common sense, whose only request is the right to earn a decent wage and live in peace with his fellow citizens. And so another man, until now *thought* to be reasonable, Justin Miller of the West Condon *Chronicle*, has presumed to answer them with wild tales (probably invented) of literally hundreds of white bird and Virgin Mary and other spectral visitations; of ecstatics who claimed to be the living incarnation of the Holy Ghost, marrying themselves to statues of the Holy Virgin, consummating it by the nearest available proxy, and substituting their own bathwater for the blood of Christ in the Eucharist; of a multitude of monks and minstrels with their own "messages from the tomb" that led thousands to their enraptured ends; of hermits who shook empires as resurrected kings; of well-to-do folks like you and me who took to whaling themselves with barbed whips and living in nude communion, the editor's descriptions of which were rather excitingly graphic, and therefore probably obscene; of "third ages," in short, at least five or ten times a century and literally dozens of times already in this one, the so-called modern or scientific age (the editor's humorous and belittling references to messianic Marxism did at least seem reasonable to these reasonable West Condoners, if little else the editor wrote about did), with a conclusion on the Saturday before Easter to the general effect that all Christians were, in truth and by definition, as mad as March Hares, proving the editor to be, in the end, the most unreasonable man of all. Which probably explains and excuses the smashing of all the *Chronicle* windows on the night of Easter Sunday, the black cross swatched on the front door.

In the confusion of escaping the Mount, Elaine Collins and her Ma have somehow got separated, and in Carl Dean's car there are only she and Colin Meredith. By some agreement Elaine has not been privy to, Carl Dean stops for a moment on a side street just inside town and Colin gets out to take a walk. "We better go on," Elaine says, feeling a little bit afraid in such dark circumstances with nothing but this thin tunic and her underwear on, and her Ma absent.

"They won't notice if we're just a couple minutes late, Elaine. Anyhow, I got a big bunch of feathers, and we can say we stayed to pick up the last one." Carl Dean's arm slides past her neck and he grips her back kind of at the armpit. "We don't never get any time alone together. Your Ma's always watching." The cloth of her tunic is such that there doesn't seem to be anything between her back and his fidgety hand, and it keeps coming to her mind about Jesus asking them to stand on the Mount with their clothes all off, and how Carl Dean had looked at her that moment. "I—I just wanted to tell you, Elaine," he stammers, "that, well, I think you're just beautiful in your tunic."

Her heart jumps in excitement and he kisses her. She is scared, but she lets him, because she loves him. From the beginning, they have been in love. They have a lot in common and have always talked together about it all. The only trouble at first was that Carl Dean said he didn't know if it was really true or not, and then both of them suffered powerful doubts. But, in the end, they both believed, and they are glad that religion has brought them together. When he puts his other hand right smack on her leg, though, she jumps back and stops him. "I don't like boys to do that," she says, a little breathlessly, though in truth no boy ever has before. Her heart is going like crazy.

"I'm sorry, Elaine . . . it's just . . . well, I love you so much . . . and now . . . with just a week . . . just seven days . . ."

An indefinable anguish wells up inside her and she kisses him again, and, even though it makes her cry, she lets him leave his hand on her leg, and it makes them kiss harder and love each other more than ever. Her Ma was a little cool on Carl Dean at first, on account of she was afraid he wasn't a true believer. And Carl Dean took more interest in Mrs. Norton than he did in her Ma, and that didn't help a whole lot either. Elaine said, if he didn't think it was true, what difference did it make if he catered to Mrs. Norton or to her Ma? But he said he didn't say it wasn't true, he just didn't *know*, that was all, and he had a lot of faith in Mrs. Norton. After all, he knew her first, and even her Ma said she was a great lady, didn't she? But finally he came to believe more in her Ma and now her Ma likes him okay. "We better go," Elaine says, partly because her leg is starting to hurt, he's grabbing it so hard, "or Ma'll be mad."

"Just kiss me one more time, Elaine," he whispers, taking his hand off her leg to wet one finger in the tears on her cheek. He looks at her extremely serious and she looks at him the same way. "So, no matter what, I'll always remember it. It may be . . . our last kiss before . . ."

And so she does and feels the anguish in her throat again, and she holds him tight and prays to God to let nothing bad ever happen to him, but suddenly Carl Dean, loving her so much, hauls her right up off the seat and pulls her hard against him and she feels everything just like they were bare naked and his hands are everywhere and not just on her leg either, and that *really* scares her and she twists away and starts to bawl and get hysterical. But he apologizes and lets go right away and doesn't do anything more except kiss her softly on her cheek, and he

401

blinks the lights, and Colin comes back, and they drive
straight to Giovanni Bruno's house. As Colin gets out
and starts up the walk, Carl Dean whispers, "I love you,
Elaine, I really do! I'm awful sorry if . . ." She smiles a
little and tells him she isn't mad. She isn't. Just scared.
And worried about what she'll say if her Ma asks her
where she's been so long and why her face is all streaked
up.

Worry: indeed, what night in West Condon ends without it? Certainly Easter Sunday looking toward the
prophesied end of the world is no exception. Worry is
the universal dread tempered by hope, prolepsis of pleasure
and pain alike, and so intrinsic to the human condition,
that humanity has on occasion been defined by it. And so,
tonight, fathers worry about their daughters, wives about
their husbands, ministers about their flocks, doctors about
their patients, Brunists about how they will meet the End,
doubters about the truth, the mayor about the embarrassment and the shame and the next elections, businessmen
about the slump and miners about the unemployment,
children about their aging parents, and just about all West
Condoners worry a moment or two, unless they have
dropped off blissfully before the TV, about their health or
their virility or their weight or their period or their happiness or when and how they're going to die. Abner
Baxter's particular worry concerns the reluctance of his
Nazarene congregation to recognize the real majesty and
breadth of his vision, their almost womanish bickering
about what to do and when to do it, instead of simply
following him in faith—in short, their galling blindness.
The newspaper publicity has frightened them. Yet, he is
grateful for it. In the end, it will inspire them. Ralph
Himebaugh, approaching total poverty—surprised to discover that it is an ascent, not a descent—also worries, like
Baxter, about the willpower of those about him, and so
he is also grateful for the publicity, much as he despises
the publicist, convinced that, in the end, it will commit

them utterly. Meanwhile, he is alert to the least sign of weakness, the least hint of retreat, the least flush of fear or faintness of heart. At night, he doesn't sleep at all. Nor, for a long time tonight anyway, does the banker Ted Cavanaugh. His dreams of a revivified community spirit, sprung from the Common Sense Committee, now seem doomed, thanks mainly to the *Chronicle* editor's ruthless and unscrupulous exploitation of this insignificant cult. Passions in the Committee, as a result, are much higher than he had ever intended, and elements are taking over that he had hoped to keep excluded, and he wonders now if anything constructive can ever be salvaged from it after next Sunday. Probably not. He would like to turn it off, but knows he is unable. He is caught like the rest, and the most he can hope to do is to moderate somewhat the Committee's zeal and pray for a small turnout next Sunday. As for the editor, on the other hand, there are some retaliatory steps that might be taken, that might even get rid of the bastard for good. Contemplating these, his other worries are momentarily forgotten, and he is able, finally, to sleep. The editor's employees also worry, torn between conflicting loyalties. The devoutly Catholic Girl Fried Egg Annie Pompa, for example, has been called upon almost daily by friends who find much to criticize in her continuing assistance in the production of that paper. And today, even the priest has spoken to her. The police chief Dee Romano is worried that he may have to use his pistol. He has spent the afternoon at target practice, now methodically cleans it. In all his years on the force, he has never fired it at a man. Barney Davis, mine supervisor at Deepwater No. 9, is worried about the announcement he must make, now that Easter week is over, ending the Company's pledge to Ted Cavanaugh. He himself has been offered a job with the Company elsewhere, yet he feels the pain of unemployment here as if it were his own personal affliction. He stares off, through his bedroom window, at the night sky. The worries of Wally Fisher, owner and operator of the West Condon Hotel and presently prostrate on his back on the floor of the Legion Hall, contrarily, are the happiest he has had in three months. Must remember to stock in some after-hours booze. Increase his fire insurance. Locate something to use as an annex, for already the room reservation requests from newsmen and TV people have surpassed the hotel's capacity. What else will these news-guys want? Get some women from Waterton lined up. Keep the coffeeshop open longer somehow. And then the brainstorm hits him. He breaks into a delirious giggle, stretched out all alone there in the Legion Hall, terminating in a coughing fit. Tomorrow, he will call Barney Davis. If he lives that long. Somehow, incredibly, Eleanor Norton has cut the Mount of Jupiter on her left hand with a paring knife, and worries about the portent of it. On Eleanor's hand, this rise is shifted toward the base of the middle finger, indicating, as one might expect, a tendency toward mystical religion, though principally, of course, it is ambition and the desire to command others that is read here. Can it omen the proximate loss of control over the movement she has mothered? Wylie asks her how she cut it, and she admits she doesn't know. Betty Wilson, poor soul, faced with imminent judgment, worries about having fallen into the sin of envy and covetousness, insofar as he covets Ben Wosznik, who seems to have become the private property of Wanda Cravens. Wanda has been taking special privileges in their group, moreover, just be-cause Lee was with Ely and Giovanni Bruno when he died, but, after all, wasn't her own Eddie a saint and prophet too? She has tried, humbly, to suggest this, but Ben seems less impressed. She is getting nowhere and is miserable. She decides to talk it over with her best friend Clara Collins the first thing tomorrow morning, and meanwhile sings herself to sleep with Ben's new ballad. Battista Baglione frets about the correctness of the excommunication pro-ceedings he has initiated against his former altar boy Giovanni Bruno. He does not doubt the heresy, of course, which he perceives as really a further fragmentation of Protestantism, heresy being, as he knows full well, a straight-line regression from the Mother Church . . . and the further, the faster. He is worried, however, about the wording, about the aptness of each charge, about the accuracy of his knowledge of pertinent Church history. His own future within God's Kingdom on Earth may well depend on it. Although most of his flock worry conventionally, one who worries hardly at all is little Angela Bonali. She is almost literally afloat. She must be about the happiest luckiest girl in the world, her only worry being that this luck and happiness might end. Perhaps, in fact, it is inevitable. And her joy is not just because Christ is risen or because her Daddy has become so important, though she's glad about these things, but because she is hopelessly beautifully unbelievably in love, and her love loves her. Ben Wosznik, in a comparable circumstance, though tempered by thirty or forty years more of experience, a man's more defensive perspective, and a lifetime of obeying his own gift for practical common sense, worries about a possible proposal of marriage in the event they are disappointed Sunday. He's afraid she may see something improper about it, though of course Christ Jesus Himself, just before His own death, emphasized that the risen dead did not live in wedlock in Heaven. And he sure does admire her, he's never met a woman her equal, yet he understands it won't be easy to make her forget. He decides, practicing his new song, that maybe he ought to talk to her about it before Sunday, so she'll know it's on his mind and won't run off afterwards without having had the opportunity at least to consider it. . . .

On a cold and wintry eighth of January,
Ninety-eight men entered into the mine;
Only one of these returned to tell the story
Of that disaster that struck Old Number Nine!

Hark ye to the White Bird of Glory!
Hark ye to the White Bird of Grace!
We shall gather at the Mount of Redemption
To meet our dear Lord there face to face!

405

As we carried out the bodies of our loved ones,
We looked up to God in Heav'n above;
We asked Him why, and He sent a man to tell us:
Hark ye to the White Bird of Love!

And from that tomb came a message of gladness,
Though its author had passed to his reward:
"Hark ye ever to the White Bird in your hearts,
And we shall all stand together 'fore the Lord!"

So, hark ye to the White Bird of Glory!
Yes, hark ye to the White Bird of Grace!
We shall gather at the Mount of Redemption
To meet our dear Lord there face to face!

Seven weeks we gathered by his bedside,
Seven weeks we knelt and prayed to the Divine,
Seven weeks, and from the Seventh Aspect,
God answered our prayers with a Sign!

(Now,) fourteen weeks will have passed since the
    Rescue,
When we gather out on the Mount that night;
We shall lift our voices then to sing God's Glory,
And await with joy the Coming of the Light!

So, hark ye to the White Bird of Glory!
Oh yes, hark ye to the White Bird of Grace!
We shall gather at the Mount of Redemption
To meet our dear Lord there face to face!

And, finally, Reverend Wesley Edwards of the First Presbyterian Church worries about his sermon for next Sunday. A touchy problem, since he feels the occasion should be utilized, yet does not want to contribute in any way to hysteria. Somehow, Mark 4:11-12 seems appropriate to him as a text, yet it is full of pitfalls. Dare he risk it?

And he said unto them: Unto you is given the mystery of the kingdom of God, but unto them that

are without, all things are done in parables: that seeing they may see, and not perceive; and hearing they
may hear, and not understand; lest haply they should
turn again, and it should be forgiven them.

What a triumph it could be! He and his wife have
turned in late, exhausted by the long week and longer
day, having suffered through just about everything from
baptisms to egghunts, from ecumenical Good Friday
services to his own jampacked flower-laden programs, even
a wedding and an afternoon children's party, and so he is
not exactly overjoyed that his wife chooses just this moment
to find fault with his sermon this morning.

"Of course, it was beautiful, dear. Don't bite your lip
like that. I don't mean that everyone didn't enjoy it
thoroughly."

"What was the matter with it?" He tries to sound
agreeable and open-minded, but he is very tired. Moreover,
undressing in the room where she lay reading idly, he was
even considering the marital sacrament this night as an appropriate climax to the joy of Christian renewal (both
students of *The Golden Bough*, they often celebrate
primitive festivals in such manner), but he has never been
able to succeed—even as a lusting boy—so long as his
mind was at work.

"I didn't say anything was the *matter* with it, dear. Only,
well, it seemed so much like the one you gave last year."

He laughs. "You want me to rewrite the Resurrection?"

"Oh no, that's not what I mean." She smiles. "But, I
don't know, it just seems like you only tell them what they
want to hear, and that doesn't seem . . ." Her voice trails
off ambiguously.

"That may be so, dear," he says, rolling his back to her.
"But if I do, it is because I believe that God's behavior is
visible in their needs. It's difficult to put it precisely, but
for some time now I've had the feeling that I am only a
passive participant in a larger drama, that by responding
to them, I respond to Divine Will, and thus fulfill what is

407

there potentially all the time. I think this is really what ritual is all about. And it seems especially right at Easter-time, which celebrates not a speech or moral judgment, but a mute action. Who am I to stand above and scold?"

"Oh, Wesley!" She laughs, switching off the bedlamp and curling around his back. "You're not a preacher, dear, you're a poet!"

He laughs in pleased response. She runs her hands down inside his pajama pants. He is still irritated with her for having turned him on, as it were, but as she scratches and burrows, the channels of his mind click closed, one by one. Visions of candy Easter eggs behind slender trees, gay flowered bonnets and starched skirts, the long green look down the No. 6 fairway toward the red flag that stabs its hole, fill the void as his mind retreats.

"Is he risen?" she asks in his ear then, astonishingly resurrecting this old premarital collegetime joke of theirs.

Click! the last channel. "Indeed," he whispers, rolling on his back to receive her: "he is risen!"

PART FOUR
The Mount

*Come, gather for the great supper of God,
to eat the flesh of kings, the flesh of captains,
the flesh of mighty men, the flesh of horses and their riders,
and the flesh of all men, both free and slave,
both small and great!*

—REVELATION TO JOHN 19:17-18

1

---

*Of every clean beast thou shalt take to thee
seven and seven, the male and his female* . . .

West Condon, as though unable to gaze any longer upon
the deep black reach of night, rolls over on its back to
receive the Monday sun, now rising, as men say, in the
eastern sky: the eye of God, the golden chariot, the communal hearthfire and source of life, the solar center that,
for all its berserk fury, still works its daily anodyne magic
on man's ultimately incurable disease of dread and despair.
Its first rays glance off the top of the West Condon Hotel,
the high school flagpole, roof and treetops, the Deepwater
No. 9 tipple and watertower, and, close by, the small
irregular rise, now internationally known as the Mount
of Redemption, where this morning occasional white
chicken feathers lie like a fall of manna, their barbs
gummed into clumps by the dew. Although no one is out
at the mine, on the flagpole, or in the treetops, and thus
no one can see the sun until at least another hour's roll has
lapsed, and though, as a matter of further fact, almost
none will bother to look at it when it can be seen, its
radiations are nevertheless early perceived: they shred
dreams, calm the sleepless, turn West Condon on: clocks
sound, radios crow, throats hack, razors buzz, frypans
heat, toilets flush, children scuffle, doors bang, church and
school bells ring, forks clink, toasters pop, motors turn
over, sweepers roar, it is Monday morning.

Justin Miller, editor and publisher of the West Condon
Chronicle, rouses himself from the jobroom sofa, where he
has spent the night, camera at his side, in a vain attempt

411

to catch further demonstrators or looters in the act. He feels, in a word, rotten. Dirty, unshaved, tired, disgusted. When there is enough light, he steps outside in the street to take photos of the broken windows, the cross on the door, then develops and prints them immediately for quick sale to the wireservices and photo magazines. He decides to leave the damages unrepaired as one further curiosity for the newshounds who will descend on the town, noses at the ready, this weekend—indeed, the back lot of the hotel is already filling up with cars—and now simply boards up the windows from the inside with cardboard ripped from packing boxes. He is still at the task when his office and advertising people begin to arrive, and, given his bearish temper this morning, he is hardly delighted to learn that his indispensable office girl, bookkeeper, librarian, classified ads chief, and social columnist Annie Pompa will not show up . . . for "religious" reasons, one of the other girls explains, then tenders her own resignation. "Ah shit!" the editor is heard to lament.

The morning does not go well. The ad force returns glumly from futile rounds, reporting they weren't even allowed in the door most places. Miller encourages them not to worry about it, he anticipated as much, didn't he? A little patience and things will return to normal. The girls up front, those who remain, receive angry phonecalls canceling subscriptions, but he tells them to accept them gracefully and to arrange for larger bundles to be left at newsstands. No one, he knows, will want to be without the paper, and after it's all over they will all renew. Without Jones, however, the pressures of the day mount. Miller attempts to gather most of the routine material by phone, but gets almost no response from anyone. Even Dee Romano at the police station hangs up on him.

Just before heading to Fisher's coffeeshop for breakfast, he hears from Barney Davis: the mine is closed. He banners that instead of the Brunists, but ties it to the Brunist story. At the coffeeshop, he finds Robbins, Elliott, and Cavanaugh already discussing the closing, the word having flown ahead of him. Cavanaugh turns his back as Miller enters. Amuses him. Cavanaugh could be like a little kid playing cops and robbers, getting mad and going home when the others wouldn't fall dead when shot.

"Highest paid industrial worker in the U.S.," Robbins is snarling. "If he had any brains, he'd take a cut in pay to keep his goddamn mines open." Cavanaugh settles into into his traditional role of defending the moderate labor movement, Elliott agreeing with everybody. Merest rituals.

"Pecan waffles, Doris," he says. They turn on him, then turn away.

"Don't get me wrong," Robbins is arguing. "I'm not saying the miners don't deserve good pay and good working conditions. I'm only saying—"

"They don't deserve good pay and good working conditions," says Cavanaugh.

"In a lot of ways now, you have to admit, Burt's right," Elliott offers by way of mediation. Right is right: he's a goddamn fascist. And so on. Over and over. "Coalmining is a marginal business these days, and the union has pretty much brought on itself the closing down of so many."

Traditionally now, it is his, the expert's, line: "That and dieselization of the railroads and strip-mining and the profit motive and the rising cost of machinery and underground gasification and rulings on—"

"Hark yc," interrupts Robbins, "to the white turd!" Not even much laughter. It is, from their end of the counter, all too true. Well, anyway, they're reading his newspaper. And, in spite of their anger, in spite of his battered plant and decimated force, even in spite of his breakup with Marcella, Miller feels oddly pleased with himself. He has not, by God, been assimilatcd.

There is an awkward silence then, and something seems to be missing. Puzzles Miller for a moment. Then he realizes it is Jones's absence. At just such moments, Jones would always grunt, cueing the others to amused attention. Time for a story. Most likely horrible, for Jones was horrible, horrible but decorated with a deathly humor, for

Jones was also funny. The Father. A reservoir of gaudy misery, he collected horror like others collect stamps. And he never failed to get them. They always attended when Papa Jones cast his bloody pearls. Now, without him, they stand, exit as a group.

"Where's Wally this morning?" Miller asks Doris, who has just cleaned the crud off the grill with a dishcloth which she is now using to dry a few coffee cups.

"Who, the boss?" She arches one penciled brow, loose-wristedly flaps a palm at him. "Spent the night on the Legion floor. Can't walk, can't turn his neck, can't talk, he's in a hell of a mess! When I seen him coming down the street like that, I thought, oh-oh! Doris, old girl, you better take the day off! But you know what?"

"What?"

"He come in giggling like a idiot!" Doris whirs one index finger around her ear. "Now he's upstairs sleeping it off."

A couple East Condoners enter the coffeeshop, take stools at the other end of the counter from him. Look at first like newsmen, but they turn out to be salesmen passing through. Newspapers—including his Saturday night edition—rattle, eggs sizzle and pop on the grill, coffee cups clank. The salesmen kid with Doris and the one reading the *Chronicle* asks if she's ready to meet her Maker.

"Which maker?" she retorts flatly, hand on grease-stained hip. "I been made by so many, I wouldn't know one from the other."

The salesmen whoop at that. Even Doris grins as she flops the eggs to platters, glances over at Miller and winks. And now, treated to this classic, they will travel and the word will be carried. Miller grins at that, as Doris turns, flips up the top of the waffle iron. Sloppy as she is, she never misses the moment: they're always golden brown.

Miller receives them. "A blessing, Doris!" he praises, pouring syrup. "You're a goddamn saint!"

The Brunist Mrs. Betty Wilson is waiting for him on his return to the office, posted plumply and skittishly in the chair by his desk, and her news depresses him deeply: Giovanni Bruno seems much stronger now, it's almost like he's suddenly come alive, but his sister, she says, hasn't eaten a bite or said a word for nigh on a week now, and she seems, well, a bit strange. "Sometimes she don't even, even take care of herself, Mr. Miller. But nobody blames you, Mr. Miller. Leastways, not me or Clara or Wanda or Mary. We know they's more to it than meets the eye." What met the eye was Marcella arriving hysterical and more or less stripped.

"Thanks, Mrs. Wilson. You're quite right."

"Clara is jist tearin' up the countryside, Mr. Miller, and now Ben Wosznik he's helpin' her, you remember Ben. Oh, the most terrible thing! Last Friday, the very day they crucified Christ Jesus, why, a whole buncha men come and beat up poor Ben, yes, that there Mr. Cavanaugh and Mr. Bonali and a whole buncha them fellas. And they drug poor Mary Harlowe right outa her own house and like to kidnap her little children, it was jist awful! They come to the Halls' place, too, I seen them, but Mabel she didn't let them in, and that's jist a good thing she didn't! And now Ben and Clara, why, they're lookin' for more folks to come next weekend and Clara she's very optimistic. Of course, you know how she is, Mr. Miller. And that Palmers boy, he's got seven or eight new members somewheres, though of course them young ones hardly ever stays on."

All good stuff. Miller gets more details on the Common Sense visits, then he tips her, and the woman leaves. Irresistibly, he opens his desk drawer, takes out Jones's photos. There you are, he says: the Tiger. Look at her face. Jones caught it all. Well, she's mad, he tells himself, and it was she, staking too much on a thin fantasy, who broke herself; he was little more than the accidental instrument . . . his audience, however, remains unconvinced. Conscience, he knows, is merely instinct socialized into guilt— Can one, knowing this, still fall prey to it? Yes, concludes this man much given to this sort of theorizing, another flaw in the evolution of mind. He dumps the photos back in the drawer, realizing the whole thing is starting to make him sick.

Then, like an act of grace, there appears in his morning mail a black-bordered envelope.

One day during the Last Judgment proceedings, there appeared before the Judge a prophet and his beautiful sister. Aha! said the Judge to the prophet: I believe I know you! Yes, smiled the prophet with modest pride: I foretold your coming. How could you have done such a thing, asked the Judge: when I didn't even know myself? Perhaps there is another, replied the prophet with a sly inscrutable wink over the Judge's shoulder: yet greater than either of us. Hmmm, said the Judge, considering that: yet it seems improbable. What is probability in a universe such as ours? asked the prophet. I don't know, I guess I was just a born skeptic, said the Judge with a wry knowing smile: But now what am I to do with you? I suppose you want to go to Heaven. Well, uh, no, Your Honor, replied the prophet: if you don't mind, I'd rather like—hee hee—to be put in charge of Hell. Hah! good boy! said the Judge: It's done! When, however, the Supreme Judge asked the prophet's sister, whose beauty might have weakened any lesser Judge, she opted for Heaven.

—And why do you wish to be admitted to Heaven, my dear?

—Because I am afraid to be where you are not.

—But you can never be where I am.

—Because . . . because I believe in you.

—And if I do not believe in myself?

—Because you are perfect.

—What is your imperfection?

—Because you are beautiful.

—You, too, are beautiful. Where is the reason?

416

—Because, then, because I need you.
—Your need is a burden, inappropriate in Heaven.
—Because I find fullness only with you.
—What do you lack?
—Because . . . because I love you.
—In Heaven, there are no transitive verbs.
—Then because I shall cry if you do not admit me!
—Your tears, my sweet, shall water Hell.
The next supplicant, a virgin who shall here be otherwise nameless, was brought before the Judge. Her virginity, of course, was not a possession (the Judgment itself made property an absurd contradiction), but rather of the essence, a thing happily forever renewable, if in fact with use it ever aged.
—And why do you wish to be admitted to Heaven?
—What is Heaven?
—Why, Heaven is where I am.
—And where are you?
—I have said.
—And so have I.
The Judge smiled and because, to tell the truth, there had never been a Heaven before, the Judge and the virgin forthwith created one and had a Hell of a good time doing it. . . .

But when he calls her, he finds her cold and indifferent, as though she might be resenting having sent him what she did, and it takes him awhile, but after all, in the end, they both have a fear of Hell, and she says finally, "Okay, Tiger. You're the Judge." And, somehow, they're both able to laugh.

Midmorning finds Eleanor Norton stopped dead in her tracks downtown at the corner of Third and Main. She has been wandering absently through the bright town, shocked that others use light without perceiving what they use, and has arrived now at this corner where suddenly

417

everything seems incredibly strange. People pass and their stares prove her corporeal existence, and yet it is as though . . .

Don't you see, dear Elan? You have passed through!

"Ah! But, but who are you?"

You know me and yet you do not know me.

"Domiron!"

I have come briefly to bring you hope and renewed assurance. Do not forsake your vision, Elan! do not forsake me!

"How could I? But where am I? I seem to be here and yet not here. Am I at the seventh aspect?"

No, we have met, let us say, halfway.

"Are you—I've always wanted to ask—are you the only God?"

Perhaps not, Elan, but such is our relationship at this level that that can be thought of as the case.

"Wait!"

Yes?

"I . . . I *love you!*"

Your love is known and dear to me. You would never have found me without it, for existence at the seventh aspect is pure love itself, without form, without object, without act.

"How strange! I seem to have known that all along!"

Is that strange?

"And am I worthy?"

Look about you at these staring faces. Do they perceive the light?

"No."

Do they hear my voice?

"No."

Do they even wish to? Do they try? Could they even dream of it?

"No."

Then you have given response to yourself, have witnessed the gulf between you and men. Yet, remember, Elan: every created thing is divine, even these stupid foolish men!

"Yes, yes! God is all that is!"

Therefore, hark ye, Elan! I say to you that a time has been ordained and a time is to come. Time is not, yet a time must end: Stand on high wthout remorse and look about thee eastward with love!

"I shall!"

You have.

"Never leave me"

As you love me, Elan, so I love you. Lo! I am with you always!

419

She returns. The objects solidify, the street hardens. She occurs before their eyes, creates ears for their laughter. She pities them. The dense ones, the lost ones. "I love you all," she says, then steps forward. Their circle rends to let her pass.

Ugly Palmers stands in the noisy melancholic corridors of old WCHS, leaning against Elaine's locker, at noon. He sees it all as if for the first time, hears only now the music in the excited voices and banging lockers, smells as though they had never before existed the dense sweaty odors of the generations which have passed through here. Nostalgically, he munches an apple, runs his fingers over the cool surface of Elaine's locker. An end to this! Sometimes it seems almost unbelievable. Already, though he still has a whole week to enjoy it here, he is feeling the pain of irrevocable loss. And yet: he is happy.

Elaine, however, arrives crying, her little face streaked with tears, blowing her nose in one of her Pa's big handkerchiefs. There's something so lovable about her blowing her nose in one of those great big handkerchiefs, something so terrible about her tears. "What's the matter, Elaine?"

She snuffles, more tears come, she opens her locker, shoves her books in, but she doesn't answer.

"What is it, Elaine? Why're you crying?"

"I cain't tell you," she whispers. She pulls out a brown paper sack, containing her lunch, from the locker, then closes it again.

"Why not?"

"It's too bad."

"Bad?" Carl Dean bristles. "You can tell me, Elaine. You still love me, don't you?"

She nods, looks up at him with reddened eyes. Her look always gets him. "It was something Junior Baxter said. In front of everybody."

Carl Dean feels his muscles tense, his back straighten, his fists ball shut. But he feels very cool now. This is something he can handle. "What was it?" he asks.

"He called me . . . he called me . . ."

"Look, why don't you write it?" he suggests. He gives her a pencil stub and she uses the paper lunchbag. Her face reddens and her eyes water up again as she writes. She turns away and he reads: HORE. He sets his teeth. Looks around. Never find him now. But Junior's first class after lunch is history. They eat their lunch in dark silence, holding hands.

He walks Elaine to her class, then goes down the hall to look for Junior. Class has already begun and Junior Baxter is on the far side of the room, next to the windows, between Joey Altoviti and Angie Bonali. Boy, what a bunch of enemies! He has no choice. He strides into the room, trying to act official about it. "Excuse me," he says, "but I have to talk with Junior Baxter a minute." Junior shrinks into his seat, toward the aisle, but Carl Dean drags him out. Books spill and girls cry out. Junior grabs onto his desk, starts whining like a baby, kicks out, but he is weaker than a girl. Carl Dean hauls him out the door, paying no mind to the teacher's protest, and in the corridor gives Junior a thrashing. Junior puts up no defense to speak of, so Carl Dean alternates his blows by whim between the boy's beanbag belly and his fat white face. When blood is running out his mouth and nose and Junior starts to vomit, Carl Dean lets up. "Now you just watch how you talk to girls from now on," he says.

He realizes then he has a considerable audience. One of them is the principal, Mr. Bradley. "Come with me, young man!" Mr. Bradley says. In the office, Carl Dean starts to explain, but Mr. Bradley cuts him off. "I know who you are," he says. "Now, you do down and clean out your locker, turn in everything you might have checked out, bring the locker key back to me . . . and get out of here!"

"Get out—?"

"You are expelled!"

So, he does what Mr. Bradley has told him to do, but in a kind of daze, wondering how it could ever have happened, how his life could have turned out this way, and altogether it takes him about forty-five minutes, so he is able to catch Elaine in the corridor between fifth and sixth hour classes. He tells her all that happened and he doesn't know exactly what he wants her to do about it, but she does it anyway. She takes ahold of his hand like she doesn't mean ever to let go and says if he has to go, then she's going too, and that's how it is that they walk out of there together, laughingly in love, and the day, crazy as it is, is beautiful.

Elaine's Ma is that moment over in Randolph Junction with another Brunist, Ben Wosznik, concluding the most successful day so far. The newspaper stories have carried their fame far and wide, and the way, she discovers, has been prepared. Naturally, there are those who scoff, there always are, but there are many who do not. Above all, she does not encounter out here that kind of implacable hostility she has run up against in West Condon. And, of course, the people with whom she speaks have, almost all of them, known and respected her and Ely for years and years, such that even the scoffers scoff gently.

The Cleggs, Hiram and Emma, to whom she and Ben now bid farewell, are two of at least fifteen people who have said they would try to come next weekend, and, what is more, they believe they can bring another half dozen or so with them. Both Hiram and Emma are important leaders of the Randolph Junction Church of the Nazarene. Clara tells them how the Spirit has truly taken on flesh, that a new day is come, brought by the White Bird, which would last to the end of the world.

"Amazing! To be sure, there is something great here!" Hiram says, nodding gravely, and Emma listens wide-eyed.

Clara recounts the prophecies and the signs, tells of Ely's premonitions and his disaster message, explains how so many folks arrived at the same truth by different paths, and mentions the secret aspects of it which of course

422

cannot be let out until they actually join. She's noticed the effect this usually has.

"And a prophetic cross, you say?"

"You mean like to tell the future?" Emma asks. "Oh, Hiram! we must go see!"

"Yes, dear, I quite agree."

Clara also is careful to mention how the Mother Mary has played a part, because she has discovered this idea has a tremendous appeal wherever she goes. Ben tells them again how he himself was attracted to the group and why he has stayed on. It's just plain common sense to come and have a look for yourself, he says.

"True! That's true!" says Hiram.

Ben's frank and earthy manner impresses people.

Driving back toward West Condon together, Clara tells Ben how big a help he has been to her. He tells her then how much he admires her, and adds surprisingly that if she ever thought of remarrying, he would like to be considered. She says she hasn't been thinking about any such thing. He tells her that he understands perfectly well and certainly he could never hope to hold a candle to so great a man as Ely Collins, but he only wanted her to know how he felt. Just like Ben, she thinks, to put it so plain like that. Anyway, he adds, there's no point even concerning themselves about it until after next Sunday, if there *is* an afterward, but he does go on to mention anyway the Bible story about the woman who was widowed seven times. Of course, that story has already occurred to her. And then something Elaine reminded her of yesterday morning, something she had almost forgot, something Ely used to say in almost every preaching, comes back to her now and it has all the ring of a prophecy to it: "Grace is not something you die to get, it is something you get to live!"

One moment, Colin Meredith is assured of the end and ecstatic with its glorious promise, the next, plunged into deepest despair in seeing it can never be, then relieved and even made joyful by the certainty of continuance, the certainty of more life, next terrorized by a sudden paralyzing vision of the final horror now upon them. For one sublime and exquisite moment, he embraces and is embraced by all, the boy of the Brunists, the loved one, he upon whom all depend, the all without whom he is forever lost; and then, suddenly, he is utterly alone, ignored, forgotten, unwanted—Eleanor is self-absorbed and impatient, Carl Dean deserts him for a girl, Giovanni does not even see him, a woman laughs cruelly in his face. Though he has willed an end to all his vices, they return to overwhelm him. Chaste in principle, he seeks lecherous solace in the act of love. Spent, he sinks miserably into self-disgust, returns repentant to his vows and to his friends, only to meet rebuff and anguish and to fail again in sin. She is beautiful, but her beauty is ultimately a terror to him; she is enormous, but her enormity protects him. She is brilliant with Mr. Himebaugh's cold true brilliance, and her passion is as spontaneous and furious as Carl Dean's temper. Her eyes are gray and wise, and her mouth is young and full and eager. Her breasts, sweet to his hungry mouth, are greater even than Mrs. Wilson's, her hips, which quiver in his grip, mightier even than Mrs. Hall's. Her arms grip with the strength of Mr. Wosznik, her hands, like Mrs. Cravens', tear at his flesh, her massive thighs squeeze and kick like a mare's, and her hair, wild as the prophet's, whirls and snarls and clings to his body. Her womb, fertile as Mrs. Harlowe's, grabs him like a fist and wrings the seed from his body and angels sing and sweat beads his forehead—"*Mother!*" he cries out, and sucks, bites, chews the hard nipple of his pillow. "Son!" she says, and sinks away from him into the dark and hollow earth.

We all were so happy there together
In our peaceful little mountain home,

424

But the Savior needed angels up in Heaven:
Now they're singin' round that great white throne!

Tommy (the Kitten) Cavanaugh has, at long last, climbed that famous furry mountain and passed into manhood. Spent, yet firm and ready as ever—a *tiger*, man!— he cuddles naked with her in a corner of the Lincoln's rangy back seat, staring out on the old ice plant, only witness to the miracle of his accomplishment. He rolls down the window, and, turning his back to her—which she kisses and softly scratches—he slips the fragile skin off: like a young snake enjoying his first molt. Taking care to hold it cuplike so as not to make an even worse mess in his Dad's car, he flips it out, regretting that it could not be kept somehow as a souvenir. He's still wet where the skin was and his hands are sticky, so he looks in the clothes on the floor for a handkerchief or something, comes across her panties. "May I?" he asks devilishly, yet at the same time with an intimacy, a camaraderie, he has never known before. She nods, takes them from him, dries him tenderly, looking down at it, her cheeks against his chest. There are dark stains, too, which cause profound pangs of compassion and gratitude to course through him.

"I can hear your heart," she whispers.

Which is cause for him to listen to hers, and he does so, staring ahead at that stupendous pink bud at the tip of his nose. The two feelings he has not anticipated are the inexpressible after-sense of well-being that now magnifies everything into such tremendous—almost unbearable— beauty, and the terrible nostalgia that goes, he supposes, with any perfect love. For love it is, no doubt about it, the greatest he has ever known and the greatest, he's sure, he'll ever know. The unexpected beauty, the excruciating sadness, the intensity of his love, all seem oddly summed up in the silly country music swimming over them from the car radio. He knows now that, though neither of them likes hillbilly stuff, it will be, in an inescapable way, their song, and that no matter where they are or who they're married to, the song will recall for them this moment. . . .

> *White dove will mourn in sorrow,*
> *And the willows bow down their heads,*
> *I live my life in sorrow,*
> *Since Mother and Daddy are dea-ea-ead!*

Sooner or later, in a sad, a terrible, yet also beautiful moment, they will have to talk about religion, that impossible thing, bigger than both of them, cruel to their love, her Catholicism and his Protestantism, and, after that, sooner or later, they will have to tear themselves apart. Forever. Tears spring to the edges of his eyes. There are tears in her eyes, too, and he wonders if her thoughts are the same as his. "I love you," he says. He kisses her long and tenderly, tragically, and though her whole body is available to him, his embrace is chaste and gentle, a promise of his eternal care for her. So beautiful is she, so virginal, so *his* . . . his white dove . . .

> *As the years roll by I often wonder,*
> *Will we all be together some day?*
> *And each night as I wander through the graveyard,*
> *Darkness hides me where I kneel to pray!*

> *White dove will mourn in sorrow* . . .

Sainthood, ultimately, is a rising above—not only God —but the Destroyer as well. Saint Rahim, rigid, hungry, but supremely at one with the All, stares meditatively in front of him at springs and the red and blue stripes of a cotton mattress. Illusion at moments of remarkable distance. A great calm. Through discipline to pattern. Distantly, a toilet lid clunks carelessly against the enameled tank. Like a bell in the mind. Shattering of peace, but still the perception of pattern. Again—as always—his childhood washes over and through him here, like an infusion of raw guilt, imprecise as ever in the imagery it calls up, yet piercing in the accuracy of emotions aroused. Panic! This dust—! He twists, squirms, chokes. Then it passes. He sighs. In truth, he feels better just now than he has felt all day, his second to go without food. Just six more days, and they say it gets easier after the third day. He believes he can make it. Abstractly, he worries about his cats. They have also been subjected to a fast, but he is not certain they will survive the week. Except for Nyx. Nyx will survive. He smiles.

Water running. Door hinges revolving. He turns his head, watches her bare feet pad wearily across the wooden floor. Poor dear child! She is very weak. He would give up speech, too, but cannot afford it, not even for her sake. He needs every word at his command to keep the others from faltering. God! he cannot stand alone! She arrives at the bed, pauses. She has forgotten to turn out the light. An urge to kiss her small toes—just a foot from his face— leaps to his lips, but he overmasters it. Discipline is his greatest virtue. She curls a toe. Oh God! He starts to cry, clamps his hand between his teeth, bites down with all his strength. She turns toward the door, hesitating, as though measuring the distance. Then, mechanically, her small feet, under the hem of her tunic, pad back to the door. The light goes off. She no longer troubles to put the hook.

Almost before he realizes it, her feet are near his face again. God! catches his breath, holds himself rigid. At last, she enters the bed. The mattress hardly sinks below her weight now, so thin is she. He reaches up, strokes the gentle depression. Calm returns. He waits for her to sleep. The perfect man is the motionless cause.

2

The news of the mine closing broke on Monday and Sal Ferrero came by Tuesday morning, the fourteenth. Vince was up on the ladder. He had stirred up the old paint, was just putting a new coat over the patch he'd started on the south side nearly a month before. He knew what Sal wanted to talk about, so he hooked the bucket on the top of the ladder, crawled down. They had known it was coming, everybody had known it for weeks, but still it had hit them hard. "It's awful," he said. He pulled out his handkerchief, wiped the paint off his hands.

"It's a real blow, Vince."

"I don't know what the hell I'm gonna do." He stuffed the handkerchief back in his pocket, shaking his head thoughtfully. "Care for a beer, Sal?"

Sal looked at his watch. Poor guy seemed lost. "Pretty early," he said. "But, hell, okay." They walked up on the porch, Vince's four-fingered hand clapped on Sal's narrow shoulders.

"How about a couple beers, chicken?" Vince called in through the screen door. They eased themselves into chairs like tired old beat-up men. Vince fumbled in his pocket, found a half-smoked cigar butt, stuck it in his cheeks. "Well, goddamn it, I knew they'd do it, Sal."

"I know." He sighed, pulling one big ear absently. Looking at his old friend closely, Vince saw for the first time that Sal was getting to be an old man.

Etta came out with the beers, but today there wasn't any of the usual kidding around. Sal and Etta looked at each other, shook their heads in troubled silence, and she went back in. Last night, she cried for over an hour; in fact, she'd hardly stopped crying since Charlie pulled out without a word Sunday afternoon. She was some better today, but still pretty glum.

"Well," said Sal, sipping at the beer, "I suppose they did what they had to do."

"I tell you what they had to do, Sal. They had to think about us, the people of this community, that's what they by God had to do! Instead of fretting how much they were gonna suck outa here—no, Sal, they ain't no excuse! It's high time we started fighting back!"

Sal nodded. Poor guy was really down in the dumps. Vince felt bad, but somehow not as bad as he probably ought to.

"Sure leaves us high and dry, Vince."

"You said it—and now with all this Brunist shit—Jesus!"

"Sure is getting wild, all right."

" 'Wild' ain't the word. Did you see that story Tiger published last night about them people who got together naked and whipped themselves all bloody, and how they got ahold of some little virgin girl and made a big mess outa her?"

"No, I musta missed that. I hardly noticed anything except about the mine closing."

"Well, there was a white bird in this story, too, or maybe they called themselves a 'White Dove Gang' or something, but the awful thing was how they take this girl and tell her she is the Mother of God, see, and they strip her naked and spread her on the altar." All the while Vince read it, he kept seeing his daughter Angie there, and it made him so mad he wanted to cry. "Then they have a big ceremony and everybody whips her and screws her, just a little virgin, see, who doesn't know what's happening."

"That's pretty awful, Vince."

"Wait! You ain't heard the worst! If she gets knocked up, they strip her again and stick her in a barrel of water. Then they chop off the little kid's left tit and close up the bloody goddamn hole with a hot iron!"

"Jesus Christ! You mean this was in the newspaper?"

"I'm telling you, Sal! But the point is, they chop this tit up and eat it, see, just like it was the Host—"

"I can't believe it!"

"Wait! That's not all! If she has a boy, why, they say that this is the Savior, and they take this little newborn baby and they stab it and drink its blood. Then they dry up the body and beat it to powder, and, Sal, they make bread outa that powder and they eat that, too"

"Have you still got that paper?"

"Sure, I saved it."

"But you mean these Brunist people are doing things like that? Why, that's horrible, Vince! I didn't realize—"

"Well, this wasn't the Brunists, this was some people in Russia a hundred years or so ago, but the point is, like Miller is virtually saying, Sal, in the end, they're all the same."

"It kinda shakes you up, doesn't it?"

"And Jesus, right there in the goddamn newspaper, Sal! I didn't see it at first, it was Angie who found it, and she got all hysterical, why, it was just awful."

"It *is* awful. Jesus, I don't think they should print stuff like that, Vince. Not where young kids can see it and get ideas."

"I'm not kidding, Sal, sometimes I feel like going down there myself and breaking that sonuvabitch Miller's neck."

"It sure seems funny how all of this is fitting together, all this horrible stuff and the mine closing down and the bad times, all that Black Hand trouble we was having, and now, Jesus, all these goddamn newspeople pouring in here, why, the streets are full of them, and they're just here to make us out a bunch of fools!"

"Don't I know it?" Vince pulled the unlit butt out of his mouth, stared at it a moment in disgust, pitched it out toward the street.

"I suppose more guys than ever will be moving on now," Sal said. "Looks like old West Condon is all washed up."

Vince slammed the rocker arm with his palm so hard

it surprised even him and made Sal nearly spill his beer. "We can't *let* it die, Sal, we just *can't*, goddamn it!" He'd show them the way, by God, he'd find it and show them all. "It's our town, Sal, and if it dies, we die with it!" Sal shrugged. "Hey! you ain't figuring on bugging out on me, too, are you?"

Sal grinned, pulled his ear. "No, I suppose not. I'm too goddamn tired to go anywhere." He sighed. "Sure is funny how a dump like this can grow on you."

"Yeah, you're right about that," Vince agreed.

"Here we are, Vince, a couple old displaced dagos who've got nothing but trouble and the runaround in this damn town, and still, when the chips are down, we can't seem to let go of it."

"I been thinking about that lately, Sal. I been thinking a man ain't born with an attachment to the soil, like they say, or even to a piece of it, he just sort of picks it up as he goes along."

"You been making too many goddamn speeches," Sal said.

Vince laughed, downed the rest of his beer. "I tell you the truth, Sal. I been enjoying this work with the Committee."

"So we've noticed."

"Go ahead, wise off, you bastard, but it's been a good thing for me. Somehow—I don't know—but somehow, growing up in an immigrant home and all, I just always had a kind of oddball idea about this place, like I was being kept here against my will and the town was a bunch of goddamn foreigners I didn't understand and never could." He paused, leaned back in the rocker, wiped the beer foam from his lip. "But I've got so I can see things better, Sal. I've caught on to what makes this town tick. Sometimes, goddamn it, I feel like I been fighting the wrong damn fights all this time."

"Well, you got the right kind of friends, Vince."

"Yeah, maybe . . . but, hell," grinned Vince, "you're one of them, ain't you?"

431

Three of his new friends came by that afternoon, Ted Cavanaugh, Burt Robbins, and Reverend Wesley Edwards of the First Presbyterian. Just in case Ted might drop over, Vince had quit the painting project and cleaned up, now felt smug about his foresight. "We don't think it will do much good frankly," Ted said, "but we thought it was at least worth a try to call on Ralph Himebaugh, Dr. Norton, and the Meredith boy. Want to come along?"

"Sure. I'll go tell Etta."

In the car, on their way downtown, Vince in the back with the minister, Robbins brown-nosing Cavanaugh up front, Ted told them about some of the latest incidents: Mrs. Norton talking to herself on the street, the Palmers boy getting thrown out of school on bad conduct yesterday, and the Easter Sunday burning of one of Widow Harlowe's cats, which looked like a revival of the Black Hand activities, maybe even an inside revenge for her having weakened last Friday.

"Oh, Jesus!" Vince said with a shudder, and his missing finger tingled. Catching himself, he started to apologize to the minister, but the guy smiled and shook his head. Likable man, small fellow with a deep hairline, piercing gaze, nervous mouth, very bright.

"We want to be reasonable," Ted was saying, "but we want them to know what the limits of our tolerance are. If they want to persist in their destructive ways, well, they're free to do so, but we'd rather they didn't do it here. We can't afford it."

That sounded more like it. Vince was in the mood to kick somebody's ass out of town. The minister had a pipe stoked up; Ted and Burt had cigarettes going. Vince regretted having forgot his cigars in the anxiety not to hold anybody up. Maybe Ted guessed it: he handed a cigar back over his shoulder. Great guy. "Thanks, Ted." The minister lit it for him.

"Why don't we just ask the Nortons to get out?" Robbins suggested. "They're outsiders anyhow."

432

"Well," the minister said, "I think we want to give them every chance to mitigate their views and become absorbed once more in the community life. Our task is not so much to chastise or threaten, as to define for them what it means to be a West Condoner."

"Exactly!" said Ted. "Whatever we do, we've got to take it easy. We don't want them to be able to use anything against us. Oh, incidentally, you fellows might like to read this," he added, passing a letter back.

It was addressed to the mayor, came from a man named Wild in a town over in the next state. The guy was bitching about his son's getting spooky letters from Mrs. Norton, trying to get the boy to leave home, come to West Condon before the nineteenth. He told how they'd had to boot her out of Carlyle about a year or so ago, and warned the mayor that she was a complete nut and had a perverted interest in young boys. "Whew! Pretty hot stuff!" Vince commented, handing the letter to the minister.

Ted parked in front of Savings and Loan, and they walked up to the second floor, where Himebaugh had his law office. "He was here about an hour ago," Ted whispered on the stairs. "If he's gone, we'll try his house."

But he was there, cleaning papers out of file cabinets and desk drawers, dumping them indiscriminately into a large trash basket. He looked up at them, smiled oddly. "Good afternoon, gentlemen! How have you been?"

"Good to see you again, Ralph!" Ted beamed. "Ralph, you know Burt, Wes. This is Vince Bonali—"

"Glad to know you, Mr. Himebaugh."

"My pleasure, I assure you."

What odd words these were! Things you said every day, but now they had such a weird ring, ghostly. "What are you throwing away there?" Vince asked, to get the ball rolling.

"Oh, damage suits, Mr. Bonali. Wills. Liquor licenses." Vince had heard the guy was shy, but if so, he hardly showed it now. Bright humorous gleam in his eyes, bold gestures, firm handshake. Kind of tremble there, though.

"Did you gentlemen ever stop to consider how inutterably absurd our legal institutions are?"

"Sure, lots of times!" laughed Ted easily. "I don't know who's more absurd, though, the institutions or the damned attorneys who invent them!"

The lawyer smiled faintly, but something seemed to give way. He sat down, motioned them to chairs. They remained standing.

"Of course, there's an element of the absurd in every institution, isn't there, Ralph?" Reverend Edwards asked. "Any society is a kind of jerryrig at best, and it's hard to think of one without the compromises that make it seem absurd."

"Yes," Himebaugh agreed. His fingers were pressed together prayerlike in front of him and they trembled. "That's how it usually seems to turn out, all right." A kind of smile jumped to his face, jumped away. "But no more."

"But that's pretty much what it means to be a man, isn't it, Ralph?" Ted asked. "Holding on to one's beliefs on the one hand, one's ideals, and on the other, accommodating oneself to the institution, making changes in it where it seems—"

"No, not at all!" snapped the lawyer. He leaned forward on one unsteady elbow, and his lips seemed to flush pink. Kind of flutter in the thick brows as he looked up at them. The guy looked in pretty bad shape, now that Vince observed more closely. Awful thin. "To be a whole man is to be at one with the—"

"Aw, come on, Ralph," Robbins cut in. "Let's talk plain. All Ted's trying to say is a guy can believe what he wants to believe, and still get along with—"

"You can't know one thing and act otherwise," the lawyer said. Precise enunciation, tremulous undercurrent. The total insane calm of the man and his weird shifty eyes were beginning to get to all four of them. "You can't know that fire burns and put your hand into it."

434

"No? Well, goddamn it, Ralph," Cavanaugh said gruffly, "that seems to me just what the hell you're doing!"

The lawyer smiled, lips quivering. "Maybe I've gone the next step. Maybe I've found out that fire doesn't burn, after all."

"Oh, hell, Himebaugh!" Robbins said. "Don't you see, we're here to help you get out of this thing."

"I don't want help. I don't need help." No smiles now. Very white. Very goddamn sick.

"Well, man, it's now or never. Don't expect us to come around Monday to give you a hand when you've got this whole town ready to ride you out on a rail—"

"There won't *be* a Monday, you *fools!*" Himebaugh cried. He leaped up, grabbed a pile of papers, heaved them at them. A folder struck Vince right on the bridge of his nose, made his eyes smart. He moved in, fists doubled, but Ted held him back. "*Get out! Get out!*" the lawyer screamed. Threw more heaps of paper. Jesus, he was really cracking up! Paper flying everywhere like a goddamn flock of mad birds let loose. "Get out, I say! *Get out, you fools, or I'll kill you!*" Banging of cabinet doors. His screams echoed. Wastebasket rattled off a wall. "*I'll kill you!*" They heard him screaming like that all the way out to the street.

On the way to the Nortons, they talked about it. Even Ted was shocked, and they all noticed how his health had deteriorated. Vince, embarrassed by the tears, repeated several times how the folder had caught him square on the nose. "I felt like laying into that guy right then and there!" he boomed. "Good thing you held me back, Ted!"

It was already dusk when they stepped heavy-footed onto the Nortons' front porch, knocked. Dr. Norton came to the door. Looked like they might have waked him up. "Hello, fellows, come on in." Soft gentle voice. You could hardly hear him. Vince started forward, but Ted, holding his ground, blocked him.

"I don't think it will take us long to say what we've come to say, Dr. Norton," Ted said.

Norton's wife, the schoolteacher Vince had driven in from the coalmine one day a couple months or so ago, stepped up behind the veterinarian. "What is it, Wylie?"

"These men . . ."

"We just came to say it might be better for you and for everybody," Robbins said, "if you just sort of moved on."

"Now, wait a moment, Mr. Robbins," the minister interrupted. "I think we want to give Dr. and Mrs. Norton every opportunity to reconsider the whole thing. You see, Dr. Norton, we—that is, all of us here in West Condon—have become concerned about certain activities which, we feel, are not in the best interests of—"

"Why, gentlemen!" laughed Mrs. Norton. "All this has happened before!"

"How's that?" asked Reverend Edwards, biting down on his lower lip.

"Look, Wylie! the dark one!" Vince broke into a strange sweat under her excited gaze. She smiled at him. "We are not going to leave."

"Well," said Reverend Edwards, "that's what I'm trying—"

"We have been expecting you. We have been pursued by you all our lives, and we knew that you would find us here. But we have been brought here to consummate our life's work, and we are never going to run again. We are not afraid."

Robbins' neck was blushing red, a sure sign. "Maybe you better think again—"

"We are going to the Mount of Redemption on Sunday to await the Coming of the Light. I hope you gentlemen will find it in your hearts to join us there. Now, go away and bother us no more. Wash the earth from your hands and feet and cast your eyes to the limitless stars!"

"That's nutty!" said Robbins. "Show 'em the letter."

"Forget it," said Cavanaugh. He showed by his look, his back turned coldly on the Nortons, that he considered it a lost cause.

436

They made one final call. And this one worked. At the orphanage, Reverend Edwards and Ted Cavanaugh pinned the Meredith kid in one lamplit corner. The old hotbox technique. Vince himself had used it in the union organizing days. Meredith was a pansy and it didn't take much to break him. Suddenly, in a flood of tears, he said he was sorry, it was all wrong, embraced Cavanaugh like a father, disclaimed the Brunists, said they'd been persecuting him from the start, hinted they might have been whipping him, and, in fear of them, he asked to be hidden away. Reverend Edwards, deeply moved, offered his home for the rest of the week. The boy wept gratefully, then cheered up, became even joyful on the ride to the Presbyterian manse, and it made them all feel good. Won one!

Or so they thought. That night, Tuesday, not only the goddamn local paper and the city papers were headlining the Brunist story, but it was even featured on the six o'clock televised newscast. Helicopter movies of West Condon and the coalmine, blown-up stills of some of Tiger Miller's photos, and the announcer saying: "In this placid little American community of West Condon, a small band of devout believers, calling themselves followers of the coalminer-prophet Giovanni Bruno, believe that on Sunday evening, the nineteenth of April, the world will end. In expectation of their own salvation, they will gather on this little knoll here, near the Deepwater Number Nine coalmine, where only three months ago an explosion and fire killed ninety-seven men. From that catastrophe, on Sunday, January eleventh, one man was rescued, this man—"

"Daddy!" Angie called out from her bedroom and he nearly went a foot up off his chair. "Listen to *this!*"

She threw open her door, the radio turned up fullblast. Cheap country-style music, badly sung. "What's that?" he asked. She'd taken lately to listening to a lot of that crap, especially the morbid ones about dead people, not excluding dead daddies.

437

"The Brunists!" she cried. "They're singing!"

> *Do not think that God's Chosen are the mighty!*
> *Do not think that God's Elect are the high!*
> *Just remember the stories in your Bible:*
> *'Tis the humble whom God doth glorify!*
>
> *Think of Moses, discovered in a river!*
> *Think of Jesus, a carpenter's son!*
> *Think of Bruno, a humble coalminer!*
> *'Tis the poor by whom God's battles are won!*
>
> *So, hark ye to the White Bird of Glory!*
> *Yes, hark ye to the White Bird of Grace!*
> *We shall gather at the Mount of Redemption*
> *To meet our dear Lord there face to face . . .*

"I'll be goddamned!" Vince said, and hurried away midchorus to the phone. "Hello, Ted? Vince here. Hey, turn on your radio! The Brunists are singing! They're on TV, too!"

"Jesus Christ, what next! Vince, I've got some bad news."

"Yeah?" Felt the hair on his neck stand up.

"The Meredith boy. Wes Edwards just phoned in a panic to tell me the kid has slashed his wrists with a razor. He's in the hospital."

"Jeee-zuss God All-*mighty!*" Took the wind right out of him. "Is it bad?"

"No, Doc Lewis told Wes it looked very much like the boy's done it before. Apparently he doesn't do it to kill himself. But we can't let go of him now. If he got back to the Brunists, he'd probably try to make murderers of us, or worse, the state of mind he's in. We're sending him up to a state hospital tonight. But, listen, Vince, not a word! Miller will probably find out, but if he or anybody asks, you know nothing, okay?"

"Sure, Ted. But Jesus, what a bad break!"

"Nobody's fault. We might even have saved the boy's life. No telling what he might have done after Sunday night. But we don't want Wes Edwards to get mixed up in this if we can help it, and so it's just as well the Brunists don't know how he ended up over there. Anyway, he'll be up there a good while, so there's no worry about him Sunday night. Just let's hope Miller doesn't get wind of it."

Fat chance. Headlines Wednesday night: BRUNIST KIDNAPPED! COLIN MEREDITH DISAPPEARS FROM WEST CONDON! TREATED AT HOSPITAL FOR INJURIES OR POSSIBLE SUICIDE! LAST SEEN AT HOME OF REV. WESLEY EDWARDS! And so on, big scare stuff. Phone rang. Thinking it was Ted, he answered it. "Mr. Bonali, this is CBS calling. We understand you were with the missing Meredith boy yesterday afternoon, just before his disappearance. Can you tell us—?" In a panic he hung up. Jesus! Kidnapping— that's FBI stuff, isn't it? He told Etta to answer the phone, ask who was calling, and if it wasn't Ted, to say he wasn't home.

He switched on the TV and—wham!—there was Mrs. Norton's funny little face. Every now and then, as she turned her head different angles, the floods beamed off her glasses and caused a kind of leap of light around her head. "We do not know what has happened to him. Our . . . sources, our sources at the higher aspects have informed us that he has fallen into the hands of the powers of darkness. We are . . . deeply hurt and concerned, but we are not surprised. We have all suffered threats upon our lives and upon our health. We are praying for his deliverance."

Announcer: "Mrs. Norton, do you have any idea who these powers, uh, these powers of darkness might be?"

Mrs. Norton: "Yes!" She paused, fingering a little medallion on her breast that flicked light back at the lens like a secret code. Vince started right up in his chair, felt a cold sweat in the small of his back. She was looking right at him. "*All* of you!" she said.

Feeling shaky, he called Ted, and Ted told him to relax, the entire story was being released, that he himself was taking all the responsibility, and that he would be by to see him the next morning. Final meeting of the Common Sense Committee tomorrow night. That calmed Vince down—Jesus! Ted was a great guy!—but he was still pretty restless. He paced the room, trapped by the Brunists: newspaper headlines black as death, their goddamn faces on television, and—blam!—Angie threw open her door again, and there they were:

> *Come all ye who seek your salvation!*
> *Come all who would stand upon God's Land!*
> *Come and march to the Mount of Redemption,*
> *For the end of all things is at hand!*
>
> *So, hark ye to the White Bird of Glory!* . . .

Ted's message the next day, the sixteenth, was to cool it. But Vince was feeling so goddamn high, he knew it wouldn't be easy. He had splurged on a bottle of whiskey, good stuff, in anticipation of Ted's visit, but Ted had turned it down. Too early in the day, he said. Vince, who had already poured his own to make the offering of it more natural, felt a little awkward himself with a glass of whiskey in his hand at ten in the goddamn morning, but he lied that he usually took a bracer in the mornings. He hoped he hadn't made some kind of mistake. Jesus! the thing hit him like seven hundred blazing biocarbonates!

Ted showed him their release on the Meredith boy. The boy had come to them, it claimed, in fear of reprisals from members of the Brunist group, whose fanaticism he had come to abhor, and had asked for protection. He had wept gratefully when Reverend Edwards, approached on the matter, had generously welcomed the boy to his own

440

home. But, evidently distraught by the experiences of the preceding weeks and fearing that attempts might be made against his life, he had cut his wrists with a razor, although not seriously. He was now being cared for in a hospital distant from West Condon, the name of which was not being divulged for the present for the boy's own protection. Hah! "That should keep them quiet!" Vince said.

"Well," said Ted, "it's mainly the truth, after all."

"Yeah," Vince said, remembering the hotbox. Swallowed down the whiskey belches. Wondered whether to suffer the stuff gradually, or just throw it down. "And so tonight at the meeting, you want me to ask everybody to stay at home."

"Right. Not much hope they will, but we can try." Ted paused, grinned. "I don't want to give you stagefright or anything, Rockduster, but I should warn you that the meeting is being covered by radio, news chains, and television across the country."

That put Vince at the verge of a bowel movement, but outwardly he remained calm. He even shrugged. And he was pleased that Ted still remembered his first CSC speech.

"You know, Vince, I'd like to make the meeting so goddamned straightforward, so goddamned plain and sensible, that it will bore those cheap corrupt headline-hunters to death, and they'll pack up and get out of here."

Vince laughed, toned it: little too harsh maybe. Didn't know why he felt so goddamn nervous today, sensation that something was—he looked out at the big red Lincoln: it was the connection. Today they broke the connection. "I wish we could've stopped it, Ted."

"So do I, Vince. But I don't see what more we could have done. We've at least contained it, and even cut them down one. I frankly doubt that that little handful of people can do us much harm, no matter how hard Tiger Miller strains. Now, our main worry is just to keep everybody calmed down, away from that hill, minimize the effect Sunday, and then try to get over it. Of course, things could get worse. If they do, I'll give you a call."

"I'll stay by the phone, Ted. Isn't there anything else we can do meanwhile?"

"I don't know what. I tried to cajole Whimple into arresting Bruno on grounds of suspected insanity, but he didn't have the nerve."

Vince glanced up, found Ted's cool eyes fixed on him. He lowered his gaze, took a slow drink of whiskey. "Not a bad idea," he said. "He should've done it." Then he added: "I sure as hell would've."

"Speaking of Whimple, Vince," Ted continued, "I wonder if you'd do us the favor of asking for a vote of thanks for him tonight at the meeting, for him and Father Baglione and Reverend Edwards."

"Sure." Fixed his jaw in a kind of mockery.

"Oh hell, I know, Vince, they're not the ones who have put out on this job, but that's the game we play." There was a pause. It was now or never. Vince gazed thoughtfully into his whiskey glass. "You might be interested in knowing, though, that they're setting up a Mayor's Special Commission on Industrial Planning. I've nominated you for a spot on it."

Vince nodded, stroked his chin, looked up at Ted. "Thanks," he said. "I'd like that."

Ted shrugged. "Nothing to thank me for, Vince. You're the right man for the job, that's all. Probably be about eight of us. Not too much in the way of rewards, twenty or so a month probably, but it might lead to some good things." Ted stood.

"Well," said Vince standing, extending his hand, "see you tonight at the adjournment."

"Let's call it a recess," Ted said with a smile.

"It was really great, Vince, you were really great!" Etta kept repeating it, over and over, all the way home from the meeting, from all those cameras, all that noise, all those assurances, all the way home and into their bedroom, where now she stood at the mirror in her slip, putting clips and curlers in her hair. Large satisfied smile on her face. "Everybody couldn't stop complimenting me afterwards."

Vince tossed his pants over a chair, sat on the edge of the bed in his shorts. "Well, chicken, you ain't got the best yet, I been saving it."

"Really? You mean there's something more?" She looked inquisitively at him through the mirror as she reached under her slip, pulled down her huge balloonlike drawers. She carried them over to the closet where her nightshirt hung on a clothes hook.

"It is my pleasure to announce that they have just set up this here mayor's special group for planning industry, and just by chance it turns out, ahem, that the old man's gonna be on it."

"*What?*" She wheeled around, face alive with a big plump happiness. "Oh, Vince, that's *swell!*" First real burst of enthusiasm he'd seen her register since he could remember.

Vince felt great, heroic in fact, but he nodded with an affected disinterest, inspected his toes. "Even gonna bring in a few coins each month. Ted'll be coming by next week, after this Bruno sideshow is closed down, to talk about it." While he was talking, she turned her broad back to him, started to hoist the slip up over her big pink body. Vince tiptoed over behind her, reached suddenly around and hugged onto both breasts.

"Vince! Help! I can't see! *Vince!*"

"*Sshh!* You'll have Angie thinking I'm committing murder instead of just friendly rape!" She giggled girlishly, twisted her three hundred pounds around, tried to work her arms free of the entangling slip, but it was wrapped around her head, caught in the curlers. There was always something wonderfully oily about her body. Vince clutched onto the far breast with one hand, slid the still-whole one down over the mountainous range of her smooth bulbous abdomen, felt the groin flesh start and tremble. A man

443

really had to stretch. "And, baby," he whispered, releasing her breast to shove his shorts down, "we're just seven short months away from city elections. . . ."

Vince was up on the ladder again Friday morning, feeling like a kind of king up there, when Burt Robbins and the shoeman Maury Castle came by. "Hey, Vince, got a minute?" Something phony in their smiles.

"Hell," Vince laughed carelessly, "this is the fifth goddamn time I've painted this same patch!" But he crawled down.

"Vince, goddamn! Good to see you!" Castle grabbed his hand and nearly tore it off. "Listen, buddy, we got a great great project!"

"Yeah?" Kept grinning, but he didn't like the looks of it.

"If you're game," Robbins added. The needle.

"Listen, Vince," said Castle, leaning forward like he was about to let go a secret, but his voice was just as loud as ever. "We got a hilarious idea—we thought we might bring the end of the world tonight. A little early."

"How's that?"

"A few of us is planning to pay a call tonight on old Ralphie—"

"You mean—?"

"Himebaugh," said Robbins. "The guy who tried to bloody your nose with a filing cabinet."

Vince grinned. "So?" He felt himself getting sucked deeper and deeper.

"So we thought we'd visit Ralphie tonight—in-cog-nito, as they say," explained Castle, "and inform him we're the Second Coming. You get the picture?"

"Yeah, I think so—"

"Well, how's it grab you?"

Vince rubbed his nose with the back of his hand, reached in his shirt pocket for a cigar. Didn't grab him at all, not at all, but he supposed he'd have to go along. "But he'll probably be over at Bruno's house—"

444

"We checked that out," Robbins said. "They've got a long weekend coming up and apparently decided to spend this night at home, getting a good rest and winding up their private affairs."

Vince tried to look amused. "I dunno, Ted said—"

"Whatsamatter?" Castle asked. "You Ted's baby?"

Vince smarted. "No, shit, but—"

"Anyway, keep it quiet," said Robbins, "but Ted's in on this. You know how he feels about Himebaugh." Robbins' eyes were nothing but slits. Vince thought about the mayor and how he hadn't had the nerve.

"Well, come on, Vince!" Castle shouted. When that man opened his mouth it really whammed out of there. "You game, goddamn it, or ain't you?"

"Hell, I'm always game. Who else—?"

"Bring anybody you want. We already talked to Cheese Johnson and Georgie Lucci, and they're coming. Anybody else you like."

Cheese. Known the bastard for years and never knew anybody called him Cheese. Maybe one of these guys thought it up. "Okay. Where do we go?"

"Over to my place first," said Castle. "We'll oil up the machinery before. I'm at 701 Elm, first white house on the corner of Elm and Seventh. Seven sharp."

"Okay," said Vince, working up a grin around the cigar. Get a free drink or two out of it anyhow.

"Oh, and Vince, bring an old sheet."

> *"Jesus loves me, this I know,*
> *Cause ole Bruno tol' me so!*
> *Little ones to him belong,*
> *His is short, but mine is long!"*

sang old Cheese Johnson at the top of his goddamn funny nasal voice.

> *"Yes, Jesus loves me!*
> *Yes, Jesus loves me . . . !"*

bellowed old Vince and old Sal Ferrero and good old Georgie Lucci.

"Hey, you guys, can it! You'll have us all in the clink!" hissed old Burt, but he was laughing, old Maury was laughing, everybody was laughing to beat hell.

"Ifn Jesus loved *you*, you wouldn' talk thetaway!" slurred old Cheese. Vince giggled.

They stopped and staggered out of the car.

"This the place?" hollered Georgie. "Looks all dark."

"*Ssst!*" That was old Burt the goddamn spoilsport. "Pipe down! We're still a block away. We'll walk the rest. Now look, you crazy bastards, calm down or you'll spoil the gag!"

"Oh, Jesus *Christ*, boys!" moaned old Cheese, falling all over himself. "*Don't* spoil the *gag!* Oh, *Jesus!*"

Arms over each other's shoulders, they careened down the street. "Hey, wait!" That goddamn Robbins again.

"Maury, old buddy, call that fucking deacon off our ass, for God's sake!"

Robbins laughed. "Shit, Vince, all I want is for you to get your goddamn sheets on. It's no party without them."

They paused for that business. Felt all stuffy inside. Vince thought he'd gag. Couldn't find the damn eyeholes. Then two fingers nearly put his eyes out. "Got it now, Vince, old buddy?" That goddamn Castle had a voice carry to Singapore.

"Now, listen," said Robbins. "Don't forget the point is this: you guys are spirits from the other world, see, and—"

"*Oh earthling Ralphus!*" cried old Cheese Johnson, staggering around in hilarious circles. "*We are spirits—*"

"Hold it! hold it! You got it, but we're not there yet. Now remember: you've come to pick Ralphie up and escort him to the spaceship."

"Spayshit," said Sal Ferrero solemnly. Castle guffawed. Sal got quieter and funnier the drunker he got.

"Tell him, above all, he's not to wear any earth clothes, nothing, just a sheet, see, and then—"

"Sheetsie," said Sal.

Robbins and Castle were laughing themselves sick. Old Burt could hardly talk. He was a lot nicer guy tonight. Maybe it just took awhile to get to know him. "And then you lead him right down to Main Street, and when you get him to city hall, you—"

"Shittyall," said Sal.

"Jesus Christ!" howled the sheet that had old Georgie in it. "Sal, you're a goddamn riot!"

"Riot!" affirmed Sal, and everybody broke up again.

Robbins hissed. "It's right there, next house! Now remember: when you get him in front of city hall, you—"

"We pull off his sheet," said Vince. Sure goddamn hard to breathe in this thing.

"You've got it!"

"Jesus, Vince!" cried the tall thin sheet with the silly-ass nasal voice. "You've *got* it!"

"But why ain't you two guys wearing sheets?"

"Hell, he'd recognize our voices in a minute, Vince, spoil the gag. Look, see that hedge just over there? Me and Maury'll wait behind that, watch how it goes. If you need us, we'll be there. Now, go to it!"

The four sheets approached old Ralphie's house.

"Damn, Sal, at least stand up right!"

"Riot!"

"Okay," announced old Cheese, "watch this!" He picked up a handful of pebbles and flung them at a window. Himebaugh's face appeared in it. "Light the torch!" Georgie struck a match to the torch, then lifted it flaming over his head. Old Ralphie's eyes nearly shot right out of their sockets. Johnson lifted his elbows, shook the sheet. The others imitated him. Himebaugh opened the door a crack, poked out his terrified white face. "*Oh earthling Ralphus! We are spirits from the upper worlds come to transport thee hither!*" Except for the twang, it was a great fucking act. Himebaugh stepped gingerly out onto the porch, dressed in one of those funny Brunist nightshirts. "*Our spaceship awaits thee!*"

447

Vince's line: *"Come, friend! Makest thee haste!"* Christ! stumbled all over the goddamn *s-t's!* *"The Destroyer cometh!"*

"B-but tonight?" whined the old guy. He was cracking all apart. Very different pose from what Vince had seen yesterday. "We thought—isn't it—?"

"Well, our plans is got changed," said old Cheese, ad-libbing it. "Now git your ass in gear, Ralphus!"

Himebaugh stiffened, eyebrows slid down off the top of his head. "I don't know who you are," he sighed, "but you're wasting your time."

"Tie 'em!" cried Sal. Georgie snickered. Vince had to piss.

"Listen, ifn you don't git comin'," hollered Johnson, sliding all the way back into his cruddy accent, "we're gonna shag off without ye!"

Himebaugh shook his head wearily, went in, shut the door. Could hear the key working in the lock.

"Jeez, Cheese, it's that goddamn hillbilly accent of yours," Vince complained. "There *ain't* no hillbillies in the other world, don't you know that?"

"Whaddaya think we oughta do, bust in an' git him?"

"Naw, what good would that do? Let's go ask old Burt and old Maury." Vince led the way to the hedge. Nobody there. "Why those goddamn sonsabitches!"

"Fairweather friends," said Cheese.

"Left us in the fucking lurch," said Georgie.

"But all is not lost!" announced old Sal, lifting off his sheet and producing a fifth of bourbon. "I borrowed this from good old faithful Maury's liquor cabinet."

"Hey! Good man, Salvo!" laughed Johnson, whipping off his sheet. "Uncork that mother!"

"Three cheers for old Sal Ferrero!" proposed Georgie, and they all hip-hip-hoorayed while pissing on a tree. Then the four of them sat down on their sheets behind the hedge and passed the bottle. "Well, what'll we do next?" asked Georgie.

448

"Let's go visit old Wosznik and spook his mutt," suggested Johnson.

"We can burn down a couple houses," Georgie offered.

"Vince has got a hand we can use." The bastard.

"Let's go hang a buncha rubbers in the little tree on Cunt Hill," Johnson said.

"Where's that?" Vince asked.

"That rise out by old Number Nine—"

"Mount of Redemption," said Sal.

"I never heard it called that," Vince said. "When did it—?"

"Tiger Miller's old buddy Lou Jones made it up."

"What's the point?"

"What's the point of any cunt?" asked Georgie, and they all laughed idiotically at that.

Vince chugalugged on the fifth, got what he supposed was more or less his quarter, then handed it to Georgie. "Think I'll bug out, fellow phantoms. Go get me some shuteye." Thrust himself to his feet, staggered away. Fact was, he'd been thinking all night about poor Wanda Cravens. She never knew why he never came back. Poor kid. Shouldn't have been that way. Man can cut out without being crude. Go tell her now. Wanda honey, I'm being a good boy now. Gonna be mayor, see, can't fuck it up. You understand, hunh? Good girl. Lotta fun, but. Meant to tell you before, but I been busy—oh yes, very very busy. Too bad. Awful sorry. You know I am. Listen, though. You're a cute kid. I'll keep my eye out for you, know what I mean? Anything you ever need. Count on me.

Yeah, this was the place okay. Stumbled up on the porch, thumped the door, then staggered on in. Whoo-ee! shouldn't have chugalugged. House dead still. All the junk gone. Jesus, maybe she'd moved. Light on in the bedroom. She was just grabbing up her ragtag robe when he reeled in. In her skivvies, snow-white, but her cute titties were flying free.

"Oh, Vince! Landsakes, you give me a fright! I was

449

takin' a bath. Didn't know *who* it could be out there bumpin' around."

"Who *else*'d it be?"

"Well, I jist didn't know, I thought maybe, you know, day after tomorra bein' the end a the world and all. I jist thought—"

"Oh yeah. That." Vince thought of old Ralphie and grinned. Lights all funny in the damn room somehow. He blew out his cheeks. "Hey, listen, Wanda, I didn't mean. to butt in or nothing, I just only came to tell you—"

"Vince, I never knowed you to drink so much."

Must really be swaying. "Well, I ain't accustomed to it." Couldn't quite see if she was all covered up with the robe or not.

"Vince, I'm sorry, but I have to ask ye to go. It's all over now, what we was—"

"All *over!*"

"Yes, for some time now. I thought you knowed or guessed. I been comin' to the light, Vince. And I gotta have my soul all clean for the end. I've sold all I had and give all the money away, and I ain't gonna do nothin' sinful. Leastways with the powers of—"

"Wanda! You ain't saying you're turning me out!"

"Vince, I gotta! It ain't what I want or don't want, things is different now. Jist one more day, Vince—"

"Wanda! How can you *do* it? I—you just—" He felt all knotted up. And she was so calm, so cold. Had she forgot how it was between them? "Please, I—"

"Vince, it was a mistake. I was lonely and you was nice to me, but we cain't go makin' that mistake all over agin."

"*Mistake!*" Jesus, she was cutting him something awful!

"Now stop it, Vince! You're drunk. Let's be honest, I was a good thing for you, somethin' for fun on the side, but—"

"*Wanda!*" He slumped to the bed by where she was standing, felt like bawling, took her hand. She didn't understand, everything was wrong, he felt awful. "Wanda,

450

Wanda, I *love* you! Couldn't you tell that? You don't know how you're hurting me!"

"Oh, really, Vince! You're gittin' silly!"

He could smell the damp fragrance of her bathed crotch. My God, what was she doing to him? "Wanda, please! Try to understand! Listen, I'm gonna be mayor here! Don't that mean nothing to you?" Maybe he should just tumble her to the sack and lay her. He worked her robe apart with his nose, pressed his face against her white-pantied groin, felt the nylon whistle along his beard.

"Vince, don't—!"

He laughed the old laugh. "The mayor, baby!" Got a wrist before she could get away."

"The baby's watchin'!"

"That never stopped us—"

"*No!*"

Shoved her hard to the bed. Springs twanged. Caught the wide-eyed drool of the baby, staring over the side of the crib. Heard Davey. She hit out, but no life in it. They all want it. "*Please, Wanda!*" he whispered hoarsely, as he wallowed down over her. "Once more, Wanda! for old times! for the old mayor!" She turned her head, wouldn't let him kiss her. He unbuckled his pants, fingers thick and fumbling, whipped the fly open, reared his rump up and shoved his pants and shorts to his knees. Couldn't bother getting the pants off her. Slide in past the legband. She squirmed—

"Please!

"Oh Wanda, you don't know how you're *hurting* me!

"I *love* you!

"One more for the old mayor!

"The mayor, baby!"

Vince lurched up off the bed, tripped over his own pants, whammed to the floor on his hands and knees. Johnson, Ferrero, and Lucci stood in the doorway splitting their goddamn drunken guts with laughter. "You goddamn sonuvabitching cocksuckers!" screamed Vince. Pants all tangled up somehow. Baby howling like a maniac. Davey padding in. Wanted to take a swing, hit anybody. But Jesus, he realized he had nothing left in him and he was going blind to boot.

"Well, so this is how we talk to the spirits!" grinned Johnson. "Well, boys, I for one am goin' to join this here religion!"

"I believe!" cried Georgie. Jesus, they could hardly stand.

"Now you two fellers take a restrainin' grip on old Dad there, so's he don't break the spell," Johnson said, then hiccupped, "and let's see ifn I cain't git a message through to the holy kingdom."

Sal and Georgie rubberlegged over. Grabbed Vince unconvincingly just as he'd got his pants up. Georgie shoved his pants down to his ankles again. "Don't want you running out on us again," he said. Vince struggled, but just didn't have any goddamn strength.

Johnson unzipped his fly and reeled forward. Wanda cowered pale against the head of the bed, clutching the robe tight around her neck, but showing a bright white glimpse of snatch. Wasn't her fault, she was too scared to realize, but still it made Vince mad, showing what she had like that. Lights were still screwed up. And he couldn't sort the noises. Like a fucking circus or something. Watched the scene, but had to think about it to be sure he was seeing it. Was Johnson into her? No, he was still standing there, showing off his instrument, pulling out his shirt, and hiccupping. "Le's git the Comin' on the road!" he was saying to Wanda.

"Please!" she whispered. "Go away!" She was scared. Vince couldn't see her good, but he knew, could tell. The poor kid. "Davey! don't look! Go to your room!"

"You let go, Sal, old buddy," Vince whispered between his teeth, "or I'll rebust that arm of yours so they'll *never* get it fixed again!" Sal relaxed his grip. Vince stepped out of one pant leg, spun, tempted to bust Georgie's nuts, but, pitying him standing there so blearily innocent, he only threw a right to the gut. Georgie whined and doubled, and Vince popped him hard as he could on the back of the neck, sent him—grateful maybe—to the floor. Johnson faced around just as Vince reached him, one leg dragging his pants on the floor, but the dumb bastard made the mistake of trying to close his fly first and caught Vince's full-bodied right square in his silly mouth. His head shot back like it was snapped and he crashed against the wall, brought down the endtable and bedlamp. Lights and shadows flew every which way, like suddenly there was a hundred people in there running around. Tried to think how to follow up. Reached for his own pants. Wanda was gone, that quick. Heard her grab up the phone in the hall. Johnson pushed confusedly up off the floor, wheeled forward, pitched himself on Vince more like a lover than a foe, and they tumbled like potato bags to the floor. Johnson kneed him in the stomach. Vince struggled. If only he could get room to swing. For a minute he thought, Aw, to hell with it. Bad dream. Wake up. Johnson was pummeling him with short weak blows to the midriff, but they felt a great distance off. They rolled and pitched drearily on the floor. Nobody seemed to get ahead.

"Vince baby," Johnson gasped, "you'll git slivers in your ass!" That lamebrain was grinning even with blood smeared all over his knobby mug—must have really opened something up with that right.

Bonali raised his hips up fast and sudden, hardly thinking about it, surprising even himself, drove Johnson off-balance headfirst into the wall, slid out fast from under the bastard and slugged him with all his might behind the ear, in the face, wherever he could make it land. He stood up, gasping for breath. Room still whipping around there, wilder than ever. "Johnson!" Coughing, could hardly breathe. Johnson out dead. "You always talk too much for your own fucking good!" Reached down, pulled up his shorts. His balls hurt him and he tried to see if they'd got busted or something.

"Police are on the way," Wanda said, watching him coldly from the doorway, dressed now in slacks and sweater, baby in her arms, holding Davey's hand.

Georgie was still groveling on the floor, holding his belly, whimpering, "Muh-*donna!*"

Sal was standing like a specter against the wall. Going green. "Sal, you better bug out, buddy," Vince gasped. "I'll be right behind." Sal was gone like a shot. Vince untwisted his pants, they were a goddamn mess, hauled them up, felt the pockets: billfold gone! Jesus, they could pin him with that! "Wanda, listen, if the cops get here before I get away, you tell them these two bastards came first, and I followed them and tried to protect you, you hear?" But he saw no response there. Searched for the billfold. Sense of not moving fast enough, limbs heavy, head—found it under the goddamn bed. Crawled under, bed above him winding like a fucking carousel, he was sweating to beat hell, and the dust under here was sticking to him. He spat, reached for the billfold—move, Dad!— had his ass out when Dee Romano and old Willie walked in, pistols cocked.

"Landsakes!" exclaimed Willie through his whistling false teeth. "Looks like they's been some party!"

Wanda stood wan and martyred with her kids. Vince tried to get her eye. Georgie squinted blearily up at Dee and Willie from the floor, as though trying to figure out who the hell they could be.

"What happened, Mrs. Cravens?" Romano asked. Kept his great big gun out, very edgy, finger on the goddamn trigger.

"Well, these guys—" Vince began, getting to his feet, but Romano waved his pistol at him menacingly.

"These here men come in drunk, just bustin' in, got in a awful fight," said Wanda dully. "They was another one, but he run off."

"Musta been that body we passed," Willie remarked.

"Yeah," said Dee.

"What'd they come for?" drawled Willie.

Romano grinned sarcastically and pointed with his gun down at Johnson, just beginning to stir: Johnson's prick was lolling limp outside his fly.

Wanda began to cry. "I don't know even who they are!" She wept. Davey started in, too. So he had a voice okay. "Maybe they come in here by mistake. I don't know why they picked on me!"

"Hey, wait—!" protested Vince, then thought better of it, cut himself off.

"Do you wanna file any charges?" asked Romano.

"No," she said, sniffling pathetically. "Please, officer, jist git 'em out!"

Johnson came around just then, sat up painfully, stared head-on into Romano's pistol barrel. "Man alive!" he exclaimed. "I'd say that one takes the prize!" Vince couldn't help grinning. Johnson got to his feet, noticed he was still open, turned his back to Wanda to zip up. "Now, how many times I told ye, Wanda, when I'm takin' a nap, not to—" He caught his bloody reflection in the mirror, stepped closer in alarm. "Jesus, men! It ain't *me!*" he cried.

"Come on, quit the clowning!" said Romano officiously. "We're all going down to the station. You can clean up there." He paused for effect. "Over the next six months or so."

"Dee baby, you been watchin' too much TV," said Johnson. The five of them filed out of the room, old Willie leading, Romano lingering fifth. "Come on, Romano," complained Johnson in a nasal nag, "ifn we cain't have none, you cain't neither."

"*You bastard!*" hissed Romano, and kicked Johnson hard in the butt. "I'm sorry, Mrs. Cravens. We'll take care of these guys. For good."

They washed up at the station. It all began to register there what had happened, what the consequences were. Several people had seen him as they drove to the station—

right down the middle of Main Street, for Christ sake—
though they might not have been able to recognize him.
Had his eyes ducked coming in, didn't know if he was
being watched out front or not. Goddamn Romano pushing them in ahead with his pistol out for the whole fucking world to see. But, hell, what did all that matter? Six
months! And Jesus, what could he even say? Caught,
man. In the act. Pants down. It would be in the newspapers. And mixed up with the Brunist mess besides. Oh
God! And Ted and his family, Etta, Angie! How the hell
had he ever—? Had to get out, *had* to, even if he had to
screw Johnson and Lucci to do it. He was nearly crying.

Johnson nudged him, washing up. "Got fifteen bucks
or so?"

"Yeah, I think so." Reached for his billfold to look.

"No, don't grab for it now," cautioned Johnson. "Jist
have it ready, and play along with ol' Chester." The
guy's face was a mess and a tooth was broken, but he could
still grin.

They went out front again to get booked. Luckily,
nobody was lounging around in the station like they usually
were. "Say, Willie, ol' man, while we're signin' ourselves
into this fine hotel here, would ye be so kind as to run out
and git ol' Chester a pack a smokes?" He handed Willie
five bucks. "Gonna be a long night. And buy some for
yourself." Willie looked questioningly at Romano, and
Romano nodded him out. "Well, now, where do we sign
this here petition?" asked Johnson, examining the book.
"Well, I'll be damned! Here's all my old very best
friends. Hell, I'd be downright honored to join this fine
company."

"Stop wising off and get it over with!" snapped Romano.

"Listen, you know, Dee baby, they ain't nothin' really
that cunt kin pin us on. Ever' sonuvabitch in this town
has been humpin' her since ol' Lee got hisself killt. Ain't
that the truth, boys?"

"Jesus, yes!" affirmed Georgie. "She asked us all over.
Last big bang before the end of the world, she thinks."

"Yeah, that's right," said Vince. "She's one of those Brunist nuts, Dee, one of those folks who's been causing this town, our community here, so much trouble." Perspiring, felt rotten about screwing her like that, but she'd screwed him first, hadn't she?

"Well, now, that's all very interesting," said Romano. "Now, sign your names here, and I'll get your new home away from home all ready for you."

"Hey, ya know, boys," said Johnson, picking up the pen and licking the point, "old Dee here's got his eye on a very fine huntin' dog. Ain't that so, Dee?" Romano grumbled again, squinted his eye warily toward Johnson. "Very purty spaniel type, useter be ol' Eddie Wilson's mutt, poor ol' Eddie, ya know."

"Oh yeah!" said Vince, getting the picture now. "Very fine dog. I'd like to have it, but I cain't afford it." Christ, he even found himself imitating Johnson's cornball cadences. Still felt pretty funny, though he thought his head was clearing some.

"How much does old Widow Wilson want for it?" asked Lucci, joining in.

"Forty," mumbled Romano, his eye on the door.

"Ya know," said Johnson, "all of us guys is so fond of our ol' buddy here, our good ol' swell ol' asshole buddy Dee, whaddaya say we all make him a little present a that there dog, whaddaya say?"

"Well, I been wanting to make a present to good old Dee for a long time now," said Vince. "This sure does look like a fine opportunity."

"Don't it though!" said Johnson. The three of them turned on Romano.

He hesitated, glanced at the door. "Well, I guess she is one a them troublemakers," he muttered and took the book back. They dropped the bills in front of him and walked out, hands in pockets.

Outside, the light blinded them. Heart jumped, because his first thought was the mine blowing up. Then he saw all the cameras, guys rushing up. Questions. Pops

457

of light. He brushed by them, but came up against Tiger Miller. "What's up, Bonali?" he asked.

Vince could tell the sonuvabitch already knew plenty. "Nothing," he said and set his jaw, ready to lay into the bastard if he had to. Felt Johnson and Lucci backing him up. "Just having a little talk with the boys here about the Brunists." Some of the cameras, he saw, were movie jobs. He wondered what brought them.

"What kind of talk?" Miller stood his ground. "Listen, Vince, you'd better cool it. You've got big ambitions here, but don't forget you can screw yourself by going too far, getting into some legal trouble, and if I ever hear about—"

"Oh yeah Jesus!" cried Johnson, his cackling laugh cutting Miller off. "Don't do nothin' as might git ye in *trouble*, Vince!"

Lucci joined the bastard in the yak-yakking. "*One more time for the ol' mayor!*" he cried.

"Don't sweat it, Miller!" growled Vince, and shoved by him. Shit. Felt like the number-one all-star ass of all time. And it was bound to get worse. All those cameras. And he knew better than to think Johnson could keep his fat mouth shut.

Four A.M. Staggered from the bed. Reached the bathroom door and up it came. Tracked through it in bare feet to the stool and got rid of the rest. Down to the bile. Sat on the side of the tub, head in hands. Sick. Not just in the gut. Sick in the heart, too. Fucked it up. End of the world. It was all over.

3

Miller listened to Hilda roar and groan, smelled her dark reek, watched his Saturday night edition, that of the eighteenth of April, *flap-flap-flap* out of her. The back shop force, faces streaked with oily black ink, looked beat, but pleased with themselves. They'd made it through the week, shy two men who had quit under Cavanaugh's pressure, stayed right on schedule, got $50 bonuses for it. Twice already tonight—God's vindictive ways—the old press had broken down, but it looked now like she'd make it through the rest of the run.

Miller tucked his hand into the parade of copies slapping out, pulled out a damp one. WE SHALL GATHER AT THE MOUNT OF REDEMPTION! Two-line banner, bigger than anything since the war. Official portrait of the whole group, now minus Colin Meredith, spanned the middle columns under the banner. Not his photo, of course. In an odd reversal of roles, he had come more and more this week to depend on the East Condon newsmen, having been cut off on all sides by his own people. The photo showed fifteen tunicked grownups, eight infants similarly dressed. He'd thought the group would have grown by now, but the Common Sensers had apparently locked them out. Widow Wilson had spoken of converts, but they hadn't shown their faces.

But they might. Certainly he'd got a lot of letters from all over the country expressing interest in and sympathy with the Brunist movement. Tonight's paper was full of these letters. A minister in Mississippi who said he'd chartered a bus for the West Condon pilgrimage. A movie actress who wrote from California that Bruno had appeared to her in her dreams, promising her salvation. A blind man in an old folks' home in New Hampshire who claimed that, hearing about Bruno on television, he had suddenly had a glimpse of light and seemed headed for a cure. That wasn't the only miracle. An invalid in Arizona had risen from his bed and begun to walk, and, if his letter could be believed, was presently hitchhiking his way across the country to West Condon. A woman in Chicago, committing suicide, had left a note behind, confirming, through her own sources, Bruno's prophecy, and explaining that she couldn't bear to face the horror that would be her sinner's lot.

The inside pages—there were now virtually no ads— were filled with a picture story of the Brunists. He was in a couple of the pictures himself. Nothing so fancy as some of the big spreads he'd helped work up for a couple of the national picture magazines, but pretty good at that. He'd filled in with a rerun of the texts of Ben Wosznik's songs, the essentials of Eleanor Norton's system, Bruno's prophecies, or "words." These last, now six in number, had been codified as: Hark ye to the White Bird; I am the One to Come; Coming of Light, Sunday week; the tomb is its message; a circle of evenings; and gather on the Mount of Redemption. He had letters he had beguiled out of several eminent churchmen, an article on the lusty response of the mass media to the event, and blunt verbatim reports of conversations he'd overheard in Mick's, the coffeeshop, in barbershops, and on the street. Miller had also taken a last-minute interest in that vast segment of the holy milieu who were simply not involved, had in- terviewed the high school track coach, a drummer in a nearby roadhouse, a bartender in Waterton, his own mentally subnormal janitor Jerry. An old woman in her nineties told him she used to expect the end of the world all the time, but it was like all of a sudden it had slipped up on her. She'd always been a decent Godfearing woman, to be sure, but now did all this mean she had to go out on that hill and sing songs and all? How big a hill was it? Could they get all the people they were going to save up on that one hill? Would there be room for her even if she went *out* there? And what if it wasn't the end of the world at all? Why, she'd probably catch her death! And surely there would be photographers and, yes, television, because she'd noticed that all her favorites this week from "Captain Kangaroo" to "What's My Line?" had got bumped by this thing. So what should she wear? She had nothing new. No, no, it was better to stay home and watch it on television, that was *almost* like being there, wasn't it? Or maybe if she broke her leg and couldn't get there, what if she did that? It'd be all the same, didn't he think so? Yes, that was a splendid idea! Watch it on television, get a slip from the doctor explaining it would be unwise for her to spend the night out in the air, call a taxi to be at her house about twenty minutes before, you see, and if things seemed to be going on, why then, trot on out. . . .

As for the Brunists, they now gave interviews freely to anyone but him, held open house daily, posed for photos, appeared gladly on radio and television. Last night, Ben Wosznik had given a touching account of his conversion, had sung a few songs he had composed, had spoken simply but convincingly of each of his fellow Brunists, and had even managed to turn so grotesque an object as that scabby bland hand—still one of their altar relics and getting them a lot of mileage in the East Condon newspapers—into a moving symbol of the persecution that besets the holy. As for Marcella, Miller, staring again at his front-page group photo, hardly recognized her. Ralph Himebaugh and Eleanor Norton were holding her up, and her head lolled foolishly on Himebaugh's shoulder. Her hair hung down haglike past her ears, past her face, now a dull matte white. Those eyes that had so captivated him now stared vapidly out past the camera, too large for this face, all their bright glitter gone. The others in the photo were pale and solemn, posed stiffly as in old daguerreotypes, heads high, hands folded, chins up . . . "such a one caught up, even to the third heaven . . ."

He realized that his own mind had also been, subtly, geared for an end tomorrow: Monday had been and still was an unreality. Projects always did that. They set up something that looked hard and real, something to aim at, but they always concealed then the thick tangle of endless ambiguities that were the one true thing of this world. For Miller, there was nothing worse than the end of a project: cold sweats, nausea, couldn't eat—like shaking a habit. Even knowing that though, he could never resist launching new ones. The reason was: it was that or nothing, and nothing was not good at all. There was, of course, the alternative of the lifetime project instead of all these short ones, but he feared a greater despair, the mid-project collapse. He could only make himself believe in a game a short time, and he preferred to take a lot of short hard falls than one long sickening and endless drop. Did Happy Bottom guess this? Did she see that Monday must come? It didn't matter; forget it. He tossed the paper in a trash barrel and went home, there to crawl in a white hole with a great white mole, split white thighs and sleep a white sleep.

Marcella wakes from a distant place. An inexplicable chill. She supposes that, kissed by Death, she is dead. Her body is still bare as He left it, the tunic rolled up to her throat. The house is filled with noise. Her wake? Yet, when she rolls her ear into the pillow, she hears the beating of a heart. Can it be hers? Has she returned?

Freshly showered, richly fed, mildly drunk, the phone unplugged, the doors locked, and the blinds pulled, Happy Bottom and the West Condon Tiger lay face to fork, listening to the merry secular twang of Yogi Bear on the bedroom television, each contemplating in his/her own way that peculiar piece of anatomy toward which he/she was so relentlessly drawn, tasting it, toying with it, slowly drifting out of this time and this place, out of particularity toward union with the One. Classical copulation, belly to belly, was of course the true magical experience: the illusion of having solved the Great Mystery, simply because the parts seemed to fit. Antipodally, on the other hand, the parts no longer fit, and analogues had to be improvised. But, thus stripped of magic, it was closer to a pure mystical experience, for contemplation of the mystery was direct, enhanced by the strange fact that one could not imagine the thoughts of one's partner, since one could not, without repugnance, imagine the partner's perspective, being able only to feel—literally—the other's hunger and excitement, the other's joy. Though each knew, better even than any part of himself/herself, that concavity/ convexity that he/she kissed, it nevertheless remained utterly unimaginable to him/her, impossible, always incredibly new. A tasty cornflakes commercial was the dingdong epithalamium that accompanied their gradual ascent into blessedness. Happy's thighs twitched, kicked, cuffed his ears, her bottom leaped, her fingers scurried, burrowed, clawed, kneaded, her mouth raged—

"This man, Giovanni Bruno, was born thirty-four years ago next November, the fourth child of five of Antonio Bruno, an immigrant Italian coalminer, and his wife Emilia. Three months ago—or to be precise, fourteen Sundays ago tomorrow—he was rescued from a mine disaster that killed ninety-seven men. Tomorrow, he and a band of devout followers anticipate the end of the world. The astonishing story of the Brunists of West Condon, after this message . . ."

Miller recognized it. He had written it. He'd forgot it was to be televised tonight. If Happy noticed his sudden distraction, she gave no sign of it. Unless an increased fervency was in fact a sign—

". . . Little is known of Giovanni Bruno's boyhood, but that is not to say that it was uneventful. It was a time of physical and psychological insecurity, a time of anti-union violence and inter-union wars, a time of Ku Klux Klan persecutions of immigrant Catholics, and particularly of Italians, of whom, by 1920, there were more than twice as many working the American coal beds as any other nationality. It was a time when coalmines were closing and jobs were few. Then came the crash of 1929, and by 1933, West Condon's largest industry was relief. West Condon then was a town of intense poverty, of hatred and suspicion, of Prohibition gangsterism, of corruption and lawlessness. The mines still operating paid fifty cents an hour at the coalface, and life at that face was miserable and precarious. Death came quickly and brutally, and families such as the Brunos lived in its shadow. It came by fire, by falling rock and coal, by powder and methane explosions, by the crushing impact of mine cars and locomotives, by falls down shafts. Knees swelled, spines were broken, arms were crushed, lungs were scarred, eyes lost their vision. Both of Giovanni Bruno's brothers were killed in the mines, and his father was made a virtual invalid the last ten years of his life . . ."

Losing it, the ascendant thrust, the flight from the immediate, Miller wondered if he should risk breaking their convulsive circle to go turn the goddamn set off. But, as he pulled his head back, Happy flashed out with her top thigh, rolled him to his back, pinning him, and down fell the mighty hero of the sun, undone by the dragon Ouroboros, primordial and true. . . .

". . . Like all his family before him, Giovanni Bruno, too, left school at an early age and entered the mines. Here you see him as he appeared in his high school class photo. He was considered, by the principal, John Bradley, a poor student, withdrawn and friendless." [*John Bradley:* "Yes, I remember the boy well. He was never in any trouble, and he seemed intelligent enough, but he was poorly adjusted. When he left school at the legal age of sixteen, he still had not completed what we consider freshman or ninth grade work. He was—how shall I put it?— he was peculiar."] "About that same time, Giovanni suffered what was apparently a sudden revolt from orthodox Roman Catholicism. Until then unusually devout, spending most of his free time in the church, serving first as an altar boy, then as lay assistant to the Right Reverend Battista Baglione here in West Condon, he suddenly separated himself from the church and has not been known to have set foot inside it during these subsequent sixteen or seventeen years." [*Father Baglione:* "Yes, I t'ink, uh, de 'eresy, yes, is cause', uh, by de, uh, de *pride.*"]

Those mountains, their valley twice pierced, now pitched, plunged, even as though angry, displaying against the gray-green wall beyond their vibrant silhouette of a rounded *M*, and in him a dark inscrutable river ran fast and deep . . .

". . . If he entered the mines to seek companionship, however, he did not find it. Deepwater Number Nine Coalmine supervisor Barney Davis recalls that he was a listless worker, did not participate in union activities or attend meetings, was not well liked." [*Barney Davis:* "He didn't get along with anybody. Nobody wanted to work with him. Even his escape from disaster last January was a sign of this isolation. There were seven guys barricaded in that room. Six of them were together and they died. Bruno lay a ways off from them, and he lived. Maybe he had more oxygen, since he didn't have to share it with anybody. The only guy in the mine who took pity on him was his working buddy Ely Collins. Reverend Collins."] "Ely Collins, an evangelist preacher of the Church of the Nazarene, was one of those six men who died, trapped in that same space with Giovanni Bruno . . . but not before he had managed to write a brief note to his wife, Mrs. Clara Collins." [*Clara Collins:* " 'I disobeyed and I know I must die. Listen always to the Holy Spirit in your hearts. Abide in grace—' "]

And then the dams began to break, the mountains to crumble, the walls to fall, all the fountains of the great deep to burst forth, and the windows of heaven to open . . .

". . . God in His mercy . . . a white bird . . . found him in a . . . Virgin Mary . . . message from the tomb . . . attractive softspoken girl born . . . unavailable for com-

465

ment . . . able to pass on this good news to all the world . . ."

Has she slept again? Was she awake before? The chill is gone, the tunic lowered. The house is silent. Silent? Marcella rises.

Miller woke, still on his back. The room was dark, but for the image pitched by the television set, enough to enable him to make out the bluish billowing terrain of Happy's bottom beside him. Something was missing. *Announcer:* "When it's time to relax, time for a smoke, enjoy the real American flavor, the natural mildness, the kingsize satisfaction . . ." He, leaning out: "Aha." She: "Don't rock the boat."

Marcella finds the house empty. Signs throughout of a sudden departure. Even her mother and brother are gone. Gone! A cry leaps to her throat. Can it be? It is coming! They forgot her! They have left her behind! She runs out the door. Gone! They have all gone! She is alone! Alone in the darkness! Wait! Wait!

The television off, bedlamp on, cold drink beside him, enjoying a smoke, belly down and Happy Bottom astride, giving him a really tremendous rubdown, he mused: "You know, the appeal of Noah is not the Ark or the rescue."
"No?"
She was being sarcastic, but he went on. "They just added that stuff to make the story credible."
"Aha."
That was worse than sarcasm, that was outright mockery, but still he went on. "No, it's the righteous destruction, that's what it's all about. We're all Noahs."
"Why"—as though astonished—"that's *true!*"
And still he went on. "So, see, the excitement of the disaster is over unless new destruction is possible. If

466

Noah has three sons, one and preferably two have to become corrupt, so that we can—"

Abruptly, she backed off and cracked his ass mightily, a kingsize belt that made him drop his smoke—grabbed it up, but not before he'd put a neat brown hole in the sheet. And then she cracked the other cheek and said, "And this is the sign of my covenant!" At which time, in view of the way things stood, he stubbed out the cigarette.

Running on the mine road, she can see their fire ahead. On the Mount. She hardly feels the ruts stabbing her bare feet, hardly notices the night's damp chill, ignores the binding cramp in her chest, the lightness in her head. Will she be on time? Oh wait! And then she seems to see light, even to feel—yes! it is coming! Surging up behind. She races desperately against its advance. The light grows, gathers, enlarges. Ahead of her, always just ahead of her, spreading, filling the—the fire on the Mount is out! She cannot make it! Oh please! She sees her shadow as the light sweeps down on her from behind. She tries to enclose herself in its sweep. She spreads wide her arms to hold it back. Suddenly: lights spring up before her! out of nowhere! lights on all sides! flooding the world! she in its center! It comes! she cries. God is here! she laughs. And she spins whirls embraces light leaps heaving her bathing in light her washes and as she flows laughs His Presence light! stars burst sky burns with absolute laugh light! and

4

For I am the least of the apostles,
that am not meet to be called an apostle,
because I persecuted the Church of God.
But by the Grace of God
               I am what I am. . . .

Abner Baxter stood brooding and crestfallen in the ditch
over the battered body. Blood glistened yet in dark drools
from mouth to ears, and the bright glitter had not yet
departed from her open eyes. How many cars had struck
her, he did not know, but he knew one that had. Lights
sliced damply now through the night air and the country
silence was laced with the shrieks and moans of men and
women alike. A doctor pronounced her dead, and a great
threnodial plaint went up. The prophet knelt to kiss her
and rose with blood staining his lips, his face drawn with
grief. A woman, the doctor's wife, indeed the very woman
who two months before had inveighed against him in the
prophet's house, now scourged him with lacerating cries of
"murderer!" and *"fiend!"* and a hostile passion smoldered
and grew in that great multitude. Compassed about with
so great a cloud of witnesses, Abner found that the will to
resist had left him utterly. He had left his wife Sarah
blubbering in the car, had marched boldly back down the
mine road, past the shocked and stricken faces, in the
ruthless beams of light, down the road to where he'd struck
her, had seen her from the lip of the ditch lying at the
bottom like a crumpled bird, lights from wrecked cars
illuminating spectrally her small body, and with strength
still, and with calm presence of mind, had strode down into
this ditch, here to arrive standing still while others bent
over her, here to see her twitch and die . . . and now it was
done. Sister Clara Collins stood there, across the body

from him, watching him. The doctor bent over the girl still, along with that Wosznik fellow and several others. Of his own people, Abner alone was there. Which was as it should be. The others wept. He would have too, perhaps, but something restrained him: a sense of propriety maybe, as though . . . as though he had no right. Those terrible texts which had been troubling him these past weeks, those passages which spoke of the rebellion which must precede Christ's return, now sprang forth in his mind, augmenting his affliction. Apologies formed on his tongue, but he seemed incapable of speech. He stood by the dead child in the midst of that mantling hysteria and execration and waited—for what? Perhaps: to be slain. *"Monster!"* shrieked that maddened woman. *"Butcher!"*

"No, friends! We're *all* murderers!" From a quarter least expected: it was Sister Clara Collins, ennobled, it would seem, by her own great griefs, and thus less undone by this present one, who now spoke forth boldly: "We *all* killed her with our hate and with our fear!" And he recognized the magnitude of it, the greatness of spirit, and he was stirred in the soul and much amazed. She stared then at his face, and Abner gave her much to read there, if she could but discern it. "Abner," she said softly, softly though her voice carried far in the night air and stilled the lamentations, "this awful thing is a judgment on us— Please! Join hands with us now and pray!"

And he reached across and accepted Clara's hand, and as he did so, a great warmth surged through him—for all things are cleansed with blood, he thought, and apart from shedding of blood there is no remission—and then, unleashed, the tears flowed.

". . . And knowin' that in the Last Days grievous times must come, help us to take heart, and, as Brother Abner hisself has taught us, Lord, to fergit the things which are behind, and stretchin' forward to the things which are before, help us to press on. . . ."

And with a great lightening of his heart, he perceived that, though a terrible thing was upon them and many

469

would despair, he, Abner Baxter, would march in the vanguard and give them strength, and he foresaw the great and holy march upon the morrow, he like these, in a pure-white tunic, foresaw the massing on the Mount of the mighty army of the sons of light, foresaw the smiting of the wicked and the destruction of the temples, foresaw the *glory*. . . .

Amens were shouted and songs were sung and people wept and embraced one another and his own tears, he saw, were dampening the shoulder of Sister Clara's tunic, and for just that moment he felt a boy again and wished to fold himself forever in her embrace, but then it was Brother Ben Wosznik whose arm was around his shoulders and then a pale stout man named Brother Hiram and he saw his own wife Sarah come running down the ditch and into Clara's arms—"Oh, Sister Clara! God help us!"

"Children!" cried Sister Clara. "It is the last hour! God has called us to redemption! The battle lines is formed and the last struggle is commenced!"

"Destroyers are come upon all the bare heights in the wilderness!" Abner cried out then through his tears, finding voice. "For the sword of God devoureth from the one end of the land even unto the other end of the land! *No flesh has got peace!*"

"The darkness is passing! the hour is at hand! and the dead they shall hark to the White Bird of Grace and Glory and them that hear shall live!"

"Amen!"

"We shall live!"

And the stout man raised his hand and lifted his soft chin, tears streaming down his round cheeks, and Sister Clara cried, "Brother Hiram Clegg!"

"And henceforth," he proclaimed, "them that have wives may be as though they had none, and them that weep as though they wept not, and them that rejoice as though they rejoiced not, and them that use the world as though they used it not, for the fashion of this world, it is passing away!"

And then up rose the woman who had so newly reviled him, and she cried out, "Go! says the prophet. Stand on high! Look thee toward the east! It comes!"
"Now"
"Christ Jesus!"
"March!"
"Repent!"
"It is coming!"
"Save us!"
They lifted up the body.

Oh the powers of darkness tremble and with fear their hearts do fill,
As the sons of light go marching out to stand upon that Hill
Beneath the Cross and Circle to fulfill God's blessèd Will!
For the end of time has come!

So come and march with us to Glory!
Oh, come and march with us to Glory!
Yes, come and march with us to Glory!
For the end of time has come!

5

Mid-Sunday dreams. Not all peaceful. Races against old deadlines. Missing trains and planes. Bags, badly packed, falling open on busy platforms. All of them lucid, but disjointed. Trying to straighten them out, he woke. Then back down again. Sounds from the television, Happy's adjacent body, daylight squeezing past the blinds, the twisted sheets, all these entered in, and though he was al-

471

ways conveniently far from this place and time, there was still a nagging need to be doing something he was neglecting, to get somewhere before it was too late, all of which, during semiconscious spells, he understood only too well. Once he was racing on a bicycle on an old dirt road. Then it was a car. Hairy turns, torn-up roads, horrible precipices, tremendous speed he couldn't seem to control. As though in the sky above there were parenthetical comments being made by a television announcer, who called him "His Eminence Justin Miller" and once "His Promontory" just for laughs. The situation of this announcer was peculiar and he woke finally in the aura of that peculiarity: for the announcer, while ostensibly describing the race, if that's what it was, neither explained accurately to the audience what "His Eminence" was doing, nor did he reveal to Miller the precise structure of the race, or how or why in fact he'd got into it. Perhaps it was night. Certainly, later, it *was* night. He was in a church-camp, having driven there perhaps, though this part was not distinct. Now he was at Inspiration Point with a blond-haired girl. Large full moon, which, however, was a bit unstable, occasionally startling him with its sudden oscillations. The girl was crying, yet they were both quite happy. They suddenly remembered the prayer meeting, raced, feeling guilty, through a dark forest, arrived late for it. Inside the church, there was crying and singing and impassioned preaching. The girl got drawn into it, soon was weeping emotionally with all the other boys and girls. He realized, within the dream, that all this had happened to him when he was in the seventh grade, and he had forgotten about this girl entirely. Her name, he recalled, was Mary. She was still the same, but he was now a grown man. The women who worked in the camp kitchen bawled and shrieked, their skirts always hiking up somehow over the roll of their stockings on their beefy thighs. He was dismayed that Mary, who had just wept for him (though exactly what he had done, he could not remember), now wept the same tears for Jesus. He turned to a companion, a large somber man whom he had

472

brought here to show this sort of behavior, perhaps a father figure of sorts, and explained: "She has been seeking God, you see, but has never found him. I have been the victim of transcendence."

He woke repeating this, correcting the last word to "transubstantiation," and, opening his eyes, found himself vis-à-vis Happy's magic bottom, a scant six inches from his nose. She stood at the edge of the bed, his robe half on, lighting a cigarette. He leaned forward, nipped one cheek with his teeth.

She squeaked, dropping the smoke, then twitched like a mare flicking a fly. "I've been standing here for three hours waiting for you to do that," she complained, covering it up now with the robe and stooping for the cigarette.

"The cross in the circle," he mused, singsonging it to a tune that seemed to be running through his mind.

"How's that?"

"The cross in the circle." He turned her backside toward the full-length mirror on the back of the door, lifted the robe. "The circle," he indicated, swooping his hand through an oval whose extremities were the small of her back and the back of her knees.

"That's an egg," she corrected.

"And the cross." He started between the knees and plowed up through the vertical that would have ended at the sacroiliac, had she not got ticklish where the thigh-wrinkle crossbeam cut across it.

"That's not a cross, either," she said. "That's a highway intersection."

He laughed and pulled her toward him, but she resisted. She looked toward the television, and he guessed what was eating her. He fell back, pretending indifference. "What time is it?"

"About two," she replied. "There they are again." She turned up the volume and left without smiling. Phony fussing noises in the kitchen.

Miller sat up and pulled on his shorts, listening to the announcer recast once more the story of the goddamn

Brunists and their march to the Mount of Redemption. In the background: the thumping strains of "The Battle Hymn of the Republic," which accounted for certain parts of dreams now coming to mind. He felt groggy from having slept too long and too hard, and he wondered what he and Happy could do this afternoon to get away from this thing altogether. Unlike the little old lady, he didn't even want to watch it on television. Room seemed dark— must be cloudy out. He smiled, thinking of the night just past, and turned toward the set to watch the Brunists advancing toward him, tunics aflutter and banners high. Looked to be Locust, about the 1500 block. The street-level angle of the camera prevented him from seeing any but the front rank, but they seemed to have grown some. What woke him up was seeing Abner Baxter: there he was, he and Ben Wosznik flanking the lean prophet at the very front of the tramping column, both carrying banners. "Hey!" he said out loud, and then the next thing he saw was Marcella's body on a kind of stretcher.

". . . Of the prophet. We still have no definite explanation of her death. Members of the cult with whom we have spoken insist only that she met her death through an act of divine providence, but refuse to release further details." Cut from Marcella to Ben Wosznik in a living room. Miller couldn't believe it. His heart pounded. Ben said, "Well, now, I don't think it's proper for me to say. I will say that it seemed as though her tragic passing from this life, just so short a time before God's Coming, before the Coming of Light, why, it did strike all of us like a message from above, not a punishment so much as an act of mercy, a kind of sacrifice, you might almost say, which brung to pass that a lot of good people who weren't getting along suddenly found that their fights was foolish, and against the Will of God." Miller crouched, in his shorts, gripping his T-shirt, before the set.

Announcer: "Excuse me, Mr. Wosznik, but do you mean to say that she met her death by some sort of sacrificial ritu—" *Wosznik:* "No, I don't mean nothing like that! What kinda stories are you boys trying to scare up?" *Announcer:* "Why has no one been permitted to examine her?" But now it was Clara Collins who replied: "Well, we got a doctor with us. He done what he could, and now his word is good enough for us. We're takin' her with us to the Mount of Redemption so's she can be received bodily unto the Lord, there to be raised from the dead. We ain't takin' no chances, deliverin' her over to the powers of darkness." *Announcer:* "Do you mean to say that you expect her to be brought back from the dead?" *Clara:* "Of course, I do. Don't *you* believe in the resurrection of the dead?" Cut to procession. Tremendous crowd, all right. Far as you could see.

Not knowing when he'd begun, Miller now was nearly dressed, frantically buttoning his shirt, stuffing his feet into shoes.

Announcer: "Earlier today, Mr. Mortimer Whimple, mayor of the city of West Condon, issued a brief statement in which he deplored the Brunist aggression against several West Condon churches this morning and the consequent increase in violence and hysteria, but discounted a persistent rumor that the girl might have been ceremoniously sacrificed or might have offered herself up in self-immolation, observing . . ." *Whimple:* "We understand it was some kind of accident. Maybe a fall or something. I think it's all too easy to jump to wild conclusions. You gotta remember that her health had got, ah, pretty precarious by going such a long time without eating, and, ah, there are none of the usual signs of violence like you might expect in a, a sacrifice, let me say." He looked shrunken and persecuted. *Announcer:* "Mr. Mayor, has any official autopsy been conducted or ordered?" *Whimple* (hesitating): "Uh, no comment." *Another voice:* "Mr. Mayor, are any arrests in connection with her death being contemplated?" *Whimple:* "Not now." *Announcer* (while Whimple talked silently on the screen to reporters): "We

475

learned about an hour ago through sources close to the mayor, however, that the governor is being kept in touch by telephone with the situation as it develops, and that elements of the state police force have been dispatched and are now on their way to West Condon." View of the Brunists, sound of their marching hymn in the background. Nearing the edge of town. "We return you to the network program now in progress."

Miller looked up from tying his shoes, saw Happy Bottom in the doorway. "Get your clothes on! Let's get going!"

"I think I'll take a shower," she said, "I'll come out later."

"We just had three showers," he argued, but he saw she was near to tears, or her equivalent of them, which was a kind a bleak wintry absence of all animation.

Announcer's voice broke through the network program again with a sudden bulletin, accompanied by a newsclip of the Brunists standing on a hill—already!—but this hill was rocky and unfamiliar. Didn't recognize any of the cultists either. Good reason: they turned out to be a group in Beirut, where, the announcer explained, night had already fallen and the end of the world was expected momentarily. Quick bulletins then of similar groups gathering in Germany, in Great Britain, in Rhodesia, Greece, Australia, Peru, Canada, and all over the United States. In Guatemala, a popular astrologist who had rightly predicted the end of the last war and the deaths of three world leaders now claimed to have verified Bruno's prediction of the Parousia, and was at this moment leading twenty-seven fat Catholic ladies, including the President's sister—all shown from the elephantine rump in the newsclip—up the side of the volcano Acatenango. Cut to Eleanor Norton reading heaps upon heaps of telegrams in the Bruno living room from people who said they were either on the way to West Condon or were organizing similar marches to hills or mountains in their vicinity. Interview with the Arizona invalid-hitchhiker, who had made it. Cut to a film of a small Cessna arriving at the county airport, its two occupants emerging dressed in Brunist tunics. Back to Eleanor and more telegrams, many of them requesting that she repeat all details over the television networks, which she willingly did. "We wish to emphasize that the exact . . . content of the Coming of Light is not known, what precisely it will be or how it will . . . take place. We do know that, whatever shape it takes, it will take place today, barring of course unforeseen obstacles caused by the powers of darkness. We are also reasonably convinced that it must take place here, in West Condon, on the Mount of Redemption, to where God, Domiron, all the higher forces of the universe, and our prophet Giovanni Bruno, the One to Come, have directed us to march. This does not . . . does not mean it will not occur simultaneously elsewhere, and we encourage all of you, elsewhere in the world, too distant to be able to reach us here . . . that all of you follow to the best of your abilities your own inspiration and sources. Those of you near enough to come, we urge you to do so, being unable to certify that this . . . this event will indeed occur in any other given place, but assured for those reasons I have so often repeated that it must surely occur at least at this Mount . . . this Mount over the Deepwater Coalmine."

Clara Collins came on, a sudden dynamic contrast: "Yessir, we are *very* excited! This sudden response around the world to our message, or messages jist like ours, why, it certainly is another sign we're on the right track. You cain't say it's jist coincidence. And you cain't say we done any missionary work. It's jist spontaneous-like, and I believe all this activity, all this here zeal for the Lord, well, it jist has *got* to *mean* something!"

Announcer: "When exactly, Mrs. Collins, do you anticipate the, eh, the end of the world?"

Clara: "Well, we don't rightly know, but if you're worryin' about it like you better be, then I'd say to you

477

you'd better come along with us right now, on account of it's apt to happen jist any moment!" Back to the network.

He wasn't able to catch them by car after all. Crowds blocked the way. People milled in every street. Mostly strangers. Lot of cars with out-of-state licenses. He parked as near to the back edge of town as he could, took up the Speedgraphic, set out in a light jog. He decided to cut across the acreage that the city had just bought for purposes of luring industry. Hoped to cut the parade off. The lope over those untended fields was not easy: irregular, high with dried grass and shrubs that bit and clutched at his ankles, lot of junk to trip him up. He saw the crowds, though, just swelling out onto the mine road from the edge of town. Helicopter circling overhead, no doubt photographing his lone gallop crosscountry toward the Brunists: lost lamb returning to the fold, or messenger with the Word. Sky beyond the helicopter was gray with fat ripe clouds.

He angled more sharply so as to get ahead of the advancing masses. Out in front: several cars, many of them with tripods and other equipment strapped on top. Big TV outfit rolled along in front, followed by an enormous crowd that just didn't seem to end. A kind of flood at that: the Brunists bubbling down the road like a spread of white foam, and at the edges, like dark scum, the welter of the curious, the doubters, the hecklers, the indignant. He aimed toward a grove of trees, saw that if his wind lasted he'd make it before the Brunists with a couple minutes to spare. The helicopter came roaring down over his head and on toward the Brunists, there to hover like a great speckled insect.

His wind lasted, but barely. He staggered up against one of the trees, gasping, pulled out a smoke. His side ached, one ankle hurt. He tucked the camera between his knees, lit up, then sighted the camera on the road in front of him, just as a couple cars shot by.

"Real scene," somebody said behind him.

Miller looked around, noticed for the first time that he shared the grove with three or four other cameramen. The guy who had addressed him had come up from behind, now stood looking over Miller's shoulder. Young kid. Shaggy. Cocky.

"Did you catch the rumpus this morning at the R.C. place?"

"Guess I missed that," Miller said, still panting.

"Apocalyptic," the kid said. "Laid into altars with mining picks, swiped a lot of stuff."

Miller could see the front ranks now: Giovanni Bruno, gaunt, lugging what did indeed look like a coal pick, head held high, hair flowing, legs kicking out vigorously against the restraint of the tunic, narrow bony feet, bare, beating down the hard ruts of the road; on either side of him, Abner Baxter and Ben Wosznik, singing lustily and bearing the two banners, a German police dog trotting at Wosznik's heels.

The photographer unwrapped a red pack of gum, shoved about half of it in his mouth, offered Miller some. "No, thanks." So, in went the rest.

Behind the three men walked the Nortons, side by side, faces collapsed in grief and maybe a kind of horror, but their step measured and determined. On either side, more or less in single file, marched the women of West Condon, led by Clara Collins and Sarah Baxter. Mixing in and trailing back down the road: scores of East Condoners, no, *hundreds!* Some wielded torches, some silver candlesticks, part of the morning's loot, no doubt. And, in the middle, borne on—

"Now you won't believe this," the photographer said, working his jaws mightily around the gum, "but you see that little Seenyora Two Hung Lo? There in the middle with the little fat fella? Well, they both been to college."

"Is that so?" Miller was getting his breath back. He dropped his butt to his feet, ground it out, pulled out another.

"Degrees and everything." The kid lifted his camera, took a photo. Somehow, his doing that made the camera in Miller's hand grow cold and heavy. The front ranks of the procession had pulled nearly abreast of them. "You wouldn't think brainy types like that could get their asses in such a silly sling, now wouldja?"

"Hard to figure."

"You said it, man." The gum cracked and popped. Miller felt chills ripple through him, seeing the thing now clearly, jogging slightly, back and forth, back and forth, to the rhythm of their song. "Now that poor little piece of dead snatch they're toting, that's a different story." On the shoulders of six men. Litter was what looked like a lawn chair, folded down flat. She was just no color at all. Something between the dull aluminum of the chair frame and the vapid gray of the darkening sky. Fresh white tunic, too big for her—a grotesquely ironic thought occurred to him, and, yes, it was probably true . . . they probably found that tunic in her closet, or a drawer, and thought . . . Her mouth gaped open, lips drawn dry; he licked his own self-consciously. One hand pointed rigidly heavenward, the other downward. Eyelids half-open over a filmy opaque surface. It was so unreal a thing, he could register no emotion except horror. Marcella! He shuddered, closed his eyes, opened them. "They say she died with her hand aimed up at the Old Man like that, and that was what made that redheaded bugger see the light." Miller just couldn't attach her to this brittle blue corpse that rocked on the road before him. The run here had weakened him, had made him sweat; now the sweat was cold as death on him and all his tendons were gone to rot. He leaned up against the tree to keep from buckling, flicked his cigarette into the ditch, lit a new one. Marcella. He saw her name on his desk blotter, heard her gay laughter, smelled her body on his, saw the intricate turn of a lightly tanned wrist, tasted the newness of her mouth. Marcella. Marcella Bruno. Was it something in her he had loved . . . or something in himself he had hated? He felt old. "Well, the word

480

is she got banged by the guy who grinds out the local scandal sheet. He was a big cat in the club, but he cut out on them and got into her. She went off her nut and, so they say, finally knocked herself off. Now that's pretty wild too, I admit, but that's something I can understand."

"Where'd you hear all that?"

"Oh, I dunno. You pick things up. You just drag in? There's a couple lambent skin pix making the rounds at the flophouse that this wiseguy took of himself laying the meat to her. Big guy, about as tall as Papa Spook out there, but twice as wide." The kid popped his gum, spat out the side of his mouth, photographed Marcella's cadaver. "Gives you a weird feeling," he said. "In one of the photos she's just like that, one arm up, one down, looking scared. Like it was all planned." Weird feeling.

Behind the body marched alternate pallbearers, large numbers of out-of-towners among them. Willie Hall and a heavyset man dragged along a little red wagon, in which, huddled miserably, sat Emilia Bruno, ancient, dark, withered, looking very ill indeed, yellowish eyes cast upward toward where her daughter rocked above her. Some of the men carried large wooden crosses at least four feet tall, roughly hewn from tree branches. Miller saw three or four of them. Then came the young, a disordered, emotional, wildly singing lot, dozens of them, all sizes. The four Baxter redheads stood out. Carl Dean Palmers hopped backward in front of them, leading them in their singing:

"O the sons of light are marching since the coming
of the dawn,
Led by Giovanni Bruno and the voice of Domiron!
We shall look upon God's Glory after all the world
is gone!
For the end of time has come!

"So come and march with us to Glory!
Oh, come and march with us to Glory!
Yes, come and march with us to Glory!
For the end of time has come!"

The helicopter lowered, cameras whirred and shutters clicked on all sides, the crowds trotted by, filling the ditches. The guys here in the grove with him folded up their gear, hiked it to their shoulders and set off, keeping pace with the procession, the vanguard of which was now virtually out of sight. The kid started to trail the others, turned around. "Hey, you coming?" He cocked his head, spat. "Say, man, you feeling okay?" Miller nodded, leaned away from the tree. Nothing to do but go on, see it out, find out what he could. "Got a little too much last night, hunh?" The kid, thank God, didn't wait for an answer.

There must have been at least three of four hundred tunicked followers in the procession, it was strung out for nearly a quarter of a mile. Others joined in, some wrapped in sheets, some merely in streetclothes, all barefoot. Behind the caravan were cars and trucks as far as the eye could see. A rumble in the sky. The singing broke off. Everyone looked up. A kind of moan or mumble rippled through the crowd, Brunists and spectators alike. Slowly, unevenly, the singing resumed:

"*O the sons of light are marching to the Mount*
    where it is said
We shall find our true Redemption from this world
    of woe and dread,
We shall see the cities crumble and the earth give up
    its dead,
        For the end of time has come!

"*So come and march with us to Glory!* . . ."

Miller trailed wearily along, the crowds ahead dissolving into a shifting white mass, bordered by browns and grays, Marcella's body floating as though on a raft. Further rumbles overhead. Nervous jokes about that, strained laughter about his ears. He heard his name on occasion, nodded to people. What if, he wondered, what if he'd deflowered her first, talked after? He shuddered, as though with a chill. Ahead of him, the procession seemed to have stopped. People butted up against one another and began to murmur. He heard whisperings of "blockades" and "powers of darkness" and "police." He edged up the slope of the ditch, made cautious inquiries of people in the rear ranks about Marcella, but they saw his camera and no one answered him. Back into the ditch then and toward the bottleneck, protected from Brunists who knew him by the thick hordes of massing spectators, staying as deep in the ditch as possible, passing under the body—he saw only the slight depression her cadaver made in the brightly striped canvas of the lawn chair—and the thick shapes of the tunicked women and the white banners, now becalmed.

At the head of it all he discovered a barricade and—goddamn!—a ticket booth! Manning it were Wally Fisher and Maury Castle and a couple guys Miller didn't know. Miller had heard rumors all week that Fisher was up to no good, and Fisher himself, with a dry cackle, had spoken of his "brainstorm." The cop Dee Romano was there, too, palm resting on his pistol butt. He was explaining that it was all legal, that Mr. Fisher had rented the premises for the day for the purpose of promoting a small carnival, and that the admission charge of one dollar was entirely legitimate—all of which meant that Romano was getting a cut of the gate.

There was a tremendous protest boiling up, and Dec couldn't cover it. His right hand grew very fidgety. Maury Castle took over. "Now, folks, we realize that there is a conflict of interests here today," he boomed out. "And we want to do everything possible to alleviate that conflict." TV and movie cameras rolled, flashguns popped, the helicopter hovered. "We respect all religions and it was not Mr. Fisher's intention to interfere with the activities of you people." Only man in West Condon who could talk to a square mile of people without a P.A. system. "Therefore, we have not bothered in any way the hill where you folks are going, and we have not mounted any of our stands up there. Moreover, we understand—" There was

483

a sudden loud clap of thunder. The helicopter lifted and soared away. Castle grinned up at the sky, then continued. "Because we understand that you folks are not really interested in our carnival, why, we thought the only courteous thing to do would be to let you pass by at no charge. But I want to ask you to please be orderly and I'm afraid we have to limit the free entrance to only those who have these here jumpers on, these—what do you call . . . ?" His voice had sunk to a consultational tone, still audible, as he leaned toward Wosznik. "Yes, these here tunics. So now, if you other folks will please step back just a minute and let these people pass through, it will make things a whole lot easier."

There was a lot of discontent, but also a lot of laughter. Good old pioneer ingenuity. Clara Collins and Ben Wosznik stood by the gate, explaining to those at the tail end what had happened, seeking to protect their people, but in effect doing Castle's work for him. They argued with Fisher and Castle about those members not in tunics, and bare feet became sufficient criteria, whereupon the Brunist fold was increased temporarily by about twenty-five young gate-crashers. Miller hung back until Clara and Wosznik had moved on. At the ticket booth, Fisher said, "One dollar, please."

"Press," said Miller sourly.

"No passes today," the old bastard said with a broad grin. "This is, in fact, hee hee, a press carnival!" And then, his dewlaps flapping, he nearly gagged with laughter.

Rather than argue, Miller fished up a buck.

"Say, you'll never guess who the hell is here today!" Fisher said.

"Jesus Christ."

Again that deep delighted wheeze. "No! Father Jones! He got a job on one of the city papers and pulled this as his first goddamn assignment!" The old man really thought that was funny, wheezed and choked so hard that tears came to his eyes. "I was so happy to see him, I even let him in for nothing!" Then he leaned forward, his face up against the ticket window, looking for a moment like an old father confessor, and whispered, "Say, Miller, you got a pretty ass!" Then back he roared again, nearly falling off his stool. "Jesus! I'm having so much fun, I'll never live out the day!"

Miller turned away from Fisher, only to confront Romano. "Take it easy today, Miller," the cop said. "We don't want no trouble."

Miller brushed by, feeling not so very great. The carnival amounted to a handful of refreshment stands, a bingo game, and a numbers game, the last already in operation and manned by Doris, the hotel coffeeshop waitress. She winked lewdly at him as he passed by. The Brunists had already arranged themselves on the hill, were busying themselves with their own circle, as though afraid to look down on the threat at the hill's foot. He saw now what the wooden crosses were for. Ben Wosznik digging and directing, they planted the crosses on the east slope, mounted Marcella's lawn-chair bier on them, each rounded aluminum corner resting on a rustic wooden crossbeam. A statue of the martyr Stephen—Miller recognized it as the patron of the Catholic church here—seemed to appear from nowhere, dressed in a Brunist tunic. Sorrowful and empty-sleeved, it was placed beside Marcella on the south slope, this side of her, as though to guard her from the powers of darkness who milled about below, eating peanuts and cotton candy, drinking bottled pop. The silver candelabra were placed at her head and feet, but efforts to light them proved futile. The two banners were set in holes already dug for them and, between, an altar was put up with all its now-familiar Brunist relics.

It started then with a kind of moan, a wail, even while the crowds of spectators who had followed them out here filed still past the ticket booth, dropping their dollars. There was thunder. The wheel of the numbers game revolved with a purring flutter. Semicircling Marcella, but each with a view of the east, the Brunists knelt. The wail mounted. Popcorn *flup-flup-flupped* in the lit-up popping

485

cage. A woman laughed. On the hill, a long dramatic prayer was commenced, led alternately by Clara Collins and Abner Baxter and a plump man with a vibrant voice who Miller learned was a Mr. Hiram Clegg from some town nearby, the man he'd seen pulling Emilia's wagon. Everyone joined in, echoing parts, chorusing familiar responses, all of it a kind of contest of Biblical knowledge and appropriate responsive ritual. Most of the new ones, apparently, were types like those of the local Church of the Nazarene; the Nortons seemed very isolated indeed. In fact, now that he thought of it, where was Himebaugh? Poor bastard didn't have it, after all.

It was growing dark, more from the clouding over than from the approach of night, but Fisher had strung lights down along the row of booths, and now the cameramen were setting up their own lamps, electricity apparently provided by the mine. Miller wandered to the eastern edge of the carnival area, found Mickey DeMars there dispensing soft drinks.

"H'lo, Tiger!" Mick squeaked. "Say, you're looking a little peakèd. You been getting enough sleep?"

"What've you got back there, Mick?"

"Jim Beam or Canadian."

"Either one."

"Say, you seen Lou?"

"No."

"Well, you never believe it, but the bastard's out here!"

"I believe it, Mick." He tossed the drink down, looked up at the soles of Marcella's blue feet. Then, suddenly remembering, he reached in his trenchcoat pocket; his fingers closed around a small cotton sock. Beyond the Brunists, over the far edge of the hill, he could see the tops of trees, then the upper flight of the tipple and the watertower with its DEEPWATER banner, thrust fatly up like a carburetor advertisement. Beyond that, a motion in the skies of mixed grays, like a photograph taking shape: photograph of a young brown-eyed girl in a shawl, the shawl slipping to her shoulders . . . and he saw then that he was

one with the Brunists: that he, too, had been brought full
circle to stand upon this place. . . .

> *We were gathered on the Mount of Redemption*
> *On the night before the Coming of the Light,*
> *Seeking peace and the path of Salvation,*
> *But hate and fear made a horror of that night!*
>
> *In faith, she came running out to save us;*
> *In faith, she came out to end our strife;*
> *And, with her hand pointing upward unto Heaven,*
> *In faith, she laid down her precious life!*
>
> *So, hark ye to the White Bird of Glory!*
> *Yes, hark ye to the White Bird of Grace!*
> *We have gathered at the Mount of Redemption*
> *To meet our dear Lord here face to face!*

He saw some of the clutch approaching, Cavanaugh,
Whimple, Elliott, and others, so he paid Mick and left. He
had to pass by them, but they either missed him or in-
tentionally ignored him. On the hill, the prayer meeting
was getting louder, and Clara and Baxter were whipping
the crowd up with challenges.
"Do you believe?"
"*Yes! Oh Lord! Yes, we believe!*"
"Does He come?"
"*He comes! Yes! Now!*"
"Are you ready?"
"*Ready, Lord! Amen! God save us! Come!*"
Severe rumbles in the sky now. Clara Collins gazed upward, lifted her fist and cried out, and they all mimed her.
What power that woman had! Miller noticed she was
wearing Ellie Norton's gold medallion: a mysterious occult
talisman on Eleanor, it became a flashing badge of hegem-
ony on Clara. Could he go directly to her? Probably not.
Not today. He looked for Betty Wilson, spied her on her
knees between a woman even fatter than herself and the
man named Clegg. Down here, the crowds were multiply-

ing by the minute, now packed the tents and booths, and swarmed densely at the base of the hill. Though amused, often giggling pointlessly, chewing gum and popcorn with exaggerated jaw motions, getting into friendly scuffles, they nevertheless seemed disinclined to aim taunts directly at the Brunists. Maybe they were afraid to. There were close to four hundred excited people up on that hill. Or maybe it was just the way they'd been brought up. This was a religious service, after all, screwball or not, and what derision could one properly hurl at a man who prayed to the Christian God? They, too, had prayed, sung, confessed. Yet, they yearned to storm that hill, Miller could feel it, they ached to obliterate that white fungus, they were hate hungry and here was something to hit out at. They waited for: the outrage.

Miller slipped into the bingo tent, arranging himself with a view out at the hill. Crowds in front of him, but the hill rose above them. He looked for Jones. Preferred to settle that business first. People pushed into the tent in fear of rain, people pushed out to take another look, jostling him. Finally, he moved back into one empty corner, took a folding chair, and cut away a flap of canvas for a window. "Under the *I: 28!*" Up on the hill, Bruno paced silently among his followers, stopping once or twice to kiss the withered forehead of his old mother, she still heaped in a sickly little mound in the wagon. The man seemed suddenly this afternoon to have acquired tremendous energy, moved with assurance and even a kind of ferocity. "Under the *O: 69!*" Ripple of giggles. Outside, they were giggling at a couple who had stripped off their streetclothes to stand with the Brunists in their white underwear. And, just in front of him through the flap, he saw a fat lady giggle when someone handed her a bag of buttered popcorn. "Under the *B: 9!*" Bruno, he noticed, repeated a peculiar gesture several times: the raising of his hand in a kind of benediction and the placing of it on a person's shoulder. At first, Miller supposed it was a way of giving encouragement, but then he observed that those

488

least in need of it received it: Eleanor, Baxter, Clara, Wosznik. "Under the B: 12!"

And then it began to rain. A cloudburst. The crowds shrieked, laughed like children at a party, pressed back against the small booths and tents, pushing for shelter. Up on the hill, the Brunists seemed to take cheer. They smiled down condescendingly upon the turmoil below them, then lifted their eyes and hands to the exploding heavens. The harder it rained, the more ecstatic they became, the more violent became the crowds at the base. Distantly, he heard the emcee calling out the bingo numbers, but could no longer distinguish them. Half-consciously he'd been waiting for 7 or 14, and knew now he'd never hear it. Behind the downpour, bullish thunder stampeded and trumpeted. Amateur photographers added their Brownies and Polaroids to the one-eyed host that encircled the worshipers, conspiring to nail them forever to this time and place, and Miller noticed that the one thing that drew the crowds' attention from the hill was the instant copies of the Polaroid cameras, exciting them even more than watching the real thing.

The rain roared on the tent, thunder crashed, the crowds screamed and shouted, now laughing less. A fight broke out in front of him, a nose was bloodied, a face pushed in the mud. Up on the Mount, people leaped up in the air as though trying to fly, ran about, rolled in the mud. Streetclothes were shed and so, in some cases, was underwear. Some of the spectators caught out in the rain screamed at that, some laughed, some only shouted meaninglessly. People pushed up against the tent, buckling its sides inward and blocking Miller's view, showing him nothing but dark wet bodies, hands feeling haunches, elbows swinging.

He stood on his chair, cut another hole higher up. The Brunists were in a frenzy. Their thin white tunics clung to their bodies, wimpling white, otherwise showing a pale flesh color, except where underclothing protected. Hair streamed over faces, hands reached upward as though clawing, naked bodies milled with tunicked ones. Lights went out, came on again, tremendous clap of thunder, everybody started, gasped en masse, cried out, laughed excitedly. Some cried. Rain blew in through his window, spraying his face. One hand gripped the Speedgraphic, the other kneaded the sock in his pocket. The emcee no longer called out numbers, seemed to be pleading for calm. Some people on the outer, wettest, fringe, frightened by the storm and lashed by the frantic press of the mass, lost their heads and ran hysterically up the hill to join the Brunists. Near the entrance to the bingo tent a woman went down, a froth on her mouth, and others, losing balance, trampled and fell over her. Women prayed and shrieked, and there were cries, some mocking, some terrifyingly real, that the end was coming. Miller's chair went out from under him, and he dropped leadenly on two men who, slugging at him, ended up at each other's throats. At the corner on the side there seemed to be no body pressed, so he slashed a full-length slit and pushed out. As he pushed out, others pushed in, kicking, bucking. He saw new holes opening up. Couldn't see the hill.

Miller bulled forward, not caring who or what he hit—what are social niceties in a stampede? Rain beat on his face and his feet slipped and skidded in the mud. People bitched. He got knocked up against the wall of a booth. But, more and more, the crowds were turning to face the Brunists. And it was a sight to see. Naked or near-naked, they leaped and groveled and embraced and rolled around in the mud. A large group danced wildly around Marcella, screaming at her, kissing her dead mouth, clearly expecting her to rise up off her litter. Women embraced the statue of Stephen and kissed its mouth. Men tore branches off the little tree until it was stripped nearly bare, and whipped themselves and each other. It was a scene to delight a Lou Jones and now Miller saw him, moving impassively up the hill, photographing them as he went, kneeling for angles, apparently steering a course toward the dead girl. Jones, in drooping fedora and glistening raincoat, shaped like a

490

big dark bag, made an odd contrast to the frenetic worshipers who performed for his lens. There was something
almost contemplative, devotional, almost satuesque about
him as he crouched to peer into the instrument in his lap.

Miller, breaking free of the crowd at last, paused just
a moment, long enough to spot the white helmets and
black uniforms of the state troopers, just arrived and in
an anxious huddle with Whimple, Cavanaugh, and
Romano, then ran for the hill, ran for Jones. Other newsmen, following Jones's lead, had ventured forward into that
belt of space that had till now separated the redeemed from
the dead. Miller slammed past them in his heavyfooted
slog up the hill, anger mounting, but a peculiar joy, too:
he was here! it was on! And a hysterical fat woman, her
tunic up under her armpits, rolled under his feet, bowled
him over, and he felt his face slap into the mud. Tried
to stand, but found himself in a swirl of wet bodies. A
man sat beating his own face with his fists, and a woman
staggering backward fell on him, their legs twining as
they rolled. Miller couldn't see Jones. Someone laid into
him with a switch and he felt a tug at his clothes. He
escaped, half running, half crawling, back downhill, then,
seeing he was cut off from retreat by an advancing singing
bloc of new and naked converts, swung around toward
where Jones now knelt, his back to the eastern sky, focusing
on the soles of Marcella's feet, his sullen face veiled by the
drip of rain off his hatbrim, plastic sack over his camera,
soggy cigar in his mouth. Charging Jones, Miller caught a
glimpse of Marcella's cadaver, the tunic pasted down
against her livid flesh, pools standing here and there, her
mouth and eyes filling with water that the rain splashed
in. Jones glanced up just as Miller leaped, a grin there,
and he turned his shoulder— It was like hitting a goddamn
ox. It pitched him right on over and, in midair, he realized
for the first time he was still carrying his own Speedgraphic— Miller felt something go, a sharp hot pain in his
left arm or shoulder, and he saw the camera just as his
own ass came crashing down on it. Hurt, but angry, hating

someone whether it was Jones or not, he stood to face the man, who now squatted, deadpan as always, cigar still in place, hat knocked a bit askew, gazing up at him.

Suddenly he heard a shrill mad shriek that carried over all the roar up there: *"That's him! He murdered her!"* It was Eleanor Norton, gray hair wild with the rain, tunic limp on her aging body, eyes fixed on him through wet lenses, arms outspread and fingers bent like claws—*"Killer! Killer! Killer!"*

It was a signal for them. All the aimless fury of the moment before suddenly discovered its object. He turned to run. They cut him off, swarmed down upon him. He dodged, spun, rolled, straight-armed, warded off blindly flung blows, but there were millions of them, and ducking one only put him in line for another. He watched feet trampling his camera as branches whaled his body, saw Jones, slyly amused, in modest retreat partway down the hill, photographing it all. He pushed downhill for Jones, but, letting down his guard, got a foot in his gut that doubled him over. He struggled to his feet, but they piled onto him. He swung at them, kicked, butted, but nothing slowed them. They covered him and their heaped flesh choked him. A fat man, that Clegg guy, an erection distorting the front of his wet tunic, leaped, came down like a mountain on Miller's head. They fought for his trench-coat and, releasing it, he somehow wriggled free. Wall of their bodies below him, so he switched strategy, bowled straight up the hill, seemed to have lost his shoes, but it helped him gain speed, dove headfirst into a cluster of bodies, felt something flatten his nose in, hit somebody hard as wood. Chorus of screams of horror—something cold struck his face—and as by the hundreds·they jumped him, he saw what it was he had knocked over and he lost heart. They dragged him away from her, kicking and punching and whipping him with branches. Distantly, he felt their blows, felt them leap and dance on him, knew he was vomiting, knew he was bleeding, but as though someone were explaining this to him. They are killing you, he said, and though it caused wonderment in him, he could not lift an arm to stop them. He felt them shred the clothes off him, saw the ax, knew, though he couldn't feel it, that his legs had been splayed and hands had been laid on him. Amazingly, just at that moment, he saw, or thought he saw, a woman giving birth: her enormous thighs were spread, drawn up in agony, and, staring up them, he saw blood burst out. "No!" he pleaded, but it sounded more like a gurgle. "Please!" and a whip lashed his mouth. Where the fuck were the troopers?

And it was done, the act was over. Through the web of pain, skies away, he recognized the tall broad-shouldered priestess with the gold medallion. She issued commands and he floated free. Rain washed over him. He seemed to be moving. The priestess was gone. And then there was a fall. Trees. Muddy cleft and a splash of water when he arrived. At which point, Tiger Miller departed from this world, passing on to his reward.

6

Vince Bonali and the only two buddies he had left in the world, old Cheese Johnson and old Georgie Lucci, sprawled, roaring drunk, upon the red wool expanse of vacant carpet in the lawyer's house, as the West Condon cops, with Whimple and Cavanaugh and God knows who else, came in and arrested them there where they lay. This time there were no bird dogs to be bought, but, since the facilities were flooded with ecstatic raving Brunists, they let them go anyway. "Listen," Vince told them. "Listen, I don't give a shit what you do. Lock me up if you wanna.

493

I don't give a shit." But they booted his ass out of there, and there was no place to go but home. Where things were not very good.

He staggered, feeling one with the scum of the earth, right down the rainsoaked middle of Main Street, telling anyone who cared to listen that he just didn't give a shit, understand? then past St. Stephen's where had a kind of grievous heart attack that didn't quite come off, past the homes of old buddies, Judases all, past the Bruno house, guarded now by burly troopers in white crash helmets, past his whole fucking life into total and eternal oblivion, reeling like an old blinded bull come mad to town.

There had been one moment today, there in the Church of the Nazarene, when, in spite of all his overcrowding misery, he'd been at peace with the world, a wild exhilarating bounce back from his notorious television appearance the night before—now, how had those TV bastards known they were going to go spooking Friday night? Robbins and Castle'd pay for that some day—the unspecified back scenes of which (were his pants zipped up? he'd been scared to look) had not escaped his wife and daughter.

It had started at Mass. His old archenemy Red Baxter, that sonuvabitch who'd once called Vince "a mealy-mouthed henchman for fascists," had stormed into the Cathedral with all those raving Brunist crackpots, had laid into the altar and organ with a mining pick, had torn down paintings, and had even seemed set to slaughter the old priest. Vince had leaped up, followed by six or seven others, formed a human wall in front of Father Baglione, and held the Brunists to a stalemate. They had finally pulled out, but not before that goddamn Bruno had spit in the Father's face. Baxter had railed at the congregated, calling the Church a whore: "I tell you, it has become a habitation of demons! and a haunt of every unclean spirit! and by the wine of her lust all the nations has *fallen!* and the kings of the earth has committed *fornication* with her, and the capitalists of the earth has *waxed rich* by the power

494

of her *wantonness!* But listen here! I tell you, they shall weep and wail over her, when they look upon the smoke of her *burning!*" Burning! that was too much! Vince had plunged for the bastard, but guys had held him back. "There's too many of them, Vince!" And Baxter, passing, had called him personally "a drunkard and a Jew and a fornicator, an intriguer dealing in the souls of men!" Vince then had seen what Bruno really was: he'd thought he was just a nut, but he was the very force of evil right in the flesh, the antichrist whose black spirit oozed out of him like an obscene vapor and penetrated all West Condon— could even penetrate the world! This was a battle of the spirit!

So, when it had broken up, they did what they had to do. Gathering up hatchets and hammers, rifles, whatever they could find, they went, Vince leading them, to the Church of the Nazarene, about a dozen of them. It was a cheap squarish dump with false brick siding, a kind of one-room schoolhouse with a high loft and a damp crotchy odor. They bashed out all the windows, knocked out the lights, broke up the pews and folding chairs, tore out the wiring, smashed the pulpit and the old upright piano, ripped the songbooks. The thing that frustrated them was that no matter what they did to this dimestore junk, it didn't compensate for the brutalizing of their Cathedral, but as they worked a kind of exhilaration did sweep over them. This was a holy thing, and they swung with the might of God empowering their bodies. Like a great horned beast in God's service, they fell upon that place of sin and crushed it. They chopped the doors off the hinges, tore the toilet out of the floor, which caused the place to start flooding, broke into a small office. In there, they found a small desk, Baxter's probably, almost nothing inside it: they chopped it up. They were sweating and they were feeling good. They dumped the books out of the shelves, heaved the shelves through the window, and tore up the books. Sal Ferrero said, "Hey, Vince! That's a Bible you're tearing up!" "But it ain't a Catholic Bible, buddy!" They

495

found two revolting paintings on the wall which they studied a moment before smashing. One was a grossly sensual male devil, bloated, cruel. The other was a hideous woman with snakes. "My God!" said Guido Mello. "What kind of place is this?" They left it nothing but rubble.

When it was done, they felt fine, they'd labored hard and had a good sweat up, they felt powerful and the axes and rifles swung firm in their hands, but they didn't feel satisfied. "What next?" they wanted to know.

"Let's go to the hill," Bonali said.

Tremendous crowds jammed all the streets, they could hardly get through. Lay down on the horn and bulled ahead. Three carloads in tandem, ax handles and rifle barrels poking out the windows. Two or three guys, seeing them, piled in with them. Vince picked up Chester Johnson, "Hey, boys! didja see me on TV?" he preened, and Vince felt his neck flush. Rough laughter, deep in the throat, from the back seat.

The going was easier once they hit the mine road. Vince, leading, gunned it, had his old crate doing eighty before they reached the mine—"Well now, goddamn, I jist don't think she's gonna take off," Johnson drawled— then saw ahead of him a barricade, slammed the brakes, skidded, nearly spun, pulled her out, shimmied to a halt, jumped out, found the cops and a bunch of shopowners off Main there.

"What the hell?" he asked, too loud, but he couldn't help it. "You not gonna let them get to the hill?" He felt cheated somehow, but his heart was racing like a sonuvabitch, and his hands were sweating.

"Aw sure," said Maury Castle, grinning at Vince—that goddamn fatface cocksucker! maybe this was the moment! "But, see, we just happened accidental-like to have scheduled our first annual spring carnival out here this weekend."

Vince didn't get it at all. "Whaddya mean, Castle?"

"Buck a head, Vince. Games and refreshments for everybody."

Vince stared at Castle. "You guys always got it figured, don't you?" Castle only shrugged, stared off. Vince went back to the boys, waiting for him there, half out of the cars. He realized then he was still swinging an ax. "Should we just bust on through?" They didn't like the idea, seeing the cops there; he felt them shrink back from him. Just then, Vince spied Cavanaugh on the other side of the barricades. Something told him not to, but he hollered out: "Hey, Ted!" He grinned at the others. "Come on, you guys. Ted'll let us in."

They all climbed out, followed him up to the barricades. Ted came over, looking like a mortgage-holder, and said, "I thought I asked you to stay clear of here today, Bonali."

Vince went cold all over. Didn't hate, just felt emptied out, brought down. "I thought you might need me," he said weakly. He felt his shame radiating behind him.

"Say, what the hell are you carrying there?"

"We just come from the—" But he decided not to mention it. Ted was a Protestant, too. He wouldn't understand.

"Romano, I don't want any goddamn weapons out here!"

Romano and Monk Wallace came out from behind the barricade, collected the rifles and axes. "Now, either pay your buck, boys, or beat it," Romano said.

Bonali, crumbling into ruins, turned to go, but some of the other guys started forking up. "Hey! you gonna go along with that shit?" he hollered at them. It was a gray muggy day and his sweat was sticky on him. Something sick was lodged in his stomach.

"Take it easy, Vince," said Mello. "This is gonna be pretty funny. I don't want to miss it."

As the other guys lined up like a bunch of fucking sheep, Mort Whimple came waddling up on the run. "I just got the word, Ted!" he gasped. "They're about two blocks from Willow. They'll hit the mine road in about ten minutes, maybe fifteen."

"Tell them to slow them down any way they can."

Cavanaugh looked irritably at his watch, then up at the sky. "Flat tire, anything."

"They tell me Himebaugh's still not with them," the mayor said.

"Good," was the first word of Ted's reply, but Vince couldn't hear the rest, because the mayor and Cavanaugh wandered off in a heads-down huddle. Something about the troopers coming by helicopter. Vince looked up. It was going to rain.

"Let's go get Himebaugh," Vince said to those who remained.

But the others split off from him. They didn't make any excuses, they just edged away like he had some goddamn disease, strolled over to the ticketbooth and paid their dollars. "Come on, Vince," said Sal Ferrero, smiling. Was he digging him? "Let's watch this awhile, get something to drink, cool off."

"You chickening out too, Sal?" Sal shrugged, looked embarrassed, wandered away. "Sal, goddamn you, man, I'm asking you for the last time! You coming, buddy, or ain't you?"

"I'm not coming, Vince."

"Well, *fuck* you then, you yellowbellied *cocksucker!*" Oh Jesus, it all boiled up in him, he was so mad he could have cried, and he could have killed Ferrero right there, could have thrown him to the dirt and battered his fucking brains out, and, trembling, he spun on Johnson and Lucci, the only two guys left—maybe they didn't have a buck on them—and cried, "Let's go, goddamn it!" And afraid they were going to bug out too, he added, "Himebaugh was a rich bastard. Maybe we'll find something." That kept them with him, okay, but he felt rotten about it. That sick thing was puffing up and filled his belly now.

They made it back to the edge of town just as the first carloads of newspaper and radio people were pulling out on the mine road. Everything was all mashed up. He blared and cursed and inched and bellowed, but finally ran into solid rivers of people who kicked his car and swore at him when he tried to move. They parked and walked, having a rough time of it against the tide, though Johnson and Lucci amused themselves feeling up every foreign female they squeezed by. It was getting dark and Vince thought he heard thunder.

At last they broke free of the mob, found their way back to Himebaugh's place. Vince felt queasy, looked about nervously for cameras, but Johnson danced around waving at all the trees and shouting out his "earthling Ralphus" lines. Himebaugh's front door was locked. Vince realized he didn't know exactly what he was going to do if he found the man inside, but he put his shoulder to the door, and in three or four heaves it gave way. The moment it broke in, a big skinny black cat came streaking out, made Vince nearly jump out of his skin. "What the hell was *that?*"

"A little good luck," said Lucci.

"That pussy looked like she might not a had no meat for a while," whined Johnson. Johnson wasn't funny today. Just nasal and grating.

The house was nearly bare. Carpets still down, matted depressions where furniture had sat. A few heavy pieces remained. A couple paintings on the walls, books in the bookshelves. But everything showed signs of a quiet but permanent departure.

While Lucci and Johnson searched for loot, Bonali hunted Himebaugh. Didn't want to find him, but he couldn't quit the idea. Tried to remember the file busting him on the nose. The empty house was getting on his nerves. "*Ho-lee shee-it!*" cried Lucci just then, and Vince nearly squeaked out loud. "Hey, come here!"

Johnson and Bonali found him in the bathroom, staring into the tub. It was full of water. It was also full of dead cats. "I never knowed you could drown a cat without tyin' a stone to him," Johnson said.

"He must've held them under," Vince reasoned. He tried to think of the antichrist, but it was getting all mixed up.

499

"Well," cackled Johnson, "the cats are all yours, boys. I got mine." He held up a bottle. Brandy.

"Jesus! Just what I need!" Vince said.

"Hunh-unh!" negated Johnson, tucking the bottle under his skinny arm and backing off.

"Unh-*hunh!*" argued Vince, and he and Lucci went for the flask.

"Okay, okay!" Johnson cried, going down hard. "Shit, boys, you're swingin' like you're mad or somethin'!"

They split it, and when it was gone, they looked for more. Lucci found half a fifth near the tub, behind the stool, and Bonali discovered a whole one in the bookshelves. Outside, a storm had commenced to blow, and there wasn't any point in going out there and getting wet, and that was how it was that the cops found them there in a state only bordering on consciousness.

There was nothing very wonderful about the days that followed either. Vince came down with the flu, which kept him in bed awhile, and Etta, in spite of everything, took care of him like always. When he could get up, he felt weak all the time, not up to anything more strenuous than sitting in his old rocker on the front porch. Ted Cavanaugh never came by about that special committee of course, though in his imaginings, Vince kept seeing that big red Lincoln pulling up at the curb. Out of boredom one morning, he did manage to drag himself back up the ladder and got the whole south side of the house painted. The paint was a little gummy. When he was through, he hardly realized he'd been painting, though he dreamed that night about falling off the ladder and woke up screaming for Angelo. Had no goddamn idea when he'd get to the other two sides.

Sal Ferrero came over while he still had the flu, and they apologized to each other. "I don't know what happened to me that day, Sal."

"I know, Vince. It was a crazy time. Anyhow, it's over."

It sure was. Sal dropped by about every second or third

day after that. They bitched together about being out of work and no prospects, or talked over old times, and sometimes the Brunists came up, though they never felt exactly comfortable speaking about that. Sal filled Vince in on all that happened out there at the hill that day, about the rain and all those naked people, and how they got old Tiger Miller before the cops moved in, how in the big fight they overturned the TV dollies and busted the lamps, and how the bingo tent fell in, crushing a little child to death. "It's awful, Sal."

"Hard to realize it ever happened here."

A lot of people got killed and hurt, and what did they do about it? Nothing. They put that old man Fisher in jail but let him right out again. Didn't touch Castle. And all they did to Bruno was send him to the looneybin, put old Emilia in a rest home. Sent one kid up for nearly killing a couple cops. But that was all. The rest: scot-free. And now they were showing up on TV and whatnot all over the country. "It *is* hard to realize, Sal. I still can't believe it."

"They say Baxter's even back in town again."

"No kidding?" He wanted to explain to Sal about the emptiness, but somehow he didn't have the words for it. Instead, Sal told him a story that was going around about how, when they still had all those wild wet Brunists packed into the jail here that night, a state trooper slipped into the women's cell to play the stud bull and got pulled out an hour later half dead and raving mad.

Vince and Etta never went up to the Eagles anymore. He hated to see those faces up there, especially Johnson's. They called him "The Mayor." Vince spent the days rocking on the porch, the nights escaping west or into crime on the TV. He wished the daytime programs were better, so he didn't ever have to do anything else. There was a strain between him and Etta most of the time, but watching TV, they were happy enough, and found themselves talking together about the programs.

They got a letter one day from the Marine Corps, inquiring into the whereabouts of their son Charles Josef, who, the letter said, had been AWOL since the seventh of April. Vince groaned and Etta bawled, but they'd both pretty much guessed as much. They wrote back that he had visited them on Easter weekend but that they had no idea where he had gone afterwards; then sent letters to the other kids in the family to let them know about it, in case he showed up with one of them. "Shit, I'm sorry," Vince said that day, rocking all alone out on the front porch, and he cried awhile by himself.

It was all empty, the town was falling all apart, soon there wouldn't be anybody left around but him. No mines, no paper, businesses closing. The clubs would go soon. He looked across the table and there was Ange Moroni, hat tipped down to his nose, grinning at his cards. Mike Strelchuk and Carlo Juliano playing with them. Why did he remember that? He didn't know, but it was plain as day. There was a big crowd, loud music, and they were winning. Where did it go: that excitement?

One evening just as the ten-o'clock newscast was coming on, all they had to keep plugged into the world now that the *Chronicle* was closed, Vince stood to stretch, chanced to gaze out the window just in time to see Ted Cavanaugh's red Lincoln swing up at the curb. He ran into the bedroom, woke Etta up. "Hey! Wake up! Ted's coming! I just saw his car out front!" Looked frantically for a tie.

"Angie's got a date with his boy," Etta replied sleepily, and rolled over hugely.

Vince went back to the door, peeked out. It was true, nobody was getting out. He went in to watch the news and sports. Began to understand a few of the remarks Angie had been making of late, why she'd seemed almost to hate him. Hours passed. He watched the midnight movie, old swashbuckler, hardly followed it. Time it was over, having watched all those flashing swords, he was in a sweat, imagining just about every grotesque perversion conceivable. When she finally came in, he called to her.

"I'm tired, Dad," she snapped, sounding tough. Whorish. "Let's have confessions tomorrow."

The kid might not have laid her, but he'd sure mussed her up. "Who you been wrestling with?" he asked dully, then saw that her face was all streaked with tears.

"Oh, *please!*" she cried, and ran into her room. For a long time, he heard her sobbing in there. It naturally occurred to him what the matter was. He'd have Etta ask tomorrow. "Ted, old buddy, I hate to tell you, but you and me is about to become related, in a manner of speaking." But shit, the bastard would find a way out of it, buy off the doctors or the judges or something. It'd be Vince who'd wind up in the jug afterwards, and little Angie to raise a bastard. Things were bad. In fact, they were so bad that when he found out the next day that this had not been the problem, that it was just a routine breakup, he almost found himself feeling let down.

That was the kind of mood he was in when Wally Brevnik and Georgie Lucci came by his house to say good-bye. They told him they were going up North together, get some kind of factory work. They'd both been in his gang at the mine, and they said they still thought he was the best goddamn faceboss that mine had ever had. They didn't say anything about mayors, but told him they sure as hell hated to say good-bye.

Vince told them it hurt him to see them go, too. Seemed like just about everybody in town was bugging out on him. Again, he wanted to tell them about the big hole he was looking into, about how afraid he was.

Wally said that by God they'd write for him when they found something good, figured it would only take them a couple weeks. "Shit, a man of your ability and experience, Vince, you'll have no trouble."

Vince got a little excited about that, said for them not to forget now, hell, it'd be just like down in the mine, all of them working together, and they all laughed about that, and then they were gone. Last thing he heard, as he walked them out to their car and saw them off, was Ben Wosznik on the car radio singing that Brunist song that was such a big hit these days. They waved at each other until they turned a corner a couple blocks down. He turned around, that hillbilly melody still ringing in his head, and there was the old house. Angie's bike up against the bright yellow porch. On the rocker: a new calico pillow that Etta had made for him. Stop kidding yourself, he said. You ain't going nowhere.

Then one night, he went for a walk. He was trying to get a new outlook. He had made mistakes, but who in this town hadn't? He walked under leafy trees, past flowering bushes and lawns with a new green nap, the air laden with vegetable renascence. This town wasn't through yet, and neither was he. Why couldn't he make a new start? The ballooning May moon smiled down on him as though to say: it goes on; only men quit.

He found he had wandered into the old housing development where Wanda lived. Quiet, empty, badly lit, yet bright in the moonlight. Decided to stop by, what the hell, make some sort of apology. She must be feeling about as cruddy as he was. It didn't matter much anymore who saw him or what they thought. And he felt like a wrong had to be righted, no matter how it was misread afterwards. He even thought about going home to get Etta and bringing her with him, but it was a long walk. He located Wanda's house, but it was dark. He didn't see curtains up, remembered then that she had given everything away. Jesus, the poor kid, all she had was the bare walls! Then he saw the FOR RENT sign sticking up in the clay of the front yard. Gone. With the rest of them. Like Sal said, hard to believe it had really happened. He felt relieved, but vaguely disappointed at the same time. "Well, God bless her," he said, not knowing quite what he meant by it.

Moseying back, he chanced to pass the old Bruno house. It sat like a spook there in a tunic of moonlight, no longer protected. They sure got Bruno and the old lady put away fast, had to give them credit for that much. Vince noticed that the windows and doors were broken. He wandered up . . . then once on the porch, on in. A pale ghostly light hung dustily throughout. Things looked pretty busted up. He stood in the front room and looked about him on the melancholy scene. Did they see it would come to this? In the dining room, a huge glass chandelier lay splattered all over the floor, so that it crunched wherever he walked. His eyes were adjusted to the dark now, and he saw that the drapes had been slashed, chairs broken up, upholstery ripped, and he remembered his own demolition of the Church of the Nazarene. "What do we do it for, God?" he asked aloud, and wouldn't have been too surprised to get an answer. "Do You understand what makes it happen? Can You forgive it?"

He felt he needed something by which to remember his coming here, to remember the whole Brunist story, and, since it was the nearest at hand, he picked up a fragment of the broken chandelier. He held it up toward the moonlight and, miraculously, a rainbow danced and shimmered in it. He wandered through the other rooms, and throughout there was the sound of glass underfoot like slate in the mine, wallpaper stripped and hanging in spectral shreds, black distorted objects silhouetted against the pallid light. In the kitchen he found a staircase, mounted it. Things upstairs were no different. In the bathroom, even the fixtures had been torn out and robbed.

He heard sirens. He thought it might be another fire. The last one had brought him so much luck, he couldn't resist chasing this one. And this time there'd be no screwing up. He started for the stairs, but realized the sirens were wailing up right out in front. No bells: must be an ambulance. Or the cops! Somebody had seen him come in! He looked frantically for a hidingplace, but the rooms were mostly barren. Heard them on the porch, heard the rattle of the door and the crunch of glass as they shoved on in. "This way!" That was Dee Romano! "The guy who called said we'd find him upstairs." Vince's

505

heart raced, his mind seemed frozen. A back window. Might be a chance. Maybe a porch roof below. Heard them rumbling up the stairs. Window in the back bedroom, big one, but also a bed. He ducked under . . . and ducked right out again. Somebody already under there. Galloped on hands and knees to a closet, rolled inside. The light came on. Closet door was half open, but he couldn't close it now. He huddled, shaking, in a corner. "I smell it," said Romano. He could hear them bumping to their knees. "And here he is!" said Monk Wallace. "Jee-ee-*zuss!*" Old Willie scrambled out of there. "Boys, I'm retirin'!" he said. "What should we do?" asked Wallace. "Not our job," said Romano. "We don't have to pick it up." They followed Willie out, leaving the light burning. Vince heard them talking down the stairs. More people down there. He supposed they'd keep coming all night. It'd be a long time before the place emptied out and he could leave. Meanwhile, he lay curled up there in a corner of the closet, bawling like a newborn baby. "Don't leave me again!" he sobbed. "Without You, God, it's horrible!" He had to still his sobs from time to time, because others, curious, came up to look, to shudder, to shrink away. "Boy, you never know, hunh?" "You said it, man!" "Like he just stretched out there and kicked off." "Really weird." "They all were." Vince fingered the small piece of glass from the chandelier, pressed shut his eyes. *Santa Maria, madre di Dio, pregate per noi peccatori, adesso e nell' ora della mostra morte. Così sia.*

When finally the tears had stopped, when he felt like all the horror had washed out of him and he could stand alone again, he stood and walked out, walked down. Somebody met him at the foot of the stairs. "Is it true, Vince?" Vince nodded, passed on. Glass crunched beneath his feet. He kept a tight grip on the piece in his pocket. "God, it's awful, isn't it, Vince?" somebody said. He shook his head in commiseration. "It couldn't be worse," he said. At the door, Dee Romano, looking washed out, nodded at him, and Vince nodded back. But it could be worse. And, walking out of the home of the prophet Giovanni Bruno on that lush night in May, Vince Bonali released at last the piece of glass (though he reached in his pocket every now and then to touch it again, make sure it was still there) and looked up at the magnitude and care of the universe and thanked God that, if no one else had, he at least had come at last to his Redemption.

7

In June, the Reformed Nazarene Followers of Giovanni Bruno all waited around the world for the Coming of the Light again. It was on a Sunday, the seventh, seven Sundays after the nineteenth of April, but they waited until midnight because the next day was the eighth of the month, and Elaine's Ma had not entirely put away that idea yet. It was an extraordinary—though, as it turned out, again somewhat symbolic—event, huge rallies everywhere, all of it covered simultaneously by world television, press, and radio: as though literally nothing else in the whole world was happening that night. In fact, it made Elaine feel funny the next day reading the newspapers and discovering that a lot of other things *did* happen. And another funny thing: as exciting as their own meeting was and as important as she was in it, she kept feeling all night like she'd rather go see it on television, as if that was where it was *really* happening.

Her Ma had changed a few things by the time of the June rallies—like wearing regular clothes under the tunics and staying in out of the weather—so things went a little more calmly most places. They read afterwards about some meetings where things got even worse than they had at the Mount of Redemption, but her Ma said those people were sensationalists and not real Christians. By letter and telephone and television appearances, her Ma and Ben organized these Bruno Follower rallies all over the world, convinced now that when it happened it would happen everywhere at once, though of course their own meeting in Randolph Junction was the most important and one of the biggest. Reverend Baxter wanted to hold it on the Mount of Redemption in West Condon, but Elaine's Ma decided against it on account of the Persecution, organized it instead of Randolph Junction, where the mayor was a friend of Brother Bishop Hiram Clegg and even became a True Follower. It was a very nice meeting, even though the newspeople were rather impolite some of the time and a few people from out of town got to acting up—in fact, though it was much bigger and there were a lot more lights, it was a great deal like the wonderful revivalist tentmeetings her Pa used to hold.

Elaine was thinking a lot about her Pa these days, not just because he had become a Saint and Martyr, or because she and her Ma sometimes talked to him, or because she might go to Heaven and see him soon, but because she had a new Pa now, Mr. Wosznik, and she couldn't help comparing. She loved them both, but the truth was, if she could choose, she would stick with the old one. Ben was very kind, but her old Pa was even kinder. Her old Pa was smarter, too, she thought, and dressed better. Ben always smelled a little bit like a farm. Of course, one thing about Ben, he sure could sing. Their ballad with him singing it was number three on the Hillbilly Hit Parade, and they were making lots of money, which Ben was giving to the movement because it had a lot of expenses now. Just what it spent on postage was something hard to believe. Of course, as her Ma said, there wasn't any need to choose: we were all God's children and, in a way, were all married to each other. Ben sometimes made Elaine think of her brother Harold, who was killed in the war, and who always used to play a banjo and sing religious songs to her when she was little, and she wondered if maybe her Ma wasn't thinking of Harold when she married Ben. Her Ma kept her old name so people would always know who she was, calling herself Mrs. Clara Collins-Wosznik.

Elaine was a much bigger help to her Ma now than she used to be. Her Ma even remarked on it several times. She wasn't afraid anymore and people looked up to her because she was one of the First Followers and might even be a Saint someday. She took up collections and typed envelopes and helped organize meetings and even gave instruction in the Creed sometimes to the younger people at Junior Evening Circle. Like everybody always agreed, the Creed was very beautiful; it was based on the Seven Words of Giovanni Bruno and Saint Paul and the Revelation to John, and contained wonderful new ideas about Mother Mary and Spiritual Communication and the God, not of Wrath or Love, but of Light. It changed from time to time because, as her Ma said, it was a *living* Creed: Domiron wasn't mentioned in it anymore, for example, though he might come back, now that Mrs. Norton's book, *The Sayings of Domiron*, was out. She and Dr. Norton had become the first Bishops of the whole state of California, and her Ma would always say how she admired that lady and still to this day wore the medallion, but as Bishops the Nortons were not very active. They seemed too inclined to go their own way and forget they were all children of the same God.

Some of the younger people Elaine instructed were boys and they paid her a lot of attention, but regardless of what her Ma said about all being married to each other, she never let things go too far. It wasn't just because she had her mind on being a Saint, but because she was going steady in a religious kind of way: ever since Carl Dean had gone to jail for trying to kill all those policemen, she had been writing letters regularly with Junior Baxter. Junior had stayed in West Condon with his folks in spite of the terrible Persecution still going on there, and they were meeting secretly now—Junior wrote "underground" and Elaine actually thought they were meeting in the mines

509

or something until her Ma explained. Her Ma didn't seem too happy about her writing to Junior, but she didn't say not to. Elaine didn't show her Ma all the letters either, because sometimes she and Junior had to discuss pretty grown-up things, considering they both wanted to be Saints.

All day long that Sunday that they went to the Mount, the Day of Redemption, she and Junior had been staring at each other. Elaine didn't know at the time if it was because they still hated each other or what, but she didn't like it. Her tunic felt funny on her all day. She even thought of asking Carl Dean to make him stop, but she was afraid of causing trouble just when everybody was so excited about all the Baxter people joining them in the Spirit. And they were so tired. Elaine thought she'd drop, and it made her kind of dizzy all day—she kept getting the funny feeling she was floating in and out of all those other people. They had been up all night watching over poor Marcella, whom she loved so—Elaine had cried and cried like a baby, and once had even kissed the cold mouth and nearly died doing it, it just didn't seem possible. All the next day, she kept waiting for Marcella to rise up and take her hand and smile. And then all the baptisms there before they went out to march, just at dawn, because Giovanni Bruno, who was heartbroken, opened his mouth in that special way of his when he wanted to say something important and said: *"Baptize . . . Light!"* It was the last thing anybody ever remembered him saying before they took him away from the Mount. Her Ma and Reverend Baxter and Mrs. Norton all agreed right away: he meant they were supposed to have a new kind of baptism, a baptism with light, and so they gave him a flashlight to hold and everybody walked under it, sniffling and bawling to beat the band. Her Ma still baptized with light in the same way, she had a special lamp for it, but Junior said his Pa had changed it a little, using real fire, and they couldn't wear anything on their shoulders. That made her Ma a little mad when she found out, just like she got upset at Mrs. Norton for saying out in California that "light" meant "television." It seemed like her Ma was always caught in the middle between those two.

But Elaine's commitment, the strangest and most important moment of her life, happened out there on the Mount of Redemption. Holding hands with Carl Dean, praying and singing and crying, Elaine had watched the lightning flash and the rain come down, had watched the terrible forces of evil gather like dirty clouds below them, had watched the worshiping multitudes rolling and dancing and beating each other, and she could tell that Carl Dean was pretty excited and not just about the End of the World. He kept looking around nervously and saying they might never see each other again after today and once he even asked her to go down in the trees with him so they could be alone a minute. But she was afraid and praying all the time, because she really believed, she really was *sure* it was going to happen and right *then*, and she kept looking for her Pa. She held on to Carl Dean's hand because she was scared, but all the time she kept feeling miles away from him: suddenly the only thing that counted was that *moment* and Carl Dean couldn't get his mind off what would happen *next*.

But then somebody came running up the Mount and he wasn't in a tunic or taking off his dark garments of the earth and they saw it was Mr. Miller and Elaine felt a great terror because he seemed to be headed right for Marcella and everybody started screaming like crazy and Carl Dean ran away, left her all alone on the top of the Mount, ran to get Mr. Miller, and Elaine saw him hit him and everybody was hitting him and it was raining something awful and Marcella seemed to get right up and throw herself into the mud and Saint Stephen went tumbling down and Elaine was on her knees in the mud and bawling and calling for her Pa and terrified to be all alone and just then something hit her—*whack!* She spun, falling into the mud, scared to death, and she saw it was Junior Baxter. He was cold white in his tunic and his head seemed like on fire. He had a long greenish-white switch and he looked very serious. Nobody had ever switched her before, her Pa, her Ma, nobody. She looked around for her Ma, but everybody was over by Mr. Miller. *"No!"* she gasped.

But Junior didn't hit her again. He looked around on the ground, found another switch somebody had dropped —the little tree there was nothing but a barbed pole now. He handed it to her. Her heart was pounding like mad, and she could hardly hold on to that greasy thing, could hardly see through the tears and rain, could hardly hear him in the rain's roar when he said, "Hit me!" His voice was soft, almost like a girl's. He turned his wet white back to her. She stood up, her knees shaky, but suddenly she wasn't afraid anymore, the conflicts were gone, the strange sense of sin she felt for not being *within* was lifted, and at last the moment was whole. She swatted him lightly. She still didn't know quite what she was doing and she was still bawling, but the sky seemed brighter even though it was still raining pitchforks and it seemed like they were suddenly all alone in the world and she thought: It's coming! *Now!* And Junior's switch whistled and bit into her side. She cried out, but the pain was a joy, strangely a joy, and the rain was right and the lightning and the frenzy, and everything was *right now:* she swung, hard— *crack!* Under his wet red hair, he smiled a little. She closed her eyes. His whip stung her legs. She lashed his legs. He whipped her tummy. She swung at his face. Faster and faster they slashed away and now the blows fell all over, on her face and chest, down her back, they didn't take turns, just gave and took with all their hearts, and she couldn't even see him, never knew when she hit him, just felt him out there, felt everything at once, and maybe she was singing, or maybe she was screaming, but it was coming, she grew a giant and lashed the world to her heart and her Pa was smiling down and the world was on her back, she stretched out her arms and dug her nails into its flesh and the rain was in her face and mud in her mouth, but she could still see Junior somehow, looking down with that serious face, the switch in his hand, and he had blood around his eye and trickling from his mouth, his hair red in the gray sky, and she stretched her limbs, north south east and west, stretched to embrace it all. *NOW!*

But when she looked again, Junior Baxter was on the ground and Carl Dean Palmers was on top of him, yelling that Junior's Ma had just had a baby in front of everybody, though it turned out it really wasn't a baby but a miscarriage, and he was hitting Junior with his fists, hitting him and hitting him and hitting him. And that was when it happened, when Elaine chose between love and sainthood: for one pitch-black moment she swooned away into the earth, to the very pit, then exploded up again into light, and the next thing she knew she was scratching and clawing Carl Dean, and screaming at him to stop, and when he did she fell down on top of Junior, all bloody and suffering, so Carl Dean couldn't hit him again, and she screamed at Carl Dean to go away, go *away!* At first, she thought Carl Dean was going to cry, but then, instead, he sort of just went crazy. He called her what Junior had called her—he didn't understand at all!—and right in front of her own Ma who had just come running up to say they had to get going because the Persecution was starting, and then, hollering like the Indians do in the movies, he went running right at all those policemen with their big white clubs. She never saw what happened because her Ma pulled her away, they had to run, they didn't have time.

Later, she learned that Carl Dean had been sent up to detention for six months to a year for nearly killing three policemen. She thought that was awful, yet she sometimes wondered if he wasn't the closest he ever got to real salvation right at that moment. He never wrote to her because of course he didn't know where she was. That suited her okay. She never saw Junior Baxter again either, but they wrote letters. Sometimes they talked in the letters about what happened that afternoon on the Mount of Redemption. They both agreed they had "grown up" that day and had taken the whole world into their hearts. In the days that followed, things got broken up again, and they lost the complete feeling, but to help them remember, they agreed to touch each sore place every night when they said their prayers. The last mark to go away was one he had made across her heart. He said he believed that was very significant, for it meant that her heart was God's, and she agreed. They both looked forward to the real and final Coming of the Light when they'd all be together in absolute union again.

Her Ma and his Pa also wrote letters, but not about the same things. Her Ma was worried, because Reverend Baxter kept insisting about having his own way on everything, and she thought maybe he tended to carry things too far sometimes. Like the baptism business, for instance, and some of the rules about the tunics. Her Ma liked to think of their Prophet as a great new spiritual force unleashed upon the world, a renovating force for all Christendom, she said, but it didn't seem like Reverend Baxter even thought of himself as a Christian anymore, and he was more excited about the way the Prophet spit in the priest's eye than in the way her Ma was helping the movement grow. Still, she went ahead and made him the Bishop of West Condon, mainly because nobody else was there anymore. Brother Willie Hall, who was *supposed* to be the Bishop, wasn't able to stay on account of the Persecution, and so he and Sister Mabel became Traveling Missionaries for the movement. Elaine followed all this very closely, for she had a very strange feeling about something: she wondered if maybe she herself hadn't come closer to Redemption that day on the Mount than her own Ma.

One very sad thing happened the Day of Redemption: Sister Emma Clegg died of a stroke. She was a very holy woman and some said afterward that God had taken her away as a Sign of His keeping His Word. Nevertheless, it was a terrible shock for Brother Hiram, who was such a nice man and loved his wife so. At first, he was put in jail with all the other menfolk, but they let him right out again to take care of burying his wife, and they never came back to get him again. For a long time, he was very depressed, and he didn't want even to think about making a new life. But her Ma, who had suffered so herself, had restored his spirit and made him get active again in the movement. He became the Bishop of Randolph Junction and, on that Sunday morning of the seventh of June, the day of the possible Midnight Coming—though by then nearly everybody was expecting it on the eighth of January, possibly next year, but more likely either seven or fourteen years from now—had married the widow Sister Betty Wilson, her Ma and her new Pa Ben standing as witnesses. As her Ma said at the little party after, it was a very poetical arrangement. A lot of people were there from all over the world, and most of them cried to think about it.

They also found poor Mr. Himebaugh, who had disappeared the Night of the Sacrifice, starved to death. Her Ma didn't find that at all poetical and, even though they made him a Martyr, she hardly ever talked about Mr. Himebaugh again. Colin Meredith wrote them from where they were keeping him that he was in continual communication with the spiritual world and would return to them one day with incredible revelations. Sister Mary Harlowe settled in Randolph Junction and kept coming to their meetings, because after all she was a First Follower and her husband was a Saint and Early Martyr, but it seemed like she was starting to get bitter and sometimes talked rudely to Elaine's Ma. Sister Wanda Cravens never got bitter and she was always very active.

Their Prophet was excommunicated by the Romanists and put in chains, and his people prayed daily for his deliverance. Really, he and his Ma were put in institutions like poor Colin, but, as her own Ma said, it was the same thing, it was all a part of the Persecution, and, as everybody knew, the mental institutions were controlled by Jews and atheists and they tortured Christians. They prayed for him to return and lead them to Light and most people believed his appearance would coincide with the real and final Coming, which meant he probably wouldn't turn up for another seven years anyway. They had to learn patience

515

and readiness, her Ma always said. Her Ma, who had run into a lot of problems talking on the phone to people where the time and even the date were completely different, had even begun to wonder if her old Pa's final message, now known as the Revelation to Saint Ely Collins, anyway that part regarding the "eighth of the month," was not to be taken symbolically instead of literally. Elaine and Junior speculated about this in their letters and talked about what they would do that day that the Prophet appeared and they were all together again.

And then one day in the middle of June, about a week after they waited for the Midnight Coming, Brother Bishop Hiram Clegg called a special meeting of all the Bishops who could come, about thirty of them by then, and he didn't tell her Ma about it. Her Ma got terribly upset when she found out, because it looked for all the world like Brother Hiram was taking things into his own hands—and after all she'd done for him! She prayed to God and got guidance from Pa, and then she took Elaine and they stormed right into the middle of that meeting. Her Ma strode right down the aisle and was just about to raise the roof, when they all stood up and clapped and clapped.

Bishop Clegg rapped a gavel and said: "Sister Clara, we have, ahem, convened here this here night to consider the future of this great movement, and we have determined that the world lies open before us and we have but begun. But to accomplish the tasks that lie ahead, we must put our house in working order. To this end, we have here gathered and here, by unanimous consent, resolved to name you, Sister Clara Collins-Wosznik, our Evangelical Leader and Organizer!" Her Ma was just stopped dead in her tracks and seemed to go white all over. "Our financial picture has, of course, ahem, not yet stabilized itself, for the core itself is smaller than the loose ends still to be tied up, so we must apologize for the modesty of our initial offer, but we do feel able at this time to, ah, to propose a commencing remuneration of seven thousand dollars a year and traveling expenses. If you could just see fit . . ." And poor Brother Hiram's voice started to break because he saw how her Ma was taking it: her Ma just broke right down and cried, and Elaine cried, and then so did a lot of other folks.

Then her Ma wiped her face with one of her old Pa's big handkerchiefs and stepped up to the front and gave the most exciting speech Elaine had ever heard. She talked of their sacred goals and the race they had to run and how God's Kingdom was not a gift to the indolent but the justifiable wages for honest hard work. "A body visited by grace must *live* by grace!" she cried, and Elaine felt a shudder run through her, tingling the place over her heart, and she started thinking about the next letter she would write to Junior Baxter. Her Ma told of all the converts and read letters from distant places and then: *"God willing,"* she shouted out, *"we will go out and win the souls of the whole wide world!"*

Everybody stood up and clapped and cheered and cried and said she'd have to give that speech on television, surely no one could resist, and then Bishop Clegg led them all in fervent prayer. They had been calling themselves the Reformed Nazarene Followers of Giovanni Bruno, but that night they decided to go back to the name Mr. Miller had given them: the Brunists.

EPILOGUE
Return

The West Condon Tiger rose from the dead, pain the only
sign of his continuance, for he was otherwise blind, deaf
to all but a distant shriek, and abidingly transfixed. There
was light, or seemed to be, more felt than seen. And down
again: into the black bowels. Later: coruscations of terrible
brilliance, an engulfing centerless agony. *"Help!"* Sounds
of the rude world—or only a dream? Then, as the earth
lazed through a few million revolutions, the pain passed,
leaving only the light, figureless and unaimed, a medium
merely: so it had come after all. And was he impressed?
Not at all. Last thoughts: obscene blasphemies, social
phalanx erected to the whole holy lot. Retributive passage
then through epochs of black nebulae that twisted into
shapes and masks of the grieving dead, scarred and sup-
plicating: he sorrowed but could not reach them in their
distress nor could they him in his. Unrepentant wrenched
back to light, torture, somebody cried out, then dropped
again to the dark company. Thus ages passed, in flickering
succession. And what would he emerge? toward what new
monster was his soul evolving? He tried to move—anything—assert his will—could not. Nailed fast to his torment, he stared out with blind eyes on the impossibility
of the cosmos, and, staring, saw what looked like a cord
with a button at the end. He tried reaching for it, realized
for perhaps the billionth time in the course of his soul's
racked passage that he could move nothing at all. Nonetheless, from nowhere, from his renascent will maybe, an
Angel of Light—*the* Angel of Light—appeared. "I thought
I died," he said and wondered who had stuffed his mouth

with rocks. "How many years have I been here?" meaning light-years.

"Some eighteen, twenty hours," said Happy Bottom drily. "And how feels today the man who redeemed the world?"

"A little while . . . ," he said, but already he was tumbling, and there were great convulsions and mountains fell, burying his words. And again a little while . . .

She came to him on the arid plain, a motion of dull white on dull white, defined by her shadows, by her shifting tunic folds, by the dark point of her head. How she moved he could not tell, if she did at all: their convergence seemed governed by some law irrelevant to willed motion. From his height he could see the smooth curve of her brow, the clasp in her loose brown hair. He sought for images there, but convulsions of pain shrank his vision. Heal me! She looked up and, smiling faintly, uncertainly, held his gaze. Now! he gasped. In her hands, she held a fading dandelion, which now she brought to her smiling lips. From his great bulge of pain hung his knees and feet, and between them he could see her upturned face. Oh damn it, Marcella! Let me in! Her smile faded, her grieving eyes drooped to the dying flower, her lowering head's delicate rotation conducting the hairclasp between his toes. In it now he saw himself, crosshung, huge below, head soaring out of sight. She turned, receding. When next he perceived her, she was kneeling, not far away, scratching a hole in the hard dead clay to plant the dandelion. Was that blood? "Please! Oh God!" But, smiling, she was patting dust around the stem. Her tunic lay limp on her spine and haunches, darkened between her thighs. A pale foot's sole showed itself below the hem: then suddenly shot out, the hem flew up—"No!" he cried, squeezing shut his eyes. Something knocked against his cross: vibrations racked him and, screaming, he fell.

It was night. He was staring straight up at the ceiling, one arm outstretched and the other folded but elevated, and both pinned to something or other. His neck ached from the weight that lay upon it, and he was unable to see lower than the tip of his enormous nose. He was breathing hard; screams echoed in his ears still, the wound in his fork screamed still. Nailed into it: a flower—but had it taken root? He was almost sure, but he'd heard of amputees who felt their fingers and toes, and so he couldn't trust the testimony of his nerve ends.

She came in then and said, "Well, the old cock crows again!"

"You mean—?"

"Does it hurt?" He heard water running, then felt the lid fly off it and a shriveling cold wrap it. Intact! "Shame to waste it," Happy said, "but I don't want any crowds forming outside your door."

He laughed around the rocks and muck. "You know, I thought I'd lost it," he said.

"You nearly did. You can thank that big horsey lady for holding back the hatchets."

"Who? Clara? No kidding?"

"I guess she knew a good thing when she saw it."

"Why didn't those goddamn cops come?"

"I don't know," Happy said flatly, a frown crossing her freckled face. "Maybe they knew a good thing when they saw it, too."

She helped him then to urinate, and though he felt like one long ravaged nerve, he was able to smile. "Take good care of it," he whispered. "God gave the greater honor to the inferior part, let us not do less." With a wink, she pierced his side with a needle, and the nerve coated over. He relaxed, and though he plunged once more toward darkness, he plunged now without dread; the nails in his palms were basketballs and his legs were lean and could run again. "I'll be back!" he said, and, distantly, he thought he heard rewarding laughter.

Judas sat in the garden, propped against the tuberous trunk of an ancient tree, and gazed wearily upon his companions. Most slept, scratching fitfully at the old itches. It would come to nothing, he knew, watching them. He fingered the moneybox. There was now almost nothing in it. Why had they trusted him with it? Because his pure hope belied their weaknesses. They trusted him because he included them all and needed none of them, but they feared him for what he wanted, and his were never the decisions made. The prophet brooded distantly. For days now, Judas had suffered the man's wretched beseeching eyes. Judas knew what he wanted, knew that the man himself nor none of these could ever do it. Simon Peter, snoring, scratched one calloused foot on a tree trunk. One of the others seemed to be making running motions with his feet. A woman, too sleepy to shuffle away the prescribed distance, squatted to piss; someone protested, and she moved on. The fattening Passover moon illuminated their fragmented pathos. Judas stood. He looked up toward where the prophet knelt, saw that the man was watching him. He'd expected that, but felt a shudder just the same. He stared out on the hard dry hills, stared ahead at the days succeeding days, the endless wearisome motions, all prospects sickened to habit, stared out on the hopeless generative and digestive processes of unnumbered generations, and thought: Well, anyway, it's something different. And he went down into the town.

"Listen, Happy," said Miller, celebrating the bath hour, "let's set up a private little cult of our own." He saw doubt cross her eyes, as she looked up from his wet belly to study his face. "Trade rings, break a pot, whatever it is they do these days, build for perpetuity." Blushing, she turned back to the belly, rained suds on it from a sponge squeezed high. "Anyway," he said, "it'd be something different."

She dipped an index finger into his navel. "And on this rock . . ." she said, and they both watched the church grow.

The Coming of the Light had been, unless one took Eleanor Norton's point of view, delayed; the Powers of

Darkness had stormed the holy Mount, throwing the Sons of Light into dungeons or dispersion, and so there were none there to whom God might, in proper glory, come. From visitors, from doctors and nurses, from others hospitalized like himself, Miller picked up the pieces, and, oddly, without hands to write it down, he seemed to enjoy it all the more. Happy, he learned, had watched it all on television—all channels carried it, in spite of the nudity, none apparently wanting to be the first to cut itself off—and though reception had been bad with the storm, she had recognized him floundering around out there in his trenchcoat and had decided he might need a little help. But by the time she had arrived, the police had at last moved in, religious freedom or no, the Brunists were being herded into school buses brought out there for the purpose, and Miller was nowhere to be seen. Overhearing lurid accounts of what had just happened and thinking him dead, she had turned her woman's wrath on the mayor, judging him guilty by negligence, and poor Mort Whimple had nearly joined the army of the blind. Then she had chased up the hill, learned from that fat boy who used to be Tiger's assistant where he thought the body had been dumped, raced there to find him in an awry heap, a public curiosity, in a puddle before the red clay cranny of Cunt Hill. A mess, dressed only in mud and blood, but alive. She had grabbed an ambulance boy she knew and made them load him up— in spite of demands already rising on the Mount, where the cops, in their inimitable manner and being perhaps just a bit excited themselves, were opening a few recalcitrant skulls—and they had rushed him off to the hospital.

Eventually, another twenty or so Brunists had joined him, a few newsmen who, curiously, got the brunt of the Brunist wrath, as well as another forty-odd who sustained injuries from getting trampled inside the bingo tent, which had suddenly collapsed. Few had died. A small child had been mashed to a pulp in the bingo tent panic and a woman

525

near the entrance had perished in a fit; somebody had had a miscarriage; an old man, with several bones shattered when the tent fell, had died in the hospital of a stroke; a lady named Clegg had apparently succumbed *in medius ritus* to a heart attack, though she, like many, Doc Lewis said, had also got knocked around a bit; a woman who had flown in all the way from the East Coast had died a week later of pneumonia, and the old man in New Hampshire whose sight, he'd said, was returning to him had, following the new light, taken abortive flight off the roof of the old folks' home; and, of course, a few weeks later they found Ralph IIimebaugh under the Bruno bed, though by then Miller was already down off his rood and out of the hospital. Other than that: only broken heads, collapsed lungs, bruised bellies, crushed spines, and the like, minor statistics.

Born to be caught and killed. Frail cages. Containing what? Staring at X rays of his fractured clavicle, right thumb and left humerus, which Happy held out for him to see one morning while one of her buddies gave him an enema, both of them joking about his torn ear, rooted-out hair, broken nose, blackened eyes, and chipped and loosened teeth, he suddenly felt himself out there on the hill again, being danced on, bedded with corpses, splayed for a good Christian gelding, saw again the massed-up nameless bodies, the mad frenzy for life, the loins giving birth, and deep despair sprayed up his ass and inundated his body. "Why did you bother, Happy?" he asked.

He expected her to make some crack, but instead she only smiled and said, "I don't know. I guess because I like the way you laugh."

Yes, there was that. Not the void within and ahead, but the immediate living space between two. The plug was pulled and the sheet lifted, and the despair, a lot of it anyway, flooded out of him with a soft gurgle. "My message to the world," he said, and if he hadn't been afraid of swallowing half his teeth in the process, he might have laughed along with them.

526

Survival of the fittest. Or was it the youngest? Or rather the one with the right connections? Jesus yelling from his cross: "Maggie! where the hell is Maggie?" Miller mused, uprighted, staring out on a balmy April afternoon. What next? He didn't know. A lot of feelers from radio and television, but all they offered him was a job and he didn't want a job. Dear Mr. Christ: In view of your experience in personnel management . . . No, it was somehow like Ox Clemens going down in the mines: a broken bird. Once Ox had scandalized a whole stadium of fans and players, those that saw and heard, when, coming into a time-out huddle just after making a brilliant drive-in shot in a whale of a game up in the state championships, face dripping sweat and eyes closed, hand on a hard-on that not even a jockstrap could hold back, he gasped, "*Oh Jesus! I jist wanna jack off!*" In the walled-in years of datelines that had followed, whenever for a moment he'd broken out of the pattern, Miller had remembered Ox's mystical moment, and he was thinking about it now.

On a table nearby sat, or stood, his old Speedgraphic. Somebody had gathered up the pieces, Jones maybe, and sent them to him. Jones's own photos, he'd learned, were being made into a book called *On the Mount of Redemption*. Happy had reassembled the whole apparatus into a kind of squatting figure with the lens for a navel, looking, not back into a dark inscrutable box, but out on West Condon, and her parabolic intent was not lost on him: shrunk and its perspective distorted, West Condon was upside down. Happy, he knew, wanted to leave West Condon. He couldn't blame her. So did he, yet at the same time he knew better than to expect too much of East Condon. A little more elbow room, of course, a little more privacy in which to nurture their nascent sect. Here, he no longer hated really, he was only tired, the spirit was gone out of him and he just felt plain cramped . . . or maybe that was only a product of his present plight. Crucifixion was a proper end for insurgents: it de-

527

humanized them. Man only felt like man when he could bring his hands together.

A lot of people had come to see him. Some of the klatch from Mick's had brought him a fifth of Canadian and some cheap bourbon, most of which they'd managed to drink up themselves at his bedside, either forgetting he had no arms to help himself with, or feeling too embarrassed about it to hold the glass for him. No one had said anything directly, but the way they'd talked, Miller had got the idea they supposed he'd be moving on when he was able. Guys on his ball team had stopped up to shoot the shit. He'd urged them to get a team up, but they seemed to have no heart for it. Most of his people from the plant had dropped by, too, sooner or later. Naturally, they'd wanted to know what was going to happen: was the *Chronicle* going to publish again? He didn't know. But he'd told them he thought it would open and he paid them their regular salaries. Sometimes, he had to admit it, the idea of working up a good layout or chasing a story appealed to him, and he longed to hear old Hilda hump again. Just the taste of a Coke stirred up the old excitement. But then somebody like Robbins or Elliott would drop in and make him want to run again. Reverend Wesley Edwards had winked at him and tossed a wave from the doorway most mornings, but he had never come in. Was he gloating? Probably.

Jesus, dying, disconnected, was shocked to find Judas at his feet. "Which . . . one of us," Jesus gasped, "is really He: I or . . . or thou?" Judas offered up a hallowing omniscient smile, shrugged, and went his way, never to be seen in these parts again. Probably best, all right.

His own connection came by then to lower him, turning a noisy crank at his feet: mechanized Descent. Later, she would prepare spices and ointments. For now, she only wrapped his body in the sterile linens, stuck a thermometer in his mouth, turned her back to pluck idly at the wandering legband. Five picas, given all stresses. And that was what he needed to know: what were the stresses? Even the thermometer was a lesson, he knew. Was he going to go on forever plucking at legbands and submitting to having his temperature pointlessly taken? Oh Christ! How he wanted to move his arms again! How he wanted to *feel!* He spat out the thermometer, careful not to dislodge any teeth, and said, "Happy, come here!" She had to stand on a phonebook because of his arm's elevation, and he could only use one hand, but she could use two. He closed his eyes and received a world of messages, and while they were plugged in like that, he worrying about whether or not his whole life until now hadn't been just one fractured waste of time, she phoned him in yet another *Judgment. . . .*

At one point during the Last Judgment, at a particularly tense and difficult moment, someone present released a thundering, monumental—if not indeed mystical—fart. It was not, however, as efficacious as its historic reputation might have led one to expect. The Divine Judge did not disappear in a cloud of crimson smoke, nor did His Judgments reflect increasing or diminishing wrath or benevolence, nor did the Devil lead a raucous dance around the Throne, nor did the Angels faint, nor did their wings quiver sensuously from suppressed giggling and set the fabled West Wind going, nor was the farter pardoned (he or she was not even recognized), nor, in the end, were the masses edified by this commentary, if it was that, on Divine Justice. In short, nothing happened at all. Nevertheless, one should not lose sight of the reality of it. . . .

Old Wally Fisher came by when he got out of jail. Because of the bingo tent scandal and his general poor attitude, he'd been jugged that night with all the Brunists. When they'd spied him in their midst, still in street-

529

clothes, they'd taken him for an envoy from the dark powers, and he would have gone the way of all poor flesh, meaning Miller, had not Dee Romano propitiously and for five bucks intervened. Fisher's account of that night's whole wild scene was hilarious, obscene but hilarious, from the no doubt apocryphal tale of the state centurion caught mixing it up in the women's cell to the description of the comedy outside, seen through the cell windows, where a wobbly-kneed scar-faced Mort Whimple and a ring of unnerved troopers had stood, weapons at the ready, to keep at bay a rollicking mob of news and cameramen, East and West Condoners, visiondrunk one and all—and Miller, hearing it, felt better than he'd felt in weeks. They had jailed the poor guy, hadn't set him free until he had agreed to turn over the entire proceeds of his First Annual Spring Carnival to the West Condon Chamber of Commerce for its industrial brochure, had brought a series of damage suits against him, and had started boycotting his coffeeshop, but the old bastard could still laugh about it, and Miller laughed with him. "Oh Jesus, Tiger, we gotta do something like that again soon!" he wheezed, dewlaps awag, old man's lowslung paunch quaking. (Jesus, crucified, had a sudden glimpse of all his end would lead to, and he began to giggle. A Roman soldier, indignant at the blasphemy, thrust his spear into Jesus' quaking side. Real blood came out, and the soldier paled. But Jesus went right on giggling: once you know you're going to die, what, really, can they do to you?)

"Well, we could run Doris for mayor," Miller suggested. The old man had a fit about that, but Miller, laughing, had a funny thought: what about running Abner Baxter?

By the time Ted Cavanaugh came to see Miller, the idea had got a pretty firm hold on him. A number of things had happened in the meantime. The article he'd set out to do on the Brunists in the first place, his study of small-group rebound in the face of public embarrassment and a description of the roots of religious motivation and commitment, his public excuse for involvement and his private antidote against the guilt he felt for the pain he'd caused, got rejected again, discouraging him from any more games-playing in that direction. On the other hand, he had received—and accepted—an offer to do a series of TV commentaries on the Brunists which, he saw, might give him a wimble into the whole world's cranny. Moreover, he could move his arms again, plug in razors, use the telephone, pinch bottoms, and piss alone: in short, felt a man again.

Abner, he knew, was still in town, only Brunist leader not to run, and Miller learned he was holding clandestine Brunist meetings with a format all his own. His church had been wrecked, his home broken into and looted, black crosses swatched on his door, his kids beaten up, all credit canceled, and he'd got a lot of anonymous phonecalls and letters telling him he'd better move on or else. But he'd stayed. And, from what Miller could pick up, he also seemed to be at odds with the rest of the Brunists by now, or at least with Clara's people, and partly, it seemed, because he still insisted louder than anybody that Bruno was a prophet and the Coming was at hand. A democratic mayoral election with the Millennium as an issue: it had a certain promise, and he could plot the documentary out from the beginning, wouldn't have to move in after it was all over.

Wes Edwards came in with Cavanaugh, crinkled up his pastoral face, and asked, "Feeling better?" and that just about decided it for Miller.

The chat with Cavanaugh went poorly from the start. Ted was talking about West Condon's troubles and "the best thing for all of us," Miller was talking about Peter who, hearing the cock crow thrice, got to like the music of it, and Edwards was speaking nervously about friends he had up in the city who might find something for Justin more suitable for his talents. "Where things are livelier," the preacher was saying, and Ted's words were "shoulder to the wheel" and "a tough ball game," while Miller, speaking of money-changers and pigeon-sellers and getting nowhere, finally interrupted and said, "I'm not going."

Cavanaugh stood. "Why not?"

Miller sighed. "Necessity is laid upon me," he said.

"I've got a buyer for you," Cavanaugh said, not getting it. He explained the details: amounted to enough to clear debts and buy gas to get out of town.

Miller listened. If he had any horse sense, he'd take it, but the recent deprivation of his senses had deprived him of that one as well. He knew, of course, that the plant was in bad shape, had been looted during his hospitalization, knew, too, that he was sick to death of deadlines and club meetings, knew that Happy wanted to get out of here and rightside-up again, but still he couldn't stop himself. "Go to hell," he said. He heard Happy outside his door, so he added as a sort of dedication: "Do not pass Go, do not collect two hundred dollars."

She came in after they'd gone and he explained it to her. "Just until November," he said. He had a lot of money just now from all those articles and the TV assignments to get the plant in shape, and for the present a weekly would do as well as a daily. Maybe he could even get ahold of the radio station somehow. He began to make plans.

Happy sighed. "Okay, but if we stay that long, we might as well stay on through January."

"Why? You mean the Brunist—?"

"I'm talking about *tigers*, man," she said, and patted her belly.

"Hey! You mean it? But when—?"

She shrugged, grinned. "Sons of Noah . . ."

"Aha! sign of the covenant!"

So they quickly signed a pact, exchanged gifts, broke a chamberpot, bought Ascension Day airline tickets for the Caribbean, and, nailed to the old tree of life and knowledge that night, she murmured in his ear one last *Last Judgment* . . .

The trial proceedings, caught up in the absurd intricacies of human ambiguity, slowed to a near standstill. Several totally unanticipated logistic problems had been run up against, and the Angels, faced at last with the actuality of this long-planned but unfortunately never practiced event, proved less resourceful and efficient than was no doubt expected. A leading American public relations agency was hired for thirty pieces of silver to provide the solution, and indeed certain gains—or at least apparent gains— were made. To be sure, the image of this sordid business was improved. A catchy slogan was introduced to help everybody remember to bring their certificates of baptism, and, to take up the slack caused by the cramming of the judicial calendar, tourism of Heaven and Hell, formerly the privilege of the sensitive few, was introduced and became a democratic commonplace. Still, in spite of the agency, or probably in the long run because of it, the whole affair bogged down entirely in bureaucracy and the impenetrable paradoxes of behavior, language, and jurisdiction, until at last one day it occurred to someone (most likely not a child, in spite of the overwhelming tradition) to ask why the whole thing was being perpetrated in the first place, and the Divine Judge found Himself hard put to provide an answer that satisfied even Himself, having to confess that He was less amused by it than He had thought He would be. It was therefore agreed to drop it, and the various Divine Substances took their leave. The only trouble was that by that time the enormity of the support organization and the goal hunger of the participants were such that the absented Divine Substances were never missed. The proceedings, indulging

*the everlasting lust for perpetuity and stage direc-
tions, dragged on happily through the centuries, the
only consolation for those who might have guessed
the true state of affairs being that which the risen
Jesus centuries ago offered to his appalled disciples. . . .*

"Come and have breakfast."